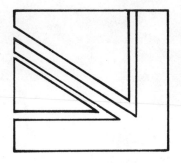

MODERN BRITISH SHORT NOVELS

Robert M. Davis
University of Oklahoma

MODERN BRITISH SHORT NOVELS

Scott, Foresman and Company
GLENVIEW, ILLINOIS   LONDON

For Jim Merritt and Arthur Oberg

Library of Congress Catalog Card Number: 75-157243

Copyright © 1972 by Scott, Foresman and Company, Glenview, Illinois 60025.
Philippines Copyright 1972 by Scott, Foresman and Company.
All Rights Reserved.
Printed in the United States of America.

Regional Offices of Scott, Foresman are located in Dallas, Oakland, N.J.,
Palo Alto, and Tucker, Ga.

ACKNOWLEDGMENTS

"The Man Who Would Be King" from *Wee Willie Winkie,* by Rudyard Kipling.
Published by Doubleday and Company. Reprinted by permission of A. P. Watt & Son
for Mrs. George Bambridge and the Macmillan Company of Canada.

Heart of Darkness, by Joseph Conrad. Reprinted by permission of J. M. Dent & Sons
Ltd. and the Trustees of the Joseph Conrad Estate.

"Concerning the Eccentricities of Cardinal Pirelli" from *Five Novels,* by Ronald
Firbank. Published by New Directions. Copyright © 1961 by Thomas Firbank.
Reprinted by permission of Collins-Knowlton-Wing, Inc. and A. P. Watt & Son for the
Estate of Ronald Firbank and Duckworth & Co. Ltd.

"After the Fireworks" from *Brief Candles,* Stories by Aldous Huxley. Copyright,
1930, 1958 by Aldous Huxley. Reprinted by permission of Harper & Row, Publishers,
Chatto & Windus Ltd., and Mrs. Laura Huxley.

"Ivy Gripped the Steps" from *Ivy Gripped the Steps,* by Elizabeth Bowen. Copyright
1941, 1946 and renewed 1969 by Elizabeth Bowen. Reprinted by permission of
Alfred A. Knopf, Inc. and Jonathan Cape Ltd.

"Love Among the Ruins" from *Tactical Exercise,* by Evelyn Waugh. Copyright 1936,
1942, 1943, 1947, 1953, 1954 by Evelyn Waugh. Reprinted by permission of
Atlantic-Little, Brown and Company and A. D. Peters & Company.

"A Contest of Ladies" from *The Stories of William Sansom,* by William Sansom.
Copyright © 1947, 1950, 1953, 1957, 1960, 1963 by William Sansom. Reprinted by
permission of Atlantic-Little, Brown and Company and the Hogarth Press.

"A Home for the Highland Cattle" from *African Stories,* by Doris Lessing. Copyright
© 1951, 1952, 1953, 1954, 1957, 1958, 1962, 1963, 1964, 1965 by Doris Lessing.
Reprinted by permission of Simon & Schuster, Inc. and Curtis Brown Ltd.

"Elephant and Colosseum" from the book, *Hear Us O Lord From Heaven Thy
Dwelling Place,* by Malcolm Lowry. Copyright © 1961 by Margerie Bonner Lowry.
Reprinted by permission of J. B. Lippincott Company.

Preface

This collection has grown out of a conviction that the usual course in the modern British novel is unduly limited by format to the discussion of a relatively few books and authors, and that the use of shorter works in a convenient format would enable teacher and student to become familiar with novelists worthy of attention but usually squeezed out because of the number of fine novels produced in the twentieth century. A few major figures—Conrad, Joyce, Lawrence, perhaps Woolf, perhaps Ford—have obvious claims to attention; thereafter, the book list of any modern novel course depends upon the teacher's estimate of his students' finances and stamina and upon the availability of certain authors' works. For example, much of the fiction of Aldous Huxley and Evelyn Waugh is available in paperback editions, but neither of the works included here is available from American publishers, and no fiction by William Sansom is listed in *Books in Print.* The stories by Elizabeth Bowen, Doris Lessing, and Malcolm Lowry are reprinted in collections of their work, but these volumes do nothing to solve the practical problem of expanded coverage of modern writers.

This anthology, then, is designed to increase the number of options available to student and teacher, not by excerpting from longer works, but by offering complete, self-contained works of art that represent each author's themes and techniques and that, hopefully, will lead the student to their other works. Most of them have been accorded high rank by critics of modern fiction; all are respected, though some in rather limited circles in this country, as masters of the art of fiction. Furthermore, these writers span the entire modern period, although more than half of them achieved their reputations after 1930 and thus represent four decades with which students of the novel have not yet come to adequate terms.

Therefore, this anthology is especially suited to courses in the modern novel or surveys of modern literature. Many features of the apparatus also make it suitable for courses in generic study of fiction, whether introductory or advanced, or for study of modern intellectual and social history, notably in courses designed to trace England's relationship with her colonies and the shifting of social distinctions within England. However, the apparatus is designed to be indicative rather than determinative. Many approaches besides the thematic-social-technical one of the Introduction are possible, and the discussions appended to each novel illustrate various ways of analyzing and understanding fiction. None is or is intended to be exhaustive, though each provides an introduction not merely to the individual work but to the body of the author's fiction, and each provides information—critical, biographical, textual—which indicates possibilities for further study on any level, from the most elementary to the most advanced. Not every student will profit by all of the apparatus, but it is there if he needs it; and recent educational theory indicates that underestimating or talking down to students or failing to provide them with as much as they can handle is always a mistake.

Like any activity, this one would have not been possible without the help of many people. A summer stipend from the National Endowment for the Humanities to study comedy and satire in modern fiction gave me the opportunity to consider a number of related topics, including the teaching of modern fiction in general. The library staff of the University of Oklahoma helped find what the library contained and acquired what it did not. As always, my wife read and rigorously edited the manuscript. And other friends and colleagues helped by being interested in and vocal about literature.

R.M.D.

Contents

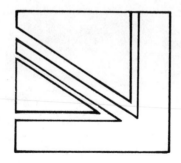

MODERN
BRITISH
SHORT
NOVELS

Introduction:
The Imagination of Defeat

Discussions of modern British fiction are likely to be as much lament as analysis. Critics deplore or bewail the decline in experiment, scope, and energy; publishers fear that rising costs will destroy the market for new writers; and literary historians are reluctant to cross the magic border of 1930 (the death of D. H. Lawrence) or 1939 (the publication of James Joyce's *Finnegan's Wake*) to explore the terra incognita of the modern novel.[1] The difficulties are obvious: once past the triple peaks of Conrad, Joyce, and Lawrence, the student encounters ranges of writers more or less equal in talent whose similarity makes them seem smaller than they really are. Evelyn Waugh, torn between pride in his craft and distaste for any products of the modern world, expressed the same idea in positive terms:

> It may happen in the next hundred years that the English novelists of the present day will come to be valued as we now value the artists and craftsmen of the late eighteenth century. The originators, the exuberant men, are extinct and in their place subsists and modestly flourishes a generation notable for elegance and variety of contrivance. It may well happen that there are lean years ahead in which our posterity will look back hungrily to this period, when there was so much will and so much ability to please.[2]

American audiences in particular are shy of "elegance and variety of contrivance" unless it can somehow be concealed by the writer's public image—Hemingway's hunting, Fitzgerald's drinking and despairing, even Truman Capote's rusticating in Kansas. Serious readers, and American literary intellectuals are among the most serious in the world, tend to regard a "desire to please" as obsequious courting of the audience or as mere entertainment.[3]

For these and for a variety of historical and broadly cultural reasons, critics of the modern British novel have focused less upon what it has done than what it does not do, condemning without understanding the limits which the artist has, willingly or not, accepted. Only when we begin to understand those limits can we begin to assess the artistic achievement within them.

To do so, it is necessary to invoke some dangerous but useful generaliza-

---

[1]For exceptions, notably the books by James Hall, whose untimely death cut short his work on the recent novel, see the bibliographical note which follows.

[2]Evelyn Waugh, *The Ordeal of Gilbert Pinfold* (Boston: Little, Brown and Company, 1957), p. 3.

[3]For example, Steven Marcus, "Evelyn Waugh and the Art of Entertainment," *Partisan Review*, 23 (Summer 1956), 348–357.

tions about the culture in which these novels were written. Critics could say, with some plausibility, that the English novel of the eighteenth and nineteenth centuries was the product of bourgeois society,[4] that its theme was "essentially that of formation, of education,"[5] or that it dealt with "learning how to dispense with fantasy."[6] These statements all presuppose a confidence in the coherence of the society and its continuation into an indefinite future. And even tragic novels like *Wuthering Heights* or *The Mayor of Casterbridge* invoke at the end a peaceful world which the survivors, lesser but more stable people than the protagonists, can gracefully inhabit. This basic optimism about the possibilities for change and development within human character and human society led critics like Lionel Trilling and W. J. Harvey to identify the novel as the characteristic form of liberalism, essentially a melioristic, humanistic philosophy.[7]

Most English novelists of the twentieth century have had bourgeois origins—if one is willing to use the considerable elasticity of that term to cover people like Elizabeth Bowen and Ronald Firbank—and many of them came from a class which was at the same time the result and the source of liberal thought. They were "the moneyless, landless, educated gentry who managed the country,"[8] oriented toward Oxford and Cambridge even if they did not attend a university and toward the Oxbridge-Bloomsbury-London West End world. Obviously, exceptions abound—Joyce was Irish lower middle class, Lawrence midlands lower class, Conrad Polish upper class, and all artists are in some fashion aliens in their worlds—but all found major sources of support and encouragement among the higher bourgeoisie. Perhaps the outsiders were the first to detect the malaise of English society, but those immersed in the culture began to recognize the signs of decay—they were unavoidable and unmistakable—and to shift the novel from its traditional orientation toward a new subject: the undermining and destruction of the middle class, or, what may amount to the same thing, of that group's conception of itself and therefore of the civilization which gave rise to it.

Inevitably, this meant a shift in the traditional treatment of the individual in relation to society. Novelists of the previous two centuries conveyed the sense that the individual could pursue his own life parallel to if not

---

[4]See especially Ian Watt, *The Rise of the Novel* (Berkeley: University of California Press, 1957).

[5]Maurice Z. Shroder, "The Novel as a Genre," *Massachusetts Review,* 4 (Winter 1963), 294. Reprinted in Robert Murray Davis, *The Novel: Modern Essays in Criticism* (Englewood Cliffs, N.J.: Prentice-Hall, Inc., 1969), p. 46.

[6]Barbara Hardy, "Towards a Poetics of Fiction: 3. An Approach through Narrative," *Novel,* 2 (Fall 1968), 12.

[7]Lionel Trilling, *The Liberal Imagination* (New York: The Viking Press, Inc., 1950) and W. J. Harvey, *Character and the Novel* (Ithaca, N.Y.: Cornell University Press, 1965).

[8]Evelyn Waugh, "Work Suspended," in *Tactical Exercise* (Boston: Little, Brown and Company, 1954), p. 135.

entirely independent of society as mechanism. Vanity Fair can continue its run while the major characters retire: Becky Sharp goes on being Becky Sharp while the Dobbin ménage retire to placid domesticity; Lady Booby returns to London and the consolations of a half-pay captain while Joseph Andrews lives the good life in the country. The conception of society which Fielding and Thackeray and most of their contemporaries shared makes not only possible but inevitable the happy ending with its "distribution at the last of prizes, pensions, husbands, wives, babies, millions, appended paragraphs, and cheerful remarks"[9]—though the last element does not adequately reflect the irony or melancholy of many endings otherwise covered by the description. In our century, however one explains the process, novelists have been much more aware of the ways in which the characters are immersed in and shaped by society, all the way from Conrad's Kurtz, to whose making "All Europe contributed," to Waugh's Miles Plastic. Many novelists shifted their focus to society, using character to illustrate the effects of society rather than for its own sake and constructing plots which led to the characters' acquiescence or rebellion rather than to triumph or self-knowledge. In part, the shift results from a loss of confidence in society as a stable and reasonable force, in part from a loss of a sense of innocence or, even more important, of immunity. The loss is treated in many ways, but pathos underlies the attitude of most authors. Even—perhaps especially—the comedians are touched by melancholy.

Like any human, historical process, the erosion of confidence and its portrayal in fiction were confused in their beginnings, intermittent in their working, and uncertain in their results. Even though authors within a period and themes within a single book overlap, the theme of preparation for defeat can be traced through several stages. At first, authors sought to undercut late Victorian and Edwardian optimism by attacking its basic assumptions. Usually regarded as the spokesman for British imperialism, Rudyard Kipling ridiculed, in prose and verse, homegrown pieties and social certainties by testing them against the oppressive climate and moral ambiguities of India and against the struggles of the people who tried to govern the empire and themselves in circumstances that were often very nearly impossible. In *Heart of Darkness,* Joseph Conrad denies that society is a civilizing force. Social forms, even laws, become nonsense in Africa, in fact serve to insulate human beings from reality. Or, what is better or worse depending upon the point of view, social restrictions can fall away completely, placing the individual in isolation, where he can appeal to nothing outside himself. Marlow compromises his principles because he comes to see that only the strong can bear reality and that the weak, ignorant, and flabby need the old concept of society. Of course, he lets the secret out, and in a way the knowledge is exhilarating: man is not determined by society; he can confront the depths within himself.

---

[9]Henry James, "The Art of Fiction," reprinted in many collections. See John Henry Raleigh, "The English Novel and the Three Kinds of Time," *Sewanee Review,* 62 (July-September 1954), 428–440, and Davis, *The Novel,* pp. 242–252.

But what if there is nothing beneath the surface; what if the primitive consciousness within man leads to minor confusion rather than to unspeakable rites; what if instead of horror there is merely nothing? Marlow's tale turns London into an immense darkness for one listener; for Saki and other writers of social satire, it becomes a tidy chessboard on which a class gone fat and soft maneuvers for illusory advantages within confines the characters do not even begin to realize. Comus Bassington, *The Unbearable Bassington* of Saki's novel, is taken like Kurtz and Marlow to central Africa, and he too begins to see that English society is only an excrescence, that not everyone necessarily has a soul, and—a step further than Marlow—that time is the nemesis of the way of life that he knows he can never escape. Kurtz at least has something to say and an audience to hear it; Comus is silent and alone.

Both Conrad and Saki predicted defeat for those strong enough or flawed enough to recognize it, but neither doubted that society would remain as a refuge for all the others. World War I moved Englishmen beyond doubting that society was coherent to being nearly certain that it was not. It literally killed Saki; figuratively, it finished off those who had attacked Edwardian complacency from a sense of liberal optimism: E. M. Forster, John Galsworthy, Bernard Shaw, and others who continued to write but who had no real contact with the new world. Those with a taste for drama can date exactly the death of British innocence and confidence and of the European dream of progress through reason: July 1, 1916, the beginning of the battle of the Somme, in which the British Army had 19,000 killed and 57,000 wounded on the first day alone. The battle lasted until November, with no gain on either side and over a million casualties.[10] One of them was Saki.

The immediate reaction of bitterness against the government and the society which for the most part supported it was expressed by poets like Wilfred Owen and Siegfried Sassoon. Some of the survivors later wrote fictional accounts, but disillusion with the war, with society, and indirectly with the novel as a liberal form found more enduring expression in the work of noncombatants like Aldous Huxley and Ronald Firbank. Disillusion became a new norm: man was flawed, government venal or blind, society doomed. In fact all human societies came to be seen as bound to a cycle, whether Vico's, Spengler's, or Yeats', doomed to decline and fall as surely as they rose. Theoretically, it is possible to be heartened by the prospect of recurrence, but only James Joyce was strong or callous enough to regard that prospect with much enthusiasm. Yeats' finest poems deal with the death throes of contemporary society rather than the prospects of the new world. Other poets and novelists imagined not simply defeat for individual man but the complete collapse of civilization. From this prospect they turned to various refuges: to an unillusioned and ironic nostalgia for a past in which dreams and confidence were possible, like the world which could allow Sir Christopher Wren at least to plan for, if not to build, a new

---

[10]See A. J. P. Taylor, *English History 1914–1945,* vol. IX of *The Oxford History of England* (New York: Oxford University Press, 1965), pp. 60–61.

London, described in Huxley's *Antic Hay,* or like the decorative and decadent quasi-Edwardian societies of Ronald Firbank's novels. Without belief in society as a force, seeing it merely as a weight, a meretricious and distracting millstone, Firbank, Huxley, and even Lawrence turned toward the individual who sought in isolation to preserve a sense of the self. Firbank was content to portray the problem; Huxley and Lawrence proposed solutions which ended in mysticism or extreme forms of personalism in works like *Those Barren Leaves* and *The Man Who Died.* In their most characteristic work, however, the endings are problematic, with more questions than answers, and a sense of unresolved, necessarily incomplete action which, if not defeat, is certainly not victory.[11]

Younger men, less able or willing to turn away from society and the possibility of action in it, were ambivalent in a different way. Acutely conscious of the identity of their generation, writers like Evelyn Waugh and Anthony Powell, who seemed to believe that to act is to live, had a strong sense, even a fear, that action was not possible, that for them there would be nothing to *do.* In novels like *A Handful of Dust* and *Afternoon Men* the young hang about the fringes of conventional society, waiting for calls that never come or going through meaningless and boring social rituals because, immersed as they are in society, they can imagine no other way of life. Like their predecessors, though on a less obviously humanistic-religious basis, the younger novelists turned inward to find meaning. Individual aberrance and vitality became proof of the individual's capacity for survival, especially survival of boredom, and characters like Waugh's Basil Seal (in *Black Mischief* and *Put Out More Flags)* and Christopher Isherwood's Mr. Norris (in *Mr. Norris Changes Trains*) enjoy flux and chaos as escapes from society. But Basil must return to an England in which everyone has grown much poorer and duller (in *Black Mischief*). He ultimately professes a kind of patriotism (in *Put Out More Flags*) because the war gives him something to do and because he or at least his creator realizes that he could indulge his private whims because society provided a context for them. And Mr. Norris is finally caught by his own machinations, lamenting his fate but learning nothing from it.

Before the Second World War, novelists like Waugh portrayed the individual in retreat from a decaying, boring society—Basil's escape to Africa and William Boot's (*Scoop*) to Boot Magna, the picturesque, moribund country house of his family, represent opposite extremes—but the war cut off both of these escapes and delivered the individual into the hands of the state. "You used to know what you were like," Elizabeth Bowen said, "from the things you liked, and chose. Now there was not what you liked, and you did not choose."[12] Reacting against the physical and emotional privations of wartime and perhaps against the belief that their world and class would not survive the war, authors like Bowen and Waugh turned toward the past,

---

[11]For a discussion of the changing conventions in novel endings, see Alan Friedman, *The Turn of the Novel* (New York: Oxford University Press, 1966).

[12]Elizabeth Bowen, "Preface to *The Demon Lover,*" in *Collected Impressions* (New York: Alfred A. Knopf, Inc., 1950), p. 49.

this time a past projected as dream, an "unconscious, instinctive, saving resort on the part of the characters" in *The Demon Lover,* or as contained within and judged by the structure of an unchanging religious faith in Waugh's *Brideshead Revisited.* With defeat imminent (and by this I do not mean military defeat), the imagination counterattacks, marks off new territories of the spirit—including madness—which the world cannot invade, and thus acknowledges defeat in the old realms.

In spite of Englishmen's conflicting hopes and fears, the war did not destroy the English class system, though education acts and changes in tax laws altered it somewhat. Everyone did get rather poorer and, from a prewar point of view, duller. Still, having accepted limitation, authors seemed disposed to agree with Angela Lyne in *Put Out More Flags:* "One can't expect anything to be perfect now. In the old days if there was one thing wrong it spoiled everything; from now on for all our lives, if there's one thing right the day is made."[13] Angela marries Basil, despite his obvious shortcomings; John Lewis gives up dreams of belonging to the middle class in Kingsley Amis' *That Uncertain Feeling;* Arthur Seaton accepts the bondage and security of marriage in Alan Sillitoe's *Saturday Night and Sunday Morning;* most of the characters in Iris Murdoch's and Muriel Spark's early novels recognize that they must be content with partial and equivocal knowledge. Some authors like Alan Sillitoe (and a number of Americans) not only accept the idea of limits but use them to outline, as in a life mask, the dimensions of man, who is defined but not determined by all that is not him, by his inherent resistance to the pressures of society and cosmos. These writers may seem to disprove the generalization that English fiction of the twentieth century explores the ways in which defeat is rendered, but in fact they accept defeat as inevitable and then go on to explore the ways in which life remains bearable.

If one agrees that valid experiment arises from new, expansive concepts of reality or of the human psyche, and certainly the experiments of the early modern novel did so, then novelists who accept the idea of defeat are unlikely to be experimental.[14] Portraying a tradition, a culture, and a class in decline, they have found traditional means adequate. To "love that well which thou must leave ere long" requires tenderness rather than movements unrecorded in the *Kama Sutra.* Most early modern experiments in technique, for example, sought to show what an exceedingly queer thing reality was—the words are Huxley's—by manipulating viewpoint from within (either the limited narrator, piecing together information and trying to reach a conclusion, or the stream of consciousness, showing that one man in time and space implied many men and many states) or from

---

[13]Evelyn Waugh, *Put Out More Flags,* new and corrected uniform edition (London: Chapman and Hall, 1967), p. 230.

[14]Some obvious exceptions are novelists like Lawrence Durrell, Samuel Beckett, and Iris Murdoch, who use the idea that language is necessarily an inaccurate reflection of reality as a basis for constructing their novels. See especially Durrell's *A Key to Modern British Poetry* (Norman, Okla.: University of Oklahoma Press, 1952), pp. 75–89.

without, on the analogy of the five blind men describing the elephant. All of these methods are calculated to unsettle the reader, to destroy his confidence in the reliability of people or impressions, flouting the "naïve ontology" of earlier fiction which was "commonsensical, positing no split between experience and reality."[15] But confusion, like innocence, is precarious and easily used up. Most British novels of the twentieth century, after the initial wave of experiment, have been narrated by an omniscient, detached author who limits his focus to a single character. The character may be and often is bewildered and uncertain, but his confusion is significant primarily as it reveals the situation, not as it reveals depth and complexity of character. With notably few exceptions—Gully Jimson in Joyce Cary's *The Horse's Mouth,* Darley in Lawrence Durrell's *Alexandria Quartet,* the narrator in Alan Sillitoe's *The Loneliness of the Long Distance Runner,* and Jake Donoghue in Iris Murdoch's *Under the Net,* all of whom transcend the limitations of the world through acceptance and through personal, aesthetic impulses or codes of behavior—characters do not have room in their worlds in which to exfoliate into complexity. The characteristic world of the British novel is neither hothouse like Alexandria nor prisonhouse like hundreds of *Bildungsroman.* Both enclosures imply worlds outside, and for most British novelists, there is no escape.[16] Yet, though the character may be confused, the author is not—at least not within the limits of the reality he has chosen to portray. Often those limits are so narrow—as in Muriel Spark's London full of old people in *Memento Mori* or of bachelors in *The Bachelors*—that the author's authority is not questioned even by those who think it "quite appropriate for modern criticism to condemn a spurious omniscience in the contemporary novel as an empty imitation of an outmoded posture."[17]

For the most part, these novelists have been impelled to make do with "an outmoded posture" to be able to see coherence and order enough for art to survive. They and their audiences are fully aware of confusion, which for them no longer seems vital or promising. Metaphysical and social structures which once provided coherence are gone; order remains possible as a product of the imagination, but of an imagination which must arrange rather than transmute the materials on which it works. These writers know that lead will not change to gold, that they will not create uncreated consciences; instead, they seek to understand what can be done with lead.

This tendency—and it is a tendency rather than a universal or a direc-

---

[15]Philip Rahv, "Fiction and the Criticism of Fiction," in *The Myth and the Powerhouse* (New York: Farrar, Straus & Giroux, Inc., 1965), p. 45. Also in Davis, *The Novel,* p. 112.

[16]See my "The Shrinking Garden and New Exits," *Kansas Quarterly,* 1 (Summer 1969), 5–16, for a more elaborate discussion of this idea.

[17]Robert Scholes and Robert Kellogg, *The Nature of Narrative* (New York: Oxford University Press, 1966), p. 278. The authors concede that omniscience may produce (presumably valid) "works which abandon the novel's traditional and representational predilections" (p. 279). In *The Fabulators* (New York: Oxford University Press, 1967), Scholes maintains that such abandonment may be a source of new vitality in prose fiction.

tive—may seem to be fatal to art, which must have energy, vitality, interest in order to thrive. However, there are different ways of achieving energy, a fact overlooked by critics for whom technical experiment is paramount and by the literary mountebanks who proclaim that their lead is gold. One kind of energy results from the struggle with limitations imposed or accepted, as in the sonnet or the miniature. In fact, most of the novelists included in this collection look for energy not to broad and sweeping subjects or to extensions into new psychic and moral areas, but to methods which harmonize style and subject so carefully that art supports vision. Thus when Evelyn Waugh praises Christopher Isherwood's writing not simply for eschewing clichés but for never seeming to avoid clichés,[18] he commends not merely craft but a habit of mind exercised in art. And when, as in the novels of Firbank, Waugh, and Bowen, art calls attention to itself, it does so intentionally and meaningfully. One might argue that this is low-risk art, and that, like William Faulkner, most of us prefer ambitious failure. But the risks of this kind of art are in a sense more perilous than those undertaken by Thomas Wolfe. Having little psychological margin, these writers work within even narrower self-chosen limits. That too is daring, an arrogance like that of the high-wire performer who disdains a pole but uses a net to keep the spectators from worrying too much about the wrong things and thus risks what for an artist is worse than death—failure.

It may be tempting, because of the lack of range and depth of these novelists, to call their work minor. Yet they conceal a breathtaking confidence in their ability to portray the contemporary situation with a control which eliminates posturing. Even done badly, epic gesture and epic sweep seldom need defense, but it is useful to remember that, as Ford Madox Ford wrote, "The death of a mouse by cancer is the whole sack of Rome by the Goths. . . . "[19]

A Selective Bibliography for Students of Modern British Fiction

Bibliography:

COURTNEY, WINIFRED F., ed. *The Reader's Adviser: A Guide to the Best in Literature.* 11th ed. New York: R. R. Bowker Co., 1968. Chapter 2,

---

[18]Evelyn Waugh, "Mr. Isherwood and Friend," *Spectator,* 162 (24 March 1939), 498.

[19]Ford Madox Ford, *The Good Soldier* (New York: Random House, Inc., Vintage Books, 1958), p. 5.

"Bibliography," and Chapter 13, "Modern British Fiction," are especially useful. The latter gives many editions of works in print and annotates listings of secondary works, though no attempt is made to give complete primary or secondary bibliographies.

HOWARD-HILL, T. H. *Bibliography of British Literary Bibliographies.* Oxford: Oxford University Press, 1969.

TEMPLE, RUTH Z., and MARTIN TUCKER. *Twentieth Century British Literature: A Reference Guide and Bibliography.* New York: Frederick Ungar Publishing Co., Inc., 1968. Lists bibliographical, biographical and critical books for all genres of the whole period in part one; part two lists what purport to be the complete works of some 400 writers. Full of minor errors: omission of titles, mislabeling of the genres of individual titles.

The following annual bibliographies supplement these two reference works:

Primary works: British National Bibliography, ed. A. J. Wells. Council of the British National Bibliography, 1950–present.
The English Catalogue of Books. Publishers Circular, 1801–present.

Secondary works: International Bibliography. Modern Language Association of America, 1922–present. Secondary material for the language and literature of many modern languages. Lists work by American scholars only from 1922–1956; since then international. Originally the May issue of *PMLA;* then the June issue; now published in volume form and in separate fascicles.
Annual Bibliography of English Language and Literature. Cambridge: Modern Humanities Research Association, 1921–present. Has fallen behind and is to some degree supplanted by the previous item after 1956, but lists some material, notably reviews of primary and secondary sources, not found therein.
The Year's Work in English Studies. London: The English Association, 1920–present. A running commentary on scholarship for the previous year.
British Humanities Index. Library Association, 1962–present. Supplants and expands upon the coverage of *Subject Index to Periodicals,* 1915–1961.
Book Review Digest. New York: H. W. Wilson Co., 1905–present.
An Index to Book Reviews in the Humanities. Detroit: Philip Thomson, 1960–present.
Book Review Index. Detroit: Gale Research Co., 1965–present.

Biography:

KUNITZ, STANLEY J., and HOWARD HAYCRAFT. *Twentieth Century Authors: A Biographical Dictionary of Modern Literature.* New York: H. W. Wilson Co., 1942. First Supplement, 1955.

Biography Index. New York: H. W. Wilson Co., 1946–present.
Current Biography. New York: H. W. Wilson Co., 1940–present.

Histories of Modern Literature:

DAICHES, DAVID. *The Present Age in British Literature.* Bloomington: Indiana University Press, 1958. Part of a series: *Introductions to English Literature.*

FORD, BORIS, ed. *The Modern Age.* Harmondsworth, England: Penguin Books, 1963. Part of *The Pelican Guide to English Literature.*

TINDALL, WILLIAM YORK. *Forces in Modern British Literature 1885–1950.* New York: Random House, Inc., Vintage Books, 1956.

Surveys of the Modern Novel:

ALLEN, WALTER. *The English Novel.* New York: E. P. Dutton & Co., Inc., 1958.

ALLEN, WALTER. *The Modern Novel in Britain and the United States.* New York: E. P. Dutton & Co., Inc., 1964.

BAKER, E. A. *The History of the English Novel.* Vol. IX: *The Day Before Yesterday.* London: H. F. & G. Witherby, Ltd., 1938; Vol. X: *Yesterday.* London: H. F. & G. Witherby, Ltd., 1939. See Stevenson for the continuation of the series.

CONNOLLY, CYRIL. *Enemies of Promise.* Rev. ed. New York: The Macmillan Company, 1948.

ELLIS, G. U. *Twilight on Parnassus: A Survey of Post-War Fiction and Pre-War Criticism.* London: Michael Joseph, Ltd., 1939.

GINDIN, JAMES. *Postwar British Fiction: New Accents and Attitudes.* Berkeley: University of California Press, 1962.

HALL, JAMES. *The Tragic Comedians.* Bloomington: Indiana University Press, 1963.

HALL, JAMES. *The Lunatic Giant in the Drawing Room: The British and American Novel Since 1930.* Bloomington: Indiana University Press, 1968.

KARL, FREDERICK R. *A Reader's Guide to the Contemporary English Novel.* New York: Farrar, Straus & Giroux, Inc., The Noonday Press, 1962.

STEVENSON, LIONEL. *The History of the English Novel.* Vol. XI: *Yesterday and After.* New York: Barnes & Noble, Inc., 1967.

WEBSTER, HARVEY CURTIS. *After the Trauma: Representative British Novelists Since 1920.* Lexington, Ky.: University Press of Kentucky, 1970.

WEST, PAUL. *The Modern Novel.* 2 vols. Vol. I: *England and France.* London: Hutchinson University Library, 1967.

Theory of the Novel:

Selections from theoretical books and essays and further bibliography can be found in the following:

DAVIS, ROBERT MURRAY, ed. *The Novel: Modern Essays in Criticism.* Englewood Cliffs, N.J.: Prentice-Hall, Inc., 1969.

STEVICK, PHILIP, ed. *Theory of the Novel.* Glencoe, Ill.: The Free Press, 1967.

RUDYARD KIPLING

The Man Who Would Be King

Brother to a Prince and fellow to a beggar if he be found worthy.

The Law, as quoted, lays down a fair conduct of life, and one not easy to follow. I have been fellow to a beggar again and again under circumstances which prevented either of us finding out whether the other was worthy. I have still to be brother to a Prince, though I once came near to kinship with what might have been a veritable King and was promised the reversion of a Kingdom—army, law-courts, revenue and policy all complete. But, to-day, I greatly fear that my King is dead, and if I want a crown I must go hunt it for myself.

The beginning of everything was in a railway train upon the road to Mhow from Ajmir. There had been a Deficit in the Budget, which necessitated travelling, not Second-class, which is only half as dear as First-class, but by Intermediate, which is very awful indeed. There are no cushions in the Intermediate class, and the population are either Intermediate, which is Eurasian, or native, which for a long night journey is nasty, or Loafer, which is amusing though intoxicated. Intermediates do not buy from refreshment-rooms. They carry their food in bundles and pots, and buy sweets from the native sweetmeat-sellers, and drink the roadside water. That is why in hot weather Intermediates are taken out of the carriages dead, and in all weathers are most properly looked down upon.

My particular Intermediate happened to be empty till I reached Nasirabad, when a big black-browed gentleman in shirt-sleeves entered, and, following the custom of Intermediates, passed the time of day. He was a wanderer and a vagabond like myself, but with an educated taste for

12

whiskey. He told tales of things he had seen and done, of out-of-the-way corners of the Empire into which he had penetrated, and of adventures in which he risked his life for a few days' food.

"If India was filled with men like you and me, not knowing more than the crows where they'd get their next day's rations, it isn't seventy millions of revenue the land would be paying—it's seven hundred millions," said he; and as I looked at his mouth and chin I was disposed to agree with him.

We talked politics—the politics of Loaferdom, that sees things from the underside where the lath and plaster are not smoothed off—and we talked postal arrangements because my friend wanted to send a telegram back from the next station to Ajmir, the turning-off place from the Bombay to the Mhow line as you travel westward. My friend had no money beyond eight annas which he wanted for dinner, and I had no money at all, owing to the hitch in the Budget before mentioned. Further, I was going into a wilderness where, though I should resume touch with the Treasury, there were no telegraph offices. I was, therefore, unable to help him in any way.

"We might threaten a Station-master, and make him send a wire on tick," said my friend, "but that'd mean enquiries for you and for me, and I've got my hands full these days. Did you say you were travelling back along this line within any days?"

"Within ten," I said.

"Can't you make it eight?" said he. "Mine is rather urgent business."

"I can send your telegram within ten days if that will serve you," I said.

"I couldn't trust the wire to fetch him now I think of it. It's this way. He leaves Delhi on the 23d for Bombay. That means he'll be running through Ajmir about the night of the 23d."

"But I'm going into the Indian Desert," I explained.

"Well *and* good," said he. "You'll be changing at Marwar Junction to get into Jodhpore territory—you must do that—and he'll be coming through Marwar Junction in the early morning of the 24th by the Bombay Mail. Can you be at Marwar Junction on that time? 'Twon't be inconveniencing you because I know that there's precious few pickings to be got out of these Central India States—even though you pretend to be correspondent of the 'Backwoodsman.'"

"Have you ever tried that trick?" I asked.

"Again and again, but the Residents find you out, and then you get escorted to the Border before you've time to get your knife into them. But about my friend here. I *must* give him a word o' mouth to tell him what's come to me, or else he won't know where to go. I would take it more than kind of you if you was to come out of Central India in time to catch him at Marwar Junction, and say to him: 'He has gone South for the week.' He'll know what that means. He's a big man with a red beard, and a great swell he is. You'll find him sleeping like a gentleman with all his luggage round him in a Second-class apartment. But don't you be afraid. Slip down the window and say: 'He has gone South for the week,' and he'll tumble. It's only cutting your time of stay in those parts by two days. I ask you as a stranger—going to the West," he said with emphasis.

"Where have *you* come from?" said I.

"From the East," said he, "and I am hoping that you will give him the message on the Square—for the sake of my Mother as well as your own."

Englishmen are not usually softened by appeals to the memory of their mothers; but for certain reasons, which will be fully apparent, I saw fit to agree.

"It's more than a little matter," said he, "and that's why I asked you to do it—and now I know that I can depend on you doing it. A Second-class carriage at Marwar Junction, and a red-haired man asleep in it. You'll be sure to remember. I get out at the next station, and I must hold on there till he comes or sends me what I want."

"I'll give the message if I catch him," I said, "and for the sake of your Mother as well as mine I'll give you a word of advice. Don't try to run the Central India States just now as the correspondent of the 'Backwoodsman.' There's a real one knocking about here, and it might lead to trouble."

"Thank you," said he simply, "and when will the swine be gone? I can't starve because he's ruining my work. I wanted to get hold of the Degumber Rajah down here about his father's widow, and give him a jump."

"What did he do to his father's widow, then?"

"Filled her up with red pepper and slippered her to death as she hung from a beam. I found that out myself, and I'm the only man that would dare going into the State to get hush-money for it. They'll try to poison me, same as they did in Chortumna when I went on the loot there. But you'll give the man at Marwar Junction my message?"

He got out at a little roadside station, and I reflected. I had heard, more than once, of men personating correspondents of newspapers and bleeding small Native States with threats of exposure, but I had never met any of the caste before. They lead a hard life, and generally die with great suddenness. The Native States have a wholesome horror of English newspapers, which may throw light on their peculiar methods of government, and do their best to choke correspondents with champagne, or drive them out of their mind with four-in-hand barouches. They do not understand that nobody cares a straw for the internal administration of Native States so long as oppression and crime are kept within decent limits, and the ruler is not drugged, drunk, or diseased from one end of the year to the other. They are the dark places of the earth, full of unimaginable cruelty, touching the Railway and the Telegraph on one side, and, on the other, the days of Harun-al-Raschid. When I left the train I did business with divers Kings, and in eight days passed through many changes of life. Sometimes I wore dress-clothes and consorted with Princes and Politicals, drinking from crystal and eating from silver. Sometimes I lay out upon the ground and devoured what I could get, from a plate made of leaves, and drank the running water, and slept under the same rug as my servant. It was all in the day's work.

Then I headed for the Great Indian Desert upon the proper date, as I had promised, and the night Mail set me down at Marwar Junction, where a funny little, happy-go-lucky, native-managed railway runs to Jodhpore. The Bombay Mail from Delhi makes a short halt at Marwar. She arrived as I got in, and I had just time to hurry to her platform and go down the carriages. There was only one Second-class on the train. I slipped the window and looked down upon a flaming red beard, half covered by a railway rug. That was my man, fast asleep, and I dug him gently in the ribs. He woke with a grunt, and I saw his face in the light of the lamps. It was a great and shining face.

"Tickets again?" said he.

"No," said I. "I am to tell you that he is gone South for the week. He has gone South for the week!"

The train had begun to move out. The red man rubbed his eyes. "He has gone South for the week," he repeated. "Now that's just like his impidence. Did he say that I was to give you anything? 'Cause I won't.'"

"He didn't," I said, and dropped away, and watched the red lights die out in the dark. It was horribly cold because the wind was blowing off the sands. I climbed into my own train—not an Intermediate carriage this time—and went to sleep.

If the man with the beard had given me a rupee I should have kept it as a memento of a rather curious affair. But the consciousness of having done my duty was my only reward.

Later on I reflected that two gentlemen like my friends could not do any good if they foregathered and personated correspondents of newspapers, and might, if they blackmailed one of the little rattrap states of Central India or Southern Rajputana, get themselves into serious difficulties. I therefore took some trouble to describe them as accurately as I could remember to people who would be interested in deporting them: and succeeded, so I was later informed, in having them headed back from the Degumber borders.

Then I became respectable, and returned to an Office where there were no Kings and no incidents outside the daily manufacture of a newspaper. A newspaper office seems to attract every conceivable sort of person, to the prejudice of discipline. Zenana-mission ladies arrive, and beg that the Editor will instantly abandon all his duties to describe a Christian prize-giving in a back slum of a perfectly inaccessible village; Colonels who have been overpassed for command sit down and sketch the outline of a series of ten, twelve, or twenty-four leading articles on Seniority *versus* Selection; missionaries wish to know why they have not been permitted to escape from their regular vehicles of abuse and swear at a brother-missionary under special patronage of the editorial We; stranded theatrical companies troop up to explain that they cannot pay for their advertisements, but on their return from New Zealand or Tahiti will do so with interest; inventors of patent punkah-pulling machines, carriage couplings and unbreakable swords and axle-trees call with specifications in their pockets and hours at their disposal; tea-companies enter and elaborate their prospectuses with the office pens; secretaries of ball-committees clamour to have the glories of their last dance more fully described; strange ladies rustle in and say: "I want a hundred lady's cards printed *at once,* please," which is manifestly part of an Editor's duty; and every dissolute ruffian that ever tramped the Grand Trunk Road makes it his business to ask for employment as a proof-reader. And, all the time, the telephone-bell is ringing madly, and

Kings are being killed on the Continent, and Empires are saying—"You're another," and Mr. Gladstone is calling down brimstone upon the British Dominions, and the little black copy-boys are whining, *"kaa-pi chay-ha-yeh"* (copy wanted) like tired bees, and most of the paper is as blank as Modred's shield.

But that is the amusing part of the year. There are six other months when none ever come to call, and the thermometer walks inch by inch up to the top of the glass, and the office is darkened to just above reading-light, and the press-machines are red-hot of touch, and nobody writes anything but accounts of amusements in the Hill-stations or obituary notices. Then the telephone becomes a tinkling terror, because it tells you of the sudden deaths of men and women that you knew intimately, and the prickly-heat covers you with a garment, and you sit down and write: "A slight increase of sickness is reported from the Khuda Janta Khan District. The outbreak is purely sporadic in its nature, and, thanks to the energetic efforts of the District authorities, is now almost at an end. It is, however, with deep regret we record the death," etc.

Then the sickness really breaks out, and the less recording and reporting the better for the peace of the subscribers. But the Empires and the Kings continue to divert themselves as selfishly as before, and the Foreman thinks that a daily paper really ought to come out once in twenty-four hours, and all the people at the Hill-stations in the middle of their amusements say: "Good gracious! Why can't the paper be sparkling? I'm sure there's plenty going on up here."

That is the dark half of the moon, and, as the advertisements say, "must be experienced to be appreciated."

It was in that season, and a remarkably evil season, that the paper began running the last issue of the week on Saturday night, which is to say Sunday morning, after the custom of a London paper. This was a great convenience, for immediately after the paper was put to bed, the dawn would lower the thermometer from 96° to almost 84° for half an hour, and in that chill—you have no idea how cold is 84° on the grass until you begin to pray for it—a very tired man could get off to sleep ere the heat roused him.

One Saturday night it was my pleasant duty to put the paper to bed alone. A King or courtier or a courtesan or a Community was going to die or get a new Constitution, or do something that was important on the other side of the world, and the paper was to be held open till the latest possible minute in order to catch the telegram.

It was a pitchy-black night, as stifling as a June night can be, and the *loo,* the red-hot wind from the westward, was booming among the tinder-dry trees and pretending that the rain was on its heels. Now and again a spot of almost boiling water would fall on the dust with the flop of a frog, but all our weary world knew that was only pretence. It was a shade cooler in the press-room than the office, so I sat there, while the type ticked and clicked, and the night-jars hooted at the windows, and the all but naked compositors wiped the sweat from their foreheads, and called for water. The thing that was keeping us back, whatever it was, would not come off, though the *loo* dropped and the last type was set, and the whole round earth stood still in the choking heat, with its finger on its lip, to wait the event. I drowsed, and wondered whether the telegraph was a blessing, and whether this dying man, or struggling people, might be aware of the inconvenience the delay was causing. There was no special reason beyond the heat and worry to make tension, but, as the clock-hands crept up to three o'clock and the machines spung their fly-wheels two and three times to see that all was in order, before I said the word that would set them off, I could have shrieked aloud.

Then the roar and rattle of the wheels shivered the quiet into little bits. I rose to go away, but two men in white clothes stood in front of me. The first one said: "It's him!" The second said: "So it is!" And they both laughed almost as loudly as the machinery roared, and mopped their foreheads. "We seed there was a light burning across the road, and we were sleeping in that ditch there for coolness, and I said to my friend here, 'The office is open. Let's come along and speak to him as turned us back from the Degumber State,'" said the smaller of the two. He was the man I had met in the Mhow train, and his fellow was the red-bearded man of Marwar Junction. There was no mistaking the eyebrows of the one or the beard of the other.

I was not pleased, because I wished to go to sleep, not to squabble with loafers. "What do you want?" I asked.

"Half an hour's talk with you, cool and comfortable, in the office," said the red-bearded man. "We'd *like* some drink—the Contrack doesn't begin yet, Peachey, so you needn't look—but what we really want is advice. We don't want money. We ask you as a favour, because we found out you did us a bad turn about Degumber State."

I led from the press-room to the stifling office with the maps on the walls, and the red-haired man rubbed his hands. "That's something like," said he. "This was the proper shop to come to. Now, Sir, let me introduce to you Brother Peachey Carnehan, that's him, and Brother Daniel Dravot, that is *me,* and the less said about our professions the better, for we have been most things in our time. Soldier, sailor, compositor, photographer, proof-reader, street-preacher, and correspondents of the 'Backwoodsman' when we thought the paper wanted one. Carnehan is sober, and so am I. Look at us first, and see that's sure. It will save you cutting into my talk. We'll take one of your cigars apiece, and you shall see us light up."

I watched the test. The men were absolutely sober, so I gave them each a tepid whiskey and soda.

"Well *and* good," said Carnehan of the eyebrows, wiping the froth from his moustache. "Let me talk now, Dan. We have been all over India, mostly on foot. We have been boiler-fitters, engine-drivers, petty contractors, and all that, and we have decided that India isn't big enough for such as us."

They certainly were too big for the office. Dravot's beard seemed to fill half the room and Carnehan's shoulders the other half, as they sat on the big table. Carnehan continued: "The country isn't half worked out because they that governs it won't let you touch it. They spend all their blessed time in governing it, and you can't lift a spade, nor chip a rock, nor look for oil, nor anything like that without all the Government saying—'Leave it alone, and let us govern.' Therefore, such *as* it is, we will let it alone, and go away to some other place where a man isn't crowded and can come to his own. We are not little men, and there is nothing that we are afraid of except Drink, and we have signed a Contrack on that. *Therefore,* we are going away to be Kings."

"Kings in our own right," muttered Dravot.

"Yes, of course," I said. "You've been tramping in the sun, and it's a very warm night, and hadn't you better sleep over the notion? Come to-morrow."

"Neither drunk nor sunstruck," said Dravot. "We have slept over the notion half a year, and require to see Books and Atlases, and we have decided that there is only one place now in the world that two strong men can Sar-a-*whack*. They call it Kafiristan. By my reckoning it's the top right-hand corner of Afghanistan, not more than three hundred miles from Peshawar. They have two-and-thirty heathen idols there, and we'll be the thirty-third and fourth. It's a mountaineous country, and the women of those parts are very beautiful."

"But that is provided against in the Contrack," said Carnehan. "Neither Woman nor Liqu-or, Daniel."

"And that's all we know, except that no one has gone there, and they fight, and in any place where they fight a man who knows how to drill men can always be a King. We shall go to those parts and say to any King we find—'D'you want to vanquish your foes?' and we will show him how to drill men; for that we know better than anything else. Then we will subvert that King and seize his Throne and establish a Dy-nasty."

"You'll be cut to pieces before you're fifty miles across the Border," I said. "You have to travel through Afghanistan to get to that country. It's one mass of mountains and peaks and glaciers, and no Englishman has been through it. The people are utter brutes, and even if you reached them you couldn't do anything."

"That's more like," said Carnehan. "If you could think us a little more mad we would be more pleased. We have come to you to know about this country, to read a book about it, and to be shown maps. We want you to tell us that we are fools and to show us your books." He turned to the book-cases.

"Are you at all in earnest?" I said.

"A little," said Dravot sweetly. "As big a map as you have got, even if it's all blank where Kafiristan is, and any books you've got. We can read, though we aren't very educated."

I uncased the big thirty-two-miles-to-the-inch map of India, and two smaller Frontier maps, hauled down volume INF–KAN of the "Encyclopaedia Britannica," and the men consulted them.

"See here!" said Dravot, his thumb on the map. "Up to Jagdallak, Peachey and me know the road. We was there with Roberts' Army. We'll have to turn off to the right at Jagdallak through Laghmann territory. Then we get among the hills—fourteen thousand feet—fifteen thousand—it will be cold work there, but it don't look very far on the map."

I handed him Wood on the "Sources of the Oxus." Carnehan was deep in the "Encyclopaedia."

"They're a mixed lot," said Dravot reflectively; "and it won't help us to know the names of their tribes. The more tribes the more they'll fight, and the better for us. From Jagdallak to Ashang. H'mm!"

"But all the information about the country is as sketchy and inaccurate as can be," I protested. "No one knows anything about it really. Here's the file of the 'United Services' Institute.' Read what Bellew says."

"Blow Bellew!" said Carnehan. "Dan, they're a stinkin' lot of heathens, but this book here says they think they're related to us English."

I smoked while the men pored over "Raverty," "Wood," the maps, and the "Encyclopaedia."

"There is no use your waiting," said Dravot politely. "It's about four o'clock now. We'll go before six o'clock if you want to sleep, and we won't steal any of the papers. Don't you sit up. We're two harmless lunatics, and if you come to-morrow evening down to the Serai we'll say good-bye to you."

"You *are* two fools," I answered. "You'll be turned back at the Frontier or cut up the minute you set foot in Afghanistan. Do you want any money or a recommendation down-country? I can help you to the chance of work next week."

"Next week we shall be hard at work ourselves, thank you," said Dravot. "It isn't so easy being a King as it looks. When we've got our Kingdom in going order we'll let you know, and you can come up and help us to govern it."

"Would two lunatics make a Contrack like that?" said Carnehan, with subdued pride, showing me a greasy half-sheet of notepaper on which was written the following. I copied it, then and there, as a curiosity—

> *This Contract between me and you persuing witnesseth in the name of God—Amen and so forth.*
>
> *(One)   That me and you will settle this matter together; i.e., to be Kings of Kafiristan.*
>
> *(Two)   That you and me will not, while this matter is being settled, look at any Liquor, nor any Woman black, white, or brown, so as to get mixed up with one or the other harmful.*
>
> *(Three) That we conduct ourselves with Dignity and Discretion, and if one of us gets into trouble the other will stay by him.*
>
> *Signed by you and me this day.*
>
> Peachey Taliaferro Carnehan.
> Daniel Dravot.
> Both Gentlemen at Large.

"There was no need for the last article," said Carnehan, blushing modestly; "but it looks regular. Now you know the sort of men that loafers are—we *are* loafers, Dan, until we get out of India—and *do* you think that we would sign a Contrack like that unless we was in earnest? We have kept away from the two things that make life worth having."

"You won't enjoy your lives much longer if you are going to try this idiotic adventure. Don't set the office on fire," I said, "and go away before nine o'clock."

I left them still poring over the maps and making notes on the back of the

"Contrack." "Be sure to come down to the Serai to-morrow," were their parting words.

The Kumharsen Serai is the great four-square sink of humanity where the strings of camels and horses from the North load and unload. All the nationalities of Central Asia may be found there, and most of the folk of India proper. Balkh and Bokhara there meet Bengal and Bombay, and try to draw eye-teeth. You can buy ponies, turquoises, Persian pussy-cats, saddle-bags, fat-tailed sheep and musk in the Kumharsen Serai, and get many strange things for nothing. In the afternoon I went down to see whether my friends intended to keep their word or were lying there drunk.

A priest attired in fragments of ribbons and rags stalked up to me, gravely twisting a child's paper whirligig. Behind him was his servant bending under the load of a crate of mud toys. The two were loading up two camels, and the inhabitants of the Serai watched them with shrieks of laughter.

"The priest is mad," said a horse-dealer to me. "He is going up to Kabul to sell toys to the Amir. He will either be raised to honour or have his head cut off. He came in here this morning and has been behaving madly ever since."

"The witless are under the protection of God," stammered a flat-cheeked Usbeg in broken Hindi. "They foretell future events."

"Would they could have foretold that my caravan would have been cut up by the Shinwaris almost within shadow of the Pass!" grunted the Eusufzai agent of a Rajputana trading-house whose goods had been diverted into the hands of other robbers just across the Border, and whose misfortunes were the laughing-stock of the bazar. "Ohé, priest, whence come you and whither do you go?"

"From Roum have I come," shouted the priest, waving his whirligig; "from Roum, blown by the breath of a hundred devils across the sea! O thieves, robbers, liars, the blessing of Pir Khan on pigs, dogs, and perjurers! Who will take the Protected of God to the North to sell charms that are never still to the Amir? The camels shall not gall, the sons shall not fall sick, and the wives shall remain faithful while they are away, of the men who give me place in their caravan. Who will assist me to slipper the King of the Roos with a golden slipper with a silver heel? The protection of Pir Khan be upon his labours!" He spread out the skirts of his gaberdine and pirouetted between the lines of tethered horses.

"There starts a caravan from Peshawar to Kabul in twenty days, *Huzrut*," said the Eusufzai trader. "My camels go therewith. Do thou also go and bring us good luck."

"I will go even now!" shouted the priest. "I will depart upon my winged camels, and be at Peshawar in a day! Ho! Hazar Mir Khan," he yelled to his servant, "drive out the camels, but let me first mount my own."

He leaped on the back of his beast as it knelt, and, turning round to me, cried: "Come thou also, Sahib, a little along the road, and I will sell thee a charm—an amulet that shall make thee King of Kafiristan."

Then the light broke upon me, and I followed the two camels out of the Serai till we reached open road and the priest halted.

"What d'you think o' that?" said he in English. "Carnehan can't talk their patter, so I've made him my servant. He makes a handsome servant. 'Tisn't for nothing that I've been knocking about the country for fourteen years. Didn't I do that talk neat? We'll hitch on to a caravan at Peshawar till we get to Jagdallak, and then we'll see if we can get donkeys for our camels, and strike into Kafiristan. Whirligigs for the Amir, O Lor! Put your hand under the camelbags and tell me what you feel."

I felt the butt of a Martini, and another and another.

"Twenty of 'em," said Dravot placidly. "Twenty of 'em and ammunition to correspond, under the whirligigs and the mud dolls."

"Heaven help you if you are caught with those things!" I said. "A Martini is worth her weight in silver among the Pathans."

"Fifteen hundred rupees of capital—every rupee we could beg, borrow, or steal—are invested on these two camels," said Dravot. "We won't get caught. We're going through the Khaiber with a regular caravan. Who'd touch a poor mad priest?"

"Have you got everything you want?" I asked, overcome with astonishment.

"Not yet, but we shall soon. Give us a memento of your kindness, *Brother.* You did me a service yesterday, and that time in Marwar. Half my Kingdom shall you have, as the saying is." I slipped a small charm compass from my watch-chain and handed it up to the priest.

"Good-bye," said Dravot, giving me his hand cautiously. "It's the last time we'll shake hands with an Englishman these many days. Shake hands with him, Carnehan," he cried, as the second camel passed me.

Carnehan leaned down and shook hands. Then the camels passed away along the dusty road, and I was left alone to wonder. My eye could detect no failure in the disguises. The scene in the Serai proved that they were complete to the native mind. There was just the chance, therefore, that Carnehan and Dravot would be able to wander through Afghanistan without detection. But, beyond, they would find death—certain and awful death.

Ten days later a native correspondent, giving me the news of the day from Peshawar, wound up his letter with: "There has been much laughter here on account of a certain mad priest who is going in his estimation to sell petty gauds and insignificant trinkets which he ascribes as great charms to H. H. the Amir of Bokhara. He passed through Peshawar and associated himself to the Second Summer caravan that goes to Kabul. The merchants are pleased because through superstition they imagine that such mad fellows bring good fortune."

The two, then, were beyond the Border. I would have prayed for them, but, that night a real King died in Europe, and demanded an obituary notice.

The wheel of the world swings through the same phases again and again. Summer passed and winter thereafter, and came and passed again. The daily paper continued, and I with it, and upon the third summer there fell a hot night, a night-issue, and a strained waiting for something to be telegraphed from the other side of the world, exactly as had happened before. A few great men had died in the past two years, the machines worked with more clatter, and some of the trees in the Office garden were a few feet taller. But that was all the difference.

I passed over to the press-room, and went through just such a scene as I have already described. The nervous tension was stronger than it had been two years before, and I felt the heat more acutely. At three o'clock I cried, "Print off," and turned to go, when there crept to my chair what was left of a man. He was bent into a circle, his head was sunk between his shoulders, and he moved his feet one over the other like a bear. I could hardly see whether he walked or crawled—this rag-wrapped, whining cripple who addressed me by name, crying that he was come back. "Can you give me a drink?" he whimpered. "For the Lord's sake, give me a drink!"

I went back to the office, the man following with groans of pain, and I turned up the lamp.

"Don't you know me?" he gasped, dropping into a chair, and he turned his drawn face, surmounted by a shock of gray hair, to the light.

I looked at him intently. Once before had I seen eyebrows that met over the nose in an inch-broad black band, but for the life of me I could not tell where.

"I don't know you," I said, handing him the whiskey. "What can I do for you?"

He took a gulp of the spirit raw, and shivered in spite of the suffocating heat.

"I've come back," he repeated; "and I was the King of Kafiristan—me and Dravot—crowned Kings we was! In this office we settled it—you setting there and giving us the books. I am Peachey—Peachey Taliaferro Carnehan, and you've been setting here ever since—O Lord!"

I was more than a little astonished, and expressed my feelings accordingly.

"It's true," said Carnehan, with a dry cackle, nursing his feet, which were wrapped in rags.

"True as gospel. Kings we were, with crowns upon our heads—me and Dravot—poor Dan—oh, poor, poor Dan, that would never take advice, not though I begged of him!"

"Take the whiskey," I said, "and take your own time. Tell me all you can recollect of everything from beginning to end. You got across the border on your camels. Dravot dressed as a mad priest and you his servant. Do you remember that?"

"I ain't mad—yet, but I shall be that way soon. Of course I remember. Keep looking at me, or maybe my words will go all to pieces. Keep looking at me in my eyes, and don't say anything."

I leaned forward and looked into his face as steadily as I could. He dropped one hand upon the table and I grasped it by the wrist. It was twisted like a bird's claw, and upon the back was a ragged, red, diamond-shaped scar.

"No, don't look there. Look at *me*," said Carnehan. "That comes afterwards, but for the Lord's sake don't distrack me! We left with that caravan, me and Dravot playing all sorts of antics to amuse the people we were with. Dravot used to make us laugh in the evenings when all the people was cooking their dinners—cooking their dinners, and . . . what did they do then? They lit little fires with sparks that went into Dravot's beard, and we all laughed—fit to die. Little red fires they was, going into Dravot's big red beard—so funny." His eyes left mine, and he smiled foolishly.

"You went as far as Jagdallak with that caravan," I said at a venture, "after you had lit those fires. To Jagdallak, where you turned off to try to get into Kafiristan."

"No, we didn't neither. What are you talking about? We turned off before Jagdallak, because we heard the roads was good. But they wasn't good enough for our two camels—mine and Dravot's. When we left the caravan, Dravot took off all his clothes and mine too, and said we would be heathen, because the Kafirs didn't allow Mohammedans to talk to them. So we dressed betwixt and between, and such a sight as Daniel Dravot I never saw yet nor expect to see again. He burned half his beard, and slung a sheep-skin over his shoulder, and shaved his head into patterns. He shaved mine, too, and made me wear outrageous things to look like a heathen. That was in a most mountaineous country, and our camels couldn't go along any more because of the mountains. They were tall and black, and coming home I saw them fight like wild goats—there are lots of goats in Kafiristan. And these mountains, they never keep still, no more than the goats. Always fighting they are, and don't let you sleep at night."

"Take some more whiskey," I said very slowly. "What did you and Daniel Dravot do when the camels could go no further because of the rough roads that led into Kafiristan?"

"What did which do? There was a party called Peachey Taliaferro Carnehan that was with Dravot. Shall I tell you about him? He died out there in the cold. Slap from the bridge fell old Peachey, turning and twisting in the air like a penny whirligig that you can sell to the Amir. No; they was two for three ha'pence, those whirligigs, or I am much mistaken and woeful sore . . . And then these camels were no use, and Peachey said to Dravot—'For the Lord's sake let's get out of this before our heads are chopped off,' and with that they killed the camels all among the mountains, not having anything in particular to eat, but first they took off the boxes with the guns and the ammunition, till two men came along driving four mules. Dravot up and dances in front of them, singing—'Sell me four mules.' Says the first man—'If you are rich enough to buy, you are rich enough to rob;' but before ever he could put his hand to his knife, Dravot breaks his neck over his knee, and the other party runs away. So Carnehan loaded the mules with the rifles that was taken off the camels, and together we starts forward into those bitter cold mountaineous parts, and never a road broader than the back of your hand."

He paused for a moment, while I asked him if he could remember the nature of the country through which he had journeyed.

"I am telling you as straight as I can, but my head isn't as good as it might be. They drove nails through it to make me hear better how Dravot died.

The country was mountaineous and the mules were most contrary, and the inhabitants was dispersed and solitary. They went up and up, and down and down, and that other party, Carnehan, was imploring of Dravot not to sing and whistle so loud, for fear of bringing down the tremenjus avalanches. But Dravot says that if a King couldn't sing it wasn't worth being King, and whacked the mules over the rump, and never took no heed for ten cold days. We came to a big level valley all among the mountains, and the mules were near dead, so we killed them, not having anything in special for them or us to eat. We sat upon the boxes, and played odd and even with the cartridges that was jolted out.

"Then ten men with bows and arrows ran down that valley, chasing twenty men with bows and arrows, and the row was tremenjus. They was fair men—fairer men than you or me—with yellow hair and remarkable well built. Says Dravot, unpacking the guns—'This is the beginning of the business. We'll fight for the ten men,' and with that he fires two rifles at the twenty men, and drops one of them at two hundred yards from the rock where he was sitting. The other men began to run, but Carnehan and Dravot sits on the boxes picking them off at all ranges, up and down the valley. Then we goes up to the ten men that had run across the snow too, and they fires a footy little arrow at us. Dravot he shoots above their heads, and they all falls down flat. Then he walks over them and kicks them, and then he lifts them up and shakes hands all round to make them friendly like. He calls them and gives them the boxes to carry, and waves his hand for all the world as though he was King already. They takes the boxes and him across the valley and up the hill into a pine wood on the top, where there was half a dozen big stone idols. Dravot he goes to the biggest—a fellow they call Imbra—and lays a rifle and a cartridge at his feet, rubbing his nose respectful with his own nose, patting him on the head, and saluting in front of it. He turns round to the men and nods his head, and says—'That's all right. I'm in the know too, and all these old jim-jams are my friends.' Then he opens his mouth and points down it, and when the first man brings him food, he says—'No;' and when the second man brings him food he says—'No;' but when one of the old priests and the boss of the village brings him food, he says—'Yes;' very haughty, and eats it slow. That was how we came to our first village, without any trouble, just as though we had tumbled from the skies. But we tumbled from one of those damned rope-bridges, you see, and—you couldn't expect a man to laugh much after that?"

"Take some more whiskey and go on," I said. "That was the first village you came into. How did you get to be King?"

"I wasn't King," said Carnehan. "Dravot he was the King, and a handsome man he looked with the gold crown on his head, and all. Him and the other party stayed in that village, and every morning Dravot sat by the side of old Imbra, and the people came and worshipped. That was Dravot's order. Then a lot of men came into the valley, and Carnehan and Dravot picks them off with the rifles before they knew where they was, and runs down into the valley and up again the other side and finds another village, same as the first one, and the people all falls down flat on their faces, and Dravot says—'Now what is the trouble between you two villages?' and the people points to a woman, as fair as you or me, that was carried off, and Dravot takes her back to the first village and counts up the dead—eight there was. For each dead man Dravot pours a little milk on the ground and waves his arms like a whirligig, and 'That's all right,' says he. Then he and Carnehan takes the big boss of each village by the arm and walks them down into the valley, and shows them how to scratch a line with a spear right down the valley, and gives each a sod of turf from both sides of the line. Then all the people comes down and shouts like the devil and all, and Dravot says—'Go and dig the land, and be fruitful and multiply,' which they did, though they didn't understand. Then we asks the names of things in their lingo—bread and water and fire and idols and such, and Dravot leads the priest of each village up to the idol, and says he must sit there and judge the people, and if anything goes wrong he is to be shot.

"Next week they was all turning up the land in the valley as quiet as bees and much prettier, and the priests heard all the complaints and told Dravot in dumb show what it was about. 'That's just the beginning,' says Dravot. 'They think we're Gods.' He and Carnehan picks out twenty good men and shows them how to click off a rifle, and form fours, and advance in line, and they was very pleased to do so, and clever to see the hang of it. Then he takes out his pipe and his baccy-pouch and leaves one at one village, and one at the other, and off we two goes to see what was to be done in the next valley. That was all rock, and there was a little village there, and Carnehan says—'Send 'em to the old valley to plant,' and takes 'em there and gives 'em some land that wasn't took before. They were a poor lot, and we blooded 'em with a kid before letting 'em into the new Kingdom. That was to impress the people, and then they settled down quiet, and Carnehan went back to Dravot, who had got into another valley, all snow and ice and most mountaineous. There was no people there, and the Army got afraid, so Dravot shoots one of them, and goes on till he finds some people in a village, and the Army explains that unless the people wants to be killed they had better not shoot their little matchlocks; for they had matchlocks. We makes friends with the priest, and I stays there alone with two of the Army, teaching the men how to drill; and a thundering big Chief comes across the snow with kettle-drums and horns twanging, because he heard there was a new God kicking about. Carnehan sights for the brown of the men half a mile across the snow and wings one of them. Then he sends a message to the Chief that, unless he wished to be killed, he must come and shake hands with me and leave his arms behind. The Chief comes alone first, and Carnehan shakes hands with him and whirls his arms about, same as Dravot used, and very much surprised that Chief was, and strokes my eyebrows. Then Carnehan goes alone to the Chief, and asks him in dumb show if he had an enemy he hated. 'I have,' says the Chief. So Carnehan weeds out the pick of his men, and sets the two of the Army to show them drill, and at the end of two weeks the men can manoeuvre about as well as Volunteers. So he marches with the Chief to a great big plain on the top of a mountain, and the Chief's men rushes into a village and takes it; we three Martinis firing into the brown of the enemy. So we took that village too, and I gives the Chief a rag from my coat and says, 'Occupy till I come;' which was scriptural. By way of a reminder, when me and the Army was eighteen hundred yards away, I drops a bullet near him standing on the snow, and all the people falls flat on their faces. Then I sends a letter to Dravot wherever he be by land or by sea."

At the risk of throwing the creature out of train, I interrupted—"How could you write a letter up yonder?"

"The letter?—Oh!—The letter! Keep looking at me between the eyes, please. It was a string-talk letter, that we'd learned the way of it from a blind beggar in the Punjab."

I remember that there had once come to the office a blind man with a knotted twig and a piece of string which he wound round the twig according to some cipher of his own. He could, after the lapse of days or hours, repeat the sentence which he had reeled up. He had reduced the alphabet to eleven primitive sounds; and he tried to teach me his method, but I could not understand.

"I sent that letter to Dravot," said Carnehan; "and told him to come back because this Kingdom was growing too big for me to handle, and then I struck for the first valley, to see how the priests were working. They called the village we took along with the Chief, Bashkai, and the first village we took, Er-Heb. The priests at Er-Heb was doing all right, but they had a lot of pending cases about land to show me, and some men from another village had been firing arrows at night. I went out and looked for that village, and fired four rounds at it from a thousand yards. That used all the cartridges I cared to spend, and I waited for Dravot, who had been away two or three months, and I kept my people quiet.

"One morning I heard the devil's own noise of drums and horns, and Dan Dravot marches down the hill with his Army and a tail of hundreds of men, and, which was the most amazing, a great gold crown on his head. 'My Gord, Carnehan,' says Daniel, 'this is a tremenjus business, and we've got the whole country as far as it's worth having. I am the son of Alexander by Queen Semiramis, and you're my younger brother and a God too! It's the biggest thing we've ever seen. I've been marching and fighting for six weeks with the Army, and every footy little village for fifty miles has come in rejoiceful; and more than that, I've got the key of the whole show, as you'll see, and I've got a crown for you! I told 'em to make two of 'em at a place called Shu, where the gold lies in the rock like suet in mutton. Gold I've seen, and turquoise I've kicked out of the cliffs, and there's garnets in the sands of the river, and here's a chunk of amber that a man brought me. Call up all the priests and, here, take your crown.'

"One of the men opens a black hair bag, and I slips the crown on. It was too small and too heavy, but I wore it for the glory. Hammered gold it was—five pound weight, like a hoop of a barrel.

" 'Peachey,' says Dravot, 'we don't want to fight no more. The Craft's the trick, so help me!' and he brings forward that same Chief that I left at Bashkai—Billy Fish we called him afterwards, because he was so like Billy

Fish that drove the big tank-engine at Mach on the Bolan in the old days. 'Shake hands with him,' says Dravot, and I shook hands and nearly dropped, for Billy Fish gave me the Grip. I said nothing, but tried him with the Fellow Craft Grip. He answers all right, and I tried the Master's Grip, but that was a slip. 'A Fellow Craft he is!' I says to Dan. 'Does he know the word?'—'He does,' says Dan, 'and all the priests know. It's a miracle! The Chiefs and the priests can work a Fellow Craft Lodge in a way that's very like ours, and they've cut the marks on the rocks, but they don't know the Third Degree, and they've come to find out. It's Gord's Truth. I've known these long years that the Afghans knew up to the Fellow Craft Degree, but this is a miracle. A God and a Grand-Master of the Craft am I, and a Lodge in the Third Degree I will open, and we'll raise the head priests and the Chiefs of the villages.'

" 'It's against all the law,' I says, 'holding a Lodge without warrant from any one; and you know we never held office in any Lodge.'

" 'It's a master-stroke o' policy,' says Dravot. 'It means running the country as easy as a four-wheeled bogie on a down grade. We can't stop to enquire now, or they'll turn against us. I've forty Chiefs at my heel, and passed and raised according to their merit they shall be. Billet these men on the villages, and see that we run up a Lodge of some kind. The temple of Imbra will do for the Lodge-room. The women must make aprons as you show them. I'll hold a levee of Chiefs to-night and Lodge to-morrow.'

"I was fair run off my legs, but I wasn't such a fool as not to see what a pull this Craft business gave us. I showed the priests' families how to make aprons of the degrees, but for Dravot's apron the blue border and marks was made of turquoise lumps on white hide, not cloth. We took a great square stone in the temple for the Master's chair, and little stones for the officers' chairs, and painted the black pavement with white squares, and did what we could to make things regular.

"At the levee which was held that night on the hillside with big bonfires, Dravot gives out that him and me were Gods and sons of Alexander, and Past Grand-Masters in the Craft, and was come to make Kafiristan a country where every man should eat in peace and drink in quiet, and specially obey us. Then the Chiefs come round to shake hands, and they were so hairy and white and fair it was just shaking hands with old friends. We gave them names according as they was like men we had known in India—Billy Fish, Holly Dilworth, Pikky Kergan, that was Bazar-master when I was at Mhow, and so on, and so on.

"*The* most amazing miracles was at Lodge next night. One of the old priests was watching us continuous, and I felt uneasy, for I knew we'd have to fudge the Ritual, and I didn't know what the men knew. The old priest was a stranger come in from beyond the village of Bashkai. The minute Dravot puts on the Master's apron that the girls had made for him, the priest fetches a whoop and a howl, and tries to overturn the stone that Dravot was sitting on. 'It's all up now,' I says. 'That comes of meddling with the Craft without warrant!' Dravot never winked an eye, not when ten priests took and tilted over the Grand-Master's chair—which was to say the stone of Imbra. The priest begins rubbing the bottom end of it to clear away the black dirt, and presently he shows all the other priests the Master's Mark, same as was on Dravot's apron, cut into the stone. Not even the priests of the temple of Imbra knew it was there. The old chap falls flat on his face at Dravot's feet and kisses 'em. 'Luck again,' says Dravot, across the Lodge to me; 'they say it's the missing Mark that no one could understand the why of. We're more than safe now.' Then he bangs the butt of his gun for a gavel and says: 'By virtue of the authority vested in me by my own right hand and the help of Peachey, I declare myself Grand-Master of all Freemasonry in Kafiristan in this the Mother Lodge o' the country, and King of Karifistan equally with Peachey!' At that he puts on his crown and I puts on mine—I was doing Senior Warden—and we opens the Lodge in most ample form. It was a amazing miracle! The priests moved in Lodge through the first two degrees almost without telling, as if the memory was coming back to them. After that, Peachey and Dravot raised such as was worthy—high priests and Chiefs of far-off villages. Billy Fish was the first, and I can tell you we scared the soul out of him. It was not in any way according to Ritual, but it served our turn. We didn't raise more than ten of the biggest men, because we didn't want to make the Degree common. And they was clamouring to be raised.

" 'In another six months,' says Dravot, 'we'll hold another Communication, and see how you are working.' Then he asks them about their villages, and learns that they was fighting one against the other, and were sick and tired of it. And when they wasn't doing that they was fighting with the Mohammedans. 'You can fight those when they come into our country,' says Dravot. 'Tell off every tenth man of your tribes for a Frontier guard, and send two hundred at a time to this valley to be drilled. Nobody is going to be shot or speared any more so long as he does well, and I know that you won't cheat me, because you're white people—sons of Alexander—and not like common, black Mohammedans. You are *my* people, and by God,' says he, running off into English at the end—'I'll make a damned fine Nation of you, or I'll die in the making!'

"I can't tell all we did for the next six months, because Dravot did a lot I couldn't see the hang of, and he learned their lingo in a way I never could. My work was to help the people plough, and now and again go out with some of the Army and see what the other villages were doing, and make 'em throw rope-bridges across the ravines which cut up the country horrid. Dravot was very kind to me, but when he walked up and down in the pine wood pulling that bloody red beard of his with both fists I knew he was thinking plans I could not advise about, and I just waited for orders.

"But Dravot never showed me disrespect before the people. They were afraid of me and the Army, but they loved Dan. He was the best of friends with the priests and the Chiefs; but any one could come across the hills with a complaint, and Dravot would hear him out fair, and call four priests together and say what was to be done. He used to call in Billy Fish from Bashkai, and Pikky Kergan from Shu, and an old Chief we called Kafuzelum—it was like enough to his real name—and hold councils with 'em when there was any fighting to be done in small villages. That was his Council of War, and the four priests of Bashkai, Shu, Khawak, and Madora was his Privy Council. Between the lot of 'em they sent me, with forty men and twenty rifles, and sixty men carrying turquoises, into the Ghorband country to buy those hand-made Martini rifles, that come out of the Amir's workshops at Kabul, from one of the Amir's Herati regiments that would have sold the very teeth out of their mouths for turquoises.

"I stayed in Ghorband a month, and gave the Governor there the pick of my baskets for hush-money, and bribed the Colonel of the regiment some more, and, between the two and the tribes-people, we got more than a hundred hand-made Martinis, a hundred good Kohat Jezails that'll throw to six hundred yards, and forty man-loads of very bad ammunition for the rifles. I came back with what I had, and distributed 'em among the men that the Chiefs sent in to me to drill. Dravot was too busy to attend to those things, but the old Army that we first made helped me, and we turned out five hundred men that could drill, and two hundred that knew how to hold arms pretty straight. Even those corkscrewed, hand-made guns was a miracle to them. Dravot talked big about powder-shops and factories, walking up and down in the pine wood when the winter was coming on.

" 'I won't make a Nation,' says he; 'I'll make an Empire! These men aren't niggers; they're English! Look at their eyes—look at their mouths. Look at the way they stand up. They sit on chairs in their own houses. They're the Lost Tribes, or something like it, and they've grown to be English. I'll take a census in the spring if the priests don't get frightened. There must be a fair two million of 'em in these hills. The villages are full o' little children. Two million people—two hundred and fifty thousand fighting men—and all English! They only want the rifles and a little drilling. Two hundred and fifty thousand men ready to cut in on Russia's right flank when she tries for India! Peachey, man,' he says, chewing his beard in great hunks, 'we shall be Emperors—Emperors of the Earth! Rajah Brooke will be a suckling to us. I'll treat with the Viceroy on equal terms. I'll ask him to send me twelve picked English—twelve that I know of—to help us govern a bit. There's Mackray, Sergeant-pensioner at Segowli—many's the good dinner he's given me, and his wife a pair of trousers. There's Donkin, the Warder of Tounghoo Jail; there's hundreds that I could lay my hand on if I was in India. The Viceroy shall do it for me; I'll send a man through in the spring for those men, and I'll write for a dispensation from the Grand Lodge for what I've done as Grand-Master. That—and all the Sniders that'll be thrown out when the native troops in India take up the Martini. They'll be worn smooth, but they'll do for fighting in these hills. Twelve English, a hundred thousand Sniders run through the Amir's country in driblets—I'd be content with twenty thousand in one year—and we'd be an Empire. When everything was shipshape, I'd hand over the crown—this crown I'm wearing now—to Queen Victoria on my knees, and she'd say: "Rise up, Sir Daniel Dravot." Oh, it's big! It's big, I tell you! But there's so much to be done in every place—Bashkai, Khawak, Shu, and everywhere else.'

" 'What is it?' I says. 'There are no more men coming in to be drilled this autumn. Look at those fat, black clouds. They're bringing the snow.'

" 'It isn't that,' says Daniel, putting his hand very hard on my shoulder; 'and I don't wish to say anything that's against you, for no other living man would have followed me and made me what I am as you have done. You're a first-class Commander-in-Chief, and the people know you; but—it's a big country, and somehow you can't help me, Peachey, in the way I want to be helped.'

" 'Go to your blasted priests, then!' I said, and I was sorry when I made that remark, but it did hurt me sore to find Daniel talking so superior when I'd drilled all the men, and done all he told me.

" 'Don't let's quarrel, Peachey,' says Daniel, without cursing. 'You're a King too, and the half of this Kingdom is yours; but can't you see, Peachey, we want cleverer men than us now—three or four of 'em, that we can scatter about for our Deputies. It's a hugeous great State, and I can't always tell the right thing to do, and I haven't time for all I want to do, and here's the winter coming on, and all.' He put half his beard into his mouth, all red like the gold of his crown.

" 'I'm sorry, Daniel,' says I. 'I've done all I could. I've drilled the men and shown the people how to stack their oats better; and I've brought in those tinware rifles from Ghorband—but I know what you're driving at. I take it Kings always feel oppressed that way.'

" 'There's another thing too,' says Dravot, walking up and down. 'The winter's coming, and these people won't be giving much trouble, and if they do we can't move about. I want a wife.'

" 'For Gord's sake leave the women alone!' I says. 'We've both got all the work we can, though I *am* a fool. Remember the Contrack, and keep clear o' women.'

" 'The Contrack only lasted till such time as we was Kings; and Kings we have been these months past,' says Dravot, weighing his crown in his hand. 'You go get a wife too, Peachey—a nice, strappin', plump girl that'll keep you warm in the winter. They're prettier than English girls, and we can take the pick of 'em. Boil 'em once or twice in hot water, and they'll come out like chicken and ham.'

" 'Don't tempt me!' I says. 'I will not have any dealings with a woman not till we are a dam' side more settled than we are now. I've been doing the work o' two men, and you've been doing the work o' three. Let's lie off a bit, and see if we can get some better tobacco from Afghan country and run in some good liquor; but no women.'

" 'Who's talking o' *women*?' says Dravot. 'I said *wife*—a Queen to breed a King's son for the King. A Queen out of the strongest tribe, that'll make them your blood-brothers, and that'll lie by your side and tell you all the people thinks about you and their own affairs. That's what I want.'

" 'Do you remember that Bengali woman I kept at Mogul Serai when I was a plate-layer?' says I. 'A fat lot o' good she was to me. She taught me the lingo and one or two other things; but what happened? She ran away with the Station-Master's servant and half my month's pay. Then she turned up at Dadur Junction in tow of a half-caste, and had the impidence to say I was her husband—all among the drivers in the running-shed too!'

" 'We've done with that,' says Dravot; 'these women are whiter than you or me, and a Queen I will have for the winter months.'

" 'For the last time o' asking, Dan, do *not*,' I says. 'It'll only bring us harm. The Bible says that Kings ain't to waste their strength on women, 'specially when they've got a new raw Kingdom to work over.'

" 'For the last time of answering, I will,' said Dravot, and he went away through the pine-trees looking like a big red devil, the sun being on his crown and beard and all.

"But getting a wife was not as easy as Dan thought. He put it before the Council, and there was no answer till Billy Fish said that he'd better ask the girls. Dravot damned them all round. 'What's wrong with me?' he shouts, standing by the idol Imbra. 'Am I a dog or am I not enough of a man for your wenches? Haven't I put the shadow of my hand over this country? Who stopped the last Afghan raid?' It was me really, but Dravot was too angry to remember. 'Who bought your guns? Who repaired the bridges? Who's the Grand-Master of the sign cut in the stone?' says he, and he thumped his hand on the block that he used to sit on in Lodge, and at Council, which opened like Lodge always. Billy Fish said nothing, and no more did the others. 'Keep your hair on, Dan,' said I; 'and ask the girls. That's how it's done at Home, and these people are quite English.'

" 'The marriage of the King is a matter of State,' says Dan, in a white-hot rage, for he could feel, I hope, that he was going against his better mind. He walked out of the Council-room, and the others sat still, looking at the ground.

" 'Billy Fish,' says I to the Chief of Bashkai, 'what's the difficulty here? A straight answer to a true friend.'

" 'You know,' says Billy Fish. 'How should a man tell you who knows everything? How can daughters of men marry Gods or Devils? It's not proper.'

"I remembered something like that in the Bible; but if, after seeing us as long as they had, they still believed we were Gods, it wasn't for me to undeceive them.

" 'A God can do anything,' says I. 'If the King is fond of a girl he'll not let her die.'

" 'She'll have to,' said Billy Fish. 'There are all sorts of Gods and Devils in these mountains, and now and again a girl marries one of them and isn't seen any more. Besides, you two know the Mark cut in the stone. Only the Gods know that. We thought you were men till you showed the sign of the Master.'

"I wished then that we had explained about the loss of the genuine secrets of a Master-Mason at the first go-off; but I said nothing. All that night there was a blowing of horns in a little dark temple half-way down the hill, and I heard a girl crying fit to die. One of the priests told us that she was being prepared to marry the King.

" 'I'll have no nonsense of that kind,' says Dan. 'I don't want to interfere with your customs, but I'll take my own wife.'

" 'The girl's a little bit afraid,' says the priest. 'She thinks she's going to die, and they are a-heartening of her up down in the temple.'

" 'Hearten her very tender, then,' says Dravot, 'or I'll hearten you with the butt of a gun so you'll never want to be heartened again.' He licked his lips, did Dan, and stayed up walking about more than half the night, thinking of the wife that he was going to get in the morning. I wasn't any means comfortable, for I knew that dealings with a woman in foreign parts, though you was a crowned King twenty times over, could not but be risky. I got up very early in the morning while Dravot was asleep, and I saw the priests talking together in whispers, and the Chiefs talking together too, and they looked at me out of the corners of their eyes.

" 'What is up, Fish?' I says to the Bashkai man, who was wrapped up in his furs and looking splendid to behold.

" 'I can't rightly say,' says he; 'but if you can make the King drop all this nonsense about marriage, you'll be doing him and me and yourself a great service.'

" 'That I do believe,' says I. 'But sure, you know, Billy, as well as me, having fought against and for us, that the King and me are nothing more than two of the finest men that God Almighty ever made. Nothing more, I do assure you.'

" 'That may be,' says Billy Fish, 'and yet I should be sorry if it was.' He sinks his head upon his great fur cloak for a minute and thinks. 'King,' says he, 'be you man or God or Devil, I'll stick by you to-day. I have twenty of my men with me, and they will follow me. We'll go to Bashkai until the storm blows over.'

"A little snow had fallen in the night, and everything was white except the greasy fat clouds that blew down and down from the north. Dravot came out with his crown on his head, swinging his arms and stamping his feet, and looking more pleased than Punch.

" 'For the last time, drop it, Dan,' says I in a whisper; 'Billy Fish here says that there will be a row.'

" 'A row among my people!' says Dravot. 'Not much. Peachey, you're a fool not to get a wife too. Where's the girl?' says he with a voice as loud as the braying of a jackass. 'Call up all the Chiefs and priests, and let the Emperor see if his wife suits him.'

"There was no need to call any one. They were all there leaning on their guns and spears round the clearing in the centre of the pine wood. A lot of priests went down to the little temple to bring up the girl, and the horns blew fit to wake the dead. Billy Fish saunters round and gets as close to Daniel as he could, and behind him stood his twenty men with matchlocks. Not a man of them under six feet. I was next to Dravot, and behind me was twenty men of the regular Army. Up comes the girl, and a strapping wench she was, covered with silver and turquoises, but white as death, and looking back every minute at the priests.

" 'She'll do,' said Dan, looking her over. 'What's to be afraid of, lass? Come and kiss me.' He puts his arm round her. She shuts her eyes, gives a bit of a squeak, and down goes her face in the side of Dan's flaming red beard.

" 'The slut's bitten me!' says he, clapping his hand to his neck, and, sure enough, his hand was red with blood. Billy Fish and two of his matchlock-men catches hold of Dan by the shoulders and drags him into the Bashkai lot, while the priests howls in their lingo—'Neither God nor Devil, but a man!' I was all taken aback, for a priest cut at me in front, and the Army behind began firing into the Bashkai men.

" 'God A'mighty!' says Dan. 'What is the meaning o' this?'

" 'Come back! Come away!' says Billy Fish. 'Ruin and Mutiny is the matter. We'll break for Bashkai if we can.'

"I tried to give some sort of orders to my men—the men o' the regular Army—but it was no use, so I fired into the brown of 'em with an English Martini and drilled three beggars in a line. The valley was full of shouting, howling creatures, and every soul was shrieking, 'Not a God nor a Devil, but only a man!' The Bashkai troops stuck to Billy Fish all they were worth, but their matchlocks wasn't half as good as the Kabul breech-loaders, and four of them dropped. Dan was bellowing like a bull, for he was very wrathy; and Billy Fish had a hard job to prevent him running out at the crowd.

" 'We can't stand,' says Billy Fish. 'Make a run for it down the valley! The whole place is against us.' The matchlock-men ran, and we went down the valley in spite of Dravot. He was swearing horrible and crying out he was a King. The priests rolled great stones on us, and the regular Army fired hard, and there wasn't more than six men, not counting Dan, Billy Fish, and Me, that came down to the bottom of the valley alive.

"Then they stopped firing, and the horns in the temple blew again. 'Come away—for Gord's sake come away!' says Billy Fish. 'They'll send runners out to all the villages before ever we get to Bashkai. I can protect you there, but I can't do anything now.'

"My own notion is that Dan began to go mad in his head from that hour. He stared up and down like a stuck pig. Then he was all for walking back alone and killing the priests with his bare hands; which he could have done. 'An Emperor am I,' says Daniel, 'and next year I shall be a Knight of the Queen.'

" 'All right, Dan,' says I; 'but come along now while there's time.'

" 'It's your fault,' says he, 'for not looking after your Army better. There was mutiny in the midst, and you didn't know—you damned engine-driving, plate-laying, missionary's-pass-hunting hound!' He sat upon a rock and called me every foul name he could lay tongue to. I was too heart-sick to care, though it was all his foolishness that brought the smash.

" 'I'm sorry, Dan,' says I, 'but there's no accounting for natives. This business is our Fifty-Seven. Maybe we'll make something out of it yet, when we've got to Bashkai.'

" 'Let's get to Bashkai, then,' says Dan, 'and, by God, when I come back here again I'll sweep the valley so there isn't a bug in a blanket left!'

"We walked all that day, and all that night Dan was stumping up and down on the snow, chewing his beard and muttering to himself.

" 'There's no hope o' getting clear,' said Billy Fish. 'The priests will have sent runners to the villages to say that you are only men. Why didn't you stick on as Gods till things was more settled? I'm a dead man,' says Billy

Fish, and he throws himself down on the snow and begins to pray to his Gods.

"Next morning we was in a cruel bad country—all up and down, no level ground at all, and no food either. The six Bashkai men looked at Billy Fish hungry-way as if they wanted to ask something, but they said never a word. At noon we came to the top of a flat mountain all covered with snow, and when we climbed up into it, behold, there was an Army in position waiting in the middle!

" 'The runners have been very quick,' says Billy Fish, with a little bit of a laugh. 'They are waiting for us.'

"Three or four men began to fire from the enemy's side, and a chance shot took Daniel in the calf of the leg. That brought him to his senses. He looks across the snow at the Army, and sees the rifles that we had brought into the country.

" 'We're done for,' says he. 'They are Englishmen, these people,—and it's my blasted nonsense that has brought you to this. Get back, Billy Fish, and take your men away; you've done what you could, and now cut for it. Carnehan,' says he, 'shake hands with me and go along with Billy. Maybe they won't kill you. I'll go and meet 'em alone. It's me that did it. Me, the King!'

" 'Go!' says I. 'Go to Hell, Dan. I'm with you here. Billy Fish, you clear out, and we two will meet those folk.'

" 'I'm a Chief,' says Billy Fish, quite quiet. 'I stay with you. My men can go.'

"The Bashkai fellows didn't wait for a second word, but ran off; and Dan and Me and Billy Fish walked across to where the drums were drumming and the horns were horning. It was cold—awful cold. I've got that cold in the back of my head now. There's a lump of it there."

The punkah-coolies had gone to sleep. Two kerosene lamps were blazing in the office, and the perspiration poured down my face and splashed on the blotter as I leaned forward. Carnehan was shivering, and I feared that his mind might go. I wiped my face, took a fresh grip of the piteously mangled hands, and said: "What happened after that?"

The momentary shift of my eyes had broken the clear current.

"What was you pleased to say?" whined Carnehan. "They took them without any sound. Not a little whisper all along the snow, not though the King knocked down the first man that set hand on him—not though old Peachey fired his last cartridge into the brown of 'em. Not a single solitary sound did those swines make. They just closed up tight, and I tell you their furs stunk. There was a man called Billy Fish, a good friend of us all, and they cut his throat, Sir, then and there, like a pig; and the King kicks up the bloody snow and says: 'We've had a dashed fine run for our money. What's coming next?' But Peachey, Peachey Taliaferro, I tell you, Sir, in confidence as betwixt two friends, he lost his head, Sir. No, he didn't neither. The King lost his head, so he did, all along o' one of those cunning rope-bridges. Kindly let me have the paper-cutter, Sir. It tilted this way. They marched him a mile across that snow to a rope-bridge over a ravine with a river at the bottom. You may have seen such. They prodded him behind like an ox. 'Damn your eyes!' says the King. 'D'you suppose I can't die like a gentleman?' He turns to Peachey—Peachey that was crying like a child. 'I've brought you to this, Peachey,' says he. 'Brought you out of your happy life to be killed in Kafiristan, where you was late Commander-in-Chief of the Emperor's forces. Say you forgive me, Peachey.'—'I do,' says Peachey. 'Fully and freely do I forgive you, Dan.'—'Shake hands, Peachey,' says he. 'I'm going now.' Out he goes, looking neither right nor left, and when he was plumb in the middle of those dizzy dancing ropes, 'Cut, you beggars,' he shouts; and they cut, and old Dan fell, turning round and round and round, twenty thousand miles, for he took half an hour to fall till he struck the water, and I could see his body caught on a rock with the gold crown close beside.

"But do you know what they did to Peachey between two pine-trees? They crucified him, Sir, as Peachey's hands will show. They used wooden pegs for his hands and his feet; and he didn't die. He hung there and screamed, and they took him down next day, and said it was a miracle that he wasn't dead. They took him down—poor old Peachey that hadn't done them any harm—that hadn't done them any—"

He rocked to and fro and wept bitterly, wiping his eyes with the back of his scarred hands and moaning like a child for some ten minutes.

"They was cruel enough to feed him up in the temple, because they said he was more of a God than old Daniel that was a man. Then they turned him out on the snow, and told him to go home, and Peachey came home in about a year, begging along the roads quite safe; for Daniel Dravot he walked before and said: 'Come along, Peachey. It's a big thing we're doing.' The mountains they danced at night, and the mountains they tried to fall on Peachey's head, but Dan he held up his hand, and Peachey came along bent double. He never let go of Dan's hand, and he never let go of Dan's head. They gave it to him as a present in the temple, to remind him not to come again, and though the crown was pure gold, and Peachey was starving, never would Peachey sell the same. You knew Dravot, Sir! You knew Right Worshipful Brother Dravot! Look at him now!"

He fumbled in the mass of rags round his bent waist; brought out a black horsehair bag embroidered with silver thread; and shook therefrom on to my table—the dried, withered head of Daniel Dravot! The morning sun that had long been paling the lamps struck the red beard and blind, sunken eyes; struck, too, a heavy circlet of gold studded with raw turquoises, that Carnehan placed tenderly on the battered temples.

"You be'old now," said Carnehan, "the Emperor in his 'abit as he lived—the King of Kafiristan with his crown upon his head. Poor old Daniel that was a monarch once!"

I shuddered, for, in spite of defacements manifold, I recognised the head of the man of Marwar Junction. Carnehan rose to go. I attempted to stop him. He was not fit to walk abroad. "Let me take away the whiskey, and give me a little money," he gasped. "I was a King once. I'll go to the Deputy Commissioner and ask to set in the Poorhouse till I get my health. No, thank you, I can't wait till you get a carriage for me. I've urgent private affairs—in the south—at Marwar."

He shambled out of the office and departed in the direction of the Deputy Commissioner's house. That day at noon I had occasion to go down the blinding hot Mall, and I saw a crooked man crawling along the white dust of the roadside, his hat in his hand, quavering dolorously after the fashion of street-singers at Home. There was not a soul in sight, and he was out of all possible earshot of the houses. And he sang through his nose, turning his head from right to left:—

> "The Son of Man goes forth to war,
>   A golden crown to gain;
> His blood-red banner streams afar—
>   Who follows in his train?"

I waited to hear no more, but put the poor wretch into my carriage and drove him off to the nearest missionary for eventual transfer to the Asylum. He repeated the hymn twice while he was with me, whom he did not in the least recognise, and I left him singing it to the missionary.

Two days later I enquired after his welfare of the Superintendent of the Asylum.

"He was admitted suffering from sun-stroke. He died early yesterday morning," said the Superintendent. "Is it true that he was half an hour bareheaded in the sun at midday?"

"Yes," said I, "but do you happen to know if he had anything upon him by any chance when he died?"

"Not to my knowledge," said the Superintendent.

And there the matter rests.

On Kipling

Both idolized and execrated in the first half of his career, given the Nobel Prize in 1907, and virtually ignored by the literary-intellectual world during the last ten years of his life, Rudyard Kipling (1865–1936) has since 1941 compelled the attention if not the entire approval of critics as diverse as T. S. Eliot, George Orwell, C. S. Lewis, Lionel Trilling, Edmund Wilson, and W. H. Auden and of many analysts, biographers, and intellectual historians. All have registered their ambivalence towards Kipling: Eliot refused him the title of poet but paid tribute to his powers as a versifier; Orwell thought that "Kipling sold out to the British governing class, not financially but emotionally," although he had the advantage of trying "to imagine what action and responsibility are like"; Trilling insisted that "Kipling belongs irretrievably to our past" and patronized him, but twenty years later asked Andrew Rutherford to note that if he were to write the essay anew that he would do so "less censuriously and with more affectionate admiration." In fact, except for uncritical devotees and wholehearted opponents, everyone who reads Kipling not only feels a bit shamefaced about it but rather ashamed of being ashamed.

A major reason for their difficulty with Kipling is that he is neither quite in nor out of the world we comprehend. His world—for most of his readers this means nineteenth-century India, where he was born and to which, after his schooling, he returned at seventeen—was dying throughout the first four and a half decades of this century, and it vanished irrecoverably with the advent of Indian independence in 1950. The Anglo-Indians who governed the country and staffed its English-oriented cultural institutions were not pioneers but an occupying force, and Kipling's portrayal, like the later and less sympathetic account by E. M. Forster in *A Passage to India* (1921), emphasized the psychological and social strains caused by their position: isolation, homesickness, being hated or ignored by the native population, subjection to what seemed to be the whims of distant policy-makers, overwork. Anglo-Indian children were doubly exiled: first from England (Kipling and many others first spoke and even thought in the language of native nurses) and then from their families when they were sent to England to escape the rigors of Indian climate and disease and, more important, to learn to be English gentlemen rather than to be absorbed into the culture in which they were born. Kipling's public school Westward Ho! taught him something about the duties of a gentleman, a good deal about the major English writers and American humorists like Bret Harte, Mark Twain, and Joel Chandler Harris, and still more about the ways of the world: discipline, punishment, incompetence, and the delights of workmanship and the companionship of one's own kind.

When he returned to India in 1882 to become half of the editorial staff of the *Civil and Military Gazette* at Lahore (where his father was principal of the school and curator of the art museum), he worked ten to fifteen hours a day, often in conditions like those described in *The Man Who Would Be King,* traversing the whole of society, from the viceroy to the opium den. In 1885, he began to write, as filler, the sketches which were collected in *Plain Tales from the Hills* and the verses which became *Departmental Ditties.* Two years later he was promoted to the *Pioneer,* a larger newspaper. Informed of a plan to buy syndicated stories by well-known authors, he offered to furnish stories himself, pleased with the chance to expand from "mere twelve-hundred Plain Tales jammed into rigid frames" to "three- or five-thousand word cartoons once a week" (*Something of Myself,* p. 77). In 1889, with eight books published, he left India. For a time he traveled in the colonies; for a time, after his marriage in 1892 to an American girl, Caroline Balastier, he lived in Vermont until a quarrel with a brother-in-law led to his return to England, where he settled for the rest of his life. He traveled, received honors, and mourned the death in World War I of his only son, but always he wrote: more than fifty titles in verse and prose, not counting numerous collected editions and anthologies, before his death in 1936. He was buried in Poet's Corner, Westminster Abbey, honored by the Establishment—the Prime Minister, military men, and scholars. No man of letters served as a pallbearer.

The critics have since come to bury and to praise. To most of them

Kipling's racial and political views are abhorrent, and only a little less so are some of the excesses in the diction and sentiment of most of his verse and a good deal of his prose. His view of imperialism seems jingoistic, his view of discipline fascist or sadistic, his acceptance of the fact of cruelty callous or masochistic, his accuracy of observation the mere facility of the trained reporter. Some of these judgments are just, but many are based on misunderstanding: Orwell pointed out that the "lesser breeds without the law" in "Recessional" were not black or brown but German, and that far from being an imperialistic paean, the poem was a warning to the British to keep their sense of purpose and discipline and to remember that excessive pride leads to downfall. And while "the white man's burden" may have rested on the natives, it also weighed down the whites. In *The Man Who Would Be King,* Dravot and Carnehan are vulgar and deluded adventurers with small regard for human life, but they reach some understanding of their errors and their fates, and pay with dignity the price they have always known might be exacted. Moreover, Kipling writes about things that interest everyone: how things work, how society works, what honor, fidelity, and dignity mean, and, as C. S. Lewis has pointed out, what it means to be a member of an Inner Group, a profession, a craft—groups without which civilization would be impossible and within which much of man's most significant experience occurs, however little other novelists treat of it.

For Kipling, of course, the group was more than a source of experience: it was a source of value because, as Alan Sandison says, it protected the individual against the kind of psychic disintegration portrayed by Conrad and by many later novelists. Kipling's experience of India, with its many castes, customs, and moralities, forced him to consider "why society still continued to hang together," and his solution, the idea of Law (Noel Annan equates it with "culture"), places him with modern sociologists like Durkheim and Weber rather than with philosophically and ethically oriented thinkers more characteristic of nineteenth-century England. The possibility of collapse, both social and personal, lies behind many of his stories and poems; like William Butler Yeats, with whom he is almost exactly contemporary, he had a peculiar point of vantage, straddling two centuries and two cultures, which enabled him to portray the malaise of a society whose certainties were collapsing in the face of increasing amounts of detail—scientific, political, psychological, anthropological.

Yeats chose the visionary path, constructing a vast and comprehensive system with which to explain each human life and all human history. Kipling was consciously less ambitious, rejecting the role of prophet or adept because "I have seen too much evil and sorrow and wreck of good minds on the road to Endor to take one step along that perilous track" (*Something of Myself,* p. 232). Instead, he believed, the individual could attain self-respect and a kind of secular salvation by mastery of one's craft. Like that of Ernest Hemingway, who resembles Kipling in a startling number of ways, this philosophy has obvious limitations, since it focuses on means rather than ends; but it has the advantage for the writer of fiction of focusing on the immediate and concrete—a major tenet of theorists who ignored Kipling and praised Hemingway. Moreover, this philosophy raises the question of the possibility of heroism in a world without coherent and established values, and Hemingway's bullfighters and Kipling's subalterns and loafers become heroic because they remain true to essentially private and self-established conceptions of themselves. The modern hero is lonely in a way that even Beowulf is not, for Beowulf at least had the support of, was in fact the embodiment of, the values of his society. Dravot and Carnehan die unheralded; Yeats' horsemen and artisans transcend rather than transform a nation of shopkeepers who can only "pray and save"; Hemingway's Maera is pelted with boos and cushions; and F. Scott Fitzgerald's Jay Gatsby is buried with only three mourners, his epitaph "The poor son of a bitch." Being private, the dream cannot be passed on: Dravot cannot found a dynasty to perpetuate his idea and his accomplishment because of the very nature of his success; the dream of Gatsby, the self-created son of God who sprang from his own Platonic conception of himself, must inevitably wither because it is wedded to the perishable flesh of Daisy Fay Buchanan.

One could draw numerous other parallels between Kipling and modern writers now considered great—with Conrad, especially in *Heart of Darkness,* for example, or, as Randall Jarrell does, with Byron and Hemingway—but while these comparisons show that Kipling's themes are complex, subtle, and specifically modern in ways that are not generally realized, it is not his abstract ideas that draw readers and critics, willingly or not, to his work. Rather, it is the tale, which, as Sir Philip Sidney wrote, "holdeth children from play, and olde men from the Chimney corner." Lionel Trilling has testified to his youthful excitement at discovering *The Jungle Book,* "my first independently chosen and avidly read book, my first literary discovery," and long before I heard of Trilling I had read the same book, with mounting excitement and absorption and a desire to prolong the experience of a fascinating, satisfying, and coherent world. Mowgli's farewell to the wolf pack was and is obviously true and necessary in a way that happy endings of children's books are not, an acknowledgment and acceptance of the realities of the world that parallels Prospero's farewell to Ariel in *The Tempest.* Trilling felt that Kipling was a writer for youth; he focuses upon Kipling's conception of society. Feeling, perhaps, that Kipling was pre-Jamesian in spirit if not chronology, he says no more about Kipling's art. But as Sidney insisted four centuries ago and modern critics like Wayne Booth and Robert Scholes are helping us to realize anew, the craft of fiction involves far more than precepts, however useful.

Many of the experiences ascribed to Kipling's characters—for example, the narrator's encounter with the loafer who asked him to carry a message—had happened to Kipling, and it is also true that reporting helped to sharpen his eye for telling detail. The dictum, "Take nothing for granted if you can check it," is good advice to the reporter, but the corollary, "Even though that seem waste-work, and has nothing to do with the essentials of things" (*Something of Myself,* p. 235), resembles in intention and sometimes in effect the theory of Hemingway, another reporter turned story-teller, that a writer could leave something out only if he knew it, because that knowledge would support and strengthen the details left in. And it was the artist rather than the ephemeral journalist who experimented with the aural and visual effects of words to "hold the ear" or "draw the eye," who read his work aloud, over and over again, to remove "the grosser superflui-ties" (*Something of Myself,* p. 78), and who learned "that a tale from which pieces have been raked out is like a fire that has been poked. One does not know that the operation has been performed, but everyone feels the effect. Note, though, that the excised stuff must have been honestly written for inclusion" (p. 224).

Moreover, it was Kipling the artist who learned the necessity "to think in another man's skin" (p. 226) in order to create rather than merely record the experiences of the newspaperman who narrates the tale and provides the framework—which, C. E. Carrington points out, was characteristic of Kipling's method and which almost inevitably contrasted with the tale it contained. The newspaperman is cynical, knowing or semi-knowing, tough or pseudo-tough, and his sense of superiority and incredulity distances the reader from the two loafers and makes us accept his valuation of them until Carnehan observes, "and you've been setting here ever since—O Lord!" Knowledge and authority then pass to Peachey, and his highly complex, contrasting narrative styles, within the larger framework, are technically as intricate as anything devised by Joseph Conrad, who was called by James the master of doing things in the way that took the most doing. In fact, Conrad's manipulation of point of view in *Heart of Darkness,* another tale of a white man who got himself adored, closely resembles Kipling's.

Dravot's course is the negative image of Conrad's Kurtz, however. He begins without the "fine sentiments" Conrad finds useless, but conceives "an idea and an unselfish belief in the idea" which develop as he acquires a sense of his own destiny and that of his people far beyond the original looter's motive. Yet, like Kurtz, he is finally a victim of his own ludicrous conception of himself turned respectable, his acts sanctioned by the sources of authority he had so long ignored. Trailing reluctantly along, his brows perpetually joined in worry, Peachey—like Marlow in *Heart of Darkness* and Nick Carraway in *The Great Gatsby*—is left to tell the tale, making it credible by his colloquial, sometimes comic understatement and his own surprise not only at the events but at himself. He remains faithful in the end to another man's conception of himself, thereby finding his own identity.

Textual Note:

First published in *The Phantom 'Rickshaw and Other Tales,* 1888 (India); first published in England and the United States in 1890; in vol. V of *The Writings in Prose and Verse of Rudyard Kipling* (New York: Charles Scribner's Sons, 1897), for which Kipling read proof and which he revised. The text printed here follows the reissue of this volume, as vol. IV, in the 1925 reprinting.

Resources for further study:

Kim, generally regarded as Kipling's only successful novel, and the various volumes of short stories, now regarded as his most significant achievement, are widely reprinted.

BIBLIOGRAPHICAL:

Primary: LIVINGSTON, FLORA V. *Bibliography of the Works of Rudyard Kipling.* New York: Burt Franklin, 1968. Originally published in 1927, it ends with 1926.
STEWART, JAMES MCG. *Rudyard Kipling: A Bibliographical Catalogue,* A. W. Yeats, ed. Toronto: Dalhousie University Press and University of Toronto Press, 1965.

Secondary: GERBER, HELMUT E., and EDWARD LAUTERBACH. "Rudyard Kipling: An Annotated Bibliography of Writings About Him," *English Fiction in Transition,* 3, Nos. 3, 4, 5 (1960), 1–235.
LAUTERBACH, EDWARD S. "An Annotated Bibliography of Writings About Rudyard Kipling: First Supplement," *English Literature in Transition* (new title of *EFT*), 8, Nos. 3, 4 (1965), 136–241.

BIOGRAPHICAL:

CARRINGTON, C. E. *The Life of Rudyard Kipling.* Garden City, N.Y.: Doubleday & Company, Inc., 1955.
KIPLING, RUDYARD. *Something of Myself for My Friends Known and Unknown.* Garden City, N.Y.: Doubleday, Doran and Co., Inc., 1937.

SELECTED CRITICAL STUDIES:

BROOKS, CLEANTH, and ROBERT PENN WARREN. *The Scope of Fiction.* New York: Appleton-Century-Crofts, 1960. See pp. 29–31.
CORNELL, LOUIS L. *Kipling in India.* New York: St. Martin's Press, 1966. A study of Kipling's literary apprenticeship.
DOBREE, BONAMY. *Rudyard Kipling: Realist and Fabulist.* London: Oxford University Press, 1967.
FUSSELL, PAUL, JR. "Irony, Freemasonry and Humane Ethics in *The Man Who Would Be King,*" *ELH (Journal of English Literary History),* 25 (September 1958), 216–233.

GILBERT, ELLIOT L., ed. *Kipling and the Critics.* New York: New York University Press, 1965. More historically oriented than Rutherford's collection: contains Randall Jarrell's essay.

HENN, T. R. *Kipling.* Edinburgh: Oliver and Boyd, 1967. A volume in the Writers and Critics Series.

LEWIS, C. S. "Kipling's World," in *They Asked for a Paper.* London: Geoffrey Bles, 1962.

MEYERS, JEFFREY. "The Idea of Moral Authority in *The Man Who Would Be King," Studies in English Literature,* 8 (Autumn 1968), 711–723.

RAO, K. BHASKARA. *Rudyard Kipling's India.* Norman, Okla.: University of Oklahoma Press, 1967.

RUTHERFORD, ANDREW, ed. *Kipling's Mind and Art: Selected Critical Essays.* Stanford, Calif.: Stanford University Press, 1964. Contains essays by Edmund Wilson, George Orwell, Lionel Trilling, and Noel Annan, among others.

SANDISON, ALAN. *The Wheel of Empire: A Study of the Imperial Idea in Some Late Nineteenth and Early Twentieth Century Fiction.* New York: St. Martin's Press, Inc., 1967. Chapters on Kipling and Conrad.

TOMKINS, J. M. S. *The Art of Rudyard Kipling.* London: Methuen and Co., 1965.

JOSEPH CONRAD

Heart of Darkness

I

The *Nellie,* a cruising yawl, swung to her anchor without a flutter of the sails, and was at rest. The flood had made, the wind was nearly calm, and being bound down the river, the only thing for it was to come to and wait for the turn of the tide.

The sea-reach of the Thames stretched before us like the beginning of an interminable waterway. In the offing the sea and the sky were welded together without a joint, and in the luminous space the tanned sails of the barges drifting up with the tide seemed to stand still in red clusters of canvas sharply peaked, with gleams of varnished sprits. A haze rested on the low shores that ran out to sea in vanishing flatness. The air was dark above Gravesend, and farther back still seemed condensed into a mournful gloom, brooding motionless over the biggest, and the greatest, town on earth.

The Director of Companies was our captain and our host. We four affectionately watched his back as he stood in the bows looking to seaward. On the whole river there was nothing that looked half so nautical. He resembled a pilot, which to a seaman is trustworthiness personified. It was difficult to realise his work was not out there in the luminous estuary, but behind him, within the brooding gloom.

Between us there was, as I have already said somewhere, the bond of the sea. Besides holding our hearts together through long periods of separation, it had the effect of making us tolerant of each other's yarns—and even convictions. The Lawyer—the best of old fellows—had, because of his many years and many virtues, the only cushion on deck, and was lying on the only rug. The Accountant had brought out already a box of dominoes, and was toying architecturally with the bones. Marlow sat cross-legged right aft, leaning against the mizzen-mast. He had sunken cheeks, a yellow complexion, a straight back, an ascetic aspect, and, with his arms dropped, the palms of hands outwards, resembled an idol. The Director, satisfied the anchor had good hold, made his way aft and sat down amongst us. We exchanged a few words lazily. Afterwards there was silence on board the yacht. For some reason or other we did not begin that game of dominoes. We felt meditative, and fit for nothing but placid staring. The day was ending in a serenity of still and exquisite brilliance. The water shone pacifically; the sky, without a speck, was a benign immensity of unstained light; the very mist on the Essex marshes was like a gauzy and radiant fabric, hung from the wooded rises inland, and draping the low shores in diaphanous folds. Only the gloom to the west, brooding over the upper reaches, became more sombre every minute, as if angered by the approach of the sun.

And at last, in its curved and imperceptible fall, the sun sank low, and from glowing white changed to a dull red without rays and without heat, as if about to go out suddenly, stricken to death by the touch of that gloom brooding over a crowd of men.

Forthwith a change came over the waters, and the serenity became less brilliant but more profound. The old river in its broad reach rested unruffled at the decline of day, after ages of good service done to the race that peopled its banks, spread out in the tranquil dignity of a waterway leading to the uttermost ends of the earth. We looked at the venerable stream not in the vivid flush of a short day that comes and departs for ever, but in the august light of abiding memories. And indeed nothing is easier for a man who has, as the phrase goes, "followed the sea" with reverence and affection, than to evoke the great spirit of the past upon the lower reaches of the Thames. The tidal current runs to and fro in its unceasing service, crowded with memories of men and ships it has borne to the rest of home or to the battles of the sea. It had known and served all the men of whom the nation is proud, from Sir Francis Drake to Sir John Franklin, knights all, titled and untitled—the great knights-errant of the sea. It had borne all the ships whose names are like jewels flashing in the night of time, from the *Golden Hind* returning with her round flanks full of treasure, to be visited by the Queen's Highness and thus pass out of the gigantic tale, to the *Erebus* and *Terror,* bound on other conquests—and that never returned. It had known the ships and the men. They had sailed from Deptford, from Greenwich, from Erith—the adventurers and the settlers; kings' ships and the ships of men on 'Change; captains, admirals, the dark "interlopers" of the Eastern trade, and the commissioned "generals" of East India fleets. Hunters for gold or pursuers of fame, they all had gone out on that stream, bearing the sword, and often the torch, messengers of the might within the land, bearers of a spark from the sacred fire. What greatness had not floated on the ebb of that river into the mystery of an unknown earth! . . . The dreams of men, the seed of commonwealths, the germs of empires.

The sun set; the dusk fell on the stream, and lights began to appear along the shore. The Chapman lighthouse, a three-legged thing erect on a mud-flat, shone strongly. Lights of ships moved in the fairway—a great stir of lights going up and going down. And farther west on the upper reaches the place of the monstrous town was still marked ominously on the sky, a brooding gloom in sunshine, a lurid glare under the stars.

"And this also," said Marlow suddenly, "has been one of the dark places of the earth."

He was the only man of us who still "followed the sea." The worst that could be said of him was that he did not represent his class. He was a seaman, but he was a wanderer too, while most seamen lead, if one may so express it, a sedentary life. Their minds are of the stay-at-home order, and their home is always with them—the ship; and so is their country—the sea. One ship is very much like another, and the sea is always the same. In the immutability of their surroundings the foreign shores, the foreign faces, the changing immensity of life, glide past, veiled not by a sense of mystery but by a slightly disdainful ignorance; for there is nothing mysterious to a seaman unless it be the sea itself, which is the mistress of his existence and as inscrutable as Destiny. For the rest, after his hours of work, a casual stroll or a casual spree on shore suffices to unfold for him the secret of a whole continent, and generally he finds the secret not worth knowing. The yarns of seamen have a direct simplicity, the whole meaning of which lies within the shell of a cracked nut. But Marlow was not typical (if his propensity to spin yarns be excepted), and to him the meaning of an episode was not inside like a kernel but outside, enveloping the tale which brought it out only as a glow brings out a haze, in the likeness of one of these misty halos that sometimes are made visible by the spectral illumination of moonshine.

His remark did not seem at all surprising. It was just like Marlow. It was accepted in silence. No one took the trouble to grunt even; and presently he said, very slow:

"I was thinking of very old times, when the Romans first came here, nineteen hundred years ago—the other day. . . . Light came out of this river since—you say Knights? Yes; but it is like a running blaze on a plain, like a flash of lightning in the clouds. We live in the flicker—may it last as long as the old earth keeps rolling! But darkness was here yesterday. Imagine the feelings of a commander of a fine—what d'ye call 'em?—trireme in the Mediterranean, ordered suddenly to the north; run overland across the Gauls in a hurry; put in charge of one of these craft the legionaries—a wonderful lot of handy men they must have been too—used to build, apparently by the hundred, in a month or two, if we may believe what we read. Imagine him here—the very end of the world, a sea the colour of lead, a sky the colour of smoke, a kind of ship about as rigid as a concertina—and going up this river with stores, or orders, or what you like. Sandbanks, marshes, forests, savages—precious little to eat fit for a civilised man, nothing but Thames water to drink. No Falernian wine here, no going ashore. Here and there a military camp lost in a wilderness, like a needle in a bundle of hay—cold, fog, tempests, disease, exile, and death—death skulking in the air, in the water, in the bush. They must have been dying like flies here. Oh yes—he did it. Did it very well, too, no doubt, and without thinking much about it either, except afterwards to brag of what he had gone through in his time, perhaps. They were men enough to face the darkness. And perhaps he was cheered by keeping his eye on a chance of promotion to the fleet at Ravenna by and by, if he had good friends in Rome and survived the awful climate. Or think of a decent young citizen in a toga—perhaps too much dice, you know—coming out here in the train of some prefect, or tax-gatherer, or trader, even, to mend his fortunes. Land in a swamp, march through the woods, and in some inland post feel the savagery, the utter savagery, had closed round him—all that mysterious life of the wilderness that stirs in the forest, in the jungles, in the hearts of wild men. There's no initiation either into such mysteries. He has to live in the midst of the incomprehensible, which is also detestable. And it has a fascination, too, that goes to work upon him. The fascination of the abomination—you know. Imagine the growing regrets, the longing to escape, the powerless disgust, the surrender, the hate."

He paused.

"Mind," he began again, lifting one arm from the elbow, the palm of the hand outwards, so that, with his legs folded before him, he had the pose of a Buddha preaching in European clothes and without a lotus-flower—"Mind, none of us would feel exactly like this. What saves us is efficiency—the devotion to efficiency. But these chaps were not much account, really. They were no colonists; their administration was merely a squeeze, and nothing more, I suspect. They were conquerors, and for that you want only brute force—nothing to boast of, when you have it, since your strength is just an accident arising from the weakness of others. They grabbed what they could get for the sake of what was to be got. It was just robbery with violence, aggravated murder on a great scale, and men going at it blind—as is very proper for those who tackle a darkness. The conquest of the earth, which mostly means the taking it away from those who have a different complexion or slightly flatter noses than ourselves, is not a pretty thing when you look into it too much. What redeems it is the idea only. An idea at the back of it; not a sentimental pretence but an idea; and an unselfish belief in the idea—something you can set up, and bow down before, and offer a sacrifice to. . . . "

He broke off. Flames glided in the river, small green flames, red flames, white flames, pursuing, overtaking, joining, crossing each other—then separating slowly or hastily. The traffic of the great city went on in the deepening night upon the sleepless river. We looked on, waiting patiently— there was nothing else to do till the end of the flood; but it was only after a long silence, when he said, in a hesitating voice, "I suppose you fellows remember I did once turn fresh-water sailor for a bit," that we knew we were fated, before the ebb began to run, to hear about one of Marlow's inconclusive experiences.

"I don't want to bother you much with what happened to me personally," he began, showing in this remark the weakness of many tellers of tales who seem so often unaware of what their audience would best like to hear; "yet to understand the effect of it on me you ought to know how I got out there, what I saw, how I went up that river to the place where I first met the poor chap. It was the farthest point of navigation and the culminating point of my experience. It seemed somehow to throw a kind of light on everything about me—and into my thoughts. It was sombre enough too—and pitiful— not extraordinary in any way—not very clear either. No, not very clear. And yet it seemed to throw a kind of light.

"I had then, as you remember, just returned to London after a lot of Indian Ocean, Pacific, China Seas—a regular dose of the East—six years or so, and I was loafing about, hindering you fellows in your work and invading your homes, just as though I had got a heavenly mission to civilise you. It was very fine for a time, but after a bit I did get tired of resting. Then I began to look for a ship—I should think the hardest work on earth. But the ships wouldn't even look at me. And I got tired of that game too.

"Now when I was a little chap I had a passion for maps. I would look for hours at South America, or Africa, or Australia, and lose myself in all the glories of exploration. At that time there were many blank spaces on the earth, and when I saw one that looked particularly inviting on a map (but they all look that) I would put my finger on it and say, When I grow up I will go there. The North Pole was one of these places, I remember. Well, I haven't been there yet, and shall not try now. The glamour's off. Other places were scattered about the Equator, and in every sort of latitude all over the two hemispheres. I have been in some of them, and . . . well, we won't talk about that. But there was one yet—the biggest, the most blank, so to speak—that I had a hankering after.

True, by this time it was not a blank space any more. It had got filled since my boyhood with rivers and lakes and names. It had ceased to be a blank space of delightful mystery—a white patch for a boy to dream gloriously over. It had become a place of darkness. But there was in it one river especially, a mighty big river, that you could see on the map, resembling an immense snake uncoiled, with its head in the sea, its body at rest curving afar over a vast country, and its tail lost in the depths of the land. And as I looked at the map of it in a shop-window, it fascinated me as a snake would a bird—a silly little bird. Then I remembered there was a big concern, a Company for trade on that river. Dash it all! I thought to myself, they can't trade without using some kind of craft on that lot of fresh water— steamboats! Why shouldn't I try to get charge of one? I went on along Fleet Street, but could not shake off the idea. The snake had charmed me.

"You understand it was a Continental concern, that Trading Society; but I have a lot of relations living on the Continent, because it's cheap and not so nasty as it looks, they say.

"I am sorry to own I began to worry them. This was already a fresh departure for me. I was not used to get things that way, you know. I always went my own road and on my own legs where I had a mind to go. I wouldn't have believed it of myself; but, then—you see—I felt somehow I must get there by hook or by crook. So I worried them. The men said, 'My dear fellow,' and did nothing. Then—would you believe it?—I tried the women. I, Charlie Marlow, set the women to work—to get a job. Heavens! Well, you see, the notion drove me. I had an aunt, a dear enthusiastic soul. She wrote: 'It will be delightful. I am ready to do anything, anything for you. It is a glorious idea. I know the wife of a very high personage in the Administration, and also a man who has lots of influence with,' etc. etc. She was determined to make no end of fuss to get me appointed skipper of a river steamboat, if such was my fancy.

"I got my appointment—of course; and I got it very quick. It appears the Company had received news that one of their captains had been killed in a scuffle with the natives. This was my chance, and it made me the more anxious to go. It was only months and months afterwards, when I made the attempt to recover what was left of the body, that I heard the original quarrel arose from a misunderstanding about some hens. Yes, two black hens. Fresleven—that was the fellow's name, a Dane—thought himself wronged somehow in the bargain, so he went ashore and started to hammer the chief of the village with a stick. Oh, it didn't surprise me in the least to hear this, and at the same time to be told that Fresleven was the gentlest, quietest creature that ever walked on two legs. No doubt he was; but he had been a couple of years already out there engaged in the noble cause, you know, and he probably felt the need at last of asserting his self-respect in some way. Therefore he whacked the old nigger mercilessly, while a big crowd of his people watched him, thunderstruck, till some man—I was told the chief's son—in desperation at hearing the old chap yell, made a tentative jab with a spear at the white man—and of course it went quite easy between the shoulder-blades. Then the whole population cleared into the forest, expecting all kinds of calamities to happen, while, on the other hand, the steamer Fresleven commanded left also in a bad panic, in charge of the engineer, I believe. Afterwards nobody seemed to trouble much about Fresleven's remains, till I got out and stepped into his shoes. I couldn't let it rest, though; but when an opportunity offered at last to meet my predecessor, the grass growing through his ribs was tall enough to hide his bones. They were all there. The supernatural being had not been touched after he fell. And the village was deserted, the huts gaped black, rotting, all askew within the fallen enclosures. A calamity had come to it, sure enough. The people had vanished. Mad terror had scattered them, men, women, and children, through the bush, and they had never returned. What became of the hens I don't know either. I should think the cause of progress got them, anyhow. However, through this glorious affair I got my appointment, before I had fairly begun to hope for it.

"I flew around like mad to get ready, and before forty-eight hours I was crossing the Channel to show myself to my employers, and sign the contract. In a very few hours I arrived in a city that always makes me think of a whited sepulchre. Prejudice no doubt. I had no difficulty in finding the Company's offices. It was the biggest thing in the town, and everybody I met was full of it. They were going to run an oversea empire, and make no end of coin by trade.

"A narrow and deserted street in deep shadow, high houses, innumerable windows with venetian blinds, a dead silence, grass sprouting between the stones, imposing carriage archways right and left, immense double doors standing ponderously ajar. I slipped through one of these cracks, went up a swept and ungarnished staircase, as arid as a desert, and opened the first door I came to. Two women, one fat and the other slim, sat on straw-bottomed chairs, knitting black wool. The slim one got up and walked straight at me—still knitting with downcast eyes—and only just as I began to think of getting out of her way, as you would for a somnambulist, stood still, and looked up. Her dress was as plain as an umbrella-cover, and she turned round without a word and preceded me into a waiting-room. I gave my name, and looked about. Deal table in the middle, plain chairs all round the walls, on one end a large shining map, marked with all the colours of a rainbow. There was a vast amount of red—good to see at any time, because one knows that some real work is done in there, a deuce of a lot of blue, a little green, smears of orange, and, on the East Coast, a purple patch, to show where the jolly pioneers of progress drink the jolly lager-beer. However, I wasn't going into any of these. I was going into the yellow. Dead in the centre. And the river was there—fascinating—deadly—like a snake. Ough! A door opened, a white-haired secretarial head, but wearing a compassionate expression, appeared, and a skinny forefinger beckoned me into the sanctuary. Its light was dim, and a heavy writing-desk squatted in the middle. From behind that structure came out an impression of pale plumpness in a frockcoat. The great man himself. He was five feet six, I should judge, and had his grip on the handle-end of ever so many millions. He shook hands, I fancy, murmured vaguely, was satisfied with my French. *Bon voyage.*

"In about forty-five seconds I found myself again in the waiting-room with the compassionate secretary, who, full of desolation and sympathy, made me sign some document. I believe I undertook amongst other things not to disclose any trade secrets. Well, I am not going to.

"I began to feel slightly uneasy. You know I am not used to such ceremonies, and there was something ominous in the atmosphere. It was just as though I had been let into some conspiracy—I don't know—something not quite right; and I was glad to get out. In the outer room the two women knitted black wool feverishly. People were arriving, and the younger one was walking back and forth introducing them. The old one sat on her chair. Her flat cloth slippers were propped up on a foot-warmer, and a cat reposed on her lap. She wore a starched white affair on her head, had a wart on one cheek, and silver-rimmed spectacles hung on the tip of her nose. She glanced at me above the glasses. The swift and indifferent placidity of that look troubled me. Two youths with foolish and cheery countenances were being piloted over, and she threw at them the same quick glance of unconcerned wisdom. She seemed to know all about them and about me too. An eerie feeling came over me. She seemed uncanny and fateful. Often far away there I thought of these two, guarding the door of Darkness, knitting black wool as for a warm pall, one introducing, introducing continuously to the unknown, the other scrutinising the cheery and foolish faces with unconcerned old eyes. *Ave!* Old knitter of black wool. *Morituri te salutant.* Not many of those she looked at ever saw her again—not half, by a long way.

"There was yet a visit to the doctor. 'A simple formality,' assured me the secretary, with an air of taking an immense part in all my sorrows. Accordingly a young chap wearing his hat over the left eyebrow, some clerk I suppose—there must have been clerks in the business, though the house was as still as a house in a city of the dead—came from somewhere upstairs, and led me forth. He was shabby and careless, with ink-stains on the sleeves of his jacket, and his cravat was large and billowy, under a chin shaped like the toe of an old boot. It was a little too early for the doctor, so I proposed a drink, and thereupon he developed a vein of joviality. As we sat over our vermuths he glorified the Company's business, and by and by I expressed casually my surprise at him not going out there. He became very cool and collected all at once. 'I am not such a fool as I look, quoth Plato to his disciples,' he said sententiously, emptied his glass with great resolution, and we rose.

"The old doctor felt my pulse, evidently thinking of something else the while. 'Good, good for there,' he mumbled, and then with a certain eagerness asked me whether I would let him measure my head. Rather surprised, I said Yes, when he produced a thing like callipers and got the dimensions back and front and every way, taking notes carefully. He was an unshaven little man in a thread-bare coat like a gaberdine, with his feet in slippers, and I thought him a harmless fool. 'I always ask leave, in the interests of science, to measure the crania of those going out there,' he said. 'And when they come back too?' I asked. 'Oh, I never see them,' he remarked; 'and, moreover, the changes take place inside, you know.' He smiled, as if at some quiet joke. 'So you are going out there. Famous. Interesting too.' He gave me a searching glance, and made another note. 'Ever any madness in your family?' he asked, in a matter-of-fact tone. I felt very annoyed. 'Is that question in the interests of science too?' 'It would be,' he said, without taking notice of my irritation, 'interesting for science to watch the mental changes of individuals, on the spot, but . . . ' 'Are you an alienist?' I interrupted. 'Every doctor should be—a little,' answered that original imperturbably. 'I have a little theory which you Messieurs who go out there must help me to prove. This is my share in the advantages my country shall reap from the possession of such a magnificent dependency. The mere wealth I leave to others. Pardon my questions, but you are the first Englishman coming under my observation . . . ' I hastened to assure him I was not in the least typical. 'If I were,' said I, 'I wouldn't be talking like this with you.' 'What you say is rather profound, and probably erroneous,' he said, with a laugh. 'Avoid irritation more than exposure to the sun. Adieu. How do you English say, eh? Good-bye. Ah! Good-bye. Adieu. In the tropics one must before everything keep calm.' . . . He lifted a warning forefinger. . . . *'Du calme, du calme. Adieu.'*

"One thing more remained to do—say good-bye to my excellent aunt. I found her triumphant. I had a cup of tea—the last decent cup of tea for many days—and in a room that most soothingly looked just as you would expect a lady's drawing-room to look, we had a long quiet chat by the fireside. In the course of these confidences it became quite plain to me I had been represented to the wife of the high dignitary, and goodness knows to how many more people besides, as an exceptional and gifted creature—a piece of good fortune for the Company—a man you don't get hold of every day. Good Heavens! and I was going to take charge of a two-penny-half-penny river-steamboat with a penny whistle attached! It appeared, how-ever, I was also one of the Workers, with a capital—you know. Something like an emissary of light, something like a lower sort of apostle. There had been a lot of such rot let loose in print and talk just about that time, and the excellent woman, living right in the rush of all that humbug, got carried off her feet. She talked about 'weaning those ignorant millions from their horrid ways,' till, upon my word, she made me quite uncomfortable. I ventured to hint that the Company was run for profit.

"'You forget, dear Charlie, that the labourer is worthy of his hire,' she said brightly. It's queer how out of touch with truth women are. They live in a world of their own, and there had never been anything like it, and never can be. It is too beautiful altogether, and if they were to set it up it would go to pieces before the first sunset. Some confounded fact we men have been living contentedly with ever since the day of creation would start up and knock the whole thing over.

"After this I got embraced, told to wear flannel, be sure to write often, and so on—and I left. In the street—I don't know why—a queer feeling came to me that I was an impostor. Odd thing that I, who used to clear out for any part of the world at twenty-four hours' notice, with less thought than most men give to the crossing of a street, had a moment—I won't say of hesitation, but of startled pause, before this commonplace affair. The best way I can explain it to you is by saying that, for a second or two, I felt as though, instead of going to the centre of a continent, I were about to set off for the centre of the earth.

"I left in a French steamer, and she called in every blamed port they have out there, for, as far as I could see, the sole purpose of landing soldiers and custom-house officers. I watched the coast. Watching a coast as it slips by the ship is like thinking about an enigma. There it is before you—smiling, frowning, inviting, grand, mean, insipid, or savage, and always mute with an air of whispering, Come and find out. This one was almost featureless, as if still in the making, with an aspect of monotonous grimness. The edge of a colossal jungle, so dark green as to be almost black, fringed with white surf, ran straight, like a ruled line, far, far away along a blue sea whose glitter was blurred by a creeping mist. The sun was fierce, the land seemed to glisten and drip with steam. Here and there greyish-whitish specks showed up clustered inside the white surf, with a flag flying above them perhaps—settlements some centuries old, and still no bigger than pin-heads on the untouched expanse of their background. We pounded along, stopped, landed soldiers; went on, landed custom-house clerks to levy toll in what looked like a God-forsaken wilderness, with a tin shed and a flag-pole lost in it; landed more soldiers—to take care of the custom-house clerks presumably. Some, I heard, got drowned in the surf; but whether they did or not, nobody seemed particularly to care. They were just flung out there, and on we went. Every day the coast looked the same, as though we had not moved; but we passed various places—trading places—with names like Gran' Bassam, Little Popo; names that seemed to belong to some sordid farce acted in front of a sinister back-cloth. The idleness of a passenger, my isolation amongst all these men with whom I had no point of contact, the oily and languid sea, the uniform sombreness of the coast, seemed to keep me away from the truth of things, within the toil of a mournful and senseless delusion. The voice of the surf heard now and then was a positive pleasure, like the speech of a brother. It was something natural, that had its reason, that had a meaning. Now and then a boat from the shore gave me a momentary contact with reality. It was paddled by black fellows. You could see from afar the white of their eyeballs glistening. They shouted, sang; their bodies streamed with perspiration; they had faces like grotesque masks—these chaps; but they had bone, muscle, a wild vitality, an intense energy of movement, that was as natural and true as the surf along their coast. They wanted no excuse for being there. They were a great comfort to look at. For a time I would feel I belonged still to a world of straightforward facts; but the feeling would not last long. Something would turn up to scare it away. Once, I remember, we came upon a man-of-war anchored off the coast. There wasn't even a shed there, and she was shelling the bush. It appears the French had one of their wars going on thereabouts. Her ensign dropped limp like a rag; the muzzles of the long six-inch guns stuck out all over the low hull; the greasy, slimy swell swung her up lazily and let her down, swaying her thin masts. In the empty immensity of earth, sky, and water, there she was, incomprehensible, firing into a continent. Pop, would go one of the six-inch guns; a small flame would dart and vanish, a little white smoke would disappear, a tiny projectile would give a feeble screech —and nothing happened. Nothing could happen. There was a touch of insanity in the proceeding, a sense of lugubrious drollery in the sight; and it was not dissipated by somebody on board assuring me earnestly there was a camp of natives—he called them enemies!—hidden out of sight somewhere.

"We gave her her letters (I heard the men in that lonely ship were dying of fever at the rate of three a day) and went on. We called at some more places with farcical names, where the merry dance of death and trade goes on in a still and earthy atmosphere as of an overheated catacomb; all along the formless coast bordered by dangerous surf, as if Nature herself had tried to ward off intruders; in and out of rivers, streams of death in life, whose banks were rotting into mud, whose waters, thickened into slime, invaded the contorted mangroves, that seemed to writhe at us in the extremity of an impotent despair. Nowhere did we stop long enough to get a particularised impression, but the general sense of vague and oppressive wonder grew upon me. It was like a weary pilgrimage amongst hints for nightmares.

"It was upward of thirty days before I saw the mouth of the big river. We anchored off the seat of the government. But my work would not begin till some two hundred miles farther on. So as soon as I could I made a start for a place thirty miles higher up.

"I had my passage on a little sea-going steamer. Her captain was a Swede, and knowing me for a seaman, invited me on the bridge. He was a young man, lean, fair, and morose, with lanky hair and a shuffling gait. As we left the miserable little wharf, he tossed his head contemptuously at the shore. 'Been living there?' he asked. I said, 'Yes.' 'Fine lot these government chaps—are they not?' he went on, speaking English with great precision and considerable bitterness. 'It is funny what some people will do for a few francs a month. I wonder what becomes of that kind when it goes up country?' I said to him I expected to see that soon. 'So-o-o!' he exclaimed. He shuffled athwart, keeping one eye ahead vigilantly. 'Don't be too sure,' he continued. 'The other day I took up a man who hanged himself on the road. He was a Swede, too.' 'Hanged himself! Why, in God's name?' I cried. He kept on looking out watchfully. 'Who knows? The sun too much for him, or the country perhaps.'

"At last we opened a reach. A rocky cliff appeared, mounds of turned-up earth by the shore, houses on a hill, others with iron roofs, amongst a waste of excavations, or hanging to the declivity. A continuous noise of the rapids above hovered over this scene of inhabited devastation. A lot of people, mostly black and naked, moved about like ants. A jetty projected into the river. A blinding sunlight drowned all this at times in a sudden recrudescence of glare. 'There's your Company's station,' said the Swede, pointing to three wooden barrack-like structures on the rocky slope. 'I will send your things up. Four boxes did you say? So. Farewell.'

"I came upon a boiler wallowing in the grass, then found a path leading up the hill. It turned aside for the boulders, and also for an undersized railway truck lying there on its back with its wheels in the air. One was off. The thing looked as dead as the carcass of some animal. I came upon more pieces of decaying machinery, a stack of rusty rails. To the left a clump of trees made a shady spot, where dark things seemed to stir feebly. I blinked, the path was steep. A horn tooted to the right, and I saw the black people run. A heavy and dull detonation shook the ground, a puff of smoke came out of the cliff, and that was all. No change appeared on the face of the rock. They were building a railway. The cliff was not in the way or anything; but this objectless blasting was all the work going on.

"A slight clinking behind me made me turn my head. Six black men advanced in a file, toiling up the path. They walked erect and slow, balancing small baskets full of earth on their heads, and the clink kept time with their footsteps. Black rags were wound round their loins, and the short ends behind waggled to and fro like tails. I could see every rib, the joints of their limbs were like knots in a rope; each had an iron collar on his neck, and all were connected together with a chain whose bights swung between them, rhythmically clinking. Another report from the cliff made me think suddenly of that ship of war I had seen firing into a continent. It was the same kind of ominous voice; but these men could by no stretch of imagination be called enemies. They were called criminals, and the outraged law, like the bursting shells, had come to them, an insoluble mystery from the sea. All their meagre breasts panted together, the violently dilated nostrils quivered, the eyes stared stonily uphill. They passed me within six inches, without a glance, with that complete, deathlike indifference of unhappy savages. Behind this raw matter one of the reclaimed, the product of the new forces at work, strolled despondently, carrying a rifle by its middle. He had a uniform jacket with one button off, and seeing a white man on the path, hoisted his weapon to his shoulder with alacrity. This was simple prudence, white men being so much alike at a distance that he could not tell who I might be. He was speedily reassured, and with a large, white, rascally grin, and a glance at his charge, seemed to take me into partnership in his exalted trust. After all, I also was a part of the great cause of these high and just proceedings.

"Instead of going up, I turned and descended to the left. My idea was to let that chain-gang get out of sight before I climbed the hill. You know I am not particularly tender; I've had to strike and to fend off. I've had to resist and to attack sometimes—that's only one way of resisting—without counting the exact cost, according to the demands of such sort of life as I had blundered into. I've seen the devil of violence, and the devil of greed, and the devil of hot desires; but, by all the stars! these were strong, lusty, red-eyed devils, that swayed and drove men—men, I tell you. But as I stood on this hillside, I foresaw that in the blinding sunshine of that land I would become acquainted with a flabby, pretending, weak-eyed devil of a rapacious and pitiless folly. How insidious he could be, too, I was only to find out several months later and a thousand miles farther. For a moment I stood appalled, as though by a warning. Finally I descended the hill, obliquely, towards the trees I had seen.

"I avoided a vast artificial hole somebody had been digging on the slope, the purpose of which I found it impossible to divine. It wasn't a quarry or a sandpit, anyhow. It was just a hole. It might have been connected with the philanthropic desire of giving the criminals something to do. I don't know. Then I nearly fell into a very narrow ravine, almost no more than a scar in the hillside. I discovered that a lot of imported drainage-pipes for the settlement had been tumbled in there. There wasn't one that was not broken. It was a wanton smash-up. At last I got under the trees. My purpose was to stroll into the shade for a moment; but no sooner within than it seemed to me I had stepped into the gloomy circle of some Inferno. The rapids were near, and an uninterrupted, uniform, headlong, rushing noise filled the mournful stillness of the grove, where not a breath stirred, not a leaf moved, with a mysterious sound—as though the tearing pace of the launched earth had suddenly become audible.

"Black shapes crouched, lay, sat between the trees, leaning against the trunks, clinging to the earth, half coming out, half effaced within the dim light, in all the attitudes of pain, abandonment, and despair. Another mine on the cliff went off, followed by a slight shudder of the soil under my feet. The work was going on. The work! And this was the place where some of the helpers had withdrawn to die.

"They were dying slowly—it was very clear. They were not enemies, they were not criminals, they were nothing earthly now—nothing but black shadows of disease and starvation, lying confusedly in the greenish gloom. Brought from all the recesses of the coast in all the legality of time contracts, lost in uncongenial surroundings, fed on unfamiliar food, they sickened, became inefficient, and were then allowed to crawl away and rest. These moribund shapes were free as air—and nearly as thin. I began to distinguish the gleam of the eyes under the trees. Then, glancing down, I saw a face near my hand. The black bones reclined at full length with one shoulder against the tree, and slowly the eyelids rose and the sunken eyes looked up at me, enormous and vacant, a kind of blind, white flicker in the depths of the orbs, which died out slowly. The man seemed young—almost a boy—but you know with them it's hard to tell. I found nothing else to do but to offer him one of my good Swede's ship's biscuits I had in my pocket. The fingers closed slowly on it and held—there was no other movement and no other glance. He had tied a bit of white worsted round his neck—Why? Where did he get it? Was it a badge—an ornament—a charm—a propitiatory act? Was there any idea at all connected with it? It looked startling round his black neck, this bit of white thread from beyond the seas.

"Near the same tree two more bundles of acute angles sat with their legs drawn up. One, with his chin propped on his knees, stared at nothing, in an intolerable and appalling manner: his brother phantom rested its forehead, as if overcome with a great weariness; and all about others were scattered in every pose of contorted collapse, as in some picture of a massacre or a pestilence. While I stood horror-struck, one of these creatures rose to his hands and knees, and went off on all-fours towards the river to drink. He lapped out of his hand, then sat up in the sunlight, crossing his shins in front of him, and after a time let his woolly head fall on his breastbone.

"I didn't want any more loitering in the shade, and I made haste towards the station. When near the buildings I met a white man, in such an unexpected elegance of get-up that in the first moment I took him for a sort of vision. I saw a high starched collar, white cuffs, a light alpaca jacket, snowy trousers, a clean necktie, and varnished boots. No hat. Hair parted, brushed, oiled, under a green-lined parasol held in a big white hand. He was amazing, and had a pen-holder behind his ear.

"I shook hands with this miracle, and I learned he was the Company's chief accountant, and that all the book-keeping was done at this station. He had come out for a moment, he said, 'to get a breath of fresh air.' The expression sounded wonderfully odd, with its suggestion of sedentary desk-life. I wouldn't have mentioned the fellow to you at all, only it was from his lips that I first heard the name of the man who is so indissolubly connected with the memories of that time. Moreover, I respected the fellow. Yes; I respected his collars, his vast cuffs, his brushed hair. His appearance was certainly that of a hairdresser's dummy; but in the great demoralisation of the land he kept up his appearance. That's backbone. His starched collars and got-up shirt-fronts were achievements of character. He had been out nearly three years; and, later, I could not help asking him how he managed to sport such linen. He had just the faintest blush, and said modestly, 'I've been teaching one of the native women about the station. It was difficult. She had a distaste for the work.' Thus this man had verily accomplished something. And he was devoted to his books, which were in apple-pie order.

"Everything else in the station was in a muddle,—heads, things, buildings. Strings of dusty niggers with splay feet arrived and departed; a stream of manufactured goods, rubbishy cottons, beads, and brass-wire set into the depths of darkness, and in return came a precious trickle of ivory.

"I had to wait in the station for ten days—an eternity. I lived in a hut in the yard, but to be out of the chaos I would sometimes get into the accountant's office. It was built of horizontal planks, and so badly put together that, as he bent over his high desk, he was barred from neck to heels with narrow strips of sunlight. There was no need to open the big shutter to see. It was hot there too; big flies buzzed fiendishly, and did not sting, but stabbed. I sat generally on the floor, while, of faultless appearance (and even slightly scented), perching on a high stool, he wrote, he wrote. Sometimes he stood up for exercise. When a truckle-bed with a sick man (some invalided agent from up-country) was put in there, he exhibited a gentle annoyance. 'The groans of this sick person,' he said, 'distract my attention. And without that it is extremely difficult to guard against clerical errors in this climate.'

"One day he remarked, without lifting his head, 'In the interior you will no doubt meet Mr. Kurtz.' On my asking who Mr. Kurtz was, he said he was a first-class agent; and seeing my disappointment at this information, he added slowly, laying down his pen, 'He is a very remarkable person.' Further questions elicited from him that Mr. Kurtz was at present in charge of a trading-post, a very important one, in the true ivory-country, at 'the very bottom of there. Sends in as much ivory as all the others put together . . . ' He began to write again. The sick man was too ill to groan. The flies buzzed in a great peace.

"Suddenly there was a growing murmur of voices and a great tramping of feet. A caravan had come in. A violent babble of uncouth sounds burst out on the other side of the planks. All the carriers were speaking together, and in the midst of the uproar the lamentable voice of the chief agent was heard 'giving it up' tearfully for the twentieth time that day. . . . He rose slowly. 'What a frightful row,' he said. He crossed the room gently to look at the sick man, and returning, said to me, 'He does not hear.' 'What! Dead?' I asked, startled. 'No, not yet,' he answered, with great composure. Then, alluding with a toss of the head to the tumult in the station-yard, 'When one has got to make correct entries, one comes to hate those savages—hate them to the death.' He remained thoughtful for a moment. 'When you see Mr. Kurtz,' he went on, 'tell him from me that everything here'—he glanced at the desk—'is very satisfactory. I don't like to write to him—with those messengers of ours you never know who may get hold of your letter—at that Central Station.' He stared at me for a moment with his mild, bulging eyes. 'Oh, he will go far, very far,' he began again. 'He will be a somebody in the

Administration before long. They, above—the Council in Europe, you know—mean him to be.'

"He turned to his work. The noise outside had ceased, and presently in going out I stopped at the door. In the steady buzz of flies the homeward-bound agent was lying flushed and insensible; the other, bent over his books, was making correct entries of perfectly correct transactions; and fifty feet below the doorstep I could see the still tree-tops of the grove of death.

"Next day I left that station at last, with a caravan of sixty men, for a two-hundred-mile tramp.

"No use telling you much about that. Paths, paths, everywhere; a stamped-in network of paths spreading over the empty land, through long grass, through burnt grass, through thickets, down and up chilly ravines, up and down stony hills ablaze with heat; and a solitude, a solitude, nobody, not a hut. The population had cleared out a long time ago. Well, if a lot of mysterious niggers armed with all kinds of fearful weapons suddenly took to travelling on the road between Deal and Gravesend, catching the yokels right and left to carry heavy loads for them, I fancy every farm and cottage thereabouts would get empty very soon. Only here the dwellings were gone too. Still, I passed through several abandoned villages. There's something pathetically childish in the ruins of grass walls. Day after day, with the stamp and shuffle of sixty pair of bare feet behind me, each pair under a 60-lb. load. Camp, cook, sleep; strike camp, march. Now and then a carrier dead in harness, at rest in the long grass near the path, with an empty water-gourd and his long staff lying by his side. A great silence around and above. Perhaps on some quiet night the tremor of far-off drums, sinking, swelling, a tremor vast, faint; a sound weird, appealing, suggestive, and wild—and perhaps with as profound a meaning as the sound of bells in a Christian country. Once a white man in an unbuttoned uniform, camping on the path with an armed escort of lank Zanzibaris, very hospitable and festive—not to say drunk. Was looking after the upkeep of the road, he declared. Can't say I saw any road or any upkeep, unless the body of a middle-aged negro, with a bullet-hole in the forehead, upon which I absolutely stumbled three miles farther on, may be considered as a permanent improvement. I had a white companion too, not a bad chap, but rather too fleshy and with the exasperating habit of fainting on the hot hillsides, miles away from the least bit of shade and water. Annoying, you know, to hold your own coat like a parasol over a man's head while he is coming to. I couldn't help asking him once what he meant by coming there at all. 'To make money, of course. What do you think?' he said scornfully. Then he got fever, and had to be carried in a hammock slung under a pole. As he weighed sixteen stone I had no end of rows with the carriers. They jibbed, ran away, sneaked off with their loads in the night—quite a mutiny. So, one evening, I made a speech in English with gestures, not one of which was lost to the sixty pairs of eyes before me, and the next morning I started the hammock off in front all right. An hour afterwards I came upon the whole concern wrecked in a bush—man, hammock, groans, blankets, horrors. The heavy pole had skinned his poor nose. He was very anxious for me to kill somebody, but there wasn't the shadow of a carrier near. I remembered the old doctor—'It would be interesting for science to watch the mental changes of individuals, on the spot.' I felt I was becoming scientifically interesting. However, all that is to no purpose. On the fifteenth day I came in sight of the big river again, and hobbled into the Central Station. It was on a back water surrounded by scrub and forest, with a pretty border of smelly mud on one side, and on the three others enclosed by a crazy fence of rushes. A neglected gap was all the gate it had, and the first glance at the place was enough to let you see the flabby devil was running that show. White men with long staves in their hands appeared languidly from amongst the buildings, strolling up to take a look at me, and then retired out of sight somewhere. One of them, a stout, excitable chap with black moustaches, informed me with great volubility and many digressions, as soon as I told him who I was, that my steamer was at the bottom of the river. I was thunderstruck. What, how, why? Oh, it was 'all right.' The 'manager himself' was there. All quite correct. 'Every-body had behaved splendidly! splendidly!'—'You must,' he said in agitation, 'go and see the general manager at once. He is waiting.'

"I did not see the real significance of that wreck at once. I fancy I see it now, but I am not sure—not at all. Certainly the affair was too stupid—when I think of it—to be altogether natural. Still . . . But at the moment it presented itself simply as a confounded nuisance. The steamer was sunk. They had started two days before in a sudden hurry up the river with the manager on board, in charge of some volunteer skipper, and before they had been out three hours they tore the bottom out of her on stones, and she sank near the south bank. I asked myself what I was to do there, now my boat was lost. As a matter of fact, I had plenty to do in fishing my command out of the river. I had to set about it the very next day. That, and the repairs when I brought the pieces to the station, took some months.

"My first interview with the manager was curious. He did not ask me to sit down after my twenty-mile walk that morning. He was commonplace in complexion, in feature, in manners, and in voice. He was of middle size and of ordinary build. His eyes, of the usual blue, were perhaps remarkably cold, and he certainly could make his glance fall on one as trenchant and heavy as an axe. But even at these times the rest of his person seemed to disclaim the intention. Otherwise there was only an indefinable, faint expression of his lips, something stealthy—a smile—not a smile—I remember it, but I can't explain. It was unconscious, this smile was, though just after he had said something it got intensified for an instant. It came at the end of his speeches like a seal applied on the words to make the meaning of the commonest phrase appear absolutely inscrutable. He was a common trader, from his youth up employed in these parts—nothing more. He was obeyed, yet he inspired neither love nor fear, nor even respect. He inspired uneasiness. That was it! Uneasiness. Not a definite mistrust—just uneasi-ness—nothing more. You have no idea how effective such a . . . a . . . faculty can be. He had no genius for organising, for initiative, or for order even. That was evident in such things as the deplorable state of the station.

He had no learning, and no intelligence. His position had come to him—why? Perhaps because he was never ill . . . He had served three terms of three years out there . . . Because triumphant health in the general rout of constitutions is a kind of power in itself. When he went home on leave he rioted on a large scale—pompously. Jack ashore—with a difference—in externals only. This one could gather from his casual talk. He originated nothing, he could keep the routine going—that's all. But he was great. He was great by this little thing that it was impossible to tell what could control such a man. He never gave that secret away. Perhaps there was nothing within him. Such a suspicion made one pause—for out there there were no external checks. Once when various tropical diseases had laid low almost every 'agent' in the station, he was heard to say, 'Men who come out here should have no entrails.' He sealed the utterance with that smile of his, as though it had been a door opening into a darkness he had in his keeping. You fancied you had seen things—but the seal was on. When annoyed at meal-times by the constant quarrels of the white men about precedence, he ordered an immense round table to be made, for which a special house had to be built. This was the station's mess-room. Where he sat was the first place—the rest were nowhere. One felt this to be his unalterable conviction. He was neither civil or uncivil. He was quiet. He allowed his 'boy'—an overfed young negro from the coast—to treat the white men, under his very eyes, with provoking insolence.

"He began to speak as soon as he saw me. I had been very long on the road. He could not wait. Had to start without me. The up-river stations had to be relieved. There had been so many delays already that he did not know who was dead and who was alive, and how they got on—and so on, and so on. He paid no attention to my explanations, and, playing with a stick of sealing-wax, repeated several times that the situation was 'very grave, very grave.' There were rumours that a very important station was in jeopardy, and its chief, Mr. Kurtz, was ill. Hoped it was not true. Mr. Kurtz was . . . I felt weary and irritable. Hang Kurtz, I thought. I interrupted him by saying I had heard of Mr. Kurtz on the coast. 'Ah! So they talk of him down there,' he murmured to himself. Then he began again, assuring me Mr. Kurtz was the best agent he had, an exceptional man, of the greatest importance to the Company; therefore I could understand his anxiety. He was, he said, 'very, very uneasy.' Certainly he fidgeted on his chair a good deal, exclaimed, 'Ah, Mr. Kurtz!' broke the stick of sealing-wax and seemed dumbfounded by the accident. Next thing he wanted to know 'how long it would take to' . . . I interrupted him again. Being hungry, you know, and kept on my feet too, I was getting savage. 'How can I tell?' I said. 'I haven't even seen the wreck yet—some months, no doubt.' All this talk seemed to me so futile. 'Some months,' he said. 'Well, let us say three months before we can make a start. Yes. That ought to do the affair.' I flung out of his hut (he lived all alone in a clay hut with a sort of verandah) muttering to myself my opinion of him. He was a chattering idiot. Afterwards I took it back when it was borne in upon me startlingly with what extreme nicety he had estimated the time requisite for the 'affair.'

"I went to work the next day, turning, so to speak, my back on that station. In that way only it seemed to me I could keep my hold on the redeeming facts of life. Still, one must look about sometimes; and then I saw this station, these men strolling aimlessly about in the sunshine of the yard. I asked myself sometimes what it all meant. They wandered here and there with their absurd long staves in their hands, like a lot of faithless pilgrims bewitched inside a rotten fence. The word 'ivory' rang in the air, was whispered, was sighed. You would think they were praying to it. A taint of imbecile rapacity blew through it all, like a whiff from some corpse. By Jove! I've never seen anything so unreal in my life. And outside, the silent wilderness surrounding this cleared speck on the earth struck me as something great and invincible, like evil or truth, waiting patiently for the passing away of this fantastic invasion.

"Oh, those months! Well, never mind. Various things happened. One evening a grass shed full of calico, cotton prints, beads, and I don't know what else, burst into a blaze so suddenly that you would have thought the earth had opened to let an avenging fire consume all that trash. I was smoking my pipe quietly by my dismantled steamer, and saw them all cutting capers in the light, with their arms lifted high, when the stout man with moustaches came tearing down to the river, a tin pail in his hand, assured me that everybody was 'behaving splendidly, splendidly,' dipped about a quart of water and tore back again. I noticed there was a hole in the bottom of his pail.

"I strolled up. There was no hurry. You see the thing had gone off like a box of matches. It had been hopeless from the very first. The flame had leaped high, driven everybody back, lighted up everything—and collapsed. The shed was already a heap of embers glowing fiercely. A nigger was being beaten near by. They said he had caused the fire in some way; be that as it may, he was screeching most horribly. I saw him, later, for several days, sitting in a bit of shade looking very sick and trying to recover himself: afterwards he arose and went out—and the wilderness without a sound took him into its bosom again. As I approached the glow from the dark I found myself at the back of two men, talking. I heard the name of Kurtz pronounced, then the words, 'take advantage of this unfortunate accident.' One of the men was the manager. I wished him a good evening. 'Did you ever see anything like it—eh? it is incredible,' he said, and walked off. The other man remained. He was a first-class agent, young, gentleman-ly, a bit reserved, with a forked little beard and a hooked nose. He was stand-offish with the other agents, and they on their side said he was the manager's spy upon them. As to me, I had hardly ever spoken to him before. We got into talk, and by and by we strolled away from the hissing ruins. Then he asked me to his room, which was in the main building of the station. He struck a match, and I perceived that this young aristocrat had not only a silver-mounted dressing-case but also a whole candle all to himself. Just at that time the manager was the only man supposed to have any right to candles. Native mats covered the clay walls; a collection of spears, assegais, shields, knives, was hung up in trophies. The business entrusted to this fellow was the making of bricks—so I had been informed;

but there wasn't a fragment of a brick anywhere in the station, and he had been there more than a year—waiting. It seems he could not make bricks without something, I don't know what—straw maybe. Anyway, it could not be found there, and as it was not likely to be sent from Europe, it did not appear clear to me what he was waiting for. An act of special creation perhaps. However, they were all waiting—all the sixteen or twenty pilgrims of them—for something; and upon my word it did not seem an uncongenial occupation, from the way they took it, though the only thing that ever came to them was disease—as far as I could see. They beguiled the time by backbiting and intriguing against each other in a foolish kind of way. There was an air of plotting about that station, but nothing came of it, of course. It was as unreal as everything else—as the philanthropic pretence of the whole concern, as their talk, as their government, as their show of work. The only real feeling was a desire to get appointed to a trading-post where ivory was to be had, so that they could earn percentages. They intrigued and slandered and hated each other only on that account—but as to effectually lifting a little finger—oh no. By Heavens! there is something after all in the world allowing one man to steal a horse while another must not look at a halter. Steal a horse straight out. Very well. He has done it. Perhaps he can ride. But there is a way of looking at a halter that would provoke the most charitable of saints into a kick.

"I had no idea why he wanted to be sociable, but as we chatted in there it suddenly occurred to me the fellow was trying to get at something—in fact, pumping me. He alluded constantly to Europe, to the people I was supposed to know there—putting leading questions as to my acquaintances in the sepulchral city, and so on. His little eyes glittered like mica discs—with curiosity—though he tried to keep up a bit of superciliousness. At first I was astonished, but very soon I became awfully curious to see what he would find out from me. I couldn't possibly imagine what I had in me to make it worth his while. It was very pretty to see how he baffled himself, for in truth my body was full only of chills, and my head had nothing in it but that wretched steamboat business. It was evident he took me for a perfectly shameless prevaricator. At last he got angry, and, to conceal a movement of furious annoyance, he yawned. I rose. Then I noticed a small sketch in oils, on a panel, representing a woman, draped and blindfolded, carrying a lighted torch. The background was sombre—almost black. The movement of the woman was stately, and the effect of the torchlight on the face was sinister.

"It arrested me, and he stood by civilly, holding an empty half-pint champagne bottle (medical comforts) with the candle stuck in it. To my question he said Mr. Kurtz had painted this—in this very station more than a year ago—while waiting for means to go to his trading-post. 'Tell me, pray,' said I, 'who is this Mr. Kurtz?'

" 'The chief of the Inner Station,' he answered in a short tone, looking away. 'Much obliged,' I said, laughing. 'And you are the brickmaker of the Central Station. Every one knows that.' He was silent for a while. 'He is a prodigy,' he said at last. 'He is an emissary of pity, and science, and progress, and devil knows what else. We want,' he began to declaim suddenly, 'for the guidance of the cause entrusted to us by Europe, so to speak, higher intelligence, wide sympathies, a singleness of purpose.' 'Who says that?' I asked. 'Lots of them,' he replied. 'Some even write that; and so *he* comes here, a special being, as you ought to know.' 'Why ought I to know?' I interrupted, really surprised. He paid no attention. 'Yes. To-day he is chief of the best station, next year he will be assistant-manager, two years more and . . . but I daresay you know what he will be in two years' time. You are of the new gang—the gang of virtue. The same people who sent him specially also recommended you. Oh, don't say no. I've my own eyes to trust.' Light dawned upon me. My dear aunt's influential acquaintances were producing an unexpected effect upon that young man. I nearly burst into a laugh. 'Do you read the Company's confidential correspondence?' I asked. He hadn't a word to say. It was great fun. 'When Mr. Kurtz,' I continued severely, 'is General Manager, you won't have the opportunity.'

"He blew the candle out suddenly, and we went outside. The moon had risen. Black figures strolled about listlessly, pouring water on the glow, whence proceeded a sound of hissing; steam ascended in the moonlight; the beaten nigger groaned somewhere. 'What a row the brute makes!' said the indefatigable man with the moustaches, appearing near us. 'Serve him right. Transgression—punishment—bang! Pitiless, pitiless. That's the only way. This will prevent all conflagrations for the future. I was just telling the manager . . . ' He noticed my companion, and became crestfallen all at once. 'Not in bed yet,' he said, with a kind of servile heartiness; 'it's so natural. Ha! Danger—agitation.' He vanished. I went on to the river-side, and the other followed me. I heard a scathing murmur at my ear, 'Heaps of muffs—go to.' The pilgrims could be seen in knots gesticulating, discussing. Several had still their staves in their hands. I verily believe they took these sticks to bed with them. Beyond the fence the forest stood up spectrally in the moonlight, and through the dim stir, through the faint sounds of that lamentable courtyard, the silence of the land went home to one's very heart—its mystery, its greatness, the amazing reality of its concealed life. The hurt nigger moaned feebly somewhere near by, and then fetched a deep sigh that made me mend my pace away from there. I felt a hand introducing itself under my arm. 'My dear sir,' said the fellow, 'I don't want to be misunderstood, and especially by you, who will see Mr. Kurtz long before I can have that pleasure. I wouldn't like him to get a false idea of my disposition. . . . '

"I let him run on, this papier-mâché Mephistopheles, and it seemed to me that if I tried I could poke my forefinger through him, and would find nothing inside but a little loose dirt, maybe. He, don't you see, had been planning to be assistant-manager by and by under the present man, and I could see that the coming of that Kurtz had upset them both not a little. He talked precipitately, and I did not try to stop him. I had my shoulders against the wreck of my steamer, hauled up on the slope like a carcass of some big river animal. The smell of mud, of primeval mud, by Jove! was in my nostrils, the high stillness of primeval forest was before my eyes; there were shiny patches on the black creek. The moon had spread over everything a thin layer of silver—over the rank grass, over the mud, upon the wall of matted vegetation standing higher than the wall of a temple, over the great river I could see through a sombre gap glittering, glittering, as it flowed broadly by without a murmur. All this was great, expectant, mute, while the man jabbered about himself. I wondered whether the stillness on the face of the immensity looking at us two were meant as an appeal or as a menace. What were we who had strayed in here? Could we handle that dumb thing, or would it handle us? I felt how big, how confoundedly big, was that thing that couldn't talk and perhaps was deaf as well. What was in there? I could see a little ivory coming out from there, and I had heard Mr. Kurtz was in there. I had heard enough about it too—God knows! Yet somehow it didn't bring any image with it—no more than if I had been told an angel or a fiend was in there. I believed it in the same way one of you might believe there are inhabitants in the planet Mars. I knew once a Scotch sailmaker who was certain, dead sure, there were people in Mars. If you asked him for some idea how they looked and behaved, he would get shy and mutter something about 'walking on all-fours.' If you as much as smiled, he would—though a man of sixty—offer to fight you. I would not have gone so far as to fight for Kurtz, but I went for him near enough to a lie. You know I hate, detest, and can't bear a lie, not because I am straighter than the rest of us, but simply because it appals me. There is a taint of death, a flavour of mortality in lies—which is exactly what I hate and detest in the world—what I want to forget. It makes me miserable and sick, like biting something rotten would do. Temperament, I suppose. Well, I went near enough to it by letting the young fool there believe anything he liked to imagine as to my influence in Europe. I became in an instant as much of a pretence as the rest of the bewitched pilgrims. This simply because I had a notion it somehow would be of help to that Kurtz whom at the time I did not see—you understand. He was just a word for me. I did not see the man in the name any more than you do. Do you see him? Do you see the story? Do you see anything? It seems to me I am trying to tell you a dream—making a vain attempt, because no relation of a dream can convey the dream-sensation, that commingling of absurdity, surprise, and bewilderment in a tremor of struggling revolt, that notion of being captured by the incredible which is of the very essence of dreams. . . . "

He was silent for a while.

" . . . No, it is impossible; it is impossible to convey the life-sensation of any given epoch of one's existence—that which makes its truth, its meaning—its subtle and penetrating essence. It is impossible. We live, as we dream—alone. . . . "

He paused again as if reflecting, then added:

"Of course in this you fellows see more than I could then. You see me, whom you know. . . . "

It had become so pitch dark that we listeners could hardly see one another. For a long time already he, sitting apart, had been no more to us than a voice. There was not a word from anybody. The others might have been asleep, but I was awake. I listened, I listened on the watch for the sentence, for the word, that would give me the clue to the faint uneasiness inspired by this narrative that seemed to shape itself without human lips in the heavy night-air of the river.

" . . . Yes—I let him run on," Marlow began again, "and think what he pleased about the powers that were behind me. I did! And there was nothing behind me! There was nothing but that wretched, old, mangled steamboat I was leaning against, while he talked fluently about 'the necessity for every man to get on.' 'And when one comes out here, you conceive, it is not to gaze at the moon.' Mr. Kurtz was a 'universal genius,' but even a genius would find it easier to work with 'adequate tools— intelligent men.' He did not make bricks—why, there was a physical impossibility in the way—as I was well aware; and if he did secretarial work for the manager, it was because 'no sensible man rejects wantonly the confidence of his superiors.' Did I see it? I saw it. What more did I want? What I really wanted was rivets, by Heaven! Rivets. To get on with the work—to stop the hole. Rivets I wanted. There were cases of them down at the coast—cases—piled up—burst—split! You kicked a loose rivet at every second step in that station yard on the hillside. Rivets had rolled into the grove of death. You could fill your pockets with rivets for the trouble of stooping down—and there wasn't one rivet to be found where it was wanted. We had plates that would do, but nothing to fasten them with. And every week the messenger, a lone negro, letter-bag on shoulder and staff in hand, left our station for the coast. And several times a week a coast caravan came in with trade goods—ghastly glazed calico that made you shudder only to look at it, glass beads value about a penny a quart, confounded spotted cotton handkerchiefs. And no rivets. Three carriers could have brought all that was wanted to set that steamboat afloat.

"He was becoming confidential now, but I fancy my unresponsive attitude must have exasperated him at last, for he judged it necessary to inform me he feared neither God nor devil, let alone any mere man. I said I could see that very well, but what I wanted was a certain quantity of rivets—and rivets were what really Mr. Kurtz wanted, if he had only known it. Now letters went to the coast every week. . . . 'My dear sir,' he cried, 'I write from dictation.' I demanded rivets. There was a way—for an intelligent man. He changed his manner; became very cold, and suddenly began to talk about a hippopotamus; wondered whether sleeping on board the steamer (I stuck to my salvage night and day) I wasn't disturbed. There was an old hippo that had the bad habit of getting out on the bank and roaming at night over the station grounds. The pilgrims used to turn out in a body and empty every rifle they could lay hands on at him. Some even had sat up o' nights for him. All this energy was wasted, though. 'That animal has a charmed life,' he said; 'but you can say this only of brutes in this country. No man—you apprehend me?—no man here bears a charmed life.' He stood there for a moment in the moonlight with his delicate hooked nose set a little askew, and his mica eyes glittering without a wink, then, with a curt Good-night, he strode off. I could see he was disturbed and considerably puzzled, which made me feel more hopeful than I had been for days. It was a great comfort to turn from that chap to my influential friend, the battered, twisted, ruined, tin-pot steamboat. I clambered on board. She rang under my feet like an empty Huntley & Palmer biscuit-tin kicked along a gutter; she was nothing so solid in make, and rather less pretty in shape, but I had expended enough hard work on her to make me love her. No influential friend would have served me better. She had given me a chance to come out a bit—to find out what I could do. No, I don't like work. I had rather laze about and think of all the fine things that can be done. I don't like work—no man does—but I like what is in the work—the chance to find yourself. Your own reality—for yourself, not for others—what no other man can ever know. They can only see the mere show, and never can tell what it really means.

"I was not surprised to see somebody sitting aft, on the deck, with his legs dangling over the mud. You see I rather chummed with the few mechanics there were in that station, whom the other pilgrims naturally despised—on account of their imperfect manners, I suppose. This was the foreman—a boiler-maker by trade—a good worker. He was a lank, bony, yellow-faced man, with big intense eyes. His aspect was worried, and his head was as bald as the palm of my hand; but his hair in falling seemed to have stuck to his chin, and had prospered in the new locality, for his beard hung down to his waist. He was a widower with six young children (he had left them in charge of a sister of his to come out there), and the passion of his life was pigeon-flying. He was an enthusiast and a connoisseur. He would rave about pigeons. After work hours he used sometimes to come over from his hut for a talk about his children and his pigeons; at work, when he had to crawl in the mud under the bottom of the steamboat, he would tie up that beard of his in a kind of white serviette he brought for the purpose. It had loops to go over his ears. In the evening he could be seen squatted on the bank rinsing that wrapper in the creek with great care, then spreading it solemnly on a bush to dry.

"I slapped him on the back and shouted 'We shall have rivets!' He scrambled to his feet exclaiming 'No! Rivets!' as though he couldn't believe his ears. Then in a low voice, 'You . . . eh?' I don't know why we behaved like lunatics. I put my finger to the side of my nose and nodded mysteriously. 'Good for you!' he cried, snapped his fingers above his head, lifting one foot. I tried a jig. We capered on the iron deck. A frightful clatter came out of that hulk, and the virgin forest on the other bank of the creek sent it back in a thundering roll upon the sleeping station. It must have made some of the pilgrims sit up in their hovels. A dark figure obscured the lighted doorway of the manager's hut, vanished, then, a second or so after, the doorway itself vanished too. We stopped, and the silence driven away by the stamping of our feet flowed back again from the recesses of the land. The great wall of vegetation, an exuberant and entangled mass of trunks, branches, leaves, boughs, festoons, motionless in the moonlight, was like a rioting invasion of soundless life, a rolling wave of plants, piled up, crested,

ready to topple over the creek, to sweep every little man of us out of his little
existence. And it moved not. A deadened burst of mighty splashes and
snorts reached us from afar, as though an ichthyosaurus had been taking a
bath of glitter in the great river. 'After all,' said the boiler-maker in a
reasonable tone, 'why shouldn't we get the rivets?' Why not, indeed! I did
not know of any reason why we shouldn't. 'They'll come in three weeks,' I
said confidently.

"But they didn't. Instead of rivets there came an invasion, an infliction, a
visitation. It came in sections during the next three weeks, each section
headed by a donkey carrying a white man in new clothes and tan shoes,
bowing from that elevation right and left to the impressed pilgrims. A
quarrelsome band of footsore sulky niggers trod on the heels of the donkey;
a lot of tents, camp-stools, tin boxes, white cases, brown bales would be
shot down in the courtyard, and the air of mystery would deepen a little over
the muddle of the station. Five such instalments came, with their absurd
air of disorderly flight with the loot of innumerable outfit shops and
provision stores, that, one would think, they were lugging, after a raid, into
the wilderness for equitable division. It was an inextricable mess of things
decent in themselves but that human folly made look like the spoils of
thieving.

"This devoted band called itself the Eldorado Exploring Expedition, and I
believe they were sworn to secrecy. Their talk, however, was the talk of
sordid buccaneers: it was reckless without hardihood, greedy without
audacity, and cruel without courage; there was not an atom of foresight or
of serious intention in the whole batch of them, and they did not seem
aware these things are wanted for the work of the world. To tear treasure
out of the bowels of the land was their desire, with no more moral purpose
at the back of it than there is in burglars breaking into a safe. Who paid the
expenses of the noble enterprise I don't know; but the uncle of our manager
was leader of that lot.

"In exterior he resembled a butcher in a poor neighbourhood, and his eyes
had a look of sleepy cunning. He carried his fat paunch with ostentation on
his short legs, and during the time his gang infested the station spoke to no
one but his nephew. You could see these two roaming about all day long
with their heads close together in an everlasting confab.

"I had given up worrying myself about the rivets. One's capacity for that
kind of folly is more limited than you would suppose. I said Hang!—and let
things slide. I had plenty of time for meditation, and now and then I would
give some thought to Kurtz. I wasn't very interested in him. No. Still, I was
curious to see whether this man, who had come out equipped with moral
ideas of some sort, would climb to the top after all, and how he would set
about his work when there."

2

"One evening as I was lying flat on the deck of my steamboat, I heard
voices approaching—and there were the nephew and the uncle strolling
along the bank. I laid my head on my arm again, and had nearly lost myself

in a doze, when somebody said in my ear, as it were: 'I am as harmless as a little child, but I don't like to be dictated to. Am I the manager—or am I not? I was ordered to send him there. It's incredible.' . . . I became aware that the two were standing on the shore alongside the forepart of the steamboat, just below my head. I did not move; it did not occur to me to move: I was sleepy. 'It *is* unpleasant,' grunted the uncle. 'He has asked the Administration to be sent there,' said the other, 'with the idea of showing what he could do; and I was instructed accordingly. Look at the influence that man must have. Is it not frightful?' They both agreed it was frightful, then made several bizarre remarks: 'Make rain and fine weather—one man—the Council—by the nose'—bits of absurd sentences that got the better of my drowsiness, so that I had pretty near the whole of my wits about me when the uncle said, 'The climate may do away with this difficulty for you. Is he alone there?' 'Yes,' answered the manager; 'he sent his assistant down the river with a note to me in these terms: "Clear this poor devil out of the country, and don't bother sending more of that sort. I had rather be alone than have the kind of men you can dispose of with me." It was more than a year ago. Can you imagine such impudence?' 'Anything since then?' asked the other hoarsely. 'Ivory,' jerked the nephew; 'lots of it—prime sort—lots—most annoying, from him.' 'And with that?' questioned the heavy rumble. 'Invoice,' was the reply fired out, so to speak. Then silence. They had been talking about Kurtz.

"I was broad awake by this time, but, lying perfectly at ease, remained still, having no inducement to change my position. 'How did that ivory come all this way?' growled the elder man, who seemed very vexed. The other explained that it had come with a fleet of canoes in charge of an English half-caste clerk Kurtz had with him; that Kurtz had apparently intended to return himself, the station being by that time bare of goods and stores, but after coming three hundred miles, had suddenly decided to go back, which he started to do alone in a small dugout with four paddlers, leaving the half-caste to continue down the river with the ivory. The two fellows there seemed astounded at anybody attempting such a thing. They were at a loss for an adequate motive. As for me, I seemed to see Kurtz for the first time. It was a distinct glimpse: the dugout, four paddling savages, and the lone white man turning his back suddenly on the headquarters, on relief, on thoughts of home—perhaps; setting his face towards the depths of the wilderness, towards his empty and desolate station. I did not know the motive. Perhaps he was just simply a fine fellow who stuck to his work for its own sake. His name, you understand, had not been pronounced once. He was 'that man.' The half-caste, who, as far as I could see, had conducted a difficult trip with great prudence and pluck, was invariably alluded to as 'that scoundrel.' The 'scoundrel' had reported that the 'man' had been very ill—had recovered imperfectly. . . . The two below me moved away then a few paces, and strolled back and forth at some little distance. I heard: 'Military post—doctor—two hundred miles—quite alone now—unavoidable delays—nine months—no news—strange rumours.' They approached again, just as the manager was saying, 'No one, as far as I know, unless a species of wandering trader—a pestilential fellow, snapping ivory from the natives.' Who was it they were talking about now? I gathered in snatches that this was some man supposed to be in Kurtz's district, and of whom the manager did not approve. 'We will not be free from unfair competition till one of these fellows is hanged for an example,' he said. 'Certainly,' grunted the other; 'get him hanged! Why not? Anything—anything can be done in this country. That's what I say; nobody here, you understand, *here,* can endanger your position. And why? You stand the climate—you outlast them all. The danger is in Europe; but there before I left I took care to——' They moved off and whispered, then their voices rose again. 'The extraordinary series of delays is not my fault. I did my possible.' The fat man sighed, 'Very sad.' 'And the pestiferous absurdity of his talk,' continued the other; 'he bothered me enough when he was here. "Each station should be like a beacon on the road towards better things, a centre for trade of course, but also for humanising, improving, instructing." Conceive you—that ass! And he wants to be manager! No, it's——' Here he got choked by excessive indignation, and I lifted my head the least bit. I was surprised to see how near they were—right under me. I could have spat upon their hats. They were looking on the ground, absorbed in thought. The manager was switching his leg with a slender twig: his sagacious relative lifted his head. 'You have been well since you came out this time?' he asked. The other gave a start. 'Who? I? Oh! Like a charm—like a charm. But the rest—oh, my goodness! All sick. They die so quick, too, that I haven't the time to send them out of the country—it's incredible!' 'H'm. Just so,' grunted the uncle. 'Ah! my boy, trust to this—I say, trust to this.' I saw him extend his short flipper of an arm for a gesture that took in the forest, the creek, the mud, the river—seemed to beckon with a dishonouring flourish before the sunlit face of the land a treacherous appeal to the lurking death, to the hidden evil, to the profound darkness of its heart. It was so startling that I leaped to my feet and looked back at the edge of the forest, as though I had expected an answer of some sort to that black display of confidence. You know the foolish notions that come to one sometimes. The high stillness confronted these two figures with its ominous patience, waiting for the passing away of a fantastic invasion.

"They swore aloud together—out of sheer fright, I believe—then, pretending not to know anything of my existence, turned back to the station. The sun was low; and leaning forward side by side, they seemed to be tugging painfully uphill their two ridiculous shadows of unequal length, that trailed behind them slowly over the tall grass without bending a single blade.

"In a few days the Eldorado Expedition went into the patient wilderness, that closed upon it as the sea closes over a diver. Long afterwards the news came that all the donkeys were dead. I know nothing as to the fate of the less valuable animals. They, no doubt, like the rest of us, found what they deserved. I did not inquire. I was then rather excited at the prospect of meeting Kurtz very soon. When I say very soon I mean it comparatively. It was just two months from the day we left the creek when we came to the bank below Kurtz's station.

"Going up that river was like travelling back to the earliest beginnings of the world, when vegetation rioted on the earth and the big trees were kings. An empty stream, a great silence, an impenetrable forest. The air was warm, thick, heavy, sluggish. There was no joy in the brilliance of sunshine. The long stretches of the waterway ran on, deserted, into the gloom of overshadowed distances. On silvery sandbanks hippos and alligators sunned themselves side by side. The broadening waters flowed through a mob of wooded islands; you lost your way on that river as you would in a desert, and butted all day long against shoals, trying to find the channel, till you thought yourself bewitched and cut off for ever from everything you had known once—somewhere—far away—in another existence perhaps. There were moments when one's past came back to one, as it will sometimes when you have not a moment to spare to yourself; but it came in the shape of an unrestful and noisy dream, remembered with wonder amongst the overwhelming realities of this strange world of plants, and water, and silence. And this stillness of life did not in the least resemble a peace. It was the stillness of an implacable force brooding over an inscrutable intention. It looked at you with a vengeful aspect. I got used to it afterwards; I did not see it any more; I had no time. I had to keep guessing at the channel; I had to discern, mostly by inspiration, the signs of hidden banks; I watched for sunken stones; I was learning to clap my teeth smartly before my heart flew out, when I shaved by a fluke some infernal sly old snag that would have ripped the life out of the tin-pot steamboat and drowned all the pilgrims; I had to keep a look-out for the signs of dead wood we could cut up in the night for next day's steaming. When you have to attend to things of that sort, to the mere incidents of the surface, the reality—the reality, I tell you—fades. The inner truth is hidden—luckily, luckily. But I felt it all the same; I felt often its mysterious stillness watching me at my monkey tricks, just as it watches you fellows performing on your respective tight-ropes for—what is it? half a crown a tumble——"

"Try to be civil, Marlow," growled a voice, and I knew there was at least one listener awake besides myself.

"I beg your pardon. I forgot the heartache which makes up the rest of the price. And indeed what does the price matter, if the trick be well done? You do your tricks very well. And I didn't do badly either, since I managed not to sink that steamboat on my first trip. It's a wonder to me yet. Imagine a blindfolded man set to drive a van over a bad road. I sweated and shivered over that business considerably, I can tell you. After all, for a seaman, to scrape the bottom of the thing that's supposed to float all the time under his care is the unpardonable sin. No one may know of it, but you never forget the thump—eh? A blow on the very heart. You remember it, you dream of it, you wake up at night and think of it—years after—and go hot and cold all over. I don't pretend to say that steamboat floated all the time. More than once she had to wade for a bit, with twenty cannibals splashing around and pushing. We had enlisted some of these chaps on the way for a crew. Fine fellows—cannibals—in their place. They were men one could work with, and I am grateful to them. And, after all, they did not eat each other before my face: they had brought along a provision of hippo-meat which went rotten, and made the mystery of the wilderness stink in my nostrils. Phoo! I can sniff it now. I had the manager on board and three or four pilgrims with their staves—all complete. Sometimes we came upon a station close by the bank, clinging to the skirts of the unknown, and the white men rushing out of a tumble-down hovel, with great gestures of joy and surprise and welcome, seemed very strange—had the appearance of being held there captive by a spell. The word 'ivory' would ring in the air for a while—and on we went again into the silence, along empty reaches, round the still bends, between the high walls of our winding way, reverberating in hollow claps the ponderous beat of the stern-wheel. Trees, trees, millions of trees, massive, immense, running up high; and at their foot, hugging the bank against the stream, crept the little begrimed steamboat, like a sluggish beetle crawling on the floor of a lofty portico. It made you feel very small, very lost, and yet it was not altogether depressing, that feeling. After all, if you were small, the grimy beetle crawled on—which was just what you wanted it to do. Where the pilgrims imagined it crawled to I don't know. To some place where they expected to get something, I bet! For me it crawled towards Kurtz—exclusively; but when the steam-pipes started leaking we crawled very slow. The reaches opened before us and closed behind, as if the forest had stepped leisurely across the water to bar the way for our return. We penetrated deeper and deeper into the heart of darkness. It was very quiet there. At night sometimes the roll of drums behind the curtain of trees would run up the river and remain sustained faintly, as if hovering in the air high over our heads, till the first break of day. Whether it meant war, peace, or prayer we could not tell. The dawns were heralded by the descent of a chill stillness; the woodcutters slept, their fires burned low; the snapping of a twig would make you start. We were wanderers on a prehistoric earth, on an earth that wore the aspect of an unknown planet. We could have fancied ourselves the first of men taking possession of an accursed inheritance, to be subdued at the cost of profound anguish and of excessive toil. But suddenly, as we struggled round a bend, there would be a glimpse of rush walls, of peaked grass-roofs, a burst of yells, a whirl of black limbs, a mass of hands clapping, of feet stamping, of bodies swaying, of eyes rolling, under the droop of heavy and motionless foliage. The steamer toiled along slowly on the edge of a black and incomprehensible frenzy. The prehistoric man was cursing us, praying to us, welcoming us—who could tell? We were cut off from the comprehension of our surroundings; we glided past like phantoms, wondering and secretly appalled, as sane men would be before an enthusiastic outbreak in a mad-house. We could not understand because we were too far and could not remember, because we were travelling in the night of first ages, of those ages that are gone, leaving hardly a sign—and no memories.

"The earth seemed unearthly. We are accustomed to look upon the shackled form of a conquered monster, but there—there you could look at a thing monstrous and free. It was unearthly, and the men—— No, they were not inhuman. Well, you know, that was the worst of it—this suspicion of their not being inhuman. It would come slowly to one. They howled and leaped, and spun, and made horrid faces; but what thrilled you was just the thought of their humanity—like yours—the thought of your remote kinship with this wild and passionate uproar. Ugly. Yes, it was ugly enough; but if you were man enough you would admit to yourself that there was in you just the faintest trace of a response to the terrible frankness of that noise, a dim suspicion of there being a meaning in it which you—you so remote from the night of first ages—could comprehend. And why not? The mind of man is capable of anything—because everything is in it, all the past as well as all the future. What was there after all? Joy, fear, sorrow, devotion, valour, rage—who can tell?—but truth—truth stripped of its cloak of time. Let the fool gape and shudder—the man knows, and can look on without a wink. But he must at least be as much of a man as these on the shore. He must meet that truth with his own true stuff—with his own inborn strength. Principles? Principles won't do. Acquisitions, clothes, pretty rags—rags that would fly off at the first good shake. No; you want a deliberate belief. An appeal to me in this fiendish row—is there? Very well; I hear; I admit, but I have a voice too, and for good or evil mine is the speech that cannot be silenced. Of course, a fool, what with sheer fright and fine sentiments, is always safe. Who's that grunting? You wonder I didn't go ashore for a howl and a dance? Well, no—I didn't. Fine sentiments, you say? Fine sentiments be hanged! I had no time. I had to mess about with white-lead and strips of woollen blanket helping to put bandages on those leaky steam-pipes—I tell you. I had to watch the steering, and circumvent those snags, and get the tin-pot along by hook or by crook. There was surface-truth enough in these things to save a wiser man. And between whiles I had to look after the savage who was fireman. He was an improved specimen; he could fire up a vertical boiler. He was there below me, and, upon my word, to look at him was as edifying as seeing a dog in a parody of breeches and a feather hat, walking on his hind legs. A few months of training had done for that really fine chap. He squinted at the steam-gauge and at the water-gauge with an evident effort of intrepidity—and he had filed teeth too, the poor devil, and the wool of his pate shaved into queer patterns, and three ornamental scars on each of his cheeks. He ought to have been clapping his hands and stamping his feet on the bank, instead of which he was hard at work, a thrall to strange witchcraft, full of improving knowledge. He was useful because he had been instructed; and what he knew was this—that should the water in that transparent thing disappear, the evil spirit inside the boiler would get angry through the greatness of his thirst, and take a terrible vengeance. So he sweated and fired up and watched the glass fearfully (with an impromptu charm, made of rags, tied to his arm, and a piece of polished bone, as big as a watch, stuck flatways through his lower lip), while the wooded banks slipped past us slowly, the short noise was left behind, the interminable miles of silence—and we crept on, towards Kurtz. But the snags were thick, the water was treacherous and shallow, the boiler seemed indeed to have a sulky devil in it, and thus neither that fireman nor I had any time to peer into our creepy thoughts.

"Some fifty miles below the Inner Station we came upon a hut of reeds, an inclined and melancholy pole, with the unrecognisable tatters of what had been a flag of some sort flying from it, and a neatly stacked wood-pile. This was unexpected. We came to the bank, and on the stack of firewood found a flat piece of board with some faded pencil-writing on it. When deciphered it said: 'Wood for you. Hurry up. Approach cautiously.' There was a signature, but it was illegible—not Kurtz—a much longer word. 'Hurry up.' Where? Up the river? 'Approach cautiously.' We had not done so. But the warning could not have been meant for the place where it could be only found after approach. Something was wrong above. But what—and how much? That was the question. We commented adversely upon the imbecility of that telegraphic style. The bush around said nothing, and would not let us look very far, either. A torn curtain of red twill hung in the doorway of the hut, and flapped sadly in our faces. The dwelling was dismantled; but we could see a white man had lived there not very long ago. There remained a rude table—a plank on two posts; a heap of rubbish reposed in a dark corner, and by the door I picked up a book. It had lost its covers, and the pages had been thumbed into a state of extremely dirty softness; but the back had been lovingly stitched afresh with white cotton thread, which looked clean yet. It was an extraordinary find. Its title was, *An Inquiry into some Points of Seamanship,* by a man Towser, Towson— some such name—Master in His Majesty's Navy. The matter looked dreary reading enough, with illustrative diagrams and repulsive tables of figures, and the copy was sixty years old. I handled this amazing antiquity with the greatest possible tenderness, lest it should dissolve in my hands. Within, Towson or Towser was inquiring earnestly into the breaking strain of ships' chains and tackle, and other such matters. Not a very enthralling book; but at the first glance you could see there a singleness of intention, an honest concern for the right way of going to work, which made these humble pages, thought out so many years ago, luminous with another than a professional light. The simple old sailor, with his talk of chains and purchases, made me forget the jungle and the pilgrims in a delicious sensation of having come upon something unmistakably real. Such a book being there was wonderful enough; but still more astounding were the notes pencilled in the margin, and plainly referring to the text. I couldn't believe my eyes! They were in cipher! Yes, it looked like cipher. Fancy a man lugging with him a book of that description into this nowhere and studying it—and making notes—in cipher at that! It was an extravagant mystery.

"I had been dimly aware for some time of a worrying noise, and when I lifted my eyes I saw the wood-pile was gone, and the manager, aided by all the pilgrims, was shouting at me from the river-side. I slipped the book into my pocket. I assure you to leave off reading was like tearing myself away from the shelter of an old and solid friendship.

"I started the lame engine ahead. 'It must be this miserable trader—this intruder,' exclaimed the manager, looking back malevolently at the place we had left. 'He must be English,' I said. 'It will not save him from getting into trouble if he is not careful,' muttered the manager darkly. I observed with assumed innocence that no man was safe from trouble in this world.

"The current was more rapid now, the steamer seemed at her last gasp, the stern-wheel flopped languidly, and I caught myself listening on tiptoe for the next beat of the float, for in sober truth I expected the wretched thing to give up every moment. It was like watching the last flickers of a life. But still we crawled. Sometimes I would pick out a tree a little way ahead to measure our progress towards Kurtz by, but I lost it invariably before we got abreast. To keep the eyes so long on one thing was too much for human patience. The manager displayed a beautiful resignation. I fretted and fumed and took to arguing with myself whether or no I would talk openly with Kurtz; but before I could come to any conclusion it occurred to me that my speech or my silence, indeed any action of mine, would be a mere futility. What did it matter what any one knew or ignored? What did it matter who was manager? One gets sometimes such a flash of insight. The essentials of this affair lay deep under the surface, beyond my reach, and beyond my power of meddling.

"Towards the evening of the second day we judged ourselves about eight miles from Kurtz's station. I wanted to push on; but the manager looked grave, and told me the navigation up there was so dangerous that it would be advisable, the sun being very low already, to wait where we were till next morning. Moreover, he pointed out that if the warning to approach cautiously were to be followed, we must approach in daylight—not at dusk, or in the dark. This was sensible enough. Eight miles meant nearly three hours' steaming for us, and I could also see suspicious ripples at the upper end of the reach. Nevertheless, I was annoyed beyond expression at the delay, and most unreasonably too, since one night more could not matter much after so many months. As we had plenty of wood, and caution was the word, I brought up in the middle of the stream. The reach was narrow, straight, with high sides like a railway cutting. The dusk came gliding into it long before the sun had set. The current ran smooth and swift, but a dumb immobility sat on the banks. The living trees, lashed together by the creepers and every living bush of the undergrowth, might have been changed into stone, even to the slenderest twig, to the lightest leaf. It was not sleep—it seemed unnatural, like a state of trance. Not the faintest sound of any kind could be heard. You looked on amazed, and began to suspect yourself of being deaf—then the night came suddenly, and struck you blind as well. About three in the morning some large fish leaped, and the loud splash made me jump as though a gun had been fired. When the sun rose there was a white fog, very warm and clammy, and more blinding than the night. It did not shift or drive; it was just there, standing all round you like something solid. At eight or nine, perhaps, it lifted as a shutter lifts. We had a glimpse of the towering multitude of trees, of the immense matted jungle, with the blazing little ball of the sun hanging over it—all perfectly still—and then the white shutter came down again, smoothly, as if sliding in greased grooves. I ordered the chain, which we had begun to heave in, to be paid out again. Before it stopped running with a muffled rattle, a cry, a very loud cry, as of infinite desolation, soared slowly in the opaque air. It ceased. A complaining clamour, modulated in savage dis-cords, filled our ears. The sheer unexpectedness of it made my hair stir under my cap. I don't know how it struck the others: to me it seemed as though the mist itself had screamed, so suddenly, and apparently from all sides at once, did this tumultuous and mournful uproar arise. It culminated in a hurried outbreak of almost intolerably excessive shrieking, which stopped short, leaving us stiffened in a variety of silly attitudes, and obstinately listening to the nearly as appalling and excessive silence. 'Good God! What is the meaning——?' stammered at my elbow one of the pilgrims—a little fat man, with sandy hair and red whiskers, who wore side-spring boots, and pink pyjamas tucked into his socks. Two others remained openmouthed a whole minute, then dashed into the little cabin, to rush out incontinently and stand darting scared glances, with Winches-ters at 'ready' in their hands. What we could see was just the steamer we were on, her outlines blurred as though she had been on the point of dissolving, and a misty strip of water, perhaps two feet broad, around her—and that was all. The rest of the world was nowhere, as far as our eyes and ears were concerned. Just nowhere. Gone, disappeared; swept off without leaving a whisper or a shadow behind.

"I went forward, and ordered the chain to be hauled in short, so as to be ready to trip the anchor and move the steamboat at once if necessary. 'Will they attack?' whispered an awed voice. 'We will all be butchered in this fog,' murmured another. The faces twitched with the strain, the hands trembled slightly, the eyes forgot to wink. It was very curious to see the contrast of expressions of the white men and of the black fellows of our crew, who were as much strangers to that part of the river as we, though their homes were only eight hundred miles away. The whites, of course greatly discomposed, had besides a curious look of being painfully shocked by such an outrageous row. The others had an alert, naturally interested expression; but their faces were essentially quiet, even those of the one or two who grinned as they hauled at the chain. Several exchanged short, grunting phrases, which seemed to settle the matter to their satisfaction. Their head-man, a young, broad-chested black, severely draped in dark-blue fringed cloths, with fierce nostrils and his hair all done up artfully in oily ringlets, stood near me. 'Aha!' I said, just for good fellowship's sake. 'Catch 'im,' he snapped, with a bloodshot widening of his eyes and a flash of sharp teeth—'catch 'im. Give 'im to us.' 'To you, eh?' I asked; 'what would you do with them?' 'Eat 'im!' he said curtly, and, leaning his elbow on the rail, looked out into the fog in a dignified and profoundly pensive attitude. I would no doubt have been properly horrified, had it not occurred to me that he and his chaps must be very hungry: that they must have been growing increasingly hungry for at least this month past. They had been engaged for six months (I don't think a single one of them had any clear idea of time, as we at the end of countless ages have. They still belonged to the beginnings of time—had no inherited experience to teach them, as it were), and of course, as long as there was a piece of paper written over in accordance with some farcical law or other made down the river, it didn't enter anybody's head to trouble how they would live. Certainly they had brought with them some rotten hippo-meat, which couldn't have lasted very long, anyway, even if the pilgrims hadn't, in the midst of a shocking hullabaloo, thrown a considerable quantity of it overboard. It looked like a high-handed proceeding; but it was really a case of legitimate self-defence. You can't breathe dead hippo waking, sleeping, and eating, and at the same time keep your precarious grip on existence. Besides that, they had given them every week three pieces of brass wire, each about nine inches long; and the theory was they were to buy their provisions with that currency in river-side villages. You can see how *that* worked. There were either no villages, or the people were hostile, or the director, who like the rest of us fed out of tins, with an occasional old he-goat thrown in, didn't want to stop the steamer for some more or less recondite reason. So, unless they swallowed the wire itself, or made loops of it to snare the fishes with, I don't see what good their extravagant salary could be to them. I must say it was paid with a regularity worthy of a large and honourable trading company. For the rest, the only thing to eat—though it didn't look eatable in the least—I saw in their possession was a few lumps of some stuff like half-cooked dough, of a dirty lavender colour, they kept wrapped in leaves, and now and then swallowed a piece of, but so small that it seemed done more for the look of the thing than for any serious purpose of sustenance. Why in the name of all the gnawing devils of hunger they didn't go for us—they were thirty to five—and have a good tuck-in for once, amazes me now when I think of it. They were big powerful men, with not much capacity to weigh the consequences, with courage, with strength, even yet, though their skins were no longer glossy and their muscles no longer hard. And I saw that something restraining, one of those human secrets that baffle probability, had come into play there. I looked at them with a swift quickening of interest—not because it occurred to me I might be eaten by them before very long, though I own to you that just then I perceived—in a new light, as it were—how unwholesome the pilgrims looked, and I hoped, yes, I positively hoped, that my aspect was not so—what shall I say?—so—unappetising: a touch of fantastic vanity which fitted well with the dream-sensation that pervaded all my days at that time. Perhaps I had a little fever too. One can't live with one's finger everlastingly on one's pulse. I had often 'a little fever,' or a little touch of other things—the playful paw-strokes of the wilderness, the preliminary trifling before the more serious onslaught which came in due course. Yes; I looked at them as you would on any human being, with a curiosity of their impulses, motives, capacities, weaknesses, when brought to the test of an inexorable physical necessity. Restraint! What possible restraint? Was it superstition, disgust, patience, fear—or some kind of primitive honour? No fear can stand up to hunger, no patience can wear it out, disgust simply does not exist where hunger is; and as to superstition, beliefs, and what you may call principles, they are less than chaff in a breeze. Don't you know the devilry of lingering starvation, its exasperating torment, its black thoughts, its sombre and brooding ferocity? Well, I do. It takes a man all his inborn strength to fight hunger properly. It's really easier to face bereavement, dishonour, and the perdition of one's soul—than this kind of prolonged hunger. Sad, but true. And these chaps too had no earthly reason for any kind of scruple. Restraint! I would just as soon have expected restraint from a hyena prowling amongst the corpses of a battlefield. But there was the fact facing me—the fact dazzling, to be seen, like the foam on the depths of the sea, like a ripple on an unfathomable enigma, a mystery greater—when I thought of it—than the curious, inexplicable note of desperate grief in this savage clamour that had swept by us on the river-bank, behind the blind whiteness of the fog.

"Two pilgrims were quarrelling in hurried whispers as to which bank. 'Left.' 'No, no; how can you? Right, right, of course.' 'It is very serious,' said the manager's voice behind me; 'I would be desolated if anything should happen to Mr. Kurtz before we came up.' I looked at him, and had not the slightest doubt he was sincere. He was just the kind of man who would wish to preserve appearances. That was his restraint. But when he muttered something about going on at once, I did not even take the trouble to answer him. I knew, and he knew, that it was impossible. Were we to let go our hold of the bottom, we would be absolutely in the air—in space. We wouldn't be able to tell where we were going to—whether up or down stream, or across—till we fetched against one bank or the other—and then we wouldn't know at first which it was. Of course I made no move. I had no mind for a smash-up. You couldn't imagine a more deadly place for a shipwreck. Whether drowned at once or not, we were sure to perish speedily in one way or another. 'I authorise you to take all the risks,' he said, after a short silence. 'I refuse to take any,' I said shortly; which was just the answer he expected, though its tone might have surprised him. 'Well, I must defer to your judgment. You are captain,' he said, with marked civility. I turned my shoulder to him in sign of my appreciation, and looked into the fog. How long would it last? It was the most hopeless look-out. The approach to this Kurtz grubbing for ivory in the wretched bush was beset by as many dangers as though he had been an enchanted princess sleeping in a fabulous castle. 'Will they attack, do you think?' asked the manager, in a confidential tone.

"I did not think they would attack, for several obvious reasons. The thick fog was one. If they left the bank in their canoes they would get lost in it, as we would be if we attempted to move. Still, I had also judged the jungle of both banks quite impenetrable—and yet eyes were in it, eyes that had seen us. The river-side bushes were certainly very thick; but the undergrowth behind was evidently penetrable. However, during the short lift I had seen no canoes anywhere in the reach—certainly not abreast of the steamer. But what made the idea of attack inconceivable to me was the nature of the noise—of the cries we had heard. They had not the fierce character boding of immediate hostile intention. Unexpected, wild, and violent as they had been, they had given me an irresistible impression of sorrow. The glimpse of the steamboat had for some reason filled those savages with un-restrained grief. The danger, if any, I expounded, was from our proximity to a great human passion let loose. Even extreme grief may ultimately vent itself in violence—but more generally takes the form of apathy. . . .

"You should have seen the pilgrims stare! They had no heart to grin, or even to revile me; but I believe they thought me gone mad—with fright, maybe. I delivered a regular lecture. My dear boys, it was no good bothering. Keep a look-out? Well, you may guess I watched the fog for the signs of lifting as a cat watches a mouse; but for anything else our eyes were of no more use to us than if we had been buried miles deep in a heap of cotton-wool. It felt like it too—choking, warm, stifling. Besides, all I said, though it sounded extravagant, was absolutely true to fact. What we afterwards alluded to as an attack was really an attempt at repulse. The action was very far from being aggressive—it was not even defensive, in the usual sense: it was undertaken under the stress of desperation, and in its essence was purely protective.

"It developed itself, I should say, two hours after the fog lifted, and its commencement was at a spot, roughly speaking, about a mile and a half below Kurtz's station. We had just floundered and flopped round a bend, when I saw an islet, a mere grassy hummock of bright green, in the middle of the stream. It was the only thing of the kind; but as we opened the reach more, I perceived it was the head of a long sandbank, or rather of a chain of shallow patches stretching down the middle of the river. They were discoloured, just awash, and the whole lot was seen just under the water, exactly as a man's backbone is seen running down the middle of his back under the skin. Now, as far as I did see, I could go to the right or to the left of this. I didn't know either channel, of course. The banks looked pretty well alike, the depth appeared the same; but as I had been informed the station was on the west side, I naturally headed for the western passage.

"No sooner had we fairly entered it than I became aware it was much narrower than I had supposed. To the left of us there was the long uninterrupted shoal, and to the right a high steep bank heavily overgrown with bushes. Above the bush the trees stood in serried ranks. The twigs overhung the current thickly, and from distance to distance a large limb of some tree projected rigidly over the stream. It was then well on in the afternoon, the face of the forest was gloomy, and a broad strip of shadow had already fallen on the water. In this shadow we steamed up—very slowly, as you may imagine. I sheered her well inshore—the water being deepest near the bank, as the sounding-pole informed me.

"One of my hungry and forbearing friends was sounding in the bows just below me. This steamboat was exactly like a decked scow. On the deck there were two little teak-wood houses, with doors and windows. The boiler was in the fore-end, and the machinery right astern. Over the whole there was a light roof, supported on stanchions. The funnel projected through that roof, and in front of the funnel a small cabin built of light planks served for a pilot-house. It contained a couch, two camp-stools, a loaded Martini-Henry leaning in one corner, a tiny table, and the steering-wheel. It had a wide door in front and a broad shutter at each side. All these were always thrown open, of course. I spent my days perched up there on the extreme fore-end of that roof, before the door. At night I slept, or tried to, on the couch. An athletic black belonging to some coast tribe, and educated by my poor predecessor, was the helmsman. He sported a pair of brass earrings, wore a blue cloth wrapper from the waist to the ankles, and thought all the world of himself. He was the most unstable kind of fool I had ever seen. He steered with no end of a swagger while you were by; but if he lost sight of you, he became instantly the prey of an abject funk, and would let that cripple of a steamboat get the upper hand of him in a minute.

"I was looking down at the sounding-pole, and feeling much annoyed to see at each try a little more of it stick out of that river, when I saw my poleman give up the business suddenly, and stretch himself flat on the deck, without even taking the trouble to haul his pole in. He kept hold on it though, and it trailed in the water. At the same time the fireman, whom I could also see below me, sat down abruptly before his furnace and ducked his head. I was amazed. Then I had to look at the river mighty quick, because there was a snag in the fairway. Sticks, little sticks, were flying about—thick: they were whizzing before my nose, dropping below me, striking behind me against my pilot-house. All this time the river, the shore, the woods, were very quiet—perfectly quiet. I could only hear the heavy splashing thump of the stern-wheel and the patter of these things. We cleared the snag clumsily. Arrows, by Jove! We were being shot at! I stepped in quickly to close the shutter on the land-side. The fool-helmsman, his hands on the spokes, was lifting his knees high, stamping his feet, champing his mouth, like a reined-in horse. Confound him! And we were staggering within ten feet of the bank. I had to lean right out to swing the heavy shutter, and I saw a face amongst the leaves on the level with my own, looking at me very fierce and steady; and then suddenly, as though a veil had been removed from my eyes, I made out, deep in the tangled gloom, naked breasts, arms, legs, glaring eyes—the bush was swarming with human limbs in movement, glistening, of bronze colour. The twigs shook, swayed, and rustled, the arrows flew out of them, and then the shutter came to. 'Steer her straight,' I said to the helmsman. He held his head rigid, face forward; but his eyes rolled, he kept on lifting and setting down his feet gently, his mouth foamed a little. 'Keep quiet!' I said in a fury. I might just as well have ordered a tree not to sway in the wind. I darted out. Below me there was a great scuffle of feet on the iron deck; confused exclamations; a voice screamed, 'Can you turn back?' I caught sight of a V-shaped ripple on the water ahead. What? Another snag! A fusillade burst out under my feet. The pilgrims had opened with their Winchesters, and were simply squirting lead into the bush. A deuce of a lot of smoke came up and drove slowly forward. I swore at it. Now I couldn't see the ripple or the snag either. I stood in the doorway, peering, and the arrows came in swarms. They might have been poisoned, but they looked as though they wouldn't kill a cat. The bush began to howl. Our wood-cutters raised a warlike whoop; the report of a rifle just at my back deafened me. I glanced over my shoulder, and the pilot-house was yet full of noise and smoke when I made a dash at the wheel. The fool-nigger had dropped everything, to throw the shutter open and let off that Martini-Henry. He stood before the wide opening, glaring, and I yelled at him to come back, while I straightened the sudden twist out of that steamboat. There was no room to turn even if I had wanted to, the snag was somewhere very near ahead in that confounded smoke, there was no time to lose, so I just crowded her into the bank—right into the bank, where I knew the water was deep.

"We tore slowly along the overhanging bushes in a whirl of broken twigs and flying leaves. The fusillade below stopped short, as I had foreseen it would when the squirts got empty. I threw my head back to a glinting whiz that traversed the pilot-house, in at one shutter-hole and out at the other. Looking past that mad helmsman, who was shaking the empty rifle and yelling at the shore, I saw vague forms of men running bent double, leaping, gliding, distinct, incomplete, evanescent. Something big appeared in the air before the shutter, the rifle went overboard, and the man stepped back swiftly, looked at me over his shoulder in an extraordinary, profound, familiar manner, and fell upon my feet. The side of his head hit the wheel twice, and the end of what appeared a long cane clattered round and knocked over a little camp-stool. It looked as though after wrenching that thing from somebody ashore he had lost his balance in the effort. The thin smoke had blown away, we were clear of the snag, and looking ahead I could see that in another hundred yards or so I would be free to sheer off, away from the bank; but my feet felt so very warm and wet that I had to look down. The man had rolled on his back and stared straight up at me; both his hands clutched that cane. It was the shaft of a spear that, either thrown or lunged through the opening, had caught him in the side just below the ribs; the blade had gone in out of sight, after making a frightful gash; my shoes were full; a pool of blood lay very still, gleaming dark-red under the wheel; his eyes shone with an amazing lustre. The fusillade burst out again. He looked at me anxiously, gripping the spear like something precious, with an air of being afraid I would try to take it away from him. I had to make an effort to free my eyes from his gaze and attend to the steering. With one hand I felt above my head for the line of the steam whistle, and jerked out screech after screech hurriedly. The tumult of angry and warlike yells was checked instantly, and then from the depths of the woods went out such a tremulous and prolonged wail of mournful fear and utter despair as may be imagined to follow the flight of the last hope from the earth. There was a great commotion in the bush; the shower of arrows stopped, a few dropping shots rang out sharply—then silence, in which the languid beat of the stern-wheel came plainly to my ears. I put the helm hard a-starboard at the moment when the pilgrim in pink pyjamas, very hot and agitated, appeared in the doorway. 'The manager sends me——' he began in an official tone, and stopped short. 'Good God!' he said, glaring at the wounded man.

"We two whites stood over him, and his lustrous and inquiring glance enveloped us both. I declare it looked as though he would presently put to us some question in an understandable language; but he died without uttering a sound, without moving a limb, without twitching a muscle. Only in the very last moment, as though in response to some sign we could not see, to some whisper we could not hear, he frowned heavily, and that frown gave to his black death-mask an inconceivably sombre, brooding, and menacing expression. The lustre of inquiring glance faded swiftly into vacant glassiness. 'Can you steer?' I asked the agent eagerly. He looked very dubious; but I made a grab at his arm, and he understood at once I meant him to steer whether or no. To tell you the truth, I was morbidly anxious to change my shoes and socks. 'He is dead,' murmured the fellow, immensely impressed. 'No doubt about it,' said I, tugging like mad at the shoe-laces. 'And by the way, I suppose Mr. Kurtz is dead as well by this time.'

"For the moment that was the dominant thought. There was a sense of extreme disappointment, as though I had found out I had been striving after something altogether without a substance. I couldn't have been more disgusted if I had travelled all this way for the sole purpose of talking with Mr. Kurtz. Talking with . . . I flung one shoe overboard, and became aware that that was exactly what I had been looking forward to—a talk with Kurtz. I made the strange discovery that I had never imagined him as doing, you know, but as discoursing. I didn't say to myself, 'Now I will never see him,' or 'Now I will never shake him by the hand,' but, 'Now I will never hear him.' The man presented himself as a voice. Not of course that I did not connect him with some sort of action. Hadn't I been told in all the tones of jealousy and admiration that he had collected, bartered, swindled, or stolen more ivory than all the other agents together? That was not the point. The point was in his being a gifted creature, and that of all his gifts the one that stood out pre-eminently, that carried with it a sense of real presence, was his ability to talk, his words—the gift of expression, the bewildering, the illuminating, the most exalted and the most contemptible, the pulsating stream of light, or the deceitful flow from the heart of an impenetrable darkness.

"The other shoe went flying unto the devil-god of that river. I thought, By Jove! it's all over. We are too late; he has vanished—the gift has vanished, by means of some spear, arrow, or club. I will never hear that chap speak after all—and my sorrow had a startling extravagance of emotion, even such as I had noticed in the howling sorrow of these savages in the bush. I couldn't have felt more of lonely desolation somehow, had I been robbed of a belief or had missed my destiny in life. . . . Why do you sigh in this beastly way, somebody? Absurd? Well, absurd. Good Lord! mustn't a man ever—— Here, give me some tobacco." . . .

There was a pause of profound stillness, then a match flared, and Marlow's lean face appeared, worn, hollow, with downward folds and dropped eyelids, with an aspect of concentrated attention; and as he took vigorous draws at his pipe, it seemed to retreat and advance out of the night in the regular flicker of the tiny flame. The match went out.

"Absurd!" he cried. "This is the worst of trying to tell . . . Here you all are, each moored with two good addresses, like a hulk with two anchors, a butcher round one corner, a policeman round another, excellent appetites, and temperature normal—you hear—normal from year's end to year's end. And you say, Absurd! Absurd be—exploded! Absurd! My dear boys, what can you expect from a man who out of sheer nervousness had just flung overboard a pair of new shoes? Now I think of it, it is amazing I did not shed tears. I am, upon the whole, proud of my fortitude. I was cut to the quick at the idea of having lost the inestimable privilege of listening to the gifted Kurtz. Of course I was wrong. The privilege was waiting for me. Oh yes, I heard more than enough. And I was right, too. A voice. He was very little more than a voice. And I heard—him—it—this voice—other voices—all of them were so little more than voices—and the memory of that time itself lingers around me, impalpable, like a dying vibration of one immense jabber, silly, atrocious, sordid, savage, or simply mean, without any kind of sense. Voices, voices—even the girl herself—now—"

He was silent for a long time.

"I laid the ghost of his gifts at last with a lie," he began suddenly. "Girl! What? Did I mention a girl? Oh, she is out of it—completely. They—the women I mean—are out of it—should be out of it. We must help them to stay in that beautiful world of their own, lest ours gets worse. Oh, she had to be out of it. You should have heard the disinterred body of Mr. Kurtz saying, 'My Intended.' You would have perceived directly then how completely she was out of it. And the lofty frontal bone of Mr. Kurtz! They say the hair goes on growing sometimes, but this—ah—specimen was impressively bald. The wilderness had patted him on the head, and, behold, it was like a ball—an ivory ball; it had caressed him, and—lo!—he had withered; it had taken him, loved him, embraced him, got into his veins, consumed his flesh, and sealed his soul to its own by the inconceivable ceremonies of some devilish initiation. He was its spoiled and pampered favourite. Ivory? I should think so. Heaps of it, stacks of it. The old mud shanty was bursting with it. You would think there was not a single tusk left either above or below the ground in the whole country. 'Mostly fossil,' the manager had remarked disparagingly. It was no more fossil than I am; but they call it fossil when it is dug up. It appears these niggers do bury the tusks sometimes—but evidently they couldn't bury this parcel deep enough to save the gifted Mr. Kurtz from his fate. We filled the steamboat with it, and had to pile a lot on the deck. Thus he could see and enjoy as long as he could see, because the appreciation of this favour had remained with him to the last. You should have heard him say, 'My ivory.' Oh yes, I heard him. 'My Intended, my ivory, my station, my river, my——' everything belonged to him. It made me hold my breath in expectation of hearing the wilderness burst into a prodigious peal of laughter that would shake the fixed stars in their places. Everything belonged to him—but that was a trifle. The thing was to know what he belonged to, how many powers of darkness claimed him for their own. That was the reflection that made you creepy all over. It was impossible—it was not good for one either—trying to imagine. He had taken a high seat amongst the devils of the land—I mean literally. You can't understand. How could you?—with solid pavement under your feet, surrounded by kind neighbours ready to cheer you or to fall on you, stepping delicately between the butcher and the policeman, in the holy terror of scandal and gallows and lunatic asylums—how can you imagine what particular region of the first ages a man's untrammelled feet may take him into by the way of solitude—utter solitude without a policeman—by the way of silence—utter silence, where no warning voice of a kind neighbour can be heard whispering of public opinion? These little things make all the great difference. When they are gone you must fall back upon your own innate strength, upon your own capacity for faithfulness. Of course you may be too much of a fool to go wrong—too dull even to know you are being assaulted by the powers of darkness. I take it, no fool ever made a bargain for his soul with the devil: the fool is too much of a fool, or the devil too much of a devil—I don't know which. Or you may be such a thunderingly exalted creature as to be altogether deaf and blind to anything but heavenly sights and sounds. Then the earth for you is only a standing place—and whether to be like this is your loss or your gain I won't pretend to say. But most of us are neither one nor the other. The earth for us is a place to live in, where we must put up with sights, with sounds, with smells, too, by Jove!—breathe dead hippo, so to speak, and not be contaminated. And there, don't you see? your strength comes in, the faith in your ability for the digging of unostentatious holes to bury the stuff in—your power of devotion, not to yourself, but to an obscure, back-breaking business. And that's difficult enough. Mind, I am not trying to excuse or even explain—I am trying to account to myself for—for—Mr. Kurtz—for the shade of Mr. Kurtz. This initiated wraith from the back of Nowhere honoured me with its amazing confidence before it vanished altogether. This was because it could speak English to me. The original Kurtz had been educated partly in England, and—as he was good enough to say himself—his sympathies were in the right place. His mother was half-English, his father was half-French. All Europe contributed to the making of Kurtz; and by and by I learned that, most appropriately, the International Society for the Suppression of Savage Customs had entrusted him with the making of a report, for its future guidance. And he had written it too. I've seen it. I've read it. It was eloquent, vibrating with eloquence, but too high-strung, I think. Seventeen pages of close writing he had found time for! But this must have been before his—let us say—nerves went wrong, and caused him to preside at certain midnight dances ending with unspeakable rites, which—as far as I reluctantly gathered from what I heard at various times—were offered up to him—do you understand?—to Mr. Kurtz himself. But it was a beautiful piece of writing. The opening paragraph, however, in the light of later information, strikes me now as ominous. He began with the argument that we whites, from the point of development we had arrived at, 'must necessarily appear to them [savages] in the nature of supernatural beings—we approach them with the might as of a deity,' and so on, and so on. 'By the simple exercise of our will we can exert a power for good practically unbounded,' etc. etc. From that point he soared and took me with him. The peroration was magnificent, though difficult to remember, you know. It gave me the notion of an exotic Immensity ruled by an august

Benevolence. It made me tingle with enthusiasm. This was the unbounded power of eloquence—of words—of burning noble words. There were no practical hints to interrupt the magic current of phrases, unless a kind of note at the foot of the last page, scrawled evidently much later, in an unsteady hand, may be regarded as the exposition of a method. It was very simple, and at the end of that moving appeal to every altruistic sentiment it blazed at you, luminous and terrifying, like a flash of lightning in a serene sky: 'Exterminate all the brutes!' The curious part was that he had apparently forgotten all about that valuable postscriptum, because, later on, when he in a sense came to himself, he repeatedly entreated me to take good care of 'my pamphlet' (he called it), as it was sure to have in the future a good influence upon his career. I had full information about all these things, and, besides, as it turned out, I was to have the care of his memory. I've done enough for it to give me the indisputable right to lay it, if I choose, for an everlasting rest in the dust-bin of progress, amongst all the sweepings and, figuratively speaking, all the dead cats of civilisation. But then, you see, I can't choose. He won't be forgotten. Whatever he was, he was not common. He had the power to charm or frighten rudimentary souls into an aggravated witch-dance in his honour; he could also fill the small souls of the pilgrims with bitter misgivings: he had one devoted friend at least, and he had conquered one soul in the world that was neither rudimentary nor tainted with self-seeking. No; I can't forget him, though I am not prepared to affirm the fellow was exactly worth the life we lost in getting to him. I missed my late helmsman awfully—I missed him even while his body was still lying in the pilot-house. Perhaps you will think it passing strange this regret for a savage who was no more account than a grain of sand in a black Sahara. Well, don't you see, he had done something, he had steered; for months I had him at my back—a help—an instrument. It was a kind of partnership. He steered for me—I had to look after him, I worried about his deficiencies, and thus a subtle bond had been created, of which I only became aware when it was suddenly broken. And the intimate profundity of that look he gave me when he received his hurt remains to this day in my memory—like a claim of distant kinship affirmed in a supreme moment.

"Poor fool! If he had only left that shutter alone. He had no restraint, no restraint—just like Kurtz—a tree swayed by the wind. As soon as I had put on a dry pair of slippers, I dragged him out, after first jerking the spear out of his side, which operation I confess I performed with my eyes shut tight. His heels leaped together over the little door-step; his shoulders were pressed to my breast; I hugged him from behind desperately. Oh! he was heavy, heavy; heavier than any man on earth, I should imagine. Then without more ado I tipped him overboard. The current snatched him as though he had been a wisp of grass, and I saw the body roll over twice before I lost sight of it for ever. All the pilgrims and the manager were then congregated on the awning-deck about the pilot-house, chattering at each other like a flock of excited magpies, and there was a scandalised murmur at my heartless promptitude. What they wanted to keep that body hanging about for I can't guess. Embalm it, maybe. But I had also heard another, and a very ominous, murmur on the deck below. My friends the wood-cutters were likewise scandalised, and with a better show of reason—though I admit that the reason itself was quite inadmissible. Oh, quite! I had made up my mind that if my late helmsman was to be eaten, the fishes alone should have him. He had been a very second-rate helmsman while alive, but now he was dead he might have become a first-class temptation, and possibly cause some startling trouble. Besides, I was anxious to take the wheel, the man in pink pyjamas showing himself a hopeless duffer at the business.

"This I did directly the simple funeral was over. We were going half-speed, keeping right in the middle of the stream, and I listened to the talk about me. They had given up Kurtz, they had given up the station; Kurtz was dead, and the station had been burnt—and so on, and so on. The red-haired pilgrim was beside himself with the thought that at least this poor Kurtz had been properly revenged. 'Say! We must have made a glorious slaughter of them in the bush. Eh? What do you think? Say?' He positively danced, the bloodthirsty little gingery beggar. And he had nearly fainted when he saw the wounded man! I could not help saying, 'You made a glorious lot of smoke, anyhow.' I had seen, from the way the tops of the bushes rustled and flew, that almost all the shots had gone too high. You can't hit anything unless you take aim and fire from the shoulder; but these chaps fired from the hip with their eyes shut. The retreat, I maintained—and I was right—was caused by the screeching of the steam-whistle. Upon this they forgot Kurtz, and began to howl at me with indignant protests.

"The manager stood by the wheel murmuring confidentially about the necessity of getting well away down the river before dark at all events, when I saw in the distance a clearing on the river-side and the outlines of some sort of building. 'What's this?' I asked. He clapped his hands in wonder. 'The station!' he cried. I edged in at once, still going half-speed.

"Through my glasses I saw the slope of a hill interspersed with rare trees and perfectly free from undergrowth. A long decaying building on the summit was half buried in the high grass; the large holes in the peaked roof gaped black from afar; the jungle and the woods made a background. There was no enclosure or fence of any kind; but there had been one apparently, for near the house half a dozen slim posts remained in a row, roughly trimmed, and with their upper ends ornamented with round carved balls. The rails, or whatever there had been between, had disappeared. Of course the forest surrounded all that. The river-bank was clear, and on the water side I saw a white man under a hat like a cart-wheel beckoning persistently with his whole arm. Examining the edge of the forest above and below, I was almost certain I could see movements—human forms gliding here and there. I steamed past prudently, then stopped the engines and let her drift down. The man on the shore began to shout, urging us to land. 'We have been attacked,' screamed the manager. 'I know—I know. It's all right,' yelled back the other, as cheerful as you please. 'Come along. It's all right. I am glad.'

"His aspect reminded me of something I had seen—something funny I had seen somewhere. As I manoeuvred to get alongside, I was asking myself, 'What does this fellow look like?' Suddenly I got it. He looked like a harlequin. His clothes had been made of some stuff that was brown holland probably, but it was covered with patches all over, with bright patches, blue, red, and yellow—patches on the back, patches on the front, patches on elbows, on knees; coloured binding round his jacket, scarlet edging at the bottom of his trousers; and the sunshine made him look extremely gay and wonderfully neat withal, because you could see how beautifully all this patching had been done. A beardless, boyish face, very fair, no features to speak of, nose peeling, little blue eyes, smiles and frowns chasing each other over that open countenance like sunshine and shadow on a wind-swept plain. 'Look out, captain!' he cried; 'there's a snag lodged in here last night.' What! Another snag? I confess I swore shamefully. I had nearly holed my cripple, to finish off that charming trip. The harlequin on the bank turned his little pug-nose up to me. 'You English?' he asked, all smiles. 'Are you?' I shouted from the wheel. The smiles vanished, and he shook his head as if sorry for my disappointment. Then he brightened up. 'Never mind!' he cried encouragingly. 'Are we in time?' I asked. 'He is up there,' he replied, with a toss of the head up the hill, and becoming gloomy all of a sudden. His face was like the autumn sky, overcast one moment and bright the next.

"When the manager, escorted by the pilgrims, all of them armed to the teeth, had gone to the house, this chap came on board. 'I say, I don't like this. These natives are in the bush,' I said. He assured me earnestly it was all right. 'They are simple people,' he added; 'well, I am glad you came. It took me all my time to keep them off.' 'But you said it was all right,' I cried. 'Oh, they meant no harm,' he said; and as I stared he corrected himself, 'Not exactly.' Then vivaciously, 'My faith, your pilot-house wants a clean-up!' In the next breath he advised me to keep enough steam on the boiler to blow the whistle in case of any trouble. 'One good screech will do more for you than all your rifles. They are simple people,' he repeated. He rattled away at such a rate he quite overwhelmed me. He seemed to be trying to make up for lots of silence, and actually hinted, laughing, that such was the case. 'Don't you talk with Mr. Kurtz?' I said. 'You don't talk with that man—you listen to him,' he exclaimed with severe exaltation. 'But now——' He waved his arm, and in the twinkling of an eye was in the uttermost depths of despondency. In a moment he came up again with a jump, possessed himself of both my hands, shook them continuously, while he gabbled: 'Brother sailor . . . honour . . . pleasure . . . delight . . . introduce myself . . . Russian . . . son of an arch-priest . . . Government of Tambov . . . What? Tobacco! English tobacco; the excellent English tobacco! Now, that's brotherly. Smoke? Where's a sailor that does not smoke?'

"The pipe soothed him, and gradually I made out he had run away from school, had gone to sea in a Russian ship; ran away again; served some time in English ships; was now reconciled with the arch-priest. He made a point of that. 'But when one is young one must see things, gather experience, ideas; enlarge the mind.' 'Here!' I interrupted. 'You can never tell! Here I met Mr. Kurtz,' he said, youthfully solemn and reproachful. I held my tongue after that. It appears he had persuaded a Dutch trading-house on the coast to fit him out with stores and goods, and had started for the interior with a light heart, and no more idea of what would happen to him than a baby. He had been wandering about that river for nearly two years alone, cut off from everybody and everything. 'I am not so young as I look. I am twenty-five,' he said. 'At first old Van Shuyten would tell me to go to the devil,' he narrated with keen enjoyment; 'but I stuck to him, and talked and talked, till at last he got afraid I would talk the hind-leg off his favourite dog, so he gave me some cheap things and a few guns, and told me he hoped he would never see my face again. Good old Dutchman, Van Shuyten. I sent him one small lot of ivory a year ago, so that he can't call me a little thief when I get back. I hope he got it. And for the rest, I don't care. I had some wood stacked for you. That was my old house. Did you see?'

"I gave him Towson's book. He made as though he would kiss me, but restrained himself. 'The only book I had left, and I thought I had lost it,' he said, looking at it ecstatically. 'So many accidents happen to a man going about alone, you know. Canoes get upset sometimes—and sometimes you've got to clear out so quick when the people get angry.' He thumbed the pages. 'You made notes in Russian?' I asked. He nodded. 'I thought they were written in cipher,' I said. He laughed, then became serious. 'I had lots of trouble to keep these people off,' he said. 'Did they want to kill you?' I asked. 'Oh no!' he cried, and checked himself. 'Why did they attack us?' I pursued. He hesitated, then said shamefacedly, 'They don't want him to go.' 'Don't they?' I said curiously. He nodded a nod full of mystery and wisdom. 'I tell you,' he cried, 'this man has enlarged my mind.' He opened his arms wide, staring at me with his little blue eyes that were perfectly round."

3

"I looked at him, lost in astonishment. There he was before me, in motley, as though he had absconded from a troupe of mimes, enthusiastic, fabulous. His very existence was improbable, inexplicable, and altogether bewildering. He was an insoluble problem. It was inconceivable how he had existed, how he had succeeded in getting so far, how he had managed to remain—why he did not instantly disappear. 'I went a little farther,' he said, 'then still a little farther—till I had gone so far that I don't know how I'll ever get back. Never mind. Plenty time. I can manage. You take Kurtz away quick—quick—I tell you.' The glamour of youth enveloped his parti-coloured rags, his destitution, his loneliness, the essential desolation of his futile wanderings. For months—for years—his life hadn't been worth a day's purchase; and there he was gallantly, thoughtlessly alive, to all appearance indestructible solely by the virtue of his few years and of his unreflecting audacity. I was seduced into something like admiration—like envy. Glamour urged him on, glamour kept him unscathed. He surely wanted nothing from the wilderness but space to breathe in and to push on through. His need was to exist, and to move onwards at the greatest possible risk, and with a maximum of privation. If the absolutely pure, uncalculating, unpractical spirit of adventure had ever ruled a human being, it ruled this be-patched youth. I almost envied him the possession of this modest and clear flame. It seemed to have consumed all thought of self so completely, that, even while he was talking to you, you forgot that it was he—the man before your eyes—who had gone through these things. I did not envy him his devotion to Kurtz, though. He had not meditated over it. It came to him, and he accepted it with a sort of eager fatalism. I must say that to me it appeared about the most dangerous thing in every way he had come upon so far.

"They had come together unavoidably, like two ships becalmed near each other, and lay rubbing sides at last. I suppose Kurtz wanted an audience, because on a certain occasion, when encamped in the forest, they had talked all night, or more probably Kurtz had talked. 'We talked of everything,' he said, quite transported at the recollection. 'I forgot there was such a thing as sleep. The night did not seem to last an hour. Everything! Everything! . . . Of love too,' 'Ah, he talked to you of love!' I said, much amused. 'It isn't what you think,' he cried, almost passionately. 'It was in general. He made me see things—things.'

"He threw his arms up. We were on deck at the time, and the head-man of my wood-cutters, lounging near by, turned upon him his heavy and glittering eyes. I looked around, and I don't know why, but I assure you that never, never before, did this land, this river, this jungle, the very arch of this blazing sky, appear to me so hopeless and so dark, so impenetrable to human thought, so pitiless to human weakness. 'And, ever since, you have been with him, of course?' I said.

"On the contrary. It appears their intercourse had been very much broken by various causes. He had, as he informed me proudly, managed to nurse Kurtz through two illnesses (he alluded to it as you would to some risky feat), but as a rule Kurtz wandered alone, far in the depths of the forest. 'Very often coming to this station, I had to wait days and days before he would turn up,' he said. 'Ah, it was worth waiting for!—sometimes.' 'What was he doing? exploring or what?' I asked. 'Oh yes, of course'; he had discovered lots of villages, a lake too—he did not know exactly in what direction; it was dangerous to inquire too much—but mostly his expeditions had been for ivory. 'But he had no goods to trade with by that time,' I objected. 'There's a good lot of cartridges left even yet,' he answered, looking away. 'To speak plainly, he raided the country,' I said. He nodded. 'Not alone, surely!' He muttered something about the villages round that lake. 'Kurtz got the tribe to follow him, did he?' I suggested. He fidgeted a little. 'They adored him,' he said. The tone of these words was so extraordinary that I looked at him searchingly. It was curious to see his mingled eagerness and reluctance to speak of Kurtz. The man filled his life, occupied his thoughts, swayed his emotions. 'What can you expect?' he burst out; 'he came to them with thunder and lightning, you know—and they had never seen anything like it—and very terrible. He could be very terrible. You can't judge Mr. Kurtz as you would an ordinary man. No, no, no! Now—just to give you an idea—I don't mind telling you, he wanted to shoot me too one day—but I don't judge him.' 'Shoot you!' I cried. 'What for?' 'Well, I had a small lot of ivory the chief of that village near my house gave me. You see I used to shoot game for them. Well, he wanted it, and wouldn't hear reason. He declared he would shoot me unless I gave him the ivory and then cleared out of the country, because he could do so, and had a fancy for it, and there was nothing on earth to prevent him killing whom he jolly well pleased. And it was true too. I gave him the ivory. What did I care! But I didn't clear out. No, no. I couldn't leave him. I had to be careful, of course, till we got friendly again for a time. He had his second illness then. Afterwards I had to keep out of the way; but I didn't mind. He was living for the most part in those villages on the lake. When he came down to the river, sometimes he would take to me, and sometimes it was better for me to be careful. This man suffered too much. He hated all this, and somehow he couldn't get away. When I had a chance I begged him to try and leave while there was time; I offered to go back with him. And he would say yes, and then he would remain; go off on another ivory hunt; disappear for weeks; forget himself amongst these people—forget himself—you know.' 'Why! he's mad,' I said. He protested indignantly. Mr. Kurtz couldn't be mad. If I had heard him talk only two days ago, I wouldn't dare hint at such a thing. . . . I had taken up my binoculars while we talked, and was looking at the shore, sweeping the limit of the forest at each side and at the back of the house. The consciousness of there being people in that bush, so silent, so quiet—as silent and quiet as the ruined house on the hill—made me uneasy. There was no sign on the face of nature of this amazing tale that was not so much told as suggested to me in desolate exclamations, completed by shrugs, in interrupted phrases, in hints ending in deep sighs. The woods were unmoved, like a mask—heavy, like the closed door of a prison—they looked with their air of hidden knowledge, of patient expectation, of unapproachable silence. The Russian was explaining to me that it was only lately that Mr. Kurtz had come down to the river, bringing along with him all the fighting men of that lake tribe. He had been absent for several months—getting himself adored, I suppose—and had come down unexpectedly, with the intention to all appearance of making a raid either across the river or down stream. Evidently the appetite for more ivory had got the better of the—what shall I say?—less material aspirations. However, he had got much worse suddenly. 'I heard he was lying helpless, and so I came up—took my chance,' said the Russian. 'Oh, he is bad, very bad.' I directed my glass to the house. There were no signs of life, but there were the ruined roof, the long mud wall peeping above the grass, with three little square window-holes, no two of the same size; all this brought within reach of my hand, as it were. And then I made a brusque movement, and one of the remaining posts of that vanished fence leaped up in the field of my glass. You remember I told you I had been struck at the distance by certain attempts at ornamentation, rather remarkable in the ruinous aspect of the place. Now I had suddenly a nearer view, and its first result was to make me throw my head back as if before a blow. Then I went carefully from post to post with my glass, and I saw my mistake. These round knobs were not ornamental but symbolic; they were expressive and puzzling, striking and disturbing—food for thought and also for vultures if there had been any looking down from the sky; but at all events for such ants as were industrious enough to ascend the pole. They would have been even more impressive, those heads on the stakes, if their faces had not been turned to the house. Only one, the first I had made out, was facing my way. I was not so shocked as you may think. The start back I had given was really nothing but a movement of surprise. I had expected to see a knob of wood there, you know. I returned deliberately to the first I had seen—and there it was, black, dried, sunken, with closed eyelids—a head that seemed to sleep at the top of that pole, and, with the shrunken dry lips showing a narrow white line of the teeth, was smiling too, smiling continuously at some endless and jocose dream of that eternal slumber.

"I am not disclosing any trade secrets. In fact the manager said afterwards that Mr. Kurtz's methods had ruined the district. I have no opinion on that point, but I want you clearly to understand that there was nothing exactly profitable in these heads being there. They only showed that Mr. Kurtz lacked restraint in the gratification of his various lusts, that there was something wanting in him—some small matter which, when the pressing need arose, could not be found under his magnificent eloquence. Whether he knew of this deficiency himself I can't say. I think the knowledge came to him at last—only at the very last. But the wilderness had found him out early, and had taken on him a terrible vengeance for the fantastic invasion. I think it had whispered to him things about himself which he did not know, things of which he had no conception till he took counsel with this great solitude—and the whisper had proved irresistibly fascinating. It echoed loudly within him because he was hollow at the core. . . . I put down the glass, and the head that had appeared near enough to be spoken to seemed at once to have leaped away from me into inaccessible distance.

"The admirer of Mr. Kurtz was a bit crestfallen. In a hurried, indistinct voice he began to assure me he had not dared to take these—say, symbols—down. He was not afraid of the natives; they would not stir till Mr. Kurtz gave the word. His ascendancy was extraordinary. The camps of these people surrounded the place, and the chiefs came every day to see him. They would crawl . . . 'I don't want to know anything of the ceremonies used when approaching Mr. Kurtz,' I shouted. Curious, this feeling that came over me that such details would be more intolerable than those heads drying on the stakes under Mr. Kurtz's windows. After all, that was only a savage sight, while I seemed at one bound to have been transported into some lightless region of subtle horrors, where pure, uncomplicated savagery was a positive relief, being something that had a right to exist—obviously—in the sunshine. The young man looked at me with surprise. I suppose it did not occur to him that Mr. Kurtz was no idol of mine. He forgot I hadn't heard any of these splendid monologues on, what was it? on love, justice, conduct of life—or what not. If it had come to crawling before Mr. Kurtz, he crawled as much as the veriest savage of them all. I had no idea of the conditions, he said: these heads were the heads of rebels. I shocked him excessively by laughing. Rebels! What would be the next definition I was to hear? There had been enemies, criminals, workers —and there were rebels. Those rebellious heads looked very subdued to me on their sticks. 'You don't know how such a life tries a man like Kurtz,' cried Kurtz's last disciple. 'Well, and you?' I said. 'I! I! I am a simple man. I have no great thoughts. I want nothing from anybody. How can you compare me to . . . ?' His feelings were too much for speech, and suddenly he broke down. 'I don't understand,' he groaned. 'I've been doing my best to keep him alive, and that's enough. I had no hand in all this. I have no abilities. There hasn't been a drop of medicine or a mouthful of invalid food for months here. He was shamefully abandoned. A man like this, with such ideas. Shamefully! Shamefully! I—I—haven't slept for the last ten nights. . . . '

"His voice lost itself in the calm of the evening. The long shadows of the forests had slipped downhill while we talked, had gone far beyond the ruined hovel, beyond the symbolic row of stakes. All this was in the gloom, while we down there were yet in the sunshine, and the stretch of the river abreast of the clearing glittered in a still and dazzling splendour, with a murky and overshadowed bend above and below. Not a living soul was seen on the shore. The bushes did not rustle.

"Suddenly round the corner of the house a group of men appeared, as though they had come up from the ground. They waded waist-deep in the grass, in a compact body, bearing an improvised stretcher in their midst. Instantly, in the emptiness of the landscape, a cry arose whose shrillness pierced the still air like a sharp arrow flying straight to the very heart of the land; and, as if by enchantment, streams of human beings—of naked human beings—with spears in their hands, with bows, with shields, with wild glances and savage movements, were poured into the clearing by the dark-faced and pensive forest. The bushes shook, the grass swayed for a time, and then everything stood still in attentive immobility.

" 'Now, if he does not say the right thing to them we are all done for,' said the Russian at my elbow. The knot of men with the stretcher had stopped too, half-way to the steamer, as if petrified. I saw the man on the stretcher sit up, lank and with an uplifted arm, above the shoulders of the bearers. 'Let us hope that the man who can talk so well of love in general will find some particular reason to spare us this time,' I said. I resented bitterly the absurd danger of our situation, as if to be at the mercy of that atrocious phantom had been a dishonouring necessity. I could not hear a sound, but through my glasses I saw the thin arm extended commandingly, the lower jaw moving, the eyes of that apparition shining darkly far in its bony head that nodded with grotesque jerks. Kurtz—Kurtz—that means 'short' in German—don't it? Well, the name was as true as everything else in his life—and death. He looked at least seven feet long. His covering had fallen off, and his body emerged from it pitiful and appalling as from a winding-sheet. I could see the cage of his ribs all astir, the bones of his arm waving. It was as though an animated image of death carved out of old ivory had been shaking its hand with menaces at a motionless crowd of men made of dark and glittering bronze. I saw him open his mouth wide—it gave him a weirdly voracious aspect, as though he had wanted to swallow all the air, all the earth, all the men before him. A deep voice reached me faintly. He must have been shouting. He fell back suddenly. The stretcher shook as the bearers staggered forward again, and almost at the same time I noticed that the crowd of savages was vanishing without any perceptible movement of retreat, as if the forest that had ejected these beings so suddenly had drawn them in again as the breath is drawn in a long aspiration.

"Some of the pilgrims behind the stretcher carried his arms—two shotguns, a heavy rifle, and a light revolver-carbine—the thunderbolts of that pitiful Jupiter. The manager bent over him murmuring as he walked beside his head. They laid him down in one of the little cabins—just a room for a bed-place and a camp-stool or two, you know. We had brought his belated correspondence, and a lot of torn envelopes and open letters littered his bed. His hand roamed feebly amongst these papers. I was struck by the fire of his eyes and the composed languor of his expression. It was not so much the exhaustion of disease. He did not seem in pain. This shadow looked satiated and calm, as though for the moment it had had its fill of all the emotions.

"He rustled one of the letters, and looking straight in my face said, 'I am glad.' Somebody had been writing to him about me. These special recommendations were turning up again. The volume of tone he emitted without effort, almost without the trouble of moving his lips, amazed me. A voice! a voice! It was grave, profound, vibrating, while the man did not seem capable of a whisper. However, he had enough strength in him—factitious no doubt—to very nearly make an end of us, as you shall hear directly.

"The manager appeared silently in the doorway; I stepped out at once and he drew the curtain after me. The Russian, eyed curiously by the pilgrims, was staring at the shore. I followed the direction of his glance.

"Dark human shapes could be made out in the distance, flitting indistinctly against the gloomy border of the forest, and near the river two bronze figures, leaning on tall spears, stood in the sunlight under fantastic head-dresses of spotted skins, warlike and still in statuesque repose. And from right to left along the lighted shore moved a wild and gorgeous apparition of a woman.

"She walked with measured steps, draped in striped and fringed cloths, treading the earth proudly, with a slight jingle and flash of barbarous ornaments. She carried her head high; her hair was done in the shape of a helmet; she had brass leggings to the knees, brass wire gauntlets to the elbow, a crimson spot on her tawny cheek, innumerable necklaces of glass beads on her neck; bizarre things, charms, gifts of witch-men, that hung about her, glittered and trembled at every step. She must have had the value of several elephant tusks upon her. She was savage and superb, wild-eyed and magnificent; there was something ominous and stately in her deliberate progress. And in the hush that had fallen suddenly upon the whole sorrowful land, the immense wilderness, the colossal body of the fecund and mysterious life seemed to look at her, pensive, as though it had been looking at the image of its own tenebrous and passionate soul.

"She came abreast of the steamer, stood still, and faced us. Her long shadow fell to the water's edge. Her face had a tragic and fierce aspect of wild sorrow and of dumb pain mingled with the fear of some struggling, half-shaped resolve. She stood looking at us without a stir, and like the wilderness itself, with an air of brooding over an inscrutable purpose. A whole minute passed, and then she made a step forward. There was a low jingle, a glint of yellow metal, a sway of fringed draperies, and she stopped as if her heart had failed her. The young fellow by my side growled. The pilgrims murmured at my back. She looked at us all as if her life had depended upon the unswerving steadiness of her glance. Suddenly she opened her bared arms and threw them up rigid above her head, as though in an uncontrollable desire to touch the sky, and at the same time the swift shadows darted out on the earth, swept around on the river, gathering the steamer in a shadowy embrace. A formidable silence hung over the scene.

"She turned away slowly, walked on, following the bank, and passed into the bushes to the left. Once only her eyes gleamed back at us in the dusk of the thickets before she disappeared.

" 'If she had offered to come aboard I really think I would have tried to shoot her,' said the man of patches nervously. 'I had been risking my life every day for the last fortnight to keep her out of the house. She got in one day and kicked up a row about those miserable rags I picked up in the storeroom to mend my clothes with. I wasn't decent. At least it must have been that, for she talked like a fury to Kurtz for an hour, pointing at me now and then. I don't understand the dialect of this tribe. Luckily for me, I fancy Kurtz felt too ill that day to care, or there would have been mischief. I don't understand. . . . No—it's too much for me. Ah, well, it's all over now.'

"At this moment I heard Kurtz's deep voice behind the curtain: 'Save me!—save the ivory, you mean. Don't tell me. Save *me!* Why, I've had to save you. You are interrupting my plans now. Sick! Sick! Not so sick as you would like to believe. Never mind. I'll carry my ideas out yet—I will return. I'll show you what can be done. You with your little peddling notions—you are interfering with me. I will return. I . . . '

"The manager came out. He did me the honour to take me under the arm and lead me aside. 'He is very low, very low,' he said. He considered it necessary to sigh, but neglected to be consistently sorrowful. 'We have done all we could for him—haven't we? But there is no disguising the fact, Mr. Kurtz has done more harm than good to the Company. He did not see the time was not ripe for vigorous action. Cautiously, cautiously—that's my principle. We must be cautious yet. The district is closed to us for a time. Deplorable! Upon the whole, the trade will suffer. I don't deny there is a remarkable quantity of ivory—mostly fossil. We must save it, at all events—but look how precarious the position is—and why? Because the method is unsound.' 'Do you,' said I, looking at the shore, 'call it "unsound method"?' 'Without doubt,' he exclaimed hotly. 'Don't you?' . . . 'No method at all,' I murmured after a while. 'Exactly,' he exulted. 'I anticipated this. Shows a complete want of judgment. It is my duty to point it out in the proper quarter.' 'Oh,' said I, 'that fellow—what's his name?—the brickmaker, will make a readable report for you.' He appeared confounded for a moment. It seemed to me I had never breathed an atmosphere so vile, and I turned mentally to Kurtz for relief—positively for relief. 'Nevertheless, I think Mr. Kurtz is a remarkable man,' I said with emphasis. He started, dropped on me a cold heavy glance, said very quietly, 'He *was*,' and turned his back on me. My hour of favour was over; I found myself lumped along with Kurtz as a partisan of methods for which the time was not ripe: I was unsound! Ah! but it was something to have at least a choice of nightmares.

"I had turned to the wilderness really, not to Mr. Kurtz, who, I was ready to admit, was as good as buried. And for a moment it seemed to me as if I also were buried in a vast grave full of unspeakable secrets. I felt an intolerable weight oppressing my breast, the smell of the damp earth, the unseen presence of victorious corruption, the darkness of an impenetrable night. . . . The Russian tapped me on the shoulder. I heard him mumbling and stammering something about 'brother seaman—couldn't conceal—knowledge of matters that would affect Mr. Kurtz's reputation.' I waited. For him evidently Mr. Kurtz was not in his grave; I suspect that for him Mr. Kurtz was one of the immortals. 'Well!' said I at last, 'speak out. As it happens, I am Mr. Kurtz's friend—in a way.'

"He stated with a good deal of formality that had we not been 'of the same profession,' he would have kept the matter to himself without regard to consequences. He suspected 'there was an active ill-will towards him on the part of these white men that——' 'You are right,' I said, remembering a certain conversation I had overheard. 'The manager thinks you ought to be hanged.' He showed a concern at this intelligence which amused me at first. 'I had better get out of the way quietly,' he said earnestly. 'I can do no more for Kurtz now, and they would soon find some excuse. What's to stop them? There's a military post three hundred miles from here.' 'Well, upon my word,' said I, 'perhaps you had better go if you have any friends amongst the savages near by.' 'Plenty,' he said. 'They are simple people—and I want nothing, you know.' He stood biting his lip, then: 'I don't want any harm to happen to these whites here, but of course I was thinking of Mr. Kurtz's reputation—but you are a brother seaman and——' 'All right,' said I, after a time. 'Mr. Kurtz's reputation is safe with me.' I did not know how truly I spoke.

"He informed me, lowering his voice, that it was Kurtz who had ordered the attack to be made on the steamer. 'He hated sometimes the idea of being taken away—and then again . . . But I don't understand these matters. I am a simple man. He thought it would scare you away—that you would give it up, thinking him dead. I could not stop him. Oh, I had an awful time of it this last month.' 'Very well,' I said. 'He is all right now.' 'Ye-e-es,' he muttered, not very convinced apparently. 'Thanks,' said I; 'I shall keep my eyes open.' 'But quiet—eh?' he urged anxiously. 'It would be awful for his reputation if anybody here——' I promised a complete discretion with great gravity. 'I have a canoe and three black fellows waiting not very far. I am off. Could you give me a few Martini-Henry cartridges?' I could, and did, with proper secrecy. He helped himself, with a wink at me, to a handful of my tobacco. 'Between sailors—you know—good

English tobacco.' At the door of the pilot-house he turned round—'I say, haven't you a pair of shoes you could spare?' He raised one leg. 'Look.' The soles were tied with knotted strings sandal-wise under his bare feet. I rooted out an old pair, at which he looked with admiration before tucking it under his left arm. One of his pockets (bright red) was bulging with cartridges, from the other (dark blue) peeped 'Towson's Inquiry,' etc. etc. He seemed to think himself excellently well equipped for a renewed encounter with the wilderness. 'Ah! I'll never, never meet such a man again. You ought to have heard him recite poetry—his own too it was, he told me. Poetry!' He rolled his eyes at the recollection of these delights. 'Oh, he enlarged my mind!' 'Good-bye,' said I. He shook hands and vanished in the night. Sometimes I ask myself whether I had ever really seen him— whether it was possible to meet such a phenomenon! . . .

"When I woke up shortly after midnight his warning came to my mind with its hint of danger that seemed, in the starred darkness, real enough to make me get up for the purpose of having a look round. On the hill a big fire burned, illuminating fitfully a crooked corner of the station-house. One of the agents with a picket of a few of our blacks, armed for the purpose, was keeping guard over the ivory; but deep within the forest, red gleams that wavered, that seemed to sink and rise from the ground amongst confused columnar shapes of intense blackness, showed the exact position of the camp where Mr. Kurtz's adorers were keeping their uneasy vigil. The monotonous beating of a big drum filled the air with muffled shocks and a lingering vibration. A steady droning sound of many men chanting each to himself some weird incantation came out from the black, flat wall of the woods as the humming of bees comes out of a hive, and had a strange narcotic effect upon my half-awake senses. I believe I dozed off leaning over the rail, till an abrupt burst of yells, an overwhelming outbreak of a pent-up and mysterious frenzy, woke me up in a bewildered wonder. It was cut short all at once, and the low droning went on with an effect of audible and soothing silence. I glanced casually into the little cabin. A light was burning within, but Mr. Kurtz was not there.

"I think I would have raised an outcry if I had believed my eyes. But I didn't believe them at first—the thing seemed so impossible. The fact is, I was completely unnerved by a sheer blank fright, pure abstract terror, unconnected with any distinct shape of physical danger. What made this emotion so overpowering was—how shall I define it?—the moral shock I received, as if something altogether monstrous, intolerable to thought and odious to the soul, had been thrust upon me unexpectedly. This lasted of course the merest fraction of a second, and then the usual sense of commonplace, deadly danger, the possibility of a sudden onslaught and massacre, or something of the kind, which I saw impending, was positively welcome and composing. It pacified me, in fact, so much, that I did not raise an alarm.

"There was an agent buttoned up inside an ulster and sleeping on a chair on deck within three feet of me. The yells had not awakened him; he snored very slightly; I left him to his slumbers and leaped ashore. I did not betray Mr. Kurtz—it was ordered I should never betray him—it was written I should be loyal to the nightmare of my choice. I was anxious to deal with this shadow by myself alone—and to this day I don't know why I was so jealous of sharing with any one the peculiar blackness of that experience.

"As soon as I got on the bank I saw a trail—a broad trail through the grass. I remember the exultation with which I said to myself, 'He can't walk—he is crawling on all-fours—I've got him.' The grass was wet with dew. I strode rapidly with clenched fists. I fancy I had some vague notion of falling upon him and giving him a drubbing. I don't know. I had some imbecile thoughts. The knitting old woman with the cat obtruded herself upon my memory as a most improper person to be sitting at the other end of such an affair. I saw a row of pilgrims squirting lead in the air out of Winchesters held to the hip. I thought I would never get back to the steamer, and imagined myself living alone and unarmed in the woods to an advanced age. Such silly things—you know. And I remember I confounded the beat of the drum with the beating of my heart, and was pleased at its calm regularity.

"I kept to the track though—then stopped to listen. The night was very clear; a dark blue space, sparkling with dew and starlight, in which black things stood very still. I thought I could see a kind of motion ahead of me. I was strangely cocksure of everything that night. I actually left the track and ran in a wide semicircle (I verily believe chuckling to myself) so as to get in front of that stir, of that motion I had seen—if indeed I had seen anything. I was circumventing Kurtz as though it had been a boyish game.

"I came upon him, and, if he had not heard me coming, I would have fallen over him too, but he got up in time. He rose, unsteady, long, pale, indistinct, like a vapour exhaled by the earth, and swayed slightly, misty and silent before me; while at my back the fires loomed between the trees, and the murmur of many voices issued from the forest. I had cut him off cleverly; but when actually confronting him I seemed to come to my senses, I saw the danger in its right proportion. It was by no means over yet. Suppose he began to shout? Though he could hardly stand, there was still plenty of vigour in his voice. 'Go away—hide yourself,' he said, in that profound tone. It was very awful. I glanced back. We were within thirty yards from the nearest fire. A black figure stood up, strode on long black legs, waving long black arms, across the glow. It had horns—antelope horns, I think—on its head. Some sorcerer, some witch-man, no doubt: it looked fiend-like enough. 'Do you know what you are doing?' I whispered. 'Perfectly,' he answered, raising his voice for that single word: it sounded to me far off and yet loud, like a hail through a speaking-trumpet. If he makes a row we are lost, I thought to myself. This clearly was not a case for fisticuffs, even apart from the very natural aversion I had to beat that Shadow—this wandering and tormented thing. 'You will be lost,' I said— 'utterly lost.' One gets sometimes such a flash of inspiration, you know. I did say the right thing, though indeed he could not have been more irretrievably lost than he was at this very moment, when the foundations of our intimacy were being laid—to endure—to endure—even to the end—even beyond.

" 'I had immense plans,' he muttered irresolutely. 'Yes,' said I; 'but if you try to shout I'll smash your head with——' There was not a stick or a stone near. 'I will throttle you for good,' I corrected myself. 'I was on the threshold of great things,' he pleaded, in a voice of longing, with a wistfulness of tone that made my blood run cold. 'And now for this stupid scoundrel——' 'Your success in Europe is assured in any case,' I affirmed steadily. I did not want to have the throttling of him, you understand—and indeed it would have been very little use for any practical purpose. I tried to break the spell—the heavy, mute spell of the wilderness—that seemed to draw him to its pitiless breast by the awakening of forgotten and brutal instincts, by the memory of gratified and monstrous passions. This alone, I was convinced, had driven him out to the edge of the forest, to the bush, towards the gleam of fires, the throb of drums, the drone of weird incantations; this alone had beguiled his unlawful soul beyond the bounds of permitted aspirations. And, don't you see, the terror of the position was not in being knocked on the head—though I had a very lively sense of that danger too—but in this, that I had to deal with a being to whom I could not appeal in the name of anything high or low. I had, even like the niggers, to invoke him—himself—his own exalted and incredible degradation. There was nothing either above or below him, and I knew it. He had kicked himself loose of the earth. Confound the man! he had kicked the very earth to pieces. He was alone, and I before him did not know whether I stood on the ground or floated in the air. I've been telling you what we said—repeating the phrases we pronounced—but what's the good? They were common everyday words—the familiar, vague sounds exchanged on every waking day of life. But what of that? They had behind them, to my mind, the terrific suggestiveness of words heard in dreams, of phrases spoken in nightmares. Soul! If anybody had ever struggled with a soul, I am the man. And I wasn't arguing with a lunatic either. Believe me or not, his intelligence was perfectly clear—concentrated, it is true, upon himself with horrible intensity, yet clear; and therein was my only chance—barring, of course, the killing him there and then, which wasn't so good, on account of unavoidable noise. But his soul was mad. Being alone in the wilderness, it had looked within itself, and by Heavens! I tell you, it had gone mad. I had—for my sins, I suppose, to go through the ordeal of looking into it myself. No eloquence could have been so withering to one's belief in mankind as his final burst of sincerity. He struggled with himself too. I saw it—I heard it. I saw the inconceivable mystery of a soul that knew no restraint, no faith, and no fear, yet struggling blindly with itself. I kept my head pretty well; but when I had him at last stretched on the couch, I wiped my forehead, while my legs shook under me as though I had carried half a ton on my back down that hill. And yet I had only supported him, his bony arm clasped round my neck—and he was not much heavier than a child.

"When next day we left at noon, the crowd, of whose presence behind the curtain of trees I had been acutely conscious all the time, flowed out of the woods again, filled the clearing, covered the slope with a mass of naked, breathing, quivering, bronze bodies. I steamed up a bit, then swung down-stream, and two thousand eyes followed the evolutions of the splashing, thumping, fierce river-demon beating the water with its terrible tail and breathing black smoke into the air. In front of the first rank, along the river, three men, plastered with bright red earth from head to foot, strutted to and fro restlessly. When we came abreast again, they faced the river, stamped their feet, nodded their horned heads, swayed their scarlet bodies; they shook towards the fierce river-demon a bunch of black feathers, a mangy skin with a pendent tail—something that looked like a dried gourd; they shouted periodically together strings of amazing words that resembled no sounds of human language; and the deep murmurs of the crowd, interrupted suddenly, were like the responses of some satanic litany.

"We had carried Kurtz into the pilot-house: there was more air there. Lying on the couch, he stared through the open shutter. There was an eddy in the mass of human bodies, and the woman with helmeted head and tawny cheeks rushed out to the very brink of the stream. She put out her hands, shouted something, and all that wild mob took up the shout in a roaring chorus of articulated, rapid, breathless utterance.

" 'Do you understand this?' I asked.

"He kept on looking out past me with fiery, longing eyes, with a mingled expression of wistfulness and hate. He made no answer, but I saw a smile, a smile of indefinable meaning, appear on his colourless lips that a moment after twitched convulsively. 'Do I not?' he said slowly, gasping, as if the words had been torn out of him by a supernatural power.

"I pulled the string of the whistle, and I did this because I saw the pilgrims on deck getting out their rifles with an air of anticipating a jolly lark. At the sudden screech there was a movement of abject terror through that wedged mass of bodies. 'Don't! don't you frighten them away,' cried some one on deck disconsolately. I pulled the string time after time. They broke and ran, they leaped, they crouched, they swerved, they dodged the flying terror of the sound. The three red chaps had fallen flat, face down on the shore, as though they had been shot dead. Only the barbarous and superb woman did not so much as flinch, and stretched tragically her bare arms after us over the sombre and glittering river.

"And then that imbecile crowd down on the deck started their little fun, and I could see nothing more for smoke.

"The brown current ran swiftly out of the heart of darkness, bearing us down towards the sea with twice the speed of our upward progress; and Kurtz's life was running swiftly too, ebbing, ebbing out of his heart into the sea of inexorable time. The manager was very placid, he had no vital anxieties now, he took us both in with a comprehensive and satisfied glance: the 'affair' had come off as well as could be wished. I saw the time approaching when I would be left alone of the party of 'unsound method.' The pilgrims looked upon me with disfavour. I was, so to speak, numbered with the dead. It is strange how I accepted this unforeseen partnership, this choice of nightmares forced upon me in the tenebrous land invaded by these mean and greedy phantoms.

"Kurtz discoursed. A voice! a voice! It rang deep to the very last. It survived his strength to hide in the magnificent folds of eloquence the barren darkness of his heart. Oh, he struggled! he struggled! The wastes of his weary brain were haunted by shadowy images now—images of wealth and fame revolving obsequiously round his unextinguishable gift of noble and lofty expression. My Intended, my station, my career, my ideas—these were the subjects for the occasional utterances of elevated sentiments. The shade of the original Kurtz frequented the bedside of the hollow sham, whose fate it was to be buried presently in the mould of primeval earth. But both the diabolic love and the unearthly hate of the mysteries it had penetrated fought for the possession of that soul satiated with primitive emotions, avid of lying fame, of sham distinction, of all the appearances of success and power.

"Sometimes he was contemptibly childish. He desired to have kings meet him at railway stations on his return from some ghastly Nowhere, where he intended to accomplish great things. 'You show them you have in you something that is really profitable, and then there will be no limits to the recognition of your ability,' he would say. 'Of course you must take care of the motives—right motives—always.' The long reaches that were like one and the same reach, monotonous bends that were exactly alike, slipped past the steamer with their multitude of secular trees looking patiently after this grimy fragment of another world, the forerunner of change, of conquest, of trade, of massacres, of blessings. I looked ahead—piloting. 'Close the shutter,' said Kurtz suddenly one day; 'I can't bear to look at this.' I did so. There was a silence. 'Oh, but I will wring your heart yet!' he cried at the invisible wilderness.

"We broke down—as I had expected—and had to lie up for repairs at the head of an island. This delay was the first thing that shook Kurtz's confidence. One morning he gave me a packet of papers and a photo-graph—the lot tied together with a shoe-string. 'Keep this for me,' he said. 'This noxious fool' (meaning the manager) 'is capable of prying into my boxes when I am not looking.' In the afternoon I saw him. He was lying on his back with closed eyes, and I withdrew quietly, but I heard him mutter, 'Live rightly, die, die . . . ' I listened. There was nothing more. Was he rehearsing some speech in his sleep, or was it a fragment of a phrase from some newspaper article? He had been writing for the papers and meant to do so again, 'for the furthering of my ideas. It's a duty.'

"His was an impenetrable darkness. I looked at him as you peer down at a man who is lying at the bottom of a precipice where the sun never shines. But I had not much time to give him, because I was helping the engine-driver to take to pieces the leaky cylinders, to straighten a bent connecting-rod, and in other such matters. I lived in an infernal mess of rust, filings, nuts, bolts, spanners, hammers, ratchet-drills—things I abominate, be-cause I don't get on with them. I tended the little forge we fortunately had aboard; I toiled wearily in a wretched scrap-heap—unless I had the shakes too bad to stand.

"One evening coming in with a candle I was startled to hear him say a little tremulously, 'I am lying here in the dark waiting for death.' The light was within a foot of his eyes. I forced myself to murmur, 'Oh, nonsense!' and stood over him as if transfixed.

"Anything approaching the change that came over his features I have never seen before, and hope never to see again. Oh, I wasn't touched. I was fascinated. It was as though a veil had been rent. I saw on that ivory face the expression of sombre pride, of ruthless power, of craven terror—of an intense and hopeless despair. Did he live his life again in every detail of desire, temptation, and surrender during that supreme moment of complete knowledge? He cried in a whisper at some image, at some vision—he cried out twice, a cry that was no more than a breath:

" 'The horror! The horror!'

"I blew the candle out and left the cabin. The pilgrims were dining in the mess-room, and I took my place opposite the manager, who lifted his eyes to give me a questioning glance, which I successfully ignored. He leaned back, serene, with that peculiar smile of his sealing the unexpressed depths of his meanness. A continuous shower of small flies streamed upon the lamp, upon the cloth, upon our hands and faces. Suddenly the manager's boy put his insolent black head in the doorway, and said in a tone of scathing contempt:

" 'Mistah Kurtz—he dead.'

"All the pilgrims rushed out to see. I remained, and went on with my dinner. I believe I was considered brutally callous. However, I did not eat much. There was a lamp in there—light, don't you know—and outside it was so beastly, beastly dark. I went no more near the remarkable man who had pronounced a judgment upon the adventures of his soul on this earth. The voice was gone. What else had been there? But I am of course aware that next day the pilgrims buried something in a muddy hole.

"And then they very nearly buried me.

"However, as you see, I did not go to join Kurtz there and then. I did not. I remained to dream the nightmare out to the end, and to show my loyalty to Kurtz once more. Destiny. My destiny! Droll thing life is—that mysterious arrangement of merciless logic for a futile purpose. The most you can hope from it is some knowledge of yourself—that comes too late—a crop of unextinguishable regrets. I have wrestled with death. It is the most unexciting contest you can imagine. It takes place in an impalpable greyness, with nothing underfoot, with nothing around, without spectators, without clamour, without glory, without the great desire of victory, without the great fear of defeat, in a sickly atmosphere of tepid scepticism, without much belief in your own right, and still less in that of your adversary. If such is the form of ultimate wisdom, then life is a greater riddle than some of us think it to be. I was within a hair's-breadth of the last opportunity for pronouncement, and I found with humiliation that probably I would have nothing to say. This is the reason why I affirm that Kurtz was a remarkable man. He had something to say. He said it. Since I had peeped over the edge myself, I understand better the meaning of his stare, that could not see the flame of the candle, but was wide enough to embrace the whole universe, piercing enough to penetrate all the hearts that beat in the darkness. He had summed up—he had judged. 'The horror!' He was a remarkable man. After all, this was the expression of some sort of belief; it had candour, it had conviction, it had a vibrating note of revolt in its whisper, it had the appalling face of a glimpsed truth—the strange commingling of desire and hate. And it is not my own extremity I remember best—a vision of greyness without form filled with physical pain, and a careless contempt for the evanescence of all things—even of this pain itself. No! It is his extremity that I seem to have lived through. True, he had made that last stride, he had stepped over the edge, while I had been permitted to draw back my hesitating foot. And perhaps in this is the whole difference; perhaps all the wisdom, and all truth, and all sincerity, are just compressed into that inappreciable moment of time in which we step over the threshold of the invisible. Perhaps! I like to think my summing-up would not have been a word of careless contempt. Better his cry—much better. It was an affirmation, a moral victory paid for by innumerable defeats, by abominable terrors, by abominable satisfactions. But it was a victory! That is why I have remained loyal to Kurtz to the last, and even beyond, when a long time after I heard once more, not his own voice, but the echo of his magnificent eloquence thrown to me from a soul as translucently pure as a cliff of crystal.

"No, they did not bury me, though there is a period of time which I remember mistily, with a shuddering wonder, like a passage through some inconceivable world that had no hope in it and no desire. I found myself back in the sepulchral city resenting the sight of people hurrying through the streets to filch a little money from each other, to devour their infamous cookery, to gulp their unwholesome beer, to dream their insignificant and silly dreams. They trespassed upon my thoughts. They were intruders whose knowledge of life was to me an irritating pretence, because I felt so sure they could not possibly know the things I knew. Their bearing, which was simply the bearing of commonplace individuals going about their business in the assurance of perfect safety, was offensive to me like the outrageous flauntings of folly in the face of a danger it is unable to comprehend. I had no particular desire to enlighten them, but I had some difficulty in restraining myself from laughing in their faces, so full of stupid importance. I daresay I was not very well at that time. I tottered about the streets—there were various affairs to settle—grinning bitterly at perfectly respectable persons. I admit my behaviour was inexcusable, but then my temperature was seldom normal in these days. My dear aunt's endeavours to 'nurse up my strength' seemed altogether beside the mark. It was not my strength that wanted nursing, it was my imagination that wanted soothing. I kept the bundle of papers given me by Kurtz, not knowing exactly what to do with it. His mother had died lately, watched over, as I was told, by his Intended. A clean-shaved man, with an official manner and wearing gold-rimmed spectacles, called on me one day and made inquiries, at first circuitous, afterwards suavely pressing, about what he was pleased to denominate certain 'documents.' I was not surprised, because I had had two rows with the manager on the subject out there. I had refused to give up the smallest scrap out of that package, and I took the same attitude with the spectacled man. He became darkly menacing at last, and with much heat argued that the Company had the right to every bit of information about its 'territories.' And, said he, 'Mr. Kurtz's knowledge of unexplored regions must have been necessarily extensive and peculiar—owing to his great abilities and to the deplorable circumstances in which he had been placed: therefore——' I assured him Mr. Kurtz's knowledge, however extensive, did not bear upon the problems of commerce or administration. He invoked then the name of science. 'It would be an incalculable loss if,' etc. etc. I offered him the report on the 'Suppression of Savage Customs,' with the postscriptum torn off. He took it up eagerly, but ended by sniffing at it with an air of contempt. 'This is not what we had a right to expect,' he remarked. 'Expect nothing else,' I said. 'There are only private letters.' He withdrew upon some threat of legal proceedings, and I saw him no more; but another fellow, calling himself Kurtz's cousin, appeared two days later, and was anxious to hear all the details about his dear relative's last moments. Incidentally he gave me to understand that Kurtz had been essentially a great musician. 'There was the making of an immense success,' said the man, who was an organist, I believe, with lank grey hair flowing over a greasy coat-collar. I had no reason to doubt his statement; and to this day I am unable to say what was Kurtz's profession, whether he ever had any—which was the greatest of his talents. I had taken him for a painter who wrote for the papers, or else for a journalist who could paint—but even the cousin (who took snuff during the interview) could not tell me what he had been—exactly. He was a universal genius—on that point I agreed with the old chap, who thereupon blew his nose noisily into a large cotton handkerchief and withdrew in senile agitation, bearing off some family letters and memoranda without importance. Ultimately a journalist anxious to know something of the fate of his 'dear colleague' turned up. This visitor informed me Kurtz's proper sphere ought to have been politics 'on the popular side.' He had furry straight eyebrows, bristly hair cropped short, an eyeglass on a broad ribbon, and, becoming expansive, confessed his opinion that Kurtz really couldn't write a bit—'but Heavens! how that man could talk! He electrified large meetings. He had faith—don't you see?—he had the faith. He could get himself to believe anything—anything. He would have been a splendid leader of an extreme party.' 'What party?' I asked. 'Any party,' answered the other. 'He was an—an—extremist.' Did I not think so? I assented. Did I know, he asked, with a sudden flash of curiosity, 'what it was that had induced him to go out there?' 'Yes,' said I, and forthwith handed him the famous Report for publication, if he thought fit. He glanced through it hurriedly, mumbling all the time, judged 'it would do,' and took himself off with this plunder.

"Thus I was left at last with a slim packet of letters and the girl's portrait. She struck me as beautiful—I mean she had a beautiful expression. I know that the sunlight can be made to lie too, yet one felt that no manipulation of light and pose could have conveyed the delicate shade of truthfulness upon those features. She seemed ready to listen without mental reservation, without suspicion, without a thought for herself. I concluded I would go and give her back her portrait and those letters myself. Curiosity? Yes; and also some other feeling perhaps. All that had been Kurtz's had passed out of my hands: his soul, his body, his station, his plans, his ivory, his career. There remained only his memory and his Intended—and I wanted to give that up too to the past, in a way—to surrender personally all that remained of him with me to that oblivion which is the last word of our common fate. I don't defend myself. I had no clear perception of what it was I really wanted. Perhaps it was an impulse of unconscious loyalty, or the fulfilment of one of those ironic necessities that lurk in the facts of human existence. I don't know. I can't tell. But I went.

"I thought his memory was like the other memories of the dead that accumulate in every man's life—a vague impress on the brain of shadows that had fallen on it in their swift and final passage; but before the high and ponderous door, between the tall houses of a street as still and decorous as a well-kept alley in a cemetery, I had a vision of him on the stretcher, opening his mouth voraciously, as if to devour all the earth with all its mankind. He lived then before me; he lived as much as he had ever lived—a shadow insatiable of splendid appearances, of frightful realities; a shadow darker than the shadow of the night, and draped nobly in the folds of a gorgeous eloquence. The vision seemed to enter the house with me—the stretcher, the phantom-bearers, the wild crowd of obedient worshippers, the gloom of the forests, the glitter of the reach between the murky bends, the beat of the drum, regular and muffled like the beating of a heart—the heart of a conquering darkness. It was a moment of triumph for the wilderness, an invading and vengeful rush which, it seemed to me, I would have to keep back alone for the salvation of another soul. And the memory of what I had heard him say afar there, with the horned shapes stirring at my back, in the glow of fires, within the patient woods, those broken phrases came back to me, were heard again in their ominous and terrifying simplicity. I remembered his abject pleading, his abject threats, the colossal scale of his vile desires, the meanness, the torment, the tempestuous anguish of his soul. And later on I seemed to see his collected languid manner, when he said one day, 'This lot of ivory now is really mine. The Company did not pay for it. I collected it myself at a very great personal risk. I am afraid they will try to claim it as theirs though. H'm. It is a difficult case. What do you think I ought to do—resist? Eh? I want no more than justice.' . . . He wanted no more than justice—no more than justice. I rang the bell before a mahogany door on the first floor, and while I waited he seemed to stare at me out of the glassy panel—stare with that wide and immense stare embracing, condemning, loathing all the universe. I seemed to hear the whispered cry, 'The horror! The horror!'

"The dusk was falling. I had to wait in a lofty drawing-room with three long windows from floor to ceiling that were like three luminous and bedraped columns. The bent gilt legs and backs of the furniture shone in indistinct curves. The tall marble fireplace had a cold and monumental whiteness. A grand piano stood massively in a corner; with dark gleams on the flat surfaces like a sombre and polished sarcophagus. A high door opened—closed. I rose.

"She came forward, all in black, with a pale head, floating towards me in the dusk. She was in mourning. It was more than a year since his death, more than a year since the news came; she seemed as though she would remember and mourn for ever. She took both my hands in hers and murmured, 'I had heard you were coming.' I noticed she was not very young—I mean not girlish. She had a mature capacity for fidelity, for belief, for suffering. The room seemed to have grown darker, as if all the sad light of the cloudy evening had taken refuge on her forehead. This fair hair, this pale visage, this pure brow, seemed surrounded by an ashy halo from which the dark eyes looked out at me. Their glance was guileless, profound, confident, and trustful. She carried her sorrowful head as though she were proud of that sorrow, as though she would say, I—I alone know how to mourn for him as he deserves. But while we were still shaking hands, such a look of awful desolation came upon her face that I perceived she was one of those creatures that are not the playthings of Time. For her he had died only yesterday. And, by Jove! the impression was so powerful that for me too he seemed to have died only yesterday—nay, this very minute. I saw her and him in the same instant of time—his death and her sorrow—I saw her sorrow in the very moment of his death. Do you understand? I saw them together—I heard them together. She had said, with a deep catch of the breath, 'I have survived'; while my strained ears seemed to hear distinctly, mingled with her tone of despairing regret, the summing-up whisper of his eternal condemnation. I asked myself what I was doing there, with a sensation of panic in my heart as though I had blundered into a place of cruel and absurd mysteries not fit for a human being to behold. She motioned me to a chair. We sat down. I laid the packet gently on the little table, and she put her hand over it. . . . 'You knew him well,' she murmured, after a moment of mourning silence.

" 'Intimacy grows quickly out there,' I said. 'I knew him as well as it is possible for one man to know another.'

" 'And you admired him,' she said. 'It was impossible to know him and not to admire him. Was it?'

" 'He was a remarkable man,' I said unsteadily. Then before the appealing fixity of her gaze, that seemed to watch for more words on my lips, I went on, 'It was impossible not to——'

" 'Love him,' she finished eagerly, silencing me into an appalled dumbness. 'How true! how true! But when you think that no one knew him so well as I! I had all his noble confidence. I knew him best.'

" 'You knew him best,' I repeated. And perhaps she did. But with every word spoken the room was growing darker, and only her forehead, smooth and white, remained illumined by the unextinguishable light of belief and love.

" 'You were his friend,' she went on. 'His friend,' she repeated, a little louder. 'You must have been, if he had given you this, and sent you to me. I feel I can speak to you—and oh! I must speak. I want you—you who have heard his last words—to know I have been worthy of him. . . . It is not pride. . . . Yes! I am proud to know I understood him better than any one on earth—he told me so himself. And since his mother died I have had no one—no one—to—to——'

"I listened. The darkness deepened. I was not even sure whether he had given me the right bundle. I rather suspect he wanted me to take care of another batch of his papers which, after his death, I saw the manager examining under the lamp. And the girl talked, easing her pain in the certitude of my sympathy; she talked as thirsty men drink. I had heard that her engagement with Kurtz had been disapproved by her people. He wasn't rich enough or something. And indeed I don't know whether he had not been a pauper all his life. He had given me some reason to infer that it was his impatience of comparative poverty that drove him out there.

" ' . . . Who was not his friend who had heard him speak once?' she was saying. 'He drew men towards him by what was best in them.' She looked at me with intensity. 'It is the gift of the great,' she went on, and the sound of her low voice seemed to have the accompaniment of all the other sounds, full of mystery, desolation, and sorrow, I had ever heard—the ripple of the river, the soughing of the trees swayed by the wind, the murmurs of the crowds, the faint ring of incomprehensible words cried from afar, the whisper of a voice speaking from beyond the threshold of an eternal darkness. 'But you have heard him! You know!' she cried.

" 'Yes, I know,' I said with something like despair in my heart, but bowing my head before the faith that was in her, before that great and saving illusion that shone with an unearthly glow in the darkness, in the triumphant darkness from which I could not have defended her—from which I could not even defend myself.

" 'What a loss to me—to us!'—she corrected herself with beautiful generosity; then added in a murmur, 'To the world.' By the last gleams of twilight I could see the glitter of her eyes, full of tears—of tears that would not fall.

" 'I have been very happy—very fortunate—very proud,' she went on. 'Too fortunate. Too happy for a little while. And now I am unhappy for—for life.'

"She stood up; her fair hair seemed to catch all the remaining light in a glimmer of gold. I rose too.

" 'And of all this,' she went on mournfully, 'of all his promise, and of all his greatness, of his generous mind, of his noble heart, nothing remains—nothing but a memory. You and I——'

" 'We shall always remember him,' I said hastily.

" 'No!' she cried. 'It is impossible that all this should be lost—that such a life should be sacrificed to leave nothing—but sorrow. You know what vast plans he had. I knew of them too—I could not perhaps understand—but others knew of them. Something must remain. His words, at least, have not died.'

" 'His words will remain,' I said.

" 'And his example,' she whispered to herself. 'Men looked up to him—his goodness shone in every act. His example——'

" 'True,' I said; 'his example too. Yes, his example. I forgot that.'

" 'But I do not. I cannot—I cannot believe—not yet. I cannot believe that I shall never see him again, that nobody will see him again, never, never, never.'

"She put out her arms as if after a retreating figure, stretching them back and with clasped pale hands across the fading and narrow sheen of the window. Never see him! I saw him clearly enough then. I shall see this eloquent phantom as long as I live, and I shall see her too, a tragic and familiar Shade, resembling in this gesture another one, tragic also, and bedecked with powerless charms, stretching bare brown arms over the glitter of the infernal stream, the stream of darkness. She said suddenly very low, 'He died as he lived.'

" 'His end,' said I, with dull anger stirring in me, 'was in every way worthy of his life.'

" 'And I was not with him,' she murmured. My anger subsided before a feeling of infinite pity.

" 'Everything that could be done——' I mumbled.

" 'Ah, but I believed in him more than any one on earth—more than his own mother, more than—himself. He needed me! Me! I would have treasured every sigh, every word, every sign, every glance.'

"I felt like a chill grip my chest. 'Don't,' I said, in a muffled voice.

" 'Forgive me. I—I—have mourned so long in silence—in silence. . . . You were with him—to the last? I think of his loneliness. Nobody near to understand him as I would have understood. Perhaps no one to hear . . . '

" 'To the very end,' I said shakily. 'I heard his very last words. . . . ' I stopped in a fright.

" 'Repeat them,' she murmured in a heart-broken tone. 'I want—I want—something—something—to—to live with.'

"I was on the point of crying at her, 'Don't you hear them?' The dusk was repeating them in a persistent whisper all around us, in a whisper that seemed to swell menacingly like the first whisper of a rising wind. 'The horror! The horror!'

" 'His last word—to live with,' she insisted. 'Don't you understand I loved him—I loved him—I loved him!'

"I pulled myself together and spoke slowly.

" 'The last word he pronounced was—your name.'

"I heard a light sigh and then my heart stood still, stopped dead short by an exulting and terrible cry, by the cry of inconceivable triumph and of unspeakable pain. 'I knew it—I was sure!' . . . She knew. She was sure. I heard her weeping; she had hidden her face in her hands. It seemed to me that the house would collapse before I could escape, that the heavens would fall upon my head. But nothing happened. The heavens do not fall for such a trifle. Would they have fallen, I wonder, if I had rendered Kurtz that justice which was his due? Hadn't he said he wanted only justice? But I couldn't. I could not tell her. It would have been too dark—too dark altogether. . . ."

Marlow ceased, and sat apart, indistinct and silent, in the pose of a meditating Buddha. Nobody moved for a time. "We have lost the first of the ebb," said the Director suddenly. I raised my head. The offing was barred by a black bank of clouds, and the tranquil waterway leading to the uttermost ends of the earth flowed sombre under an overcast sky—seemed to lead into the heart of an immense darkness.

On Conrad

Perhaps it is less surprising that Joseph Conrad became a writer—his father was a translator and editor—even a writer in English, than that he became a seaman. Born in 1857 in landlocked Poland (then under Russian rule) and christened Josef Tedor Konrad Nalecz Korzeniowski, he went to Russia with his family when his father was exiled for political activities in 1862. Twelve years later, he left Poland for Marseilles to become a sailor in the French merchant marine. After journeys to the Caribbean, he became a gun-runner for the Spanish Carlists, fell in love, debt, and despair, and apparently tried to shoot himself. In 1878, he joined the crew of an English ship, began to learn the language, and embarked seriously on a career at sea, rising to third mate and finally, in 1888, to master of a ship. Two years later he voyaged up the Congo as captain of a river steamer. He was disliked by and was contemptuous of a manager who threatened to keep him from promotion and increase in salary, and he fell ill with dysentery and the inevitable malaria. In his luggage he carried the uncompleted manuscript of a novel. It was the turning point in his life; until then, he said, "I was a perfect animal" (Garnett, "Introduction," *Letters from Conrad*). Moreover, the diseases incurred there forced him to consider another profession, and by 1893, he had finished enough of *Almayer's Folly* to show to a passenger, John Galsworthy. The novel was published in 1895, and though for several years Conrad tried to obtain a command, his career as a writer was under way.

Until 1912, he prospered only in the artistic sense, and even then in the face of family cares (he married Jessie George in 1896), of illness, of torturous difficulty in writing, and of the collapse of various financial and literary schemes to improve his lot. In 1898 occurred what Jocelyn Baines calls "the most important event in Conrad's literary career": meeting and eventually collaborating with Ford Madox Ford (then Heuffer). The association was begun with the hope of making money; it continued because of a mutual interest in the art of fiction, especially as practiced by Flaubert and his successors. The meeting took place at a crucial point in Conrad's career. He had published three novels of increasing quality (*Almayer, An Outcast of the Islands, The Nigger of the Narcissus*) and a collection, *Tales of Unrest;* had recently completed "Youth," in which Marlow serves as narrator; and had begun and temporarily abandoned "Jim, a Sketch," a short story which was to evolve into *Lord Jim.* This body of work would have given him an honorable if not distinguished place as a novelist. Two months after he met Ford, Conrad was at work on "a short story for Blackwood which I must turn out for the sake of shekels" *(Letters from Conrad);* it became *Heart of Darkness. Lord Jim* followed in 1900, and his reputation as an artist was firmly established. The year after *Nostromo* (1904), he was granted a Civil List pension by the government, and his financial situation was made somewhat easier. With the publication of *Chance* (1913) came wider recognition and financial rewards—and, according to some critics, the beginning of the decline in powers that marked his later works. By the 1920's, he had become a public figure and was offered a knighthood, which he declined. Less than three months later, on August 3, 1924, he died.

In the preface to *Youth,* the volume containing *Heart of Darkness,* Conrad wrote that the story "is experience pushed a little (and only very little) beyond the actual facts of the case for the perfectly legitimate, I believe, purpose of bringing it home to the minds and bosoms of the readers. . . . That sombre theme had to be given a sinister resonance, a tonality of its own, a continued vibration that, I hoped, would hang in the air and dwell on the ear after the last note had been struck." In the concern for the audience as well as for the essential rather than the surface truth of a situation, this echoes the most famous announcement of his artistic intentions, the Preface to *The Nigger of the Narcissus* (1897):

> . . . art itself may be defined as a single-minded attempt to render the highest kind of justice to the visible universe, by bringing to light the truth, manifold and one, underlying its every aspect. It is an attempt to find in its forms, its colors, in its light, in its shadows, in the aspects of matter and the facts of life, what of each is fundamental, what is enduring and essential—their one illuminating and convincing quality—the very truth of their existence. . . . All art . . . appeals primarily to the senses, and the artistic aim when expressing itself in written words must also make its appeal through the senses, if its high desire is to reach the secret spring of responsive emotions. It must strenuously aspire to the plasticity of sculpture, to the color of painting, and to the magic suggestiveness of music—which is the art of arts. And it is only through complete, unswerving devotion to the perfect blending of form and substance; it is only through an unremitting, never-discouraged care for the shape and ring of sentences that an approach can be made to plasticity, to color, and that the light of magic suggestiveness may be brought to play for an evanescent instant over the commonplace surface of words: of the old, old words, worn thin, defaced by ages of careless usage. . . . My task which I am trying to achieve is, by the power of the written word, to make you hear, to make you feel—it is, before all, to make you *see.* That—and no more, and it is everything. If I succeed, you shall find there, according to your

deserts, encouragement, consolation, fear, charm, all you demand—and, perhaps, also that glimpse of truth for which you have
forgotten to ask.

A full commentary on these excerpts would stretch into a history of the
modern movement in literature; here, a few easy dichotomies will have to
suffice. Conrad is announcing a departure from the English novel of the
immediate past, choosing to re-create rather than narrate, to explore depths
rather than surfaces, to become an artist rather than a novelist in the old
sense, and to be esoteric rather than popular. Such distinctions are clearly
oversimplified, but it is true that after Conrad, James, and other practicion-
ers of the art (rather than the craft) of fiction, the novel became more
self-conscious in method and the novel intended as art sought a different
audience from the popular novel.

Conrad's announcement that he wished to make us "see" draws upon an
ancient distinction between perception of surfaces and the penetration of
surfaces to reach understanding. His "Congo Diary," published in *Last
Essays,* records many events and sensations which found their way into the
novel, and the facts of Belgian exploitation of the natives are if anything
worse than Conrad's portrait. However, Conrad chose to deemphasize
autobiography and social protest, just as he chose to avoid the conventions
of the mere adventure story: hardship, danger, and, except for the night
encounter with Kurtz, dramatic confrontation, all are underplayed. Thus
Marlow interrupts his account of the native attack to light his pipe and
digress, works casually (or seems to) toward the fact that the post ornaments are human heads, and dismisses as not worthy of comment his
struggle to live and his return to the sepulchral city. Furthermore, Conrad's
fidelity to the impression as received by the senses, before the mind fixes
and interprets it, leads to a disorientation (in "Arrows, by Jove!" to comic
incongruity) because, anticipating Ernest Hemingway, he attempted to
show what one really saw and felt rather than what one was taught to see
and feel. In the interests of making the reader understand rather than
simply react, he is doubly distanced from the events: first, by the reminis-
cent, ironic tone of Marlow, telling of "the farthest point of navigation and
the culmination of my experience" long after the fact; second, by the
unnamed narrator who listens to Marlow and indicates, by his changes in
attitude towards teller, tale, and situation, the effect that the yarn should
have on the attentive listener.

This distancing is one of the devices which makes possible the dreamlike
quality of the story: the sudden shifts in time and space and the portentous
images and situations whose significance looms on the periphery of consciousness, each containing in itself the meaning of the whole. Marlow's
memory controls the way that the audience experiences and remembers the
story: a series of vivid pictures of a battleship firing into a continent, of
skeletal forms moving in semidarkness, of blind movement in the fog. Yet
the story is far from shapeless. Its external form was in part influenced by
the original circumstances of serial publication; the three chapters correspond to the three parts, and Conrad took care to end the first two with a

hook for the reader's curiosity. Internal form is provided by the frame (the listeners on the *Nellie*), by the thread of the journey to encounter Kurtz, and by the numerous parallels in situation and character and the recurrent images. Some, like the Intended and the savage woman or the battleship and the pilgrims firing into the brush, are fairly obvious; others, like the recurrent mention of shoes, are more obscure.

What Conrad was attempting to bring home to his readers, to make them *see,* has been the object of considerable discussion and disagreement. Some critics regard Marlow as a stoic, some as a Buddha, some as a surrogate for Conrad, some as protagonist, some as interpreter. The disagreement is itself an indication of the richness and complexity of the story. Perhaps it would be profitable, at least initially, to see the story as about process—not so much man's place in the universe, which is a static conception, but the way in which man is to live in the universe and the shifts and expedients to which he is forced in the process of constructing a world about himself. A fuller understanding of the story demands careful reading and rereading, as well as study of the growth of its text, of the biographical, intellectual, and literary contexts in which it was written, and of the insights or instructive misreadings of the critics. Valid interpretation—which is not to say complete or final interpretation—must come from this kind of evidence. (See E. D. Hirsch, *Validity in Interpretation* [New Haven: Yale University Press, 1967.]) Response to the story may be another matter—we can feel before we can understand—but ultimately, some responses are more informed and have the potentiality for being richer and more rewarding than others, and these responses are or should be the end of all literary study, whether bibliographical, biographical, or critical.

Textual note:

First published as "The Heart of Darkness" in the February, March, and April 1899 issues of *Blackwood's Magazine;* revised for the collection *Youth and Two Other Stories,* 1902; further revised for the Heinemann *Collected Works* in 1921. See Kimbrough's edition for a discussion of the textual history and a list of variants. The text printed here follows the 1921 Heinemann edition.

Resources for further study:

By general consent, Conrad's finest novels are *Lord Jim* and *Nostromo.* Marlow serves as narrator of *Lord Jim,* "Youth," and *Chance.* "The Secret Sharer" is often ranked with *Heart of Darkness.*

Conrad's essays and letters throw considerable light on his fiction. Collections of essays are: *The Mirror of the Sea* (1906), *A Personal Record* (1912), *Within the Tides* (1915), *Notes on My Books* (1921), *Notes on Life*

and Letters (1921), *Last Essays* (1926), and *Conrad's Prefaces* (1927).
Collections of letters: G. Jean-Aubry, *Joseph Conrad: Life and Letters,* 2
vols. (Garden City, N.Y.: Doubleday & Company, Inc., 1927); *Conrad to a
Friend,* Richard Curle, ed. (London: Sampson Low, Marston and Co.,
1928); *Letters from Conrad,* Edward Garnett, ed. (Indianapolis: The
Bobbs-Merrill Co., Inc., 1928); *Lettres Françaises,* G. Jean-Aubrey, ed.
(Paris: Gallimard, 1929); *Letters of Joseph Conrad to Marguerite Pora-
dowska, 1890–1920,* John A. Gee and Paul J. Sturm, eds. (New Haven: Yale
University Press, 1940); *Joseph Conrad: Letters to William Blackwood
and David S. Meldrum,* William Blackburn, ed. (Durham, N.C.: Duke
University Press, 1958); Zdistaw Najder, *Conrad's Polish Background:
Letters to and from Polish Friends* (London: Oxford University Press,
1964); *Joseph Conrad's Letters to R. B. Cunninghame Graham,* C. T.
Watts, ed. (Cambridge: Cambridge University Press, 1969).

BIBLIOGRAPHICAL:

BEEBE, MAURICE. "Criticism of Joseph Conrad: A Selected Checklist,"
  Modern Fiction Studies, 10 (Spring 1964), 81–106. See the earlier
  checklist in *Modern Fiction Studies,* 1 (Fall 1955); these two issues are
  devoted entirely to Conrad.
ERSHAM, THEODORE G. *A Bibliography of Joseph Conrad.* Metuchen, N.J.:
  Scarecrow Press, Inc., 1969. The most thorough primary and secondary
  listings available.
LOHF, KENNETH A., and EUGENE P. SHEEHY. *Joseph Conrad at Mid-
  Century: Editions and Studies,* 1895–1955. Minneapolis: University of
  Minnesota Press, 1957.
Conradiana, a journal published at McMurry College, prints bibliographi-
  cal, biographical, and critical essays on Conrad.

BIOGRAPHICAL:

AUBRY, G. JEAN. *The Sea-Dreamer: A Definitive Biography of Joseph
  Conrad,* trans. Helen Sebba. Garden City, N.Y.: Doubleday & Company,
  Inc., 1927.
BAINES, JOCELYN. *Joseph Conrad.* New York: McGraw-Hill Book Company,
  1960.
MEYER, BERNARD. *Joseph Conrad: A Psychoanalytic Biography.* Prince-
  ton: Princeton University Press, 1967.

CRITICAL:

FORD, FORD MADOX. *Joseph Conrad: A Personal Remembrance.* London:
  Duckworth, 1924. More important for critical insight than for biographical fact.

GORDAN, JOHN DOZIER. *Joseph Conrad: The Making of a Novelist.* Cambridge, Mass.: Harvard University Press, 1940.

GUERARD, ALBERT. *Conrad the Novelist.* Cambridge, Mass.: Harvard University Press, 1958.

KIMBROUGH, ROBERT, ed. *Heart of Darkness: An Authoritative Text, Backgrounds and Sources, Essays in Criticism.* New York: W. W. Norton and Company, Inc., 1963.

MUDRICK, MARVIN, ed. *Conrad: A Collection of Critical Essays.* Englewood Cliffs, N.J.: Prentice-Hall, Inc., 1966.

HARKNESS, BRUCE, ed. *Conrad's "Heart of Darkness" and the Critics.* San Francisco: Wadsworth Publishing Co., Inc., 1960.

LEE, ROBERT F. *Conrad's Colonialism.* The Hague: Mouton, 1969.

SANDISON, ALAN. *The Wheel of Empire.* NewYork: St. Martin's Press, Inc., 1967.

RONALD FIRBANK

Concerning the
Eccentricities
of Cardinal Pirelli

1

Huddled up in a cope of gold wrought silk he peered around. Society had rallied in force. A christening—and not a child's.

Rarely had he witnessed, before the font, so many brilliant people. Were it an heir to the DunEden acres (instead of what it *was*) the ceremony could have hardly drawn together a more distinguished throng.

Monsignor Silex moved a finger from forehead to chin, and from ear to ear. The Duquesa DunEden's escapades, if continued, would certainly cost the Cardinal his hat.

"And ease my heart by splashing fountains,"

From the choir loft a boy's young voice was evoking Heaven.

"His hat!" Monsignor Silex exclaimed aloud, blinking a little at the immemorial font of black Macael marble that had provoked the screams of pale numberless babies.

Here Saints and Kings had been baptized, and royal Infantas, and sweet Poets, whose high names thrilled the heart.

Monsignor Silex crossed his breast. He must gather force to look about him. Frame a close report. The Pontiff, in far-off Italy, would expect precision.

112

Beneath the state baldequin, or Grand Xaymaca, his Eminence sat enthroned ogled by the wives of a dozen grandees. The Altamissals, the Villarasas (their grandeeships approving glances, indeed, almost eclipsed their wives'), and Catherine, Countess of Constantine, the most talked-of beauty in the Realm, looking like some wild limb of Astaroth in a little crushed "toreador" hat round as an athlete's coit with hanging silken balls, while beside her, a stout, dumpish dame, of enormous persuasion, was joggling, solicitously, an object that was of the liveliest interest to all.

Head archly bent, her fine arms divined through darkling laces, the Duquesa stood, clasping closely a week-old police-dog in the ripple of her gown.

"Mother's pet!" she cooed, as the imperious creature passed his tongue across the splendid uncertainty of her chin.

Monsignor Silex's large, livid face grew grim.

What,—disquieting doubt,—if it were her Grace's offspring after all? Praise heaven, he was ignorant enough regarding the schemes of nature, but in an old lutrin once he had read of a young woman engendering a missel-thrush through the channel of her nose. It had created a good deal of scandal to be sure at the time: the Holy Inquisition, indeed, had condemned the impudent baggage, in consequence, to the stake.

"That was the style to treat them," he murmured, appraising the assembly with no kindly eye. The presence of Madame San Seymour surprised him; one habitually so set apart and devout! And Madame La Urench, too, gurgling away freely to the four-legged Father: "No, my naughty Blessing; no, not now! . . . By and by, a *bone*."

Words which brought the warm saliva to the expectant parent's mouth.

Tail awag, sex apparent (to the affected slight confusion of the Infanta Eulalia-Irene), he crouched, his eyes fixed wistfully upon the nozzle of his son.

Ah, happy delirium of first parenthood! Adoring pride! Since Times primaeval by what masonry does it knit together those that have succeeded in establishing, here, on earth, the vital bonds of a family's claim? Even the modest sacristan, at attention by the font, felt himself to be superior of parts to a certain unproductive chieftain of a princely House, who had lately undergone a course of asses' milk in the surrounding mountains—all in vain!

But, supported by the Prior of the Cartuja, the Cardinal had arisen for the act of Immersion.

Of unusual elegance, and with the remains, moreover, of perfect looks, he was as wooed and run after by the ladies as any *matador*.

"And thus being cleansed and purified, I do call thee 'Crack'!" he addressed the Duquesa's captive burden.

Tail sheathed with legs "in master's drawers," ears cocked, tongue pendent. . . .

"Mother's mascot!"

"Oh, take care, dear; he's removing all your rouge!"

"*What?*"

"He's spoilt, I fear, your roses": the Countess of Constantine tittered.

The duquesa's grasp relaxed. To be seen by all the world at this disadvantage.

"Both?" she asked distressed, disregarding the culprit, who sprang from her breast with a sharp, sportive bark.

What rapture, what freedom.

"Misericordia!" Monsignor Silex exclaimed, staring aghast at a leg poised, inconsequently, against the mural-tablet of the widowed duchess of Charona—a woman, who, in her lifetime, had given over thirty million pezos to the poor!

Ave Maria purissima! What challenging snarls and measured mystery marked the elaborate recognition of father and son, and would no one then forbid their incestuous frolics?

In agitation Monsignor Silex sought fortitude from the storied windows overhead, aglow in the ambered light as some radiant missal.

It was Saint Eufraxia's Eve, she of Egypt, a frail unit numbered above among the train of the Eleven Thousand Virgins: an immaturish schoolgirl of a saint, unskilled, inexperienced in handling a prayer, lacking the vim and native astuteness of the incomparable Theresa.

Yes, divine interference, 'twixt father and son, was hardly to be looked for, and Eufraxia (she, of Egypt) had failed too often before. . . .

Monsignor Silex started slightly, as from the estrade beneath the dome, a choir-boy let fall a little white spit.

Dear child, as though *that* would part them!

"Things must be allowed to take their 'natural' course," he concluded, following the esoteric antics of the reunited pair.

Out into the open, over the Lapis Lazuli of the floor, they flashed, with stifled yelps like things possessed.

"He'll tear my husband's drawers!" the duquesa lamented.

"The duque's legs, Poor Decima." The Infanta fell quietly to her knees.

"Fortify . . . asses . . . " the royal lips moved.

"Brave darling," she murmured gently rising.

But the duquesa had withdrawn it seemed to repair her ravaged roses, and from the obscurity of an adjacent confessional-box, was calling to order Crack.

"Come, Crack!"

And to the Mauro-Hispanic rafters the echo rose.

"Crack, Crack, Crack, Crack. . . . "

2

From the Calle de la Pasión, beneath the blue-tiled mirador of the garden wall, came the soft brooding sound of a seguidilla. It was a twilight planned for wooing, unbending, consent; many, before now, had come to grief on an evening such. "It was the moon."

Pacing a cloistered walk, laden with the odour of sun-tired flowers, the Cardinal could not but feel the insidious influences astir. The bells of the institutions of the *Encarnacion* and the Immaculate Conception, joined in confirming Angelus, had put on tones half-bridal, enough to create vague longings, or sudden tears, among the young patrician boarders.

"Their parents' daughters—convent-bred," the Cardinal sighed.

At the Immaculate Conception, dubbed by the Queen, in irony, once "The school for harlots" the little Infanta Maria-Paz must be lusting for her Mamma and the Court, and the lilac carnage of the ring, while chafing also in the same loose captivity would be the roguish *niñas* of the pleasure-loving duchess of Sarmento, girls whose Hellenic ethics had given the good Abbess more than one attack of fullness.

Morality. Poise! For without temperance and equilibrium—— The Cardinal halted.

But in the shifting underlight about him the flushed camellias and the sweet Night-jasmines suggested none; neither did the shape of a garden-Eros pointing radiantly the dusk.

"For unless we have balance—" the Cardinal murmured, distraught, admiring against the elusive nuances of the afterglow the cupid's voluptuous hams.

It was against these, once, in a tempestuous mood, that his mistress had smashed her fan-sticks.

"Would that all liaisons would break as easily!" his Eminence framed the prayer: and musing on the appalling constancy of a certain type, he sauntered leisurely on. Yes, enveloping women like Luna Sainz, with their lachrymose tactless, "mys'," how shake them off? "My" Saviour, "my" lover, "my" parasol—and, even, "my" virtue. . . .

"Poor dearie."

The Cardinal smiled.

Yet once in a way, perhaps, he was not averse to being favoured by a glimpse of her: "A little visit on a night like this"—Don Alvaro Narciso Hernando Pirelli, Cardinal-Archbishop of Clemenza, smiled again.

In the gloom there, among the high thickets of bay and flowering-myrtle. . . . For, after all, bless her, one could not well deny she possessed the chief essentials: "such, poor soul, as they are!" he reflected, turning about at the sound of the neigh of a horse.

"Monseigneur. . . . "

Bearing a biretta and a silver shawl, Madame Poco, the venerable Superintendent-of-the-palace, looking, in the blue moonlight, like some whiskered skull, emerged, after inconceivable peepings, from among the leafy limbo of the trees.

"Ah, Don Alvaro, sir! Come here."

"Pest?" His Eminence evinced a touch of asperity.

"Ah, Don, Don, . . . " and skimming forward with the grace of a Torero, lassoing a bull, she slipped the scintillating fabric about the prelate's neck.

"Such nights breed fever, Don Alvaro, and there is mischief in the air."

"Mischief?"

"In certain quarters of the city you would take it almost for some sortilege."

"What next."

"At the *Encarnacion,* there's nothing, of late, but seedyness. Sister Engracia with the chickenpox, and Mother Claridad with the itch, while at the College of Noble Damosels in the Calle Santa Fé, I hear a daughter of Don José Illescas, in a fit of caprice, has set a match to her coronet."

"A match to her what?"

"And how explain, Don Alvaro of my heart, these constant shots in the Cortès? Ah *sangre mio* in what Times we live!"

Ambling a few steps pensively side by side, they moved through the brilliant moonlight. It was the hour when the awakening fireflies are first seen like atoms of rosy flame floating from flower to flower.

"Singular times, sure enough," the Cardinal answered, pausing to enjoy the transparent beauty of the white dripping water of a flowing fountain.

"And ease my heart by splashing—tum-tiddly-um-tum," he hummed: "I trust the choir-boys, Dame, are all in health?"

"Ah, Don Alvaro, no, sir!"

"Eh?"

"No, sir," Madame Poco murmured, taking up a thousand golden poses.

"Why, how's that?"

"But few now seem keen on Leapfrog, or Bossage, and when a boy shows no wish for a game of Leap, sir, or Bossage——"

"Exactly," his Eminence nodded.

"I'm told it's some time, young cubs, since they've played pranks on Tourists! Though only this afternoon little Ramón Ragatta came over queazy while demonstrating before foreigners the Dance of the Arc, which should teach him in future not to be so profane: and as to the acolytes, Don Alvaro, at least half of them are absent, confined to their cots, in the wards of the pistache Fathers!"

"To-morrow, all well, I'll take them some melons."

"Ah, Don, Don!!"

"And, perhaps, a cucumber," the Cardinal added, turning valedictionally away.

The tones of the seguidilla had deepened and from the remote recesses of the garden arose a bedlam of nightingales and frogs.

It was certainly incredible how he felt immured.

Yet to forsake the Palace for the Plaza he was obliged to stoop to creep.

With the Pirelli pride, with resourceful intimacy he communed with his heart: deception is a humiliation; but humiliation is a Virtue—a Cardinal, like myself, and one of the delicate violets of our Lady's crown. . . . Incontestably, too,—he had a flash of inconsequent insight, many a prod to a discourse, many a sapient thrust, delivered ex-cathedra, amid the broken sobs of either sex, had been inspired, before now, by what prurient persons might term, perhaps, a "frolic." But away with all scruples! Once in the street in mufti, how foolish they became.

The dear street. The adorable Avenidas. The quickening stimulus of the crowd: Truly it was exhilarating to mingle freely with the throng!

Disguised as a cabellero from the provinces or as a matron (disliking to forego altogether the militant bravoura of a skirt), it became possible to combine philosophy, equally, with pleasure.

The promenade at the Trinidades seldom failed to be diverting, especially when the brown Bettita or the Ortiz danced! *Olé*, he swayed his shawl. The Argentina with Blanca Sanchez was amusing too; her ear-tickling little song "Madrid is on the Manzanares," trailing the " 'ares" indefinitely, was sure, in due course, to reach the Cloisters.

Deliberating critically on the numerous actresses of his diocese, he traversed lightly a path all enclosed by pots of bergamot.

And how entrancing to perch on a barstool, over a glass of old golden sherry!

"Ah Jesus-Maria," he addressed the dancing lightning in the sky.

Purring to himself, and frequently pausing, he made his way, by ecstatic degrees, towards the mirador on the garden wall.

Although a mortification, it was imperative to bear in mind the consequences of cutting a too dashing figure. Beware display. Vanity once had proved all but fatal: "I remember it was the night I wore ringlets, and was called 'my queen.' "

And with a fleeting smile, Don Alvaro Pirelli recalled the persistent officer who had had the effrontery to attempt to molest him: "Stalked me the whole length of the Avenue Isadora!" It had been a lesson. "Better to be on the drab side," he reflected, turning the key of the garden tower.

Dating from the period of the Reformation of the Nunneries, it commanded the privacy of many a drowsy patio.

"I see the Infanta has begun her Tuesdays!" he serenely noted sweeping the panorama with a glance.

It was a delightful prospect.

Like some great guitar the city lay engirdled ethereally by the snowy Sierras.

"Foolish featherhead," he murmured, his glance falling upon a sunshade of sapphire chiffon, left by Luna: " 'my' parasol!" he twirled the crystal hilt.

"Everything she forgets, bless her," he breathed, lifting his gaze towards the Magnolia blossom cups that overtopped the tower, stained by the eternal treachery of the night to the azure of the Saint Virgin. Suspended in the miracle of the moonlight their elfin globes were at their zenith.

"Madrid is on the Manzan-ares," he intoned.

But "Clemenza," of course, is in white Andalucia.

3

After the tobacco-factory and the railway-station, quite the liveliest spot in all the city was the cathedral-sacristia. In the interim of an Office it would be besieged by the laity, often to the point of scrimmage: aristocrats and mendicants, relatives of acolytes—each had some truck or other in the long lofty room. Here the secretary of the chapter, a burly little man, a sound judge of women and bulls, might be consulted gratis, preferably, before the supreme heat of day. Seated beneath a sombre study of the Magdaline waylaying our Lord (a work of wistful interest ascribed to

Valdés Leal), he was, with tactful courtesy, at the disposal of anyone soliciting information as to "vacant dates," or "hours available," for some impromptu function. Indulgences, novenas, terms for special masses— with flowers and music? Or, just plain; the expense, it varied! Bookings for baptisms, it was certainly advisable to book well ahead; some mothers booked before the birth—; Ah-hah, the little Juans and Juanas; the angelic babies! And arrangements for a Corpse's lying-in-state: "Leave it to me." These, and such things, were in his province.

But the secretarial bureau was but merely a speck in the vast shuttered room. As a rule, it was by the old pagan sarcophaguses, outside the vestry-door, "waiting for Father," that *aficianados* of the cult liked best to foregather.

It was the morning of the Feast of San Antolin of Panticosa, a morning so sweet, and blue and luminous, and many were waiting.

"It's queer the time a man takes to slip on a frilly!" the laundress of the Basilica, Doña Consolacion, observed, through her fansticks, to Tomás the beadle.

"Got up as you get them. . . . "

"It's true, indeed, I've a knack with a rochet!"

"Temperament will out, Doña Consolacion; it cannot be hid."

The laundress beamed.

"Mine's the French."

"It's God's will *whatever* it is."

"It's the French," she lisped, considering the silver rings on her honey-brown hands. Of distinguished presence, with dark matted curls at either ear, she was the apotheosis of flesh triumphant.

But the entry from the vestry of a file of monsignore imposed a transient silence—a silence which was broken only by the murmur of passing mule bells along the street.

Tingaling, tingaling: evocative of grain and harvest the sylvan sound of mule bells came and went.

Doña Consolacion flapped her fan.

There was to be question directly of a Maiden Mass.

With his family all about him, the celebrant, a youth of the People, looking childishly happy in his first broidered cope, had bent, more than once, his good-natured head, to allow some small brothers and sisters to inspect his tonsure.

"Like a little, little star!"

"No. Like a *perrá gordá.*"

"No, like a little star," they fluted, while an irrepressible grandmother, moved to tears and laughter, insisted on planting a kiss on the old "Christian" symbol: "He'll be a Pope some day, if he's spared!" she sobbed transported.

"Not he, the big burly bull," Mother Garcia of the Company of Jesus addressed Doña Consolacion with a mellifluent chuckle.

Holding a bouquet of sunflowers and a basket of eggs she had just looked in from Market.

"Who knows, my dear?" Doña Consolacion returned, fixing her gaze upon an Epitaph on a vault beneath her feet: " 'He was a boy and she dazzled him.' Heigh-ho! Heysey-ho . . . ! Yes, as I was saying."

"Pho: I'd like to see him in a Papal tiara."

"It's mostly luck. I well recall his Eminence when he was nothing but a trumpery curate," Doña Consolacion declared, turning to admire the jewelled studs in the ears of the President of the College of Noble Damosels.

"Faugh!" Mother Garcia spat.

"It's all luck."

"There's luck and luck," the beadle put in. Once he had confined by accident a lady in the souterrains of the cathedral, and only many days later had her bones and a diary, a diary documenting the most delicate phases of solitude and loneliness, *a woman's contribution to Science,* come to light; a piece of carelessness that had gone against the old man in his preferment.

"Some careers are less fortunate than others," Mother Garcia exclaimed, appraising the sleek silhouette of Monsignor Silex, then precipitantly issuing from the Muniment-Room.

It was known he was not averse to a little stimulant in the bright middle of the morning.

"He has the evil Eye, dear, he has the evil Eye," Doña Consolacion murmured, averting her head. Above her hung a sombre Ribera, in a frame of elaborate, blackened gilding.

"Ah, well, I do not fear it," the Companion of Jesus answered, making way for a dark, heavy belle in a handkerchief and shawl.

"Has any one seen Jositto, my little José?"

Mother Garcia waved with her bouquet towards an adjacent portal, surmounted, with cool sobriety, by a long, lavender marble cross: "I expect he's through there."

"In the cathedral?"

"How pretty you look, dear, and what a very gay shawl!"

"Pure silk."

"I don't *doubt* it!"

Few women, however, are indifferent to the seduction of a Maiden mass, and all in a second there was scarcely one to be found in the whole sacristia.

The secretary at his bureau looked about him: without the presence of *las mujares* the atmosphere seemed to weigh a little, still, being a Holiday of Obligation, a fair sprinkling of boys, youthful chapter hands whom he would sometimes designate as the "lesser delights," relieved the place of its austerity.

Through the heraldic windows, swathed in straw-mats to shut out the heat, the sun-rays entered, tattooing with piquant freckles the pampered faces of the choir.

A request for a permit to view the fabled Orangery in the cloisters, interrupted his siestose fancies.

Like luxurious cygnets in their cloudy lawn, a score of young singing-boys were awaiting their cue: Low-masses, cheapness, and economy, how they despised them, and how they would laugh at "Old Ends" who snuffed out the candles.

"Why should the Church charge *higher* for a short *Magnificat* than for a long *Miserere?*"

The question had just been put by the owner of a dawning moustache and a snub, though expressive nose.

"Because happiness makes people generous, stupid, and often as not they'll squander, boom, but unhappiness makes them calculate. People grudge spending much on a snivel—even if it lasts an hour."

"It's the choir that suffers."

"This profiteering . . . The Chapter . . . " there was a confusion of voices.

"Order!" A slim lad, of an ambered paleness, raised a protesting hand: Indulged, and made much-of by the hierarchy, he was Felix Ganay, known as Chief-dancing-choir-boy to the cathedral of Clemenza.

"Aren't they awful?" he addressed a child with a very finished small head. Fingering a score of music he had been taking lead in a mass of Palestrina, and had the vaguely distraught air of a kitten that had seen visions.

"After that, I've not a dry stitch on me," he murmured, with a glance towards the secretary, who was making lost grimaces at the Magdalen's portrait.

A lively controversy (becoming increasingly more shrill) was dividing the acolytes and choir.

"Tiny and Tibi! Enough." The intervention came from the full-voiced Christobal, a youngster of fifteen, with soft, peach-textured cheeks, and a tongue never far away. Considered an opportunist, he was one of the privileged six dancing-boys of the cathedral.

"Order!" Felix enjoined anew. Finely sensitive as to his prerogatives, the interference of his colleague was apt to vex him. He would be trying to clip an altar pose next. Indeed, it was a matter of scandal already, how he was attempting to attract attention, in influential places, by the unnecessary undulation of his loins, and by affecting strong scents and attars, such as Egyptian Tahetant, or Long flirt through the violet Hours. Himself, Felix, he was faithful to Royal Florida, or even to plain *eau-de-Cologne,* and to those slow Mozarabic movements which alone are seemly to the Church.

"You may mind your business, young Christobal," Felix murmured, turning towards a big, serious, melancholy boy, who was describing a cigarette-case he had received as fee for singing "Say it with Edelweiss" at a society wedding.

"Say it with what?" the cry came from an oncoming-looking child, with caressing liquid eyes, and a little tongue the colour of raspberry-cream—*so bright.* Friand of all sweets and dainties, he held San Antolin's day chiefly notable for the Saint's sweet biscuits, made of sugar and white-of-egg.

"And you, too, Chicklet. Mind your business, can't you?" Felix exclaimed, appraising in some dismay a big, bland woman, then descending upon the secretary at his desk, with a slow, but determined, waddle.

Amalia Bermudez, the fashionable Actress-manageress of the Teatro

Victoria Eugenia, was becoming a source of terror to the chapter of Clemenza. Every morning, with fatal persistence, she would aboard the half-hypnotised secretary with the request that the Church should make "a little christian" of her blue-chow, for unless it could be done it seemed the poor thing wasn't *chic*. To be *chic* and among the foremost vanward, this apart from the Theatre meant all to her in life, and since the unorthodox affair of "the DunEdens," she had been quite upset by the chapter's evasive refusals.

"If a police-dog, then why not a chow?" she would ask: "Why not my little Whisky? Little devil. Ah, believe me, Father, she has need of it; For she's supposed to have had a snake by my old dog Conqueror! . . . And yet you won't receive her? Oh, it's heartless. Men are cruel. . . . "

"There she is! Amalia—the Bermudez": the whisper spread, arresting the story of the black Bishop of Bechuanaland, just begun by the roguish Ramón.

And in the passing silence the treble voice of Tiny was left talking all alone.

" . . . frightened me like Father did, when he kissed me in the dark like a lion":—a remark that was greeted by an explosion of coughs.

But this morning the clear, light laugh of the comedienne rang out merrily: "No, no, *hombre*," she exclaimed (tapping the secretary upon the cheek, archly with her fan), "now don't, don't stare at me, and intimidate me like that! I desire only to offer 'a Mass of Intention,' fully choral, *that the Church may change her mind."*

And when the cannon that told of Noon was fired from the white fortress by the river far away, she was still considering programmes of music by Rossini and Cimarosa, and the colour of the chasubles which the clergy should wear.

4

At the season when the Oleanders are in their full perfection, at the season when the oleanders are in their choicest bloom, it was the Pontiff's innovation to install his American type-writing apparatus in the long Loggie of the Apostolic Palace that had been in disuse since the demise of Innocent XVI. Out-of-doorish, as Neapolitans usually are, Pope Tertius II. was no exception to the rule, preferring blue skies to golden ceilings—a taste for which indeed many were inclined to blame him. A compromise between the state-saloons and the modest suite occupied by his Holiness from choice, these open Loggie, adorned with the radiant frescoes of Luca Signorelli, would be frequently the scene of some particular Audience, granted after the exacting press of official routine.

Late one afternoon the Pontiff after an eventful and arduous day was walking thoughtfully here alone. Participating no longer in the joys of the world, it was, however, charming to catch, from time to time, the distant sound of Rome—the fitful clamour of trams and cabs, and the plash of the great twin-fountains in the court of Saint Damascus.

Wrapped in grave absorption, with level gaze, the lips slightly pinched, Pope Tertius II. paced to and fro, occasionally raising a well-formed (though hairy) hand, as though to dismiss his thoughts with a benediction. The nomination of two Vacant Hats, the marriage annulment of an exhereditary Grand Duchess, and the "scandals of Clemenza," were equally claiming his attention and ruffling his serenity.

He had the head of an elderly lady's-maid, and an expression concealed by lairs of tactful caution.

"Why can't they all behave?" he asked himself, plaintively, descrying Lucrezia, his prized white squirrel, sidling shyly towards him.

She was the gift of the Archbishop of Trebizond who had found her in the region of the Coelian hill.

"Slyboots, slyboots," Pope Tertius exclaimed, as she skipped from reach. It was incredible with what playful zest she would spring from statue to statue; and it would have amused the Vicar of Christ to watch her slip and slide, had it not suggested many a profound moral metaphor applicable to the Church: "Gently, gently," he enjoined; for once, in her struggles, she had robbed *a fig-leaf* off a "Moses."

"Yes, why can't they all behave?" he murmured, gazing up into the far pale-blueness.

He stood a brief moment transfixed, as if in prayer, oblivious of two whispering chamberlains.

It was the turn-in-waiting of Baron Oschatz, a man of engaging exquisite manners, and of Count Cuenca, an individual who seemed to be in perpetual consternation.

Depositing a few of the most recent camera portraits of the Pontiff requiring autograph in a spot where he could not fail but see them, they formally withdrew.

It had been a day distinguished by innumerable Audiences, several not uninteresting to recall. . . .

Certainly the increasing numbers of English were decidedly promising, and bore out the sibylline predictions of their late great and sagacious ruler—that of Queen Victoria.

"The dear *santissima* woman," the Pontiff sighed, for he entertained a sincere, if brackish, enthusiasm for the lady who for so many years had corresponded with the Holy See under the signature of *the Countess of Lostwaters.*

"Anglicans . . . ? Heliolatries and sunworshippers," she had written in her most masterful hand, "and your Holiness may believe us," she had added, "when we say especially our beloved Scotch."

"I shouldn't wonder enormously if it were true," the Pope exclaimed, catching through a half-shut door a glimpse of violet stockings.

Such a display of old, out-at-heel hose could but belong to Cardinal Robin.

There had been a meeting of the board for Extraordinary Ecclesiastical Affairs, and when shortly afterwards the Cardinal was admitted, he bore still about him some remote trace of faction.

He had the air of a cuttle-fish, and an inquiring voice. Inclined to gesture, how many miles must his hands have moved in the course of the sermons that he had preached!

Saluting the sovereign Pontiff with a deep obeisance, the Cardinal came directly to the point.

"These schisms in Spain . . . "

"They are ever before me," his Holiness confessed.

"With priests like Pirelli, the Church is in peril!" the Cardinal declared, with a short, abysmal laugh.

"Does he suppose we are in the Times of Bâal and Moloch?" the Pope asked, pressing a harassed hand to his head. A Neapolitan of Naples (oh, Bay of Napoli. See Vesuvius, *and die*), he had curly hair that seemed to grow visibly; every few hours his tonsure would threaten to disappear.

The Cardinal sent up his brows a little.

"If I may tender the advice of the secret Consistory," he said, "your Holiness should Listen in."

"To what end?"

"A snarl, a growl, a bark, a yelp, coming from the font, would be quite enough to condemn . . . "

"Per Bacco. I should take it for a baby."

" . . . condemn," the Cardinal pursued, "this Perelli for a *maleficus pastor*. In which case, the earlier, the better, the unfrocking. . . . "

The Pontiff sighed.

The excellent Cardinal was as fatiguing as a mission from Salt Lake City.

"Evidently," he murmured, detecting traces of rats among the papyrus plants in the long walk below.

"They come up from the Tiber!" he exclaimed, piloting the Cardinal dexterously towards a flight of footworn steps leading to the Court of Bramante.

"It's a bore there being no lift!" he commented (the remark was Vatican cliché), dismissing the Cardinal with a benediction.

"A painful interview," the Holy Father reflected, regarding the Western sky. An evening rose and radiant altogether. . . .

Turning sadly, he perceived Count Cuenca.

A nephew of the Dean of the Sacred College, it was rumoured that he was addicted, in his "home" above Frascati, to the last excesses of the pre-Adamite Sultans.

"A dozen blessings, for a dozen Hymens—but only eleven were sent," he was babbling distractedly to himself. He had been unstrung all day, "just a mass of foolish nerves," owing to a woman, an American, it seemed, coming for her Audience in a *hat* edged with white and yellow water-lilies. She had been repulsed successfully by the Papal Guard, but it had left an unpleasant impression.

"How's that?" the Vicar of Christ exclaimed: he enjoyed to tease his Chamberlains—especially Count Cuenca.

The Count turned pale.

"——," he replied inaudibly rolling eyes at Lucrezia.

Baron Oshatz had "deserted" him; and what is one Chamberlain, alas, without another?

"The photographs of your Holiness are beside the bust of Bernini!" he stammered out, beating a diplomatic retreat.

Pope Tertius II. addressed his squirrel.

"Little slyboots," he said, "I often laugh when I'm alone."

5

Before the white façade of the DunEden Palace, commanding the long, palm-shaded Paseo del Violón, an array of carriages and limousines was waiting, while passing, in brisk succession, beneath the portico, like a swarm of brilliant butterflies, each instant was bringing more. Dating from the period of Don Pedro *el cruel,* the palace had been once the residence of the famous Princesse des Ursins, who had left behind something of her conviviality and glamour. But it is unlikely that the soirées of the exuberant and fanciful Princesse eclipsed those of the no less exuberant Duquesa DunEden. It was to be an evening (flavoured with rich heroics) in honour of the convalescence of several great ladies, from an attack of "Boheara," the new, and fashionable epidemic, diagnosed by the medical faculty, as "hyperaesthesia with complications"; a welcoming back to the world in fact of several despotic dowagers, not one perhaps of whom had she departed this life would have been really much missed or mourned! And thus, in deference to the intimate nature of the occasion, it was felt by the solicitous hostess, that a Tertulia (that mutual exchange of familiar, or intellectual ideas) would make less demand, on arms and legs, than would a ball: just the mind and lips . . . a skilful rounding-off here, developing there, chiselling, and putting-out feelers; an evening dedicated to the furtherance of intrigue, scandal, love, beneath the eager eyes of a few young girls, still at school, to whom a quiet party was permitted now and then.

Fingering a knotted-scapular beneath a windy arch, Mother Saint-Mary-of-the-Angels was asking God His will. Should she wait for Gloria and Clyte (they might be some time) or return to the convent and come back again at twelve? "The dear girls are with their mother," she informed her Maker, inclining respectfully before the Princess Aurora of the Asturias, who had just arrived attended by two bearded gentlemen with tummies.

Hopeful of glimpsing perhaps a colleague, Mother Saint-Mary moved a few steps impulsively in their wake. It was known that Monseigneur the Cardinal-Archbishop himself was expected, and not infrequently one ecclesiastic will beget another.

The crimson saloon, with its scattered groups of chairs, was waxing cheery.

Being the day it was, and the social round never but slightly varying, most of the guests had flocked earlier in the evening to the self-same place (*i.e.*), the Circus, or *Arena Amanda,* where it was subscription night, and where, at present, there was an irresistibly comic clown.

"One has only to think of him to——" the wife of the Minister of Public Instruction exclaimed, going off into a fit of wheezy laughter.

"What power, what genius, what——!" the young wife of the Inspector of Rivers and Forests was at a loss. Wedded to one of the handsomest, though dullest of men, Marvilla de Las Espinafre's perfervid and exalted nature kept her little circle in constant awe, and she would be often jealous of the Forests (chiefly scrub) which her husband, in his official capacity, was called upon to survey. "Don't lie to me. I know it! You've been to the woods." And after his inspection of the aromatic groves of Lograno, Phaedra in full fury tearing her pillow with her teeth was nothing to Marvilla. "Why, dear? Because you've been *among the Myrtles,"* was the explanation she chose to give for severing conjugal relations.

"Vittorio forbids the circus, on account of germs," the wife of the President of the National Society of Public Morals murmured momentously.

"Really with this ghastly Boheara, I shall not be grieved when the time comes to set out for dear Santander!" a woman with dog-rose cheeks, and puffed, wrinkled eyes, exclaimed, focusing languishingly the Cardinal.

"He is delicious in handsomeness tonight!"

"A shade battered. But a lover's none the worse in my opinion for acquiring technique," the Duchess of Sarmento declared.

"A lover; what? His Eminence . . . ? ?"

The duchess tittered.

"Why not? I expect he has a little woman to whom he takes off his clothes," she murmured, turning to admire the wondrous *Madonna of the Mule-mill* attributed to Murillo.

On a wall-sofa just beneath crowned with flowers and aigrettes sat Conca, Marchioness of Macarnudo.

"Que tal?"

"My joie de vivre is finished; still, it's amazing how I go on!" the Marchioness answered, making a corner for the duchess. She had known her "dearest Luiza" since the summer the sun melted the church bells and their rakish, pleasure-loving, affectionate hearts had dissolved together. But this had not been yesterday; no; for the Marchioness was a *grandmother* now.

"Conca, Conca: one sees you're in love."

"He's from *Avila,* dear—the footman."

"What!"

"Nothing *classic*—But, *oh!"*

"Fresh and blonde? I've seen him."

"Such sep . . . "

"Santiago be praised!"

The Marchioness of Macarnudo plied her fan.

"Our hands first met at table . . . yes, dear; but what I always say is, one spark explodes the mine!" And with a sigh she glanced rhapsodically at her fingers, powdered and manicured and encrusted with rings: "Our hands met first at table," she repeated.

"And . . . and the rest?" the duchess gasped.

"I sometimes wish though I resembled my sister more, who cares only for amorous, 'delicate' men—the Claudes, so to speak. But there it is! And, anyway, dear," the Marchioness dropped her voice, "he keeps me from thinking (ah perhaps more than I should) of my little grandson. Imagine, Luiza . . . Fifteen, white and vivid rose, and ink-black hair. . . . " And the Marchioness cast a long, pencilled eye towards the world-famous Pietà above her head. "Queen of Heaven, defend a weak woman from *that!*" she besought.

Surprised, and considerably edified, by the sight of the dowager in prayer, Mother Saint-Mary-of-the-Angels was emboldened to advance: The lovely, self-willed donkey (or was it a mule?) that Our Lady was prodding, one could almost stroke it, hear it bray. . . .

Mother Saint-Mary-of-the-Angels could have almost laughed.

But the recollection of the presence of royalty steadied her.

Behind pink lowered portières it had retired, escorted by the mistress of the house. She wore a gown of ivory-black with heavy golden roses and a few of her large diamonds of ceremony.

"I love your Englishy-Moorishy cosy comfort, Decima, and, I love——" the Princess Aurora had started to rave.

"An hyperaesthesia injection? . . . a beaten egg?" her hostess solicitously asked.

"*Per caritad!*" the Princess fluted, stooping to examine a voluptuous small *terre cuite,* depicting a pair of hermaphrodites amusing themselves.

She was looking like the ghost in the Ballet of Ghislaine, after an unusually sharp touch of Boheara; eight-and-forty hours in bed, and scandal declared not alone.

"A Cognac? . . . a crème de Chile? . . . "

"Nothing, nothing," the Princess negligently answered, sweeping her long, primrose trailing skirts, across the floor.

It was the boudoir of the Winterhalters and Isabeys, once the bright glory of the Radziwollowna collection, and which, after several decades of disesteem, were returning to fashion and favour.

"And I love——" she broke off, nearly stumbling over an old blind spaniel, that resided in a basket behind the "supposed original" of the *Lesbia of Lysippus.*

"Clapsey, Clapsey!" her mistress admonished. The gift of a dear, and once intimate friend, the dog seemed inclined to outlive itself and become a nuisance.

Alas, poor, fawning Clapsey! Fond, toothless bitch. Return to your broken doze, and dream again of days of leafy days in leafy Parks, and comfy drives and escapades long ago. What sights you saw when you could see; fountains, and kneeling kings, and grim beggars at Church doors (those at

San Eusebio were the worst). And sheltered spas by glittering seas: Santander! And dark adulteries and dim woods at night.

"And I love your Winterhalters!"

Beneath one of these, like a red geranium, was Cardinal Pirelli.

"Oh, your Eminence, the utter forlornness of Society! . . . Besides, (oh, my God!) to be the *one* Intellectual of a Town . . . " a wizened little woman, mistaken, not infrequently, for "Bob Foy," the jockey, was exclaiming plaintively.

"I suppose?" Monseigneur nodded. He was looking rather Richelieu, draped in ermines and some old lace of a beautiful fineness.

"It's pathetic how entertaining is done now. Each year meaner. There was a time when the DunEdens gave balls, and one could count, as a rule, on supper. To-night, there's nothing but a miserable Buffet, with flies trimming themselves on the food; and the champagne that I tasted, well, I can assure your Eminence it was more like foul flower-water than Mumm."

"Disgraceful," the Cardinal murmured, surrendering with suave dignity his hand to the lips of a pale youth all mouchoir and waist.

These kisses of young men, ravished from greedy Royalty, had a delicate savour.

The One Intellectual smiled obliquely.

"Your Eminence I notice has several devout salve-stains already," she murmured, defending her face with her fan.

"Believe me, not all these imprints were left by men!"

The One Intellectual glanced away.

"The poor Princess, I ask you, has one the right to look *so* dying!"

"Probably not," the Cardinal answered, following her ethereal transit.

It was the turn of the tide, and soon admittance to the boudoir had ceased causing "heartburnings."

Nevertheless, some few late sirens were only arriving.

Conspicuous among these was Catherine (the ideal-questing, God-groping and insouciant), Countess of Constantine, the aristocratic heroine of the capital, looking half-charmed to be naked and alive. Possessing but indifferent powers of conversation—at Tertulias and dinners she seldom shone—it was yet she who had coined that felicitous phrase: *Some men's eyes are sweet to rest in.*

Limping a little, she had sprained her foot, alas, while turning backward somersaults to a negro band in the Black Ballroom of the Infanta Eulalia-Irene, her reappearance on her misadventure was a triumph.

"Poor Kitty: It's a shame to ask her, if it's not a ball!" the Inspector of Rivers and Forests exclaimed, fondling the silvery branches of his moustache.

But, at least, a Muse, if not musicians, was at hand.

Clasping a large bouquet of American Beauty-roses, the Poetess Diana Beira Baixa was being besieged by admirers, to "give them something; just something! *Anything* of her own." Wedded, and proclaiming (*in vers libres*) her lawful love, it was whispered she had written a paean to her husband's " . . . " beginning: *Thou glorious wonder!* which was altogether too conjugal and intimate for recitation in society.

"They say I utter the cry of sex throughout the Ages," she murmured, resting her free hand idly on a table of gold and lilac lacquer beside her.

The Duchess-Dowager of Vizeu spread prudishly her fan.

"Since me maid set me muskito net afire, I'm just a bunch, me dear, of hysterics," she declared.

But requests for "something; just something!" were becoming insistent, and indeed the Muse seemed about to comply, when, overtaken by the first alarming symptoms of "Boheara," she fell with a longdrawn sigh to the floor.

6

Repairing the vast armholes of a chasuble, Madame Poco, the venerable Superintendent-of-the-palace, considered, as she worked, the social status of a Spy. It was not without a fleeting qualm that she had crossed the borderland that divides mere curiosity from professional vigilance, but having succumbed to the profitable proposals of certain monsignori, she had grown as keen on her quarry as a tigress on the track.

"It's a wearing life you're leading me, don Alvaro; but I'll have you," she murmured, singling out a thread.

For indeed the Higher-curiosity is inexorably exacting, encroaching, all too often, on the hours of slumber and rest.

"It's not the door-listening," she decided, "so much as the garden, and when he goes awenching Calle Nabuchodonosor."

She was seated by an open window, commanding the patio and the gate.

"Vamos, vamos!" Madame Poco sighed, her thoughts straying to the pontifical supremacy of Tertius II., for already she was the Pope's Poco, his devoted Phoebe, his own true girl: "I'm true blue, dear. True blue."

Forgetful of her needle, she peered interestedly on her image in a mirror on the neighbouring wall. It was a sensation of pleasant novelty to feel between her skull and her mantilla the notes of the first instalment of her bribe.

"Earned, every *perra' gorda',* earned!" she exclaimed, rising and pirouetting in elation before the glass.

Since becoming the courted favourite of the chapter, she had taken to strutting-and-languishing in private before her mirrors, improvising occult dance-steps, semi-sacred in character, modelled on those of Felix Ganay at white Easter, all in the flowery Spring. Ceremonial poses such as may be observed in storied-windows and olden *pietàs* in churches (Dalilaesque, or Shulamitish, as the case might be) were her especial delight, and from these had been evolved an eerie "Dance of Indictment."

Finger rigid, she would advance ominously with slow, Salomé-like liftings of the knees upon a phantom Cardinal: "And thus I accuse thee!" or, "I denounce thee, Don Alvaro, for," etc.

"*Dalila!* You old sly gooseberry," she chuckled, gloating on herself in the greenish spotted-depth of a tall, time-corroded glass.

Punch and late hours had left their mark.

"All this Porto and stuff to keep awake make a woman liverish," she commented, examining critically her tongue.

It was a Sunday evening of *corrida,* towards the Feast of Corpus, and through the wide open window came the near sound of bells.

Madame Poco crossed and recrossed her breast.

They were ringing "Paula," a bell which, tradition said, had fused into its metal one of the thirty pieces of silver received by the Iscariot for the betrayal of Christ.

"They seem to have asked small fees in those days," she reflected, continuing her work.

It was her resolution to divide her reward on masses for herself and the repose and "release" (from Purgatory) of her husband's soul, while anything over should be laid-out on finery for a favourite niece, the little Leonora, away in the far Americas.

Madame Poco plied pensively her needle.

She was growing increasingly conscious of the physical demands made by the Higher-curiosity upon a constitution already considerably far-through, and the need of an auxiliary caused her to regret her niece. More than once, indeed, she had been near the point of asking Charlotte Chiemsee, the maid of the Duchess of Vizeu, to assist her. It was Charlotte who had set the duchess's bed-veils on fire while attempting to nip a romance.

But alone and unaided it was astonishing the evidence Madame Poco had gained, and she smiled, as she sewed, at the recollection of her latest capture—the handkerchief of Luna Sainz.

"These hennaed heifers that come to confess! . . . " she scoffed sceptically: For Madame Poco had some experience of men—those brown humbugs (so delicious in tenderness)—in her time: "Poor soul! He had the prettiest teeth . . . " she murmured, visualising forlornly her husband's face. He had been coachman for many years to the sainted Countess of Triana, and he would tell the story of the pious countess and the vermin she had turned to flowers of flame while foraging one day among some sacks before a secondhand-clothes shop. It was she, too, who, on another occasion, had changed a handful of marsh-slush into fine slabs of chocolate, each slab engraved with the insignia of a Countess and the sign of the Cross.

"Still, she didn't change *him,* though!" Madame Poco reflected dryly, lifting the lid to her work-box.

Concealed among its contents was a copy of the gay and curious *Memoirs of Mlle. Emma Crunch,* so famous as "Cora Pearl"—; a confiscated bedside-book once belonging to the Cardinal-Archbishop.

"Ps, ps!" she purred, feeling amorously for her scissors beneath the sumptuous oddments of old church velvet and brocade that she loved to ruffle and ruck.

"Ps."

She had been freshening a little the chasuble worn last by his Eminence at the baptism of the blue-eyed police-pup of the Duquesa DunEden, and which bore still the primrose trace of an innocent insult.

"A disgraceful business altogether," Madame Poco sighed.

Not everyone knew the dog was christened in *white menthe*. . . .

"Sticky stuff," she brooded: "and a liqueur I never cared for! It takes a lot to beat Aniseed brandy; when it's old. Manzanilla runs it close; but it's odd how a glass or two turns me muzzy."

She remained a moment lost in idle reverie before the brilliant embroideries in her basket. Bits of choice beflowered brocade, multi-tinted, inimitably faded silks of the epoca of Theresa de Ahumada, exquisite tatters, telling of the Basilica's noble past, it gladdened the eyes to gaze on. What garden of Granada could show a pink to match that rose, or what sky show a blue as tenderly serene as that azure of the Saint Virgin?

"*Vamos*," she exclaimed rising: "it's time I took a toddle to know what he's about."

She had last seen the Cardinal coming from the orange orchard with a dancing-boy and Father Fadrique, who had a mark on his cheek left by a woman's fan.

Her mind still dwelling on *men* (those divine humbugs), Madame Poco stepped outside.

Traversing a white-walled corridor, with the chasuble on her arm, her silhouette, illumined by the splendour of the evening sun, all but caused her to start.

It was in a wing built in the troublous reign of Alfonso the Androgoyne that the vestments were kept. Whisking by a decayed and ancient painting, representing "Beelzebub" at Home, she passed slowly through a little closet supposed to be frequented by the ghosts of evil persons long since dead. Just off it was the vestry, gay with blue azulejos-tiles of an admirable lustre.

They were sounding Matteo now, a little bell with a passionate voice.

"The pet!" Madame Poco paused to listen. She had her "favourites" among the bells, and Matteo was one of them. Passiaflora, too:—but Anna, a slithery bell, "like a housemaid in hysterics," offended her ear by lack of tone; Sebastian, a complaining, excitable bell, was scarcely better—; "a fretful lover!" She preferred old "Wanda" the Death-bell, a trifle monotonous, and fanatical perhaps, but "interesting," and opening up vistas to varied thought and speculation.

Lifting a rosary from a linen-chest, Madame Poco laid the chasuble within. It was towards this season she would usually renew the bags of bergamot among the Primate's robes.

"This espionage sets a woman all behindhand," she commented to Tobit, the vestry cat.

Black as the Evil One, perched upon a Confessional's ledge, cleansing its belly, the sleek thing sat.

It was the "ledge of Forgotten fans," where privileged Penitents would bring their tales of vanity, infidelity and uncharitableness to the Cardinal once a week.

"Directing half-a-dozen duchesses must be frequently a strain!" Madame Poco deliberated, picking up a discarded mitre and trying it absently on.

With a plume at the side or a cluster of balls, it would make quite a striking toque, she decided, casting a fluttered glance on the male effigy of a pale-faced member of the Quesada family, hewn in marble by the door.

"*Caramba!* I thought it was the Cardinal; it gave me quite a turn," she murmured, pursuing lightly her way.

Being a Sunday evening of corrida, it was probable the Cardinal had mounted to his aerie, to enjoy the glimpse of Beauty returning from the fight.

Oh, mandolines of the South, warm throats, and winged songs, winging . . .

Following a darkened corridor with lofty windows closely barred, Madame Poco gained an ambulatory, terminated by a fresco of Our Lady, ascending to heaven in a fury of paint.

"These damp flags'll be the death of me," she complained, talking with herself, turning towards the garden.

Already the blue pushing shadows were beguiling from the shelter of the cloister eaves the rueful owls. A few flittermice, too, were revolving around the long apricot chimneys of the Palace, that, towards sunset, looked like the enchanted castle of some sleeping Princess.

"Bits of pests," she crooned, taking a neglected alley of old bay-tree laurels, presided over by a plashing fountain comprised of a Cupid sneezing. Wary of mole-hills and treacherous roots, she roamed along, preceded by the floating whiteness of a Persian peacock, mistrustful of the intentions of a Goat-sucker owl. Rounding a sequestered garden seat, beneath an aged cypress, the bark all scented knots, Madame Poco halted.

Kneeling before an altar raised to the cult of Our Lady of Dew, Cardinal Pirelli was plunged in prayer.

"Salve. Salve Regina. . . . " Above the tree-tops, a bird was singing.

7

The College of Noble Damosels in the Calle Santa Fé was in a whirl. It was "Foundation" day, an event annually celebrated with considerable fanfaronade and social éclat. Founded during the internecine wars of the Middle Age, the College, according to early records, had suffered rapine on the first day of term. Hardly it seemed had the last scholar's box been carried upstairs, than a troop of military had made its appearance at the Pension gate demanding, with "male peremptoriness," a billet. "I, alone," the Abbess ingeniously states, in relating the poignant affair in her unpublished diary: "I alone did all I was able to keep them from them, for which they (the scholars) called me 'greedy.' " Adding, not without a touch of modern socialism in disdain for titles, that she had preferred "the staff-officers to the Field-Marshal," while as to ensigns, in her estimation, why, "one was worth the lot."

Polishing urbanely her delicate nails, the actual President, a staid, pale woman with a peacock nose, recalled the chequered past. She hoped his Eminence when he addressed the girls, on handing them their prizes, would refer to the occasion with all the tactfulness required.

"When I think of the horrid jokes the old Marqués of Illescas made last year," she murmured, bestowing a harrowed smile on a passing pupil.

She was ensconced in a ponderous fauteuil of figured velvet (intended for the plump posterior of Royalty), beneath the incomparable "azulejos" ceiling of the Concert-room, awaiting the return of Madame Always Alemtejo, the English governess, from the printers, in the Plaza de Jesus, with the little silver-printed programmes (so like the paste-board cards of brides!), and which, as usual, were late.

"Another year we'll type them," she determined, awed by the ardent tones of a young girl rehearsing an aria from the new opera, *Leda*—"Gaze not on Swans."

"Ah, gaze not so on Swan-zzz! . . . "

"Crisper, child. Distinction. Don't exaggerate," the President enjoined, raising a hand to the diamonds on her heavy, lead-white cheeks.

Née an Arroyolo, and allied by marriage with the noble house of Salvaterra, the head mistress in private life was the Dowager-Marchioness of Pennisflores.

"*Nosotros,* you know, are not candidates for the stage! Bear in mind your moral," she begged, with a lingering glance at her robe of grey georgette.

The word "moral," never long from the President's lips, seemed, with her, to take on an intimate tinge, a sensitiveness of its own. She would invest the word at times with an organic significance, a mysterious dignity, that resembled an avowal made usually only in solemn confidence to a doctor or a priest.

The severity of my moral. The prestige of my moral. The perfection of my moral. She has no dignity of moral. I fear a person of no positive moral. Nothing to injure the freshness of her moral. A difficulty of moral. The etiquette of my moral. The majesty of my moral, etc., etc.—as uttered by the President, became, psychologically, interesting *data.*

"Beware of a facile moral!" she added, for the benefit of the singer's accompanist, a young nun with a face like some strange white rock, who was inclined to give herself married airs, since she had been debauched, one otiose noon, by a demon.

"Ah, Madame Always." The President swam to meet her.

British born, hailing from fairy Lisbon, Madame Always Alemtejo seemed resigned to live and die in a land of hitches.

"The delay is owing to the Printers' strike," she announced. "The Plaza's thronged: the Cigar factory girls, and all the rag-tag and bobtail, from the Alcazaba to the Puerta del Mar, are going out in sympathy, and——"

"The tarts?"

"The t's from Chamont are on the way."

It was the President's custom to lay all vexations before Nostra Señora de los Remedios, the college's divine Protectress, with whose gracious image she was on the closest footing.

Consulting her now as to the concert-programmes, the President recalled that no remedy yet had been found for Señorita Violeta de las Cubas, who had thrown her engagement ring into a place of less dignity than convenience, and refused to draw it out.

"Sapphires, my favourite stones," the President reflected, wondering if she should ask "la Inglése" to recover it with the asparagus-tongs.

But already a few *novios,* eager to behold their *novias* again, were in the Patio beneath the "Heiresses' Wing," exciting the connoisseurship of a bevy of early freshness.

"You can tell *that* by his eyebrows!" a girl of thirteen and just beginning as a woman, remarked.

"Que barbaridad."

"Last summer at Santander I and Maria-Manuela bathed with him, and one morning there was a tremendous sea, with *terrific* waves, and we noticed unmistakably."

"I can't explain; but I adore all that mauvishness about him!"

"I prefer Manolito to Gonzalito, though neither thrill me like the Toreador Tancos."

Assisted by Fräulein Pappenheim and Muley, the President's negress maid, they were putting the final touches to their vestal frocks.

"Men are my raging disgust," a florid girl of stupendous beauty declared, saturating with a flacon of *Parfum cruel* her prematurely formed silhouette.

"Nsa, nsa, señorita," Muley mumbled. "Some know better dan dat!"

"To hell with them!"

"Adios, Carlo. *Adios,* Juan. Join you down dah in one minute." The negress chuckled jauntily.

"Muley, Muley." Fräulein chided.

"What wonder next I 'bout to hear?"

Delighting in the tender ferocities of Aphrodite, she was ever ready to unite the *novio* to the *novia.* For window-vigils (where all is hand play), few could contrive more ingeniously than she those fans of fresh decapitated flowers, tuberose punctuated with inebriating jasmine, so beloved in the East by the dark children of the sun. Beyond Cadiz the blue, the Beautiful, in palm-girt Marrakech, across the sea, she had learnt other arts besides . . .

"Since seeing Peter Prettylips on the screen the Spanish type means nothing to me," Señorita Soledad, a daughter of the first Marqués of Belluga, the greatest orange-king in the Peninsula, remarked.

"How low. She is not noble."

"I *am* noble."

"Oh no; you're not."

"Cease wrangling," Fräulein exclaimed, "and enough of that," she added sharply, addressing a *novio*less little girl looking altogether bewitching of naughtiness as she tried her ablest to seduce by her crude manoeuvres the fiancé of a friend. Endowed with the lively temperament of her grand-mother, Conca, Marchioness of Macarnudo, the impressionable, highly amative nature of the little Obdulia gave her governesses some grounds for alarm. At the Post Office one day she had watched a young man lick a stamp. His rosy tongue had vanquished her. In fact, at present, she and a class-chum, Milagros, were "collecting petals" together—and much to the bewilderment of those about them, they might be heard on occasion to exclaim, at Mass, or in the street: "Quick, did you see it?" "No." "Santis-sima! *I* did!"

"Shrimp. As if Gerardo would look at her!" his *novia* scoffed: "But let me tell you, young woman," she turned upon the shrinking Obdulia, "that social ostracism, and even, in certain cases" (she slapped and pinched her), "*assassination* attends those that thieve or tamper with another's lover! And Fräulein will correct me if I exaggerate."

Fräulein Pappenheim was a little woman already drifting towards the sad far shores of forty, with no experience of the pains of Aphrodite caused by men; only at times she would complain of stomach aches in the head.

"Dat is so," Muley struck in sententiously for her: "Dair was once a young lady ob Fez——"

But from the Patio the college chaplain, Father Damien Forment, known as "Shineynose" was beckoning to the heiresses to join their relatives in the reception-hall below.

Since that sanguinary period of Christianity, synchronising with the foundation of the institution of learning in the Calle Santa Fé, what changes in skirts and trousers the world has seen. Alone unchanging are women's ambitions and men's desires.

"Dear child. . . . She accepts him . . . but a little à contre-coeur," the President was saying to the Marchioness of las Cubas, an impoverished society belle, who went often without bread, in order to buy lip-sticks and rouge.

"With Violeta off my hands. . . . Ah, President, if only Cecilio could be suitably *casada*."

"In my little garden I sometimes work a brother. The heiresses' windows are all opening to the flowers and trees. . . . The boy should be in Polo kit. A uniform interests girls," the President murmured, turning with an urbane smile to welcome the Duquesa DunEden.

She had a frock of black kasha, signed Paul Orna, with a cluster of brown-and-pink orchids, like sheep's kidneys, and a huge feather hat.

"I'm here for my God-girl, Gloria," she murmured, glancing mildly round.

Incongruous that this robust, rich woman should have brought to the light of heaven no heir, while the unfortunate Marchioness needy, and frail of physique, a wraith, did not know what to do with them!

The President dropped a sigh.

She was prepared to take a dog of the daughterless Duquesa. A bitch, of course. . . . But let it be Police, or Poodle! It would lodge with the girls. A cubicle to itself in the heiresses' wing; and since there would be no extra class-charge for dancing or drawing, no course *in belli arti,* some reduction of fees might be arranged. . . . "We would turn her out a creature of breeding. . . . An eloquent tail-wave, a disciplined moral, and with a reverence moreover for house-mats and carpets." The President decided to draw up the particulars of the prospectus by and by.

"Your Goddaughter is quite one of our most promising exhibitioners," she exclaimed, indicating with her fan some water-colour studies exposed upon the walls.

"She comes of a mother with a mania for painting," the Duquesa declared, raising a lorgnon, critically, before the portrait of a Lesbian, with dying, fabulous eyes.

"Really?"

"A positive passion," the Duquesa answered, with a swift, discerning glance at an evasive "nude," showing the posterior poudredarizé of a Saint.

"I had no idea," the President purred, drawing attention to a silvery streetscape.

"It's the Rambla from the back of Our Lady of the Pillar! It was rare fun doing it, on account of the *pirapos* of the passers-by," the artist, joining them, explained.

"Dear child, I predict for her a great deal of admiration very soon," the President murmured, with a look of reproach at a youthful pupil as she plied her boy-Father with embarrassing questions: "Who are the chief society women in the moon? What are their names? Have they got motor-cars there? Is there an Opera-House? Are there bulls?"

When the leering aspect of a lady in a costume of blonde Guadalmedina lace and a hat wreathed with clipped black cocks' feathers arrested her.

Illusion-proof, with a long and undismayed service in Love's House (sorry brutes, all the same, though, these men, with their selfishness, fickleness and lies!), the Marchioness of Macarnudo with her mysterious "legend" (unscrupulous minxes, all the same, though, these women, with their pettiness, vanity and . . . !), was too temperamentally intriguing, a type, to be ignored.

"Isn't that little Marie Dorothy with the rosebuds stuck all over her?" she asked her granddaughter who was teasing her brother on his moustache.

"To improve the growth, the massage of a *novia's* hand," she fluted, provoking the marchioness to an involuntary nervous gesture. Exasperated by resistance, struggling against an impossible infatuation, her Spanish ladyship was becoming increasingly subject to passing starts. Indeed only in excitement and dissipation could her unsatisfied longings find relief. Sometimes she would run out in her car to where the men bathe at Ponte Delgado, and one morning, after a ball, she had been seen standing on the main road to Cadiz in a cabuchon tiara, watching the antics of some nude muleteers: *Black as young Indians*—she had described them later.

"My sweet butterfly! What next?" she exclaimed, ogling Obdulia, whose elusive resemblance to her brother was really curiously disturbing.

Averting a filmy eye, she recognised Marvilla de las Espinafres, airing antipatriotic views on Birth control, her arms about an adopted daughter: "Certainly not; most decidedly *no*! I should scream!" she was saying as from the Concert-room the overture began thinning the crowd.

"It's nothing else than a National disaster," the marchioness declared to her grandson, "how many women nowadays seem to shirk their duty!"

"Well the de las Cubas hasn't anyway," he demurred.

"Poor thing. They say she jobs her mules," the marchioness murmured, exchanging a nod with the passing President.

Something, manifestly, had occurred to disturb the equilibrium of her moral.

"Such a disappointment, *Nostra Señora!*" she exclaimed. "Monseigneur, it seems, has thrown me over."

"Indeed; how awkward!"

"I fear though even more so for his chapter."

"He is not ill?"

"Cardinal Pirelli has fled the capital!"

8

Standing amid gardens made for suffering and delight, is the disestablished, and, *sic transit,* slowly decaying monastery of the Desierto. Lovely as Paradise, oppressive perhaps as Eden, it had been since the days of the mystic Luigi of Granada a site well suited to meditation and retreat. Here, in the stilly cypress-court, beneath the snowy sierras of Santa Maria la Blanca, Theresa of Avila, worn and ill, though sublime in laughter, exquisite in beatitude, had composed a part of the *Way of Perfection,* and, here, in these same realms of peace, dominating the distant city of Clemenza and the fertile plains of Andalucia, Cardinal Pirelli, one blue midday towards the close of summer, was idly considering his Defence: "*Apologia,* no; merely a defence," he mused: "Merely," he flicked the ash-tip of a cigar: "a defence! I defend myself, that's all! . . . "

A sigh escaped him.

Divided by tranquil vineyards and orange-gardens from the malice and vindictiveness of men it was difficult to experience emotions other than of forgiveness and love.

"Come, dears, and kiss me," he murmured, closing consentingly his eyes.

It was the forgetful hour of noon, when Hesperus from his heavens confers on his pet Peninsula the boon of sleep.

"A nice nap he's having, poor old gentleman," Madame Poco surveyed her master.

Ill-at-ease and lonely in the austere dismantled house, she would keep an eye on him at present almost as much for company as for gain.

As handsome and as elegant as ever, his physiognomy in repose revealed a thousand strange fine lines, suggestive subtleties, intermingled with less ambiguous signs, denoting stress and care.

"He's growing almost huntedish," she observed, casting a brief glance at the literature beside him—The Trial of Don Fernando de la Cerde, Bishop of Barcelona, defrocked for putting young men to improper uses; a treatise on The Value of Smiles; an old volume of Songs, by Sà de Miranda; The Lives of Five Negro Saints, from which escaped a bookmark of a dancer in a manton.

"Everything but his Breviary," she commented, perceiving a soutaned form through the old flowered ironwork of the courtyard gateway.

Regretting her better gown of hooped watered-silk, set aside while in retreat (for economy's sake), Madame Poco fled to put it on, leaving the visitor to announce himself.

The padre of Our Lady of the Valley, the poor padre of Our Lady, would the Primate know? Oh, every bird, every rose, could have told him that: the padre of Our Lady bringing a blue trout for his Eminence's supper from the limpid waters of Lake Orense.

Respecting the Primate's rest Father Felicitas, for so, also, was he named, sat down discreetly to await his awakening.

It was a rare sweetness to have the Cardinal to himself thus intimately. Mostly, in the city, he would be closely surrounded. Not that Father Felicitas went very much to town; no; he disliked the confusion of the streets, and even the glories of the blessed basilicas made him scarcely amends for the quiet shelter of his hills.

The blessed basilicas, you could see them well from here. The giralda of Saint Xarifa, and the twin august towers of the cathedral, and the azulejos dome of Saint Eusebio, that was once a pagan mosque; while in Santissima Marias, Maria del Carmen, Maria del Rosario, Maria de la Soledad, Maria del Dolores, Maria de las Nieves, few cities in all the wide world could show as many.

"To be sure, to be sure," he exclaimed absently, lifting his eyes to a cloudlet leisurely pointing above the lofty spur of the Pico del Mediodia. "To be sure," he added, seeking to descry the flower-like bellcot of Our Lady of the Valley just beneath.

But before he had discovered it, half concealed by trees, he was reminded by the sound of a longdrawn, love-sick wail, issuing out of the very entrails of the singer, of the lad left in charge of his rod by the gate.

"On the Bridge to Alcantara."

With its protracted cadences and doleful, vain-yearning reaches, the voice, submerged in all the anguish of a Malagueña, troubled, nostalgically, the stillness.

God's will be done. It was enough to awaken the Primate. Not everyone relished a Malagueña, a dirgeful form of melody introduced, tradition said, and made popular in the land, long, long ago, beneath the occupation of the Moors.

Father Felicitas could almost feel the sin of envy as he thought of the flawless choir and noble triumphal organ of the cathedral yonder.

Possessed of no other instrument, Our Lady of the Valley depended at present on a humble guitar. Not that the blessed guitar, with its capacity for emotion, is unworthy to please God's listening ear, but Pepe, the lad appointed to play it, would fall all too easily into those Jotas, Tangos, and Cuban Habaneiras, learnt in wayside fondas and fairs. Some day, Father Felicitas did not doubt, Our Lady would have an organ, an organ with pipes. He had prayed for it so often; oh, so often; and once, quite in the late of twilight while coming through the church, he had seen her it seemed standing just where it should be. It had been as though a blinding whiteness.

"A blinding whiteness," he murmured, trembling a little at the recollection of the radiant vision.

Across the tranquil court a rose-red butterfly pursued a blue. "I believe the world is all love, only no one understands," he meditated, contemplating the resplendent harvest plains steeped in the warm sweet sunlight.

"My infinite contrition!" The Cardinal spoke.

A rare occurrence in these days was a visitor, and now with authority ebbing, or in the balance at least, it was singular how he felt a new interest in the concerns of the diocese. The birth-rate and the death-rate and the super-rate, which it was to be feared that the *Cortès*——

Sailing down the courtyard in her watered-silken gown, Madame Poco approached with Xeres and Manzanilla, fresh from the shuttered snowery or nieveria.

"And I've just buried a bottle of champagne, in case your Eminence should want it," she announced as she inviolably withdrew.

"As devoted a soul as ever there was, and loyal to all my interests," the Primate exclaimed, touched.

"God be praised!"

"An excellent creature," the Cardinal added, focusing on the grey high road beyond the gate two youths on assback, seated close.

"Andalucians, though of another parish."

"I should like much to visit my diocese again; it's some while since I did," the Cardinal observed, filling the Padre's glass.

"You'd find up at Sodré a good many changes."

"Have they still the same little maid at the Posada de la Melodia?"

"Carmencita?"

"A dainty thing."

"She went Therewards about the month of Mary."

"America? It's where they all go."

"She made a ravishing corpse."

"Ahi."

And Doña Beatriz too had died; either in March or May. It was she who would bake the old Greek Sun-bread, and although her heirs had sought high and low, no one could find the receipt.

The Cardinal expressed satisfaction.

"Bestimina," he breathed, "and I trust they never may; for on the Feast of the Circumcision she invariably caused to be laid before the high-altar of the cathedral a peculiarly shaped loaf to the confusion of all who saw it."

And the Alcalde of Ayamonte, Don Deniz, had died on the eve of the bachelor's party he usually gave, when he took off his winter beard.

"Ahi; this death . . . "

Ah, yes, and since the delicacies ordered by the corpse could not well be countermanded, they had been divided among Christ's poor.

Left to himself once more Cardinal Pirelli returned reluctantly to his Defence.

Half the diocese it seemed had gone "Therewards," while the rest were at Biarritz or Santander. . . .

"A nice cheery time this is!" he murmured, oppressed by the silent cypress-court. Among the blue, pointing shadows, a few frail Oleanders in their blood-rose ruby invoked warm brief life and earth's desires.

"A nice cheery time," he repeated, rising and going within.

The forsaken splendour of the vast closed cloisters seemed almost to augur the waning of a cult. Likewise the decline of Apollo, Diana, Isis, with the gradual downfall of their Temples, had been heralded, in past times, by the dispersal of their priests. It looked as though Mother Church, like Venus, or Diana, was making way in due turn for the beliefs that should follow: "and we shall begin again with intolerance, martyrdom and converts," the Cardinal ruminated, pausing before an ancient fresco depicting the eleven thousand virgins, or as many as there was room for.

Playing a lonely ball game against them was the disrespectful Chicklet.

"Young vandal," the Cardinal chided, caressing the little acolyte's lustrous locks.

"Monseigneur? . . . "

"There: Run along; and say a fragrant prayer for me, Child."

Flinging back a shutter drawn fast against the sun, the boundless prospect from the balcony of his cell recalled the royal Escorial. The white scattered terraces of villas set in dark deeps of trees, tall palms, and parasol-pines so shady, and almost indistinguishable the white outline of the sea, made insensibly for company.

Changing into a creation of dull scarlet crêpe, a cobweb dubbed "summer-exile," Cardinal Pirelli felt decidedly less oppressed: "Madrid is on the Manzanares," he vociferated, catching sight of the diligence from Sodré. Frequently it would bring Frasquito, the postman—a big tawny boy overgiven to passing the day in the woods with his gun and his guitar.

"The mail bag is most irregular," he complained, fastening a few dark red, almost black, roses, to his cincture. It was Cardinal Pirelli's fancy while in retreat to assume his triple-Abraham, or mitre, and with staff in hand to roam abroad as in the militant Springtide of the Church.

"When kings were cardinals," he murmured quietly as he left the room.

It was around the Moorish water-garden towards shut of day he liked most to wander, seeking like some Adept to interpret in the still, deep pools, the mirrored music of the sky.

All, was it vanity; these pointing stars and spectral leaning towers, this mitre, this jewelled ring, these trembling hands, these sweet reflected colours, white of daffodil and golden rose. All, was it vanity?

Circling the tortuous paths like some hectic wingless bird, he was called to the refectory by the tintinnabulation of a bell.

In the deep gloominous room despoiled of all splendour but for a dozen old Zurbarans flapping in their frames, a board, set out with manifest care, was prepared for the evening meal.

Serving both at Mass and table, it was the impish Chicklet who, with a zealous napkin-flick (modelled on the *mozos* of the little café-cum-restaurant "As in Ancient Andalucia" patronised by rising toreadors and *aficianados* of the Ring), showed the Primate to his chair.

Having promised José the chef a handsome indulgence, absolved him from bigamy, and raised his wages, Cardinal Pirelli, in gastronomy nothing if not fastidious, had succeeded in inducing him to brave the ghostly basements of the monastery on the mount.

Perhaps of the many charges brought against the Primate by his traducers, that of making the sign of the cross with his left foot at meals was the most utterly unfounded—looking for a foot-cushion would have been nearer the truth.

Addressing the table briefly in the harmonious Latin tongue, his Eminence sat down with an impenetrable sigh.

With vine-sprays clinging languorously to the candle-stands, rising from a bed of nespoles, tulips, and a species of wild orchid known as Devil's-balls, the Chicklet, to judge from his floral caprices, possessed a little brain of some ambition, not incapable of excess.

"I thought you were tired of jasmine, sir, and th'orange bloom's getting on," he chirruped, coming forward with a cup of cold, clear consommé, containing hearts, coronets, and most of the alphabet in vermicelli.

"I'm tired, true, child; but not of jasmine," the Primate returned, following a little contretemps of a marqués' crown, sinking amid a frolicsome bevy of *O's.*

"I hope it's right, sir?"

"Particularly excellent, child—tell José so."

"Will I bring the trout, sir?"

"Go, boy," the Cardinal bade him, opening a volume by the menu-stand formed of a satyr, sentimentalising over a wood-nymph's breasts.

While in retreat it was his fancy, while supping, to pursue some standard work of devotion, such as Orthodoxy so often encourages or allows: it was with just such a golden fairy-tale as this that he had once won a convert: Poor woman. What had become of her? Her enthusiasm, had it lasted? She had been very ardent. Perfervid! "Instruction" would quite wear it out of them. Saint Xarifa's at fall of day; . . . an Autumn affair! Chrysanthemums; big bronze frizzlies. A Mrs Mandarin Dove. American. Ninety million sterling. Social pride and religious humility, how can I reconcile? The women in Chicago. My God!!! My little stepdaughter. . . . Her Father, fortunately. . . . Yes, your Eminence, he's dead. And, oh, I'm *glad.* Is it naughty? And then her photograph à la Mary of Magdala, her hair unbound, décolletée, with a dozen long strands of pearls. "Ever penitently yours, Stella Mandarin Dove."

"I'd rather have had the blonde Ambassadress to the Court of St James," he reflected, toying with the fine table-glass of an old rich glamour. A fluted bell cup sadly chipped provoked a criticism and a citation from Cassiodorus on the "rude" ways of boys.

Revolving around an austere piece of furniture, that resembled a Coffin-upon-six-legs, the Chicklet appeared absorbed.

"I hear it's the Hebrew in heaven, sir. Spanish is seldom spoken," he exclaimed seraphically.

"Tut, dear child. Who says so?" the Primate wondered, his eyes wandering in melancholy towards the whitest of moons illumining elusively the room—illumining a long, sexless face with large, mauve, heroic lips in a falling frame, and an "apachey," blue-cheeked, Christ, the Cardinal noticed.

"Who, sir? Why, a gentleman I was guide to once!"

The Cardinal chuckled comprehensively.

"I should surmise, dear child, there was little to show."

"What, not the crypt, sir? Or the tomb of the beautiful Princess Eboli, the beloved of Philip II., sir?"

"Jewel boy. Yum-yum," the Cardinal raised his glass.

"And the bells, sir? Last night, I'll tell you, sir. I thought I heard old 'Wanda' on the wind."

"Old Wanda, boy."

"She rings for deaths, sir."

"Nonsense, child; your little ears could never hear as far," the Cardinal answered, deliberating if a lad of such alertness and perception might be entrusted to give him a henna shampoo: it was easy enough to remove the towels before it got too red. The difficulty was to apply the henna; evenly everywhere; fair play all round; no favouring the right side more than the left, but golden Justice for each grey hair. Impartiality: proportion! "Fatal, otherwise," the Primate reasoned.

"Are you ready for your Quail, sir?"

"Quail, quail? Bring on the *dulces,* boy," his Eminence murmured, regarding absently through the window the flickering arc-lights of Clemenza far away. Dear beckoning lamps, dear calling lamps; lamps of theatres, cinemas, cabarets, bars and dancings; lamps of railway-termini, and excessively lit hotels, *olé* to you, enchantress lights!

"And, after all, dears, if I did," the Cardinal breathed, tracing a caricature of his Holiness upon the table-cloth lightly with a dessert-fork. ("Which I certainly deny" . . .), he brooded, disregarding the dissolving Orange ice *à la* Marchioness of Macarnudo."

"Had you anything in the Lottery, sir?"

"Mind your business, boy, and remove this ball-room nastiness," the Primate snapped.

It was while lingering, after dinner, over some choice vintage, that he oftenest would develop the outline of his Defence. To escape the irate horns of the Pontiff's bull (Die, dull beast) he proposed pressing the "Pauline Privilege," unassailable, and confirmed A.D. *1590* by Pope Sixtus V., home to the battered beauty of the Renaissance hilt: "With the elegance and science," he murmured, "of a *matador.*"

"I have the honour to wish you, sir, a good, and pleasant night."

"Thanks, boy."

"And if you should want me, sir" . . . the youthful acolyte possessed the power to convey the unuttered.

"If?? . . . And say a fragrant prayer for me, child," the Cardinal enjoined.

Resting an elbow among the nespoles and tulips (dawn-pink and scarlet, awakening sensitively in the candle-glow), he refilled reflectively his glass.

"God's providence is over all," he told himself, considering dreamfully a cornucopia heaped with fruit. Being just then the gracious Autumn, a sweet golden-plum called "Don Jaime of Castille" was in great perfection. It had been for the Southern orchards a singularly fertile year. Never were seen such gaily rouged peaches, such sleek, violet cherries, such immensest white grapes. Nestling delectably amid its long, deeply lobed leaves, a pomegranate (fruit of joy) attracted the Cardinal's hand.

Its seeds, round and firm as castanets, evoked the Ortiz. "Ah, Jesus-Maria. The evening she waved her breasts at me!" he sighed, attempting to locate the distant lights of the Teatro Trinidades. Interpreting God's world, with her roguish limbs and voice, how witching the Child had been but lately in *The Cistus of Venus.* Her valse-refrain "Green Fairy Absinthe" (with a full chorus in tights), had been certainly, theatrically (if, perhaps, not socially), the hit of the season.

"The oleanders come between us," he deliberated, oppressed by the amative complaint of some sweet-throated, summer night-bird.

"It's queer, dears, how I'm lonely!" he exclaimed, addressing the ancient Zurbarans flapping austerely in their frames.

The Archbishop of Archidona, for all his air of pomposity, looked not unsympathetic, neither, indeed, did a little lady with a nimbus, casting melting glances through the spokes of a mystic wheel.

"It's queer—; you'd be surprised!" he murmured, rising and setting an oval moon-backed chair beside his own.

As usual the fanciful watch-dogs in the hills had begun their disquieting barking.

"The evenings are suicide," he ruminated, idly replenishing his glass.

Sometimes, after the fifth, or sixth, bumper, the great Theresa herself would flit in from the garden. Long had her radiant spirit "walked" the Desierto, seeking, it was supposed, a lost sheet of the manuscript of her *Way of Perfection.* It may have been following on the seventh, or, even, the eighth bumper, that the Primate remarked he was not alone.

She was standing by the window in the fluttered moonshine, holding a knot of whitish heliotropes.

"Mother?"

Saint John of the Cross could scarcely have pronounced the name with more wistful ecstasy.

Worn and ill, though sublime in laughter, exquisite in tenderness she came towards him.

" . . . Child?"

"Teach me, oh, teach me, dear Mother, the Way of Perfection."

9

Verifying private dates, revising here and there the cathedral list of charges, Don Moscosco, the secretary of the chapter seated before his usual bureau, was at the disposal of the public. A ministerial crisis had brought scattered Fashion home to town with a rush, and the pressure of work was enormous. "Business" indeed had seldom been livelier, and chapels for Masses of special intention were being booked in advance as eagerly as opera-boxes for a Première, or seaside-villas in the season.

"If the boys are brisk we might work in Joseph," he mused, consulting with closely buttoned lips his Tarifa and plan; "although I'd rather not risk a clash."

Unknown to double-let like his compères on occasion outside, the swarthy little man was a master organiser, never forgetting that the chapter's welfare and prestige were inseparable from his own. Before allotting a chapel for a mass of Intent, it was his rule to analyse and classify the "purity" of the intention (adding five per cent. where it seemed not altogether to be chaste, or where the purpose was "obscure").

"I see no inconvenience," he murmured, gauging delicately the motif of a couple of great ladies of the bluest blood in Spain who were commissioning masses for the safety of a favourite toreador in an approaching *corrida.*

"Five hundred flambeaux, at least, between them," the secretary, negligently, spat.

It was the twenty-first day of September (which is the Feast of Saint Firmin), and the sacristia, thronged with mantons and monsignori, resembled some vast shifting parterre of garden-flowers. Having a little altercation together, Mother Mary of the Holy Face and Mother Garcia of the Company of Jesus, alone, seemed stable. In honour of Saint Firmin the door of Pardon (closed half the year) had just been thrown open, bringing from the basilica an odour of burning incense and the strains of a nuptial march.

How many of the bridal guests knew of the coffin installed in the next chapel but one? the little man wondered, rising gallantly to receive a client.

She wore no hat but a loose veil of gold and purple enveloped her hair and face.

"I fear for him!"

"There, there. What is it?"

"I fear for him"—a man and the stars, nights of sweet love, oleander flowers were in her voice.

By her immense hooped earrings, as large as armlets, he knew her for the Adonira, the mistress of the toreador Tancos.

"Come to me after the Friday miserere," the official objected: "let me entreat an appointment."

"No. Now."

"Well."

"I want a Mass."

"The intention being . . . ?" the secretary sent up his brows a little.

"His safety."

"Whose?"

"My lover's."

"But, señorita, it's all done! It's all *done,* dear lady," the words were on Don Moscosco's lips. Still, being the pink of chivalry with *las mujares* and a man of business, he murmured: "With what quantity of lights?"

"Two. Just for him and me."

"Tell me how you would prefer them," he exclaimed, glancing whimsically towards the canvas of the Magdalen waylaying our Lord.

"How I would——" she stammered, opening and closing the fansticks in her painted, love-tired hands.

"You would like them long and, I dare say, gross?"

"The best," she breathed, almost fainting as though from some fleeting delicious vision in the air.

"Leave it to me," Don Moscosco said, and dropping expressively his voice he added: "Come, señorita; won't you make a date with me?"

"A date with you?"

"Ah-hah, the little Juans and Juanas; the charming cherubs!" the secretary archly laughed.

Returning however no answer she moved distractedly away.

"Two tapers! *Two.* As many only as the animal's horns. It's amazing how some women stint," he reflected, faintly nettled.

The marriage ceremony was over. From the summit of the giralda, volley on volley, the vibrant bells proclaimed the consummation.

"It was all so quick; I hope it's valid?" Madame la Horra, the mother of the "Bride," looked in to say. With a rose mole here and a strawberry mole there, men (those adorable monsters) accounted her entirely attractive.

"As *though* we should hurry, as *though* we should clip!"

"Eh?"

"As though we were San Eusebio, or the Pilar!"

"Forgive me, I came only to—I, . . . I, . . . I, . . . I think I cried. The first Spring flowers looked so beautiful."

A mother's love, and contrition, perhaps, for her own shortcomings, the secretary brooded: 'I shall knock her off five per cent."

Lost in bland speculation Don Moscosco considered the assembly collected outside the curtained *camarin* of the Virgin, where the gowns of the Image were dusted and changed.

For Firmin she usually wore an osprey or two and perfumed ball-gloves of Cordoba, and carried a spread fan of gold Guadalmedina lace. Among devotees of the sacristia it was a perpetual wonder to observe how her costumes altered her. Sometimes she would appear quite small, dainty and French, at others she would recall the sumptuous women of the Argentine and the New World, and aficianados would lament their fairy isle of Cuba in the far-off Caribbean Sea.

Traversing imperiously the throng, Don Moscosco beheld the Duquesa DunEden.

Despite the optimism of the gazettes it looked as though the Government must indeed be tottering, since the Duquesa too was up from her Country quinta.

"I have a request to make," she began, sinking gratefully to a chair.

"And charmed, in advance, to grant it."

"I suppose you will have forgotten my old spaniel Clapsey?"

"Ah, no more dogs!"

"She is passing-out, poor darling; and if the Church could spare her some trifling favour——"

"Impossible."

"She is the first toy tail for my little cemetery!"

"Quite impossible."

"Poor pet," the Duquesa exclaimed undaunted: "she has shared in her time my most intimate secrets: she stands for early memories; what rambles we'd go together, she and I, at Santander long ago! I remember Santander, Don Moscosco (imagine), when there was not even a hotel! A little fishing-village, so quiet, so quiet; ah, it was nicer, far, and more exclusive then. . . . "

"I dare say."

"You know my old, blind and devoted friend was a gift from the king; and this morning I said to her: 'Clapsey! Clapsey!' I said: 'where's Carlos? Car-los . . . ?' And I'll take my oath she rallied."

Don Moscosco unbent a shade: "A token, is she, of royalty?"

"He also gave me 'Flirt'!"

"Perhaps a brief mass . . . "

"Poor dearest: you'll keep it quiet and black?"

"We say all but the Black."

"Oh?"

"One must draw the line somewhere!" Don Moscosco declared, his eye roving towards a sacristan piloting a party of travel-stained tourists, anxious to inspect the casket containing a feather from the Archangel Gabriel's wing.

"I know your creative taste! I rely on you," the Duquesa rose remarking.

Nevertheless, beneath the routine of the sacristia, the air was surcharged with tension. Rival groups, pro- or anti-Pirellian, formed almost irreconcilable camps, and partisanship ran high. Not a few among the cathedral staff had remained true to his Eminence, and Mother Sunlight, a charwoman, (who sometimes performed odd jobs at the Palace) had taught her infant in arms to cry: "Long live Spain and Cardinal Pirelli!"

Enough, according to some extreme anti-Pirellians, to be detrimental to her milk.

"I'm told the Pope has sent for him at last," the laundress of the Basilica, Doña Consolacion, remarked to Sister June of the Way Dolorous.

"Indeed, indeed; it scarcely does to think!"

"Does anyone call to mind a bit of a girl (from Bilbao she was) that came once to stop as his niece?"

"Inclined to a moustache! Perfectly."

"Phoebe Poco protests she wasn't."

"Ah, well; a little *Don Juanism* is good," the laundress said, and sighed. "She declares . . . "

"She tells the truest lies, dear, of anyone I know!"

"Be that as it may it's certain he's getting increasingly eccentric. But Sunday last, entertaining his solicitor, it seems he ordered coffee after the merienda to be served in two chamber-pots."

"Shameful—and he in his sunset years!" Mother Mary of the Holy Face commented, coming up with Tomás the beadle.

"It wouldn't surprise me," he declared, drowsily shaking a heavy bouquet of keys, "if the thread of his life was about to break."

"*Hombre . . . "* The laundress expressed alarm.

"Often now, towards Angelus, as I climb the tower, I hear the bell Herod talking with old Wanda in the loft. Eeeeeee! Eeeeeee! Horrible things they keep saying. Horrible things they keep saying."

"Nonsense," Doña Consolacion exclaimed, bestowing a smile on Monsignor Cuxa. Old, and did-did-doddery, how frail he seemed beside Father Fadrique, the splendid swagger of whose chasuble every woman must admire.

"Sent for to Rome; ah, sangre mio, I wish someone would send for me," a girl with a rose in the hair beautifully placed sighed romantically.

"Be satisfied with Spain, my dear, and remember that no other country can compare with it!" Doña Generosa, an Aunt of one of the cathedral dancing-boys (who drew a small pension as the widow of the late Leader of applause at the Opera-house) remonstrated.

"I've never travelled," Doña Consolacion blandly confessed: "but I dare say, dear, you can't judge of Egypt by *Aïda.*"

"Oh, can't I, though," Doña Generosa sniffed, as the Father of an acolyte raised his voice.

"Spain!" he exclaimed exalted, throwing a lover's kiss to the air: "Spain! The most glorious country in God's universe, His admitted masterpiece, His gem, His——" He broke off, his eloquence dashed by the sad music of Monsignor Cuxa's haemorrhage.

An office in the Chapel of the Crucifix was about to begin, recalling to their duties the scattered employees of the staff.

Hovering by the collection-box for the Souls in Hades, the Moorish maid from the College of Noble Damosels, bound on an errand of trust as ancient as the world, was growing weary of watching the people come and go.

"I must have missed him beneath the trees of the Market Place," she ruminated, straightening on her head a turban wreathed in blossoms.

It was the matter of a message from Obdulia and Milagros to the radiant youth whose lips they were so idyllically (if perhaps somewhat licentiously) sharing.

"Fo' sh'o dis goin' to put dose heiresses in a quandry," she deliberated, oppressed by her surroundings.

Eastern in origin like the Mesquita of Cordoba, it was impossible to forget that the great basilica of Clemenza was a Mosque profaned.

Designed for the cult of Islam, it made her African's warm heart bleed to behold it now. Would it were reconverted to its virginal state, and the cry of the muezzin be heard again summoning men to Muhammad's house! Yes, the restitution of the cathedral to Allah was Muley's cherished dream, and it consoled her, on certain days when she was homesick, to stand before the desecrated mihrab in worship, her face turned towards Africa, and palm-girt Marrakech across the sea.

"I almost inclined to slip across to de Café Goya," she breathed, moving aside for a shuffling acolyte, bearing a crucifix on a salver.

Led by the pious sisters of the noble order of the Flaming Hood, the Virgin was returning to her niche.

She was arrayed as though bound for the Bull-ring, in a robe of peacock silk, and a mantilla of black lace.

"Santissima! . . . "

"Elegantissima!" Devotees dropped adoring to the floor.

Alone, the African remained erect.

"Muhammad mine, how long?" she sighed, turning entreating eyes to the cabbalistic letters and Saracenic tracings of the azulejos arabesques.

10

Midnight had ceased chiming from the Belfry tower, and the last seguidilla had died away. Looking fresh as a rose, and incredibly juvenile in his pyjamas of silver-grey and scarlet (the racing colours of Vittoria, Duchess of Vizeu), the Cardinal seemed disinclined for bed.

Surveying in detachment the preparatives for his journey (set out beneath an El Greco Christ, with outspread, delicate hands), he was in the mood to dawdle.

"These for the Frontier. Those for the train," he exclaimed aloud, addressing a phantom porter.

Among the personalia was a Passport, the likeness of identity showing him in a mitre, cute to tears, though, essentially, orthodox; a flask of Napoleon Brandy, to be "declared" if not consumed before leaving the Peninsula; and a novel, *Self-Essence,* on the Index, or about to be.

"A coin, child, and put them for me on the rack," he enjoined the wraith, regarding through the window the large and radiant stars.

The rhythmic murmur of a weeping fountain filled momentously the night.

Its lament evoked the Chicklet's sobs.

"Did I so wrong my God to punish him? Was I too hasty?" the Primate asked, repairing towards an ivory crucifix by Cano, "yet, Thou knowest, I adore the boy!"

He paused a moment astonished by the revelation of his heart.

"It must have been love that made me do it," he smiled, considering the incident in his mind. Assuredly the rebuff was unpremeditated, springing directly from the boy's behaviour, spoiling what might have been a ceremony of something more than ordinary poignance.

It had come about so.

There had been held previously during the evening, after the Basilica's scheduled closing hour, a service of "Departure," fastidiously private, in the presence only of the little Ostensoir-swinger "Chicklet," who, missing all the responses, had rushed about the cathedral after mice; for which the Cardinal, his sensitiveness hurt by the lad's disdain and frivolity, had afterwards confined him alone with them in the dark.

"Had it been Miguilito or Joaquin, I should not have cared a straw for their interest in the mice! But somehow this one——" the Cardinal sighed.

Adjusting in capricious abstraction his cincture, he turned towards the window.

It was a night like most.

Uranus, Venus, Saturn showed overhead their wonted lights, while in the sun-weary cloisters, brightly blue-drenched by the moon, the oleanders in all their wonder—(how swiftly fleeting is terrestrial life)—were over, and the bougainvillaeas reigned instead.

"It must have been that," he murmured, smiling up at the cathedral towers.

Poor little Don Wilful. The chapter-mice, were they something so amusing to pursue? "I've a mind, do you know, to join you, boy; I declare I feel quite rompish!" he told himself, gathering up, with a jocund pounce, a heavy mantle of violet cloth-of-gold.

"Tu-whit, tu-whoo."

Two ominous owls answered one another across the troubled garden.

"I declare I feel——" his hand sought vaguely his heart: it went pit-a-pat for almost nothing now! "The strain of the diocese," he breathed, consulting a pier-glass of the period of Queen Isabella "the Ironical."

"The Court may favour Paul Orna, but in my opinion no one can rival Joey Paquin's 'line'; I should like to see him 'tailor' our Madonna; one of the worst and most expensively dressed little saints in the world," his Eminence commented, folding toga-wise the obedient tissues about his slender form.

An aspect so correctly classic evoked the golden Rome of the Imperial Caesars rather than the so tedious Popes.

Repeating a sonorous line from Macrobius, the Cardinal measured himself a liqueur-glass of brandy.

Poor little Don Bright-eyes, alone in the obscurity. It was said a black dervish "walked" the Coro—one of the old habitués of the Mosque.

"Jewel boy. Yum-yum," he murmured, setting a mitre like a wondrous mustard-pot upon his head. *Omnia vanitas*; it was intended for Saint Peter's.

"Tu-whit, tu-whoo!"

Grasping a Bishop's stave, remotely shepherdessy, his Eminence opened softly the door.

Olé, the Styx!

Lit by Uranus, Venus, and Saturn only, the consummate tapestries on the stairs recording the Annunciation, Conception, Nativity, Presentation, Visitation, Purification and Ascension of the Virgin made welcome milestones.

" . . . Visitation, Purification," the Primate paused on the penultimate step.

On a turn of the stair by the "Conception," a sensitive panel, chiefly white, he had the impression of a wavering shadow, as of someone following close behind.

Continuing, preoccupied, his descent, he gained a postern door. A few deal cases, stoutly corded for departure, were heaped about it: "His Holiness, I venture to predict, will appreciate the excellence of our home-grown oranges, not to be surpassed by those of any land," the Primate purred, sailing forth into the garden.

Oh, the lovely night. Oh, the lovely night. He stood, leaning on his wand, lost in contemplation of the miracle of it.

"Kek, kex, kex."

In the old lead aqua-butt, by the Chapterhouse, the gossiping bull-frogs were discussing their great horned and hoofed relations. . . .

"There was never yet one that didn't bellow!"

"Kek, kek, kek."

"*Los toros*, forsooth!"

"A blessed climate. . . . " The Primate pursued his way.

It was in the face of a little door like the door of a tomb in the cathedral's bare façade (troubled only by the fanciful shadows of the trees) that he presently slipped his key.

Olé, the Styx!

He could distinguish nothing clearly at first beyond the pale forked fugitive lightning through the triple titanic windows of the chancel.

"Sunny-locks, Don Sunny-locks?" the Cardinal cooed, advancing diffidently, as though mistrustful of meeting some Charwoman's pail.

Life had prepared him for these surprises.

Traversing on his crozier a spectral aisle, he emerged upon the nave.

Flanked by the chapels of the Crucifix, of the Virgin, of the Eldest Son of God, and of divers others, it was here as bright as day.

Presumably Don April-showers was too self-abashed to answer, perhaps too much afraid. . . . "If I recollect, the last time I preached was on the theme of Flagellation," the Primate mused, considering where it caught the moon the face of a fakir in ecstasy carved amid the corbels.

"A sermon I propose to publish," he resolved, peering into the chapel of Santa Lucia. It was prepared, it seemed, in anticipation of a wedding, for stately palms and branches of waxen peach-bloom stood all about: "Making circulation perilous," the Primate mused, arrested by the determined sound of a tenacious mouse gnawing at a taper-box.

"An admirable example in perseverance!" he mentally told himself, blinking at the flickering mauve flowers of light in the sanctuary lamps.

Philosophising, he penetrated the engrailed silver doors connecting the chapel of the Magdalen.

The chapel was but seldom without a coffin, and it was not without one now.

Since the obsequies of the brilliant Princess Eboli, it had enjoyed an unbroken vogue.

Besides the triumphal monument of the beloved of Philip II., the happy (though, perhaps, not the happiest) achievement of Jacinto Bisquert, there were also mural tablets to the Duchesses of Pampeluna (*née* Mattosinhos), Polonio (*née* Charona), and Sarmento (*née* Tizzi-Azza), while the urn and ashes of the Marchioness of Orcasitas (*née* Ivy Harris) were to be found here too, far from the race and turmoil of her native New York.

"Misericordia! Are you there, boy?" the Cardinal asked, eyeing abstractedly the twin-hooded carytides that bore the fragile casket white as frozen snow containing the remains of the all-amiable princess.

Folded in dainty sleep below, he perceived the lad.

Witching as Eros, in his loose-flowing alb, it seemed profane to wake him!

" . . . And lead us not into temptation," the Primate murmured, stooping to gaze on him.

Age of bloom and fleeting folly: Don Apple-cheeks!

Hovering in benison he had almost a mind to adopt the boy, enter him for Salamanca or, remoter, Oxford, and perhaps (by some bombshell codicil) even make him his heir.

"How would you like my Velasquez, boy? . . . " his Eminence's hand framed an airy caress. "Eh, child? Or my Cano Crucifix? . . . I know of more than one bottle-nosed dowager who thinks she'll get it! . . . You know my Venetian-glass, Don Endymion, is among the choicest in Spain. . . . "

There was a spell of singing silence, while the dove-grey mystic lightning waxed and waned.

Aroused as much by it as the Primate's hand, the boy started up with a scream of terror.

"Ouch, sir!"

"Olé, boy?"

The panic appeared to be mutual.

"Oufarella! . . . " With the bound of a young faun the lad was enskied amid the urns and friezes.

The heart in painful riot, the Primate dropped to a chair.

Ouching, Oléing and Oufarellaing it, would they never have done? Paternostering Phoebe Poco (shadowing her master) believed they never would. "Old ogre: why can't he be brisk about it and let a woman back to bed?" she wondered.

Thus will egotism, upon occasion, eclipse morality outright.

"And always be obedient, dear child," the Cardinal was saying; "it is one of the five things in Life that matter most."

"Which are the others, sir?"

"What others, boy?"

"Why, the other four!"

"Never mind now. Come here."

"Oh, Tral-a-la, sir." Laughing like some wild spirit, the lad leapt (Don Venturesome, Don Venturesome, his Eminence trembled) from the ledge of A Virtuous Wife and Mother (Sarmento, *née* Tizzi-Azza) to the urn of Ivy, the American marchioness.

"You'd not do that if you were fond of me, boy!" The Cardinal's cheek had paled.

"But I *am* fond of you, sir! Very. Caring without caring: don't you know?"

"So you do care something, child?"

"I care a lot! . . . "

Astride the urn of Ivy—poised in air—the Chicklet pellucidly laughed.

"Tell me so again," the Cardinal begged, as some convent-bell near by commenced sounding for office before aurora.

For behind the big windows the stars were fading.

"It's to-day they draw the Lottery, sir."

"Ah; well, I had nothing in it. . . . "

"00050—that's me!"

The Cardinal fetched a breath.

"Whose is it, boy?" he pointed towards the bier.

"A Poet, sir."

"A Poet?"

"The name though he had escapes me. . . . "

"No matter then."

"Where would his soul be now, sir?"

"Never mind, boy; come here."

"In the next world I should like to meet the Cid, and Christopher Columbus!"

"Break your neck, lad, and so you will."

"Pablo Pedraza too. . . . "

"Who's that, boy?"

"He was once the flower of the ring, sir; superior even to Tancos; you may recollect he was tossed and ruptured at Ronda; the press at the time was full of it."

"Our press, dear youth, our press!!! . . . " the Primate was about to lament, but an apologetic sneeze from a chapel somewhere in the neighbourhood of the Eldest Son of God arrested him.

It seemed almost to confirm the legend of old, Mosque-sick "Suliman," said to stalk the temple aisles.

The Cardinal twirled challengingly his stave—*Bible* v. *Koran*; a family case; cousins; Eastern, equally, each; hardy, old perennials, no less equivocal and extravagant often, than the ever-adorable *Arabian Nights*! "If only Oriental literature *sprawled* less, was more concise! It should concentrate its roses," he told himself, glancing out, inquiringly, into the nave.

Profoundly soft and effaced it was a place full of strange suggestion. Intersecting avenues of pillared arches, upbearing waving banners, seemed to beckon towards the Infinite.

"Will you be obliged to change, sir; or shall you go straight through?"

"Straight through, boy."

"I suppose, as you cross the border, they'll want to know what you have to declare."

"I have nothing, child, but myself."

"If 00050 is fortunate, sir, I hope to travel, too—India, Persia, Peru!! . . . Ah, it's El Dorado, then."

"El Dorado, boy?" The Cardinal risked an incautious gesture.

"Oh, Tral-a-la, sir." Quick as Cupid the lad eluded him on the evasive wings of a laugh; an unsparing little laugh, sharp and mocking, that aroused the Primate like the thong of a lash.

Of a long warrior line, he had always regarded disobedience (in others) as an inexcusable offence. What would have happened before the ramparts of Zaragoza, Valladolid, Leon, Burgos, had the men commanded by Ipolito Pirelli in the Peninsular War refused to obey! To be set at defiance by a youngster, a mere cock-robin, kindled elementary ancestral instincts in the Primate's veins.

"Don't provoke me, child, again."

From pillared ambush Don Prudent saw well, however, to effect a bargain.

"You'd do the handsome by me, sir; you'd not be mean?"

"Eh? . . . "

"The Fathers only give us texts; you'd be surprised, your Greatness, at the stinginess of some!"

" . . . ?"

"You'd run to something better, sir; you'd give me something more substantial?"

"I'll give you my slipper, child, if you don't come here!" his Eminence warned him.

"Oufarella. . . . "

Sarabandish and semi-mythic was the dance that ensued. Leading by a dozen derisive steps Don Light-of-limb took the nave. In the dusk of the dawn it seemed to await the quickening blush of day like a white-veiled negress.

"Olé, your Purpleship!"

Men (eternal hunters, novelty seekers, insatiable beings), men in their natural lives, pursue the concrete no less than the ideal—qualities not inseldom found combined in fairy childhood.

"Olé."

Oblivious of sliding mantle the Primate swooped.

Up and down, in and out, round and round "the Virgin," over the worn tombed paving, through Saint Joseph, beneath the cobweb banners from Barocco to purest Moorish, by early Philip, back to Turân-Shâh: "Don't exasperate me, boy"—along the raised tribunes of the choristers and the echoing coro—the great fane (after all) was nothing but a cage; God's cage; the cage of God! . . .

Through the chancel windows the day was newly breaking as the Oleanders will in Spring.

Dispossessed of everything but his fabulous mitre, the Primate was nude and elementary now as Adam himself.

"As you can perfectly see, I have nothing but myself to declare," he addressed some phantom image in the air.

With advancing day Don Skylark *alias* Bright-eyes *alias* Don Temptation it seemed had contrived an exit, for the cathedral was become a place of tranquillity and stillness.

"Only myself," he had dropped before a painting of old Dominic Theotocópuli, the Greek, showing the splendour of Christ's martyrdom.

Peering expectantly from the silken parted curtains of a confessional, paternostering Phoebe Poco caught her breath.

Confused not a little at the sight before her, her equilibrium was only maintained by the recollection of her status: "I'm an honest widow; so I know what men are, bless them!" And stirred to romantic memories she added: "Poor soul, he had the prettiest teeth. . . . "

Fired by fundamental curiosity, the dame, by degrees, was emboldened to advance. All over, was it with him, then? It looked as though his Eminence was far beyond Rome already.

"May God show His pity on you, Don Alvaro of my heart."

She remained a short while lost in mingled conjecture. It was certain no morning bell would wake him.

"So": she stopped to coil her brier-wood chaplet about him in order that he might be less uncovered. "It's wonderful what us bits of women do with a string of beads, but they don't go far with a gentleman."

Now that the ache of life, with its fevers, passions, doubts, its routine, vulgarity, and boredom was over, his serene, unclouded face was a marvelment to behold. Very great distinction and sweetness was visible there, together with much nobility, and love, all magnified, and commingled.

"*Adios,* Don Alvaro of my heart," she sighed, turning away towards the little garden door ajar.

Through the triple windows of the chancel the sky was clear and blue—a blue like the blue of lupins. Above him stirred the windblown banners in the Nave.

On Firbank

Arthur Annesley Ronald Firbank (he dropped the first two names when publishing his first novel) was born in 1886, forty-five years after his grandfather began his rise from a mining background much like D. H. Lawrence's to great wealth as a railway contractor. In fact, the Firbank family story is much like an upper middle class version of *Sons and Lovers*. Joseph, the grandfather, seemed to have at the same time focused and depleted the energy of the stock. Thomas, his son, was apparently negligible—first under the direction of a powerful father, then under that of a wife several inches taller and generations superior in social connections. She furnished the motive power which put him into politics, where he became a member of parliament and later a knight; she encouraged his purchases of a rich variety of *objets d'art* which were in daily use by their growing family; she provided the center of the country home which was, she thought, like a paradise. As Miriam Benkovitz demonstrates in her biography, the family life, at least on the surface, "takes on the conventional and sugary quality of popular Victorian fiction."

Judging from the results, the reality must have been quite another thing. None of the four children finished school and most of them never finished anything. Writers a generation earlier—Samuel Butler and Edmund Grosse among others—had felt the need to shake off the forceful dominance of their fathers. Those of Firbank's era, including D. H. Lawrence and, he said, most of his contemporaries, had to come to terms with their emotional submission to their mothers. Lady Firbank was even tougher and more voracious than Mrs. Lawrence: she long outlived her husband and two of her sons; Ronald, left desolate and almost incapacitated by her death, lived two years longer; Heather, the "Baby" and the only girl, outlived them all, unmarried, reclusive, eccentric.

Those with a taste for drama can see Lady Firbank and her spiritual peers as unconscious spiritual vampires, drawing and draining vitality from their progeny. Shorn of drama, the facts are that Ronald was delicate in health from his childhood and flamboyant in his habits from early manhood. No one could remember him very well—his tutors misdated his stay with them or wrote standardized commendations; he was not even persecuted for his tastes and habits in a hearty college at Cambridge. According to Professor Benkovitz, he was always surprised and gratified that anyone should recognize him. He began to seek attention in ways open to him that his mother could accept, writing and illustrating poems, later professing to live for Beauty. In that period, *beauty* meant the langours and lilies of the aesthetic and decadent movements and the less abstruse branches of the symbolist movement on the continent—Maeterlinck and Huysmans rather than Baudelaire and Mallarme. Oscar Wilde and Aubrey Beardsley he revered, collected, and imitated in a series of juvenile pastiches.

At Cambridge he took no examinations, but read widely, became a Roman Catholic, and abandoned whatever hopes he had for a career in the English diplomatic corps or in the service of the Vatican. He had already begun to cultivate the acquaintance of the great or at least the notorious. After leaving Cambridge he traveled and became a habitué of the Café Royal in London. This is the Ronald Firbank of many anecdotes, the character, like Jay Gatsby, "leaking sawdust at every pore," horrified at butcher's shops and the slaughter of flowers for Covent Garden, frequenting the Eiffel Tower restaurant, the Russian ballet, the opera, and the fringes of a crowd of artists, writers, and beauties of both sexes. Until 1914, he was having all the fun of being a writer without doing any of the actual work, but in that year he began *Vainglory* and, with the outbreak of war—he called it "that awful persecution"—changed into a productive recluse in Oxford, publishing four novels in five years. *Valmouth,* the fifth, was intended to be his last and his best. After the war ended, he resumed his travels—to North Africa, Cuba, the Continent—interrupting them sporadically by visits to the England he had come to despise. All of his remaining work is set outside England. Some fame and a little money—he subsidized all of his work in England—came to him from America in 1924, largely through the efforts of Carl Van Vechten. But his health failed as his reputation grew, and he died, alone, in Rome, in May 1926. *Concerning the Eccentricities of Cardinal Pirelli* was published the following month.

Many critics have been hostile to Firbank; they do not find him funny, perhaps because they classify him with the decadents with whom he has superficial affinities. No one who reads Aubrey Beardsley's *Under the Hill* or the anonymous homosexual tragedy "The Priest and the Acolyte" with any care is likely to confuse them with Firbank's tone and method, but not everyone does read carefully, including some who would make Firbank a cult figure of high camp. Even critics disposed to be friendly have confessed their bewilderment at the plotlessness and apparent pointlessness of his novels. Yet those novels have never been out of print since 1929; reissues are widely reviewed; and they have been praised by such critics as Evelyn Waugh, E. M. Forster, W. H. Auden, V. S. Pritchett, and, rather surprisingly, Edmund Wilson and even Ernest Jones, most famous for his *Hamlet and Oedipus.* Wilson, in fact, called Firbank a pure artist whose air of ephemerality was quite misleading. Firbank himself maintained that "I am all design, once I get going," and his continuing, if limited, popularity can be attributed to a genuinely original pathetic-comic vision conveyed in a form as revolutionary as anything by his more famous contemporaries.

Like Wilde and Beardsley, Firbank desired to believe in a purely aesthetic world; like Wilde, he gained some of his most telling effects from the conflict between aesthetics, mundane reality (a term Firbank loathed), and morality. There the resemblance ends, for Wilde did not finally have the courage of his ambivalences—"I did but touch the honey of Romance," he mourned in "Helas," "And must I lose a soul's inheritance?"—that Firbank retained and made the central conflict of his late works. In the novels through *Valmouth* (1919), he permitted the comic triumph of "decorative, self-entranced persons" (the phrase is from *Vainglory*) who become saints of the ego, enshrining themselves in cathedral stained glass or rising (and literally falling) meteorlike in the London theatrical world. In *Valmouth* and the remaining novels, however, a somber undercurrent becomes more and more prominent. Firbank does not prophesy Armageddon; only once, and then tangentially and comically, does he mention World War i and its effects. His fictional world, though beautiful and without the whimper of world's end, is winding down, decaying picturesquely, or gaining energy at the cost of distinction, beauty, grace, and complexity. In *The Flower Beneath the Foot,* for example, the stolid and banal Princess Elsie of England displaces Laura de Nazianzi as the bride of Prince Yousef of Pisuerga, bringing with her money, the hope of a large and healthy family, and a whole ruck of opportunistic hacks who will dominate her husband's country, as if Ruritania were to be overrun by the Rotary Club. However, and this distinguishes Firbank from the sentimental aesthetes, Laura is partly to blame for her own plight: too delicate to endure the idea of the Prince's sexuality, she takes refuge in a fashionable convent and in what she hopes will be the delicate sympathy of Sister Ursula, who had once declared that "marriage was obscene." At the end, however, Laura realizes the cost of her action. Though she will ultimately become a saint, she is left pounding her hands in anguished frustration on the broken glass atop the convent wall as the novel ends.

Cardinal Pirelli differs from Laura primarily in his inability or refusal to make any decision between world and spirit. The world may be all love, as Father Felicitas says, but no one does understand, least of all Pirelli. However, he is instinctively drawn to life and beauty against what Firbank called in a note for the novel, "The need of a fuller life, the narrow exclusion/the Church—heart-racked." Pirelli cannot live within these limits, but he loves them for the order and tradition they imply. At the same time, he loves the decaying, autumnal social world, competing with royalty for homage, competing with matadors for the attention of women. Like the Duquesa's dog Clapsey, with whom he is subtly paralleled, he has grown old as the pet of society women. At rare moments he attains the quiet necessary to confront his essential self, only to find a tangle of contradictions. And though he sometimes wishes to escape the social and ecclesiastical worlds which enmesh him, he can envision no destination or refuge: "Thitherwards" has no attraction for him, either as America or as eternity. The most complex of Firbank's characters, Pirelli is, seen rightly, comic and sympathetic, corrupt and holy, ludicrous and dignified, all at the same time. Firbank manages a final equilibrium of these conflicting qualities by piling up and precariously balancing extremes of diction and viewpoint. Pirelli's meditations are often comic in their tortuous self-justification, but his direct and simple self-revelation at the end is foreshadowed by several episodes, notably his vinous vision and his plea for guidance in Chapter 8—at once bibulous and sincere. In similar fashion, the author balances the attitudes of those who view Pirelli: Monsignor Silex and Father Felicitas, Mother Saint Mary of the Angels and Madam Poco, the ladies of the upper classes and women of the people.

Firbank gives order to this as to most of his novels by rhythmic contrasts. The bustle and dismay of Chapter 1, for example, are set off by the Cardinal's solitary meditations in Chapter 2, and this kind of contrast is maintained throughout the novel, underlining the contrasts between the world of society and world of nature or God which is the world of love and between indoors—confining, almost stifling, a series of cages—and the beauty and sense of release in the garden scenes. In fact, the principle of recurrence is as important to the novel's structure as the principle of contrast, for by this means Firbank is able to give a broad portrait of society as well as to deepen understanding of Pirelli. The parties in Chapters 5 and 7 show the young and the old, shading toward neurasthenia and collapse; Chapters 3 and 9 show the Cathedral open for business, with an emphasis in 9 on ceremonies of death rather than life. Most striking of all is the parallel between the first and last chapters: the pursuit of Crack and the pursuit of Chicklet; the physical, canine father in trousers before the horrified gaze of Silex and all of society, the human, spiritual father nude before the tolerant gaze of Madam Poco. However, parallels are not identities, and Firbank has ordered his episodes to show the Cardinal's nobility as well as his foolishness and to move from vanity and disorder to a balanced confrontation between the sweetness and the riotous impulses of life on the one hand and, on the other, the mystery of eternity. Even the most obvious numerological division, and Firbank used such divisions to structure many of his novels, supports the basic themes and movements of the book. The first five chapters reveal Pirelli's worldliness triumphant; even the tranquil garden scenes focus on his misdeeds. The second five emphasize the inner Pirelli, for Chapter 6 begins not with a prank or a social function but with Pirelli praying and ends not in social triumph but in death. And the society and the world itself seem increasingly transient: religious decline, decay of aristocratic tradition, political turmoil, flowers succeeding one another, in contrast to the enduring planets. In these circumstances, Firbank implies, freedom and love may be unattainable because of the contradictions in human nature and in the very nature of things. The result, however, is not despair but a resigned comic vision. Pirelli's refusal to shrink from life or contradiction has a certain comic nobility, and when he stands nude below the El Greco crucifixion, he is not just parodying St. Francis of Assisi or St. Joseph of Cupertino, who also appeared nude before images of Christ, but presenting himself to God as he is.

Textual note:

First edition, London: Grant Richards, 1926. Published with some editorial meddling by Duckworth in the collected edition, 1929; the same text reproduced through photocopying in *Five Novels,* issued in England by Duckworth (1949) and in the United States by New Directions Pub. Corp. (1949); with further minor emendations in *The Complete Ronald Firbank* (1961). Any novel published after Firbank's death will be full of so-called improvements in diction and punctuation; many of these changes alter tone or meaning. The present text is based on that of the first edition and retains Firbank's idiosyncratic spelling and punctuation.

Resources for further study:

Besides the novels and play in *The Complete Ronald Firbank,* see *The New Rythum and Other Pieces* (New York: New Directions Pub. Corp., 1963). Firbank published only one preface—to the American edition of *The Flower Beneath the Foot* (1924)—and one essay; neither is essential for an understanding of his fiction.

BIBLIOGRAPHICAL:

BENKOVITZ, MIRIAM J. *A Bibliography of Ronald Firbank.* London: Rupert Hart-Davis, 1963.

DAVIS, ROBERT MURRAY. "Ronald Firbank: A Selected Checklist of Criticism," *Bulletin of Bibliography,* 26 (October-December 1969), 108–111.

BIOGRAPHICAL:

BENKOVITZ, MIRIAM J. *Ronald Firbank: A Biography.* New York: Alfred A. Knopf, Inc., 1969.

FLETCHER, IFAN KYRLE, and others. *Ronald Firbank: A Memoir.* New York: Brentano's, 1932.

CRITICAL:

BROOKE, JOCELYN. *Ronald Firbank.* New York: Roy Publishing Co., 1952.

DAVIS, ROBERT MURRAY. "From Artifice to Art: The Technique of Firbank's Novels," *Style,* 2 (Winter 1968), 33–47.

MERRITT, JAMES DOUGLAS. *Ronald Firbank.* New York: Twayne Publishers, Inc., 1969.

POTOKER, EDWARD M. *Ronald Firbank.* New York: Columbia Essays on Modern Writers, 1969.

WAUGH, EVELYN. "Ronald Firbank," *Life and Letters,* 2 (March 1929), 191–196.

WILSON, EDMUND. *Classics and Commercials.* New York: Random House, Inc., Vintage Books, 1962. See also Wilson's *The Shores of Light.* New York: Farrar, Straus and Young, 1952.

ALDOUS HUXLEY

After the Fireworks

1

"Late as usual. Late." Judd's voice was censorious. The words fell sharp, like beak-blows. "As though I were a nut," Miles Fanning thought resentfully, "and he were a woodpecker. And yet he's devotion itself, he'd do anything for me. Which is why, I suppose, he feels entitled to crack my shell each time he sees me." And he came to the conclusion, as he had so often come before, that he really didn't like Colin Judd at all. "My oldest friend, whom I quite definitely don't like. Still . . . " Still, Judd was an asset, Judd was worth it.

"Here are your letters," the sharp voice continued.

Fanning groaned as he took them. "Can't one ever escape from letters? Even here, in Rome? They seem to get through everything. Like filter-passing bacteria. Those blessed days before post offices!" Sipping, he examined, over the rim of his coffee cup, the addresses on the envelopes.

"You'd be the first to complain if people didn't write," Judd rapped out. "Here's your egg. Boiled for three minutes exactly. I saw to it myself."

Taking his egg, "On the contrary," Fanning answered, "I'd be the first to rejoice. If people write it means they exist; and all I ask for is to be able to pretend that the world doesn't exist. The wicked flee when no man pursueth. How well I understand them! But letters don't allow you to be an ostrich. The Freudians say . . . " He broke off suddenly. After all he was talking to Colin—to *Colin*. The confessional, self-accusatory manner was wholly misplaced. Pointless to give Colin the excuse to say something disagreeable. But what he had been going to say about the Freudians was amusing. "The Freudians," he began again.

159

But taking advantage of forty years of intimacy, Judd had already started to be disagreeable. "But you'd be miserable," he was saying, "if the post didn't bring you your regular dose of praise and admiration and sympathy and . . ."

"And humiliation," added Fanning, who had opened one of the envelopes and was looking at the letter within. "Listen to this. From my American publishers. Sales and Publicity Department. 'My dear Mr. Fanning.' *My* dear, mark you. Wilbur F. Schmalz's dear. 'My dear Mr. Fanning,—Won't you take us into your confidence with regard to your plans for the Summer Vacation? What aspect of the Great Outdoors are you favouring this year? Ocean or Mountain, Woodland or purling Lake? I would esteem it a great privilege if you would inform me, as I am preparing a series of notes for the Literary Editors of our leading journals, who are, as I have often found in the past, exceedingly receptive to such personal material, particularly when accompanied by well-chosen snapshots. So won't you co-operate with us in providing this service? Very cordially yours, Wilbur F. Schmalz.' Well, what do you think of that?"

"I think you'll answer him," said Judd. "Charmingly," he added, envenoming his malice. Fanning gave a laugh, whose very ease and heartiness betrayed his discomfort. "And you'll even send him a snapshot."

Contemptuously—too contemptuously (he felt it at the time)—Fanning crumpled up the letter and threw it into the fireplace. The really humiliating thing, he reflected, was that Judd was quite right: he *would* write to Mr. Schmalz about the Great Outdoors, he *would* send the first snapshot anybody took of him. There was a silence. Fanning ate two or three spoonfuls of egg. Perfectly boiled, for once. But still, what a relief that Colin was going away! After all, he reflected, there's a great deal to be said for a friend who has a house in Rome and who invites you to stay, even when he isn't there. To such a man much must be forgiven—even his infernal habit of being a woodpecker. He opened another envelope and began to read.

Possessive and preoccupied, like an anxious mother, Judd watched him. With all his talents and intelligence, Miles wasn't fit to face the world alone. Judd had told him so (peck, peck!) again and again. "You're a child!" He had said it a thousand times. "You ought to have somebody to look after you." But if any one other than himself offered to do it, how bitterly jealous and resentful he became! And the trouble was that there were always so many applicants for the post of Fanning's bear-leader. Foolish men or, worse and more frequently, foolish women, attracted to him by his reputation and then conquered by his charm. Judd hated and professed to be loftily contemptuous of them. And the more Fanning liked his admiring bear-leaders, the loftier Judd's contempt became. For that was the bitter and unforgivable thing: Fanning manifestly preferred their bear-leading to Judd's. They flattered the bear, they caressed and even worshipped him; and the bear, of course, was charming to them, until such time as he growled, or bit, or, more often, quietly slunk away. Then they were surprised, they were pained. Because, as Judd would say with a grim satisfaction, they didn't know what Fanning was *really* like. Whereas he did know and had known since they were schoolboys together, nearly forty years before. Therefore he had a right to like him—a right and, at the same time, a duty to tell him all the reasons why he ought not to like him. Fanning didn't much enjoy listening to these reasons; he preferred to go where the bear was a sacred animal. With that air, which seemed so natural on his grey sharp face, of being dispassionately impersonal, "You're afraid of healthy criticism," Judd would tell him. "You always were, even as a boy."

"He's Jehovah," Fanning would complain. "Life with Judd is one long Old Testament. Being one of the Chosen People must have been bad enough. But to be *the* Chosen Person, in the singular . . . " And he would shake his head. "Terrible!"

And yet he had never seriously quarrelled with Colin Judd. Active unpleasantness was something which Fanning avoided as much as possible. He had never even made any determined attempt to fade out of Judd's existence as he had faded, at one time or another, out of the existence of so many once intimate bear-leaders. The habit of their intimacy was of too long standing and, besides, old Colin was so useful, so bottomlessly reliable. So Judd remained for him the Oldest Friend whom one definitely dislikes; while for Judd, he was the Oldest Friend whom one adores and at the same time hates for not adoring back, the Oldest Friend whom one never sees enough of, but whom, when he *is* there, one finds insufferably exasperating, the Oldest Friend whom, in spite of all one's efforts, one is always getting on the nerves of.

"If only," Judd was thinking, "he could have faith!" The Catholic Church was there to help him. (Judd himself was a convert of more than twenty years' standing.) But the trouble was that Fanning didn't want to be helped by the Church; he could only see the comic side of Judd's religion. Judd was reserving his missionary efforts till his friend should be old or ill. But if only, meanwhile, if only, by some miracle of grace . . . So thought the good Catholic; but it was the jealous friend who felt and who obscurely schemed. Converted, Miles Fanning would be separated from his other friends and brought, Judd realized, nearer to himself.

Watching him, as he read his letter, Judd noticed, all at once, that Fanning's lips were twitching involuntarily into a smile. They were full lips, well cut, sensitive and sensual; his smiles were a little crooked. A dark fury suddenly fell on Colin Judd.

"Telling *me* that you'd like to get no letters!" he said with an icy vehemence. "When you sit there grinning to yourself over some silly woman's flatteries."

Amazed, amused, "But what an outburst!" said Fanning, looking up from his letter.

Judd swallowed his rage; he had made a fool of himself. It was in a tone of calm dispassionate flatness that he spoke. Only his eyes remained angry. "Was I right?" he asked.

"So far as the woman was concerned," Fanning answered. "But wrong about the flattery. Women have no time nowadays to talk about anything except themselves."

"Which is only another way of flattering," said Judd obstinately. "They confide in you, because they think you'll like being treated as a person who understands."

"Which is what, after all, I am. By profession even." Fanning spoke with an exasperating mildness. "What *is* a novelist, unless he's a person who understands?" He paused; but Judd made no answer, for the only words he could have uttered would have been whirling words of rage and jealousy. He was jealous not only of the friends, the lovers, the admiring correspondents; he was jealous of a part of Fanning himself, of the artist, the public personage; for the artist, the public personage seemed so often to stand between his friend and himself. He hated, while he gloried in them.

Fanning looked at him for a moment, expectantly; but the other kept his mouth tight shut, his eyes averted. In the same exasperatingly gentle tone, "And flattery or no flattery," Fanning went on, "this is a charming letter. And the girl's adorable."

He was having his revenge. Nothing upset poor Colin Judd so much as having to listen to talk about women or love. He had a horror of anything connected with the act, the mere thought, of sex. Fanning called it his perversion. "You're one of those unspeakable chastity-perverts," he would say, when he wanted to get his own back after a bout of pecking. "If I had children, I'd never allow them to frequent your company. Too dangerous." When he spoke of the forbidden subject, Judd would either writhe, a martyr, or else unchristianly explode. On this occasion he writhed and was silent. "Adorable," Fanning repeated, provocatively. "A ravishing little creature. Though of course she *may* be a huge great camel. That's the danger of unknown correspondents. The best letter-writers are often camels. It's a piece of natural history I've learned by the bitterest experience." Looking back at the letter, "All the same," he went on, "when a young girl writes to one that she's sure one's the only person in the world who can tell her exactly who and what (both heavily underlined) she is—well, one's rather tempted, I must confess, to try yet once more. Because even if she were a camel she'd be a very young one. Twenty-one—isn't that what she says?" He turned over a page of the letter. "Yes; twenty-one. Also she writes in orange ink. And doesn't like the Botticelli's at the Uffizi. But I hadn't told you; she's at Florence. This letter has been to London and back. We're practically neighbours. And here's something that's really rather good. Listen. 'What I like about the Italian women is that they don't seem to be rather ashamed of being women, like so many English girls are, because English girls seem to go about apologizing for their figures, as though they were punctured, the way they hold themselves—it's really rather abject. But here they're all pleased and proud and not a bit apologetic or punctured, but just the opposite, which I really like, don't you?' Yes, I do," Fanning answered, looking up from the letter. "I like it very much indeed. I've always been opposed to these modern *Ars est celare arsem* fashions. I like unpuncturedness and I'm charmed by the letter. Yes, charmed. Aren't you?"

In a voice that trembled with hardly-restrained indignation, "No, I'm not!" Judd answered; and without looking at Fanning, he got up and walked quickly out of the room.

2

Judd had gone to stay with his old Aunt Caroline at Montreux. It was an annual affair; for Judd lived chronometrically. Most of June and the first half of July were always devoted to Aunt Caroline and devoted, invariably, at Montreux. On the fifteenth of July, Aunt Caroline was rejoined by her friend Miss Gaskin and Judd was free to proceed to England. In England he stayed till September the thirteenth, when he returned to Rome—"for the praying season," as Fanning irreverently put it. The beautiful regularity of poor Colin's existence was a source of endless amusement to his friend. Fanning never had any plans. "I just accept what turns up," he would explain. "Heads or tails—it's the only rational way of living. Chance generally knows so much better than we do. The Greeks elected most of their officials by lot—how wisely! Why shouldn't we toss up for Prime Ministers? We'd be much better governed. Or a sort of Calcutta Sweep for all the responsible posts in Church and State. The only horror would be if one were to win the sweep oneself. Imagine drawing the Permanent Under-Secretaryship for Education! Or the Archbishopric of Canterbury! Or the Vice-royalty of India! One would just have to drink weed-killer. But as things are, luckily . . . "

Luckily, he was at liberty, under the present dispensation, to stroll, very slowly, in a suit of cream-coloured silk, down the shady side of the Via Condotti towards the Spanish Steps. Slowly, slowly. The air was streaked with invisible bars of heat and cold. Coolness came flowing out of shadowed doorways, and at every transverse street the sun breathed fiercely. Like walking through the ghost of a zebra, he thought.

Three beautiful young women passed him, talking and laughing together. Like laughing flowers, like deer, like little horses. And of course absolutely unpunctured, unapologetic. He smiled to himself, thinking of the letter and also of his own reply to it.

A pair of pink and white monsters loomed up, as though from behind the glass of an aquarium. But not speechless. For *"Grossartig!"* fell enthusiastically on Fanning's ear as they passed, and *"Fabelhaft!"* These Nordics! He shook his head. Time they were put a stop to.

In the looking-glasses of a milliner's window a tall man in creamy-white walked slowly to meet him, hat in hand. The face was aquiline and eager, brown with much exposure to the sun. The waved, rather wiry hair was dark almost to blackness. It grew thickly, and the height of the forehead owed nothing to the approach of baldness. But what pleased Fanning most was the slimness and straightness of the tall figure. Those sedentary men of letters, with their sagging tremulous paunches—they were enough to make one hate the very thought of literature. What had been Fanning's horror when, a year before, he had realized that his own paunch was showing the first preliminary signs of sagging! But Mr. Hornibrooke's exercises had been wonderful. "The Culture of the Abdomen." So much more important, as he had remarked in the course of the last few months at so many dinner tables, than the culture of the mind! For of course he had taken everybody into his confidence about the paunch. He took everybody into his confidence about almost everything. About his love-affairs and his literary projects; about his illnesses and his philosophy; his vices and his bank balance. He lived a rich and variegated private life in public; it was one of the secrets of his charm. To the indignant protests of poor jealous Colin, who reproached him with being an exhibitionist, shameless, a self-exploiter, "You take everything so moralistically," he had answered. "You seem to imagine people do everything on purpose. But people do hardly anything on purpose. They behave as they do because they can't help it; that's what they happen to be like. 'I am that I am'; Jehovah's is the last word in realistic psychology. I am what *I* am—a sort of soft transparent jelly-fish. While you're what *you* are—very tightly shut, opaque, heavily armoured: in a word, a giant clam. Morality doesn't enter; it's a case for scientific classification. You should be more of a Linnaeus, Colin, and less the Samuel Smiles." Judd had been reduced to a grumbling silence. What he really resented was the fact that Fanning's confidences were given to upstart friends, to strangers even, before they were given to him. It was only to be expected. The clam's shell keeps the outside things out as effectually as it keeps the inside things in. In Judd's case, moreover, the shell served as an instrument of reproachful pinching.

From his cool street Fanning emerged into the Piazza di Spagna. The sunlight was stinging hot and dazzling. The flower venders on the steps sat in the midst of great explosions of colour. He bought a gardenia from one of them and stuck it in his buttonhole. From the windows of the English bookshop "*The Return of Eurydice,* by Miles Fanning" stared at him again and again. They were making a regular display of his latest volume in Tauchnitz. Satisfactory, no doubt; but also, of course, rather ridiculous and even humiliating, when one reflected that the book would be read by people like that estimable upper middle-class couple there, with their noses at the next window—that Civil Servant, he guessed, with the sweet little artistic wife and the artistic little house on Campden Hill—would be read by them dutifully (for of course they worked hard to keep abreast of everything) and discussed at their charming little dinner parties and finally condemned as "extraordinarily brilliant, but . . . " Yes, but, but, but. For they were obviously regular subscribers to *Punch,* were vertebrae in the backbone of England, were upholders of all that was depressingly finest, all that was lifelessly and genteelly best in the English upper-class tradition. And when they recognized him (as it was obvious to Fanning, in spite of their discreet politeness, that they did) his vanity, instead of being flattered, was hurt. Being recognized by people like that—such was fame! What a humiliation, what a personal insult!

At Cook's, where he now went to draw some money on his letter of credit, Fame still pursued him, trumpeting. From behind the brass bars of his cage the cashier smiled knowingly as he counted out the bank-notes.

"Of course your name's very familiar to me, Mr. Fanning," he said; and his tone was at once ingratiating and self-satisfied; the compliment to Fanning was at the same time a compliment to himself. "And if I may be permitted to say so," he went on, pushing the money through the bars, as one might offer a piece of bread to an ape, "gratters on your last book. Gratters," he repeated, evidently delighted with his very public-schooly colloquialism.

"All gratitude for gratters," Fanning answered and turned away. He was half amused, half annoyed. Amused by the absurdity of those more than Etonian congratulations, annoyed at the damned impertinence of the congratulator. So intolerably patronizing! he grumbled to himself. But most admirers were like that; they thought they were doing you an enormous favour by admiring you. And how much more they admired themselves for being capable of appreciating than they admired the object of their appreciation! And then there were the earnest ones who thanked you for giving such a perfect expression to their ideas and sentiments. They were the worst of all. For, after all, what were they thanking you for? For being *their* interpreter, *their* dragoman, for playing John the Baptist to *their* Messiah. Damn their impertinence! Yes, damn their impertinence!

"Mr. Fanning." A hand touched his elbow.

Still indignant with the thought of damned impertinences, Fanning turned round with an expression of such ferocity on his face, that the young woman who had addressed him involuntarily fell back.

"Oh . . . I'm so sorry," she stammered; and her face, which had been bright, deliberately, with just such an impertinence as Fanning was damning, was discomposed into a child-like embarrassment. The blood tingled painfully in her cheeks. Oh, what a fool, she thought, what a fool she was making of herself! This idiotic blushing! But the way he had turned round on her, as if he were going to bite . . . Still, even that was no excuse for blushing and saying she was sorry, as though she were still at school and he were Miss Huss. Idiot! she inwardly shouted at herself. And making an enormous effort, she readjusted her still scarlet face, giving it as good an expression of smiling nonchalance as she could summon up. "I'm sorry," she repeated, in a voice that was meant to be light, easy, ironically polite, but which came out (oh, idiot, idiot!) nervously shaky and uneven. "I'm afraid I disturbed you. But I just wanted to introduce . . . I mean, as you were passing . . . "

"But how charming of you!" said Fanning, who had had time to realize that this latest piece of impertinence was one to be blessed, not damned. "Charming!" Yes, charming it was, that young face with the grey eyes and the little straight nose, like a cat's, and the rather short upper lip. And the heroic way she had tried, through all her blushes, to be the accomplished woman of the world—that too was charming. And touchingly charming even were those rather red, large-wristed English hands, which she wasn't yet old enough to have learnt the importance of tending into whiteness and softness. They were still the hands of a child, a tomboy. He gave her one of those quick, those brilliantly and yet mysteriously significant smiles of his;

those smiles that were still so youthfully beautiful when they came spontaneously. But they could also be put on; he knew how to exploit their fabricated charm, deliberately. To a sensitive eye, the beauty of his expression was, on these occasions, subtly repulsive.

Reassured, "I'm Pamela Tarn," said the young girl, feeling warm with gratitude for the smile. He was handsomer, she was thinking, than in his photographs. And much more fascinating. It was a face that had to be seen in movement.

"Pamela Tarn?" he repeated questioningly.

"The one who wrote you a letter." Her blush began to deepen again. "You answered so nicely. I mean, it was so kind . . . I thought . . . "

"But of course!" he cried, so loudly, that people looked round, startled. "Of course!" He took her hand and held it, shaking it from time to time, for what seemed to Pamela hours. "The most enchanting letter. Only I'm so bad at names. So you're Pamela Tarn." He looked at her appraisingly. She returned his look for a moment, then flinched away in confusion from his bright dark eyes.

"Excuse me," said a chilly voice; and a very large suit of plus-fours edged past them to the door.

"I like you," Fanning concluded, ignoring the plus-fours; she uttered an embarrassed little laugh. "But then, I liked you before. You don't know how pleased I was with what you said about the difference between English and Italian women." The colour rose once more into Pamela's cheeks. She had only written those sentences after long hesitation, and had written them then recklessly, dashing them down with a kind of anger, just because Miss Huss would have been horrified by their unwomanliness, just because Aunt Edith would have found them so distressing, just because they had, when she spoke them aloud one day in the streets of Florence, so shocked the two schoolmistresses from Boston whom she had met at the pension and was doing the sights with. Fanning's mention of them pleased her and at the same time made her feel dreadfully guilty. She hoped he wouldn't be too specific about those differences; it seemed to her that every one was listening. "So profound," he went on in his musical ringing voice. "But out of the mouths of babes, with all due respect." He smiled again, "And 'punctured'—that was really the *mot juste*. I shall steal it and use it as my own."

"*Permesso.*" This time it was a spotted muslin and brown arms and a whiff of synthetic carnations.

"I think we're rather in the way," said Pamela, who was becoming more and more uncomfortably aware of being conspicuous. And the spirit presences of Miss Huss, of Aunt Edith, of the two American ladies at Florence seemed to hang about her, hauntingly. "Perhaps we'd better . . . I mean . . . " And, turning, she almost ran to the door.

"Punctured, punctured," repeated his pursuing voice behind her. "Punctured with the shame of being warm-blooded mammals. Like those poor lank creatures that were standing at the counter in there," he added, coming abreast with her, as they stepped over the threshold into the heat and glare. "Did you see them? So pathetic. But, oh dear!" he shook his head. "Oh dear, oh dear!"

She looked at him, and Fanning saw in her face a new expression, an expression of mischief and laughing malice and youthful impertinence. Even her breasts, he now noticed with an amused appreciation, even her breasts were impertinent. Small, but beneath the pale blue stuff of her dress, pointed, firm, almost comically insistent. No ashamed deflation here.

"Pathetic," she mockingly echoed, "but, oh dear, how horrible, how disgusting! Because they *are* disgusting," she added defiantly, in answer to his look of humorous protest. Here in the sunlight and with the noise of the town isolating her from every one except Fanning, she had lost her embarrassment and her sense of guilt. The spiritual presences had evaporated. Pamela was annoyed with herself for having felt so uncomfortable among those awful old English cats at Cook's. She thought of her mother; her mother had never been embarrassed, or at any rate she had always managed to turn her embarrassment into something else. Which was what Pamela was doing now. "Really disgusting," she almost truculently insisted. She was reasserting herself, she was taking a revenge.

"You're very ruthless to the poor old things," said Fanning. "So worthy in spite of their mangy dimness, so obviously good."

"I hate goodness," said Pamela with decision, speeding the parting ghosts of Miss Huss and Aunt Edith and the two ladies from Boston.

Fanning laughed aloud. "Ah, if only we all had the courage to say so, like you, my child!" And with a familiar affectionate gesture, as though she were indeed a child and he had known her from the cradle, he dropped a hand on her shoulder. "To say so and to act up to our beliefs. As you do, I'm sure." And he gave the slim hard little shoulder a pat. "A world without goodness—it'd be Paradise."

They walked some steps in silence. His hand lay heavy and strong on her shoulder, and a strange warmth that was somehow intenser than the warmth of mere flesh and blood seemed to radiate through her whole body. Her heart quickened its beating; an anxiety oppressed her lungs; her very mind was as though breathless.

"Putting his hand on my shoulder like that!" she was thinking. "It would have been cheek if some one else . . . Perhaps I ought to have been angry, perhaps . . . " No, that would have been silly. "It's silly to take things like that too seriously, as though one were Aunt Edith." But meanwhile his hand lay heavy on her shoulder, broodingly hot, its weight, its warmth insistently present in her consciousness.

She remembered characters in his books. Her namesake Pamela in *Pastures New*. Pamela the cold, but for that very reason an experimenter with passion; cold and therefore dangerous, full of power, fatal. Was she like Pamela? She had often thought so. But more recently she had often thought she was like Joan in *The Return of Eurydice*—Joan, who had emerged from the wintry dark underworld of an unawakened life with her husband (that awful, good, disinterested husband—so like Aunt Edith) into the warmth and brilliance of that transfiguring passion for Walter, for the

adorable Walter whom she had always imagined must be so like Miles
Fanning himself. She was sure of it now. But what of her own identity?
Was she Joan, or was she Pamela? And which of the two would it be nicer to
be? Warm Joan, with her happiness—but at the price of surrender? Or the
cold, the unhappy, but conquering, dangerous Pamela? Or wouldn't it
perhaps be best to be a little of both at once? Or first one and then the other?
And in any case there was to be no goodness in the Aunt Edith style; he had
been sure she wasn't good.

In her memory the voice of Aunt Edith sounded, as it had actually
sounded only a few weeks before, in disapproving comment on her reference to the passionless, experimental Pamela of *Pastures New.* "It's a book
I don't like. A most unnecessary book." And then, laying her hand on
Pamela's, "Dear child," she had added, with that earnest, that dutifully
willed affectionateness, which Pamela so bitterly resented, "I'd rather you
didn't read any of Miles Fanning's books."

"Mother never objected to my reading them. So I don't see . . . " The
triumphant consciousness of having at this very moment the hand that had
written those unnecessary books upon her shoulder was promising to
enrich her share of the remembered dialogue with a lofty impertinence
which the original had hardly possessed. "I don't see that you have the
smallest right . . . "

Fanning's voice fell startlingly across the eloquent silence. "A penny for
your thoughts, Miss Pamela," it said.

He had been for some obscure reason suddenly depressed by his own last
words. "A world without goodness—it'd be Paradise." But it wouldn't, no
more than now. The only paradises were fools' paradises, ostriches' paradises. It was as though he had suddenly lifted his head out of the sand and
seen time bleeding away—like the stabbed bull at the end of a bull-fight,
swaying on his legs and soundlessly spouting the red blood from his
nostrils—bleeding, bleeding away stanchlessly into the darkness. And it
was all, even the loveliness and the laughter and the sunlight, finally
pointless. This young girl at his side, this beautiful pointless creature
pointlessly walking down the Via del Babuino . . . The feelings crystallized
themselves, as usual, into whole phrases in his mind, and suddenly the
phrases were metrical.

> Pointless and arm in arm with pointlessness,
> I pace and pace the Street of the Baboon.

Imbecile! Annoyed with himself, he tried to shake off his mood of maudlin
depression, he tried to force his spirit back into the ridiculous and charming
universe it had inhabited, on the whole so happily, all the morning.

"A penny for your thoughts," he said, with a certain rather forced
jocularity, giving her shoulder a little clap. "Or forty centesimi, if you
prefer them." And, dropping his hand to his side, "In Germany," he went
on, "just after the War one could afford to be more munificent. There was a
time when I regularly offered a hundred and ninety million marks for a
thought—yes, and gained on the exchange. But now . . . "

"Well, if you really want to know," said Pamela, deciding to be bold, "I was thinking how much my Aunt Edith disapproved of your books."

"Did she? I suppose it was only to be expected. Seeing that I don't write for aunts—at any rate, not for aunts in their specifically auntly capacity. Though, of course, when they're off duty . . . "

"Aunt Edith's never off duty."

"And I'm never on. So you see." He shrugged his shoulders. "But I'm sure," he added, "you never paid much attention to her disapproval."

"None," she answered, playing the un-good part for all it was worth. "I read Freud this spring," she boasted, "and Gide's autobiography, and Krafft-Ebbing. . . . "

"Which is more than I've ever done," he laughed.

The laugh encouraged her. "Not to mention all *your* books, years ago. You see," she added, suddenly fearful lest she might have said something to offend him, "my mother never minded my reading your books. I mean, she really encouraged me, even when I was only seventeen or eighteen. My mother died last year," she explained. There was a silence. "I've lived with Aunt Edith ever since," she went on. "Aunt Edith's my father's sister. Older than he was. Father died in 1923."

"So you're all alone now?" he questioned. "Except, of course, for Aunt Edith."

"Whom I've now left." She was almost boasting again. "Because when I was twenty-one . . . "

"You stuck out your tongue at her and ran away. Poor Aunt Edith!"

"I won't have you being sorry for her," Pamela answered hotly. "She's really awful, you know. Like poor Joan's husband in *The Return of Eurydice.*" How easy it was to talk to him!

"So you even know," said Fanning, laughing, "what it's like to be unhappily married. Already. Indissolubly wedded to a virtuous aunt."

"No joke, I can tell you. *I'm* the one to be sorry for. Besides, she didn't mind my going away, whatever she might say."

"She did say something, then?"

"Oh yes. She always says things. More in sorrow than in anger, you know. Like headmistresses. So gentle and good, I mean. When all the time she really thought me too awful. I used to call her Hippo, because she was such a hypocrite—*and* so fat. Enormous. Don't you *hate* enormous people? No, she's really delighted to get rid of me," Pamela concluded, "simply delighted." Her face was flushed and as though luminously alive; she spoke with a quick eagerness.

"What a tremendous hurry she's in," he was thinking, "to tell me all about herself. If she were older or uglier, what an intolerable egotism it would be! As intolerable as mine would be if I happened to be less intelligent. But as it is . . . " His face, as he listened to her, expressed a sympathetic attention.

"She always disliked me," Pamela had gone on. "Mother too. She couldn't abide my mother, though she was always sweetly hippo-ish with her."

"And your mother—how did she respond?"

"Well, not hippo-ishly, of course. She couldn't be that. She treated Aunt

Edith—well, how *did* she treat Aunt Edith?" Pamela hesitated, frowning. "Well, I suppose you'd say she was just natural with the Hippo. I mean . . ." She bit her lip. "Well, if she ever *was* really natural. *I* don't know. Is anybody natural?" She looked up questioningly at Fanning. "Am I natural, for example?"

Smiling a little at her choice of an example, "I should think almost certainly not," Fanning answered, more or less at random.

"You're right, of course," she said despairingly, and her face was suddenly tragic, almost there were tears in her eyes. "But isn't it awful? I mean, isn't it simply hopeless?"

Pleased that his chance shot should have gone home, "At your age," he said consolingly, "you can hardly expect to be natural. Naturalness is something you learn, painfully, by trial and error. Besides," he added, "there are some people who are unnatural by nature."

"Unnatural by nature." Pamela nodded, as she repeated the words, as though she were inwardly marshalling evidence to confirm their truth. "Yes, I believe that's us," she concluded. "Mother and me. Not hippos, I mean, not *poseuses,* but just unnatural by nature. You're quite right. As usual," she added with something that was almost resentment in her voice.

"I'm sorry," he apologized.

"How is it you manage to know so much?" Pamela asked in the same resentful tone. By what right was he so easily omniscient, when she could only grope and guess in the dark?

Taking to himself a credit that belonged, in his case, to chance, "Child's play, my dear Watson," he answered banteringly. "But I suppose you're too young to have heard of Sherlock Holmes. And anyhow," he added, with an ironical seriousness, "don't let's waste any more time talking about me."

Pamela wasted no more time. "I get so depressed with myself," she said with a sigh. "And after what you've told me I shall get still more depressed. Unnatural by nature. And by upbringing too. Because I see now that my mother was like that. I mean, she was unnatural by nature too."

"Even with you?" he asked, thinking that this was becoming interesting. She nodded without speaking. He looked at her closely. "Were you very fond of her?" was the question that now suggested itself.

After a moment of silence, "I loved my father more," she answered slowly. "He was more . . . more reliable. I mean, you never quite knew where you were with my mother. Sometimes she almost forgot about me; or else she didn't forget me enough and spoiled me. And then sometimes she used to get into the most terrible rages with me. She really frightened me then. And said such terribly hurting things. But you mustn't think I didn't love her. I did." The words seemed to release a spring; she was suddenly moved. There was a little silence. Making an effort, "But that's what she was like," she concluded at last.

"But I don't see," said Fanning gently, "that there was anything specially unnatural in spoiling you and then getting cross with you." They were crossing the Piazza del Popolo; the traffic of four thronged streets intricately merged and parted in the open space. "You must have been a charming child. And also . . . Look out!" He laid a hand on her arm. An electric bus passed noiselessly, a whispering monster. "Also maddeningly exasperating. So where the unnaturalness came in . . . "

"But if you'd known her," Pamela interrupted, "you'd have seen exactly where the unnaturalness . . . "

"Forward!" he called and, still holding her arm, he steered her on across the Piazza.

She suffered herself to be conducted blindly. "It came out in the way she spoiled me," she explained, raising her voice against the clatter of a passing lorry. "It's so difficult to explain, though; because it's something I felt. I mean, I've never really tried to put it into words till now. But it was as if . . . as if she weren't just herself spoiling me, but the picture of a young mother—do you see what I mean?—spoiling the picture of a little girl. Even as a child I kind of felt it wasn't quite as it should be. Later on I began to *know* it too, here." She tapped her forehead. "Particularly after father's death, when I was beginning to grow up. There were times when it was almost like listening to recitations—dreadful. One feels so blushy and prickly; you know the feeling."

He nodded. "Yes, I know. Awful!"

"Awful," she repeated. "So you can understand what a beast I felt, when it took me that way. So disloyal, I mean. So ungrateful. Because she was being so wonderfully sweet to me. You've no idea. But it was just when she was being her sweetest that I got the feeling worst. I shall never forget when she made me call her Clare—that was her Christian name. 'Because we're going to be companions,' she said, and all that sort of thing. Which was simply too sweet and too nice of her. But if you'd heard the way she said it! So dreadfully unnatural. I mean, it was almost as bad as Aunt Edith reading *Prospice*. And yet I know she meant it, I know she wanted me to be her companion. But somehow something kind of went wrong on the way between the wanting and the saying. And then the doing seemed to go just as wrong as the saying. She always wanted to do things excitingly, romantically, like in a play. But you can't *make* things be exciting and romantic, can you?" Fanning shook his head. "She wanted to kind of force things to be thrilling by thinking and wishing, like Christian Science. But it doesn't work. We had wonderful times together; but she always tried to make out that they were more wonderful than they really were. Which only made them less wonderful. Going to the Paris Opera on a gala night is wonderful; but it's never as wonderful as when Rastignac goes, is it?"

"I should think it wasn't!" he agreed. "What an insult to Balzac to imagine that it could be!"

"And the real thing's less wonderful," she went on, "when you're being asked all the time to see it as Balzac, and to *be* Balzac yourself. When you aren't anything of the kind. Because, after all, what am I? Just good, ordinary, middle-class English."

She pronounced the words with a kind of defiance. Fanning imagined that the defiance was for him and, laughing, prepared to pick up the ridiculous little glove. But the glove was not for him; Pamela had thrown it down to a memory, to a ghost, to one of her own sceptical and mocking selves. It had been on the last day of their last stay together in Paris—that exciting, exotic Paris of poor Clare's imagination, to which their tickets from London never seemed quite to take them. They had gone to lunch at La Pérouse. "Such a marvellous, *fantastic* restaurant! It makes you feel as though you were back in the Second Empire." (Or was it the First Empire? Pamela could not exactly remember.) The rooms were so crowded with Americans, that it was with some difficulty that they secured a table. "We'll have a marvellous lunch," Clare had said, as she unfolded her napkin. "And some day, when you're in Paris with your lover, you'll come here and order just the same things as we're having to-day. And perhaps you'll think of me. Will you, darling?" And she had smiled at her daughter with that intense, expectant expression that was so often on her face, and the very memory of which made Pamela feel subtly uncomfortable. "How should I ever forget?" she had answered, laying her hand on her mother's and smiling. But after a second her eyes had wavered away from that fixed look, in which the intensity had remained as desperately on the stretch, the expectancy as wholly unsatisfied, as hungrily insatiable as ever. The waiter, thank goodness, had created a timely diversion; smiling at him confidentially, almost amorously, Clare had ordered like a princess in a novel of high life. The bill, when it came, was enormous. Clare had had to scratch the bottom of her purse for the last stray piece of nickel. "It looks as though we should have to carry our own bags at Calais and Dover. I didn't realize I'd run things so fine." Pamela had looked at the bill. "But, Clare," she had protested, looking up again at her mother with an expression of genuine horror, "it's wicked! Two hundred and sixty francs for a lunch! It wasn't worth it." The blood had risen darkly into Clare's face. "How can you be so disgustingly *bourgeoise,* Pamela? So crass, so crawling?" Incensed by the heaping up of this abuse, "I think it's stupid to do things one can't afford," the girl had answered; "stupid and vulgar." Trembling with rage, Clare had risen to her feet. "I'll never take you out again. Never." (How often since then Pamela had recalled that terribly prophetic word!) "You'll never understand life, you'll never be anything but a sordid little middle-class Englishwoman. Never, never." And she had swept out of the room, like an insulted queen. Overheard by Pamela, as she undignifiedly followed, "Gee!" an American voice had remarked, "it's a regular cat-fight."

The sound of another, real voice overlaid the remembered Middle Western accents.

"But after all," Fanning was saying, "it's better to be a good ordinary bourgeois than a bad ordinary bohemian, or a sham aristocrat, or a second-rate intellectual. . . . "

"I'm not even third-rate," said Pamela mournfully. There had been a time when, under the influence of the now abhorred Miss Huss, she had thought she would like to go up to Oxford and read Greats. But Greek grammar was so awful . . . "Not even fourth-rate."

"Thank goodness" said Fanning. "Do you know what third- and fourth-rate intellectuals are? They're professors of philology and organic chemistry at the minor universities, they're founders and honorary life presidents of the Nuneaton Poetry Society and the Baron's Court Debating Society; they're the people who organize and sedulously attend all those Conferences for promoting international goodwill and the spread of culture that are perpetually being held at Buda-Pesth and Prague and Stockholm. Admirable and indispensable creatures, of course! But impossibly dreary; one simply cannot have any relations with them. And how virtuously they disapprove of those of us who have something better to do than disseminate culture or foster goodwill—those of us who are concerned, for example, with creating beauty—like me; or, like you, my child, in deliciously *being* beauty."

Pamela blushed with pleasure, and for that reason felt it necessary immediately to protest. "All the same," she said, "it's rather humiliating not to be able to do anything but be. I mean, even a cow can be."

"Damned well, too," said Fanning. "If I *were* as intensely as a cow *is,* I'd be uncommonly pleased with myself. But this is getting almost too metaphysical. And do you realize what the time is?" He held out his watch; it was ten past one. "And where we are? At the Tiber. We've walked miles." He waved his hand; a passing taxi swerved in to the pavement beside them. "Let's go and eat some lunch. You're free?"

"Well . . . " She hesitated. It was marvellous, of course; so marvellous that she felt she ought to refuse. "If I'm not a bore. I mean, I don't want to impose . . . I mean . . . "

"You mean you'll come and have lunch. Good. Do you like marble halls and bands? Or local colour?"

Pamela hesitated. She remembered her mother once saying that Valadier and the Ulpia were the *only* two restaurants in Rome.

"Personally," Fanning went on, "I'm slightly avaricious about marble halls. I rather resent spending four times as much as eating about two-thirds as well. But I'll overcome my avarice if you prefer them."

Pamela duly voted for local colour; he gave an address to the driver and they climbed into the cab.

"It's a genuinely Roman place," Fanning explained. "I hope you'll like it."

"Oh, I'm sure I shall." All the same, she did rather wish they were going to Valadier's.

3

Fanning's old friend, Dodo del Grillo, was in Rome for that one night and had urgently summoned him to dine. His arrival was loud and exclamatory.

"Best of all possible Dodos!" he cried, as he advanced with outstretched hands across the enormous baroque saloon. "What an age! But what a pleasure!"

"At last, Miles," she said reproachfully; he was twenty minutes late.

"But I know you'll forgive me." And laying his two hands on her shoulders he bent down and kissed her. He made a habit of kissing all his women friends.

"And even if I didn't forgive, you wouldn't care two pins."

"Not one." He smiled his most charming smile. "But if it gives you the smallest pleasure, I'm ready to say I'd be inconsolable." His hands still resting on her shoulders, he looked at her searchingly, at arm's length. "Younger than ever," he concluded.

"I couldn't look as young as you do," she answered. "You know, Miles, you're positively indecent. Like Dorian Gray. What's your horrible secret?"

"Simply Mr. Hornibrooke," he explained. "The culture of the abdomen. So much more important than the culture of the mind." Dodo only faintly smiled; she had heard the joke before. Fanning was sensitive to smiles; he changed the subject. "And where's the marquis?" he asked.

The marchesa shrugged her shoulders. Her husband was one of those dear old friends whom somehow one doesn't manage to see anything of nowadays. "Filippo's in Tanganyika," she explained. "Hunting lions."

"While you hunt them at home. And with what success! You've bagged what's probably the finest specimen in Europe this evening. Congratulations!"

"*Merci, cher maître!*" she laughed. "Shall we go in to dinner?"

The words invited, irresistibly. "If only I had the right to answer: *Oui, chère maîtresse!*" Though as a matter of fact, he reflected, he had never really found her at all interesting in that way. A woman without temperament. But very pretty once—that time (how many years ago?) when there had been that picnic on the river at Bray, and he had drunk a little too much champagne. "If only!" he repeated; and then was suddenly struck by a grotesque thought. Suppose she were to say yes, now—now! "If only I had the right!"

"But luckily," said Dodo, turning back towards him, as she passed through the monumental door into the dining-room, "luckily you haven't the right. You ought to congratulate me on my immense good sense. Will you sit there?"

"Oh, I'll congratulate. I'm always ready to congratulate people who have sense." He unfolded his napkin. "And to condole." Now that he knew himself safe, he could condole as much as he liked. "What you must have suffered, my poor sensible Dodo, what you must have missed!"

"Suffered less," she answered, "and missed more unpleasantnesses than the women who didn't have the sense to say no."

"What a mouthful of negatives! But that's how sensible people always talk about love—in terms of negatives. Never of positives; they ignore those and go about sensibly avoiding the discomforts. Avoiding the pleasures and exultations too, poor sensible idiots! Avoiding all that's valuable and significant. But it's always like that. The human soul is a fried whiting. (What excellent red mullet this is, by the way! Really excellent.) Its tail is in its mouth. All progress finally leads back to the beginning again. The most sensible people—dearest Dodo, believe me—are the most foolish. The most intellectual are the stupidest. I've never met a really good metaphysician, for example, who wasn't in one way or another bottomlessly stupid. And as for the really spiritual people, look what they revert to. Not merely to silliness and stupidity, but finally to crass non-existence. The highest spiritual state is ecstasy, which is just not being there at all. No, no; we're all fried whitings. Heads are invariably tails."

"In which case," said Dodo, "tails must also be heads. So that if you want to make intellectual or spiritual progress, you must behave like a beast—is that it?"

Fanning held up his hand. "Not at all. If you rush too violently towards the tail, you run the risk of shooting down the whiting's open mouth into its stomach, and even further. The wise man . . . "

"So the whitings are fried without being cleaned?"

"In parables," Fanning answered reprovingly, "whitings are always fried that way. The wise man, as I was saying, oscillates lightly from head to tail and back again. His whole existence—or shall we be more frank and say 'my' whole existence?—is one continual oscillation. I am never too consistently sensible, like you; or too consistently feather-headed like some of my other friends. In a word," he wagged a finger, "I oscillate."

Tired of generalizations, "And where exactly," Dodo enquired, "have you oscillated to at the moment? You've left me without your news so long. . . . "

"Well, at the moment," he reflected aloud, "I suppose you might say I was at a dead point between desire and renunciation, between sense and sensuality."

"Again?" She shook her head. "And who is she this time?"

Fanning helped himself to asparagus before replying, "Who is she?" he echoed. "Well, to begin with, she's the writer of admiring letters."

Dodo made a grimace of disgust. "What a horror!" For some reason she felt it necessary to be rather venomous about this new usurper of Fanning's heart. "Vamping by correspondence—it's really the lowest . . . "

"Oh, I agree," he said. "On principle and in theory I entirely agree."

"Then why . . . " she began, annoyed by his agreement; but he interrupted her.

"Spiritual adventuresses," he said. "That's what they generally are, the women who write you letters. Spiritual adventuresses. I've suffered a lot from them in my time."

"I'm sure you have."

"They're a curious type," he went on, ignoring her sarcasms. "Curious and rather horrible. I prefer the good old-fashioned vampire. At least one knew where one stood with her. There she was—out for money, for power, for a good time, occasionally, perhaps, for sensual satisfactions. It was all entirely above-board and obvious. But with the spiritual adventuress, on the contrary, everything's most horribly turbid and obscure and slimy. You see, she doesn't want money or the commonplace good time. She wants Higher Things—damn her neck! Not large pearls and a large motor-car, but a large soul—that's what she pines for: a large soul and a large intellect, and a huge philosophy, and enormous culture, and out sizes in great thoughts."

Dodo laughed. "You're fiendishly cruel, Miles."

"Cruelty can be a sacred duty," he answered. "Besides, I'm getting a little of my own back. If you knew what these spiritual vamps had done to me! I've been one of their appointed victims. Yes, appointed; for, you see, they can't have their Higher Things without attaching themselves to a Higher Person."

"And are you one of the Higher People, Miles?"

"Should I be dining here with you, my dear, if I weren't?" And without waiting for Dodo's answer, "They attach themselves like lice," he went on. "The contact with the Higher Person makes them feel high themselves; it magnifies them, it gives them significance, it satisfies their parasitic will to power. In the past they could have gone to religion—fastened themselves on the nearest priest (that's what the priest was there for), or sucked the spiritual blood of some saint. Nowadays they've got no professional victims; only a few charlatans and swamis and higher-thought-mongers. Or alternatively the artists. Yes, the artists. They find our souls particularly juicy. What I've suffered! Shall I ever forget that American woman who got so excited by my book on Blake that she came specially to Tunis to see me? She had an awful way of opening her mouth very wide when she talked, like a fish. You were perpetually seeing her tongue; and, what made it worse, her tongue was generally white. Most distressing. And how the tongue wagged! In spite of its whiteness. Wagged like mad, and mostly about the Divine Mind."

"The Divine Mind?"

He nodded. "It was her speciality. In Rochester, N.Y., where she lived, she was never out of touch with it. You've no idea what a lot of Divine Mind there is floating about in Rochester, particularly in the neighbourhood of women with busy husbands and incomes of over fifteen thousand dollars. If only she could have stuck to the Divine Mind! But the Divine Mind has one grave defect: it won't make love to you. That was why she'd come all the way to Tunis in search of a merely human specimen."

"And what did you do about it?"

"Stood it nine days and then took the boat to Sicily. Like a thief in the night. The wicked flee, you know. God, how they can flee!"

"And she?"

"Went back to Rochester, I suppose. But I never opened any more of her letters. Just dropped them into the fire whenever I saw the writing. Ostrichism—it's the only rational philosophy of conduct. According to the Freudians we're all unconsciously trying to get back to . . . "

"But poor woman!" Dodo burst out. "She must have suffered."

"Nothing like what I suffered. Besides, she had the Divine Mind to go back to; which was her version of the Freudians' pre-natal . . . "

"But I suppose you'd encouraged her to come to Tunis?"

Reluctantly, Fanning gave up his Freudians. "She could write good letters," he admitted. "Inexplicably good, considering what she was at close range."

"But then you treated her abominably."

"But if you'd seen her, you'd realize how abominably she'd treated me."

"You?"

"Yes, abominably—by merely existing. She taught me to be very shy of letters. That was why I was so pleasantly surprised this morning when my latest correspondent suddenly materialized at Cook's. Really ravishing. One could forgive her everything for the sake of her face and that charming body. Everything, even the vamping. For a vamp I suppose she is, even this one. That is, if a woman *can* be a spiritual adventuress when she's so young and pretty and well-made. Absolutely and *sub specie aeternitatis,* I suppose she can. But from the very sublunary point of view of the male victim, I doubt whether, at twenty-one . . . "

"Only twenty-one?" Dodo was disapproving. "But Miles!"

Fanning ignored her interruption. "And another thing you must remember," he went on, "is that the spiritual vamp who's come of age this year is not at all the same as the spiritual vamp who came of age fifteen, twenty, twenty-five years ago. She doesn't bother much about Mysticism, or the Lower Classes, or the Divine Mind, or any nonsense of that sort. No, she goes straight to the real point—the point which the older vamps approached in such a tiresomely circuitous fashion—she goes straight to herself. But straight!" He stabbed the air with his fruit-knife. "A bee-line. Oh, it has a certain charm that directness. But whether it won't be rather frightful when they're older is another question. But then almost everything is rather frightful when people are older."

"Thank you," said Dodo. "And what about you?"

"Oh, an old satyr," he answered with that quick, brilliantly mysterious smile of his. "A superannuated faun. I know it; only too well. But at the same time, most intolerably, a Higher Person. Which is what draws the spiritual vamps. Even the youngest ones. Not to talk to me about the Divine Mind, of course, or their views about Social Reform. But about themselves. Their Individualities, their Souls, their Inhibitions, their Unconsciouses, their Pasts, their Futures. For them, the Higher Things are all frankly and nakedly personal. And the function of the Higher Person is to act as a sort of psychoanalytical father confessor. He exists to tell them all about their strange and wonderful psyches. And meanwhile, of course, his friendship inflates their egotism. And if there should be any question of love, what a personal triumph!"

"Which is all very well," objected Dodo. "But what about the old satyr? Wouldn't it also be a bit of a triumph for him? You know, Miles," she added gravely, "it would really be scandalous if you were to take advantage . . . "

"But I haven't the slightest intention of taking any advantages. If only for my own sake. Besides, the child is too ingenuously absurd. The most hair-raising theoretical knowledge of life, out of books. You should hear her prattling away about inverts and perverts and birth control—but prattling from unplumbed depths of innocence and practical ignorance. Very queer. And touching too. Much more touching than the old-fashioned innocences of the young creatures who thought babies were brought by storks. Knowing all about love and lust, but in the same way as one knows all about quadratic equations. And her knowledge of the other aspects of life is really of the same kind. What she's seen of the world she's seen in her mother's company. The worst guide imaginable, to judge from the child's account. (Dead now, incidentally.) The sort of woman who could never live on top gear, so to speak—only at one or two imaginative removes from the facts. So that, in her company, what was nominally real life became actually just literature—yet more literature. Bad, inadequate Balzac in flesh and blood instead of genuine, good Balzac out of a set of nice green volumes. The child realizes it herself. Obscurely, of course; but distressfully. It's one of the reasons why she's applied to me: she hopes I can explain what's wrong. And correct it in practice. Which I won't do in any drastic manner, I promise you. Only mildly, by precept—that is, if I'm not too bored to do it at all."

"What's the child's name?" Dodo asked.

"Pamela Tarn."

"Tarn? But was her mother by any chance Clare Tarn?"

He nodded. "That was it. She even made her daughter call her by her Christian name. The companion stunt."

"But I used to know Clare Tarn quite well," said Dodo in an astonished, feeling voice. "These last years I'd hardly seen her. But when I was more in London just after the War . . . "

"But this begins to be interesting," said Fanning. "New light on my little friend. . . . "

"Whom I absolutely forbid you," said Dodo emphatically, "to . . . "

"Tamper with the honour of," he suggested. "Let's phrase it as nobly as possible."

"No, seriously, Miles. I really won't have it. Poor Clare Tarn's daughter. If I didn't have to rush off to-morrow I'd ask her to come and see me, so as to warn her."

Fanning laughed. "She wouldn't thank you. And besides, if any one is to be warned, I'm the one who's in danger. But I shall be firm, Dodo—a rock. I won't allow her to seduce me."

"You're incorrigible, Miles. But mind, if you dare . . . "

"But I won't. Definitely." His tone was reassuring. "Meanwhile I must hear something about the mother."

The marchesa shrugged her shoulders. "A woman who couldn't live on top gear. You've really said the last word."

"But I want first words," he answered. "It's not the verdict that's interesting. It's the whole case, it's all the evidence. You're *sub-poenaed,* my dear. Speak up."

"Poor Clare!"

"Oh, *nil nisi bonum,* of course, if that's what disturbs you."

"She'd have so loved it to be not *bonum,* poor dear!" said the marchesa, tempering her look of vague condolence with a little smile. "That was her great ambition—to be thought rather wicked. She'd have liked to have the reputation of a vampire. Not a spiritual one, mind you. The other sort. Lola Montes—that was her ideal."

"It's an ideal," said Fanning, "that takes some realizing, I can tell you."

Dodo nodded. "And that's what she must have found out, pretty soon. She wasn't born to be a fatal woman; she lacked the gifts. No staggering beauty, no mysterious fascination or intoxicating vitality. She was just very charming, that was all; and at the same time rather impossible and absurd. So that there weren't any aspiring victims to be fatal to. And a vampire without victims is—well, *what*?"

"Certainly not a vampire," he concluded.

"Except, of course, in her own imagination, if she chooses to think so. In her own imagination Clare certainly was a vampire."

"Reduced, in fact, to being her own favourite character in fiction."

"Precisely. You always find the phrase."

"Only too fatally!" He made a little grimace. "I often wish I didn't. The luxury of being inarticulate! To be able to wallow indefinitely long in every feeling and sensation, instead of having to clamber out at once on to a hard, dry, definite phrase. But what about your Clare?"

"Well, she started, of course, by being a riddle to me. Unanswerable, or rather answerable, answered, but so very strangely that I was still left wondering. I shall never forget the first time Filippo and I went to dine there. Poor Roger Tarn was still alive then. While the men were drinking their port, Clare and I were alone in the drawing-room. There was a little chit-chat, I remember, and then, with a kind of determined desperation, as though she'd that second screwed herself up to jumping off the Eiffel Tower, suddenly, out of the blue, she asked me if I'd ever had one of those *wonderful* Sicilian peasants—I can't possibly reproduce the tone, the expression—as a lover. I was a bit taken aback, I must confess. 'But we don't live in Sicily,' was the only thing I could think of answering—too idiotically! 'Our estates are all in Umbria and Tuscany.' 'But the Tuscans are *superb* creatures too,' she insisted. Superb, I agreed. But, as it happens, I don't have affairs with even the superbest peasants. Nor with anybody else, for that matter. Clare was dreadfully disappointed. I think she'd expected the most romantic confidences—moonlight and mandolines and *stretti, stretti, nell'estasì d'amor.* She was really very ingenuous. 'Do you mean to say you've really never . . . ' she insisted. I ought to have got angry, I suppose; but it was all so ridiculous, that I never thought of it. I just said, 'Never,' and felt as though I were refusing her a favour. But she made up for my churlishness by being lavish to herself. But lavish! You can't imagine what a tirade she let fly at me. How *wonderful* it was to get away from self-conscious, complicated, sentimental love! How profoundly *satisfying* to feel oneself at the mercy of the dumb, dark forces of physical passion! How *intoxicating* to humiliate one's culture and one's class feeling before some *magnificent* primitive, some *earthily* beautiful satyr, some *divine* animal! And so on, *crescendo*. And it ended with her telling me the story of her *extraordinary* affair with—was it a gamekeeper? or a young farmer? I forget. But there was something about rabbit-shooting in it, I know."

"It sounds like a chapter out of George Sand."

"It was."

"Or still more, I'm afraid," he said, making a wry face, "like a most deplorable parody of my *Endymion and the Moon*."

"Which I've never read, I'm ashamed to say."

"You should, if only to understand this Clare of yours."

"I will. Perhaps I'd have solved her more quickly, if I'd read it at the time. As it was I could only be amazed—and a little horrified. That rabbit-shooter!" She shook her head. "He ought to have been so romantic. But I could only think of that awful yellow kitchen soap he'd be sure to wash himself with, or perhaps carbolic, so that he'd smell like washed dogs— dreadful! And the flannel shirts, not changed quite often enough. And the hands, so horny, with very short nails, perhaps broken. No, I simply couldn't understand her."

"Which is to your discredit, Dodo, if I may say so."

"Perhaps. But you must admit, I never pretended to be anything but what I am—a perfectly frivolous and respectable member of the upper classes. With a taste, I must confess, for the scandalous. Which was one of the reasons, I suppose, why I became so intimate with poor Clare. I was really fascinated by her confidences."

"Going on the tiles vicariously, eh?"

"Well, if you choose to put it grossly and vulgarly. . . . "

"Which I *do* choose," he interposed. "To be tactfully gross and appositely vulgar—that, my dear, is one of the ultimate artistic refinements. One day I shall write a monograph on the aesthetics of vulgarity. But meanwhile shall we say that you were inspired by an intense scientific curiosity to . . . "

Dodo laughed. "One of the tiresome things about you, Miles, is that one can never go on being angry with you."

"Yet another subject for a monograph!" he answered, and his smile was at once confidential and ironical, affectionate and full of mockery. "But let's hear what the scientific curiosity elicited?"

"Well, to begin with, a lot of really rather embarrassingly intimate confidences and questions, which I needn't repeat."

"No, don't. I know what those feminine conversations are. I have a native modesty. . . . "

"Oh, so have I. And, strangely enough, so had Clare. But somehow she wanted to outrage herself. You felt it all the time. She always had that desperate jumping-off-the-Eiffel-Tower manner, when she began to talk like that. It was a kind of martyrdom. But enjoyable. Perversely." Dodo shook her head. "Very puzzling. I used to have to make quite an effort to change the conversation from gynaecology to romance. Oh, those lovers of hers! Such stories! The most fantastic adventures in East End opium dens, in aeroplanes, and even, I remember (it was that very hot summer of 'twenty-two), even in a refrigerator!"

"My dear!" protested Fanning.

"Honestly! I'm only repeating what she told me."

"But do you mean to say you believed her?"

"Well, by that time, I must admit, I was beginning to be rather sceptical.

You see, I could never elicit the names of these creatures. Nor any detail. It was as though they didn't exist outside the refrigerator and the aeroplane."

"How many of them were there?"

"Only two at that particular moment. One was a Grand Passion, and the other a Caprice. A Caprrice," she repeated, rolling the r. "It was one of poor Clare's favourite words. I used to try and pump her. But she was mum. 'I want them to be *mysterious,'* she told me the last time I pressed her for details, 'anonymous, without an *état civil*. Why should I show you their passports and identity cards?' 'Perhaps they haven't got any,' I suggested. Which was malicious. I could see she was annoyed. But a week later she showed me their photographs. There they were; the camera cannot lie; I had to be convinced. The Grand Passion, I must say, was a very striking-looking creature. Thin-faced, worn, a bit Roman and sinister. The Caprice was more ordinarily the nice young Englishman. Rather childish and simple, Clare explained; and she gave me to understand that she was initiating him. It was the other, the Grand P., who thought of such refinements as the refrigerator. Also, she now confided to me for the first time, he was mildly a sadist. Having seen his face, I could believe it. 'Am I ever likely to meet him?' I asked. She shook her head. He moved in a very different world from mine."

"A rabbit-shooter?" Fanning asked.

"No: an intellectual. That's what I gathered."

"Golly!"

"So there was not the slightest probability, as you can see, that *I* should ever meet him," Dodo laughed. "And yet almost the first face I saw on leaving Clare that afternoon was the Grand P.'s."

"Coming to pay his sadistic respects?"

"Alas for poor Clare, no. He was behind glass in the show-case of a photographer in the Brompton Road, not a hundred yards from the Tarns' house in Ovington Square. The identical portrait. I marched straight in. 'Can you tell me who that is?' But it appears that photography is done under the seal of confession. They wouldn't say. Could I order a copy? Well, yes, as a favour, they'd let me have one. Curiously enough, they told me, as they were taking down my name and address, another lady had come in only two or three days before and also ordered a copy. 'Not by any chance a rather tall lady with light auburn hair and a rather amusing mole on the left cheek?' That did sound rather like the lady. 'And with a very confidential manner,' I suggested, 'as though you were her oldest friends?' Exactly, exactly; they were unanimous. That clinched it. Poor Clare, I thought, as I walked on towards the Park, poor, poor Clare!"

There was a silence.

"Which only shows," said Fanning at last, "how right the Church has always been to persecute literature. The harm we imaginative writers do! Enormous! We ought all to be on the Index, every one. Consider your Clare, for example. If it hadn't been for books, she'd never have known that such things as passion and sensuality and perversity even existed. Never."

"Come, come," she protested.

But, "Never," Fanning repeated. "She was congenitally as cold as a fish; it's obvious. Never had a spontaneous, untutored desire in her life. But she'd read a lot of books. Out of which she'd fabricated a theory of passion and perversity. Which she then consciously put into practice."

"Or rather didn't put into practice. Only day-dreamed that she did."

He nodded. "For the most part. But sometimes, I don't mind betting, she realized the day-dreams in actual life. Desperately, as you so well described it, with her teeth clenched and her eyes shut, as though she were jumping off the Eiffel Tower. That rabbit-shooter, for instance. . . . "

"But do you think the rabbit-shooter really existed?"

"Perhaps not that particular one. But *a* rabbit-shooter, perhaps several rabbit-shooters—at one time or another, I'm sure, they genuinely existed. Though never *genuinely,* of course, for her. For her, it's obvious, they were just phantoms, like the other inhabitants of her dreamery. Phantoms of flesh and blood, but still phantoms. I see her as a kind of Midas, turning everything she touched into imagination. Even in the embraces of a genuine, solid rabbit-shooter, she was still only indulging in her solitary sultry dream—a dream inspired by Shakespeare, or Mrs. Barclay, or the Chevalier de Nerciat, or D'Annunzio, or whoever her favourite author may have been."

"Miles Fanning, perhaps," Dodo mockingly suggested.

"Yes, I feared as much."

"What a responsibility!"

"Which I absolutely refuse to accept. What have I ever written but solemn warnings against the vice of imagination? Sermons against mental licentiousness of every kind—intellectual licentiousness, mystical licentiousness, fantastic-amorous licentiousness. No, no. I'll accept no responsibility. Or at least no special responsibility—only the generic responsibility of being an imaginative author, the original sin of writing in such a way as to influence people. And when I say 'influence,' of course I don't really mean *influence.* Because a writer can't influence people, in the sense of making them think and feel and act as he does. He can only influence them to be more, or less, like one of their own selves. In other words, he's never understood. (Thank goodness! because it would be very humiliating to be really understood by one's readers.) What readers get out of him is never, finally, *his* ideas, but theirs. And when they try to imitate him or his creations, all that they can ever do is to act one of their own potential rôles. Take this particular case. Clare read and, I take it, was impressed. She took my warnings against mental licentiousness to heart and proceeded to do—what? Not to become a creature of spontaneous, unvitiated impulses—for the good reason that that wasn't in her power—but only to imagine that she was such a creature. She imagined herself a woman like the one I put into *Endymion and the Moon* and acted accordingly—or else didn't act, only dreamed; it makes very little difference. In a word, she did exactly what all my books told her not to do. Inevitably; it was her nature. I'd influenced her, yes. But she didn't become more like one of my heroines. She only became more intensely like herself. And then, you must remember, mine weren't the only books on her shelves. I think we can take it that she'd read *Les Liaisons Dangereuses* and Casanova and some biography, shall we say, of the Maréchal de Richelieu. So that those spontaneous unvitiated impulses—how ludicrous they are, anyhow, when you *talk* about them!—became identified in her mind with the most elegant forms of 'caprice'—wasn't that the word? She was a child of nature—but with qualifications. The kind of child of nature that lived at Versailles or on the Grand Canal about 1760. Hence those rabbit-shooters and hence those sadistic intellectuals, whether real or imaginary—and imaginary even when real. I may have been a favourite author. But I'm not responsible for the rabbit-shooters or the Grand Ps. Not more responsible than any one else. She'd heard of the existence of love before she'd read me. We're all equally to blame, from Homer downwards. Plato wouldn't have any of us in his Republic. He was quite right, I believe. Quite right."

"And what about the daughter?" Dodo asked, after a silence.

He shrugged his shoulders. "In reaction against the mother, so far as I could judge. In reaction, but also influenced by her, unconsciously. And the influence is effective because, after all, she's her mother's daughter and probably resembles her mother, congenitally. But consciously, on the surface, she knows she doesn't want to live as though she were in a novel. And yet can't help it, because that's her nature, that's how she was brought up. But she's miserable, because she realizes that fiction-life *is* fiction. Miserable and very anxious to get out—out through the covers of the novel into the real world."

"And are you her idea of the real world?" Dodo enquired.

He laughed, "Yes, I'm the real world. Strange as it may seem. And also, of course, pure fiction. The Writer, the Great Man—the Official Biographer's fiction, in a word. Or, better still, the autobiographer's fiction. Chateaubriand, shall we say. And her breaking out—that's fiction too. A pure Miles Fanningism, if ever there was one. And, poor child, she knows it. Which makes her so cross with herself. Cross with me too, in a curious obscure way. But at the same time she's thrilled. What a thrilling situation! And herself walking about in the middle of it. She looks on and wonders and wonders what the next instalment of the feuilleton's going to contain."

"Well, there's one thing we're quite certain it's not going to contain, aren't we? Remember your promise, Miles."

"I think of nothing else," he bantered.

"Seriously, Miles, seriously."

"I think of nothing else," he repeated in a voice that was the parody of a Shakespearean actor's.

Dodo shook her finger at him. "Mind," she said, "mind!" Then, pushing back her chair, "Let's move into the drawing-room," she went on. "We shall be more comfortable there."

4

"And to think," Pamela was writing in her diary, "how nervous I'd been beforehand, and the trouble I'd taken to work out the whole of our first meeting, question and answer, like the Shorter Catechism, instead of which I was like a fish in water, really at home, for the first time in my life, I believe. No, perhaps not more at home than with Ruth and Phyllis, but then they're girls, so they hardly count. Besides, when you've once been at home in the sea, it doesn't seem much fun being at home in a little glass bowl, which is rather unfair to Ruth and Phyllis, but after all it's not their fault and they can't help being little bowls, just as M. F. can't help being a sea, and when you've swum about a bit in all that intelligence and knowledge and really *devilish* understanding, well, you find the bowls rather narrow, though of course they're sweet little bowls and I shall always be very fond of them, especially Ruth. Which makes me wonder if what he said about Clare and me—unnatural by nature—is always true, because hasn't every unnatural person got somebody she can be natural with, or even that she can't help being natural with, like oxygen and that other stuff making water? Of course it's not guaranteed that you find the other person who makes you natural, and I think perhaps Clare never did find her person, because I don't believe it was Daddy. But in my case there's Ruth and Phyllis and now to-day M. F.; and he really proves it, because I *was* natural with him more than with any one, even though he did say I was unnatural by nature. No, I feel that if I were with him always, I should always be my *real* self, just kind of easily spouting, like those lovely fountains we went to look at this afternoon, not all tied up in knots and squirting about vaguely in every kind of direction, and muddy at that, but beautifully clear in a big gushing spout, like what Joan in *The Return of Eurydice* finally became when she'd escaped from that awful, awful man and found Walter. But does that mean I'm in love with him?"

Pamela bit the end of her pen and stared, frowning, at the page before her. Scrawled large in orange ink, the question stared back. Disquietingly and insistently stared. She remembered a phrase of her mother's. "But if you knew," Clare had cried (Pamela could *see* her, wearing the black afternoon dress from Patou, and there were yellow roses in the bowl on the table under the window), "if you knew what certain writers were to me! *Shrines*—there's no other word. I could worship the Tolstoy of Anna Karenina." But Harry Braddon, to whom the words were addressed, had laughed at her. And, though she hated Harry Braddon, so had Pamela, mockingly. For it was absurd; nobody was a shrine, nobody. And anyhow, what *was* a shrine? Nothing. Not nowadays, not when one had stopped being a child. She told herself these things with a rather unnecessary emphasis, almost truculently, in the style of the professional atheists in Hyde Park. One didn't worship—for the good reason that she herself once had worshipped. Miss Figgis, the classical mistress, had been her pash for more than a year. Which was why she had gone to Early Service so frequently in those days and been so keen to go up to Oxford and take Greats. (Besides, she had even, at that time, rather liked and admired Miss Huss. Ghastly old Hussy! It seemed incredible now.) But oh, that grammar! And Caesar was such a bore, and Livy still worse, and as for Greek . . . She had tried very hard for a time. But when Miss Figgis so obviously preferred that priggish little beast Kathleen, Pamela had just let things slide. The bad marks had come in torrents and old Hussy had begun being more sorrowful than angry, and finally more angry than sorrowful. But she hadn't cared. What made not caring easier was that she had her mother behind her. "I'm so delighted," was what Clare had said when she heard that Pamela had given up wanting to go to Oxford. "I'd have felt so terribly inferior if you'd turned out a blue-stocking. Having my frivolity rebuked by my own daughter!" Clare had always boasted of her frivolity. Once, under the influence of old Hussy and for the love of Miss Figgis, an earnest disapprover, Pamela had become an apostle of her mother's gospel. "After all," she had pointed out to Miss Figgis, "Cleopatra didn't learn Greek." And though Miss Figgis was able to point out, snubbingly, that the last of the Ptolemies had probably spoken nothing but Greek, Pamela could still insist that in principle she was quite right: Cleopatra hadn't learnt Greek, or what, if you were a Greek, corresponded to Greek. So why should she? She began to parade a violent and childish cynicism, a cynicism which was still (though she had learnt, since leaving school, to temper the ridiculous expression of it) her official creed. There were no shrines—though she sometimes, wistfully and rather shamefacedly, wished there were. One didn't, determinedly didn't worship. She herself might admire Fanning's books, *did* admire them, enormously. But as for worshipping—no, she absolutely declined. Clare had overdone it all somehow—as usual. Pamela was resolved that there should be no nonsense about *her* feelings.

"But does that mean I'm in love with him?" insisted the orange scrawl.

As though in search of an answer, Pamela turned back the pages of her diary (she had already covered nearly eight of them with her account of this memorable twelfth of June). "His face," she read, "is very brown, almost like an Arab's, except that he has blue eyes, as he lives mostly in the South, because he says that if you don't live in the sun, you go slightly mad, which is why people in the North, like us and the Germans and the Americans, are so tiresome, though of course you go still madder where there's too much sun, like in India, where they're even more hopeless. He's very good-looking and you don't think of him as being either old or young, but as just being there, like that, and the way he smiles is really very extraordinary, and so are his eyes, and I simply *adored* his white silk suit." But the question was not yet answered. His silk suit wasn't him, nor was his voice, even though he had "an awfully nice one, rather like that man who talks about books on the wireless, only nicer." She turned over a page. "But M. F. is different from most clever people," the orange scrawl proclaimed, "because he doesn't make you feel a fool, even when he does laugh at you, and never, which is so *ghastly* with men like Professor Cobley, talks down to you in that awful patient, gentle way, which makes you feel a million times more of a worm than being snubbed or ignored, because, if you have any pride, that sort of intelligence without tears is just loathsome, as though you were being given milk pudding out of charity. No, M. F. talks to you on the level, and the extraordinary thing is that, while he's talking to you and you're talking to him, you *are* on a level with him, or at any rate you feel as though you were, which comes to the same thing. He's like influenza, you catch his intelligence." Pamela let the leaves of the notebook flick past, one by one, under her thumb. The final words on the half-blank page once more stared at her, questioningly. "But does that mean I'm in love with him?" Taking her pen from between her teeth, "Certainly," she wrote, "I do find him terribly attractive physically." She paused for a moment to reflect, then added, frowning as though with the effort of raising an elusive fact from the depths of memory, of solving a difficult problem in algebra: "Because really, when he puts his hand on my shoulder, which would have been simply intolerable if any one else had done it, but somehow with him I didn't mind, I felt all thrilled with an absolute frisson." She ran her pen through the last word and substituted "thrill," which she underlined to make it seem less lamely a repetition. "Frisson" had been one of Clare's favourite words; hearing it pronounced in her mother's remembered voice, Pamela had felt a sudden mistrust of it; it seemed to cast a kind of doubt on the feelings it stood for, a doubt of which she was ashamed—it seemed so disloyal and the voice had sounded so startlingly, so heart-rendingly clear and near—but which she still couldn't help experiencing. She defended herself; "frisson" had simply had to go, because the thrill was genuine, absolutely genuine, she insisted. "For a moment," she went on, writing very fast, as though she were trying to run away from the sad, disagreeable thoughts that had intruded upon her, "I thought I was going to faint when he touched me, like when one's coming to after chloroform, which I've certainly never felt like with any one else." As a protest against the doubts inspired by that unfortunate frisson she underlined "never," heavily. Never; it was quite true. When Harry Braddon had tried to kiss her, she had been furious and disgusted—disgusting beast! Saddening and reproachful, Clare's presence hovered round her once more; Clare had liked Harry Braddon. Still, he was a beast. Pamela had never told her mother about that kiss. She shut her eyes excludingly and thought instead of Cecil Rudge, poor, timid, unhappy little Cecil, whom she liked so much, was so genuinely sorry for. But when, that afternoon at Aunt Edith's, when at last, after an hour's visibly laborious screwing to the sticking point, he had had the courage to take her hand and say "Pamela" and kiss it, she had just laughed, oh! unforgivably, but she simply couldn't help it; he was so ridiculous. Poor lamb, he had been terribly upset. "But I'm so sorry," she had gasped between the bursts of her laughter, "so dreadfully sorry. Please don't be hurt." But his face, she could see, was agonized. "Please! Oh, I feel so miserable." And she had gone off into another explosion of laughter which almost choked her. But when she could breathe again, she had run to him where he stood, averted and utterly unhappy, by the window, she had taken his hand and, when he still refused to look at her, had put her arm round his neck and kissed him. But the emotion that had filled her eyes with tears was nothing like passion. As for Hugh Davies—why, it certainly had been rather thrilling when Hugh kissed her. It had been thrilling, but certainly not to fainting point. But then had she *really* felt like fainting to-day? a small voice questioned. She drowned the small voice with the scratching of her pen. "Consult the oracles of passion," she wrote and, laying down her pen, got up and crossed the room. A copy of *The Return of Eurydice* was lying on the bed; she picked it up and turned over the pages. Here it was! "Consult the oracles of passion," she read aloud, and her own voice sounded, she thought, strangely oracular in the solitude. "A god speaks in them, or else a devil, one can never tell which beforehand, nor even, in most cases, afterwards. And, when all is said, does it very much matter? God and devil are equally supernatural, that is the important thing; equally supernatural and therefore, in this all too flatly natural world of sense and science and society, equally desirable, equally significant." She shut the book and walked back to the table. "Which is what he said this afternoon," she went on writing, "but in that laughing way, when I said I could never see why one shouldn't do what one liked, instead of all this Hussy and Hippo rigmarole about service and duty, and he said yes, that was what Rabelais had said" (there seemed to be an awful lot of "saids" in this sentence, but it couldn't be helped; she scrawled on); "which I pretended I'd read—why can't one tell the truth? particularly as I'd just been saying at the same time that one ought to say what one thinks as well as do what one likes; but it seems to be hopeless—and he said he entirely agreed, it was perfect, so long as you had the luck to like the sort of things that kept you on the right side of the prison bars and think the sort of things that don't get you murdered when you say them. And I said I'd rather say what I thought and do what I liked and be murdered and put in gaol than be a Hippo, and he said I was an idealist, which annoyed me and I said I certainly wasn't, all I was was some one who didn't want to go mad with inhibitions. And he laughed, and I wanted to quote him his own words about the oracles, but somehow it was so shy-making that I didn't. All the same, it's what I intensely feel, that one *ought* to consult the oracles of passion. And I shall consult them." She leaned back in her chair and shut her eyes. The orange question floated across the darkness: "But does that mean I'm in love with him?" The oracle seemed to be saying yes. But oracles, she resolutely refused to remember, can be rigged to suit the interests of the questioner. Didn't the admirer of *The Return of Eurydice* secretly *want* the oracle to say yes? Didn't she think she'd almost fainted, because she'd wished she'd almost fainted, because she'd come desiring to faint? Pamela sighed; then, with a gesture of decision, she slapped her notebook to and put away her pen. It was time to get ready for dinner; she bustled about efficiently and distractingly among her trunks. But the question returned to her as she lay soaking in the warm other-world of her bath. By the time she got out she had boiled herself to such a pitch of giddiness that she could hardly stand.

For Pamela, dinner in solitude, especially the public solitude of hotels, was a punishment. Companionlessness and compulsory silence depressed her. Besides, she never felt quite eye-proof; she could never escape from the obsession that every one was looking at her, judging, criticizing. Under a carapace of rather impertinent uncaringness she writhed distressfully. At Florence her loneliness had driven her to make friends with two not very young American women who were staying in her hotel. They were a bit earnest and good and dreary. But Pamela preferred even dreariness to solitude. She attached herself to them inseparably. They were touched. When she left for Rome, they promised to write to her, they made her promise to write to them. She was so young; they felt responsible; a steadying hand, the counsel of older friends. . . . Pamela had already received two steadying letters. But she hadn't answered them, never would answer them. The horrors of lonely dining cannot be alleviated by correspondence.

Walking down to her ordeal in the restaurant, she positively yearned for her dreary friends. But the hall was a desert of alien eyes and faces; and the waiter who led her through the hostile dining-room, had bowed, it seemed to her, with an ironical politeness, had mockingly smiled. She sat down haughtily at her table and almost wished she were under it. When the *sommelier* appeared with his list, she ordered half a bottle of something absurdly expensive, for fear he might think she didn't know anything about wine.

She had got as far as the fruit, when a presence loomed over her; she looked up. "You?" Her delight was an illumination; the young man was dazzled. "What marvellous luck!" Yet it was only Guy Browne, Guy whom she had met a few times at dances and found quite pleasant—that was all. "Think of your being in Rome!" She made him sit down at her table. When she had finished her coffee, Guy suggested that they should go and dance somewhere. They went. It was nearly three when Pamela got to bed. She had had a most enjoyable evening.

5

But how ungratefully she treated poor Guy when, next day at lunch, Fanning asked her how she had spent the evening! True, there were extenuating circumstances, chief among which was the fact that Fanning had kissed her when they met. By force of habit, he himself would have explained, if any one had asked him why, because he kissed every presentable face. Kissing was in the great English tradition. "It's the only way I can be like Chaucer," he liked to affirm. "Just as knowing a little Latin and less Greek is my only claim to resembling Shakespeare and as lying in bed till ten's the nearest I get to Descartes." In this particular case, as perhaps in every other particular case, the force of habit had been seconded by a deliberate intention; he was accustomed to women being rather in love with him, he liked the amorous atmosphere and could use the simplest as well as the most complicated methods to create it. Moreover he was an experimentalist, he genuinely wanted to see what would happen. What happened was that Pamela was astonished, embarrassed, thrilled, delighted, bewildered. And what with her confused excitement and the enormous effort she had made to take it all as naturally and easily as he had done, she was betrayed into what, in other circumstances, would have been a scandalous ingratitude. But when one has just been kissed, for the first time and at one's second meeting with him, kissed offhandedly and yet (she felt it) significantly, by Miles Fanning—actually Miles Fanning!—little men like Guy Browne do seem rather negligible, even though one did have a very good time with them the evening before.

"I'm afraid you must have been rather lonely last night," said Fanning, as they sat down to lunch. His sympathy hypocritically covered a certain satisfaction that it should be his absence that had condemned her to dreariness.

"No, I met a friend," Pamela answered with a smile which the inward comparison of Guy with the author of *The Return of Eurydice* had tinged with a certain amused condescendingness.

"A friend?" He raised his eyebrows. "*Amico* or *amica?* Our English is so discreetly equivocal. With this key Bowdler locked up his heart. But I apologize. *Co* or *ca?*"

"*Co.* He's called Guy Browne and he's here learning Italian to get into the Foreign Office. He's a nice boy." Pamela might have been talking about a favourite, or even not quite favourite, retriever. "Nice; but nothing very special. I mean, not in the way of intelligence." She shook her head patronizingly over Guy's very creditable First in History as a guttersnipe capriciously favoured by an archduke might learn in his protector's company to shake his head and patronizingly smile at the name of a marquis of only four or five centuries' standing. "He can dance, though," she admitted.

"So I suppose you danced with him?" said Fanning in a tone which, in spite of his amusement at the child's assumption of an aged superiority, he couldn't help making rather disobligingly sarcastic. It annoyed him to think that Pamela should have spent an evening, which he had pictured as dismally lonely, dancing with a young man.

"Yes, we danced," said Pamela, nodding.

"Where?"

"Don't ask me. We went to about six different places in the course of the evening."

"Of course you did," said Fanning almost bitterly. "Moving rapidly from one place to another and doing exactly the same thing in each—that seems to be the young's ideal of bliss."

Speaking as a young who had risen above such things, but who still had to suffer from the folly of her unregenerate contemporaries, "It's quite true," Pamela gravely confirmed.

"They go to Pekin to listen to the wireless and to Benares to dance the fox-trot. I've seen them at it. It's incomprehensible. And then the tooting up and down in automobiles, and the roaring up and down in aeroplanes, and the stinking up and down in motorboats. Up and down, up and down, just for the sake of not sitting still, of having never time to think or feel. No, I give them up, these young of yours." He shook his head. "But I'm becoming a minor prophet," he added; his good humour was beginning to return.

"But after all," said Pamela, "we're not *all* like that."

Her gravity made him laugh. "There's at least one who's ready to let herself be bored by a tiresome survivor from another civilization. Thank you, Pamela." Leaning across the table, he took her hand and kissed it. "I've been horribly ungrateful," he went on, and his face as he looked at her was suddenly transfigured by the bright enigmatic beauty of his smile. "If you knew how charming you looked!" he said; and it was true. That ingenuous face, those impertinent little breasts—charming. "And how charming you *were*! But of course you *do* know," a little demon prompted him to add: "no doubt Mr. Browne told you last night."

Pamela had blushed—a blush of pleasure, and embarrassed shyness, and excitement. What he had just said and done was more significant, she felt, even than the kiss he had given her when they met. Her cheeks burned; but she managed, with an effort, to keep her eyes unwaveringly on his. His last words made her frown. "He certainly didn't," she answered. "He'd have got his face smacked."

"Is that a delicate hint?" he asked. "If so," and he leaned forward, "here's the other cheek."

Her face went redder than ever. She felt suddenly miserable; he was only laughing at her. "Why do you laugh at me?" she said aloud, unhappily.

"But I wasn't," he protested. "I really did think you were annoyed."

"But why should I have been?"

"I can't imagine." He smiled. "But if you would have smacked Mr. Browne's face . . . "

"But Guy's quite different."

It was Fanning's turn to wince. "You mean he's young, while I'm only a poor old imbecile who needn't be taken seriously?"

"Why are you so stupid?" Pamela asked almost fiercely. "No, but I mean," she added in quick apology, "I mean . . . well, I don't care two pins about Guy. So you see, it would annoy me if he tried to push in, like that. Whereas with somebody who does mean something to me . . . " Pamela hesitated. "With *you*," she specified in a rather harsh, strained voice and with just that look of despairing determination, Fanning imagined, just that jumping-off-the-Eiffel-Tower expression, which her mother's face must have assumed in moments such as this, "it's quite different. I mean, with you of course I'm not annoyed. I'm pleased. Or at least I *was* pleased, till I saw you were just making a fool of me."

Touched and flattered, "But, my dear child," Fanning protested, "I wasn't doing anything of the kind. I meant what I said. And much more than I said," he added, in the teeth of the warning and reproachful outcry raised by his common sense. It was amusing to experiment, it was pleasant to be adored, exciting to be tempted (and how young she was, how perversely fresh!) There was even something quite agreeable in resisting temptation; it had the charms of a strenuous and difficult sport. Like mountain climbing. He smiled once more, consciously brilliant.

This time Pamela dropped her eyes. There was a silence which might have protracted itself uncomfortably, if the waiter had not broken it by bringing the *tagliatelle*. They began to eat. Pamela was all at once exuberantly gay.

After coffee they took a taxi and drove to the Villa Giulia. "For we mustn't," Fanning explained, "neglect your education."

"Mustn't we?" she asked. "I often wonder why we mustn't. Truthfully now, I mean without any hippoing and all that—why shouldn't I neglect it? Why should I go to this beastly museum?" She was preparing to play the cynical, boastfully unintellectual part which she had made her own. "Why?" she repeated truculently. Behind the rather vulgar lowbrow mask she cultivated wistful yearnings and concealed the uneasy consciousness of inferiority. "A lot of beastly old Roman odds and ends!" she grumbled; that was one for Miss Figgis.

"Roman?" said Fanning. "God forbid! Etruscan."

"Well, Etruscan, then; it's all the same, anyhow. Why shouldn't I neglect the Etruscans? I mean, what have they got to do with me—*me*?" And she gave her chest two or three little taps with the tip of a crooked forefinger.

"Nothing, my child," he answered. "Thank goodness, they've got absolutely nothing to do with you, or me, or anybody else."

"Then why . . . ?"

"Precisely for that reason. That's the definition of culture—knowing and thinking about things that have absolutely nothing to do with us. About Etruscans, for example; or the mountains on the moon; or cat's-cradle among the Chinese; or the Universe at large."

"All the same," she insisted, "I still don't see."

"Because you've never known people who weren't cultured. But make the acquaintance of a few practical business-men—the kind who have no time to be anything but alternately efficient and tired. Or of a few workmen from the big towns. (Country people are different; they still have the remains of the old substitutes for culture—religion, folk-lore, tradition. The town fellows have lost the substitutes without acquiring the genuine article.) Get to know those people; *they'll* make you see the point of culture. Just as the Sahara'll make you see the point of water. And for the same reason: they're arid."

"That's all very well; but what about people like Professor Cobley?"

"Whom I've happily never met," he said, "but can reconstruct from the expression on your face. Well, all that can be said about those people is: just try to imagine them if they'd never been irrigated. Gobi or Shamo."

"Well, perhaps." She was dubious.

"And anyhow the biggest testimony to culture isn't the soulless philistines—it's the soulful ones. My sweet Pamela," he implored, laying a hand on her bare brown arm, "for heaven's sake don't run the risk of becoming a soulful philistine."

"But as I don't know what that is," she answered, trying to persuade herself, as she spoke, that the touch of his hand was giving her a tremendous frisson—but it really wasn't.

"It's what the name implies," he said. "A person without culture who goes in for having a soul. An illiterate idealist. A Higher Thinker with nothing to think about but his—or more often, I'm afraid, *her*—beastly little personal feelings and sensations. They spend their lives staring at their own navels and in the intervals trying to find other people who'll take an interest and come and stare too. Oh, figuratively," he added, noticing the expression of astonishment which had passed across her face. "*En tout* bien, tout honneur. At least, sometimes and to begin with. Though I've known cases . . . " But he decided it would be better not to speak about the lady from Rochester, N.Y. Pamela might be made to feel that the cap fitted. Which it did, except that her little head was such a charming one. "In the end," he said, "they go mad, these soulful philistines. Mad with self-consciousness and vanity and egotism and a kind of hopeless bewilderment; for when you're utterly without culture, every fact's an isolated, unconnected fact, every experience is unique and unprecedented. Your world's made up of a few bright points floating about inexplicably in the midst of an unfathomable darkness. Terrifying! It's enough to drive any one mad. I've seen them, lots of them, gone utterly crazy. In the past they had organized religion, which meant that somebody had once been cultured for them, vicariously. But what with protestantism and the modernists, their philistinism's absolute now. They're alone with their own souls. Which is the worst companionship a human being can have. So bad that it sends you dotty. So beware, Pamela, beware! You'll go mad if you think only of what has something to do with you. The Etruscans will keep you sane." ˙

"Let's hope so." She laughed. "But aren't we there?"

The cab drew up at the door of the villa; they got out.

"And remember that the things that start with having nothing to do with you," said Fanning, as he counted out the money for the entrance tickets, "turn out in the long run to have a great deal to do with you. Because they become a part of you and you of them. A soul can't know or fully become itself without knowing and therefore to some extent becoming what isn't itself. Which it does in various ways. By loving, for example."

"You mean . . . ?" The flame of interest brightened in her eyes.

But he went on remorselessly. "And by thinking of things that have nothing to do with you."

"Yes, I see." The flame had dimmed again.

"Hence my concern about your education." He beckoned her through the turnstile into the museum. "A purely selfish concern," he added, smiling down at her. "Because I don't want the most charming of my young friends to grow into a monster, whom I shall be compelled to flee from. So resign yourself to the Etruscans."

"I resign myself," said Pamela, laughing. His words had made her feel happy and excited. "You can begin." And in a theatrical voice, like that which used to make Ruth go off into such fits of laughter, "I am all ears," she added, "as they say in the Best Books." She pulled off her hat and shook out the imprisoned hair.

To Fanning, as he watched her, the gesture brought a sudden shock of pleasure. The impatient, exuberant youthfulness of it! And the little head, so beautifully shaped, so gracefully and proudly poised on its long neck! And her hair was drawn back smoothly from the face to explode in a thick tangle of curls on the nape of the neck. Ravishing!

"All ears," she repeated, delightedly conscious of the admiration she was receiving.

"All ears." And almost meditatively, "But do you know," he went on,

"I've never even seen your ears. May I?" And without waiting for her permission, he lifted up the soft, goldy-brown hair that lay in a curve, drooping, along the side of her head.

Pamela's face violently reddened; but she managed none the less to laugh. "Are they as long and furry as you expected?" she asked.

He allowed the lifted hair to fall back into its place and, without answering her question, "I've always," he said, looking at her with a smile which she found disquietingly enigmatic and remote, "I've always had a certain fellow-feeling for those savages who collect ears and thread them on strings, as necklaces."

"But what a horror!" she cried out.

"You think so?" He raised his eyebrows.

But perhaps, Pamela was thinking, he was a sadist. In that book of Krafft-Ebbing's there had been a lot about sadists. It would be queer if he were . . .

"But what's certain," Fanning went on in another, business-like voice, "what's only too certain is that ears aren't culture. They've got too much to do with us. With me, at any rate. Much too much." He smiled at her again. Pamela smiled back at him, fascinated and obscurely a little frightened; but the fright was an element in the fascination. She dropped her eyes. "So don't let's waste any more time," his voice went on. "Culture to right of us, culture to left of us. Let's begin with this culture on the left. With the vases. They really have absolutely nothing to do with us."

He began and Pamela listened. Not very attentively, however. She lifted her hand and, under the hair, touched her ear. "A fellow-feeling for those savages." She remembered his words with a little shudder. He'd almost meant them. And "ears aren't culture. Too much to do with us. With me. Much too much." He'd meant that too, genuinely and whole-heartedly. And his smile had been a confirmation of the words; yes, and a comment, full of mysterious significance. What *had* he meant? But surely it was obvious what he had meant. Or wasn't it obvious?

The face she turned towards him wore an expression of grave attention. And when he pointed to a vase and said, "Look," she looked, with what an air of concentrated intelligence! But as for knowing what he was talking about! She went on confusedly thinking that he had a fellow-feeling for those savages, and that her ears had too much to do with him, much too much, and that perhaps he was in love with her, perhaps also that he was like those people in Krafft-Ebbing, perhaps . . . ; and it seemed to her that her blood must have turned into a kind of hot, red soda-water, all fizzy with little bubbles of fear and excitement.

She emerged, partially at least, out of this bubbly and agitated trance to hear him say, "Look at that, now." A tall statue towered over her. "The Apollo of Veii," he explained. "And really, you know, it *is* the most beautiful statue in the world. Each time I see it, I'm more firmly convinced of that."

Dutifully, Pamela stared. The God stood there on his pedestal, one foot advanced, erect in his draperies. He had lost his arms, but the head was intact and the strange Etruscan face was smiling, enigmatically smiling. Rather like *him,* it suddenly occurred to her.

"What's it made of?" she asked; for it was time to be intelligent.

"Terracotta. Originally coloured."

"And what date?"

"Late sixth century."

"B.C.?" she queried, a little dubiously, and was relieved when he nodded. It really would have been rather awful if it had been A.D. "Who by?"

"By Vulca, they say. But as that's the only Etruscan sculptor they know the name of . . . " He shrugged his shoulders, and the gesture expressed a double doubt—doubt whether the archaeologists were right and doubt whether it was really much good talking about Etruscan art to some one who didn't feel quite certain whether the Apollo of Veii was made in the sixth century before or after Christ.

There was a long silence. Fanning looked at the statue. So did Pamela, who also, from time to time, looked at Fanning. She was on the point, more than once, of saying something; but his face was so meditatively glum that, on each occasion, she changed her mind. In the end, however, the silence became intolerable.

"I think it's extraordinarily fine," she announced in the rather religious voice that seemed appropriate. He only nodded. The silence prolonged itself, more oppressive and embarrassing than ever. She made another and despairing effort. "Do you know, I think he's really rather like you. I mean, the way he smiles. . . . "

Fanning's petrified immobility broke once more into life. He turned towards her, laughing. "You're irresistible, Pamela."

"Am I?" Her tone was cold; she was offended. To be told you were irresistible always meant that you'd behaved like an imbecile child. But her conscience was clear; it was a gratuitous insult—the more intolerable since it had been offered by the man who, a moment before, had been saying that he had a fellow-feeling for those savages and that her ears had altogether *too* much to do with him.

Fanning noticed her sudden change of humour and obscurely divined the cause. "You've paid me the most irresistible compliment you could have invented," he said, doing his best to undo the effect of his words. For after all what did it matter, with little breasts like that and thin brown arms, if she did mix up the millenniums a bit? "You could hardly have pleased me more if you'd said I was another Rudolph Valentino."

Pamela had to laugh.

"But seriously," he said, "if you knew what this lovely God means to me, how much . . . "

Mollified by being once more spoken to seriously, "I think I can understand," she said in her most understanding voice.

"No, I doubt if you can." He shook his head. "It's a question of age, of the experience of a particular time that's not your time. I shall never forget when I came back to Rome for the first time after the War and found this marvellous creature standing here. They only dug him up in 'sixteen, you see. So there it was, a brand new experience, a new and apocalyptic voice out of the past. Some day I shall try to get it on to paper, all that this God has taught me." He gave a little sigh; she could see that he wasn't thinking about her any more; he was talking for himself. "Some day," he repeated. "But it's not ripe yet. You can't write a thing before it's ripe, before it wants to be written. But you can talk about it, you can take your mind for walks all round it and through it." He paused and, stretching out a hand, touched a fold of the God's sculptured garment, as though he were trying to establish a more intimate, more real connection with the beauty before him. "Not that what he taught me was fundamentally new," he went on slowly. "It's all in Homer, of course. It's even partially expressed in the archaic Greek sculpture. Partially. But Apollo here expresses it wholly. He's *all* Homer, *all* the ancient world, concentrated in a single lump of terracotta. That's his novelty. And then the circumstances gave him a special point. It was just after the War that I first saw him—just after the apotheosis and the logical conclusion of all the things Apollo *didn't* stand for. You can imagine how marvellously new he seemed by contrast. After that horrible enormity, he was a lovely symbol of the small, the local, the kindly. After all that extravagance of beastliness—yes, and all that extravagance of heroism and self-sacrifice—he seemed so beautifully sane. A God who doesn't admit the separate existence of either heroics or diabolics, but somehow includes them in his own nature and turns them into something else—like two gases combining to make a liquid. Look at him," Fanning insisted. "Look at his face, look at his body, see how he stands. It's obvious. He's neither the God of heroics, nor the God of diabolics. And yet it's equally obvious that he knows all about both, that he includes them, that he combines them into a third essence. It's the same with Homer. There's no tragedy in Homer. He's pessimistic, yes; but never tragic. His heroes aren't heroic in our sense of the word; they're men." (Pamela took a very deep breath; if she had opened her mouth, it would have been a yawn.) "In fact, you can say there aren't any heroes in Homer. Nor devils, nor sins. And none of our aspiring spiritualities, and, of course, none of our horrible, nauseating disgusts— because they're the complement of being spiritual, they're the tails to its heads. You couldn't have had Homer writing 'the expense spirit in a waste of shame.' Though, of course, with Shakespeare, it may have been physio- logical; the passion violent and brief, and then the most terrible reaction. It's the sort of thing that colours a whole life, a whole work. Only of course one's never allowed to say so. All that one isn't allowed to say!" He laughed. Pamela also laughed. "But physiology or no physiology," Fanning went on, "he couldn't have written like that if he'd lived before the great split—the great split that broke life into spirit and matter, heroics and diabolics, virtue and sin and all the other accursed antitheses. Homer lived before the split; life hadn't been broken when he wrote. They're complete, his men and women, complete and real; for he leaves nothing out, he shirks no issue, even though there is no tragedy. He knows all about it—*all*." He laid his hand again on the statue. "And this God's his portrait. He's Homer, but with the Etruscan smile. Homer smiling at the sad, mysterious, beautiful absurdity of the world. The Greeks didn't see that divine absurdity as clearly as the Etruscans. Not even in Homer's day; and by the time you get to any sculptor who was anything like as accomplished as the man who made this, you'll find that they've lost it altogether. True, the earliest Greeks' God used to smile all right—or rather grin; for subtlety wasn't their strong point. But by the end of the sixth century they were already becoming a bit too heroic; they were developing those athlete's muscles and those tiresomely noble poses and damned superior faces. But our God here refused to be a prize-fighter or an actor-manager. There's no *terribiltà* about him, no priggishness, no sentimentality. And yet without being in the least pretentious, he's beautiful, he's grand, he's authentically divine. The Greeks took the road that led to Michelangelo and Bernini and Thorwaldsen and Rodin. A rake's progress. These Etruscans were on a better track. If only people had had the sense to follow it! Or at least get back to it. But nobody has, except perhaps old Maillol. They've all allowed themselves to be lured away. Plato was the arch-seducer. It was he who first sent us whoring after spirituality and heroics, whoring after the complementary demons of disgust and sin. We needs must love—well, not the highest, except sometimes by accident—but always the most extravagant and exciting. Tragedy was much more exciting than Homer's luminous pessimism, than this God's smiling awareness of the divine absurdity. Being alternately a hero and a sinner is much more sensational than being an integrated man. So as men seem to have the Yellow Press in the blood, like syphilis, they went back on Homer and Apollo; they followed Plato and Euripides. And Plato and Euripides handed them over to the Stoics and the Neo-Platonists. And these in turn handed humanity over to the Christians. And the Christians have handed us over to Henry Ford and the machines. So here we are."

Pamela nodded intelligently. But what she was chiefly conscious of was the ache in her feet. If only she could sit down!

But, "How poetical and appropriate," Fanning began again, "that the God should have risen from the grave exactly when he did, in 1916! Rising up in the midst of the insanity, like a beautiful, smiling reproach from another world. It was dramatic. At least I felt it so, when I saw him for the first time just after the War. The resurrection of Apollo, the Etruscan Apollo. I've been his worshipper and self-appointed priest ever since. Or at any rate I've tried to be. But it's difficult." He shook his head. "Perhaps it's even impossible for us to recapture . . . " He left the sentence unfinished and, taking her arm, led her out into the great courtyard of the Villa. Under the arcades was a bench. Thank goodness, said Pamela inwardly. They sat down.

"You see," he went on, leaning forward, his elbows on his knees, his hands clasped, "you can't get away from the things that the God protests against. Because they've become a part of you. Tradition and education have driven them into your very bones. It's a case of what I was speaking about just now—of the things that have nothing to do with you coming by force of habit to have everything to do with you. Which is why I'd like you to get Apollo and his Etruscans into your system while you're still young. It may save you trouble. Or on the other hand," he added with a rueful little laugh, "it may not. Because I really don't know if he's everybody's God. He may do for me—and do, only because I've got Plato and Jesus in my bones. But does he do for you? *Chi lo sa?* The older one grows, the more often one asks that question. Until, of course, one's arteries begin to harden, and then one's opinions begin to harden too, harden till they fossilize into certainty. But meanwhile, *chi lo sa? chi lo sa?* And after all it's quite agreeable, not knowing. And knowing, and at the same time knowing that it's no practical use knowing—that's not disagreeable either. Knowing, for example, that it would be good to live according to this God's commandments, but knowing at the same time that one couldn't do it even if one tried, because one's very guts and skeleton are already pledged to other Gods."

"I should have thought that was awful," said Pamela.

"For you, perhaps. But I happen to have a certain natural affection for the accomplished fact. I like and respect it, even when it is a bit depressing. Thus, it's a fact that I'd like to think and live in the unsplit, Apollonian way. But it's also a fact—and the fact as such is lovable—that I can't help indulging in aspirations and disgusts; I can't help thinking in terms of heroics and diabolics. Because the division, the splitness, has been worked right into my bones. So has the microbe of sensationalism; I can't help wallowing in the excitements of mysticism and the tragic sense. Can't help it." He shook his head. "Though perhaps I've wallowed in them rather more than I was justified in wallowing—justified by my upbringing, I mean. There was a time when I was really quite perversely preoccupied with mystical experiences and ecstasies and private universes."

"Private universes?" she questioned.

"Yes, private, not shared. You create one, you live in it, each time you're in love, for example." (Brightly serious, Pamela nodded her understanding and agreement; yes, yes, she knew all about *that*.) "Each time you're spiritually exalted," he went on, "each time you're drunk, even. Everybody has his own favourite short cuts to the other world. Mine, in those days, was opium."

"Opium?" She opened her eyes very wide. "Do you mean to say you smoked opium?" She was thrilled. Opium was a vice of the first order.

"It's as good a way of becoming supernatural," he answered, "as looking at one's nose or one's navel, or not eating, or repeating a word over and over again, till it loses its sense and you forget how to think. All roads lead to Rome. The only bother about opium is that it's rather an unwholesome road. I had to go to a nursing home in Cannes to get disintoxicated."

"All the same," said Pamela, doing her best to imitate the quiet casualness of his manner, "it must be rather delicious, isn't it? Awfully exciting, I mean," she added, forgetting not to be thrilled.

"*Too* exciting." He shook his head. "That's the trouble. We needs must love the excitingest when we see it. The supernatural *is* exciting. But I don't want to love the supernatural, I want to love the natural. Not that a little supernaturalness isn't, of course, perfectly natural and necessary. But you can overdo it. I overdid it then. I was all the time in t'other world, never here. I stopped smoking because I was ill. But even if I hadn't been, I'd have stopped sooner or later for aesthetic reasons. The supernatural world is so terribly baroque—altogether too Counter-Reformation and Bernini. At its best it can be Greco. But you can have too much even of Greco. A big dose of him makes you begin to pine for Vulca and his Apollo."

"But doesn't it work the other way too?" she asked. "I mean, don't you sometimes *long* to start smoking again?" She was secretly hoping that he'd let her try a pipe or two.

Fanning shook his head. "One doesn't get tired of very good bread," he answered. "Apollo's like that. I don't pine for supernatural excitements. Which doesn't mean," he added, "that I don't in practice run after them. You can't disintoxicate yourself of your culture. That sticks deeper than a mere taste for opium. I'd like to be able to think and live in the spirit of the God. But the fact remains that I can't."

"Can't you?" said Pamela with a polite sympathy. She was more interested in the opium.

"No, no, you can't entirely disintoxicate yourself of mysticism and the tragic sense. You can't take a Turvey treatment for spirituality and disgust. You can't. Not nowadays. Acceptance is impossible in a split world like ours. You've got to recoil. In the circumstances it's right and proper. But absolutely it's wrong. If only one could accept as this God accepts, smiling like that . . . "

"But you *do* smile like that," she insisted.

He laughed and, unclasping his hands, straightened himself up in his seat. "But unhappily," he said, "a man can smile and smile and not be Apollo. Meanwhile, what's becoming of your education? Shouldn't we . . . ?"

"Well, if you like," she assented dubiously. "Only my feet are rather tired. I mean, there's something about sight-seeing . . . "

"There is indeed," said Fanning. "But I was prepared to be a martyr to culture. Still, I'm thankful you're not." He smiled at her, and Pamela was pleased to find herself once more at the focus of his attention. It had been very interesting to hear him talk about his philosophy and all that. But all the same . . .

"Twenty to four," said Fanning, looking at his watch. "I've an idea; shouldn't we drive out to Monte Cavo and spend the evening up there in the cool? There's a view. And a really very eatable dinner."

"I'd love to. But . . . " Pamela hesitated. "Well, you see I did tell Guy I'd go out with him this evening."

He was annoyed. "Well, if you prefer . . . "

"But I don't prefer," she answered hastily. "I mean, I'd much rather go with you. Only I wondered how I'd let Guy know I wasn't . . . "

"Don't let him know," Fanning answered, abusing his victory. "After all, what are young men there for, except to wait when young women don't keep their appointments? It's their function in life."

Pamela laughed. His words had given her a pleasing sense of importance and power. "Poor Guy!" she said through her laughter, and her eyes were insolently bright.

"You little hypocrite."

"I'm not," she protested. "I really *am* sorry for him."

"A little hypocrite *and* a little devil," was his verdict. He rose to his feet. "If you could see your own eyes now! But *andiamo.*" He held out his hand to help her up. "I'm beginning to be rather afraid of you."

"What nonsense!" She was delighted. They walked together towards the door.

Fanning made the driver go out by the Appian Way. "For the sake of your education," he explained, pointing at the ruined tombs, "which we can continue, thank heaven, in comfort, and at twenty miles an hour."

Leaning back luxuriously in her corner, Pamela laughed. "But I must say," she had to admit, "it is really rather lovely."

From Albano the road mounted through the chestnut woods towards Rocca di Papa. A few miles brought them to a turning on the right; the car came to a halt.

"It's barred," said Pamela, looking out of the window. Fanning had taken out his pocket-book and was hunting among the bank-notes and the old letters. "The road's private," he explained. "They ask for your card— heaven knows why. The only trouble being, of course, that I've never possessed such a thing as a visiting-card in my life. Still, I generally have one or two belonging to other people. Ah, here we are! Good!" He produced two pieces of pasteboard. A gatekeeper had appeared and was waiting by the door of the car. "Shall we say we're Count Keyserling?" said Fanning, handing her the count's card. "Or alternatively," he read from the other, "that we're Herbert Watson, Funeral Furnisher, Funerals conducted with Efficiency and Reverence, Motor Hearses for use in every part of the Country." He shook his head. "The last relic of my poor old friend Tom Hatchard. Died last year. I had to bury him. Poor Tom! On the whole I think we'd better be Herbert Watson. *Ecco!*" He handed out the card; the man saluted and went to open the gate. "But give me back Count Keyserling." Fanning stretched out his hand. "He'll come in useful another time."

The car started and went roaring up the zig-zag ascent. Lying back in her corner, Pamela laughed and laughed, inextinguishably.

"But what *is* the joke?" he asked.

She didn't know herself. Mr. Watson and the Count had only been a pretext; this enormous laughter, which they had released, sprang from some other, deeper source. And perhaps it was a mere accident that it should be laughter at all. Another pretext, a different finger on the trigger, and it might have been tears, or anger, or singing "Constantinople" at the top of her voice—anything.

She was limp when they reached the top. Fanning made her sit down where she could see the view and himself went off to order cold drinks at the bar of the little inn that had once been the monastery of Monte Cavo.

Pamela sat where he had left her. The wooded slopes fell steeply away beneath her, down, down to the blue shining of the Alban Lake; and that toy palace perched on the hill beyond was the Pope's, that tiny city in a picture-book, Marino. Beyond a dark ridge on the left the round eye of Nemi looked up from its crater. Far off, behind Albano an expanse of blue steel, burnished beneath the sun, was the Tyrrhenian, and flat like the sea, but golden with ripening corn and powdered goldenly with a haze of dust, the Campagna stretched away from the feet of the subsiding hills, away and up towards a fading horizon, on which the blue ghosts of mountains floated on a level with her eyes. In the midst of the expanse a half-seen golden chaos was Rome. Through the haze the dome of St. Peter's shone faintly in the sun with a glitter as of muted glass. There was an enormous silence, sad, sad but somehow consoling. A sacred silence. And yet when, coming up from behind her, Fanning broke it, his voice, for Pamela, committed no iconoclasm; for it seemed, in the world of her feelings, to belong to the silence, it was made, as it were, of the same intimate and friendly substance. He squatted down on his heels beside her, laying a hand on her shoulder to steady himself.

"What a panorama of space and time!" he said. "So many miles, such an expanse of centuries! You can still walk on the paved road that led to the temple here. The generals used to march up sometimes in triumph. With elephants."

The silence enveloped them again, bringing them together; and they were alone and as though conspiratorially isolated in an atmosphere of solemn amorousness.

"*I signori son serviti,*" said a slightly ironic voice behind them.

"That's our drinks," said Fanning. "Perhaps we'd better . . . " He got up and, as he unbent them, his knees cracked stiffly. He stooped to rub them, for they ached; his joints were old. "Fool!" he said to himself, and decided that to-morrow he'd go to Venice. She was too young, too dangerously and perversely fresh.

They drank their lemonade in silence. Pamela's face wore an expression of grave serenity which it touched and flattered and moved him to see. Still, he was a fool to be touched and flattered and moved.

"Let's go for a bit of a stroll," he said, when they had slaked their thirst. She got up without a word, obediently, as though she had become his slave.

It was breathless under the trees and there was a smell of damp, hot greenness, a hum and flicker of insects in the probing slants of sunlight. But in the open spaces the air of the heights was quick and nimble, in spite of the sun; the broom-flower blazed among the rocks; and round the bushes where the honeysuckle had clambered, there hung invisible islands of perfume, cool and fresh in the midst of the hot sea of bracken smell. Pamela moved here and there with little exclamations of delight, pulling at the tough sprays of honeysuckle. "Oh, look!" she called to him in her rapturous voice. "Come and look!"

"I'm looking," he shouted back across the intervening space. "With a telescope. With the eye of faith," he corrected; for she had moved out of sight. He sat down on a smooth rock and lighted a cigarette. Venice, he reflected, would be rather boring at this particular season. In a few minutes Pamela came back to him, flushed, with a great bunch of honeysuckle between her hands.

"You know, you ought to have come," she said reproachfully. "There were such *lovely* pieces I couldn't reach."

Fanning shook his head. "He also serves who only sits and smokes," he said, and made room for her on the stone beside him. "And what's more," he went on, " 'let Austin have his swink to him reserved.' Yes, let him. How wholeheartedly I've always agreed with Chaucer's Monk! Besides, you seem to forget, my child, that I'm an old, old gentleman." He was playing the safe, the prudent part. Perhaps if he played it hard enough, it wouldn't be necessary to go to Venice.

Pamela paid no attention to what he was saying. "Would you like this one for your buttonhole, Miles?" she asked, holding up a many-trumpeted flower. It was the first time she had called him by his Christian name, and the accomplishment of this much-meditated act of daring made her blush. "I'll stick it in," she added, leaning forward, so that he shouldn't see her reddened cheeks, till her face was almost touching his coat.

Near and thus offered (for it was an offer, he had no doubt of that, a deliberate offer) why shouldn't he take this lovely, this terribly and desperately tempting freshness? It was a matter of stretching out one's hands. But no; it would be too insane. She was near, this warm young flesh, this scent of her hair, near and offered—with what an innocent perversity, what a touchingly ingenuous and uncomprehending shamelessness! But he sat woodenly still, feeling all of a sudden as he had felt when, a lanky boy, he had been too shy, too utterly terrified, in spite of his longings, to kiss that Jenny—what on earth was her name?—that Jenny Something-or-Other he had danced the polka with at Uncle Fred's one Christmas, how many centuries ago!—and yet only yesterday, only this instant.

"There!" said Pamela, and drew back. Her cheeks had had time to cool a little.

"Thank you." There was a silence.

"Do you know," she said at last, efficiently, "you've got a button loose on your coat."

He fingered the hanging button. "What a damning proof of celibacy!"

"If only I had a needle and thread . . . "

"Don't make your offer too lightly. If you knew what a quantity of unmended stuff I've got at home . . . "

"I'll come and do it all to-morrow," she promised, feeling delightfully protective and important.

"Beware," he said. "I'll take you at your word. It's sweated labour."

"I don't mind. I'll come."

"Punctually at ten-thirty, then." He had forgotten about Venice. "I shall be a ruthless taskmaster."

Nemi was already in shadow when they walked back; but the higher slopes were transfigured with the setting sunlight. Pamela halted at a twist of the path and turned back towards the western sky. Looking up, Fanning saw her standing there, goldenly flushed, the colours of her skin, her hair, her dress, the flowers in her hands, supernaturally heightened and intensified in the almost level light.

"I think this is the most lovely place I've ever seen." Her voice was solemn with a natural piety. "But you're not looking," she added in a different tone, reproachfully.

"I'm looking at you," he answered. After all, if he stopped in time, it didn't matter his behaving like a fool—it didn't finally matter and, meanwhile, was very agreeable.

An expression of impertinent mischief chased away the solemnity from her face. "Trying to see my ears again?" she asked; and, breaking off a honeysuckle blossom, she threw it down in his face, then turned and ran up the steep path.

"Don't imagine I'm going to pursue," he called after her. "The Pan and Syrinx business is a winter pastime. Like football."

Her laughter came down to him from among the trees; he followed the retreating sound. Pamela waited for him at the top of the hill and they walked back together towards the inn.

"Aren't there any ruins here?" she asked. "I mean, for my education."

He shook his head. "The Young Pretender's brother pulled them all down and built a monastery with them. For the Passionist Fathers," he added after a little pause. "I feel rather like a Passionist Father myself at the moment." They walked on without speaking, enveloped by the huge, the amorously significant silence.

But a few minutes later, at the dinner table, they were exuberantly gay. The food was well cooked, the wine an admirable Falernian. Fanning began to talk about his early loves. Vaguely at first, but later, under Pamela's questioning, with an ever-increasing wealth of specific detail. They were indiscreet, impudent questions, which at ordinary times she couldn't have uttered, or at least have only despairingly forced out, with a suicide's determination. But she was a little tipsy now, tipsy with the wine and her own laughing exultation; she rapped them out easily, without a tremor. "As though you were the immortal Sigmund himself," he assured her, laughing. Her impudence and that knowledgeable, scientific ingenuousness amused him, rather perversely; he told her everything she asked.

When she had finished with his early loves, she questioned him about the opium. Fanning described his private universes and that charming nurse who had looked after him while he was being disintoxicated. He went on to talk about the black poverty he'd been reduced to by the drug. "Because you can't do journalism or write novels in the other world," he explained. "At least I never could." And he told her of the debts he still owed and of his present arrangements with his publishers.

Almost suddenly the night was cold and Fanning became aware that the bottle had been empty for a long time. He threw away the stump of his cigar. "Let's go." They took their seats and the car set off, carrying with it the narrow world of form and colour created by its head-lamps. They were alone in the darkness of their padded box. An hour before Fanning had decided that he would take this opportunity to kiss her. But he was haunted suddenly by the memory of an Australian who had once complained to him of the sufferings of a young colonial in England. "In Sydney," he had said, "when I get into a taxi with a nice girl, I know exactly what to do. And I know exactly what to do when I'm in an American taxi. But when I apply my knowledge in London—God, isn't there a row!" How vulgar and stupid it all was! Not merely a fool, but a vulgar, stupid fool. He sat unmoving in his corner. When the lights of Rome were round them, he took her hand and kissed it.

"Good-night."

She thanked him. "I've had the loveliest day." But her eyes were puzzled and unhappy. Meeting them, Fanning suddenly regretted his self-restraint, wished that he had been stupid and vulgar. And, after all, would it have been so stupid and vulgar? You could make any action seem anything you liked, from saintly to disgusting, by describing it in the appropriate words. But his regrets had come too late. Here was her hotel. He drove home to his solitude feeling exceedingly depressed.

6

June 14th. Spent the morning with M., who lives in a house belonging to a friend of his who is a Catholic and lives in Rome, M. says, because he likes to get his popery straight from the horse's mouth. A nice house, old, standing just back from the Forum, which I said I thought was like a rubbish heap and he agreed with me, in spite of my education, and said he always preferred live dogs to dead lions and thinks it's awful the way the Fascists are pulling down nice ordinary houses and making holes to find more of these beastly pillars and things. I sewed on a lot of buttons, etc., as he's living in only two rooms on the ground floor and the servants are on their holiday, so he eats out and an old woman comes to clean up in the afternoons, but doesn't do any mending, which meant a lot for me, but I liked doing it, in spite of the darning, because he sat with me all the time, sometimes talking, sometimes just working. When he's writing or sitting with his pen in his hand thinking, his face is quite still and *terribly* serious and far, far away, as though he were a picture, or more like some sort of not human person, a sort of angel, if one can imagine them without night-dresses and long hair, really rather frightening, so that one longed to shout or throw a reel of cotton at him so as to change him back again into a man. He has very beautiful hands, rather long and bony, but strong. Sometimes, after he'd sat thinking for a long time, he'd get up and walk about the room, frowning and looking kind of angry, which was still more terrifying— sitting there while he walked up and down quite close to me, as though he were absolutely alone. But one time he suddenly stopped his walking up and down and said how profusely he apologized for his toes, because I was darning, and it was really very wonderful to see him suddenly changed back from that picture-angel sort of creature into a human being. Then he sat down by me and said he'd been spending the morning wrestling with the problem of speaking the truth in books; so I said, but haven't you always spoken it? because that always seemed to me the chief point of M.'s books. But he said, not much, because most of it was quite unspeakable in our world, as we found it too shocking and humiliating. So I said, all the same I didn't see why it shouldn't be spoken, and he said, nor did he in theory, but in practice he didn't want to be lynched. And he said, look for example at those advertisements in American magazines with the photos and life stories of people with unpleasant breath. So I said, yes, aren't they simply *too* awful. Because they really do make one shudder. And he said, precisely, there you are, and they're so successful because every one thinks them so perfectly awful. They're outraged by them, he said, just as you're outraged, and they rush off and buy the stuff in sheer terror, because they're so terrified of being an outrage physically to other people. And he said, that's only one small sample of all the class of truths, pleasant and unpleasant, that you can't speak, except in scientific books, but that doesn't count, because you deliberately leave your feelings outside in the cloak-room when you're being scientific. And just because they're unspeakable, we pretend they're unimportant, but they aren't, on the contrary, they're terribly important, and he said, you've only got to examine your memory quite sincerely for five minutes to realize it, and of course he's quite right. When I think of Miss Poole giving me piano lessons—but no, really, one *can't* write these things, and yet one obviously ought to, because they *are* so important, the humiliating physical facts, both pleasant and unpleasant (though I must say, most of the ones I can think of seem to be unpleasant), so important in all human relationships, he says, even in love, which is really rather awful, but of course one must admit it. And M. said it would take a whole generation of being shocked and humiliated and lynching the shockers and humiliators before people could settle down to listening to that sort of truth calmly, which they did do, he says, at certain times in the past, at any rate much more so than now. And he says that when they can listen to it completely calmly, the world will be quite different from what it is now, so I asked, in what way? but he said he couldn't clearly imagine, only he knew it would be different. After that he went back to his table and wrote very quickly for about half an hour without stopping, and I longed to ask him if he'd been writing the truth, and if so, what about, but I didn't have the nerve, which was stupid.

We lunched at our usual place, which I really don't much like, as who wants to look at fat business-men and farmers from the country simply *drinking* spaghetti? even if the spaghetti *is* good, but M. prefers it to the big places, because he says that in Rome one must do as the Romans do, not as the Americans. Still, I must say I do like looking at people who dress well and have good manners and nice jewels and things, which I told him, so he said all right, we'd go to Valadier tomorrow to see how the rich ate macaroni, which made me wretched, as it looked as though I'd been cadging, and of course that's the last thing in the world I meant to do, to make him waste a lot of money on me, particularly after what he told me yesterday about his debts and what he made on the average, which still seems to me shockingly little, considering who he is, so I said no, wouldn't he lunch with *me* at Valadier's, and he laughed and said it was the first time he'd heard of a gigolo of fifty being taken out by a woman of twenty. That rather upset me—the way it seemed to bring what we are to each other on to the wrong level, making it all a sort of joke and sniggery, like something in *Punch*. Which is hateful, I can't bear it. And I have the feeling that he does it on purpose, as a kind of protection, because he doesn't want to care too much, and that's why he's always saying he's so old, which is all nonsense, because you're only as old as you feel, and sometimes I even feel older than he does, like when he gets so amused and interested with little boys in the street playing that game of sticking out your fingers and calling a number, or when he talks about that awful old Dickens. Which I told him, but he only laughed and said age is a circle and you grow into a lot of the things you grew out of, because the whole world is a fried whiting with its tail in its mouth, which only confirms what I said about his saying he was old being all nonsense. Which I told him and he said, quite right, he only *said* he felt old when he *wished* that he felt old. Which made me see still more clearly that it was just a defence. A defence of *me,* I suppose, and all that sort of nonsense. What I'd have liked to say, only I didn't, was that I don't want to be defended, particularly if being defended means his defending himself against me and making stupid jokes about gigolos and old gentlemen. Because I think he really does rather care underneath—from the way he looks at me sometimes—and he'd like to say so and act so, but he won't on principle, which is really against all *his* principles, and some time I *shall* tell him so. I insisted he should lunch with me and in the end he said he would, and then he was suddenly very silent and, I thought, glum and unhappy, and after coffee he said he'd have to go home and write all the rest of the day. So I came back to the hotel and had a rest and wrote this, and now it's nearly seven and I feel terribly sad, almost like crying. *Next day.* Rang up Guy and had less difficulty than I expected getting him to forgive me for yesterday, in fact he almost apologized himself. Danced till 2.15.

June 15th. M. still sad and didn't kiss me when we met, *on purpose,* which made me angry, it's so humiliating to be defended. He was wearing an open shirt, like Byron, which suited him; but I told him, you look like the devil when you're sad (which is true, because his face ought to move, not be still), and he said that was what came of feeling and behaving like an angel; so of course I asked why he didn't behave like a devil, because in that case he'd look like an angel, and I preferred his looks to his morals, and then I blushed, like an idiot. But really it is too stupid that women aren't supposed to say what they think. Why can't we say, I like you, or whatever it is, without being thought a kind of monster, if we say it first, and even thinking ourselves monsters? Because one ought to say what one thinks and do what one likes, or else one becomes like Aunt Edith, hippo-ish and dead inside. Which is after all what M.'s constantly saying in his books, so he oughtn't to humiliate me with his beastly defendings. Lunch at Valadier's was really rather a bore. Afterwards we went and sat in a church, because it was so hot, a huge affair full of pink marble and frescoes and marble babies and gold. M. says that the modern equivalent is Lyons' Corner House, and that the Jesuits were so successful because they gave the poor a chance of feeling what it was like to live in a palace, or something better than a palace, because he says the chief difference between a Corner House and the state rooms at Buckingham Palace is that the Corner House is so much more sumptuous, almost as sumptuous as these Jesuit churches. I asked him if he believed in God and he said he believed in a great many gods, it depended on what he was doing, or being, or feeling at the moment. He said he believed in Apollo when he was working, and in Bacchus when he was drinking, and in Buddha when he felt depressed, and in Venus when he was making love, and in the Devil when he was afraid or angry, and in the Categorical Imperative when he had to do his duty. I asked him which he believed in now and he said he didn't quite know, but he thought it was the Categorical Imperative, which really made me furious, so I answered that I only believed in the Devil and Venus, which made him laugh, and he said I looked as though I were going to jump off the Eiffel Tower, and I was just going to say what I thought of his hippo-ishness, I mean I'd really made up my mind, when a most horrible old verger rushed up and said we must leave the church, because it seems the Pope doesn't allow you to be in a church with bare arms, which is really *too* indecent. But M. said that after all it wasn't surprising, because every god has to protect himself against hostile gods, and the gods of bare skin *are* hostile to the gods of souls and clothes, and he made me stop in front of a shop window where there were some mirrors and said, you can see for yourself, and I must say I really did look very nice in that pale green linen which goes so awfully well with the skin, when one's a bit sunburnt. But he said, it's not merely a question of seeing, you must touch too, so I stroked my arms and said yes, they were nice and smooth, and he said, precisely, and then he stroked my arm very lightly, like a moth crawling, agonizingly creepy but delicious, once or twice, looking very serious and attentive, as though he were tuning a piano, which made me laugh, and I said I supposed he was experimenting to see if the Pope was in the right, and then he gave me the most horrible pinch and said, yes, the Pope was quite right and I ought to be muffled in Jaeger from top to toe. But I was so angry with the pain, because he pinched me really terribly, that I just rushed off without saying anything and jumped into a cab that was passing and drove straight to the hotel. But I was so wretched by the time I got there that I started crying in the lift and the lift man said he hoped I hadn't had any *dispiacere di famiglia,* which made me laugh and that made the crying much worse, and then I suddenly thought of Clare and felt such a horrible beast, so I lay on my bed and simply howled for about an hour, and then I got up and wrote a letter and sent one of the hotel boys with it to M.'s address, saying I was so sorry and would he come at once. But he didn't come, not for hours and hours, and it was simply too awful, because I thought he was offended, or despising, because I'd been such a fool, and I wondered whether he really did like me at all and whether this defending theory wasn't just my imagination. But at last, when I'd quite given him up and was so miserable I didn't know what I should do, he suddenly appeared—because he'd only that moment gone back to the house and found my note—and was too wonderfully sweet to me, and said he was so sorry, but he'd been on edge (though he didn't say why, but I know now that the defending theory wasn't just imagination) and I said I was so sorry and I cried, but I was happy, and then we laughed because it had all been so stupid and then M. quoted a bit of Homer which meant that after they'd eaten and drunk they wept for their friends and after they'd wept a little they went to sleep, so we went out and had dinner and after dinner we went and danced, and he dances really very well, but we stopped before midnight, because he said the noise of the jazz would drive him crazy. He was perfectly sweet, but though he didn't say anything sniggery, I could feel he was on the defensive all the time, sweetly and friendly on the defensive, and when he said good-night he only kissed my hand.

June 18th. Stayed in bed till lunch re-reading *The Return of Eurydice.* I understand Joan so well now, better and better, she's *so* like me in all she feels and thinks. M. went to Tivoli for the day to see some Italian friends who have a house there. What is he like with other people, I wonder? Got two tickets for the fireworks to-morrow night, the hotel porter says they'll be good, because it's the first Girandola since the War. Went to the Villa Borghese in the afternoon for my education, to give M. a surprise when he comes back, and I must say some of the pictures and statues were very lovely, but the most awful looking fat man would follow me round all the time, and finally the old beast even had the impertinence to speak to me, so I just said, *Lei è un porco,* which I must say was very effective. But it's extraordinary how things do just depend on looks and being sympathique, because if he hadn't looked such a pig, I shouldn't have thought him so piggish, which shows again what rot hippo-ism is. Went to bed early and finished *Eurydice.* This is the fifth time I've read it.

7

"Oh, it was marvellous before the War, the Girandola. Really marvellous."

"But then what wasn't *marvellous* before the War?" said Pamela sarcastically. These references to a Golden Age in which she had had no part always annoyed her.

Fanning laughed. "Another one in the eye for the aged gentleman!"

There, he had slipped back again behind his defences! She did not answer for fear of giving him some excuse to dig himself in, impregnably. This hateful bantering with feelings! They walked on in silence. The night was breathlessly warm; the sounds of brassy music came to them faintly through the dim enormous noise of a crowd that thickened with every step they took towards the Piazza del Popolo. In the end they had to shove their way by main force.

Sunk head over ears in this vast sea of animal contacts, animal smells and noise, Pamela was afraid. "Isn't it awful?" she said, looking up at him over her shoulder; and she shuddered. But at the same time she rather liked her fear, because it seemed in some way to break down the barriers that separated them, to bring him closer to her—close with a physical closeness of protective contact that was also, increasingly, a closeness of thought and feeling.

"You're all right," he reassured her through the tumult. He was standing behind her, encircling her with his arms. "I won't let you be squashed"; and as he spoke he fended off the menacing lurch of a large back. "*Ignorante!*" he shouted at it.

A terrific explosion interrupted the distant selections from *Rigoletto* and the sky was suddenly full of coloured lights; the Girandola had begun. A wave of impatience ran through the advancing crowd; they were violently pushed and jostled. But, "It's all right," Fanning kept repeating, "it's all right." They were squeezed together in a staggering embrace. Pamela was terrified, but it was with a kind of swooning pleasure that she shut her eyes and abandoned herself limply in his arms.

"*Ma piano!*" shouted Fanning at the nearest jostlers. "*Piano!*" and "'Sblood!" he said in English, for he had the affectation of using literary oaths. "Hell and Death!" But in the tumult his words were as though unspoken. He was silent; and suddenly, in the midst of that heaving chaos of noise and rough contacts, of movement and heat and smell, suddenly he became aware that his lips were almost touching her hair, and that under his right hand was the firm resilience of her breast. He hesitated for a moment on the threshold of his sensuality, then averted his face, shifted the position of his hand.

"At last!"

The haven to which their tickets admitted them was a little garden on the western side of the Piazza, opposite the Pincio and the source of the fireworks. The place was crowded, but not oppressively. Fanning was tall enough to overlook the interposed heads, and when Pamela had climbed on to a little parapet that separated one terrace of the garden from another, she too could see perfectly.

"But you'll let me lean on you," she said, laying a hand on his shoulder, "because there's a fat woman next me who's steadily squeezing me off. I think she's expanding with the heat."

"And she almost certainly understands English. So for heaven's sake . . . "

A fresh volley of explosions from the other side of the great square interrupted him and drowned the answering mockery of her laughter. "Ooh! ooh!" the crowd was moaning in a kind of amorous agony. Magical flowers in a delirium of growth, the rockets mounted on their slender stalks and, ah! high up above the Pincian hill, dazzlingly, deafeningly, in a bunch of stars and a thunder-clap, they blossomed.

"Isn't it marvellous?" said Pamela, looking down at him with shining eyes. "Oh God!" she added, in another voice. "She's expanding again. Help!" And for a moment she was on the verge of falling. She leaned on him so heavily that he had to make an effort not to be pushed sideways. She managed to straighten herself up again into equilibrium.

"I've got you in case . . . " He put his arm round her knees to steady her.

"Shall I see if I can puncture the old beast with a pin?" And Fanning knew, by the tone of her voice, that she was genuinely prepared to make the experiment.

"If you do," he said, "I shall leave you to be lynched alone."

Pamela felt his arm tighten a little about her thighs. "Coward!" she mocked and pulled his hair.

"Martyrdom's not in my line," he laughed back. "Not even martyrdom for your sake." But her youth was a perversity, her freshness a kind of provocative vice. He had taken a step across that supernatural threshold. He had given—after all, why not?—a certain license to his desires. Amid their multitudinous uncoiling, his body seemed to be coming to a new and obscure life of its own. When the time came he would revoke the license, step back again into the daily world.

There was another bang, another, and the obelisk at the centre of the Piazza leapt out sharp and black against apocalypse after apocalypse of jewelled light. And through the now flushed, now pearly-brilliant, now emerald-shining smoke-clouds, a pine tree, a palm, a stretch of grass emerged, like strange unearthly visions of pine and palm and grass, from the darkness of the else invisible gardens.

There was an interval of mere lamplight—like sobriety, said Fanning, between two pipes of opium, like daily life after an ecstasy. And perhaps, he was thinking, the time to step back again had already come. "If only one could live without any lucid intervals," he concluded.

"I don't see why not." She spoke with a kind of provocative defiance, as though challenging him to contradict her. Her heart beat very fast, exultantly. "I mean, why shouldn't it be fireworks all the time?"

"Because it just isn't, that's all. Unhappily." It was time to step back again; but he didn't step back.

"Well, then, it's a case of damn the intervals and enjoy . . . Oh!" She started. That prodigious bang had sent a large red moon sailing almost slowly into the sky. It burst into a shower of meteors that whistled as they fell, expiringly.

Fanning imitated their plaintive noise. "Sad, sad," he commented. "Even the fireworks can be sad."

She turned on him fiercely. "Only because you want them to be sad. Yes, you want them to be. Why do you want them to be sad?"

Yes, why? It was a pertinent question. She felt his arm tighten again round her knees and was triumphant. He was defending himself no more, he was listening to those oracles. But at the root of his deliberate reckless-ness, its contradiction and its cause, his sadness obscurely persisted. "But I *don't* want them to be sad," he protested.

Another garden of rockets began to blossom. Laughing, triumphant, Pamela laid her hand on his head.

"I feel so superior up here," she said.

"On a pedestal, what?" He laughed. "'*Guardami ben; ben son, ben son Beatrice!*'"

"Such a comfort you're not bald," she said, her fingers in his hair. "That must be a great disadvantage of pedestals—I mean, seeing the baldness of the men down below."

"But the great advantage of pedestals, as I now suddenly see for the first time . . . " Another explosion covered his voice. " . . . make it possible . . . " Bang!

"Oh, look!" A bluish light was brightening, brightening.

" . . . possible for even the baldest . . . " There was a continuous uninterrupted rattle of detonations. Fanning gave it up. What he had meant to say was that pedestals gave even the baldest men unrivalled opportunities for pinching the idol's legs.

"What were you saying?" she shouted through the battle.

"Nothing," he yelled back. He had meant, of course, to suit the action to the word, playfully. But the fates had decided otherwise and he wasn't really sorry. For he was tired; he had realized it almost suddenly. All this standing. He was no good at standing nowadays.

A cataract of silver fire was pouring down the slopes of the Pincian Hill, and the shining smoke-clouds rolled away from it like the spray from a tumbling river. And suddenly, above it, the eagle of Savoy emerged from the darkness, enormous, perched on the lictor's axe and rods. There was applause and patriotic music. Then, gradually, the brightness of the cataract grew dim; the sources of its silver streaming were one by one dried up. The eagle moulted its shining plumage, the axe and rods faded, faded and at last were gone. Lit faintly by only the common lamplight, the smoke drifted slowly away towards the north. A spasm of motion ran through the huge crowd in the square below them. The show was over.

"But I feel," said Pamela, as they shoved their way back towards the open streets, "I feel as though the rockets were still popping off inside me." And she began to sing to herself as she walked.

Fanning made no comment. He was thinking of that Girandola he'd seen with Alice and Tony and Laurina Frescobaldi—was it in 1907 or 1908? Tony was an ambassador now, and Alice was dead, and one of Laurina's sons (he recalled the expression of despair on that worn, but still handsome face, when she had told him yesterday, at Tivoli) was already old enough to be getting housemaids into trouble.

"Not only rockets," Pamela went on, interrupting her singing, "but even catherine-wheels. I feel all catherine-wheely. You know, like when one's a little drunk." And she went on again with "Old Man River," tipsily happy and excited.

The crowd grew thinner around them and at last they were almost alone. Pamela's singing abruptly ceased. Here, in the open, in the cool of the dark night it had suddenly become inappropriate, a little shameful. She glanced anxiously at her companion; had he too remarked that inappropriateness, been shocked by it? But Fanning had noticed nothing; she wished he had. Head bent, his hands behind his back, he was walking at her side, but in another universe. When had his spirit gone away from her, and why? She didn't know, hadn't noticed. Those inward fireworks, that private festival of exultation had occupied her whole attention. She had been too excitedly happy with being in love to be able to think of the object of that love. But now, abruptly sobered, she had become aware of him again, repentantly at first, and then, as she realized his new remoteness, with a sinking of the heart. What had happened in these few moments? She was on the point of addressing him, then checked herself. Her apprehension grew and grew till it became a kind of terrified certainty that he'd never loved her at all, that he'd suddenly begun to hate her. But why, but why? They walked on.

"How lovely it is here!" she said at last. Her voice was timid and unnatural. "And so deliciously cool." They had emerged on to the embankment of the Tiber. Above the river, a second invisible river of air flowed softly through the hot night. "Shall we stop for a moment?" He nodded without speaking. "I mean, only if you want to," she added. He nodded again.

They stood, leaning on the parapet, looking down at the black water. There was a long, long silence. Pamela waited for him to say something, to make a gesture; but he did not stir, the word never came. It was as though he were at the other end of the world. She felt almost sick with unhappiness. Heart-beat after heart-beat, the silence prolonged itself.

Fanning was thinking of to-morrow's journey. How he hated the train! And in this heat. . . . But it was necessary. The wicked flee, and in this case the fleeing would be an act of virtue—painful. Was it love? Or just an itch of desire, of the rather crazy, dirty desire of an ageing man? "*A cinquant' anni si diventa un po' pazzo.*" He heard his own voice speaking, laughingly, mournfully, to Laurina. "*Pazzo e porco. Si, anch' io divento un porco. Le minorenni—a cinquant' anni, sa, sono un ossessione. Proprio un ossessione.*" Was that all—just an obsession of crazy desire? Or was it love? Or wasn't there any difference, was it just a question of names and approving or disapproving tones of voice? What was certain was that you could be as desperately unhappy when you were robbed of your crazy desire as when you were robbed of your love. A *porco* suffers as much as Dante. And perhaps Beatrice too was lovely, in Dante's memory, with the perversity of youth, the shamelessness of innocence, the vice of freshness. Still, the wicked flee, the wicked flee. If only he'd had the strength of mind to flee before! A touch made him start. Pamela had taken his hand.

"Miles!" Her voice was strained and abnormal. Fanning turned towards her and was almost frightened by the look of determined despair he saw on her face. The Eiffel Tower . . . "Miles!"

"What is it?"

"Why don't you speak to me?"

He shrugged his shoulders. "I didn't happen to be feeling very loquacious. For a change," he added, self-mockingly, in the hope (he knew it for a vain one) of being able to turn away her desperate attack with a counter-attack of laughter.

She ignored his counter-attack. "Why do you shut yourself away from me like this?" she asked. "Why do you hate me."

"But, my sweet child . . . "

"Yes, you hate me. You shut me away. Why are you so cruel, Miles?" Her voice broke; she was crying. Lifting his hand, she kissed it, passionately, despairingly. "I love you so much, Miles. I love you." His hand was wet with her tears when, almost by force, he managed to draw it away from her.

He put his arm round her, comfortingly. But he was annoyed as well as touched, annoyed by her despairing determination, by the way she had made up her mind to jump off the Eiffel Tower, screwed up her courage turn by turn. And now she was jumping—but how gracelessly! The way he had positively had to struggle for his hand! There was something forced and unnatural about the whole scene. She was being a character in fiction. But characters in fiction suffer. He patted her shoulder, he made consolatory murmurs. Consoling her for being in love with him! But the idea of explaining and protesting and being lucidly reasonable was appalling to him at the moment, absolutely appalling. He hoped that she'd just permit herself to be consoled and ask no further questions, just leave the whole situation comfortably inarticulate. But his hope was again disappointed.

"Why do you hate me, Miles?" she insisted.

"But, Pamela . . . "

"Because you did care a little, you did. I mean, I could see you cared. And now, suddenly . . . What have I done, Miles?"

"But nothing, my child, nothing." He could not keep a note of exasperation out of his voice. If only she'd allow him to be silent!

"Nothing? But I can hear from the way you speak that there's something." She returned to her old refrain. "Because you did care, Miles; a little, you did." She looked up at him, but he had moved away from her, he had averted his eyes towards the street. "You did, Miles."

Oh God! he was groaning to himself, God! And aloud (for she had made his silence untenable, she had driven him out into articulateness), "I cared too much," he said. "It would be so easy to do something stupid and irreparable, something mad, yes and bad, bad. I like you too much in other ways to want to run that risk. Perhaps, if I were twenty years younger . . . But I'm too old. It wouldn't do. And you're too young, you can't really understand, you . . . Oh, thank God, there's a taxi." And he darted forward, waving and shouting. Saved! But when they had shut themselves into the cab, he found that the new situation was even more perilous than the old.

"Miles!" A flash of lamplight through the window of the cab revealed her face to him. His words had consoled her; she was smiling, was trying to look happy; but under the attempted happiness her expression was more desperately determined than ever. She was not yet at the bottom of her Tower. "Miles!" And sliding across the seat towards him, she threw her arms round his neck and kissed him. "Take me, Miles," she said, speaking in quick abrupt little spurts, as though she were forcing the words out with violence against a resistance. He recognized the suicide's voice, despairing, strained, and at the same time, flat, lifeless. "Take me. If you want me . . . "

Fanning tried to protest, to disengage himself, gently, from her embrace.

"But I want you to take me, Miles," she insisted. "I want you . . . " She kissed him again, she pressed herself against his hard body. "I want you,

Miles. Even if it is stupid and mad," she added in another little spurt of desperation, making answer to the expression on his face, to the words she wouldn't permit him to utter. "And it isn't: I mean, love isn't stupid or mad. And even if it were, I don't care. Yes, I want to be stupid and mad. Even if it were to kill me. So take me, Miles." She kissed him again. "Take me."

He turned away his mouth from those soft lips. She was forcing him back across the threshold. His body was uneasy with awakenings and supernatural dawn.

Held up by a tram at the corner of a narrow street, the cab was at a standstill. With quick strong gestures Fanning unclasped her arms from round his neck and, taking her two hands in his, he kissed first one and then the other. "Good-bye, Pamela," he whispered, and, throwing open the door, he was half out of the cab before she realized what he was doing.

"But what are you doing, Miles? Where . . . " The door slammed. He thrust some money into the driver's hand and almost ran. Pamela rose to her feet to follow him, but the cab started with a sudden jerk that threw her off her balance, and she fell back on to the seat.

"Miles!" she called, and then, "Stop!"

But the driver either didn't hear, or else paid no attention. She did not call again, but sat, covering her face with her hands, crying and feeling so agonizingly unhappy that she thought she would die of it.

8

"By the time you receive this letter, I shall be—no, not dead, Pamela, though I know how thrilled and proud you'd be, through your temporary inconsolability, if I were to blow my brains out—not dead, but (what will be almost worse in these dog-days) in the train, bound for some anonymous refuge. Yes, a refuge, as though you were my worst enemy. Which in fact you almost are at the moment, for the good reason that you're acting as your own enemy. If I were less fond of you, I'd stay and join forces with you against yourself. And, frankly, I wish I were less fond of you. Do you know how desirable you are? Not yet, I suppose, not consciously, in spite of Prof. Krafft-Ebbing and the novels of Miles F. You can't yet know what a terrible army with banners you are, you and your eyes and your laughter and your impertinent breasts, like La Maja's, and those anti-educational ears in ambush under the hair. You can't know. But I know. Only too well. Just *how* well you'll realize, perhaps, fifteen or twenty years from now. For a time will come when the freshness of young bodies, the ingenuousness of young minds will begin to strike you as a scandal of shining beauty and attractiveness, and then finally as a kind of maddeningly alluring perversity, as the exhibition of a kind of irresistibly dangerous vice. The madness of the desirer—for middle-aged desires are mostly more or less mad desires—comes off on the desired object, staining it, degrading it. Which isn't agreeable if you happen to be fond of the object, as well as desiring. Dear object, let's be a little reasonable—oh, entirely against all my principles; I accept all the reproaches you made me the other day. But what are principles for but to be gone against in moments of crisis? And this *is* a moment of crisis. Consider: I'm thirty years older than you are; and even if one doesn't look one's age, one is one's age, somehow, somewhere; and even if one doesn't feel it, fifty's always fifty and twenty-one's twenty-one. And when you've considered that, let me put a few questions. First: are you prepared to be a disreputable woman? To which, of course, you answer yes, because you don't care two pins about what the old cats say. But I put another question: Do you know, by experience, what it's like to be a disreputable woman? And you must answer, no. Whereupon I retort: If you can't answer yes to the second, you've got no right to answer yes to the first. And I don't intend to give you the opportunity of answering yes to the second question. Which is all pure Podsnapism. But there are certain circumstances in which Podsnap is quite right.

"Sweet Pamela, believe me when I say it would be fatal. For when you say you love me, what do you mean? Who and what is it you love? I'll tell you. You love the author of *Eurydice* and of all those portraits of yourself he's filled his books with. You love the celebrated man, who was not only unsnubbing and attentive, but obviously admiring. Even before you saw him, you vaguely loved his reputation, and now you love his odd confidences. You love a kind of conversation you haven't heard before. You love a weakness in him which you think you can dominate and protect. You love—as I, of course, intended you to love—a certain fascinating manner. You even love a rather romantic and still youthful appearance. And when I say (which as yet, you know, I haven't said) that I love you, what do *I* mean? That I'm amused, and charmed, and flattered, and touched, and puzzled, and affectionate, in a word, a Passionist Father. But chiefly that I find you terribly desirable—an army with banners. Bring these two loves together and what's the result? A manifold disaster. To begin with, the nearer you come to me and the longer you remain with me, the more alien you'll find me, the more fundamentally remote. Inevitably. For you and I are foreigners to one another, foreigners in time. Which is a greater foreignness than the foreignness of space and language. You don't realize it now, because you don't know me—you're only in love, at first sight (like Joan in *Eurydice*!) and, what's more, not really with me, with your imagination of me. When you come to know me better—well, you'll find that you know me much worse. And then one day you'll be attracted by a temporal compatriot. Perhaps, indeed, you're attracted already, only your imagination won't allow you to admit it. What about that long-suffering Guy of yours? Of whom I was, and am, so horribly jealous—jealous with the malignity of a weaker for a stronger rival; for though I seem to hold all the cards at the moment, the ace of trumps is his: he's young. And one day, when you're tired of living at cross-purposes with me, you'll suddenly realize it; you'll perceive that he speaks your language, that he inhabits your world of thought and feeling, that he belongs, in a word, to your nation—that great and terrible nation, which I love and fear and hate, the nation of Youth. In the end, of course, you'll leave the foreigner for the compatriot. But not before you've inflicted a good deal of suffering on every one concerned, including yourself. And meanwhile, what about me? Shall I be still there for you to leave? Who knows? Not I, at any rate. I can no more answer for my future desires than for the Shah of Persia. For my future affection, yes. But it may last (how often, alas, affections do last that way!) only on condition of its object being absent. There are so many friends whom one's fond of when they're not there. Will you be one of them? It's the more possible since, after all, you're just as alien to me as I am to you. My country's called Middle-Ageia and every one who was out of the egg of childhood before 1914 is my compatriot. Through all my desires, shouldn't I also pine to hear my own language, to speak with those who share the national traditions? Of course. But the tragedy of middle-aged life is that its army with banners is hardly ever captained by a compatriot. Passion is divorced from understanding, and the ageing man's desire attaches itself with an almost insane violence to precisely those outrageously fresh young bodies that house the most alien souls. Conversely, for the body of an understood and understanding soul, he seldom feels desire. And now, Pamela, suppose that my sentiment of your alienness should come to be stronger (as sometime it must) than my desire for the lovely scandal of your young body. What then? This time I can answer; for I am answering for a self that changes very little through every change of circumstances—the self that doesn't intend to put up with more discomfort than it can possibly avoid; the self that, as the Freudians tell us, is homesick for that earthly paradise from which we've all been banished, our mother's womb, the only place on earth where man is genuinely omnipotent, where his every desire is satisfied, where he is perfectly at home and adapted to his surroundings, and therefore perfectly happy. Out of the womb we're in an unfriendly world, in which our wishes aren't anticipated, where we're no longer magically omnipotent, where we don't fit, where we're not snugly at home. What's to be done in this world? Either face out the reality, fight with it, resignedly or heroically accept to suffer or struggle. Or else flee. In practice even the strongest heroes do a bit of fleeing—away from responsibility into deliberate ignorance, away from uncomfortable fact into imagination. Even the strongest. And conversely even the weakest fleers can make themselves strong. No, not the weakest; that's a mistake. The weakest become day-dreamers, masturbators, paranoiacs. The strong fleer is one who starts with considerable advantages. Take my case. I'm so endowed by nature that I can have a great many of the prizes of life for the asking— success, money in reasonable quantities, love. In other words I'm not entirely out of the womb; I can still, even in the extra-uterine world, have at least some of my desires magically satisfied. To have my wishes fulfilled I don't have to rush off every time to some imaginary womb-substitute. I have the power to construct a womb for myself out of the materials of the real world. But of course it's not a completely perfect and watertight womb; no post-natal uterus can ever in the nature of things be that. It lets in a lot of unpleasantness and alienness and obstruction to wishes. Which I deal with by flight, systematic flight into unawareness, into deliberate ignorance, into irresponsibility. It's a weakness which is a source of strength.

For when you can flee at will and with success (which is only possible if nature has granted you, as she has to me, the possibility of anarchic independence of society), what quantities of energy you save, what an enormous amount of emotional and mental wear and tear is spared you? I flee from business by leaving all my affairs in the hands of lawyers and agents, I flee from criticism (both from the humiliations of misplaced and wrongly motivated praise and from the pain of even the most contemptible vermin's blame) by simply not reading what anybody writes of me. I flee from time by living as far as possible only in and for the present. I flee from cold weather by taking the train or ship to places where it's warm. And from women I don't love any more, I flee by just silently vanishing. For, like Palmerston, I never explain and never apologize. I just fade out. I decline to admit their existence. I consign their letters to the waste-paper basket, along with the press cuttings. Simple, crude even, but incredibly effective, if one's ready to be ruthless in one's weakness, as I am. Yes, quite ruthless, Pamela. If my desire grew weary or I felt homesick for the company of my compatriots, I'd just run away, determinedly, however painfully much you might still be in love with me, or your imagination, or your own hurt pride and humiliated self-love. And you, I fancy, would have as little mercy on my desires if they should happen to outlive what you imagine to be your passion for me. So that our love-affair, if we were fools enough to embark on it, would be a race towards a series of successive goals—a race through boredom, misunderstanding, disillusion, towards the final winning-post of cruelty and betrayal. Which of us is likely to win the race? The betting, I should say, is about even, with a slight tendency in favour of myself. But there's not going to be a winner or a loser, for the good reason that there's not going to be any race. I'm too fond of you, Pamela, to . . . "

"Miles!"

Fanning started so violently that a drop of ink was jerked from his pen on to the paper. He felt as though his heart had fallen into an awful gulf of emptiness.

"Miles!"

He looked round. Two hands were clutching the bars of the unshuttered window and, as though desperately essaying to emerge from a subterranean captivity, the upper part of a face was peering in, over the high sill, with wide unhappy eyes.

"But Pamela!" There was reproach in his astonishment.

It was to the implied rebuke that she penitently answered. "I couldn't help it, Miles," she said; and, behind the bars, he saw her reddened eyes suddenly brighten and overflow with tears. "I simply had to come." Her voice trembled on the verge of breaking. "*Had* to."

The tears, her words and that unhappy voice were moving. But he didn't want to be moved, he was angry with himself for feeling the emotion, with her for inspiring it. "But, my dear child!" he began, and the reproach in his voice had shrilled to a kind of exasperation—the exasperation of one who feels himself hemmed in and helpless, increasingly helpless, against circumstances. "But I thought we'd settled," he began and broke off. He rose, and walked agitatedly towards the fireplace, agitatedly back again, like a beast in a cage; he was caught, hemmed in between those tearful eyes behind the bars and his own pity, with all those dangerous feelings that have their root in pity. "I thought," he began once more.

But, "Oh!" came her sharp cry, and looking again towards the window he saw that only the two small hands and a pair of straining wrists were visible. The tragical face had vanished.

"Pamela?"

"It's all right." Her voice came rather muffled and remote. "I slipped. I was standing on a little kind of ledge affair. The window's so high from the ground," she added plaintively.

"My poor child!" he said on a little laugh of amused commiseration. The reproach, the exasperation had gone out of his voice. He was conquered by the comic patheticness of her. Hanging on to the bars with those small, those rather red and childishly untended hands! And tumbling off the perch she had had to climb on, because the window was so high from the ground! A wave of sentimentality submerged him. "I'll come and open the door." He ran into the hall.

Waiting outside in the darkness, she heard the bolts being shot back, one by one. Clank, clank! and then "Damn!" came his voice from the other side of the door. "These things are so stiff. . . . I'm barricaded up as though I were in a safe." She stood there waiting. The door shook as he tugged at the recalcitrant bolt. The waiting seemed interminable. And all at once a huge, black weariness settled on her. The energy of wrought-up despair deserted her and she was left empty of everything but a tired misery. What was the good, what was the good of coming like this to be turned away again? For he *would* turn her away; he didn't want her. What was the good of renewing suffering, of once more dying?

"Hell and death!" On the other side of the door Fanning was cursing like an Elizabethan.

Hell and Death. The words reverberated in Pamela's mind. The pains of Hell, the darkness and dissolution of Death. What was the good?

Clank! Another bolt had gone back. "Thank goodness. We're almost . . . " A chain rattled. At the sound Pamela turned and ran in a blind terror down the dimly lighted street.

"At last!" The door swung back and Fanning stepped out. But the sentimental tenderness of his outstretched hands wasted itself on empty night. Twenty yards away a pair of pale legs twinkled in the darkness. "Pamela!" he called in astonishment. "What the devil . . . ?" The wasting on emptiness of his feelings had startled him into annoyance. He felt like one who has put forth all his strength to strike something and, missing his aim, swipes the unresisting air, grotesquely. "Pamela!" he called again, yet louder.

She did not turn at the sound of his voice, but ran on. These wretched high-heeled shoes! "Pamela!" And then came the sound of his pursuing footsteps. She tried to run faster. But the pursuing footsteps came nearer and nearer. It was no good. Nothing was any good. She slackened her speed to a walk.

"But what on earth?" he asked from just behind her, almost angrily.

Pursuing, he had called up within him the soul of a pursuer, angry and desirous. "What on earth?" And suddenly his hand was on her shoulder. She trembled a little at the touch. "But why?" he insisted. "Why do you suddenly run away?"

But Pamela only shook her averted head. She wouldn't speak, wouldn't meet his eyes. Fanning looked down at her intently, questioningly. Why? And as he looked at that weary hopeless face, he began to divine the reason. The anger of the pursuit subsided in him. Respecting her dumb, averted misery, he too was silent. He drew her comfortingly towards him. His arm round her shoulders, Pamela suffered herself to be led back towards the house.

Which would be best, he was wondering with the surface of his mind: to telephone for a taxi to take her back to the hotel, or to see if he could make up a bed for her in one of the upstairs rooms? But in the depths of his being he knew quite well that he would do neither of these things. He knew that he would be her lover. And yet, in spite of this deep knowledge, the surface mind still continued to discuss its little problem of cabs and bed-linen. Discussed it sensibly, discussed it dutifully. Because it would be a madness, he told himself, a criminal madness if he didn't send for the taxi or prepare that upstairs room. But the dark certainty of the depths rose suddenly and exploded at the surface in a bubble of ironic laughter, in a brutal and cynical word. "Comedian!" he said to himself, to the self that agitatedly thought of telephones and taxis and pillow-slips. "Seeing that it's obvious I'm going to have her." And, rising from the depths, her nakedness presented itself to him palpably in an integral and immediate contact with his whole being. But this was shameful, shameful. He pushed the naked Anadyomene back into the depths. Very well, then, (his surface mind resumed its busy efficient rattle), seeing that it was perhaps rather late to start telephoning for taxis, he'd rig up one of the rooms on the first floor. But if he couldn't find any sheets . . . ? But here was the house, the open door.

Pamela stepped across the threshold. The hall was almost dark. Through a curtained doorway on the left issued a thin blade of yellow light. Passive in her tired misery, she waited. Behind her the chain rattled, as it had rattled only a few moments before, when she had fled from the ominous sound, and clank, clank! the bolts were thrust back into place.

"There," said Fanning's voice. "And now . . . " With a click, the darkness yielded suddenly to brilliant light.

Pamela uttered a little cry and covered her face with her hands. "Oh, please," she begged, "please." The light hurt her, was a sort of outrage. She didn't want to see, couldn't bear to be seen.

"I'm sorry," he said, and the comforting darkness returned. "This way." Taking her arm he led her towards the lighted doorway on the left. "Shut your eyes," he commanded, as they approached the curtain. "We've got to go into the light again; but I'll turn it out the moment I can get to the switch. Now!" She shut her eyes and suddenly, as the curtain rings rattled, she saw, through her closed eyelids, the red shining of transparent blood. Still holding her arm, he led her forward into the room.

Pamela lifted her free hand to her face. "Please don't look at me," she whispered. "I don't want you to see me like this. I mean, I couldn't bear . . . " Her voice faded to silence.

"I won't look," he assured her. "And anyhow," he added, when they had taken two or three more steps across the room, "now I can't." And he turned the switch.

The pale translucent red went black again before her eyes. Pamela sighed. "I'm so tired," she whispered. Her eyes were still shut; she was too tired to open them.

"Take off your coat." A hand pulled at her sleeve. First one bare arm, then the other slipped out into the coolness.

Fanning threw the coat over a chair. Turning back, he could see her, by the tempered darkness that entered through the window, standing motionless before him, passive, wearily waiting, her face, her limp arms pale against the shadowy blackness.

"Poor Pamela," she heard him say, and then suddenly light finger-tips were sliding in a moth-winged caress along her arm. "You'd better lie down and rest." The hand closed round her arm, she was pushed gently forward. That taxi, he was still thinking, the upstairs room . . . But his fingers preserved the silky memory of her skin, the flesh of her arm was warm and firm against his palm. In the darkness, the supernatural world was coming mysteriously, thrillingly into existence; he was once more standing upon its threshold.

"There, sit down," came his voice. She obeyed; a low divan received her. "Lean back." She let herself fall on to pillows. Her feet were lifted on to the couch. She lay quite still. "As though I were dead," she thought, "as though I were dead." She was aware, through the darkness of her closed eyes, of his warm breathing presence, impending and very near. "As though I were dead," she inwardly repeated with a kind of pleasure. For the pain of her misery had ebbed away into the warm darkness, and to be tired, she found, to be utterly tired and to lie there utterly still were pleasures. "As though I were dead." And the light reiterated touch of his finger-tips along her arm—what were those caresses but another mode, a soothing and delicious mode, of gently dying?

In the morning, on his way to the kitchen to prepare their coffee, Fanning caught sight of his littered writing-table. He halted to collect the scattered sheets. Waiting for the water to boil, he read. "By the time you receive this letter, I shall be—no, not dead, Pamela . . . " He crumpled up each page as he had finished reading it and threw it into the dust-bin.

9

The architectural background was like something out of Alma Tadema. But the figures that moved across the sunlit atrium, that lingered beneath the colonnades and in the coloured shadow of the awnings, the figures were Hogarthian and Rowlandsonian, were the ferocious satires of Daumier and Rouveyre. Huge jellied females overflowed the chairs on which they sat.

Sagging and with the gait of gorged bears, old men went slowly shambling down the porticoes. Like princes preceded by their outriders, the rich fat burgesses strutted with dignity behind their bellies. There was a hungry prowling of gaunt emaciated men and women, yellow-skinned and with tragical, bile-injected eyes. And, conspicuous by their trailing blackness, these bloated or cadaverous pencillings from an anti-clerical notebook were priests.

In the midst of so many monsters Pamela was a lovely miracle of health and beauty. These three months had subtly transformed her. The rather wavering and intermittent *savoir-vivre,* the child's forced easiness of manner, had given place to a woman's certainty, to that repose even in action, that decision even in repose, which are the ordinary fruits of the intimate knowledge, the physical understanding of love.

"For it isn't only murder that will out," as Fanning had remarked some few days after the evening of the fireworks. "It isn't only murder. If you could see yourself, my child! It's almost indecent. Any one could tell that you'd been in bed with your lover. Could tell in the dark, even; you're luminous, positively luminous. All shining and smooth and pearly with love-making. It's really an embarrassment to walk about with you. I've a good mind to make you wear a veil."

She had laughed, delightedly. "But I don't mind them seeing. I *want* them to see. I mean, why should one be ashamed of being happy?"

That had been three months since. At present she had no happiness to be ashamed of. It was by no shining of eyes, no luminous soft pearliness of smoothed and rounded contour that she now betrayed herself. All that her manner, her pose, her gestures proclaimed was the fact that there *had* been such shinings and pearly smoothings, once. As for the present, her shut and sullen face announced only that she was discontented with it and with the man who, sitting beside her, was the symbol and the embodiment of that unsatisfactory present. A rather sickly embodiment at the moment, a thin and jaundiced symbol. For Fanning was hollow-cheeked, his eyes darkly ringed, his skin pale and sallow under the yellowed tan. He was on his way to becoming one of those pump-room monsters at whom they were now looking, almost incredulously. For, "Incredible!" was Fanning's comment. "Didn't I tell you that they simply weren't to be believed?"

Pamela shrugged her shoulders, almost imperceptibly, and did not answer. She did not feel like answering, she wanted to be uninterested, sullen, bored.

"How right old Butler was!" he went on, rousing himself by the stimulus of his own talk from the depression into which his liver and Pamela had plunged him. "Making the Erewhonians punish illness as a crime—how right! Because they *are* criminals, all these people. Criminally ugly and deformed, criminally incapable of enjoyment. Look at them. It's a caution. And when I think that I'm one of them . . . " He shook his head. "But let's hope this will make me a reformed character." And he emptied, with a grimace of disgust, his glass of tepid salt water. "Revolting! But I suppose it's right that Montecatini should be a place of punishment as well as cure.

One can't be allowed to commit jaundice with impunity. I must go and get another glass of my punishment—my purgatory, in every sense of the word," he added, smiling at his own joke. He rose to his feet painfully (every movement was now a painful effort for him) and left her, threading his way through the crowd to where, behind their marble counters, the pump-room barmaids dispensed warm laxatives from rows of polished brass taps.

The animation had died out of Fanning's face as he turned away. No longer distracted and self-stimulated by talk, he relapsed at once into melancholy. Waiting his turn behind two bulging monsignori at the pump, he looked so gloomily wretched, that a passing connoisseur of the waters pointed him out to his companion as a typical example of the hepatic pessimist. But bile, as a matter of fact, was not the only cause of Fanning's depression. There was also Pamela. And Pamela—he admitted it, though the fact belonged to that great class of humiliating phenomena whose existence we are always trying to ignore—Pamela, after all, was the cause of the bile. For if he had not been so extenuated by that crazy love-making in the narrow cells of the Passionist Fathers at Monte Cavo, he would never have taken chill and the chill would never have settled on his liver and turned to jaundice. As it was, however, that night of the full moon had finished him. They had gone out, groping their way through the terrors of the nocturnal woods, to a little grassy terrace among the bushes, from which there was a view of Nemi. Deep sunk in its socket of impenetrable darkness and more than half eclipsed by shadow, the eye of water gleamed up at them secretly, as though through eyelids almost closed. Under the brightness of the moon, the hills, the woods seemed to be struggling out of ghostly greyness towards colour, towards the warmth of life. They had sat there for a while, in silence, looking. Then, taking her in his arms, " '*Ceda al tatto la vista, al labro il lume'*" he had quoted with a kind of mockery—mocking her for the surrender to which he knew he could bring her, even against her will, even though, as he could see, she had made up her mind to sulk at him, mocking himself at the same time for the folly which drove him, weary and undesiring, to make the gesture. "'*Al labro il lume,*' " he repeated with that undercurrent of derision in his voice, and leaned towards her. Desire returned to him as he touched her, and with it a kind of exultation, a renewal (temporary, he knew, and illusory) of all his energies.

"No, Miles. Don't. I don't want . . . " And she had averted her face, for she was angry, resentful, she wanted to sulk. Fanning knew it, mockingly, and mockingly he had turned back her face towards him—*"al labro il lume"*—and found her lips. She struggled a little in his arms, protested and then was silent, lay still. His kisses had had the power to transform her. She was another person, different from the one who had sulked and been resentful. Or rather she was two people—the sulky and resentful one, with another person superimposed, a person who quiveringly sank and melted under his kisses, melted and sank down, down towards that mystical death, that apocalypse, that almost terrible transfiguration. But beneath, to one side, stood always the angry sulker, unappeased, unreconciled, ready to emerge again (full of a new resentment for the way she had been undignifiedly hustled off the stage) the moment the other should have retired. His realization of this made Fanning all the more perversely ardent, quickened the folly of his passion with a kind of derisive hostility. He drew his lips across her cheek, and suddenly their soft electrical touch on her ear made her shudder. "Don't!" she implored, dreading and yet desiring what was to come. Gently, inexorably his teeth closed, and the petal of cartilage was a firm elastic resistance between them. She shuddered yet more violently. Fanning relaxed the muscles of his jaws, then tightened them once more, gently, against that exquisite resistance. The felt beauty of rounded warmth and resilience was under his hand. In the darkness they were inhabitants of the supernatural world.

But at midnight they had found themselves, almost suddenly, on earth again, shiveringly cold under the moon. Cold, cold to the quick, Fanning had picked himself up. They stumbled homewards through the woods, in silence. It was in a kind of trance of chilled and sickened exhaustion that he had at last dropped down on his bed in the convent cell. Next morning he was ill. The liver was always his weak point. That had been nearly three weeks ago.

The second of the two monsignori moved away; Fanning stepped into his place. The barmaid handed him his hot dilute sulphate of soda. He deposited fifty centesimi as a largesse and walked off, meditatively sipping. But returning to the place from which he had come, he found their chairs occupied by a pair of obese Milanese business-men. Pamela had gone. He explored the Alma Tadema background; but there was no sign of her. She had evidently gone back to the hotel. Fanning, who still had five more glasses of water to get through, took his place among the monsters round the band-stand.

In her room at the hotel Pamela was writing up her diary. "September 20th. Montecatini seems a beastly sort of hole, particularly if you come to a wretched little hotel like this, which M. insisted on doing, because he knows the proprietor, who is an old drunkard and also cooks the meals, and M. has long talks with him and says he's like a character in Shakespeare, which is all very well, but I'd prefer better food and a room with a bath, not to mention the awfulness of the other people in the hotel, one of whom is the chief undertaker in Florence, who's always boasting to the other people at meal times about his business and what a fine motor hearse with gilded angels he's got and the number of counts and dukes he's buried. M. had a long conversation with him and the old drunkard after dinner yesterday evening about how you preserve corpses on ice and the way to make money by buying up the best sites at the cemetery and holding them till you could ask five times as much as you paid, and it was the first time I'd seen him looking cheerful and amused since his illness and even for some time before, but I was so horrified that I went off to bed. This morning at eight to the pump-room, where M. has to drink eight glasses of different kinds of water before breakfast and there are hundreds of hideous people all carrying mugs, and huge fountains of purgatives, and a band playing the 'Geisha,' so I came away after half an hour, leaving M. to his waters, because I really can't be expected to watch him drinking, and it appears there are six hundred W.C.s."

She laid down her pen and, turning round in her chair, sat for some time pensively staring at her own reflection in the wardrobe mirror. "If you look long enough," (she heard Clare's voice, she saw Clare, inwardly, sitting at her dressing-table), "you begin to wonder if it isn't somebody else. And perhaps, after all, one *is* somebody else, all the time." Somebody else, Pamela repeated to herself, somebody else. But was that a spot on her cheek, or a mosquito bite? A mosquito, thank goodness. "Oh God," she said aloud, and in the looking-glass somebody else moved her lips, "if only I knew what to do! If only I were dead!" She touched wood hastily. Stupid to say such things. But if only one knew, one were certain! All at once she gave a little stiff sharp shudder of disgust, she grimaced as though she had bitten on something sour. Oh, oh! she groaned; for she had suddenly seen herself in the act of dressing, there, in that moon-flecked darkness, among the bushes, that hateful night just before Miles fell ill. Furious because he'd humiliated her, hating him; she hadn't wanted to and he'd made her. Somebody else had enjoyed beyond the limits of enjoyment, had suffered a pleasure transmuted into its opposite. Or rather *she* had done the suffering. And then that further humiliation of having to ask him to help her look for her suspender belt! And there were leaves in her hair. And when she got back to the hotel, she found a spider squashed against her skin under the chemise. Yes, *she* had found the spider, not somebody else.

Between the brackish sips Fanning was reading in his pocket edition of the *Paradiso.* "*L'acqua che prendo giammai non si corse,*" he murmured;

> "*Minerva spira e conducemi Apollo,
> e nove Muse mi dimostran l'Orse.*"

He closed his eyes. "*E nove Muse mi dimostran l'Orse.*" What a marvel! "And the nine Muses point me to the Bears." Even translated the spell did not entirely lose its potency. "How glad I shall be," he thought, "to be able to do a little work again."

"*Il caffè?*" said a voice at his elbow. "*Non lo bevo mai, mai. Per il fegato, sa, è pessimo. Si dice anche che per gl'intestini . . .*" The voice receded out of hearing.

Fanning took another gulp of salt water and resumed his reading.

> *Voi altri pochi che drizzante il collo
> per tempo al pan degli angeli, del quale
> vivesi qui ma non sen vien satollo . . .*

The voice had returned. "*Pesce bollito, carne ai ferri o arrostita, patate lesse . . .*"

He shut his ears and continued. But when he came to

> *La concreata e perpetua sete*
>   *del deiforme regno,*

he had to stop again. This craning for angels' bread, this thirsting for the god-like kingdom . . . The words reverberated questioningly in his mind. After all, why not? Particularly when man's bread made you sick (he thought with horror of that dreadful vomiting of bile), when it was a case of *pesce bollito* and you weren't allowed to thirst for anything more palatable than this stuff. (He swigged again.) These were the circumstances when Christianity became appropriate. Christians, according to Pascal, ought to live like sick men; conversely, sick men can hardly escape being Christians. How pleased Colin Judd would be! But the thought of Colin was depressing, if only all Christians were like Dante! But in that case, what a frightful world it would be! Frightful.

> *La concreata e perpetua sete*
>   *del deiforme regno cen portava*
>   *Veloci, quasi come il ciel vedete.*
>   *Beatrice in suso ed io in lei guardava.* . . .

He thought of Pamela at the fireworks. On that pedestal. *Ben son, ben son Beatrice* on that pedestal. He remembered what he had said beneath the blossoming of the rockets; and also what he had meant to say about those legs which the pedestal made it so easy for the worshipper to pinch. Those legs, how remote now, how utterly irrelevant! He finished off his third glass of Torretta and, rising, made his way to the bar for his first of Regina. Yes, how utterly irrelevant! he thought. A complete solution of continuity. You were on the leg level, then you vomited bile, and as soon as you were able to think of anything but vomiting, you found yourself on the Dante level. He handed his mug to the barmaid. She rolled black eyes at him as she filled it. Some liverish gentlemen, it seemed, could still feel amorous. Or perhaps it was only the obese ones. Fanning deposited his offering and retired. Irrelevant, irrelevant. It seemed, now, the unlikeliest story. And yet there it was, a fact. And Pamela was solid, too, too solid.

Phrases floated up, neat and ready-made, to the surface of his mind.
"What does he see in her? What on earth can she see in him?"
"But it's not a question of sight, it's a question of touch."
And he remembered—*sentiments-centimètres*—that French pun about love, so appallingly cynical, so humiliatingly true. "But only humiliating," he assured himself, "because we choose to think it so, arbitrarily, only cynical because *Beatrice in suso ed io in lei guardava;* only appalling because we're creatures who sometimes vomit bile and because, even without vomiting, we sometimes feel ourselves naturally Christians." But in any case, *nove Muse mi dimostran l'Orse.* Meanwhile, however . . . He tilted another gill of water down his throat. And when he was well enough to work, wouldn't he also be well enough to thirst again for that other god-like kingdom, with its different ecstasies, its other peace beyond all

understanding? But *tant mieux, tant mieux,* so long as the Bears remained unmoved and the Muses went on pointing.

Pamela was looking through her diary. "June 24th," she read. "Spent the evening with M. and afterwards he said how lucky it was for me that I'd been seduced by him, which hurt my feelings (that word, I mean) and also rather annoyed me, so I said he certainly hadn't seduced me, and he said, all right, if I liked to say that I'd seduced him, he didn't mind, but anyhow it was lucky because almost anybody else wouldn't have been such a good psychologist as he, not to mention physiologist, and I should have hated it. But I said, how could he say such things? because it wasn't that at all and I was happy because I loved him, but M. laughed and said, you don't, and I said, I do, and he said, you don't, but if it gives you any pleasure to imagine you do, imagine, which upset me still more, his not believing, which is due to his not wanting to love himself, because I *do* love . . . "

Pamela quickly turned the page. She couldn't read that sort of thing now.

"June 25th. Went to the Vatican where M. . . . " She skipped nearly a page of Miles's remarks on classical art and the significance of orgies in the ancient religions; on the duty of being happy and having the sun inside you, like a bunch of ripe grapes; on making the world appear infinite and holy by an improvement of sensual enjoyment; on taking things untragically, unponderously.

"M. dined out and I spent the evening with Guy, the first time since the night of the fireworks, and he asked me what I'd been doing all this time, so I said, nothing in particular, but I felt myself blushing, and he said, anyhow you look extraordinarily well and happy and pretty, which also made me rather uncomfortable, because of what M. said the other day about murder will out, but then I laughed, because it was the only thing to do, and Guy asked what I was laughing about, so I said, nothing, but I could see by the way he looked at me that he was rather thrilled, which pleased me, and we had a very nice dinner and he told me about a girl he'd been in love with in Ireland and it seems they went camping together for a week, but he was never her lover because she had a kind of terror of being touched, but afterwards she went to America and got married. Later on, in the taxi, he took my hand and even tried to kiss me, but I laughed, because it was somehow very funny, I don't know why, but afterwards, when he persisted, I got angry with him.

"June 27th. Went to look at mosaics to-day, rather fine, but what a pity they're all in churches and always pictures of Jesus and sheep and apostles and so forth. On the way home we passed a wine shop and M. went in and ordered a dozen bottles of champagne, because he said that love can exist without passion, or understanding, or respect, but not without champagne. So I asked him if he really loved me, and he said, *Je t'adore,* in French, but I said, no, do you really *love* me? But he said, silence is golden and it's better to use one's mouth for kissing and drinking champagne and eating caviar, because he'd also bought some caviar; and if you start talking about love and thinking about love, you get everything wrong, because it's not *meant* to be talked about, but acted, and if people want to talk and think, they'd better talk about mosaics and that sort of thing. But I still went on asking him if he loved me. . . . "

"Fool, fool!" said Pamela aloud. She was ashamed of herself. Dithering on like that! At any rate Miles had been honest; she had to admit that. He'd taken care to keep the thing on the champagne level. And he'd always told her that she was imagining it all. Which had been intolerable, of course; he'd been wrong to be so right. She remembered how she had cried when he refused to answer her insistent question; had cried and afterwards allowed herself to be consoled. They went back to his house for supper; he opened a bottle of champagne, they ate the caviar. Next day he sent her that poem. It had arrived at the same time as some flowers from Guy. She reopened her notebook. Here it was.

> At the red fountain's core the thud of drums
> Quickens; for hairy-footed moths explore
> This aviary of nerves; the woken birds
> Flutter and cry in the branched blood; a bee
> Hums with his million-times-repeated stroke
> On lips your breast promotes geometers
> To measure curves, to take the height of mountains,
> The depth and silken slant of dells unseen.
>
> I read your youth, as the blind student spells
> With finger-tips the song from *Cymbeline.*
> Caressing and caressed, my hands perceive
> (In lieu of eyes) old Titian's paradise
> With Eve unaproned; and the Maja dressed
> Whisks off her muslins, that my skin may know
> The blind night's beauty of brooding heat and cool,
> Of silk and fibre, of molten-moist and dry,
> Resistance and resilience.
>   But the drum
> Throbs with yet faster beat, the wild birds go
> Through their red liquid sky with wings yet more
> Frantic and yet more desperate crying. Come!
> The magical door its soft and breathing valves
> Has set ajar. Beyond the threshold lie
> Worlds after worlds receding into light,
> As rare old wines on the ravished tongue renew
> A miracle that deepens, that expands,
> Blossoms, and changes hue, and chimes, and shines.
> Birds in the blood and doubled drums incite
> Us to the conquest of these new, strange lands
> Beyond the threshold, where all common times,

Things, places, thoughts, events expire, and life
Enters eternity.

The darkness stirs, the trees are wet with rain;
Knock and it shall be opened, oh, again,
Again! The child is eager for its dam
And I the mother am of thirsty lips,
Oh, knock again!
Wild darkness wets this sound of strings.
How smooth it slides among the clarinets,
How easily slips through the trumpetings!
Sound glides through sound, and lo! the apocalypse,
The burst of wings above a sunlit sea.
Must this eternal music make an end?
Prolong, prolong these all but final chords!
Oh, wounded sevenths, breathlessly suspend
Our fear of dying, our desire to know
The song's last words!
Almost Bethesda sleeps, uneasily.
A bubble domes the flatness; gyre on gyre,
The waves expand, expire, as in the deeps
The woken spring subsides
                  Play, music, play!
Reckless of death, a singing giant rides
His storm of music, rides; and suddenly
The tremulous mirror of the moon is broken;
On the farthest beaches of our soul, our flesh,
The tides of pleasure foaming into pain
Mount, hugely mount; break; and retire again.
The final word is sung, the last word spoken.

"Do I like it, or do I rather hate it? I don't know.

"June 28th. When I saw M. at lunch to-day, I told him I didn't really know if I liked his poem, I mean apart from literature, and he said, yes, perhaps the young *are* more romantic than they think, which rather annoyed me, because I believe he imagined I was shocked, which is too ridiculous. All the same, I *don't* like it."

Pamela sighed and shut her eyes, so as to be able to think more privately, without distractions. From this distance of time she could see all that had happened in perspective, as it were, and as a whole. It was her pride, she could see, her fear of looking ridiculously romantic that had changed the quality of her feelings towards Miles—a pride and a fear on which he had played, deliberately. She had given herself with passion and desperately, tragically, as she imagined that Joan would have desperately given herself, at first sight, to a reluctant Walter. But the love he had offered her in return was a thing of laughter and frank, admitted sensuality, was a gay and easy companionship enriched, but uncomplicated, by pleasure. From the first he had refused to come up to her emotional level. From the first he had taken it for granted—and his taking it for granted was in itself an act of moral compulsion—that she should descend to his. And she had descended—reluctantly at first, but afterwards without a struggle. For she came to realize, almost suddenly, that after all she didn't really love him in the tragically passionate way she had supposed she loved him. In a propitious emotional climate her belief that she was a despairing Joan might perhaps have survived, at any rate for a time. But it was a hot-house growth of the imagination; in the cool dry air of his laughter and cheerfully cynical frankness it had withered. And all at once she had found herself, not satisfied, indeed, with what he offered, but superficially content. She returned him what he gave. Less even than he gave. For soon it became apparent to her that their rôles were being reversed, that the desperate one was no longer herself, but Miles. For "desperate"—that was the only word to describe the quality of his desires. From light and gay—and perhaps, she thought, the lightness had been forced, the gaiety fabricated for the occasion as a defence against the tragical vehemence of her attack and of his own desires—his sensuality had become heavy, serious, intense. She had found herself the object of a kind of focused rage. It had been frightening sometimes, frightening and rather humiliating; for she had often felt that, so far as he was concerned, she wasn't there at all; that the body between those strong, those ruthless and yet delicate, erudite, subtly intelligent hands of his, that were like a surgeon's or a sculptor's hands, was not her body, was no one's body, indeed, but a kind of abstraction, tangible, yes, desperately tangible, but still an abstraction. She would have liked to rebel; but the surgeon was a master of his craft, the sculptor's fingers were delicately learned and intelligent. He had the art to overcome her reluctances, to infect her with some of his strange, concentrated seriousness. Against her will. In the intervals he resumed his old manner; but the laughter was apt to be bitter and spiteful, there was a mocking brutality in the frankness.

Pamela squeezed her eyes more tightly shut and shook her head, frowning at her memories. For distraction she turned back to her diary.

"June 30th. Lunched with Guy, who was really rather tiresome, because what is more boring than somebody being in love with you, when you're not in love with them? Which I told him quite frankly, and I could see he was dreadfully upset, but what was I to do?"

Poor Guy! she thought, and she was indignant, not with herself, but with Fanning. She turned over several pages. It was July now and they were at Ostia for the bathing. It was at Ostia that that desperate seriousness had come into his desire. The long hot hours of the siesta were propitious to his earnest madness. Propitious also to his talents, for he worked well in the heat. Behind her lowered eyelids Pamela had a vision of him sitting at his table, stripped to a pair of shorts, sitting there, pen in hand, in the next room and with an open door between them, but somehow at an infinite distance. Terrifyingly remote, a stranger more foreign for being known so well, the inhabitant of other worlds to which she had no access. They were worlds which she was already beginning to hate. His books were splendid, of course; still, it wasn't much fun being with a man who, for half the time, wasn't there at all. She saw him sitting there, a beautiful naked stranger, brown and wiry, with a face like brown marble, stonily focused on his paper. And then suddenly this stranger rose and came towards her through the door, across the room. "Well?" she heard herself saying. But the stranger did not answer. Sitting down on the edge of her bed, he took the sewing out of her hands and threw it aside on to the dressing-table. She tried to protest, but he laid a hand on her mouth. Wordlessly he shook his head. Then, uncovering her mouth, he kissed her. Under his surgeon's, his sculptor's hands, her body was moulded to a symbol of pleasure. His face was focused and intent, but not on her, on something else, and serious, serious, like a martyr's, like a mathematician's, like a criminal's. An hour later he was back at his table in the next room, in the next world, remote, a stranger once again—but he had never ceased to be a stranger.

Pamela turned over two or three more pages. On July 12th they went sailing and she had felt sick; Miles had been provokingly well all the time. The whole of the sixteenth had been spent in Rome. On the nineteenth they drove to Cerveteri to see the Etruscan tombs. She had been furious with him, because he had put out the lamp and made horrible noises in the cold sepulchral darkness, underground—furious with terror, for she hated the dark.

Impatiently Pamela went on turning the pages. There was no point in reading; none of the really important things were recorded. Of the earnest madness of his love-making, of those hands, that reluctantly suffered pleasure she hadn't been able to bring herself to write. And yet those were the things that mattered. She remembered how she had tried to imagine that she was like her namesake of *Pastures New*—the fatal woman whose cool detachment gives her such power over her lovers. But the facts had proved too stubborn; it was simply impossible for her to pretend that this handsome fancy-picture was her portrait. The days flicked past under her thumb.

"July 30th. On the beach this morning we met some friends of M.'s, a journalist called Pedder, who has just come to Rome as correspondent for some paper or other, and his wife, rather awful, I thought, both of them, but M. seemed to be extraordinarily pleased to see them, and they bathed with us and afterwards came and had lunch at our hotel, which was rather boring so far as I was concerned, because they talked a lot about people I didn't know, and then there was a long discussion about politics and history and so forth, *too* highbrow, but what was intolerable was that the woman thought she ought to be kind and talk to me meanwhile about something I could understand, so she talked about shops in Rome and the best places for getting clothes, which was rather ridiculous, as she's obviously one of those absurd arty women, who appeared in M.'s novels as young girls just before and during the War, so advanced in those days, with extraordinary coloured stockings and frocks like pictures by Augustus John. Anyhow, what she was wearing at lunch was really too fancy-dress, and really at her age one ought to have a little more sense of the decencies, because she must have been quite thirty-five. So that the idea of talking about smart shops in Rome was quite ludicrous to start with, and anyhow it was so insulting to me, because it implied that I was too young and half-witted to be able to take an interest in their beastly conversation. But afterwards, apropos of some philosophical theory or other, M. began talking about his opium smoking, and he told them all the things he'd told me and a lot more besides, and it made me feel very uncomfortable and then miserable and rather angry, because I thought it was only me he talked to like that, so confidentially, but now I see he makes confidences to everybody and it's not a sign of his being particularly fond of a person, or in love with them, or anything like that. Which made me realize that I'm even less important to him than I thought, and I found I minded much more than I expected I should mind, because I thought I'd got past minding. But I *do* mind."

Pamela shut her eyes again. "I ought to have gone away then," she said to herself. "Gone straight away." But instead of retiring, she had tried to come closer. Her resentment—for oh, how bitterly she resented those Pedders and his confidential manner towards them!—had quickened her love. She wanted to insist on being more specially favoured than a mere Pedder; and, loving him, she had the right to insist. By a process of imaginative incubation, she managed to revive some of the emotions she had felt before the night of the fireworks. Tragically, with a suicide's determination, she tried to force herself upon him. Fanning fought a retreating battle, ruthlessly. Oh, how cruel he could be, Pamela was thinking, how pitilessly cruel! The way he could shut himself up as though in an iron box of indifference! The way he could just fade out into absent silence, into another world! The way he could flutter out of an embarrassing emotional situation on the wings of some brilliant irrelevance! And the way he could flutter back again, the way he could compel you, with his charm, with the touch of his hands, to reopen the gates of your life to him, when you'd made up your mind to shut them against him for ever! And not content with forcing you to yield, he would mock you for your surrender, mock himself too for having attacked—jeering, but without seeming to jeer, indirectly, in some terrible little generalization about the weakness of the human soul, the follies and insanities of the body. Yes, how cruel he could be! She reopened her eyes.

"August 10th. M. still very glum and depressed and silent, like a wall when I come near. I think he sometimes hates me for loving him. At lunch he said he'd got to go into Rome this afternoon, and he went and didn't come back till late, almost midnight. Waiting for him, I couldn't help crying.

"August 11th. Those Pedders came to lunch again to-day and all M.'s glumness vanished the moment he saw them and he was charming all through lunch and so amusing, that I couldn't help laughing, though I felt more like crying, because why should he be so much nicer and more *friendly* with them than with me? After lunch, when we went to rest, he came into my room and wanted to kiss me, but I wouldn't let him, because I said, I don't want to owe your fits of niceness to somebody else, and I asked him, why? why was he so much nicer to them than to me? And he said they were his people, they belonged to the same time as he did and meeting them was like meeting another Englishman in the middle of a crowd of Kaffirs in Africa. So I said, I suppose I'm the Kaffirs, and he laughed and said, no, not quite Kaffirs, not more than a Rotary Club dinner in Kansas City, with the Pedders playing the part of a man one had known at Balliol in 'ninety-nine. Which made me cry, and he sat on the edge of the bed and took my hand and said he was very sorry, but that's what life was like, and it couldn't be helped, because time was always time, but people weren't always the same people, but sometimes one person and sometimes another, sometimes Pedder-fanciers and sometimes Pamela-fanciers, and it wasn't my fault that I hadn't heard the first performance of *Pelléas* in 1902 and it wasn't Pedder's fault that he had, and therefore Pedder was his compatriot and I wasn't. But I said, after all, Miles, you're my lover, doesn't that make any difference? But he said, it's a question of speech, and bodies don't speak, only minds, and when two minds are of different ages it's hard for them to understand each other when they speak, but bodies can understand each other, because they don't talk, thank God, he said, because it's such a comfort to stop talking sometimes, to stop thinking and just *be,* for a change. But I said that might be all right for him, but just *being* was my ordinary life and the change for me was talking, was being friends with somebody who knew how to talk and do all the other things talking implies, and I'd imagined I was that, besides just being somebody he went to bed with, and that was why I was so miserable, because I found I wasn't, and those beastly Pedders were. But he said, damn the Pedders, damn the Pedders for making you cry! and he was so *divinely* sweet and gentle that it was like gradually sinking, sinking and being drowned. But afterwards he began laughing again in that rather hurting way, and he said, your body's so much more beautiful than their minds—that is, so long as one's a Pamela-fancier; which I am, he said, or rather was and shall be, but now I must go and work, and he got up and went to his room, and I was wretched again."

The entries of a few days later were dated from Monte Cavo. A superstitious belief in the genius of place had made Pamela insist on the change of quarters. They had been happy on Monte Cavo; perhaps they would be happy there again. And so, suddenly, the sea didn't suit her, she needed mountain air. But the genius of place is an unreliable deity. She had been as unhappy on the hill-top as by the sea. No, not quite so unhappy, perhaps. In the absence of the Pedders, the passion which their coming had renewed declined again. Perhaps it would have declined even if they had still been there. For the tissue of her imagination was, at the best of times, but a ragged curtain. Every now and then she came to a hole and through the hole she could see a fragment of reality, such as the bald and obvious fact that she didn't love Miles Fanning. True, after a peep through one of these indiscreet holes she felt it necessary to repent for having seen the facts, she would work herself up again into believing her fancies. But her faith was never entirely whole-hearted. Under the superficial layer of imaginative suffering lay a fundamental and real indifference. Looking back now, from the further shore of his illness, Pamela felt astonished that she could have gone on obstinately imagining, in spite of those loop-holes on reality, that she loved him. "Because I didn't," she said to herself, clear-sighted, weeks too late. "I didn't." But the belief that she did had continued, even on Monte Cavo, to envenom those genuinely painful wounds inflicted by him on her pride, her self-respect, inflicted with a strange malice that seemed to grow on him with the passage of the days.

"August 23rd." She had turned again to the notebook. "M. gave me this at lunch to-day.

> Sensual heat and sorrow cold
>   Are undivided twins;
> For there where sorrow ends, consoled,
>   Lubricity begins.

I told him I didn't exactly see what the point of it was, but I supposed it was meant to be hurting, because he's always trying to be hurting now, but he said, no, it was just a Great Thought for putting into Christmas crackers. But he did mean to hurt, and yet in one way he's crazy about me, he's . . . "

Yes, crazy was the right word. The more and the more crazily he had desired her, the more he had seemed to want to hurt her, to hurt himself too—for every wound he inflicted on her was inflicted at the same time on himself. "Why on earth didn't I leave him?" she wondered as she allowed a few more days to flick past.

"August 29th. A letter this morning from Guy in Scotland, so no wonder he took such an endless time to answer mine, which is a relief in one way, because I was beginning to wonder if he wasn't answering on purpose, but also rather depressing, as he says he isn't coming back to Rome till after the middle of September and goodness knows what will have happened by that time. So I felt very melancholy all the morning, sitting under the big tree in front of the monastery, such a marvellous huge old tree with very bright bits of sky between the leaves and bits of sun on the ground and moving across my frock, so that the sadness somehow got mixed up with the loveliness, which it often does do in a queer way, I find. M. came out unexpectedly and suggested going for a little walk before lunch, and he was very sweet for a change, but I dare say it was because he'd worked well. And I said, do you remember the first time we came up to Monte Cavo? and we talked about that afternoon and what fun it had been, even the museum, I said, even my education, because the Apollo was lovely. But he shook his head and said, *Apollo, Apollo, lama sabachthani,* and when

I asked why he thought his Apollo had abandoned him he said it was because of Jesus and the Devil, and you're the Devil, I'm afraid, and he laughed and kissed my hand, but I ought to wring your neck, he said. For something that's *your* fault, I said, because it's you who make me a Devil for yourself. But he said it was me who made him make me into a Devil. So I asked how? And he said just by existing, just by having my particular shape, size, colour, and consistency, because if I'd looked like a beetle and felt like wood, I'd have never made him make me into a Devil. So I asked him why he didn't just go away seeing that what was wrong with me was that I was there at all. But that's easier said than done, he said, because a Devil's one of the very few things you can't run away from. And I asked why not? And he said because you can't run away from yourself and a Devil is at least half you. Besides, he said, the essence of a vice is that it *is* a vice—it holds you. Unless it unscrews itself, I said, because I'd made up my mind that minute that I'd go away, and it was such a relief having made up my mind, that I wasn't furious or miserable any more, and when M. smiled and said, if it *can* unscrew itself, I just laughed."

A little too early, she reflected, as she read the words; she had laughed too early. That night had been the night of the full moon (oh, the humiliation of that lost suspender belt, the horror of that spider squashed against her skin!) and the next day he had begun to be ill. It had been impossible, morally impossible to leave him while he was ill. But how ghastly illness was! She shuddered with horror. Ghastly! "I'm sorry to be so repulsive," he had said to her one day, and from her place at his bedside she had protested, but hypocritically, hypocritically. As Aunt Edith might have protested. Still, one's *got* to be hippo-ish, she excused herself, simply *got* to be sometimes. "But, thank goodness," she thought, "he's better now." In a day or two he'd be quite fit to look after himself. These waters were supposed to be miraculous.

She took a sheet of writing-paper from the box on the table and uncorked the bottle of ink.

"Dear Guy," she began, "I wonder if you're back in Rome yet?"

On Huxley

One of the more remarkable members of a remarkable family, Aldous Huxley (born July 26, 1894) seemed destined to take a place in English intellectual and public life at least equal to that of his brother Julian. Grandson of the famous Victorian scientist and educator Thomas Henry Huxley, great-nephew of Thomas's occasional adversary Matthew Arnold, son of Leonard Huxley (editor of the *Cornhill Magazine*), Aldous planned to specialize in biology. He had spent two years at Eton, first major step toward entering the Establishment, when in 1910 a sudden attack of blindness forced him to abandon the study of science and the idea of a conventional career and to study literature, taking a First Class degree in

English literature at Balliol College, Oxford, in 1916. During the First World War he was unfit for military service but taught and continued to write and publish poetry (four volumes by 1920) and to meet many prominent writers and philosophers, most of them through Lady Ottoline Morrell. Like hers, his taste was then and continued to be broad: Sitwells and members of Bloomsbury, deadly literary antagonists; D. H. Lawrence, author of *Lady Chatterly's Lover,* and Anita Loos, author of *Gentlemen Prefer Blondes.* After the war he became a literary journalist, first with John Middleton Murry's short-lived but influential *Athenaeum* as reviewer and columnist, then with the *Westminster Gazette* as drama critic, finally with Condé Nast's publications, first *Vogue* and *Vanity Fair,* and then *House and Garden,* which he helped to found, as general factotum, including advertising copywriter. These jobs and a vast flow of independent journalism helped to support him and his wife, Maria Nys, until 1923, when income from his writing helped to free him from steady employment—"honest work," he sardonically called it in essays and in mocking portraits of his various jobs in his early novels. Not that he grew lazy. In a life filled with frequent illnesses and even more frequent moves, he managed to produce well over 1300 items by the time of his death: occasional regular columns—for the *Chicago Herald and Examiner* in the thirties, for *Esquire* in the fifties—a steady flow of essays and books—on poetry, religion, art, mysticism, science, psychedelic drugs, eyesight—as well as novels, biographies, introductions to books, and occasional film and play scripts. From 1923 to 1937 the Huxleys lived abroad, more or less based in Italy but traveling extensively. In 1937, they moved to California, their home until Huxley's death from cancer on November 22, 1963—a few hours after the assassination of President John F. Kennedy.

Recurrent in criticism of Huxley is the charge that he was more essayist than novelist. He obliquely admitted this charge in the confession of Philip Quarles, novelist within the novel *Point Counter Point,* that he was not a congenital novelist. Many years later Huxley admitted in an interview that he had trouble "inventing plots" and integrating "the essay element" and "the fictional element." He was obviously as much interested in ideas as in situations, in history as in the contemporary scene, and he delighted in juxtaposing characters drawn from historical personages with others drawn from his immediate acquaintance. Thus, in *Antic Hay* the diabolist Coleman is based on Philip Heseltine, alias Peter Warlock, while Casimir Lypiatt is drawn from the nineteenth-century English painter, poet, failure, and suicide, Benjamin Robert Haydon. In *Point Counter Point,* Denis Burlap and Mark Rampion owe much to Murry and Lawrence, while Spandrell exhibits many of the characteristics described in Huxley's essay on Charles Baudelaire, published a year later. Conversely, Huxley's biographical sketches, like that of Maine de Biran in *Themes and Variations* (1950), owe their creation of the atmosphere of the times and the conflict of motives within the individual to the novelist's skill.

"After the Fireworks" is typical of Huxley's blend of fact and fiction. The basic situation, a young girl throwing herself at a famous older man, was drawn, he said, from the letters of Chateaubriand, who wrote the girl but fended her off when she invaded his house. "With my usual sadism," Huxley added, "I thought it would be amusing to give it the cruel ending. And as one couldn't use Chateaubriand himself—that monstrous pride, and loneliness, and underneath the burning imagination, that emotional aridity would have been impracticable to handle—I made the hero one of those people (they have always fascinated me and provoked a certain envy) who know how to shirk natural consequences and get something for nothing, give Nemesis the slip" (*Letters of Aldous Huxley,* p. 338).

However, as Huxley knew, but as many early readers who were misled by his apparent cynicism failed to recognize, Nemesis cannot be escaped, even though her operation might be unrecognizable or, to the imperceptive, rather pleasant. "After the Fireworks" was published in 1930, two years after *Point Counter Point* and two years before *Brave New World,* two of his most famous novels. During this period Huxley was beginning to move away from the influence of D. H. Lawrence toward a more skeptical philosophical position, but he retained the Laurentian idea that failure to integrate all aspects of one's personality led to imbalance and that the exclusive or discontinuous development of these aspects led to a perversion of the self and a kind of nemesis, an inexorable operation of cause and effect in both physical and psychological realms. In earlier works, especially *Do What You Will* and *Proper Studies,* he attempted to find a means of integration, but his most memorable and most characteristic fiction dealt with the unresolvable divisions in man between his passion and his reason and between his desire for good and his accomplishment of ill. Miles Fanning resembles many of Huxley's characters: Theodore Gumbril of *Antic Hay,* who tries to see the link between God seen as a warm feeling and God as an equation, and who finally abdicates his moral responsibility; Calamy of *Those Barren Leaves,* who vacillates between sensual indulgence and ascetic search for self-knowledge; and Anthony Beavis of *Eyeless in Gaza* and Dr. Sigmund Obispo of *After Many a Summer Dies the Swan,* who at least in part are detached sensualists. Pamela Tarn is a somewhat younger version of one type of Huxleyan female who attracts men and leads them to destroy themselves: Myra Viveash in *Antic Hay* and Lucy Tantamount in *Point Counter Point* are the most notable.

Like Huxley's other novels, "After the Fireworks" supports by its technique the theme that people are parallel straight lines that never meet, that true communication is almost impossible. As in *Point Counter Point,* though on a smaller scale, Huxley refuses to let a single character's viewpoint dominate or even to let a character rest secure in his analysis of motives and events. Pamela and Miles see the same events from different angles, and the poems and diaries underscore the fact that one's interpretation of events changes with time. Furthermore, Huxley contrasts ideas by embodying them in characters or underlines a theme by introducing a character to make a specific point. Miles and Colin are an example of the first, Guy of the second.

After this short novel, Huxley continued to employ the same themes and character types, but increasingly he felt the necessity to resolve the conflicts instead of merely stating them. In the novels written after *Brave New World,* he advocated self-transcendence through religious and even mystical discipline which drew heavily upon Oriental sources as well as upon the findings of modern science, especially pharmacology.

Textual note:

In *Brief Candles* (London: Chatto and Windus, 1930), the text followed here; in America published by Doubleday, Doran. The pagination of the limited edition follows the American first. After 1930, published in various editions, including an Avon paperback retitled *After the Fireworks.*

It has also appeared in the following collections: *Retrospect: An Omnibus of Aldous Huxley's Books* (Garden City, N.Y.: Doubleday, Doran, 1933); *Rotunda: A Selection from the Works of Aldous Huxley* (London: Chatto and Windus, 1933); *The World of Aldous Huxley: An Omnibus of His Fiction and Non-Fiction over Three Decades,* ed. Charles J. Rolo (New York:Harper & Row, Publishers, 1947; New York: Grosset & Dunlap, Inc., 1957).

Resources for further study:

All of Huxley's novels, especially *Antic Hay* (1923), *Those Barren Leaves* (1925) (set in Italy), *Point Counter Point* (1928), and *Brave New World* (1932). His collected stories, including all but the longest, were published in 1957.

Most useful among the nonfiction are the volumes of essays from this period: *Proper Studies* (1927), *Do What You Will,* (1929), and *Music at Night* (1931). The collected essays (in fact, a selection) were published in 1959. Huxley's last two volumes of poetry, *Arabia Infelix* (1929), and *The Cicadas* (1931), deal with many of the same themes as his fiction. See also the interview in *Writers at Work: Second Series,* ed. Van Wyck Brooks (New York: The Viking Press, Inc., 1963), pp. 193–214. And see *Letters,* below.

BIBLIOGRAPHICAL:

DUVAL, HANSON R. *Aldous Huxley: A Bibliography,* New York: Arrow Editions, 1939. A descriptive bibliography.

ESCHELBACH, CLAIRE JOHN, and JOYCE LEE SHOBER. *Aldous Huxley: A Bibliography 1916–1959.* Berkeley, Calif.: University of California Press, 1961. More enumerative than descriptive. Contains a preface by Huxley, and compiled with his assistance.

CLARESON, THOMAS D., and CAROLYN S. ANDREWS. "Aldous Huxley: A Bibliography, 1960–64," *Extrapolation,* 6 (1964), 2–21.

BIOGRAPHICAL:

CLARK, RONALD W. *The Huxleys.* New York: McGraw-Hill Book Company, 1968. Clearest and most straightforward account of Aldous Huxley's life, interspersed with information about other descendants of Thomas Henry Huxley. Many pictures and a genealogy.

HUXLEY, ALDOUS. *The Letters of Aldous Huxley,* ed. Grover Smith. New York: Harper and Row, 1969. Contains a detailed chronology by Smith. The letters themselves contain a wealth of biographical detail.

HUXLEY, JULIAN, ed. *Aldous Huxley, 1894–1963: A Memorial Volume.* New York: Harper & Row, Publishers, 1965. Memoirs by many friends of Huxley.

HUXLEY, LAURA ARCHERA. *This Timeless Moment.* New York: Farrar, Straus & Giroux, Inc., 1968. A memoir by Huxley's second wife, focusing on the years after 1955.

CRITICAL:

ATKINS, JOHN ALFRED. *Aldous Huxley: A Literary Study.* New York: Grossman Publishers, Inc., Orion Press, 1968. Revised edition.

BOWERING, PETER. *Aldous Huxley: A Study of the Major Novels.* New York: Oxford University Press, 1969.

WATTS, HAROLD W. *Aldous Huxley.* New York: Twayne Publishers, Inc., 1969. Like the other volumes in Twayne's various series, consciously an introduction.

ELIZABETH BOWEN
Ivy Gripped the Steps

Ivy gripped and sucked at the flight of steps, down which with such a deceptive wildness it seemed to be flowing like a cascade. Ivy matted the door at the top and amassed in bushes above and below the porch. More, it had covered, or one might feel consumed, one entire half of the high, double-fronted house, from the basement up to a spiked gable: it had attained about half-way up to the girth and more than the density of a tree, and was sagging outward under its own weight. One was left to guess at the size and the number of windows hidden by looking at those in the other side. But these, though in sight, had been made effectively sightless: sheets of some dark composition that looked like metal were sealed closely into their frames. The house, not old, was of dull red brick with stone trimmings.

To crown all, the ivy was now in fruit, clustered over with fleshy pale green berries. There was something brutal about its fecundity. It was hard to credit that such a harvest could have been nourished only on brick and stone. Had not reason insisted that the lost windows must, like their fellows, have been made fast, so that the suckers for all their seeking voracity could not enter, one could have convinced oneself that the ivy must be feeding on something inside the house.

The process of strangulation could be felt; one wondered how many more years of war would be necessary for this to complete itself. And, the conventionality of the house, the remains, at least, of order in its surroundings made what was happening more and more an anomaly. Mrs. Nicholson's house had always enjoyed distinction—that of being detached, while its neighbours, though equally "good," had been erected in couples or even in blocks of four; that of being the last in the avenue; that of having on one hand as neighbour the theatre, to whose façade its front was at right angles. The theatre, set back behind shallow semi-circular gardens, at once crowned and terminated the avenue, which ran from it to the Promenade overhanging the sea. And the house, apart from the prestige of standing just where it stood, had had the air of reserving something quite of its own. It was thus perhaps just, or not unfitting, that it should have been singled out for this gothic fate.

This was, or had been, one of the best residential avenues in Southstone, into which private hotels intruded only with the most breathless, costly discretion: if it was not that now it was nothing else, for there was nothing else for it to be. Lines of chestnut trees had been planted along the pavements, along the railed strip of lawn that divided the avenue down the middle—now, the railings were, with all other ironwork, gone; and where the lawn was very long rusty grass grew up into the tangles of rusty barbed wire. On to this, as on to the concrete pyramids—which, in the course of four years of waiting to be pushed out to obstruct the invader, had sunk some inches into the soil—the chestnuts were now dropping their leaves.

The decline dated from the exodus of the summer of 1940, when Southstone had been declared in the front line. The houses at the sea end of the avenue had, like those on the Promenade, been requisitioned; but some of those at the theatre end stayed empty. Here and there, portions of porches or balustrades had fallen into front gardens, crushing their over-growth; but there were no complete ruins; no bomb or shell had arrived immediately here, and effects of blast, though common to all of Southstone, were less evident than desuetude and decay. It was now the September of 1944; and, for some reason, the turn of the tide of war, the accumulation of the Invasion victories, gave Southstone its final air of defeat. The with-drawal of most of the soldiers, during the summer, had drained off adventitious vitality. The A.A. batteries, this month, were on the move to another part of the coast. And, within the very last few days, the silencing of the guns across the Channel had ended the tentative love affair with death: Southstone's life, no longer kept to at least a pitch by shelling warnings, now had nothing but an etiolated slowness. In the shuttered shopping streets along the Promenade, in the intersecting avenues, squares and crescents, vacuum mounted up. The lifting of the ban on the area had, so far, brought few visitors in.

This afternoon, for minutes together, not a soul, not even a soldier, crossed the avenue: Gavin Doddington stood to regard the ivy in what was, virtually, solitude. The sky being clouded, though not dark, a timeless flat light fell on to everything. Outside the theatre a very few soldiers stood grouped about; some moodily, some in no more than apathy. The theatre gardens had been cemented over to make a lorry park; and the engine of one of the lorries was being run.

Mrs. Nicholson could not be blamed for the ivy: *her* absence from Southstone was of long standing, for she had died in 1912—two years before the outbreak of what Gavin still thought of as Admiral Concannon's war. After her death, the house had been put up for auction by her executors: since then, it might well have changed hands two or three times. Probably few of the residents dislodged in 1940 had so much as heard Mrs. Nicholson's name. In its condition, today, the house was a paradox: having been closed and sealed up with extreme care, it had been abandoned in a manner no less extreme. It had been nobody's business to check the ivy. Nor, apparently, had there been anybody to authorize a patriotic sacrifice of the railings—Gavin Doddington, prodding between the strands of ivy, confirmed his impression that that iron lacework still topped the parapet of the front garden. He could pursue with his finger, though not see, the pattern that with other details of the house, outside and in, had long ago been branded into his memory. Looking up at the windows in the exposed half he saw, still in position along the sills, miniature reproductions of this pattern, for the support of window boxes. Those, which were gone, had been flowery in her day.

The assumption was that, as lately as 1940, Mrs. Nicholson's house *had* belonged to someone, but that it belonged to nobody now. The late owner's death in some other part of England must have given effect to a will not brought up to date, by which the property passed to an heir who could not be found—to somebody not heard of since Singapore fell or not yet reported anything more than "missing" after a raid on London or a battle abroad. Legal hold-ups dotted the worldwide mess . . . So reasoning, Gavin Doddington gave rein to what had been his infant and was now his infantile passion for explanation. But also he attached himself to the story as to something nothing to do with him; and did so with the intensity of a person who must think lest he should begin to feel.

His passion for explanation had been, when he knew Mrs. Nicholson, raised by her power of silently baulking it into the principal reason for suffering. It had been among the stigmata of his extreme youth—he had been eight when he met her, ten when she died. He had not been back to Southstone since his last stay with her.

Now, the lifting of the official ban on the area had had the effect of bringing him straight back—why? When what one has refused is put out of reach, when what one has avoided becomes forbidden, some lessening of the inhibition may well occur. The ban had so acted on his reluctance that, when the one was removed, the other came away with it—as a scab, adhering, comes off with a wad of lint. The transmutation, due to the fall of France, of his "*I* cannot go back to Southstone," into "*One* cannot go there" must have been salutary, or, at least, exteriorizing. It so happened that when the ban came off he had been due for a few days' leave from the Ministry. He had at once booked a room at one of the few hotels that remained at the visitor's disposition.

Arriving at Southstone yesterday evening, he had confined his stroll in the hazy marine dusk to the cracked, vacant and wire-looped Promenade— from which he returned with little more than the wish that he had, after all, brought somebody down here with him. Amorist since his 'teens, he had not often set off on a holiday uncompanioned. The idea of this as a pilgrimage revolted him: he remained in the bar till the bar closed. This morning he had no more than stalked the house, approaching it in wavering closing circles through the vaguer Southstone areas of association. He had fixed for the actual confrontation that hour, deadline for feeling, immediately after lunch.

The story originated in a friendship between two young girls in their Dresden finishing year. Edith and Lilian had kept in touch throughout later lives that ran very widely apart—their letters, regularly exchanged, were perhaps more confidential than their infrequent meetings. Edith had married a country gentleman, Lilian a business man. Jimmie Nicholson had bought the Southstone house for his wife in 1907, not long before his death, which had been the result of a stroke. He had been senior by about fifteen years: their one child, a daughter, had died at birth.

Edith Doddington, who had never been quite at ease on the subject of Lilian's marriage, came to stay more often now her friend was a widow, but still could not come as often as both would have liked. Edith's own married life was one of contrivance and of anxiety. After money, the most pressing of Edith's worries centred round the health of her second son: Gavin had been from birth a delicate little boy. The damp of his native county, inland and low-lying, did not suit him: there was the constant question of change of air—till his health stabilized, he could not go away to school. It was natural that Lilian, upon discovering this, should write inviting Gavin to stay at Southstone—ideally, of course, let his mother bring him; but if Edith could not be free, let him come alone. Mrs. Nicholson hoped he and she, who had not yet met, would not, or would not for long, be shy of each other. Her maid Rockham was, at any rate, good with children.

Gavin had heard of Southstone as the scene of his mother's only exotic pleasures. The maid Rockham was sent to London to meet him: the two concluded their journey with the absurdly short drive, in an open victoria, from the station to Mrs. Nicholson's house. It was early in what was a blazing June: the awnings over the windows rippled, the marguerites in the window-boxes undulated, in a hot breeze coming down the avenue from the sea. From the awnings the rooms inside took a tense bright dusk. In the sea-blue drawing-room, up whose walls reared mirrors framed in ivory brackets, Gavin was left to await Mrs. Nicholson. He had time to marvel at the variety of the bric-à-brac crowding brackets and tables, the manyness of the cut-crystal vases, the earliness of the purple and white sweet pea—at the Doddingtons', sweet pea did not flower before July. Mrs. Nicholson then entered: to his surprise she did not kiss him.

Instead, she stood looking down at him—she was tall—with a glittering, charming uncertainty. Her head bent a little lower, during consideration not so much of Gavin as of the moment. Her *coiffeur* was like spun sugar: that its crisp upward waves should seem to have been splashed with silvery powder added, only, marquise-like glowing youth to her face.

The summery light-like fullness of her dress was accentuated by the taut belt with coral-inlaid clasp: from that small start the skirts flowed down to dissipate and spread where they touched the floor. Tentatively she extended her right hand, which he, without again raising his eyes, shook. "Well . . . Gavin," she said. "I hope you had a good journey? I am so very glad you could come."

He said: "And my mother sends you her love."

"Does she?" Sitting down, sinking an elbow into the sofa cushions, she added: "How *is* Edith—how is your mother?"

"Oh, she is very well."

She vaguely glanced round her drawing-room, as though seeing it from his angle, and, therefore, herself seeing it for the first time. The alternatives it offered could be distracting: she soon asked him her first intimate question—"Where do you think you would like to sit?"

Not that afternoon, nor, indeed, until some way on into this first visit did Gavin distinguish at all sharply between Mrs. Nicholson and her life. Not till the knife of love gained sufficient edge could he cut out her figure from its surroundings. Southstone was, for the poor landowner's son, the first glimpse of the enchanted existence of the *rentier*. Everything was effortless; and, to him, consequently, seemed stamped with style. This society gained by smallness: it could be comprehended. People here, the company that she kept, commanded everything they desired, were charged with nothing they did not. The expenditure of their incomes—expenditure calculated so long ago and so nicely that it could now seem artless—occupied them. What there was to show for it showed at every turn; though at no turn too much, for it was not too much. Such light, lofty, smooth-running houses were to be found, quite likely, in no capital city. A word to the livery stables brought an imposing carriage to any door: in the afternoons one drove, in a little party, to reflect on a Roman ruin or to admire a village church. In the Promenade's glare, at the end of the shaded avenue, parasols passed and repassed in a rhythm of leisure. Just inland were the attentive shops. There were meetings for good causes in cool drawing-rooms, afternoon concerts in the hotel ballrooms; and there was always the theatre, where applause continued long after Gavin had gone to bed. Best of all, there were no poor to be seen.

The plan of this part of Southstone (a plateau backed by the downs and overhanging the sea) was masterful. Its architecture was ostentatious, fiddling, bulky and mixed. Gavin was happy enough to be at an age to admire the one, to be unaware of the other—he was elated, rather than not, by this exhibition of gimcrack size; and bows, bays, balustrades, glazed-in balconies and French-type mansardes not slowly took up their parts in the fairy tale. As strongly was he impressed by the strong raying out, from such points as station and theatre, of avenues; each of which crossed, obliquely, just less wide residential roads. Lavishness appeared in the public flowers, the municipal seats with their sofa-like curving backs, the flagpoles, cliff grottoes, perspectives of lawn. There was a climate here that change from season to season, the roughest Channel gale blowing, could not disturb. This town without function fascinated him—outside it, down to the port or into the fishing quarter, "old Southstone," he did not attempt to stray. Such tameness might have been found odd in a little boy: Mrs. Nicholson never thought of it twice.

Gavin's estimation of Southstone—as he understood much later—coincided with that of a dead man. When Jimmie Nicholson bought the house for his wife here, Southstone was the high dream of his particular world. It was as Lilian's husband he made the choice: alone, he might not have felt capable of this polished leisure. His death left it uncertain whether, even *as* Lilian's husband, he could have made the grade. The golf course had been his object: failing that he was not, perhaps, so badly placed in the cemetery, which was also outside the town. For, for Southstone dividends kept their mystic origin: they were as punctual as Divine grace, as unmentioned as children still in wombs. Thickset Jimmie, with his pursuant reek of the City, could have been a distasteful reminder of money's source.

Gavin, like his dead host, beheld Southstone with all the ardour of an outsider. His own family had a touch of the brutishness that comes from any dependence upon land. Mr. and Mrs. Doddington were constantly in wet clothes, constantly fatigued, constantly depressed. Nothing new appeared in the squire's home; and what was old had acquired a sort of fog from being ignored. An austere, religious idea of their own standing not so much inspired as preyed upon Gavin's parents. Caps touched to them in the village could not console them for the letters they got from their bank. Money for them was like a spring in a marsh, feebly thrusting its way up to be absorbed again: any profit forced from the home farm, any rents received for outlying lands went back again into upkeep, rates, gates, hedging, draining, repairs to cottages and renewal of stock. There was nothing, no nothing ever, to show. In the society round them they played no part to which their position did not compel them: they were poor gentry, in fact, at a period when poverty could not be laughed away. Their lot was less enviable than that of any of their employees or tenants, whose faces, naked in their dejection, and voices pitched to complaints they could at least utter, had disconcerted Gavin, since babyhood, at the Hall door. Had the Doddingtons been told that their kind would die out, they would have expressed little more than surprise that such complicated troubles could end so simply.

Always towards the end of a stay at Southstone Gavin's senses began to be haunted by the anticipation of going back. So much so that to tread the heat-softened asphalt was to feel once more the suck of a sticky lane. *Here,* day and night he breathed with ease that was still a subconscious joy: the thought of the Midlands made his lungs contract and deaden—such was the old cold air, sequestered by musty baize doors, of the corridors all the way to his room at home.

His room *here* was on the second floor, in front, looking on to the avenue. It had a frieze of violets knotted along a ribbon: as dusk deepened, these turned gradually black. Later, a lamp from the avenue cast a tree's shifting shadow on to the ceiling above his bed; and the same light pierced the Swiss skirts of the dressing-table. Mrs. Nicholson, on the first occasion when she came as far as his door to say good night, deprecated the "silliness" of this little room. Rockham, it seemed, had thought it suitable for his age—she, Rockham, had her quarters on the same floor—Mrs.

Nicholson, though she did not say so, seemed to feel it to be unsuitable for his sex. "Because I don't suppose," she said, "that you really ever *are* lonely in the night?"

Propped upright against his pillows, gripping his glass of milk, he replied: "I am never frightened."

"But, lonely—what makes you lonely, then?"

"I don't know. I suppose, thoughts."

"Oh, but why," she said, "don't you like them?"

"When I am here the night seems a sort of waste, and I don't like to think what a waste it is."

Mrs. Nicholson, who was on her way out to dinner, paused in the act of looping a gauze scarf over her hair and once again round her throat. "Only tell me," she said, "that you're not more lonely, Gavin, because I am going out? Up here, you don't know if I am in the house or not."

"I do know."

"Perhaps," she suggested humbly, "you'll go to sleep? They all say it is right for you, going to bed so early, but I wish it did not make days so short.—I must go."

"The carriage hasn't come round yet."

"No, it won't: it hasn't been ordered. It is so lovely this evening, I thought I would like to walk." She spoke, though, as though the project were spoiled for her: she could not help seeing, as much as he did, the unkindness of leaving him with this picture. She came even further into the room to adjust her scarf at his mirror, for it was not yet dark. "Just once, one evening perhaps, you could stay up late. Do you think it would matter? I'll ask Rockham."

Rockham remained the arbiter: it was she who was left to exercise anything so nearly harsh as authority. In even the affairs of her own house Mrs. Nicholson was not heard giving an order: what could not be thought to be conjured into existence must be part of the clockwork wound up at the start by Jimmie and showing no sign of beginning to run down yet. The dishes that came to table seemed to surprise her as much, and as pleasingly, as they did Gavin. Yet the effect she gave was not of idleness but of preoccupation: what she did with her days Gavin did not ask himself— when he did ask himself, later, it was too late. They continued to take her colour—those days she did nothing with.

It was Rockham who worked out the daily programme, devised to keep the little boy out of Madam's way. "Because Madam," she said, "is not accustomed to children." It was by Rockham that, every morning, he was taken down to play by the sea: the beach, undulations of orange shingle, was fine-combed with breakwaters, against one of which sat Rockham, reading a magazine. Now and then she would look up, now and then she would call. These relegations to Rockham sent Gavin to angry extremes of infantilism: he tried to drape seaweed streamers around her hat; he plagued to have pebbles taken out of his shoe. There was a literal feeling of degradation about this descent from the plateau to the cliff's foot. From close up, the sea, with its heaving mackerel vacancy, bored him—most of the time he stood with his back to it, shading his eyes and staring up at the heights. From right down here, though Southstone could not be seen—any more than objects set back on a high shelf can be seen by somebody standing immediately underneath it—its illusion, its magical artificiality, was to be savoured as from nowhere else. Tiny, the flags of the Promenade's edge, the figures leaning along the railings, stood out against a dazzle of sky. And he never looked up at these looking down without an interrupted heartbeat—might she not be among them?

The rule was that they, Rockham and Gavin, walked zigzag down by the cliff path, but travelled up in the lift. But one day fate made Rockham forget her purse. They had therefore to undertake the ascent. The path's artful gradients, hand-railed, were broken by flights of steps and by niched seats, upon every one of which Rockham plumped herself down to regain breath. The heat of midday, the glare from the flowered cliff beat up Gavin into a sort of fever. As though a dropped plummet had struck him between the eyes he looked up, to see Mrs. Nicholson's face above him against the blue. The face, its colour rendered transparent by the transparent silk of a parasol, was inclined forward: he had the experience of seeing straight up into eyes that did not see him. Her look was pitched into space: she was not only not seeing him, she was seeing nothing. She was listening, but not attending, while someone talked.

Gavin, gripping the handrail, bracing his spine against it, leaned out backwards over the handrail into the void, in the hopes of intercepting her line of view. But in vain. He tore off clumps of sea pinks and cast the too-light flowers outwards into the air, but her pupils never once flickered down. Despair, the idea that his doom must be never, never to reach her, not only now but ever, gripped him and gripped his limbs as he took the rest of the path—the two more bends and few more steps to the top. He clawed his way up the rail, which shook in its socket.

The path, when it landed Gavin on to the Promenade, did so some yards from where Mrs. Nicholson and her companion stood. Her companion was Admiral Concannon. "Hello, hello!" said the Admiral, stepping back to see clear of the parasol. "Where have *you* sprung from?"

"Oh, but Gavin," exclaimed Mrs. Nicholson, also turning, "why not come up in the lift? I thought you liked it."

"Lift?" said the Admiral. "Lift, at his age? What, has the boy got a dicky heart?"

"No indeed!" she said, and looked at Gavin so proudly that he became the image of health and strength.

"In that case," said the Admiral, "do him good." There was something, in the main, not unflattering about this co-equal masculine brusqueness. Mrs. Nicholson, looking over the railings, perceived the labouring top of her maid's hat. "It's poor Rockham," she said, "that I am thinking about; she hasn't got a heart but she has attacks.—How hazy it is!" she said, indicating the horizon with a gloved hand. "It seems to be days since we saw France. I don't believe Gavin believes it is really there."

"It is there all right," said the Admiral, frowning slightly.

"Why, Rockham," she interposed, "you look hot. Whatever made you walk up on a day like this?"

"Well, I cannot fly, can I, madam; and I overlooked my purse."

"Admiral Concannon says we may all be flying.—What are you waiting for?"

"I was waiting for Master Gavin to come along."

"I don't see why he should, really—which would you rather, Gavin?"

Admiral Concannon's expression did not easily change, and did not change now. His features were severely clear cut; his figure was nervy and spare; and he had an air of eating himself—due, possibly, to his retirement. His manners of walking, talking and standing, though all to be recognized at a distance, were vehemently impersonal. When in anything that could be called repose he usually kept his hands in his pockets—the abrupt extraction of one hand, for the purpose of clicking thumb and finger together, was the nearest thing to a gesture he ever made. His voice and step had become familiar, among the few nocturnal sounds of the avenue, some time before Gavin had seen his face; for he escorted Mrs. Nicholson home from parties to which she had been wilful enough to walk. Looking out one night, after the hall door shut, Gavin had seen the head of a cigarette, immobile, pulsating sharply under the dark trees. The Concannons had settled at Southstone for Mrs. Concannon's health's sake: their two daughters attended one of the schools.

Liberated into this blue height, Gavin could afford to look down in triumph at the sea by whose edge he had lately stood. But the Admiral said: "Another short turn, perhaps?"—since they were to *be* three, they had better be three in motion. Mrs. Nicholson raised her parasol, and the three moved off down the Promenade with the dignified aimlessness of swans. Ahead, the distance dissolved, the asphalt quivered in heat; and she, by walking between her two companions, produced a democracy of masculine trouble into which age did not enter at all. As they passed the bandstand she said to Gavin: "Admiral Concannon has just been saying that there is going to be a war."

Gavin glanced across at the Admiral, who remained in profile. Unassisted and puzzled, he said: "Why?"

"Why indeed?" she agreed.—"There!" she said to the Admiral. "It's no good trying to tease me, because I never believe you." She glanced around her and added: "After all, we live in the present day! History is quite far back; it is sad, of course, but it does seem silly. I never even cared for history at school; I was glad when we came to the end of it."

"And when, my dear, did you come to the end of history?"

"The year I put up my hair. It had begun to be not so bad from the time we started catching up with the present; and I was glad I had stayed at school long enough to be sure that it had all ended happily. But oh, those unfortunate people in the past! It seems unkind to say so, but can it have been their faults? They can have been no more like us than cats and dogs. I suppose there *is* one reason for learning history—one sees how long it has taken to make the world nice. Who on earth could want to upset things now?—No one could want to," she said to the Admiral. "You forget the way we behave now, and there's no other way. Civilized countries are polite to each other, just as you and I are to the people we know, and uncivilized countries are put down—but, if one thinks, there are beautifully few of those. Even savages really prefer wearing hats and coats. Once people wear hats and coats and can turn on electric light, they would no more want to be silly than you or I do.—Or *do* you want to be silly?" she said to the Admiral.

He said: "I did not mean to upset you."

"You don't," she said. "I should not dream of suspecting *any* civilized country!"

"Which civilized country?" said Gavin. "France?"

"For your information," said the Admiral coldly, "it is Germany we should be preparing to fight, for the reason that she is preparing to fight us."

"I have never been happier anywhere," said Mrs. Nicholson, more nearly definitely than usual. "Why," she added, turning to Gavin, "if it were not for Germany, now I come to think of it, you would not be here!"

The Admiral, meanwhile, had become intent on spearing on the tip of his cane a straying fragment of paper, two inches torn off a letter, that was defiling the Promenade. Lips compressed, he crossed to a litter basket (which had till then stood empty, there being no litter) and knocked the fragment into it off his cane. He burst out: "I should like to know what this place is coming to—we shall have trippers next!"

This concern his beautiful friend *could* share—and did so share that harmony was restored. Gavin, left to stare out to sea, reflected on one point in the conversation: he could never forget that the Admiral had called Mrs. Nicholson, "My dear."

Also, under what provocation had the Admiral threatened Mrs. Nicholson with war? . . . Back at Gavin's home again, once more with his parents, nothing was, after all, so impossible: this was outside the zone of electric light. As late summer wore slowly over the Midlands, the elms in the Doddingtons' park casting lifeless slate-coloured shadows over sorrel, dung, thistles and tufted grass, it was born in on Gavin that this existence belonged, by its nature, to *any* century. It was unprogressive. It had stayed as it was while, elsewhere, history jerked itself painfully off the spool; it could hardly be more depressed by the fateful passage of armies than by the flooding of tillage or the failure of crops: it was hardly capable, really, of being depressed further. It was an existence mortgaged to necessity; it was an inheritance of uneasiness, tension and suspicion. One could preassume the enmity of weather, prices, mankind, cattle. It was this dead weight of existence that had supplied to history not so much the violence or the futility that had been, as she said, apparent to Mrs. Nicholson, but its repetitive harshness and its power to scar. This existence had no volition, but could not stop; and its never stopping, because it could not, made history's ever stopping the less likely. No signs of even an agreeable pause were to be seen round Doddington Hall. Nor could one, at such a distance from Southstone, agree that time had laboured to make the world nice.

Gavin now saw his mother as Mrs. Nicholson's friend. Indeed, the best of the gowns in which Edith went out to dinner, when forced to go out to dinner, had been Lilian's once, and once or twice worn by her. Worn by Edith, they still had the exoticism of gifts, and dispelled from their folds not only the giver's sachets but the easy pitiful lovingness of the giver's mood. In them, Gavin's mother's thin figure assumed a grace whose pathos was lost to him at the time. While the brown-yellow upward light of the table oil-lamp unkindly sharpened the hollows in Mrs. Doddington's face and throat, Gavin, thrown sideways out of his bed, fingered the mousseline or caressed the satin of the skirts with an adoring absorption that made his mother uneasy—for fetishism is still to be apprehended by these for whom it has never had any name. She would venture: "You like, then, to see me in pretty clothes?" . . . It was, too, in the first of these intermissions between his visits to Southstone that he, for the first time, took stock of himself, of his assets—the evident pleasingness of his manner; his looks—he could take in better and better part his elder brother's jibes at his pretty-prettiness—his quickness of mind, which at times made even his father smile; and his masculinity, which, now he tried it out, gave him unexpected command of small situations. At home, nights were not a waste: he attached himself to his thoughts, which took him, by seven-league strides, onward to his next visit. He rehearsed, using his mother, all sorts of little gratuities of behaviour, till she exclaimed: "Why, Lilian has made quite a little page of you!" At her heels round the garden or damp extensive offices of the Hall, at her elbow as she peered through her letters or resignedly settled to her accounts, he reiterated: "Tell me about Germany."

"Why Germany?"

"I mean, the year you were there."

A gale tore the slates from the Hall stables, brought one tree down on to a fence and another to block the drive, the night before Gavin left for Southstone. This time he travelled alone. At Southstone, dull shingly roaring thumps from the beach travelled as far inland as the railway station; from the Promenade—on which, someone said, it was all but impossible to stand upright—there came a whistling strain down the avenues. It was early January. Rockham was kept to the house by a nasty cold; so it was Mrs. Nicholson who, with brilliantly heightened colour, holding her muff to the cheek on which the wind blew, was on the station platform to meet Gavin. A porter, tucking the two of them into the waiting carriage, replaced the foot-warmer under the fur rug. She said: "How different this is from when you were with me last. Or do you like winter?"

"I like anything, really."

"I remember one thing you don't like: you said you didn't like thoughts." As they drove past a lighted house from which music came to be torn about by the wind, she remembered: "You've been invited to several parties."

He was wary: "Shall you be going to them?"

"Why, yes; I'm sure I *could* go," she said.

Her house was hermetic against the storm: in the drawing-room, heat drew out the smell of violets. She dropped her muff on the sofa, and Gavin stroked it—"It's like a cat," he said quickly, as she turned round. "Shall I have a cat?" she said. "Would you like me to have a cat?" All the other rooms, as they went upstairs, were tawny with fires that did not smoke.

Next morning, the wind had dropped; the sky reflected on everything its mild brightness; trees, houses and pavements glistened like washed glass. Rockham, puffy and with a glazed upper lip, said: "Baster Gavid, you've brought us better weather." Having blown her nose with what she seemed to hope was exhaustive thoroughness, she concealed her handkerchief in her bosom as guiltily as though it had been a dagger. "Badam," she said, "doesn't like be to have a cold.—Poor Bisses Codcaddod," she added, "has been laid up agaid."

Mrs. Concannon's recovery must be timed for the little dinner party that they were giving. Her friends agreed that she ought to reserve her strength. On the morning of what was to be the day, it was, therefore, the Admiral whom one met out shopping: Gavin and Mrs. Nicholson came on him moodily selecting flowers and fruit. Delayed late autumn and forced early spring flowers blazed, under artificial light, against the milder daylight outside the florist's plate glass. "For tonight, for the party?" exclaimed Mrs. Nicholson. "Oh, let us have carnations, scarlet carnations!"

The Admiral hesitated. "I think Constance spoke of chrysanthemums, white chrysanthemums."

"Oh, but these are so washy, so like funerals. They will do poor Constance no good, if she still feels ill."

Gavin, who had examined the prices closely, in parenthesis said: "Carnations are more expensive."

"No, wait!" cried Mrs. Nicholson, gathering from their buckets all the scarlet carnations that were in reach, and gaily shaking the water from their stems, "you must let me send these to Constance, because I am so much looking forward to tonight. It will be delightful."

"I hope so," the Admiral said. "But I'm sorry to say we shall be an uneven number: we have just heard that poor Massingham has dropped out. Influenza."

"Bachelors shouldn't have influenza, should they.—But then, why not ask somebody else?"

"So very much at the last moment, that might seem a bit—informal."

"Dear me," she teased, "have you really *no* old friend?"

"Constance does not feel . . . "

Mrs. Nicholson's eyebrows rose: she looked at the Admiral over the carnations. This was one of the moments when the Admiral could be heard to click his finger and thumb. "What a pity," she said. "I don't care for lopsided parties. *I* have one friend who is not touchy—invite Gavin!"

To a suggestion so completely outrageous, who was to think of any reply? It was a *coup*. She completed, swiftly: "Tonight, then? We shall be with you at about eight."

Gavin's squiring Mrs. Nicholson to the Concannons' party symptomized this phase of their intimacy; without being, necessarily, its highest point. Rockham's cold had imperilled Rockham's prestige: as intervener or arbiter she could be counted out. There being no more talk of these odious drops to the beach, Gavin exercised over Mrs. Nicholson's mornings what seemed a conqueror's rights to a terrain; while with regard to her afternoons she showed a flattering indecision as to what might not please him or what he could not share. At her tea-table, his position was made subtly manifest to her guests. His bedtime was becoming later and later; in vain did Rockham stand and cough in the hall; more than once or twice he had dined downstairs. When the curtains were drawn, it was he who lit the piano candles, then stood beside her as she played—ostensibly to turn over the music, but forgetting the score to watch her hands. At the same time, he envisaged their two figures as they would appear to someone—his other self—standing out there in the cold dark of the avenue, looking between the curtains into the glowing room. One evening, she sang "Two Eyes of Grey that used to be so Bright."

At the end, he said: "But that's supposed to be a song sung by a man to a woman."

Turning on the stool, she said: "Then you must learn it."

He objected: "But your eyes are not grey."

Indeed they were never neutral eyes. Their sapphire darkness, with that of the sapphire pendant she was wearing, was struck into by the Concannons' electric light. That round fitment on pulleys, with a red silk frill, had been so adjusted above the dinner table as to cast down a vivid circle, in which the guests sat. The stare and sheen of the cloth directly under the light appeared supernatural. The centrepiece was a silver or plated pheasant, around whose base the carnations—slightly but strikingly "off" the red of the shade, but pre-eminently flattering in their contrast to Mrs. Nicholson's orchid *glacé* gown—were bunched in four silver cornets. This was a party of eight: if the Concannons had insisted on stressing its "littleness," it was, still, the largest that they could hope to give. The evident choiceness of the guests, the glitter and the mathematical placing of the silver and glass, the prompt, meticulous service of the dishes by maids whose suspended breath could be heard—all, all bespoke art and care. Gavin and Mrs. Nicholson were so placed as to face one another across the table: her glance contained him, from time to time, in its leisurely, not quite attentive play. He wondered whether she felt, and supposed she must, how great had been the effrontery of their entrance.

For this dinner-party lost all point if it were not *de rigueur*. The Concannon daughters, even (big girls, but with hair still down their backs) had, as not qualified for it, been sent out for the evening. It, the party, had been balanced up and up on itself like a house of cards: built, it remained as precarious. Now the structure trembled, down to its base, from one contemptuous flip at its top story—Mrs. Nicholson's caprice of bringing a little boy. Gavin perceived that night what he was not to forget: the helplessness, in the last resort, of society—which he was never, later, to be able to think of as a force. The pianola-like play of the conversation did not drown the nervousness round the table.

At the head of the table the Admiral leaned just forward, as though pedalling the pianola. At the far end, an irrepressible cough from time to time shook Mrs. Concannon's decolletage and the crystal pince-nez which, balanced high on her face, gave her a sensitive blankness. She had the *dévote* air of some sailors' wives; and was heroic in pale blue without a wrap—arguably, nothing could make her iller. The Admiral's pride in his wife's courage passed like a current over the silver pheasant. For Mrs. Concannon, joy in sustaining all this for his sake, and confidence in him, provided a light armour: she possibly did not feel what was felt for her. To Gavin she could not have been kinder; to Mrs. Nicholson she had only and mildly said: "He will not be shy, I hope, if he does not sit beside you?"

Rearrangement of the table at the last moment could not but have disappointed one or other of the two gentlemen who had expected to sit, and were now sitting, at Mrs. Nicholson's right and left hand. More and more, as course followed course, these two showed how highly they rated their good fortune—indeed, the censure around the rest of the table only acted for them, like heat drawing out scent, to heighten the headiness of her immediate aura. Like the quick stuff of her dress her delinquency, even, gave out a sort of shimmer: while she, neither arch nor indolent, turned from one to the other her look—if you like, melting; for it dissolved her pupils, which had never been so dilated, dark, as tonight. In this look, as dinner proceeded, the two flies, ceasing to struggle, drowned.

The reckoning would be on the way home. Silent between the flies' wives, hypnotized by the rise and fall of Mrs. Nicholson's pendant, Gavin ate on and on. The ladies' move to the drawing-room sucked him along with it in the wake of the last skirt . . . It was without a word that, at the end of the evening, the Admiral saw Mrs. Nicholson to her carriage—Gavin, like an afterthought or a monkey, nipping in under his host's arm extended to hold open the carriage door. Light from the porch, as they drove off, fell for a moment longer on that erect form and implacable hatchet face. Mrs. Nicholson seemed to be occupied in gathering up her skirts to make room for Gavin. She then leaned back in her corner, and he in his: not a word broke the tension of the short dark drive home. Not till she had dropped her cloak in front of her drawing-room fire did she remark: "The Admiral's angry with me."

"Because of me?"

"Oh dear no; because of her. If I did not think to be angry was very silly, I'd almost be a little angry with him."

"But you meant to make him angry, didn't you?" Gavin said.

"Only because he's silly," said Mrs. Nicholson. "If he were not so silly, that poor unfortunate creature would stop coughing: she would either get better or die." Still standing before her mantelpiece, she studied some freesias in a vase—dispassionately, she pinched off one fading bloom, rolled it into a wax pill between her thumb and finger, then flicked it away to sizzle in the heart of the fire. "If people," she said, "give a party for no other reason but to show off their marriage, what kind of evening can one expect?—However, I quite enjoyed myself. I hope you did?"

Gavin said: "Mrs. Concannon's quite old. But then, so's the Admiral."

"He quite soon will be, at this rate," said Mrs. Nicholson. "That's why he's so anxious to have that war. One would have thought a man could just be a man.—What's the matter, Gavin; what are you staring at?"

"That is your most beautiful dress."

"Yes; that's why I put it on." Mrs. Nicholson sat down on a low blue velvet chair and drew the chair to the fire: she shivered slightly. "You say such sweet things, Gavin: what fun we have!" Then, as though, within the seconds of silence ticked off over her head by the little Dresden clock, her own words had taken effect with her, she turned and, with an impulsive movement, invited him closer to her side. Her arm stayed round him; her short puffed sleeve, disturbed by the movement, rustled down into silence. In the fire a coal fell apart, releasing a seam of gas from which spurted a pale tense quivering flame. "Aren't you glad we are back?" she said, "that we are only you and me?—Oh, why endure such people when all the time there is the whole world! Why do I stay on and on here; what am I doing? Why don't we go right away somewhere, Gavin; you and I? To Germany, or into the sun? Would that make you happy?"

"That—that flame's so funny," he said, not shifting his eyes from it.

She dropped her arm and cried, in despair: "After all, what a child you are!"

. "I am not."

"Anyhow, it's late; you must go to bed."

She transmuted the rise of another shiver into a slight yawn.

Overcharged and trembling, he gripped his way, flight by flight, up the polished banister rail, on which his palms left patches of mist; pulling himself away from her up the staircase as he had pulled himself towards her up the face of the cliff.

After that midwinter visit there were two changes: Mrs. Nicholson went abroad, Gavin went to school. He overheard his mother say to his father that Lilian found Southstone this winter really too cold to stay in. "Or, has made it too hot to stay in?" said Mr. Doddington, from whose disapproval the story of Gavin and the Concannons' party had not been able to be kept. Edith Doddington coloured, loyal, and said no more. During his first term Gavin received at school one bright picture postcard of Mentone. The carefully chosen small preparatory school confronted him, after all, with fewer trials than his parents had feared and his brother hoped. His protective adaptability worked quickly; he took enough colour, or colourlessness, from where he was to pass among the others, and along with them—a civil and indifferent little boy. His improved but never quite certain health got him out of some things and secured others—rests from time to time in the sick-room, teas by the matron's fire. This spectacled woman was not quite unlike Rockham; also, she was the most approachable edge of the grown-up ambience that connected him, however remotely, with Mrs. Nicholson. At school, his assets of feeling remained, one would now say, frozen.

His Easter holidays had to be spent at home; his summer holidays exhausted their greater part in the same concession to a supposed attachment. Not until September was he dispatched to Southstone, for a week, to be set up before his return to school.

That September was an extension of summer. An admirable company continued its season of light opera at the theatre, in whose gardens salvias blazed. The lawns, shorn to the roots after weeks of mowing, were faintly blond after weeks of heat. Visitors were still many; and residents, after the fastidious retreat of August, were returning—along the Promenade, all day long, parasols, boater hats and light dresses flickered against the dense blue gauze backdrop that seldom let France be seen. In the evenings the head of the pier was a lighted musical box above the not yet cooling sea. Rare was the blade of chill, the too crystal morning or breathlike blur on the distance that announced autumn. Down the avenues the dark green trees hardened but did not change: if a leaf did fall, it was brushed away before anyone woke.

If Rockham remarked that Gavin was now quite a little man, her mistress made no reference to his schoolboy state. She did once ask whether the norfolk jacket that had succeeded his sailor blouse were not, in this weather, a little hot; but that he might be expected to be more gruff, mum, standoffish or awkward than formerly did not appear to strike her. The change, if any, was in her. He failed to connect—why should he?—her new languor, her more marked contrarieties and her odd little periods of askance musing with the illness that was to be her death. She only said, the summer had been too long. Until the evenings she and Gavin were less alone, for she rose late; and, on their afternoon drives through the country, inland from the coast or towards the downs, they were as often as not accompanied by, of all persons, Mrs. Concannon. On occasions when Mrs. Concannon returned to Mrs. Nicholson's house for tea, the Admiral made it his practice to call for her. The Concannons were very much occupied with preparations for another social event: a Southstone branch of the Awaken Britannia League was to be inaugurated by a drawing-room meeting at their house. The daughters were busy folding and posting leaflets. Mrs. Nicholson, so far, could be pinned down to nothing more than a promise to send cakes from her own, or rather her cook's, kitchen.

"But at least," pleaded Mrs. Concannon, at tea one afternoon, "you should come if only to hear what it is about."

By five o'clock, in September, Mrs. Nicholson's house cast its shadow across the avenue on to the houses opposite, which should otherwise have received the descending sun. In revenge, they cast shadow back through her bow window: everything in the drawing-room seemed to exist in copper-mauve glass, or as though reflected into a tarnished mirror. At this hour, Gavin saw the pale walls, the silver lamp stems, the transparent frills of the cushions with a prophetic feeling of their impermanence. At her friend's words, Mrs. Nicholson's hand, extended, paused for a moment over the cream jug. Turning her head she said: "But I know what it is about; and I don't approve."

With so little reference to the Admiral were these words spoken that he might not have been there. There, however, he was, standing drawn up above the low tea table, cup and saucer in hand. For a moment, not speaking, he weighed his cup with a frown that seemed to ponder its exact weight. He then said: "Then, logically, you should not be sending cakes."

"Lilian," said Constance Concannon fondly, "is never logical with regard to her friends."

"Aren't I?" said Mrs. Nicholson.—"But cake, don't you think, makes everything so much nicer? You can't offer people nothing but disagreeable ideas."

"You are too naughty, Lilian. All the League wants is that we should be alert and thoughtful.—Perhaps Gavin would like to come?"

Mrs. Nicholson turned on Gavin a considering look from which complicity seemed to be quite absent; she appeared, if anything, to be trying to envisage him as alert and thoughtful. And the Admiral, at the same moment, fixed the candidate with a measuring eye. "What may come," he said, "is bound, before it is done, to be his affair." Gavin made no reply to the proposition—and it was found, a minute or two later, that the day fixed for the drawing-room meeting was the day fixed for his return home. School began again after that. "Well, what a pity," Mrs. Concannon said.

The day approached. The evenings were wholly theirs, for Mrs. Nicholson dined out less. Always, from after tea, when any guests had gone, he began to reign. The apartnesses and frustrations of the preceding hours, and, most of all, the occasional dissonances that those could but produce between him and her, sent him pitching towards the twilight in a fever that rose as the week went on. This fever, every time, was confounded by the sweet pointlessness of the actual hour when it came. The warmth that lingered in the exhausted daylight made it possible for Mrs. Nicholson to extend herself on the *chaise longue* in the bow window. Seated on a stool at the foot of the *chaise longue,* leaning back against the frame of the window, Gavin could see, through the side pane of the glass projection in which they sat, the salvias smouldering in the theatre gardens. As it was towards these that her chair faced, in looking at them he was looking away from her. On the other hand, they were looking at the same thing. So they were on the evening that was his last. At the end of a minute or two of silence she exclaimed: "No, I don't care, really, for scarlet flowers.—You do?"

"Except carnations?"

"I don't care for public flowers. And you look and look at them till I feel quite lonely."

"I was only thinking, *they* will be here tomorrow."

"Have you been happy this time, Gavin? I haven't sometimes thought you've been quite so happy. Has it been my fault?"

He turned, but only to finger the fringe of the Kashmir shawl that had been spread by Rockham across her feet. Not looking up, he said: "I have not seen you so much."

"There are times," she said, "when one seems to be at the other side of glass. One sees what is going on, but one cannot help it. It may be what one does not like, but one cannot feel."

"Here, I always feel."

"Always feel what?" she remotely and idly asked.

"I just mean, here, I feel. I don't feel, anywhere else."

"And what is 'here'?" she said, with tender mocking obtuseness. "South-stone? What do you mean by 'here'?"

"Near you."

Mrs. Nicholson's attitude, her repose, had not been come at carelessly. Apparently relaxed, but not supine, she was supported by six or seven cushions—behind her head, at the nape of her neck, between her shoulders, under her elbows and in the small of her back. The slipperiness of this architecture of comfort enjoined stillness—her repose depended on each cushion staying just where it was. Up to now, she had lain with her wrists crossed on her dress: a random turn of the wrist, or flexing of fingers, were the nearest things to gestures she permitted herself—and, indeed, these had been enough. *Now,* her beginning to say, "I wonder if they were right . . . " must, though it sounded nothing more than reflective, have been accompanied by an incautious movement, for a cushion fell with a plump to the ground. Gavin went round, recovered the cushion and stood beside her: they eyed one another with communicative amazement, as though a third person had spoken and they were uncertain if they had heard aright. She arched her waist up and Gavin replaced the cushion. He said: "If who were right?"

"Rockham . . . The Admiral. She's always hinting, he's always saying, that I'm in some way thoughtless and wrong with you."

"Oh, him."

"I know," she said. "But you'll say goodbye to him nicely?"

He shrugged. "I shan't see him again—this time."

She hesitated. She was about to bring out something that, though slight, must be unacceptable. "He *is* coming in," she said, "for a moment, just after dinner, to fetch the cakes."

"Which cakes?"

"The cakes for tomorrow. I had arranged to send them round in the morning, but that would not do; no, that would not be soon enough. Everything is for the Admiral's meeting to make us ready, so everything must be ready in good time."

When, at nine o'clock, the Admiral's ring was heard, Mrs. Nicholson, indecisively, put down her coffee cup. A wood fire, lit while they were at dinner, was blazing languidly in the already warm air: it was necessary to sit at a distance from it. While the bell still rang, Gavin rose, as though he had forgotten something, and left the drawing-room. Passing the maid on her way to open the front door, he made a bolt upstairs. In his bedroom, Rockham was in possession: his trunk waited, open, bottom layer packed; her mending-basket was on the bureau; she was taking a final look through his things—his departure was to be early tomorrow morning. "Time flies," she said. "You're no sooner come than you're gone." She continued to count handkerchiefs, to stack up shirts. "I'd have thought," she said, "you'd have wanted to bring your school cap."

"Why? Anyway, it's a silly beastly old colour."

"You're too old-fashioned," she said sharply. "It was high time somebody went to school.—Now you *have* come up, just run down again, there's a good boy, and ask Madam if there's anything for your mother. If it's books, they ought to go in here among your boots."

"The Admiral's there."

"Well, my goodness, you know the Admiral."

Gavin played for time, on the way down, by looking into the rooms on every floor. Their still only partial familiarity, their fullness with objects that, in the half light coming in from the landing, he could only half perceive and did not yet dare touch, made him feel he was still only at the first chapter of the mystery of the house. He wondered how long it would be before he saw them again. Fear of Rockham's impatience, of her calling down to ask what he was up to, made him tread cautiously on the thickly carpeted stairs; he gained the hall without having made a sound. Here he smelled the fresh-baked cakes, waiting in a hamper on the hall table. The drawing-room door stood ajar, on, for a minute, dead silence. The Admiral must have gone, without the cakes.

But then the Admiral spoke. "You must see, there is nothing more to be said. I am only sorry I came. I did not expect you to be alone."

"For once, that is not my fault," replied Mrs. Nicholson, unsteadily. "I do not even know where the child is." In a voice that hardly seemed to be hers she cried out softly: "Then this is to go on always? What more do you ask? What else am I to be or do?"

"There's nothing more you can do. And all you must be is, happy."

"How easy," Mrs. Nicholson said.

"You have always said that that was easy, for you. For my own part, I have never considered happiness. There you misunderstood me, quite from the first."

"Not quite. Was I wrong in thinking you were a man?"

"I'm a man, yes. But I'm not that sort."

"That is too subtle for me," said Mrs. Nicholson.

"On the contrary, it is too simple for you. You ignore the greater part of my life. You cannot be blamed, perhaps; you have only known me since I was cursed with too much time on my hands. Your—your looks, charm and gaiety, my dear Lilian, I'd have been a fool not to salute at their full worth. Beyond that, I'm not such a fool as I may have seemed. Fool?—all things considered, I could not have been simply that without being something a good deal viler."

"I have been nice to Constance," said Mrs. Nicholson.

"Vile in my own eyes."

"I know, that is all you think of."

"I see, now, where you are in your element. You know as well as I do what your element is; which is why there's nothing more to be said. Flirtation's always been off my beat—so far off my beat, as a matter of fact, that I didn't know what it was when I first saw it. There, no doubt, I was wrong. If you can't live without it, you cannot, and that is that. If you have to be dangled after, you no doubt will be. But don't, my dear girl, go for that to the wrong shop. It would have been enough, where I am concerned, to watch you making a ninnie of that unfortunate boy."

"Who, poor little funny Gavin?" said Mrs. Nicholson. "Must I have nothing?—I have no little dog. You would not like it, even, if I had a real little dog. And you expect me to think that you do not care. . . . "

The two voices, which intensity more than caution kept pitched low, ceased. Gavin pushed open the drawing-room door.

The room, as can happen, had elongated. Like figures at the end of a telescope the Admiral and Mrs. Nicholson were to be seen standing before the fire. Of this, not a glint had room to appear between the figures of the antagonists. Mrs. Nicholson, head bent as though to examine the setting of the diamond, was twisting round a ring on her raised left hand—a lace-edged handkerchief, like an abandoned piece of stage property, had been dropped and lay on the hearthrug near the hem of her skirts. She gave the impression of having not moved: if they had not, throughout, been speaking from this distance, the Admiral must have taken a step forward. But this, on his part, must have been, and must be, all—his head was averted from her, his shoulders were braced back, and behind his back he imprisoned one of his own wrists in a handcuff grip that shifted only to tighten. The heat from the fire must have made necessary, probably for the Admiral when he came, the opening of a window behind the curtains; for, as Gavin advanced into the drawing-room, a burst of applause entered from the theatre, and continued, drowning the music which had begun again.

Not a tremor recorded the moment when Mrs. Nicholson knew Gavin was in the room. Obliquely and vaguely turning her bowed head she extended to him, in an unchanged look, what might have been no more than an invitation to listen, also, to the music. "Why, Gavin," she said at last, "we were wondering where you were."

Here he was. From outside the theatre, stink still travelled to him from the lorry whose engine was being run. Nothing had changed in the colourless afternoon. Without knowing, he had plucked a leaf of the ivy which now bred and fed upon her house. A soldier, passing behind him to join the others, must have noticed his immobility all the way down the avenue; for the soldier said, out of the side of his mouth: "Annie doesn't live here any more." Gavin Doddington, humiliated, affected to study the ivy leaf, whose veins were like arbitrary vulgar fate-lines. He thought he remembered hearing of metal ivy; he knew he had seen ivy carved round marble monuments to signify fidelity, regret, or the tomb-defying tenaciousness of memory—what you liked. Watched by the soldiers, he did not care to make the gesture involving the throwing away of the leaf: instead, he shut his hand on it, as he turned from the house. Should he go straight to the station, straight back to London? Not while the impression remained so strong. On the other hand, it would be a long time before the bars opened.

Another walk round Southstone, this afternoon, was necessary: there must be a decrescendo. From his tour of annihilation, nothing out of the story was to be missed. He walked as though he were carrying a guide-book.

Once or twice he caught sight of the immune downs, on the ascent to whose contours war had halted the villas. The most open view was, still, from the gates of the cemetery, past which he and she had so often driven without a thought. Through those gates, the extended dulling white marble vista said to him, only, that the multiplicity of the new graves, in thirty years, was enough in itself to make the position of hers indifferent—she might, once more, be lying beside her husband. On the return through the town towards the lip of the plateau overhanging the sea, the voidness and the air of concluded meaning about the plan of Southstone seemed to confirm her theory: history, after this last galvanized movement forward, had come, as she expected, to a full stop. It had only not stopped where or as she foresaw. Crossing the Promenade obliquely, he made, between wire entanglements, for the railings; to become one more of the spaced-out people who leaned along them, willing to see a convoy or gazing with indifference towards liberated France. The path and steps up the cliff face had been destroyed; the handrail hung out rotting into the air.

Back in the shopping centre, he turned a quickening step, past the shuttered, boarded or concave windows, towards the corner florist's where Mrs. Nicholson had insisted on the carnations. But this had received a direct hit: the entire corner was gone. When time takes our revenges out of our hands it is, usually, to execute them more slowly: her vindictiveness, more thorough than ours, might satisfy us, if, in the course of her slowness, we did not forget. In this case, however, she had worked in the less than a second of detonation. Gavin Doddington paused where there was no florist—was he not, none the less, entitled to draw a line through this?

Not until after some time back in the bar did it strike him—there had been one omission. He had not yet been to the Concannons'. He pushed his way out: it was about seven o'clock, twenty minutes or so before the black-out. They had lived in a crescent set just back from a less expensive reach of the Promenade. On his way, he passed houses and former hotels occupied by soldiers or A. T. S. who had not yet gone. These, from top to basement, were in a state of naked, hard, lemon-yellow illumination. Interposing dark hulks gave you the feeling of nothing more than their recent military occupation. The front doors of the Concannons' crescent opened, on the inland side, into a curved street, which, for some military reason now probably out of date, had been blocked at the near end: Gavin had to go round. Along the pavements under the front doorsteps there was so much wire that he was thrust out into the road—opposite only one house was there an inviting gap in the loops. Akmiral Concannon, having died in the last war, could not have obtained this as a concession—all the same this *was,* as the numbeer faintly confirmed, his house. Nobody now but Gavin recognized its identity or its importance. Here had dwelled, and here continued to dwell, the genius of the Southstone that now was. Twice over had there been realized the Admiral's alternative to love.

The Concannon's dining-room window, with its high triple sashes, was raised some distance above the street. Gavin, standing opposite it, looked in at an A.T.S. girl seated at a table. She faced the window, the dusk and him. From above her head, a naked electric light bulb, on a flex shortened by being knotted, glared on the stripped, whitish walls of the room and emphasized the fact that she was alone. In her khaki shirt, sleeves rolled up, she sat leaning her bare elbows on the bare table. Her face was abrupt with youth. She turned one wrist, glanced at the watch on it, then resumed her steady stare through the window, downwards at the dusk in which Gavin stood.

It was thus that, for the second time in his life, he saw straight up into the eyes that did not see him. The intervening years had given him words for trouble: a phrase, *"l'horreur de mon néant,"* darted across his mind.

At any minute, the girl would have to approach the window to do the black-out—for that, along this coast, was still strictly enforced. It was worth waiting. He lighted a cigarette: she looked at her watch again. When she did rise it was, first, to unhook from a peg beside the dining-room door not only her tunic but her cap. Her being dressed for the street, when she did reach up and, with a succession of movements he liked to watch, begin to twitch the black stuff across the window, made it his object *not* to be seen—just yet. Light staggered, a moment longer, on the desiccated pods of the wallflowers that, seeded from the front garden, had sprung up between the cracks of the pavement, and on the continuous regular loops or hoops of barbed wire, through all of which, by a sufficiently long leap, one *could* have projected oneself head foremost, unhurt. At last she had stopped the last crack of light. She had now nothing to do but to come out.

Coming smartly down the Concannons' steps, she may just have seen the outline of the civilian waiting, smoking a cigarette. She swerved impassively, if at all. He said: "A penny for your thoughts." She might not have heard. He fell into step beside her. Next, appearing to hear what he had not said, she replied: "No, I'm *not* going your way."

"Too bad. But there's only one way out—can't get out, you know, at the other end. What have *I* got to do, then—stay here all night?"

"*I* don't know, I'm sure." Unconcernedly humming, she did not even quicken her light but ringing tramp on the curved street. If he kept abreast with her, it was casually, and at an unpressing distance: this, and the widening sky that announced the open end of the crescent, must have been reassuring. He called across to her. "That house you came out of, I used to know people who lived there. I was just looking round."

She turned, for the first time—she could not help it. "People lived there?" she said. "Just fancy. I know I'd sooner live in a tomb. And that goes for all this place. Imagine anyone coming here on a holiday!"

"I'm on a holiday."

"Goodness. What do you do with yourself?"

"Just look round."

"Well, I wonder how long you stick it out—Here's where we go different ways. Good night."

"I've got nobody to talk to," Gavin said, suddenly standing still in the dark. A leaf flittered past. She was woman enough to halt, to listen, because this had not been said to her. If her "Oh yes, we girls have heard that before" was automatic, it was, still more, wavering. He cast away the end of one cigarette and started lighting another: the flame of the lighter, cupped inside his hands, jumped for a moment over his features. Her first thought was: yes, he's quite old—that went along with his desperate jauntiness. Civilian, yes: too young for the last war, too old for this. A gentleman—they were the clever ones. But he had, she perceived, forgotten about her thoughts—what she saw, in that moment before he snapped down the lighter, stayed on the darkness, puzzling her somewhere outside the compass of her own youth. She had seen the face of somebody dead who was still there—"old" because of the presence, under an icy screen, of a whole stopped mechanism for feeling. Those features had been framed, long ago, for hope. The dints above the nostrils, the lines extending the eyes, the lips' grimacing grip on the cigarette—all completed the picture of someone wolfish. A preyer. But who had said, preyers are preyed upon?

His lower lip came out, thrusting the cigarette up at a debonair angle towards his eyes. "Not a soul," he added—this time with calculation, and to her.

"Anyway," she said sharply, "I've got a date. Anyway, what made you pick on this dead place? Why not pick on some place where you know someone?"

On Bowen

Elizabeth Dorothea Cole Bowen was born in 1899 to an Anglo-Irish family whose country house, Bowen's Court, had been given to an ancestor by Oliver Cromwell. The Anglo-Irish position in Ireland was ambiguous: it was the country of their birth and the source of their income, but they never could be natives because the Irish saw them as a conquering and occupying force and because they remained, in language, in culture, and in their aspirations for careers, primarily oriented toward England. London rather than Dublin was capital in the imaginations of the long and brilliant succession of Anglo-Irish writers stretching from Swift and Congreve through Wilde and Yeats to Miss Bowen and some of her contemporaries. With the advent of Irish independence in 1922, the succession may have been ended or at least diminished, for the obviously fruitful ambiguities have ceased to exist in quite the same ways. Bowen's Court was sold in 1960.

Educated at Downe House, Kent, which she describes in "The Mulberry Tree," Miss Bowen was allowed considerable freedom by her father to live, travel, and work where she wished. After teaching and working as nurse in a shell-shock hospital and while living in various places in England and on the continent, she began to write at the age of twenty. In 1923, the year in which her first book, *Encounters,* was published, she married Alan Cameron (who died in 1952). After her marriage she continued to write fiction, and in 1937 served as theater critic for the short-lived *Night and Day* (Evelyn Waugh reviewed books; Graham Greene, films). During the Second World War she worked by day at the Ministry of Information and by night as an air-raid warden, writing all the while: reviews for the *Tatler,* radio scripts for the B.B.C., the stories in *The Demon Lover,* including "Ivy Gripped the Steps." After the war came increasing prominence as a writer—her position had been assured since *The Heat of the Day* in 1939—and attendant honors. In 1948, she was made a Companion of the British Empire; a year later, Trinity College, Dublin, gave her an honorary doctorate, as did Oxford in 1956; and in 1965 she was named a Companion of Literature.

Despite the official recognition, Miss Bowen has said that only in her books does she have a real relationship to society, perhaps a substitute for a normal relationship. One might argue that this is true of all artists; certainly her belief that "I am fully intelligent only when I write" (*Why Do I Write?*) could apply to authors of all schools and shades of opinion. By this she means that only in writing does she bring to bear her complete attention or consciousness to discover and then to work out the "poetic truth" inherent in the material. For her, attention is almost synonymous with inspiration, for she has consistently maintained that writing is a process of discovery. Plot, for example, is not a matter of choice but of necessity, the discovery of what, for that story or novel, is inevitable ("Notes on Writing a Novel," 1945). The original conception of the best stories, she said in 1936, is involuntary, "a vital fortuity" (Preface to *The Faber Book of Modern Short Stories*). Dealing with her own work she said that "It could seem to me that stories, with their *dramatis personae,* pre-exist, only wait to be come upon. I know I do not invent them; I discover them" (Preface to *Stories by Elizabeth Bowen,* 1959). This does not mean that she works automatically or easily—the artist must struggle to realize the story—and like her predecessor Henry James, her remarks on writing are as often concerned with craft as with more rarefied elements of theme and vision.

"Ivy Gripped the Steps" is, in genesis and execution, a typical example of her work. Like all of the stories in *The Demon Lover,* it was inspired as well as informed by "the overcharged consciousness" of wartime England. She had no sense of inventing this or any of the stories; rather she seemed to tap a source of material which she had to control and direct. "Ivy Gripped the Steps" was triggered by a scene—an ivy-covered house in a sea-side resort. The scene affected her, but, she felt, "it would affect 'X' more. Under what circumstances; for what reason? And who is 'X'?" (*Stories by Elizabeth Bowen*) In this case, 'X' became "a man in the early 40's who peers through the rusted fortifications and down the dusty empty perspectives of a seaside town at an Edwardian episode that has crippled his faculty for love."

Summarized thus baldly, the story sounds like a hundred other accounts of the destruction of childish innocence familiar to the reader of modern fiction. (Graham Greene's "The Basement Room" parallels this story in many aspects of structure and theme.) Miss Bowen obviously encompasses a far wider range: she has written what Joyce called "A chapter in the moral history" of her country and she presents a conflict in which the question of moral responsibility is quite complex. Gavin's family, Mrs. Nicholson, and Admiral Concannon are in part representative of English types made familiar by social history and such fiction as Ford Madox Ford's *The Good Soldier* and Evelyn Waugh's *A Handful of Dust:* the decaying gentry, chained to their land, feeling history as a never-ending weight; the rentier, genteel end of the capitalist process, decorative, idle, self-conscious, and rather bored; and the disciplined, puritan-military man who would like the world to be at permanent moral attention to prepare for war and honor. Among these conflicting people Gavin is placed, to find his own way. In a sense, he is denied choice, for he can choose in no other way. His family's way of life is so bleak and moribund as to affect his health (for if Southstone cripples him spiritually it also enables him to lead a physically normal life), and Mrs. Nicholson's house seems in contrast a secular paradise where history is a story with a happy ending. Like the ivy which overruns the house, Mrs. Nicholson is a parasite, living through efforts not her own, and the Admiral's judgment of her seems accurate: she is mischievous and irresponsible. Yet, in a startling reversal which forces a revaluation of much of the action, two disastrous wars are described as "the Admiral's alternative to love," echoing, consciously or not, the old statesman's bromide about "the moral equivalent of war." As with some of the greatest plots, the question "what if" is inadmissible; only the "how" is permitted to exist in the confines of the story. Gavin is left alone, marred by his experience, turned away by the pert and rather shabby modern enchantress who replaces Mrs. Nicholson. Like many of the characters in Miss Bowen's fiction, he is fascinated by a world he cannot enter; like many of her children, he enables her to secure an "immediacy and purity of sensation, [for] . . . the young are unspoiled instruments" (*Stories by Elizabeth Bowen*). The last word is revealing: no one is guiltless of molding or using the young—not the young themselves, not the author who uses them to discover and reveal the poetic truth for which the story exists.

Indeed, every element of the story—point of view, narrative structure, sentence structure, setting, imagery—serves to support the whole. The point of view, third person reinforced by the greater knowledge of the omniscient author, is flexible enough to bring the reader close to Gavin as a child, to distance the reader from him as adult, and to keep the other characters' motives and reactions mysterious and portentous, as they would be to a child or in the perspective of adult memory. The narrative, a three-act flashback enclosed in the framework of the present physical and spiritual desolation, reveals the growing dependence of Gavin on Mrs. Nicholson even as he comes to regard himself as a conqueror and the growing complication of her relations with the Admiral, culminating in the consciously theatrical scene in which she rejects Gavin and is rejected by the Admiral. The movement of the language—formal, elegantly hesitant, self-encumbered—serves, like that of Henry James, to describe an elegant, static, formalized, and precariously balanced world—Mrs. Nicholson on her cushions—which real movement or real emotion would unsettle and destroy. Physical description, imagery, and tropes highlight the theme—the house itself, before and after the two wars, the contrast of electric lamp and oil lamp, the lifemanship of Mrs. Nicholson's gift of carnations to Mrs. Concannon, the similes describing Mrs. Nicholson's and the Doddington's money, the recurring references to France and Germany that grow into complex symbols of a troubling real world and of a dream world that produces a nightmare. In the Southstone of 1944, simplicity, beauty, and confidence are gone: Gavin wanders the barricaded streets in a maze of barbed wire and of memory, predator and prey, failing once again to make contact.

Textual note:

First published in *Horizon* (London), 12 (September 1945), 179–208. First edition, in *The Demon Lover and Other Stories* (London: Jonathan Cape, 1945). First American edition in *Ivy Gripped the Steps* (New York: Alfred A. Knopf, Inc., 1946). Published in *The Demon Lover and Other Stories* in the collected edition of Miss Bowen's fiction (London: Jonathan Cape, 1952). The present text follows that of the collected edition.

Resources for further study:

Miss Bowen's novels *The House in Paris* (1936) and *The Death of the Heart* (1939) deal with children caught in the world of adult complexity; *The Heat of the Day* (1949) is set in wartime England; *The Little Girls* (1964) involves an excursion into prewar England in a search for the meaning of the characters' lives. The first three are generally acknowledged to be her finest novels, and many of her short stories have been widely praised and anthologized.

   Collected Impressions (New York: Alfred A. Knopf, Inc., 1950) includes the Preface to *The Faber Book of Modern Short Stories,* the Postscript to *Ivy Gripped the Steps* (reprinted also in the collected edition of *The Demon Lover*), and "Notes on Writing a Novel." *Seven Winters and Afterthoughts* (New York: Alfred A. Knopf, Inc., 1962) includes the Preface to *Stories by Elizabeth Bowen.* Also useful is *Why Do I Write? An Exchange of Views between Elizabeth Bowen, Graham Greene, and V. S. Pritchett* (London: Percival Marshall, 1948). *Collected Impressions, Seven Winters,* and *A Time in Rome* (New York: Alfred A. Knopf, Inc., 1960), contain autobiographical material.

CRITICAL:

BROOKE, JOCELYN. *Elizabeth Bowen.* London: Longmans, Green and Co. for the British Book Council, 1952. A pamphlet.

HALL, JAMES. *The Lunatic Giant in the Drawing Room: The British and American Novel Since 1930.* Bloomington, Indiana: Indiana University Press, 1968. The title is misleadingly broad. A good brief discussion of Miss Bowen as an innovator.

HEATH, WILLIAM WEBSTER. *Elizabeth Bowen: An Introduction to Her Novels.* Madison, Wisconsin: University of Wisconsin Press, 1961. The only full-length study includes some biographical material and the most complete bibliography to date.

MITCHELL, EDWARD. "Themes in Elizabeth Bowen's Short Stories," *Critique,* 8 (Spring-Summer 1966), 41–54.

O'FAOLAIN, SEAN. *The Vanishing Hero: Studies in Novelists of the Twenties.* Boston: Little, Brown and Company, 1957. A chapter on Miss Bowen.

EVELYN WAUGH
Love Among the Ruins

Despite their promises at the last election, the politicians had not yet changed the climate. The State Meteorological Institute had so far produced only an unseasonable fall of snow and two little thunderbolts no larger than apricots. The weather varied from day to day and from county to county as it had done of old, most anomalously.

This was a rich, old-fashioned Tennysonian night.

Strains of a string quartet floated out from the drawing-room windows and were lost amid the splash and murmur of the gardens. In the basin the folded lilies had left a brooding sweetness over the water. No gold fin winked in the porphyry font and any peacock which seemed to be milkily drooping in the moon-shadows was indeed a ghost, for the whole flock of them had been found mysteriously and rudely slaughtered a day or two ago in the first disturbing flush of this sudden summer.

Miles, sauntering among the sleeping flowers, was suffused with melancholy. He did not much care for music and this was his last evening at Mountjoy. Never again, perhaps, would he be free to roam these walks.

Mountjoy had been planned and planted in the years of which he knew nothing; generations of skilled and patient husbandmen had weeded and dunged and pruned; generations of dilettanti had watered it with cascades and jets, generations of collectors had lugged statuary here; all, it seemed, for his enjoyment this very night under this huge moon. Miles knew nothing of such periods and processes, but he felt an incomprehensible tidal pull towards the circumjacent splendours.

Eleven struck from the stables. The music ceased. Miles turned back, and as he reached the terrace, the shutters began to close and the great chandeliers were one by one extinguished. By the light of the sconces which still shone on their panels of faded satin and clouded gold, he joined the company dispersing to bed through the islands of old furniture.

His room was not one of the grand succession which lay along the garden front. Those were reserved for murderers. Nor was it on the floor above, tenanted mostly by sexual offenders. His was a humbler wing. Indeed he overlooked the luggage porch and the coal bunker. Only professional men visiting Mountjoy on professional business and very poor relations had been put here in the old days. But Miles was attached to this room, which was the first he had ever called his own in all his twenty years of Progress.

His next-door neighbour, a Mr. Sweat, paused at his door to say good-night. It was only now after twenty months' proximity, when Miles's time was up, that this veteran had begun to unbend. He and a man named Soapy, survivals of another age, had kept themselves to themselves, talking wistfully of cribs they had cracked, of sparklers, of snug bar-parlours where they had met their favourite fences, of strenuous penal days at the Scrubs and on the Moor. They had small use for the younger generation; crime, calvinism and classical music were their interests. But at last Mr. Sweat had taken to nodding, to grunting, and finally, too late for friendship, to speaking to Miles.

"What price the old strings tonight, chum?" he asked.

"I wasn't there, Mr. Sweat."

"You missed a treat. Of course nothing's ever good enough for old Soapy. Made me fair sick to hear Soapy going on all the time. The viola was scratchy, Soapy says. They played the Mozart just like it was Haydn. No feeling in the Debussy pizzicato, says Soapy."

"Soapy knows too much."

"Soapy knows a lot more than some I could mention, schooling or no schooling. Next time they're going to do the Grosse Fugue as the last movement of the B flat. That's something to look forward to, that is, though Soapy says no late Beethoven comes off. We'll see. Leastways, me and Soapy will; *you* won't. You're off tomorrow. Pleased?"

"Not particularly."

"No, no more wouldn't I be. It's a funny thing but I've settled down here wonderful. Never thought I should. It all seemed a bit too posh at first. Not like the old Scrubs. But it's a real pretty place once you're used to it. Wouldn't mind settling here for a lifer if they'd let me. The trouble is there's no security in crime these days. Time was, you knew just what a job was worth, six months, three years; whatever it was, you knew where you were. Now what with prison commissioners and Preventative Custody and Corrective Treatment they can keep you in or push you out just as it suits them. It's not right.

"I'll tell you what it is, chum," continued Mr. Sweat. "There's no understanding of crime these days like what there was. I remember when I was a nipper, the first time I came up before the beak, he spoke up straight: 'My lad,' he says, 'you are embarking upon a course of life that can only lead to disaster and degradation in this world and everlasting damnation in the next.' Now that's talking. It's plain sense and it shows a personal interest.

But last time I was up, when they sent me here, they called me an 'antisocial phenomenon'; said I was 'maladjusted.' That's no way to speak of a man what was doing time before they was in long trousers, now is it?"

"They said something of the same kind to me."

"Yes and now they're giving you the push, just like you hadn't no Rights. I tell you it's made a lot of the boys uncomfortable your going out all of a sudden like this. Who'll it be next time, that's what we're wondering?

"I tell you where you went wrong, chum. You didn't give enough trouble. You made it too easy for them to say you was cured. Soapy and me got wise to that. You remember them birds as got done in? That was Soapy and me. They took a lot of killing too; powerful great bastards. But we got the evidence all hid away tidy and if there's ever any talk of me and Soapy being 'rehabilitated' we'll lay it out conspicuous.

"Well, so long, chum. Tomorrow's my morning for Remedial Repose so I daresay you'll be off before I get down. Come back soon."

"I hope so," said Miles and turned alone into his own room.

He stood briefly at the window and gazed his last on the cobbled-yard. He made a good figure of a man, for he came of handsome parents and all his life had been carefully fed and doctored and exercised; well clothed too. He wore the drab serge dress that was the normal garb of the period—only certified homosexuals wore colours—but there were differences of fit and condition among these uniforms. Miles displayed the handiwork of tailor and valet. He belonged to a privileged class.

The State had made him.

No clean-living, God-fearing, Victorian gentleman, he; no complete man of the Renaissance; no gentil knight nor dutiful pagan nor, even, noble savage. All that succession of past worthies had gone its way, content to play a prelude to Miles. He was the Modern Man.

His history, as it appeared in multuplet in the filing cabinets of numberless State departments, was typical of a thousand others. Before his birth the politicians had succeeded in bringing down his father and mother to penury; they, destitute, had thrown themselves into the simple diversions of the very poor and thus, between one war and the next, set in motion a chain-reaction of divorces which scattered them and their various associates in forlorn couples all over the Free World. The aunt on whom the infant Miles had been quartered was conscribed for work in a factory and shortly afterwards died of boredom at the conveyer-belt. The child was put to safety in an orphanage.

Huge sums were thenceforward spent upon him; sums which, fifty years earlier, would have sent whole quiversful of boys to Winchester and New College and established them in the learned professions. In halls adorned with Picassos and Legers he yawned through long periods of Constructive Play. He never lacked the requisite cubic feet of air. His diet was balanced and on the first Friday of every month he was psycho-analysed. Every detail of his adolescence was recorded and microfilmed and filed, until at the appropriate age he was transferred to the Air Force.

There were no aeroplanes at the station to which he was posted. It was an institution to train instructors to train instructors to train instructors in Personal Recreation.

There for some weeks he tended a dish-washing machine and tended it, as his adjutant testified at his trial, in an exemplary fashion. The work in itself lacked glory, but it was the normal novitiate. Men from the orphanages provided the hard core of the Forces, a caste apart which united the formidable qualities of Janissary and Junker. Miles had been picked early for high command. Dish-washing was only the beginning. The adjutant, an orphan too, had himself washed both dishes and officers' underclothes, he testified, before rising to his present position.

Courts martial had been abolished some years before this. The Forces handed their defaulters over to the civil arm for treatment. Miles came up at quarter sessions. It was plain from the start, when Arson, Wilful Damage, Manslaughter, Prejudicial Conduct and Treason were struck out of the Indictment and the whole reduced to a simple charge of Antisocial Activity, that the sympathies of the Court were with the prisoner.

The Station Psychologist gave his opinion that an element of incendiarism was inseparable from adolescence. Indeed, if checked, it might produce morbid neurosis. For his part he thought the prisoner had performed a perfectly normal act and, moreover, had shown more than normal intelligence in its execution.

At this point some widows, mothers and orphans of the incinerated airmen set up an outcry from the public gallery and were sharply reminded from the Bench that this was a Court of Welfare and not a meeting of the Housewives' Union.

The case developed into a concerted eulogy of the accused. An attempt by the prosecution to emphasise the extent of the damage was rebuked from the Bench.

"The jury," he said, "will expunge from their memories these sentimental details which have been most improperly introduced."

"May be a detail to you," said a voice from the gallery. "He was a good husband to me."

"Arrest that woman," said the Judge.

Order was restored and the panegyrics continued.

At last the Bench summed up. He reminded the jury that it was a first principle of the New Law that no man could be held responsible for the consequences of his own acts. The jury must dismiss from their minds the consideration that much valuable property and many valuable lives had been lost and the cause of Personal Recreation gravely retarded. They had merely to decide whether in fact the prisoner had arranged inflammable material at various judiciously selected points in the Institution and had ignited them. If he had done so, and the evidence plainly indicated that he had, he contravened the Standing Orders of the Institution and was thereby liable to the appropriate penalties.

Thus directed the jury brought in a verdict of guilty coupled with a recommendation of mercy towards the various bereaved persons who from time to time in the course of the hearing had been committed for contempt. The Bench reprimanded the jury for presumption and impertinence in the matter of the prisoners held in contempt, and sentenced Miles to residence during the State's pleasure at Mountjoy Castle (the ancestral seat of a maimed V.C. of the Second World War, who had been sent to a Home for the Handicapped when the place was converted into a gaol).

The State was capricious in her pleasures. For nearly two years Miles enjoyed her particular favours. Every agreeable remedial device was applied to him and applied, it was now proclaimed, successfully. Then without warning a few days back, while he lay dozing under a mulberry tree, the unexpected blow had fallen; they had come to him, the Deputy Chief-Guide and the sub-Deputy, and told him bluntly and brutally that he was rehabilitated.

Now on this last night he knew he was to wake tomorrow on a harsh world. Nevertheless he slept and was gently awoken for the last time to the familiar scent of china tea on his bed table, the thin bread and butter, the curtains drawn above the luggage porch, the sunlit kitchen-yard and the stable clock just visible behind the cut-leaf copper beech.

He breakfasted late and alone. The rest of the household were already engaged in the first community-songs of the day. Presently he was called to the Guidance Office.

Since his first day at Mountjoy, when with other entrants Miles had been addressed at length by the Chief Guide on the Aims and Achievements of the New Penology, they had seldom met. The Chief Guide was almost always addressing penological conferences.

The Guidance Office was the former house-keeper's room stripped now of its plush and patriotic pictures; sadly tricked out instead with standard civil-service equipment, class A.

It was full of people.

"This is Miles Plastic," said the Chief Guide. "Sit down, Miles. You can see from the presence of our visitors this morning what an important occasion this is."

Miles took a chair and looked and saw seated beside the Chief Guide two elderly men whose faces were familiar from the television screen as prominent colleagues in the Coalition Government. They wore open flannel shirts, blazers with numerous pens and pencils protruding from the breast pocket, and baggy trousers. This was the dress of very high politicians.

"The Minister of Welfare and the Minister of Rest and Culture," continued the Chief Guide. "The stars to which we have hitched our waggon. Have the press got the hand-out?"

"Yes, Chief."

"And the photographers are all ready?"

"Yes, Chief."

"Then I can proceed."

He proceeded as he had done at countless congresses, at countless spas and university cities. He concluded, as he always did: "In the New Britain which we are building, there are no criminals. There are only the victims of inadequate social services."

The Minister of Welfare, who had not reached his present eminence without the help of a certain sharpness in debate, remarked: "But I understood that Plastic is from one of our own orphanages . . . "

"Plastic is recognised as a Special Case," said the Chief Guide.

The Minister of Rest and Culture, who in the old days had more than once done time himself, said: "Well, Plastic, lad, from all they do say I reckon you've been uncommon smart."

"Exactly," said the Chief Guide. "Miles is our first success, the vindication of the Method."

"Of all the new prisons established in the first glorious wave of Reform, Mountjoy alone has produced a complete case of rehabilitation," the Minister of Welfare said. "You may or may not be aware that the Method has come in for a good deal of criticism both in Parliament and outside. There are a lot of young hot-heads who take their inspiration from our Great Neighbour in the East. You can quote the authorities to them till you're black in the face, but they are always pressing for all the latest gadgets of capital and corporal punishment, for chain gangs and solitary confinement, bread and water, the cat-o'-nine-tails, the rope and the block, and all manner of new-fangled nonsense. They think we're a lot of old fogeys. Thank goodness we've still got the solid sense of the people behind us, but we're on the defensive now. We have to show results. That's why we're here this morning. To show them results. *You* are our Result."

These were solemn words and Miles in some measure responded to the occasion. He gazed before him blankly with an expression that might seem to be awe.

"You'd best watch your step now, lad," said the Minister of Rest and Culture.

"Photographs," said the Minister of Welfare. "Yes, shake *my* hand. Turn towards the cameras. Try to smile."

Bulbs flashed all over the dreary little room.

"State be with you," said the Minister of Welfare.

"Give us a paw, lad," said the Minister of Rest and Culture, taking Miles's hand in his turn. "And no funny business, mind."

Then the politicians departed.

"The Deputy-Chief will attend to all the practical matters," said the Chief wearily. "Go and see him now."

Miles went.

"Well, Miles, from now on I must call you Mr. Plastic," said the Deputy-Chief. "In less than a minute you become a Citizen. This little pile of papers is *You*. When I stamp them, Miles the Problem ceases to exist and Mr. Plastic the Citizen is born. We are sending you to Satellite City, the nearest Population Centre, where you will be attached to the Ministry of Welfare as a sub-official. In view of your special training you are not being classified as a Worker. The immediate material rewards, of course, are not as great. But you are definitely in the Service. We have set your foot on the bottom rung of the non-competitive ladder."

The Deputy Chief Guide picked up the rubber stamp and proceeded to his work of creation. Flip-thump, flip-thump the papers were turned and stained.

"There you are, Mr. Plastic," said the Deputy-Chief handing Miles, as it were, the baby.

At last Miles spoke: "What must I do to get back here?" he asked.

"Come, come, you're rehabilitated now, remember. It is your turn to give back to the State some of the service the State has given you. You will report this morning to the Area Progressive. Transport has been laid on. State be with you, Mr. Plastic. Be careful, that's your Certificate of Human Personality you've dropped—a *vital* document."

2

Satellite City, one of a hundred such grand conceptions, was not yet in its teens, but already the Dome of Security showed signs of wear. This was the name of the great municipal edifice about which the city was planned. The eponymous dome had looked well enough in the architect's model, shallow certainly but amply making up in girth what it lacked in height, the daring exercise of some new trick of construction. But to the surprise of all, when the building arose and was seen from the ground, the dome blandly vanished. It was hidden for ever among the roofs and butting shoulders of the ancillary wings and was never seen again from the outside except by airmen and steeplejacks. Only the name remained. On the day of its dedication, among massed politicians and People's Choirs the great lump of building materials had shone fine as a factory in all its brilliance of glass and new concrete. Since then, during one of the rather frequent weekends of international panic, it had been camouflaged and its windows blackened. Cleaners were few and usually on strike. So the Dome of Security remained blotched and dingy, the sole permanent building of Satellite City. There were no workers' flats, no officials' garden suburb, no parks, no playgrounds yet. These were all on the drawing-boards in the surveyor's office, tattered at the edges, ringed by tea-cups; their designer long since cremated and his ashes scattered among the docks and nettles. Thus the Dome of Security comprised, even more than had been intended, all the aspirations and amenities of the city.

The officials subsisted in perpetual twilight. Great sheets of glass planned to "trap" the sun, admitted few gleams from scratches in their coat of tar. At evening when the electric light came on, there was a faint glow, here and there. When, as often, the power-station was "shedding its load" the officials stopped work early and groped their way back to their darkened huts where in the useless refrigerators their tiny rations were quietly putrefying. On working days the officials, male and female, trudged through cigarette ends round and round, up and down what had once been lift-shafts, in a silent, shabby, shadowy procession.

Among these pilgrims of the dusk, in the weeks that followed his discharge from Mountjoy, moved the exiled Miles Plastic.

He was in a key department.

Euthanasia had not been part of the original 1945 Health Service; it was a Tory measure designed to attract votes from the aged and the mortally sick. Under the Bevan-Eden Coalition the Service came into general use and won instant popularity. The Union of Teachers was pressing for its application to difficult children. Foreigners came in such numbers to take advantage of the service that immigration authorities now turned back the bearers of single tickets.

Miles recognised the importance of his appointment even before he began work. On his first evening in the hostel his fellow sub-officials gathered round to question him.

"Euthanasia? I say, you're in luck. They work you jolly hard, of course, but it's the one department that's expanding."

"You'll get promoted before you know your way about."

"Great State! You *must* have pull. Only the very bright boys get posted to Euthanasia."

"I've been in Contraception for five years. It's a blind alley."

"They say that in a year or two Euthanasia will have taken over Pensions."

"You must be an orphan."

"Yes, I am."

"That accounts for it. Orphans get all the plums. I had a Full Family Life, State help me."

It was gratifying, of course, this respect and envy. It was well to have fine prospects; but for the time being Miles's duties were humble enough.

He was junior sub-official in a staff of half a dozen. The Director was an elderly man called Dr. Beamish, a man whose character had been formed in the nervous thirties, now much embittered, like many of his contemporaries, by the fulfillment of his early hopes. He had signed manifestos in his hot youth, had raised his fist in Barcelona and had painted abstractedly for *Horizon;* he had stood beside Spender at great concourses of Youth, and written "publicity" for the Last Viceroy. Now his reward had come to him. He held the most envied post in Satellite City and, sardonically, he was making the worst of it. Dr. Beamish rejoiced in every attenuation of official difficulties.

Satellite City was said to be the worst served Euthanasia Centre in the State. Dr. Beamish's patients were kept waiting so long that often they died natural deaths before he found it convenient to poison them.

His small staff respected Dr. Beamish. They were all of the official class, for it was part of the grim little game which Dr. Beamish played with the higher authorities to economise extravagantly. His department, he maintained, could not, on its present allotment, afford workers. Even the furnace-man and the girl who despatched unwanted false teeth to the Dental Redistribution Centre were sub-officials.

Sub-officials were cheap and plentiful. The universities turned them out in thousands every year. Indeed, ever since the Incitement to Industry Act of 1955, which exempted workers from taxation—that great and popular measure of reform which had consolidated the now permanent Coalition

Government—there had been a nefarious one-way traffic of expensively State-educated officials "passing," as it was called, into the ranks of the workers.

Miles's duties required no special skill. Daily at ten the Service opened its doors to welfare-weary citizens. Miles was the man who opened them, stemmed the too eager rush and admitted the first half-dozen; then he closed the doors on the waiting multitude until a Higher Official gave the signal for the admission of another batch.

Once inside they came briefly under his charge; he set them in order, saw that they did not press ahead of their turn, and adjusted the television-set for their amusement. A Higher Official interviewed them, checked their papers and arranged for the confiscation of their property. Miles never passed the door through which they were finally one by one conducted. A faint whiff of cyanide sometimes gave a hint of the mysteries beyond. Meanwhile he swept the waiting room, emptied the waste-paper basket and brewed tea—a worker's job, for which the refinements of Mountjoy proved a too rich apprenticeship.

In his hostel the same reproductions of Leger and Picasso as had haunted his childhood still stared down on him. At the cinema, to which he could afford, at the best, a weekly visit, the same films as he had seen free at orphanage, Air Force station and prison, flickered and drawled before him. He was a child of Welfare, strictly schooled to a life of boredom, but he had known better than this. He had known the tranquil melancholy of the gardens at Mountjoy. He had known ecstasy when the Air Force Training School had whirled to the stars in a typhoon of flame. And as he moved sluggishly between Dome and hostel there rang in his ears the words of the old lag: "You didn't give enough trouble."

Then one day, in the least expected quarter, in his own drab department, hope appeared.

Miles later remembered every detail of that morning. It had started in the normal way; rather below normal indeed, for they were reopening after a week's enforced idleness. There had been a strike among the coal-miners and Euthanasia had been at a standstill. Now the necessary capitulations had been signed, the ovens glowed again, and the queue at the patients' entrance stretched halfway round the dome. Dr. Beamish squinted at the waiting crowd through the periscope and said with some satisfaction: "It will take months to catch up on the waiting list now. We shall have to start making a charge for the service. It's the only way to keep down the demand."

"The Ministry will never agree to that, surely, sir?"

"Damned sentimentalists. My father and mother hanged themselves in their own back-yard with their own clothesline. Now no one will lift a finger to help himself. There's something wrong in the system, Plastic. There are still rivers to drown in, trains—every now and then—to put your head under; gasfires in some of the huts. The country is full of the natural resources of death, but everyone has to come to us."

It was not often he spoke so frankly before his subordinates. He had overspent during the week's holiday, drunk too much at his hostel with other unemployed colleagues. Always after a strike the senior officials returned to work in low spirits.

"Shall I let the first batch in, sir?"

"Not for the moment," said Dr. Beamish. "There's a priority case to see first, sent over with a pink chit from Drama. She's in the private waiting-room now. Fetch her in."

Miles went to the room reserved for patients of importance. All one wall was of glass. Pressed to it a girl was standing, turned away from him, looking out at the glum queue below. Miles stood, the light in his eyes, conscious only of a shadow which stirred at the sound of the latch and turned, still a shadow merely but of exquisite grace, to meet him. He stood at the door, momentarily struck silent at this blind glance of beauty. Then he said: "We're quite ready for you now, miss."

The girl came nearer. Miles's eyes adjusted themselves to the light. The shadow took form. The full vision was all that the first glance had hinted; more than all, for every slight movement revealed perfection. One feature only broke the canon of pure beauty; a long, silken, corn-gold beard.

She said, with a deep, sweet tone, all unlike the flat conventional accent of the age: "Let it be quite understood that I don't want anything done to me. I consented to come here. The Director of Drama and the Director of Health were so pathetic about it all that I thought it was the least I could do. I said I was quite willing to hear about your service, but I do *not* want anything *done*."

"Better tell him inside," said Miles.

He led her to Dr. Beamish's room.

"Great State!" said Dr. Beamish, with eyes for the beard alone.

"Yes," she said. "It is a shock, isn't it? I've got used to it by now, but I can understand how people feel seeing it for the first time."

"Is it real?"

"Pull."

"It *is* strong. Can't they do anything about it?"

"Oh they've tried everything."

Dr. Beamish was so deeply interested that he forgot Miles's presence. "Klugmann's Operation, I suppose?"

"Yes."

"It does go wrong like that every now and then. They had two or three cases at Cambridge."

"I never wanted it done. I never want anything done. It was the Head of the Ballet. He insists on all the girls being sterilized. Apparently you can never dance really well again after you've had a baby. And I did want to dance really well. Now this is what's happened."

"Yes," said Dr. Beamish. "Yes. They're far too slap-dash. They had to put down those girls at Cambridge, too. There was no cure. Well, we'll attend to you, young lady. Have you any arrangements to make or shall I take you straight away?"

"But I don't want to be put down. I told your assistant here, I've simply consented to come at all, because the Director of Drama cried so, and he's rather a darling. I've not the smallest intention of letting you kill me."

While she spoke, Dr. Beamish's geniality froze. He looked at her with hatred, not speaking. Then he picked up the pink form. "Then this no longer applies?"

"No."

"Then for State's sake," said Dr. Beamish, very angry, "what are you wasting my time for? I've got more than a hundred urgent cases waiting outside and you come in here to tell me that the Director of Drama is a darling. I know the Director of Drama. We live side by side in the same ghastly hostel. He's a pest. And I'm going to write a report to the Ministry about this tomfoolery which will make him, and the lunatic who thinks he can perform a Klugmann, come round to me begging for extermination. And then I'll put them at the bottom of the queue. Get her out of here, Plastic, and let some sane people in."

Miles led her into the public waiting-room. "What an old beast," she said. "What a perfect beast. I've never been spoken to like that before even in the ballet-school. He seemed so nice at first."

"It's his professional feeling," said Miles. "He was naturally put out at losing such an attractive patient."

She smiled. Her beard was not so thick as quite to obscure her delicate ovoid of cheek and chin. She might have been peeping at him over ripe heads of barley.

Her smile started in her wide grey eyes. Her lips under her golden moustachios were unpainted, tactile. A line of pale down sprang below them and ran through the centre of the chin, spreading and thickening and growing richer in colour till it met the full flow of the whiskers, but leaving on either side, clear and tender, two symmetrical zones, naked and provocative. So might have smiled some carefree deacon in the colonnaded schools of fifth-century Alexandria and struck dumb the heresiarchs.

"I think your beard is beautiful."

"Do you really? I can't help liking it too. I can't help liking anything about myself, can you?"

"Yes. Oh, yes."

"That's not natural."

Clamour at the outer door interrupted the talk. Like gulls round a lighthouse the impatient victims kept up an irregular flap and slap on the panels.

"We're all ready, Plastic," said a senior official. "What's going on this morning?"

What was going on? Miles could not answer. Turbulent sea birds seemed to be dashing themselves against the light in his own heart.

"Don't go," he said to the girl. "Please, I shan't be a minute."

"Oh, I've nothing to take me away. My department all think I'm half dead by now."

Miles opened the door and admitted an indignant half-dozen. He directed them to their chairs, to the registry. Then he went back to the girl who had turned away slightly from the crowd and drawn a scarf peasantwise round her head, hiding her beard.

"I still don't quite like people staring," she said.

"Our patients are far too busy with their own affairs to notice anyone else," said Miles. "Besides you'd have been stared at all right if you'd stayed on in ballet."

Miles adjusted the television but few eyes in the waiting-room glanced towards it; all were fixed on the registrar's table and the doors beyond.

"Think of them all coming here," said the bearded girl.

"We give them the best service we can," said Miles.

"Yes, of course, I know you do. Please don't think I was finding fault. I only meant, fancy wanting to die."

"One or two have good reasons."

"I suppose you would say that I had. Everyone has been trying to persuade me, since my operation. The medical officials were the worst. They're afraid they may get into trouble for doing it wrong. And then the ballet people were almost as bad. They are so keen on Art that they say: 'You were the best of your class. You can never dance again. How can life be worth living?' What I try to explain is that it's just because I could dance that I *know* life is worth living. That's what Art means to me. Does that sound very silly?"

"It sounds unorthodox."

"Ah, but you're not an artist."

"Oh, I've danced all right. Twice a week all through my time at the orphanage."

"Therapeutic dancing?"

"That's what they called it."

"But, you see, that's quite different from Art."

"Why?"

"Oh," she said with a sudden full intimacy, with fondness, "oh what a lot you don't know."

The dancer's name was Clara.

3

Courtship was free and easy in this epoch, but Miles was Clara's first lover. The strenuous exercises of her training, the austere standards of the corps-de-ballet and her devotion to her art had kept her body and soul unencumbered.

For Miles, child of the State, sex had been part of the curriculum at every stage of his education; first in diagrams, then in demonstrations, then in application, he had mastered all the antics of procreation. Love was a word seldom used except by politicians and by them only in moments of pure fatuity. Nothing that he had been taught prepared him for Clara.

Once in drama, always in drama. Clara now spent her days mending ballet shoes and helping neophytes on the wall bars. She had a cubicle in a Nissen hut and it was there that she and Miles spent most of their evenings. It was unlike anyone else's quarters in Satellite City.

Two little paintings hung on the walls, unlike any paintings Miles had seen before, unlike anything approved by the Ministry of Art. One represented a goddess of antiquity, naked and rosy, fondling a peacock on a bank of flowers; the other a vast, tree-fringed lake and a party in spreading silken clothes embarking in a pleasure boat under a broken arch. The gilt frames were much chipped, but what remained of them was elaborately foliated.

"They're French," said Clara. "More than two hundred years old. My mother left them to me."

All her possessions had come from her mother, nearly enough of them to furnish the little room—a looking glass framed in porcelain flowers, a gilt, irregular clock. She and Miles drank their sad, officially compounded coffee out of brilliant, riveted cups.

"It reminds me of prison," said Miles when he was first admitted there. It was the highest praise he knew.

On the first evening among this delicate bric-a-brac his lips found the bare twin spaces of her chin.

"I knew it would be a mistake to let the beastly doctor poison me," said Clara complacently.

Full summer came. Another moon waxed over these rare lovers. Once they sought coolness and secrecy among the high cow-parsley and willow-herb of the waste building sites. Clara's beard was all silvered like a patriarch's in the midnight radiance.

"On such a night as this," said Miles, supine, gazing into the face of the moon, "on such a night as this I burned an Air Force Station and half its occupants."

Clara sat up and began lazily smoothing her whiskers, then more vigorously tugged the comb through the thicker, tangled growth of her head, dragging it from her forehead; re-ordered the clothing which their embraces had loosed. She was full of womanly content and ready to go home. But Miles, all male, *post coitum tristis,* was struck by a chill sense of loss. No demonstration or exercise had prepared him for this strange new experience of the sudden loneliness that follows requited love.

Walking home they talked casually and rather crossly.

"You never go to the ballet now."

"No."

"Won't they give you seats?"

"I suppose they would."

"Then why don't you go?"

"I don't think I should like it. I see them often rehearsing. I don't like it."

"But you lived for it."

"Other interests now."

"Me?"

"Of course."

"You love me more than the ballet?"

"I am very happy."

"Happier than if you were dancing?"

"I can't tell, can I? You're all I've got now."

"But if you could change?"

"I can't."

"If?"

"There's no 'if'."

"Damn."

"Don't fret, darling. It's only the moon."

And they parted in silence.

November came, a season of strikes; leisure for Miles, unsought and unvalued; lonely periods when the ballet school worked on and the death house stood cold and empty.

Clara began to complain of ill health. She was growing stout.

"Just contentment," she said at first, but the change worried her. "Can it be that beastly operation?" she asked. "I heard the reason they put down one of the Cambridge girls was that she kept growing fatter and fatter."

"She weighed nineteen stone," said Miles. "I know because Dr. Beamish mentioned it. He has strong professional objections to the Klugmann operation."

"I'm going to see the Director of Medicine. There's a new one now."

When she returned from her appointment, Miles, still left idle by the strikers, was waiting for her among her pictures and china. She sat beside him on the bed.

"Let's have a drink," she said.

They had taken to drinking wine together, very rarely because of the expense. The State chose and named the vintage. This month the issue was "Progress Port." Clara kept it in a crimson, white-cut, Bohemian flagon. The glasses were modern, unbreakable and unsightly.

"What did the doctor say?"

"He's very sweet."

"Well?"

"Much cleverer than the one before."

"Did he say it was anything to do with your operation?"

"Oh, yes. Everything to do with it."

"Can he put you right?"

"Yes, he thinks so."

"Good."

They drank their wine.

"That first doctor did make a mess of the operation, didn't he?"

"Such a mess. The new doctor says I'm a unique case. You see, I'm pregnant."

"*Clara.*"

"Yes, it is a surprise, isn't it?"

"This needs thinking about," said Miles.

He thought.

He refilled their glasses.

He said: "It's hard luck on the poor little beast not being an orphan. Not much opportunity for it. If he's a boy we must try and get him registered as a worker. Of course it might be a girl. Then"—brightly—"we could make her a dancer."

"Oh, don't mention dancing," cried Clara, and suddenly began weeping. "Don't speak to me of dancing."

Her tears fell fast. No tantrum this, but deep uncontrolled inconsolable sorrow.

And next day she disappeared.

4

Santa-Claus-Tide was near. Shops were full of shoddy little dolls. Children in the schools sang old ditties about peace and goodwill. Strikers went back to work in order to qualify for their seasonal bonus. Electric bulbs were hung in the conifers, and the furnaces in the Dome of Security roared again. Miles had been promoted. He now sat beside the assistant registrar and helped stamp and file the documents of the dead. It was harder work than he was used to and Miles was hungry for Clara's company. The lights were going out in the Dome and on the Goodwill Tree in the car park. He walked the half-mile of hutments to Clara's quarters. Other girls were waiting for their consorts or setting out to find them in the Recreatorium, but Clara's door was locked. A note, pinned to it, read: *Miles, Going away for a bit. C.* Angry and puzzled he returned to his hostel.

Clara, unlike himself, had uncles and cousins scattered about the country. Since her operation she had been shy of visiting them. Now, Miles supposed, she was taking cover among them. It was the manner of her flight, so unlike her gentle ways, that tortured him. For a busy week he thought of nothing else. His reproaches sang in his head as the undertone to all the activities of the day and at night he lay sleepless repeating in his mind every word spoken between them and every act of intimacy.

After a week the thought of her became spasmodic and regular. The subject bored him unendurably. He strove to keep it out of his mind as a man might strive to control an attack of hiccups, and as impotently. Spasmodically, mechanically, the thought of Clara returned. He timed it and found that it came every $7^1/_2$ minutes. He went to sleep thinking of her, he woke up thinking of her. But between times he slept. He consulted the departmental psychiatrist who told him that he was burdened by the responsibility of parentage. But it was not Clara the mother who haunted him, but Clara the betrayer.

Next week he thought of her every twenty minutes. The week after that he thought of her irregularly, though often; only when something outside himself reminded him of her. He began to look at other girls and considered himself cured.

He looked hard at other girls as he passed them in the dim corridors of the Dome and they looked boldly back at him. Then one of them stopped him and said: "I've seen you before with Clara," and at the mention of her name all interest in the other girl ceased in pain. "I went to visit her yesterday."

"Where?"

"In hospital, of course. Didn't you know?"

"What's the matter with her?"

"She won't say. Nor will anyone else at the hospital. She's top secret. If you ask me she's been in an accident and there's some politician involved. I can't think of any other reason for all the fuss. She's covered in bandages and gay as a lark."

Next day, December 25, was Santa Claus Day; no holiday in the department of Euthanasia, which was an essential service. At dusk Miles walked to the hospital, one of the unfinished edifices, all concrete and steel and glass in front and a jumble of huts behind. The hall porter was engrossed in the television, which was performing an old obscure folk play which past generations had performed on Santa Claus Day, and was now revived and revised as a matter of historical interest.

It was of professional interest to the porter for it dealt with maternity services before the days of Welfare. He gave the number of Clara's room without glancing up from the strange spectacle of an ox and an ass, an old man with a lantern, and a young mother. "People here are always complaining," he said. "They ought to realize what things were like before Progress."

The corridors were loud with relayed music. Miles found the hut he sought. It was marked "Experimental Surgery. Health Officers Only." He found the cubicle. He found Clara sleeping, the sheet pulled up to her eyes, her hair loose on the pillow. She had brought some of her property with her. An old shawl lay across the bed-table. A painted fan stood against the television set. She awoke, her eyes full of frank welcome and pulled the sheet higher, speaking through it.

"Darling, you shouldn't have come. I was keeping it for a surprise."

Miles sat by the bed and thought of nothing to say except: "How are you?"

"Wonderful. They've taken the bandages off today. They won't let me have a looking glass yet, but they say everything has been a tremendous success. I'm something very special, Miles—a new chapter in surgical progress."

"But what has happened to you. Is it something to do with the baby?"

"Oh no. At least, it was. That was the first operation. But that's all over now."

"You mean our child?"

"Yes, that had to go. I should never have been able to dance afterwards. I told you all about it. That was why I had the Klugmann operation, don't you remember?"

"But you gave up dancing."

"That's where they've been so clever. Didn't I tell you about the sweet, clever new medical director? He's cured all that."

"Your dear beard."

"Quite gone. An operation the new director invented himself. It's going to be named after him or even perhaps after me. He's so unselfish he wants to call it the Clara Operation. He's taken off all the skin and put on a wonderful new substance, a sort of synthetic rubber that takes grease-paint perfectly. He says the colour isn't perfect, but that it will never show on the stage. Look, feel it."

She sat up in bed, joyful and proud.

Her eyes and brow were all that was left of the loved face. Below it something quite inhuman, a tight, slippery mask, salmon pink.

Miles stared. In the television screen by the bed further characters had appeared—Food Production Workers. They seemed to declare a sudden strike, left their sheep and ran off at the bidding of some kind of shop-steward in fantastic dress. The machine by the bedside broke into song, an old, forgotten ditty: "O tidings of comfort and joy, comfort and joy, O tidings of comfort and joy."

Miles retched unobtrusively. The ghastly face regarded him with fondness and pride. At length the right words came to him; the trite, the traditional sentence uttered by countless lips of generations of baffled and impassioned Englishmen: "I think I shall go for a short walk."

But first he walked only as far as his hostel. There he lay down until the moon moved to his window and fell across his sleepless face. Then he set out, walking far into the fields, out of sight of the Dome of Security, for two hours until the moon was near setting.

He had travelled at random, but now the white rays fell on a signpost and he read: *"Mountjoy* ¾.*"* He strode on with only the stars to light his way till he came to the castle gates.

They stood open as always, gracious symbol of the new penology. He followed the drive. The whole lightless face of the old house stared at him silently, without rebuke. He knew now what was needed. He carried in his pocket a cigarette lighter which often worked. It worked for him now.

No need for oil here. The dry old silk of the drawing-room curtains lit like paper. Paint and panelling, plaster and tapestry and gilding bowed to the embrace of the leaping flames. He stepped outside. Soon it was too hot on the terrace and he retreated further, to the marble temple at the end of the long walk. The murderers were leaping from the first storey windows, but the sexual offenders, trapped above, set up a wail of terror. He heard the chandeliers fall and saw the boiling lead cascading from the roof. This was something altogether finer than the strangulation of a few peacocks. He watched exultant as minute by minute the scene disclosed fresh wonders. Great timbers crashed within; outside the lily-pond hissed with falling brands; a vast ceiling of smoke shut out the stars and under it tongues of flame floated away into the tree tops.

Two hours later when the first engine arrived, the force of the fiery storm was already spent. Miles rose from his marble throne and began the long walk home. But he was no longer at all fatigued. He strode out cheerfully with his shadow, cast by the dying blaze, stretching before him along the lane.

On the main road a motorist stopped him and asked: "What's that over there? A house on fire?"

"It was," said Miles. "It's almost out now."

"Looks like a big place. Only Government property, I suppose?"

"That's all," said Miles.

"Well hop in if you want a lift."

"Thanks," said Miles, "I'm walking for pleasure."

5

Miles rose after two hours in bed. The hostel was alive with all the normal activity of morning. The wireless was playing; the sub-officials were coughing over their wash-basins; the reek of State sausages frying in State grease filled the asbestos cubicle. He was slightly stiff after his long walk and slightly footsore, but his mind was as calm and empty as the sleep from which he had awoken. The scorched-earth policy had succeeded. He had made a desert in his imagination which he might call peace. Once before he had burned his childhood. Now his brief adult life lay in ashes; the enchantments that surrounded Clara were one with the splendours of Mountjoy; her great golden beard, one with the tongues of flame that had leaped and expired among the stars; her fans and pictures and scraps of old embroidery, one with the gilded cornices and silk hangings, black, cold and sodden. He ate his sausage with keen appetite and went to work.

All was quiet too at the Department of Euthanasia.

The first announcement of the Mountjoy disaster had been on the early news. Its proximity to Satellite City gave it a special poignancy there.

"It is a significant phenomenon," said Dr. Beamish, "that any bad news has an immediate effect on our service. You see it whenever there is an international crisis. Sometimes I think people only come to us when they have nothing to talk about. Have you looked at our queue today?"

Miles turned to the periscope. Only one man waited outside, old Parsnip, a poet of the thirties who came daily but was usually jostled to the back of the crowd. He was a comic character in the department, this veteran poet. Twice in Miles's short term he had succeeded in gaining admission, but on both occasions had suddenly taken fright and bolted.

"It's a lucky day for Parsnip," said Miles.

"Yes. He deserves some luck. I knew him well once, him and his friend Pimpernell. *New Writing,* the Left Book Club, they were all the rage. Pimpernell was one of my first patients. Hand Parsnip in and we'll finish him off."

So old Parsnip was summoned and that day his nerve stood firm. He passed fairly calmly through the gas chamber on his way to rejoin Pimpernell.

"We might as well knock off for the day," said Dr. Beamish. "We shall be busy again soon when the excitement dies down."

But the politicians seemed determined to keep the excitement up. All the normal features of television were interrupted and curtailed to give place to Mountjoy. Survivors appeared on the screen, among them Soapy, who described how long practice as a cat burglar had enabled him to escape. Mr. Sweat, he remarked with respect, had got clear away. The ruins were surveyed by the apparatus. A sexual maniac with broken legs gave audience from his hospital bed. The Minister of Welfare, it was announced, would make a special appearance that evening to comment on the disaster.

Miles dozed intermittently beside the hostel set and at dusk rose, still calm and free; so purged of emotion that he made his way once more to the hospital and called on Clara.

She had spent the afternoon with looking-glass and make-up box. The new substance of her face fulfilled all the surgeon's promises. It took paint to perfection. Clara had given herself a full mask as though for the lights of the stage; an even creamy white with sudden high spots of crimson on the cheek bones, huge hard crimson lips, eye brows extended and turned up catwise, the eyes shaded all round with ultramarine and dotted at the corners with crimson.

"You're the first to see me," she said. "I was half afraid you wouldn't come. You seemed cross yesterday."

"I wanted to see the television," said Miles. "It's so crowded at the hostel."

"So dull today. Nothing except this prison that has been burned down."

"I was there myself. Don't you remember? I often talked of it."

"Did you, Miles? Perhaps so. I've such a bad memory for things that don't concern me. Do you really want to hear the Minister? It would be much cosier to talk."

"It's him I've come for."

And presently the Minister appeared, open-necked as always, but without his usual smile; grave to the verge of tears. He spoke for twenty minutes. " . . . The great experiment must go on . . . the martyrs of maladjustment shall not have died in vain . . . A greater, new Mountjoy shall rise from the ashes of the old . . . " Eventually tears came—real tears for he held an invisible onion—and trickled down his cheeks. So the speech ended.

"That's all I came for," said Miles, and left Clara to her cocoa-butter and face-towel.

Next day all the organs of public information were still piping the theme of Mountjoy. Two or three patients, already bored with the entertainment, presented themselves for extermination and were happily despatched. Then a message came from the Regional Director, official-in-chief of Satellite City. He required the immediate presence of Miles in his office.

"I have a move order for you, Mr. Plastic. You are to report to the Ministers of Welfare and Rest and Culture. You will be issued with a Grade-A hat, umbrella and brief case for the journey. My congratulations."

Equipped with these insignia of sudden, dizzy promotion, Miles travelled to the capital leaving behind a domeful of sub-officials chattering with envy.

At the terminus an official met him. Together in an official car they drove to Whitehall.

"Let me carry your brief case, Mr. Plastic."

"There's nothing in it."

Miles's escort laughed obsequiously at this risqué joke.

At the Ministry the lifts were in working order. It was a new and alarming experience to enter the little cage and rise to the top of the great building.

"Do they always work here?"

"Not *always,* but very very often."

Miles realised that he was indeed at the heart of things.

"Wait here. I will call you when the Ministers are ready."

Miles looked from the waiting-room window at the slow streams of traffic. Just below him stood a strange, purposeless obstruction of stone. A very old man, walking by, removed his hat to it as though saluting an acquaintance. Why? Miles wondered. Then he was summoned to the politicians.

They were alone in their office save for a gruesome young woman. The Minister of Rest and Culture said: "Ease your feet, lad," and indicated a large leatherette armchair.

"Not such a happy occasion, alas, as our last meeting," said the Minister of Welfare.

"Oh, I don't know," said Miles. He was enjoying the outing.

"The tragedy at Mountjoy Castle was a grievous loss to the cause of penology."

"But the great work of Rehabilitation will continue," said the gruesome young woman.

"A greater Mountjoy will arise from the ashes," said the Minister.

"Those noble criminal lives have not been lost in vain."

"Their memory will inspire us."

"Yes," said Miles. "I heard the broadcast."

"Exactly," said the Minister. "Precisely. Then you appreciate, perhaps, what a change the occurrence makes in your own position. From being, as we hoped, the first of a continuous series of successes, you are our only one. It would not be too much to say that the whole future of penology is in your hands. The destruction of Mountjoy Castle by itself was merely a set-back. A sad one, of course, but something which might be described as the growing pains of a great movement. But there is a darker side. I told you, I think, that our great experiment had been made only against considerable opposition. Now—I speak confidentially—that opposition has become vocal and unscrupulous. There is, in fact, a whispering campaign that the fire was no accident but the act of one of the very men whom we were seeking to serve. That campaign must be scotched."

"They can't do us down as easy as they think," said the Minister of Rest and Culture. "Us old dogs know a trick or two."

"Exactly. Counter-propaganda. You are our Exhibit A. The irrefutable evidence of the triumph of our system. We are going to send you up and down the country to lecture. My colleagues have already written your speech. You will be accompanied by Miss Flower here, who will show and explain the model of the new Mountjoy. Perhaps you will care to see it yourself. Miss Flower, the model please."

All the time they were speaking Miles had been aware of a bulky, sheeted object on a table in the window. Miss Flower now unveiled it. Miles gazed in awe.

The object displayed was a familiar, standard packingcase, set on end.

"A rush job," said the Minister of Welfare. "You will be provided with something more elaborate for your tour."

Miles gazed at the box.

It fitted. It fell into place precisely in the void of his mind, satisfying all the needs for which his education had prepared him. The conditioned personality recognized its proper pre-ordained environment. All else was insubstantial; the gardens of Mountjoy, Clara's cracked Crown Derby and her enveloping beard were trophies of a fading dream.

The Modern Man was home.

"There is one further point," continued the Minister of Welfare. "A domestic one but not as irrelevant as it may seem. Have you by any chance formed an attachment in Satellite City? Your dossier suggests that you have."

"Any woman trouble?" explained the Minister of Rest and Culture.

"Oh, yes," said Miles. "Great trouble. But that is over."

"You see, perfect rehabilitation, complete citizenship should include marriage."

"It has not," said Miles.

"That should be rectified."

"Folks like a bloke to be spliced," said the Minister of Rest and Culture. "With a couple of kids."

"There is hardly time for *them*," said the Minister of Welfare. "But we think that psychologically you will have more appeal if you have a wife by your side. Miss Flower here has every qualification."

"Looks are only skin deep, lad," said the Minister of Rest and Culture.

"So if you have no preferable alternative to offer . . . ?"

"None," said Miles.

"Spoken like an orphan. I see a splendid career ahead of the pair of you."

"When can we get divorced?"

"Come, come, Plastic. You mustn't look too far ahead. First things first. You have already obtained the necessary leave from your Director, Miss Flower?"

"Yes, Minister."

"Then off you both go. And State be with you."

In perfect peace of heart Miles followed Miss Flower to the Registrar's office.

Then the mood veered.

Miles felt ill at ease during the ceremony and fidgeted with something small and hard which he found in his pocket. It proved to be his cigarette lighter, a most uncertain apparatus. He pressed the catch and instantly, surprisingly there burst out a tiny flame—gemlike, hymeneal, auspicious.

On Waugh

Unlike most English boys of his class and time, who were sent away to private boarding schools at an early age, Evelyn Waugh (1903–1966) spent a happy childhood with his family until, at the age of twelve, he was sent to a hastily chosen public school, Lancing. The haste was due to his older brother Alec's novel *The Loom of Youth,* sensational for its time, which so roused the anger of the officials of Sherborne that both Alec and the boys' father Arthur (managing director of Chapman and Hall, Ltd., publishing company) resigned from membership in the alumni association. The suddenness of the change must have added to the younger Waugh's sense of disorientation at leaving home. The shock was more severe because of the anxieties about the war and increasing privations due to the German submarine blockade. At any rate, like many otherwise dissimilar contemporaries, Waugh always looked back to the Edwardian age as a time of peace, plenty, and security; later he could find explanations for the process of despoilation; at twelve, his knowledge of the loss of a material and maternal Eden was visceral and emotional. Even more than other contemporaries who shared his feelings, Waugh desired a refuge from the horrors of modern life, a major theme in his novels.

There was, however, an aggressive streak in Waugh's character which brought him to a position of influence at Lancing and later at Oxford, where he attended Hertford College on a history scholarship. Winning the scholarship was for him an end to, rather than an earnest of, further study; he spent his time in extracurricular writing and film production and in leading a very full and raffish social life. In 1924 he went down without a degree and spent the next few years trying to evade "the family trade of literature" by teaching, attending art school and carpentry classes, and distressing his parents by his idleness and dissipation. In 1927, hoping to marry, he secured a commission to write a biography of Dante Gabriel Rossetti and began a comic novel. On the strength of these, he married Evelyn Gardner the following year. The literary career long survived the marriage: his wife left him as he was half-way through *Vile Bodies,* his second novel. The divorce suit was filed on the same day the novel was published, and nine months later Waugh was received into the Roman Catholic Church.

In the thirties Waugh traveled extensively: to Abyssinia to cover Haile Selassie's coronation for the *Times;* to British Guiana; to Spitzbergen; to Abyssinia to cover the war with Italy for the *Daily Mail;* to Mexico to gather material about a book on the expropriation of British oil companies. These trips furnished material for a series of travel books and novels, interspersed with a biography and numerous book reviews and articles. In 1937, having obtained an annulment which permitted him to remarry as a Catholic, he married Laura Herbert and settled down to become a family man and country squire. With the outbreak of the Second World War, he joined the Royal Marines and later the Commandos, seeing action in Crete and North Africa and later serving with the British mission to the Yugoslav partisans. In the last year of the war he wrote *Brideshead Revisited,* which brought him to the attention of a popular audience through the Book-of-the-Month Club and publicity in *Life* and other magazines. After the war he continued to travel, though in less vigorous fashion, and resumed his country life, emerging from time to time to engage in controversy, file a libel suit, or publish a novel. By his own admission and intention, he grew increasingly eccentric, fighting a rear-guard action against politicians and all kinds of reform and change, especially in the Catholic liturgy. He died on Easter Sunday, 1966.

Like many novels set in the future—Aldous Huxley's *Brave New World,* George Orwell's *1984,* and Henry Green's *Concluding* are but a few examples—*Love Among the Ruins* is really about contemporary society. This is Waugh's nonlove letter to Welfare State England, bleak and unlovely under the postwar austerity program instituted by Atlee's Labour government. Orwell's *1984* gives an exaggerated picture of wartime England, and conditions were not much happier in succeeding years. The Festival of Britain in 1951 was intended to announce to the world that England had recovered its finances and its morale, and a central feature of the exposition was the Dome of Discovery—which Waugh converts into the Dome of Security. After he finished *Love Among the Ruins,* he took pains to have it published the day before the coronation of Queen Elizabeth II as a coronation present from a loyal though mischievous subject. This, he implied, was what Elizabeth was inheriting and promising to cherish and defend.

However, Waugh had a purpose underlying the teasing, and, though disguised, that purpose is moral. Ten years earlier he became involved in a controversy, conducted in the *New Statesman and Nation,* the leading Left weekly, with Dr. Marie C. Stopes over "Religion in State Schools." Dr. Stopes pointed to the higher percentage of juvenile delinquency among products of Roman Catholic schools than among those of other schools and deplored the use of tax money to subsidize institutions which produce social deviants. Waugh replied that he "was not brought up to regard the evasion of the police as the prime aim of education, nor has my subsequent observation of the world given me any reason to think that either the wickedest men or even the worst citizens are to be found in prison. The real enemies of society are sitting snug behind typewriters and microphones, pursuing their work of destruction amid popular applause. . . . No doubt by bringing my children up Catholics I am putting them in appreciable danger of imprisonment, but they must not reproach me with it. They belong to a church whose most illustrious figures in any age and country have suffered the extremities of the law. Moreover, sir, a regular perusal of your own pages gives me the impression that, if things go as you wish, by the time they are hardened in crime, gaols will have grown so congenial and the rest of the country so heavy with restraints, that they will have the laugh on their innocent old father whom a Protestant education keeps on the right side of the law."

Ten years later, the conceit of prisons more pleasant than the outside world flowered in *Love Among the Ruins,* but in a deeper sense the novella grew out of Waugh's life and works. Inversion, he implies, is perversion, and its end is madness, destruction, death—or, what he feared far more than any of these, boredom. Boredom is largely an aesthetic rather than a moral consideration, but Waugh had read enough theology to know that, besides *accide,* which is defined as "sadness in the face of spiritual good," and is allied to despair, there is an allied condition, common among people ignorant of the very existence of spiritual good and therefore outside the economy of salvation and damnation: "*pigritia,* plain slackness, which is a deflexion from, if not an outrage against, the divine order." Idleness and boredom led to apathy, resentment, and "a sense of abandonment" (from "Sloth").

Waugh's friend and contemporary, Graham Greene, once maintained that an obsession was helpful to a writer, for it alone could unify a whole body of work. In Waugh's case, the obsession took the form of a belief that Western civilization was in an advanced state of decay. His early experience with the change, privation, and decay in his own private universe was reinforced not only by ensuing events but by the cyclic theories of history he read at Lancing and Oxford. Like many of his immediate predecessors—James Joyce, W. B. Yeats, and F. Scott Fitzgerald among the best known—he had no difficulty in bringing experience and theory to bear on the modern world in fiction and nonfiction. Sometimes the theme is mentioned overtly, as in the title of *Decline and Fall* or in the short story "Out of Depth," which dramatizes English decline into barbarism and the rise to dominance of the black races. Sometimes it is less obvious, but like atmospheric pressure it is always present, a condition of the world in which his characters live and move.

Waugh and his characters found two ways of dealing with change and decay: counterattack and acceptance. The first method involves a political and ethical approach to modern ills: " . . . the spirit of the age," he once wrote, "is the spirits of those who compose it and the stronger the expressions of discontent from prevailing fashion, the higher the possibility of diverting it from its ruinous course." For this purpose he wrote *Mexico: An Object Lesson* and other pronouncements which affirmed civilization as a difficult achievement which is maintained "only by unremitting, concerted defence and counterattack." Acceptance of the modern world, on the other hand, involves what ultimately are spiritual values, not simply the long view of history but man and society considered under the aspect of eternity. Critics who accused him of cruelty and, more frequently, of nostalgic snobbery for an aristocratic society, miss the importance of this distinction. Waugh might seem to long for the stable and ordered world of the past, but he knew that the society he desired "never existed in history nor ever will" and that "One is naturally inclined to regard every period but one's own as a Conservative Utopia, where everything was tranquilly rooted in tradition, the rich respected, the poor contented, and everyone slept well and ate with a hearty appetite." Tony Last's fate in *A Handful of Dust* demonstrates Waugh's awareness that attempts to preserve an old way of life for its own sake were futile, foolish, and sentimental, however touching they might be. Hoping to find the embodiment of his Victorian Gothic dream, Tony stumbles into a microcosm of feudal society without God, based on force, slavery, and ties of blood. This basically spiritual theme is stated even more clearly in *Sword of Honour,* in which Guy Crouchback learns that "quantitative judgments don't apply" and that, in his modest way, he must return good for evil. This is another way of saying that Waugh differed from other cyclical theorists because he was a Christian, specifically a Catholic: St. Augustine's "Here we have no continuing city" echoes through all of his novels, in which he admits and almost rejoices in secular disasters and defeats. Something of this spirit lies behind his denial that he was a satirist; satire, he said, depends upon accepted social norms to induce shame in those who violate them. Amid the shameless chaos of the modern world, he maintained, the artist could only attempt "to create little independent systems of order of his own" and imitate the monks who preserved through the barbarian invasions the spark of learning.

Belief in a divine order does not necessarily mean a solemn approach to experience. Waugh could see the contemporary world outside theological and moral confines, amusing in its aberrancy, and his lack of hope for the modern world made him less censorious than those who believed improvement possible. Like G. K. Chesterton, Joseph Conrad, Rudyard Kipling, and others, he did not assume that not to be good was automatically to be evil. Besides heaven and hell, Catholic theology provides limbo for those invincibly ignorant of the truth. Waugh's limbo could be a lively place, inhabited by characters like Captain Grimes, Basil Seal, Mr. Youkoumian, and Mr. Baldwin—so lively that Edmund Wilson could argue convincingly that Waugh loved anarchic energy for its own sake and that his attempts to subdue it to theological orthodoxy led to his decline as a novelist. Yet the early novels are filled with characters who fear that there will be nothing for them to do. John Beaver, the spiritless demi-villain of *A Handful of Dust,* has no function in society, and neither do any of the other male characters. It is true that Beaver has no talents, but meaningful careers are not open to men like Basil Seal who have both talent and energy. In fact, much of the energy exhibited in Waugh's early novels is motion for its own sake or for the sake of destruction. Without vital connection with the society they inhabit, the characters must be wild particles like Basil or, like Adam Fenwich-Symes, they suffer entropic loss of energy to their environment. One significant exception is *Black Mischief,* which demonstrates and in part celebrates the vitality of natives who live in an amoral but coherent and traditional society. The Emperor Seth, wishing to modernize his island, can only destroy; energetic, almost prelapsarian barbarism, like that of the Earl of Ngumo, seems far more desirable. The Earl enters his master's victory ball in "a lion's-mane busby; on his shoulders a shapeless fur mantle; a red satin skirt; brass bangles and a necklace of lion's teeth; a long, ornamental sword hung at his side; two bandoliers of brass cartridges circled his great girth; he had small bloodshot eyes and a tousle of black wool over his cheeks and chin." Besides his picturesque appearance, the Earl exhibits a lively sense of survival: he has delayed his march until the civil war has been settled, and he and his cohorts organize a successful revolution in defence of traditional values and their own prerogatives. Even then, Waugh showed, the traditional candidate for the throne, hopelessly gaga, offers no viable alternative: he dies as the crown is placed on his head. The resulting vacuum leads to European occupation, with an increase of officialdom and dull uniformity. In *Love Among the Ruins,* the process has gone twenty-five years further. Programmed sterility has reduced politics, art, private life, even dress, to gray and spiritless norms. The slogan of Liberty, Equality, Fraternity had, in Waugh's view, been a will-of-the-wisp which led to a slough of despond. For this slogan he proposed to substitute "Liberty, Diversity, Privacy" to foster the spirit as well as the body.

Confronted with a dull and mechanical world, some of Waugh's heroes, like Paul Pennyfeather and William Boot (both, like Miles, victims of their women) find in privacy their greatest good. Less passive characters like Basil and Dennis Barlow seek diversity in odd corners of the world and in even odder pursuits: revolutions, a cannibal feast with one's mistress the main course, a job in a pet's cemetery, and the impromptu cremation of one's loved one. Basil and Dennis both combat the modern world, but differ in the women they consort with: Basil's Prudence is silly, and Basil is attracted to silly women because he can dominate them; Dennis is attracted to Aimée Thanatogenos because, "sole Eve in a bustling hygienic Eden, this girl was a decadent," with "a rich glint of lunacy" in her eyes. In fact, most of Waugh's heroes, active or passive, seek escape or consolation in their women. All, like Miles Plastic, are disappointed.

Denied any outlet, formed on no idea, given no goal, Miles Plastic becomes a pyromaniac, a scourge of the packing-case, sterile world which shaped him. Like Aimée, only in destruction can he assert and assuage the demands of his spirit. Like Waugh, he both loves the past and hates it for what it has allowed the present to become; like Waugh, he denies Browning's assertion in his "Love Among the Ruins" and the implications of other romantic poetry that love can survive the ruins of the civilization which fostered the very idea of romance.

Textual note:

In *Lilliput,* 31 (May-June 1953), 73–96; in *Commonweal,* 58 (31 July 1953), 410–412. Published separately by Chapman and Hall, 1953; included in *Tactical Exercise* (Boston: Little, Brown and Company, 1954). Except for accidentals (punctuation and capitalization), in which the second and third and frequently the first agree against the fourth, the last three versions are almost identical. The *Tactical Exercise* text has been followed here.

Resources for further study:

Among Waugh's novels, especially *Decline and Fall* (1928), *Vile Bodies* (1930), *Black Mischief* (1932), *A Handful of Dust* (1934), "Out of Depth," in *Mr. Loveday's Little Outing and Other Sad Stories* (1936), *Brideshead Revisited* (1945), and the "war trilogy," *Sword of Honour* (1952, 1955,

1961; in one volume form, 1965). All except *Mr. Loveday* are available in paperback editions.

For the study of *Love Among the Ruins,* the most useful nonfiction is *Mexico: An Object Lesson* (1939); "Religion in State Schools," *New Statesman and Nation,* 26 (2 October 1943), 217, and (16 October 1943), 251; "Fan-Fare," *Life,* 20 (3 April 1946), 53, 54, 56, 58, 60; "What to Do with the Upper Classes," *Town and Country,* 101 (1 September 1946), 141, 260–261; "Mr. Waugh Replies," *Spectator,* 191 (3 July 1953), 23–24; "Sloth," in *The Seven Deadly Sins* (1962); "Preface," Timothy McInerny, *The Private Man* (New York: Ivan Obolensky, 1962); *A Little Learning: An Autobiography: The Early Years* (1964).

BIBLIOGRAPHICAL:

DOYLE, PAUL A. "Evelyn Waugh: A Bibliography," *Bulletin of Bibliography,* 22 (May-August 1957), 57–62. Includes both primary and secondary sources.

FARR, D. PAUL. "Evelyn Waugh: A Supplemental Bibliography," *Bulletin of Bibliography,* 26 (July-September 1969), 67–68, 87. Primary materials.

KOSOK, HEINZ. "Evelyn Waugh: A Checklist of Criticism," *Twentieth Century Literature,* 11 (January 1960), 211–215.

———. "Evelyn Waugh: A Supplementary Checklist of Criticism," *Evelyn Waugh Newsletter,* 2 (Spring 1968), 1–3. The newsletter continues to add items to primary and secondary bibliography.

LINCK, CHARLES E., JR. "Works of Evelyn Waugh, 1910 to 1930," *Twentieth Century Literature,* 10 (April 1964), 19–25. Linck's Dissertation, "The Development of Evelyn Waugh's Career, 1903–1939," University of Kansas, 1963, lists a number of items not recorded elsewhere.

BIOGRAPHICAL:

A Little Learning covers Waugh's life until 1925.

DONALDSON, FRANCES. *Evelyn Waugh: Portrait of a Country Neighbor.* Philadelphia: Chilton Book Company, 1967. Deals with the period 1947–1966.

WAUGH, ALEC. *My Brother Evelyn and Other Portraits.* New York: Farrar, Straus & Giroux, 1967. Deals mostly with the period 1922–1932.

CRITICAL:

BRADBURY, MALCOLM. *Evelyn Waugh.* Edinburgh: Oliver and Boyd, 1964.

CARENS, JAMES F. *The Satiric Art of Evelyn Waugh.* Seattle: University of Washington Press, 1964.

DAVIS, ROBERT MURRAY, ed. *Evelyn Waugh.* St. Louis: B. Herder Book Co., 1969. A collection of reprinted essays.

———. "The Mind and Art of Evelyn Waugh," *Papers on Language and Literature,* 3 (Summer 1967), 270–287.

HALL, JAMES. *The Tragic Comedians: Some Modern British Novelists.* Bloomington: Indiana University Press, 1963.

JEBB, JULIAN. "The Art of Fiction XXX: Evelyn Waugh," *Paris Review,* no. 30 (Summer-Fall 1963), 72–85.

KERNAN, ALVIN. *The Plot of Satire.* New Haven: Yale University Press, 1965.

STOPP, FREDERICK J. *Evelyn Waugh: Portrait of an Artist.* Boston: Little, Brown and Company, 1958.

WASSON, RICHARD. *"A Handful of Dust: Critique of Victorianism,"* Modern Fiction Studies, 7 (Winter 1961–1962), 327–337.

WILSON, EDMUND. *Classics and Commercials.* New York: Random House, Inc., Vintage Books, 1962.

WILLIAM SANSOM
A Contest of Ladies

Fred Morley might easily have been mistaken for something of an eccentric. He was a "bachelor," he was "wealthy," he was "retired from the stage." It was not held unusual for such a man to be somewhat out of line with the rest of the world.

Nor, because he was a bachelor, was it unusual that a certain July evening found him in his bedroom wandering from door to window, from bed to fireplace, wondering what to do. Many evenings found him so—with the warm nights and in the dangerous flush of middle-age.

He looked at the metal plaque of bells by his bed. "Chambermaid." "Waiter." But he knew that if he rang, neither would come. His eye dropped to the telephone beneath—there were buttons which led to "Reception" and "Restaurant" and "Toilet Saloon": again he knew there would be no response. He wondered—as he had done so very often in the past—whether he really would have liked a response, had this been possible. But he quickly put that old idea from his mind, he was much happier as things were.

Up on the pink satin wall-paper, in a discreet position, was inset a white celluloid notice: a scramble of black lettering begged visitors to do this or not to do that. Morley's empty mind passed to all the other empty rooms around and above him, all with the same small notice bowing and begging—for the wording of these notices was polite and obsequious, a cut above the terse commercial command—by each closed door.

Downstairs the lounge would be empty. Magazines would be arranged neatly on a central table—*Country Life, The Gas Times, The Tatler*—and the curtains would be still undrawn to let a blue evening light through on to a great splay of fresh-bought lupins. Across from the empty lounge the bar would stand open and brightly polished—and empty too. At this thought old Morley brightened. Thank goodness—no one in the best chair, no chattering gin-groups, no idle guests to be sauntered into. No porter on the doorstep to mar the evening with a "Good evening" and a searching eye. Fred Morley knew he could stand alone on the step and survey what he wished, undisturbed and in silence. He brightened. Such people might have meant company. But was such company preferable to his own selected privacy? By all means no.

By what means? What sort of hotel was this—all trim and in working order, yet absolutely empty of people? Not empty as death, not dust-covered and cobweb-hung—but fresh-swept, with the feeling that a dozen servants had only a moment before left. It was as one might imagine a live hotel struck by plague, or conjured up in some ghost-tale, or in some unknown way emptied yet sailing equipped on its course like the maddening *Mary Celeste.*

A hotel bought by Morley? A hotel occupied entirely by Morley?

Almost. But in fact it was not a hotel at all. It was Morley's private house—decorated, in many of its more obvious features, like a hotel. This was Morley's "eccentricity." But was it, on closer consideration, so very eccentric? It is commonly a habit of furnishers and decorators to make things appear what they are not. Rooms—particularly of the well-to-do— have become escapes. The *chinoiserie* of Chippendale, sea-shell lairs of the rococo nymph, even the Greek revival—all have succeeded to make rooms what they are not. There have been Tudor cocktail-bars and Eliza-bethan garages, ship's-cabin beer-houses land-locked in a city street, chintzy cottage-rooms whose spinning-wheels shudder as the underground trains worm their way beneath. All of them studios of desire, each room an escape from four walls.

Morley's fancy to make his house look like a hotel was in fact less exotic than these. He had no vague wish to be different, it was a practical planned escape. A deep disaffection in him—the same that had left him a bache-lor—had revolted against the idea of house-and-home. Given a homely looking home he would feel home-bound, anchored, done. But hotels! These he loved—he felt in them adventure, the passage of possibility, a lovely rootless going and coming, excitement stalking the corridors, sin lurking in the shadows of the fire extinguishers. They reminded him, too, of his touring days in the theatre. But against this stood the truth that hotels were in fact dreadfully uncomfortable: and homes were not. Hence—most reasonably—the transposition. He had dressed his seven-bedroomed man-sion on the front of this rakish Channel seaside resort in a glamorous nostalgia for no-home.

Thus at six-thirty he sat and gazed his handsome eyes about the room and wondered what to do. Six-thirty is a bad hour. Hour of sundowners. Hour when the human beast, old moon-monkey, awakes to the idea of night. Hour of day's death and dark's beginning, uneasy hour of change. Bed-rooms stalk with people changing clothes, drinks are drunk, high teas eaten, limbs washed fresh of used daylight. No wonder Fred Morley wondered, like millions around him, what to do. A stall at the Hippodrome? A sole at the Ship? Oysters at Macey's? A glass with old Burgess? A stroll by the Band—strains of the *Rosenkavalier* across green breakwaters, the dying sands? A tinkle to Mrs Vereker—though it wasn't really His Night?

But none of these appealed. So, old bachelor that he was, he decided to pamper himself. His hand, strong, freckled, mildly arthritic, flashed its opal ring round the telephone dial. To a waiter at a real hotel some doors away his actor's accent, from between handsome curling lips and through teeth white and strong, ordered oysters and mulligatawny soup and what— oh, pigeon pie? Excellent. And a good dollop of Stilton, thank you. Wine he had, and plenty of port. Down went the receiver—above his clean square jaws the lips silently smacked—and with erect leisurely stride his legs took him over to the bathroom. A good hot bath, plenty of lather. Then, in grace to a good quiet evening at home, the raisin-red frogged smoking jacket.

Morley had played the romantic lead in most of the more robust musical comedies. He had toured for twenty years the length and breadth of the Isles in the boots of a Hussar, the breeches of a Desert Hero, the golden robes of Baghdad. He had made his money, saved it, and retired. Now as he strode his ample carpets he was still every inch a baritone. The theatrical years had stylized every manly gesture, incised surety into every feature of his square strong face, greyed not at all the good brown curly hair brushed suavely back and half sideways. And now as he undid his stays the deep and tuneful voice that had quickened hearths throughout the land broke into satisfied strains that declared how Maud was to come into the garden since the Black Bat Night had flown.

But, of course, the Black Bat Night was really at that time flying in: and with it, on the evening train, there had flown in six ladies new to the town—a Miss Clermont-Ferrand, the Misses Amsterdam and Rotterdam, Miss Sauerkraut of Nuremburg, Miss Civitavecchia and Miss Great-Belt of Denmark. Every summer the Town Corporation organized a Contest of Beauty. This year, spreading its festive wings, it had decided to make the Contest international. Invitations had been despatched. In some cases accepted. Part of the result, who had been rallied in London by their various agencies, had been sent down by the evening train.

Now they stood in the Railway Buffet studying little lists of recommended hotels and sipping, with wonder and weary enthusiasm, their watery-milked sweet cups of railway tea. The names of the hotels stared up at them with promise but nonentity. There were no Ritzes, no Savoys, none of the ordinary run. There were Ships and Crescents and Royals and many lesser establishments, listed as Boarding Houses, with Gaelic, Celtic and some-times Malayan names. All the ladies had different ideas and different purses, and all talked at once.

A group of local gentlemen sat drinking whisky and listening. These were a convivial lot, mixed commercials and retired front-walkers, black trilbies or stiff-collar tweeds. They spent most of the time ponderously pulling each other's legs; but now, with such a sudden advent of beautiful ladies, they went further. They went a bit silly. They giggled, they whispered, they mouthed and winked—the ladies, accompanied by the whisky, went straight to their heads.

Thus it was inevitable that sooner or later a sally would arch itself out at the ladies. It came very soon: an idea not indeed original, for it involved a well-tried local joke, flashed through the black trilby, the hair-grease, the hair and into the little grey cells of one of the fat red-faced commercials.

Lifting his hat, he sweated towards the ladies:

"Excuse my intruding upon yourselves, ladies—but I cannot help but see where you're not fixed up with your hotel. Now if you was to ask me—that is as I am the local man, I've lived here thirty years now—I wonder if you'd know where I'd say you'd be as best fixed up?"

He paused and looked from one to the other of those girls, eyebrows raised in huge surprise. These various girls winced, or looked away, or primped fascinated at him. He then said, sharply, with lips terse to keep a straight face:

"I'd say you'd best go to Morley's."

A gasp, quickly suppressed, from the other men. They were adept at the grave concealing face.

The ladies looked from one to the other, then at their lists. They said there was no mention of Morley's.

The man in the trilby rose instantly to this:

"And that's where you ladies hit the nail on its head. Morley's you won't find on no list. Morley's is more . . . " he waved his hands, screwing up his eyes and searching for just that one word which would do justice to the exquisition he proposed " . . . more what you call *select.*"

One of the tweeded gentlemen, removing his pipe from his mouth like a stopper, said gravely: "Morley's is a *private* hotel."

"Number Thirty-two, Marine Parade," another said. "Not five minutes."

Those jolly men then fell to in earnest. Morley's was this, Morley's was that. Once warmed up they discovered subtleties of compliment one would never have suspected; they even began to argue among themselves. In short, the ladies were at length convinced, a streetplan was quickly sketched showing the way to Number Thirty-two, and, gamely swallowing their tea, they left for Fred Morley's house.

One or two, Miss Great-Belt for one, wished inwardly to show her personal superiority by choosing a more grandly named hotel (there was indeed a Bristol, a name as hallowed as the Ritz), but on practical thought it seemed wiser in a strange land at first to stick together.

One of the gentlemen started up to escort them: but was quickly dissuaded by a furtive shake of the head from the ringleader. Let matters take their course. It might be tempting to watch old Fred Morley's face; but if any one of them were seen the game would be given away.

Such was the preposterous situation when those six Beauty Queens rang the bell of Mr Morley's house. That fact is stranger than fiction has been often observed—but seldom believed. We like the ordinary, it is more restful, and liking it tend to close our eyes to the bewilderment of chance and coincidence that otherwise would strike us every minute of the day.

In the case of these six Beauty Queens, the glove of coincidence might have fitted all the more neatly if, for instance, the waiter who had brought Fred Morley's supper had just at that moment been about to leave the house. A uniformed servant would have perfected an otherwise passable illusion. But in fact that waiter had not even arrived by the time those girls pulled the bell. And it was Morley himself, in his raisin-red smoking jacket, who finally opened the door.

"*Come* into the gar—den M—" he still sang, and then stood stupefied.

"We would like some rooms," said Miss Great-Belt, who like many Danes spoke English well. "Have you any to spare?"

Since those girls were Beauty Queens, they were passably beautiful. To Fred Morley the vision of their six faces framed in his doorway like singers at some strange summer carol-feast both bewildered him and set his mind working at an unusual rate.

The Misses Amsterdam and Rotterdam, and the two Latins Civitavecchia and Clermont-Ferrand, now followed by saying in many mixed words that for their part double rooms would do. Morley had a further second's freedom for thought. It did not occur to him that these girls were part of a joke that had in fact been played once or twice before. Beauty seldom suggests fun. His mind instead remembered that the town was full, that these girls were probably tramping from door to door hoping for rooms in a private house, that this was difficult since they were so large a party, that it was pitiable that people should be in such a predicament, that it was the more so since they were beautiful people, that he had a large house, that it was largely empty, and . . . why not?

He bowed and opened the door wider for the ladies to pass:

"Certainly, Madame," he said, wondering what the plural could be, " . . . I should be delighted to accommodate you."

They scarcely bothered to thank him, but moved brusquely into what was patently the vestibule of a hotel. In fact, that eccentric decoration hardly mattered. As foreign visitors they would never have questioned an ordinary homely hall: it would simply have looked part of the mad English scene.

"La fiche?" asked Miss Clermont-Ferrand.

"Oh, oui," Morley smiled, having no idea what this could mean. And added, as a pleasantry: "Sanfaryan."

"Vraiement?" smiled back Miss Clermont-Ferrand, impressed by such liberty.

But Morley then thought: By Jiminy I'll have to get moving. And raised his hand to command attention, and asked them kindly to wait a moment, and scuttled upstairs. He ran—striding now no longer—to the telephone by his bed and breathlessly called the restaurant to order not one but seven dinners. In half an hour. And then raced round the bedrooms. Fortunately these were kept made up: two double rooms, a good single room and a single dressing-room. One of these had already been slept in by guests on the previous weekend. He pulled the sheets back, smoothed out a crease or two, decided to risk it. But airing? Six hot-water bottles? Impossible. He ran round lighting with little pops gas-fire after gas-fire. Then he thought: Bathrooms! And banged open the door of the second bathroom, removing his rowing machine, a Hoover, some dirty linen and his golf clubs: then rushed to his own to wipe off the comfortable soap-ring left only half an hour before.

In that fine old actor's frame there coursed a sort of boyish exaltation. For nearly nothing would he have disturbed the repose of his calm dinner alone: but for such a six . . . well, it hardly happened every night. He had no designs. He was simply exhilarated, flowing with the good red blush of boyishness. He felt chivalrous, too. No snake of desire but simply the flushes of virtue filled him.

He descended to take the ladies up to their rooms.

The oysters were laid out on seven plates, the ladies had been allocated their seats round the large table in the dining-room, and he himself, having seen that seven portions of pigeon pie were keeping hot in the kitchen, was at last on the point of sitting himself down—when, in the general delight at the sight of oysters, Miss Great-Belt spoke out:

"Oysters! This is very good!" she said, wondering at the same time what the charges of so considerable a hotel might be. "But it was good luck indeed those gentlemen recommended us such a hotel!"

Morley's hand was actually on his chair to pull it back. Instead, he pulled back his hand.

"Recommended? Hotel?"

A sudden spasm gripped him where a moment before the gastric juices had begun to play.

"Surely yes," Miss Great-Belt smiled. "Some gentlemen in the railway bar. They said this is the best hotel we can have." Then she added with a knowing smile, a condescension to the servant standing above her, "But they will come quick enough for their percentage, no?"

"No?" Morley stuttered. "Oh, yes, yes."

The old joke! This time it had come off? His chivalry blew away like old hot air. He saw suddenly that he was in a very difficult position—he was a fraud. These ladies were deceived. They might be very angry. And more. He was a bachelor. Alone in his house, he had induced them to come inside. What would the world make of *that?* What would the neighbours, what would the Town Council, what would even the Court of Law think? Was it legal? Were there seduction laws? Certainly there were Boarding House Licences.

These and more terrors mounted in his mind. With regret he let his hand fall absolutely from the chair, then sculpted it round towards his plate of oysters, already beginning to act the part of a real hotel employee. He muttered that he did not know why an extra place had been laid and began to withdraw the oysters to take and to eat them in the sanctity of the kitchen, in what now must be his right and proper place. For he had decided to play the rôle out. For the moment it was the only thing to do. At all costs avert suspicion, a scene, the full fury of these now formidable girls.

His hand was about to grasp the plate—but Miss Civitavecchia's, lizard-like, was quicker:

"Piacere—do not trouble. It is plain," she said, smiling round at the others, "that we can eat some more?"

"Please place this on the bill," she added.

Morley tried to smile and withdrew, oysterless, to the empty kitchen. Some minutes later he took care to bring only six soup-platesful of mulligatawny into the dining-room.

The dining-table had been laid with only one pepper-pot, one salt-cellar. The ladies required more. Morley, his soup and now his lonely pigeon growing cold, had to search for, fill, and serve others. Vinegar was required. And oil. And in the matter of drinks there was white wine, red wine, beer and water to be found for different tastes. Morley was run off his feet. His hurriedly gulped pigeon flew instantly back at him. And on top of all this he found it necessary, on being questioned, to invent excuses for the quietness of the "hotel" and for the non-appearance of other servants.

Only later, when at last he had seen the last of the ladies mount the stairs—tired from their travels, they all went up early—only later when the front door was locked and with waiter-tired feet he lay in bed, did he allow himself at last a great retrogressive chuckle.

He saw suddenly how he lay there on his back like a dear old daddy-keeper, with his six young charges all tucked safely up sleeping blissfully on their six pillows. Six sudden beautiful girls at first look all of a piece. Only after a while, when the first endazzlement is over, can one distinguish between them. Now still to Morley they were banded indistinguishable, six little beauties all in a row, as if that beauty itself served the uniform purpose of a school hat and a gym frock.

And so there he lay, hoary old guardian of his exquisite crocodile, and chuckled, and gradually—not knowing what might happen in the morning, too tired now to care—fell asleep.

In the morning, reason asserted itself. Such a fantastic situation could not be allowed to continue. He considered for a moment applying for a boarding-house licence, hiring servants: but this was plainly too much trouble. And plainly it extended the falsity of the situation.

His daily housekeeper supplied the answer. He rose early to intercept her. He explained that he had given sanctuary the night before to six roofless ladies. The housekeeper froze. Morley pretended not to notice and asked her to prepare six breakfasts. The housekeeper pressed her lips together. Morley acted a laugh.

"An—er—equivocal position for an old bachelor, eh, Mrs Laidlaw?" his lips laughed. "But safety in numbers, Mrs L., safety in numbers."

This simple remark had a far greater effect than Morley could have hoped for. The word "equivocal" put Mrs Laidlaw momentarily off her balance, it rescued Morley again into the status of the Master. But then that "safety in numbers" in its turn saved her own comfort of mind, it sank her happily to earth, it was comfortable and what it said was what other people said all the world over. She served the breakfasts, hypnotized by the saying, muttering it over and over to herself. Only some hours later, when she had digested the good looks and the alien chic of the ladies' clothes, whorish to her woollen eyes, did she give notice.

But long before that Morley had waylaid Miss Amsterdam, who was first down. Miss Amsterdam was a dark-haired Hollander, possibly a descendant of the Spanish occupation. Most of her was covered with long dark hairs—but her face shone out from among the cropping like a lovely pale brown moon. She came hurrying down the stairs, and was already across the hall, between the ever-open cocktail-bar and the ever-empty lounge, almost to the door, handbag swinging like a third buttock, before Morley could stop her. But he came striding on with great actor's strides, calling: "Excuse me! Miss . . . Miss . . . ?"

"Call me Amsterdam."

"Oh? . . . Well, by all means . . . "

Leading her aside into the lupined lounge, he made an unclean breast of it all. The word "roofless" that he had by chance brought up to thaw Mrs Laidlaw provided his key to a happy simulation of the truth. It conjured the pitiful idea of "roofless" ladies, it implied an open door and an open heart to all the travel-stained abroad in the night in this his native country. He explained the hotel furnishings as mementoes of his own travels, his tours—off-handedly stressing as a condiment of glamour, his place in the theatre—and finally begged Miss Amsterdam to excuse this whole misunderstanding that might so easily be taken as an impertinence on his, a bachelor's part. Would she convey this to the other ladies, would they understand?

Miss Amsterdam's brown round lovely face went this way and that, it made shapes of surprise and petulance and tenderness and excitement—then finally all broke up into a wild pudding of laughter. Brown pudge of cheeks crinkling, eyes gone, brows ridged, red mouth neighing never-seen underteeth—no more now than a big brown baby howling agonies of wind.

Slapping one hand across that mouth, and the other over her stomach, she tripped her lovely legs upstairs. And Fred Morley was left waiting—for was this laughter or hysteria?—on his uneasy tenterhooks.

From upstairs silence.

A long silence. A silence in a lonely downstairs when the upstairs is full but behind closed doors. Creaks of silence, rafters loaded with words.

But—ten minutes later all was over. On the landing a door burst open and laughter, like water from a thirsty tap, laved out and down the stairs. Morley heaved a long and blessed relief.

With the laughter came the ladies—all six, all smiles. They milled in and stood in a semicircle round old Fred Morley, who rose and gravely bowed. Miss Amsterdam broke instantly.

"Mr Morley—I have told all the girls all you have told me and all of us girls have agreed together you are a kind and a big sweet."

"We thank you," dimpled Miss Rotterdam, a round blonde cheese of a girl.

"Comme c'est infiniment drôle . . . " giggled Clermont-Ferrand, who, in trousers and a checked shirt, but with a wicked fringe and a golden anklet, appeared to be a woman on two levels or layers—a check-shirt cowgirl of St Germain enclosing a Nana of more liberal boulevards.

"Such a dinner!" sighed with wondering shakes of her head the practical Miss Nuremburg. This one, who held the annual title, comic to the English but a beautiful reality to the German, of Miss Sauerkraut, had in her pallid tall glory exactly the texture of that well-prepared vegetable. A dab of rotkohl would not have harmed her cheeks.

Miss Civitavecchia took a deep breath and began, palms outstretched: "Ma—ma Mi—a!" And went on, for a long time, expending in a tumult of Italian the full breath of her bosom. On the solid foundations of a Roman body she carried the small head of a snake: it was as if some Laocoon had been fused with the bust—the bust is meant—of a great—and great is intended—Roman Empress.

So Fred Morley stood overwhelmed by this crescent before him of beauty, smiles and gratitude. He felt, and for the moment was, loved. A pleasant sensation. But, as an Englishman, he was embarrassed . . . and through the glow of pleasure his instinct was to escape by offering them all a drink. This last was on his lips—when Miss Great-Belt at last spoke up.

Miss Great-Belt was plainly the most beautiful of all. Her present title embraced that royal reach of sea separating the Danish islands of Fünen and Zealand, and no dimension of her own. She was a dark red-head. Her skin white over lilac. Her eyes deep dark blue. Her whole face the face of a cat—round high cheekbones, nearly no nose, many small teeth curving in a long smile like the dream of a bite: yet all squared into the face of a girl. How could she have become so? Copenhagen is a great seaport through which have passed many strange fathers. Whatever . . . there she was, a brilliant cat-faced red-head, who might bite, who might smile, and who now was the only one to say a disaffected word:

"How much do we owe?" she said.

Practical? Or battle-cry? Fred Morley's interest quickened. Confused by the compliments of the others, which made those ladies into no more than lovely willing sisters, his well-tried nose sniffed Woman. For the first time one among those beauties stood out separate.

"I had hoped," he instantly said, "that in the circumstances you would accept my hospitality?"

Miss Great-Belt looked him calmly in the eye.

"Thank you," she said, serene and ominously composed, "but that is impossible. Would you please be so kind as to tell us the charge?"

Of course, all the others had now to agree with her. All their various voices rose to insist. They chattered to each other and at Morley and he could not say a word. But he kept his eye on Miss Great-Belt. She had taken out her powder-puff and with aggravated unconcern dabbed her nose: he noticed with rising spirits that she used no mirror. It was a gesture. It meant war.

Finally it was settled that the ladies paid Morley a reasonable sum per day. Later he telephoned the Town Hall to ask whether he might take in paying-guests. The clerks, for the town was overcrowded, were delighted. He arranged for service and food—after all, he said to himself, it would only be for two or three days. Then, much later, when all this was fixed, asked Miss Great-Belt personally whether he might escort her round the town.

"No," was the answer. With a straight look between the eyes.

All that was on the Thursday. The Contest was scheduled for the Saturday. For three in the afternoon at the Pier Aquadrome.

Thus, for these girls, there was much to be done. Much final furbishing. Polishing, paring, depilating and all the other many measures of massage and exercise necessary to bring tissues of flesh and hair—Fred Morley was heard with a weary chuckle later to say—to scratch. For in the course of these operations old Morley's eyes were opened.

Overnight the calm of his bachelor ménage was transformed. Those girls worked themselves hard. The rooms, the corridors, the bathrooms drifted in a dry flood of cosmetic cartons: balls of cotton-wool and paper tissues mated with blonde, brunette and auburn curlings in every corner: powder flew everywhere, made solid marble shafts of the sunbeams: oil and cream made each empty surface—every table, every shelf—a viscous adventure.

Masseuses and masseurs—brisk women and strange men—came and went: Morley, to lighten the load on his new temporary staff, and because he spent much time nervously wandering and waiting downstairs, answered the door to a ceaseless stream of such visitors and the slick peremptory drivers of delivery vans. He tried as far as possible to avoid going upstairs. Things upstairs were too strange. He had found Miss Clermont-Ferrand sitting with her head in her beautiful hands and each elbow cupped in the half of a lemon. Across the landing there had whisked a blue kimono topped by a face plastered livid dry pink, with hollows it seemed where the eyes might be and naked lips huge now as a clown's, a face terribly faceless—too late he had seen that this might be Miss Great-Belt. Then Miss Rotterdam, in a bathing-dress, had come bumping across the landing on her bottom, and vanished into the bathroom: no hands nor legs, she had explained *en route*—a question of stomach muscles. Miss Sauerkraut liked to lie on the balcony on half a ping-pong table, head-downwards. Miss Civitavecchia he had found carefully combing the long black beards that hung from her armpits, a peninsular speciality: unlike Miss Amsterdam, who took no such Latin pride in the strong growth of dark hair that covered most of her—it seemed that whenever he asked for her the answer came: "Upstairs shaving."

So Morley remained downstairs.

He sat there with a whisky and soda, half impatient, half-amused, but more simply apprehensive of what else might come. He sat listening, cocking his head anxiously at the bumps and scufflings that came from above, and answering the doorbell.

But above all the question of Miss Great-Belt lightly, but persistently, tormented him. He was quite conscious of his middle years, and of her youth—yet after all was he not Frederick Morley, the idol of a thousand hearts? He felt affronted: a smile perhaps, a gracious gesture would have been enough to appease him. But this—what was it called—*snootiness!* Beyond the Fred Morley in him, the male rose in combat. Something must be done.

Yet was this attitude of hers exactly *snooty*? He wondered whether it might run deeper. It lacked the proper coquetry. It was the result, perhaps, more of a solid and almost matronly composure unusual in a so strikingly beautiful young girl. She had an air of remarkable self-containedness. When she walked, it was always with a sense of destination: she knew where she was going. When she carried parcels, one felt those parcels would never be undone in a flurry but would each await its proper time. There was a feeling of unhurried *process* about her. Though she bore the fiercely beautiful face of a cat, she was phlegmatic—but then perhaps a cat is, despite some appearances, the most phlegmatic of animals?

Later that evening—it had been a beautiful, if indeed a long day—he watched her leave the house arm-in-arm with Miss Sauerkraut. Their summer dresses clung coolly in the evening air to what must have been naked bodies, and the tall swanlike Sauerkraut served only to emphasize Miss Great-Belt's warm pliabilities. The two paused outside the door, then turned one way down the westering front. Two youths in padded flannels detached themselves from the group that lounged now always discreetly over the road from his front door, and at a suitable distance followed, eyes intent, mouths whetting for the whistles that would come.

The cavalier rose in Morley; but he quieted it. Then, pair by pair, he watched the others go. Each was followed by two, sometimes three, of the watching gentlemen. And then he was left alone in the house. At last— peace. He breathed a great sigh of peace. But to himself, and for himself. It was a false sigh. He knew that in a very few minutes the house would feel too empty. And so it did. He wandered for some time from room to room fingering things, sitting for a while here and then there. But he kept thinking of all those who had left, so young and expectant, to enjoy the evening—and he began to feel his years. That would never do. His bachelordom had taught him all about self-commiseration—and it was his custom to guard against it. He selected a hat, a curl-brimmed panama, pale but not too pale for evening wear, and left for the Club. The stolid usuality, the pot-belly of male companionship was what he needed.

The Yacht Club was not much frequented by yachtsmen. A few faded photographs of old racing-cutters spinnakered across the cream-painted, nautically planked walls. Well-polished brass shone here and there, and to seaward one wall of the lounge was given to good white-framed observatory glass. However, it was now a place mostly of comfortable horsehair where members, the elect of the town, might come and drink.

The warm fruity smell of gentlemen at ease greeted Fred Morley as he entered the lounge: tobacco smoke, fumes of whisky and port, horsehair and something else—starch, red flesh, woollen underpants?—ballooned out its bouquet of security across the Turkey carpet. Here at last was escape from all feminine essences! He rang the bell for a drink and, giving a wink or a nod to various members couched in the horsehair, joined a group at the further end.

"Why if it isn't Fred!"

"Come in, Fred—we was just about to 'ave a round of Kiss-in-the-Ring."

For it had already got about that Fred Morley had some young ladies staying in his house. Young ladies of the theatrical profession, it was presumed.

Those who now addressed Fred were a mixed bag of the livelier, wealthier citizens of the town—a couple of aldermen, a big butcher, a retired military man well-invested in beach and fairground concessions, the local brewer's brother-in-law. They were an affable, energetic, powerful lot. As far as they were allowed, they ran the town—not too unfairly. Mixed of the professional and tradesmen's classes, they forgot such differences in a close-masonry of well-to-do malehood; they even included some of the now not so well-to-do, on grounds that they had once been so—those only were excluded who had not yet come solidly up in the world. They were a cut above those other bantering gentlemen who in the first place had sent his six guests to Morley—yet they too always affected a jovial banter among themselves.

For some time Fred Morley sipped his whisky and warmed his marrow at the hands of these gentlemen. Then a Mr Everett Evans came in. Everett Evans, since he was an alderman, a prosperous draper and a local bright spark, had been appointed chairman of the judicial committee that was to sit upon the Beauty Queens. Conversation had already turned upon this coming event. Morley had kept his mouth immaculately shut. But now Evans himself had come in.

"Hallo, hallo—look who comes here!" called this group of men.

"What you having, Everett?" they then said.

"Large bicarbonate and soda, thank you," answered Mr Evans.

"For Evans' sake!"

"That's just what. For the sake of poor Evans' poor belly, that's what." He paused and looked mystified. Then: "Know what I've been drinking last twenty-four hours?"

They had fallen into amused, expectant silence. Evans' chin went out, he looked at each of them accusingly, then let his eyes bulge as he blurted:

"Barium."

"Barium?"

"No lie. Barium. Little white glassfuls of bloody barium."

"What the hell . . . ?"

"First they strip you. Then they put you in a kind of a smock affair, apron you might call it—with bloody lacing up the back. They let you keep your socks on—but them laces! Bows all down the back, bows all over your arse come to that." He paused for breath, the others were looking startled.

And then he went on: "That's the start of it. So you're left there all buttons and bows reading your old copy of *Punch.* Then they say come in, and in you go in a big dark black room and then you get your barium. Whole glassful. First thing down your gullet for twelve hours. Metal, it is. Tastes like ice-cream carton."

Another breath:

"Then they do you."

"Do you?" The gentlemen leaned forward, uneasy. "*Do* you?"

"Take your photo. The old X-ray."

Now breaths of relief, tittering. But Evans raised his hand.

"No laughing matter, I tell you. Ulcers, that's what I've got. Stomach ulcers. You know when I've been feeling bad these last months—since Christmas like? The old sawbones says he's worried I might have something proper dicky down below and sends me along to this hospital for the photo. Well, they found 'em all right. Ulcers. No lie.

"And what's more I got more photos to be took—taken like. And 'ow the 'ell I'm going to look all these bathing bellies in the face I don't know."

Everett Evans looked down sadly into his glass of soda. Little bubbles raced up at him, burst at him.

"Day after tomorrow it is. I can't do it. Someone'll 'ave to stand in for me."

He looked up suddenly and glared round the company.

"Well?" he said vicious, "any offers?"

All those men now looked at each other nervously. They simpered. Not one but secretly would have loved being up lording it over so many Beauties. But there had been too many jokes about the "Bellies" already, each man saw himself up there on the platform blushing and being laughed at. So now all began rapidly to mumble excuses—jolly excuses, for seriousness would be suspect. "The old woman'd never forgive me." "What—me with a grown-up daughter?" "Think of my poor old heart."

Except for Morley. Through Morley's mind there flashed a sudden sunlight. Here it was—on a platter! Here was the prize for Miss Great-Belt! And he—with a courteous smile—presenting it! She'd eat out of his hand! He gave a great cough.

They all looked at him. He said nothing, coughed again, looked particularly at no one and nothing.

It worked.

"The very man! Why did no one think?"

"Love's young dream! Be like falling off a log, eh, Fred? Busman's holiday."

Everett frowned at him, the only one severe: "Well, Fred—how about it? I can fix it—"

"Mm," Fred said, looking out through the big marine windows. The sea was dotted here and there with little boats. Their sails took the last evening sun. He did not see them. "I don't know that I'm doing anything that afternoon, nothing special . . . "

"I'll fix it then, Fred." Everett pressed his lips, fixing, together.

"We—ell—," mused Fred.

"*But,*" said the one man there who knew, "is this right? With some of them staying there in his house?"

"What!" This was news. They all dug him in the ribs—with their eyes, their great laughing teeth. "Old rascal!" "There's a dark horse!"

"Yes," Fred sighed, more than ever casual, "I've got six of them."

"Safety in numbers then," hissed Everett Evans, "that fixes it."

"*But*," said that one man again.

"Now look 'ere," Evans exploded, "Fred's had more skirt in 'is life than you've 'ad 'ot dinners. Think six little bellies mean a thing to Fred? You're off your rocker! I tell you I can fix this easy."

In any case those other men, accustomed to the pulling of wires, were hardly worried by prospects of collusion. This now suited them. It made things easy. Fred was the man. They all agreed.

"Well, Fred, shall I fix it?" said Everett.

Morley made one final hesitation, for form's sake. He pursed his lips, ruminated, then suddenly sharply nodded. "All right then. I'll do it."

"Good boy," rose ulcerous Evans. "Lead me to the blower. This needs fixing right now."

And so it was fixed.

It was a different Fred Morley who sat downstairs the next morning in deference to the upstairs pandemonium. From bar to lounge to front door he walked—but this time with a glint in his eye, a chuckling of hands together, sometimes the tum-tumty-tum of a little song. She may touch her toes and waggle herself and knead herself like dough, he thought—ha, *knead* herself, who'll she be needing next, eh? He blew a kiss upstairs to the invisibly exercising Great-Belt. Old Fred Morley and none other! Tum-ti-tumty-tum. And outside it was a beautiful morning, the sun shone. Old Fred Morley? Old me Aunt Fanny! Forty-eight if a day. Middle-age. And no spread.

Nor was it quite the same upstairs that morning as the day before. Those girls had had their bikinis delivered: some were too big, some too small. Tall pale Sauerkraut became too huge a goddess in hers too big: Miss Amsterdam, her brown skin cooing against the new white slips ordained by the Council but also too small, went into a corner and attached with the vigour of a true Hollander various appealing frills of her own—and of course there was a row about that. And of course the girls had by now survived their first affability—they were getting each other's measure. Some had seen others at something, others had heard some say this or that. Sides were taken, embattlements formed. But between squalls and bickering a sense of dignity prevailed. No one actually touched anyone else.

Meanwhile out on the front, on the sea—all was plain sailing. It was lovely weather and the sea lay smoothly sparkling blue. White paint of pier and railing stood freshly deadly clean against all that blue and the colours of people, boats, cars, kites—and Fred Morley had an idea. He sent, by the new and overpaid and delighted maid, messages up to the ladies Rotterdam and Clermont-Ferrand. Would they do him the honour of a stroll and an apéritif before luncheon?

All he thought was: "They're nice girls. I'd like a stroll. I've better plans for the Danish lass, let her bide (and it'll perhaps do her good)."

Rotterdam and Clermont-Ferrand—the one butterflying her arms to raise further her already sturdy breasts, the other sitting in front of a mirror practising "facial yoga"—that is making grotesque narcissist kisses at herself to exercise the mouth, then pecking her head forward twenty times a minute like a little hen on her bright young egg—read their messages with approval and half an hour later those two were one on each of Fred Morley's arms strolling the Front. Morley in a faultlessly raffish suit of biscuit tussore, with a high stiff collar, a pin in his tie and a curl to his hat: Miss Rotterdam blonde in flowered silk that wisped round her so closely in the breeze that those following could see not only the lovely knobbles of her vertebrae but the knobbles of her suspender-belt too: Miss Clermont-Ferrand in high white shoes and a strange white belt almost taller than its breadth round her no-waist, black hair flowing, black silk buttocks a-swing, preposterously and magnificently French.

Rotterdam in her friendly Dutch way, which concealed heaven knew what guile, had taken Morley's arm to draw his attention to a group of young men playing cricket on the sands below. "You English," she had laughed, pressing her round lips back on to her teeth, making enormous dimples, and giving Morley's arm a niecely squeeze. All of which Clermont-Ferrand immediately, and fiercely, noticed—so that not to be outdone she had taken the other arm, pulling Fred's interest towards a sombre green-painted glass wind shelter: "Why do you have autobus shelters," she asked, in innocence of the normal weather prevailing on such a parade, "when you have no autobuses?" And panted up a charming little laugh to him that also implied "Oh, you dear mad Englishman." But at the same time panted her mouth itself, open and eager, red-lipped and wetly pink inside, teeth laughing wide and tongue-tip pointing right out at him very close to his startled eyes.

So Fred had them both hugged on his arms. He puffed his chest with a deep breath of the good clear sea-air of morning and felt, there in the sunlight with sea to the left and bright traffic to the right, with the Cliff Memorial Gardens pine-green ahead and the white pier-dome flashing all holiday joy, good to be alive.

It was in such style that he was observed, a little further on, by those same local gentlemen who had first sent him the girls. These locals moved in a group: just then they had moved that group, bellies eased and jolly with good morning beer, from the brass-flashing doors of a near-by saloon to take a breather of sea-air before the next. But when they saw Fred they gaped, their spirits gravened and sank. For they were in that least enviable of situations—that of the practical joker who slips on his own banana-skin, that of him who is laughed at last. Yes, it had gone wrong all right. There was Fred sitting pretty, with *two,* with a blondie and a blackie, one of each kind, one to suit whatever his fancy was, turn and turn about—and they had put this in his way! They had actually been such damned idiots as to send him that choice handful he had there! Not thinking, not dreaming to keep the handful for themselves, and send it somewhere quiet round the corner where they might call later to pass the time of day. . . . Oh well, they supposed it was the booze again, that's what it was. Can't have everything. But—that it should be Fred! Fred whom always secretly they had envied,

Fred who'd had it on a platter all his life, bags of it, oodles of it there on his stage-doorstep whichever way he might turn . . . while *they*. . . .

Now to Fred passing with a beauty on each arm they raised their hats and gave grim fixed smiles, new white teeth and old yellow ones flashing in the sun: to which Fred Morley, deeply satisfied, bowed and passed on his triumphant way.

Yet those gentlemen would not have been so discomforted had they seen him an hour hence. For matters did not continue so well. In the first place, those girls were young and active, they were out to enjoy themselves and not content at all simply to take the morning air. Also, as foreigners, they were inquisitive, they wanted to taste the oddities of this strange new country. So that soon Clermont-Ferrand had dragged them to a fish-and-chip booth that lay just below down some steps: and she walked now with newspaper in one hand and a chip in the other, fish-oil lustrous all over her lipstick and powdered chin. And Rotterdam had asked for a small propeller on a coloured stick, which she waved fluttering high, while firmly her other fist clasped a long thick truncheon of pink peppermint rock. They giggled bending, pointing, nudging, giving high shrieks of awe and shock at so many strange things to see. With rock and fish-and-chips they had settled their feminine differences, now they were all for fun. And having discovered the livelier scenes of stalls and crowds beneath the arches of the Parade they dragged Morley from sweet-shop to pin-table, from whelk to winkle stand, from jellied-eel to ice-cream barrow. They took him on the Dodgem cars and they had him photographed with them in sailor hats standing in front of a huge cardboard fishing-smack. (The photographer, giving his rump a resounding whack, had cried: "Another good smack gone to the bottom!") Loudly as Morley protested, the louder they laughed and the further they dragged him. They thought these were no more than the coy protestations of an elderly man enjoying himself.

Fred Morley had planned an apértif on the terrace of the best hotel in the town, a terrace just overlooking the street and readily seen from there: he would have sat with his two beautiful guests and from that eminence with a drink in hand and a naughty glint in his eye enjoyed the envy of passers-by for the half-hour until luncheon. And then luncheon. Cold salmon, a bottle of the best, the white clean cloth, the silver and the laughter of these two pairs of lovely red lips. This had all gone wrong. Those girls had no time for luncheon. He was tired, jolted, hungry, thirsty. And he did not wish to be seen even up on the Marine Parade itself with two such high-spirited girls—who now wore each a hat with a large motto printed on it. Yet of course, when they had had enough of the beach, up they had to go.

And there, to cap everything, he saw approaching him Miss Great-Belt. Miss Great-Belt with her fine red hair and in an orange dress holding in one hand a towering stick of electric pink candy-floss, a wild mane of strident sugar which every so often she kissed with her bright carmine lips. In the other hand—and still she managed all this with no lessening of self-composure—she held the arm of a sleek young giant in a shirt of flowered American silk.

He nearly hated her. And it was then, at a moment of shame and dislike, that she made towards him her first affable gesture. She waved her great pink floss-stick with the benign gesture of passing royalty—then gave him a huge, long, tranquil wink! And passed on.

When at last he was safely home, and when thus in comfort and at ease his temper had subsided—he still remembered that wink, reviewed it in a more benevolent light, and began to build up implications for it. Hope flowered. Wish welcomed fulfillment. It was plain her mood had turned, she had completed her feminine duties—the period of cat-and-mouse play laid down in the rules—and now she was blossomed and waiting. It only remained for him to pluck her.

So that an hour later, when he met her in the hall, he mentioned that he had a box at the Hippodrome that night. And she charmingly agreed to be his guest. At the theatre? At seven-thirty? Most kind. And supper afterwards. Delightful.

But at seven-thirty she was not at the theatre, nor at eight-thirty. He telephoned home. No, she was not in. She had gone out—to what? *What?* To a *dance?*

He slammed down the receiver and left, furious.

When she came in that night he was waiting for her. She came in early—for the next day was the day of the Contest, and she had to enjoy a long night's sleep—she came in a little breathless, her lovely red hair ablaze in the light, now with no pink candyfloss but in an evening dress the colour of the night sky. For a second when she saw him she hesitated: but instantly then gathered herself and came flouncing, almost on those tall legs bouncing, along the hall, unperturbed as usual, a glint of disdain in her navy eyes, but her lips pouted to smile. And as she came up to him she did smile.

"Good evening."

Now it was he who played with composure.

"Good evening," he said coldly. "I missed you at the theatre."

"The theatre? Of course—I'm so sorry. But you know—I really felt I could not come. To sit about all evening in a stuffy box! I needed exercise, you know. The great day tomorrow!"

"Indeed? And it was nothing that I waited a full hour for you?"

"I've said I am sorry."

"And that is all?"

She said nothing. But looked at him curiously.

Then she asked: "You really expected me?"

He looked surprised. "Naturally."

"Well *really*. You spend the morning with not one but *two* of these . . . these *women* upstairs. And then you expect to spend the evening with *me?* What do you think I am? What next? Shall I tell you what *you* are—you're an old satyr, that is what. A wolf! With pointed ears! With *hoofs!*"

She had raised her voice—he was so surprised he put up a hand to feel his ears—and then, having reached her climax with the word "hoofs," which she blew at him with a mouth shaped for whoofing whole houses down, she was gone.

He stood there a moment amazed. Then his lips snapped shut. "The Great Day tomorrow?" he said to himself. "So be it."

The Great Day dawned differently to those preceding. In the early hours, as from nowhere, big clouds blacker than the night had loomed up, flashed into fire, burst into water. Straight down, as if some celestial bucket had slopped over, the rains had fallen. Summer hails had swept the front. The temperature had fallen a swift ten degrees: then more. A wind had sprung up, gathering into a light steady gale. Until when dawn finally broke the Marine Parade lay drenched and grey, chilled and windy and drizzled, deserted and to remain so throughout a long wet cold day.

Morley had awoken in the night to hear the hailstones drumming and booming on the glass verandah roof below his window: and when at nine o'clock he went downstairs not at all well-slept, the house was grey and dead, no shafts of summer light livened the rooms, the blue lupins sat dusty like drab flowers in the corner of a dull boarding-house. Which this is, he savagely thought.

Yet it was hardly dull—for throughout the morning the sounds upstairs rose to a climax. Most of the girls were now not speaking to each other. But those who did yelled at the tops of their voices. Their frenzy in these last hours of preparation rose to new and furious levels. By twelve o'clock Morley could bear it no longer, he took his mackintosh off the peg and went out.

The air on the Parade was pleasanter than he had supposed. Forlorn, perhaps, the look of things—but there was a stimulating clarity abroad, a briskness of new air blown in from the sea. He looked across at the scudding waves, took deep breaths, and in between puddles stepped out briskly. Rain-soaked boats lay about the deserted beach like wrecks, a solitary figure in a mackintosh came swept by the wind down one street and disappeared up another.

This was exactly what Morley needed. He needed a change, he needed a breath of air. He was no longer angry with that Miss Great-Belt—he had lived too long to stay too deeply perturbed by such events—but only irritated: and that irritation included Miss Rotterdam and Miss Clermont-Ferrand as well, in fact the whole lot of them. He wanted his peace back. And now as he stepped out against the rain he reflected with pleasure that in a few hours it would in fact be all over. The Contest would be done and won. Not won by Miss Great-Belt, though—and a sense of justice rather than rancour filled him as he made this reservation. Yet after the Contest would they really leave? Probably—they were mostly subsidized. And certainly—if the weather held. "Blow, blow, thou winter wind—" he hummed more cheerfully to himself as he paced along.

He went to the Club and refreshed himself. Everett Evans wished him a gloomy "best of luck" for the afternoon—but left before the eating. Morley then had a good luncheon in the company of his fellows.

The Contest had been scheduled to take place in the open-air salt-water pool—the Pier Aquadrome, a place of civic pride. Now it had to be removed inside, into the Aquadrome's Winter Garden. This was a large white concrete modern building set like a plate-glassy liner, all decks and terraces, astern the paddle-boat old Pier.

By half-past two, in spite of the weather, quite a queue had assembled. Most of those that formed it, men and women alike, wore pixie-hoods. Tall-pointed heads leaned this way and that, chattering like a troop of fairies drenched with harebell dew—the women like wet narcissus petals in their grey-white plastics, the men in duffle-hoods like hairy great gnomes. All these were admitted slowly into a bare concrete hall brilliantly shadowed by mauve strip-lighting.

This ominous form of illumination has been called "daylight" lighting. Yes—but it is the light of the worst day of the worst month of the year, the lilac light of a raw February afternoon. Faces everywhere lost their colour, lips turned purple-black and skins took on the pallor of long illness. Nevertheless, though soaked and drained of colour, the audience managed a certain cheerfulness: it was the cheerfulness particular to a wet seaside afternoon, when spirits soaked by the rain dribbling down windows of boarding-houses and hotels eventually make a burst for freedom—to batter along against rain and sea-wind, and thence to commingle at some echoing hall of entertainment with a cluttering of umbrellas, a thumping of boots, a wet rubber smell, a draughty gusto of raised voices.

So that now, sodden but heady with relief to be taken out of themselves on this stolen day of their holiday, the pixie audience gradually massed into seats set in amphitheatrical style round a semi-circular raised platform. On this the Beauties were to parade. And on its straight side there were ranged the judges' chairs, and their long table draped with Union Jacks.

A roar of laughter went up as Fred Morley and his four fellow-adjudicators entered. They were a great joke. Five portly gentlemen, wrested from their everyday dignities and their all-embracing wives, put to the task of examining pretty girls with hardly anything on! . . . Watch that professional eye glaze over. Watch blood pressures rise and pulses quicken! Five fat ruddy genial lambs up there on their altar . . . it was slaughter, it was murder, it was *killing!* "Hooooo," roared the crowd.

Dressed in their best suits, the judges simpered and blushed, dug each other in their ribs and whispered wicked chuckles in each other's ears as they settled down. One made an over-courtly gesture ushering his neighbour to his chair; another made for a brief two steps the motion so beloved of hefty hearties in their cups, he put one hand on a hip and lumbered along mincing like what he thought was a lady. Only old Fred, who was accustomed to an audience, retained his composure. He contented himself with a short, but most telling, twirl of his silken moustache-end.

Then the uniformed Silver Band at the other end of the hall struck up—what but *A Pretty Girl is like a Melody?*—and a door opened at one side and up a long inclined gang-plank came the girls.

They came first jostling, then as they reached the raised parade spaced themselves out—a plump, slender, tall, short, round forty of them. In slow measure, with short proud steps, pausing almost at each step, hesitating just as heel touched passing heel, like primping prancing two-legged ponies they passed round the ring.

All wore the same small costume. That had been one of the rules. It had been adopted because it was time the proposer had one of his ideas accepted, so that he might remain quiet in other matters. The Contest Organization bore the cost, which in terms of the area of material needed had been slight. White rayon had been chosen—a remnant from Everett Evans's Drapery Store. Now each girl wore at her loins a close-fitting triangle, and at her breasts two discreetly billowing moons. No more. And, for sure, no less.

Each carried in her hand a card with a number. Only their shoes were their own, and these were in every case the highest they had—from great clobbering wedges to elegancies of the white summer, from shoes tasselled and curiously strapped to patent black evening shoes that quarrelled painfully with the naked flesh pressed into them. One girl, hard put, had come in a pair of tennis plimsols: she went round balancing avidly on her toes, a Shetland among the Shires.

The five judges leaned forward or sat back, pretending thus either keen judicial interest or recessive judicial wisdom. At first they were simply bewildered by so much sudden beauty. They sat in a fog of arms, legs, eyes, teeth, hair and all else. From bubble-bath and mud-tub, from pummelling-board and rubber roller came those fleshlings shining and smiling. Some had enclosed their legs in whole sheets of hot wax, from which they came hairless as ivory; others had forgone the luxuriance of mascara and instead brushed their eye-lashes with black boot polish to get a stronger set, a more lustrous shine. All smiled largely—though some by lowering their eyes achieved a sort of modesty at the same time, a redoubtable feat. All seemed not only to be following in each other's footsteps but in their own as well—this because their high heels forced their knees forward, so that they hung back on themselves, as if searching out the ground before the main upperwork should follow: bended knees, mad knees stealing on tiptoe to unheard-of larders.

Miss Great-Belt hung just behind such knees when she first passed the judge's stand. Then she saw Frederick Morley—and nearly fell on them. For a second she lost her composure. Her face had been stretched into a design of radiant happy loveliness—eyes stretched wide yet with slightly lowered lids, lips stretched ovalling round their last liquid teeth. Now as she saw Morley there, Morley whom she had never expected, Morley whom she had told off only the night before, that expression did not leave her face—but in every feature it contracted, it grew smaller for a moment into an exactly reduced replica of itself. Heavens, her first thought was, what a stupid girl I am! Never to have known! (It never occurred to her how she could ever have known, she instantly blamed herself.) . . . But what a monster he is not to have told me! Then, as she transferred the blame to him, her self-esteem came flooding back, the eyes and lips opened again like the flesh of a startled anemone flowering for the attack, and never having really faltered and now with new aplomb she passed on. He would be feeling sorry, she thought, and wish to expiate his deception. Besides, deep down he's fallen for me. Besides, there are four other judges. Besides, whatever the odds I'm good enough to beat the lot of them.

As she passed him and for a moment their eyes met, Morley was able to look as though he was looking right through her.

And then round and round the girls paraded. Sometimes the band changed its tune, broke into a dreamy waltz, and then all the girls broke step, bewildered in their dancing blood by the change of tempo: they quickly regained themselves and went kneeing on.

The vast hall echoed to laughter, catcalls, whistles and sighs from the crowd. "Irene!" some called: "Doreen!" others. "Git up them stairs," yelled the lustier members, and one man throughout the long parade repeated over and over again, at most regular intervals, and on a note of despair: "Roll me over."

But despite such convivialities—how misfortunate those girls were! It was cold there in that hall. They shivered, and many arms and legs so smoothly cared for now erupted into gooseflesh. In the changing room the six foreign girls had shivered with cold—and with anger. They had combined in wholehearted vituperation of the English weather, and finally all things English. When they had exhausted everything else—food, clothes, weather and so on—Miss Clermont-Ferrand had summed the matter up with the irrelevant, but emphatic and somehow damning words: "Double-decker Buses!"

Not only was it cold, but it looked cold. That hard mauve light stared down from the ceiling with the glare of arc-lamps on arterial concrete, rinsing all in varying shades of its mauve, killing all other colour. Lilac flesh, lavender crannies, purple lips, night-shade eyes—it became a circumambulation of the dead: corpsy smiles lurked the way, rigor mortis was on the move, it was a dream parade of maidens killed before their time. And far away, like an old grey wardress, Life still drizzled a dustbin blessing from the windowed world outside.

The judges, first dazzled, then surfeited, had now become so used to the bodies before them that their minds, obeying the laws of curiosity and creation, began to work on them afresh. Their eyes searched those bodies as a prisoner may search his cell and find in such bareness a new world of hidden detail. Thus they began to notice that where the spine of one girl snuggled like a long and lovely dimple, the next protruded in a sweet and charming ladder of little knobs. Where one naked torso showed a broad squarish form moulded like Greek armour, the next was softly shapeless as the ribless tube of an odalisque.

Moles took on a new presence, they grew insistent as flies on a bare ceiling. Bruises—wide brown smudges and little purple nips—showed clearer and clearer, freckles came into their own, and in that light the yellowing of armpits took on a new and virulent lilac life. So too the flushed pork-crackling, the armadillo flesh at the backs of heels—this turned deep purple, so that sometimes it looked as if a girl wore the kind of stocking that had a dark reinforcement above the back of her shoe. And the light made Miss Sauerkraut's ears, which with her blonde pallor were normally bright red, black.

The veins of auburn girls stood out like nests of rivers on maps and the lines that others wore from navel to pudenda split like cheesewire. But the navels themselves were a study on their own—dear little buttons, wicked forget-me-knots like cropped pink piglet tails, fingertip holes and penny-size pits and sometimes none at all but simply a recessive folding of modest flesh: one alderman, who had a compulsion complex, who normally had to walk between the lines of pavement stones or make countings of objects in rooms, found himself muttering a kind of permutation gamble to himself as the navels passed: "Button-Putton. Holey-Poley. Button-Put—no, damn, Holey-Poley. . . . "

And there were the operation scars, the appendix marks. And the vaccination marks, brown cornflowers on arm and thigh. And where some had taken the sun, the criss-cross of bathing-costume straps white on brown; and the cabalist label on the wrist where a watch and strap had been. And then all the other little marks, the little creases, and the wobbling and swinging of this and of that—all of these and so much more came to the fascinated eyes of the five startled gentlemen as that blanched and black-lipped procession passed before them.

(Yet how much more startled they would have been had their ears grown as alert as their eyes—for then they would have heard the ceaseless silent song whispered on the lips of every one of those priestesses as they marched, a song of one word only, the lip-stretched litany: "Cheese.")

Even Fred Morley, accustomed to rub shoulders with so many ladies of the chorus, was surprised. In the theatre the light was kinder, and there was powder and paint. Here, he found himself thinking, they were like medical samples, girls in bottles, selected picklings.

Finally the moment for judgment arrived. The judges whispered to each other, passed little scraps of paper. The band stopped playing. The great hall was hushed—a murmur of whispering and tittering only, the sound of a hive of waiting bees. The girls stood in a long line in front of the judges, their hands to their sides, defenceless, offered.

Three of Morley's co-judges elected immediately and unreservedly for Miss Great-Belt. It took him some time to disenchant them. But he did. To them he stood as something of an expert, a professional man: he played on this, ironically arguing their lack of taste, making them feel silly. But instantly he raised their esteem by congratulating them on their second and third choices—with raised eyebrows and a knowing wink: "Ho, I see you *do* know a thing or two!"

Finally a decision was taken.

Miss Amsterdam was awarded the first prize. A local lady, a blonde Miss Browne, came second, and long pale Miss Sauerkraut romped in third. Miss Great-Belt came nowhere at all.

The crowd cheered and booed, cheered for Miss Browne, and booed for Miss Great-Belt. But the judges' decision was final. There was no going back. And now Fred Morley rose to present the prizes.

A fine crocodile dressing-case for Number One, a portable wireless for Number Two, and oddly a set of pressure cookers for Miss Sauerkraut. And cheques for all. And for everybody present a few words from Frederick Morley.

"Ladies," he began, and gave a great sigh, rolling his eyes. Roars of laughter.

"And Gentlemen," he continued, with a sniff, as though he disbelieved in the presence of these. Redoubled laughter.

But then he silenced the laughter with measured and grave opening words. He made one of those speeches that keep the audience well on their toes—as soon as he got them uncomfortable and guilty with a passage of great gravity, he let fall a howling joke (and he was careful to make it a howler, not to serve wit in that most mixed hall). And as soon as they were howling, down he came on them hard with a passage of such stony grandeur that the air echoed a susurrus of shoe shufflings and coughs as presenceful as the laughter itself.

He had prepared this. And the reason he had taken so much trouble was to introduce a more personal condiment addressed to Miss Great-Belt. It was an address of omission. He made particular reference to the other international visitors—but not to her: and to make this the more striking he made it the less pointed by omitting one of the others, Miss Rotterdam, as well. He expressed on behalf of all present his gratitude to these ladies of lands across the sea for the honour of their visit—and then brought out some personal whoppers: of the lady from Rome's seaside, "all roads lead to Miss Civitavecchia"; of Miss Sauerkraut, "my little cabbage—and not so sour at that"; of the first prize-winner, "not only a fair damsel but a veritable *Amster*-damsel," and so on, whoppers that issuing from his presidential mouth achieved an arch and fearful force.

And that, all but the shouting, was that. There was nothing left but to go off into the drizzle.

Except—for a brief moment, but a moment which was to have great repercussion—for Miss Great-Belt.

Miss Great-Belt had her place, like all the others, in the line of girls listening to Morley's speech. But with a difference—she was the only one who somehow appeared thoroughly and properly dressed. It was as usual— her self-containedness at its magic work again. There she stood in her little triangle and her two small moons, nothing else, with her hands to her sides. She should have stood as sacrificially slavishly offered as all the others. Instead she remained composed and remote. She stood on her own legs, in her own right, occupied only by herself.

But when the speech ended, and the line of girls broke up, she simply stood on.

For only a few seconds—yet seconds at such a time that stretched in the eyes of the onlookers into statuesque minutes—she stood alone exactly as she had stood for the previous quarter-hour, her eyes fixed vaguely on the platform of judges.

Then her eyes woke up, startled. She looked around her. For a moment she hesitated. She seemed even to totter, not knowing which way she had to go. Then she saw, regained herself, turned and walked with all composure down the gangplank.

Miss Great-Belt had been thinking.

That moment of action, or of inaction, had not gone unperceived by Fred Morley. He had noticed it from the corner of his eye, not then wishing to turn his full face upon her, and had triumphantly noted it as an expression of her discomfort at losing the prize. But intuition is not a monopoly of the feminine, and far back and vaguely through his jubiliation a bell of unease had tolled. An intuitive woman, in his place, would have sought for an immediate solution, right or wrong, to such a problematic sound; but Fred Morley had preferred to shut his ears to it, it was uncomfortable, he had done a good day's work and wished to relax upon his laurels.

Relaxation took the form of a visit to the Yacht Club. There, again in manly company, again among the chaffing· and congratulations of his fellows, there was every hope of a pleasant end to a perfect day. But the opposite occurred. As the conviviality compounded, so did the tolling of that small bell of unease. It rang louder and louder. He tried to be, but he could not remain, deaf to it. And as the sound grew louder it took shape—from a vague unease it invented form. What—he began to consider—would be her real reaction to the afternoon's happening? How on earth could—he thought between drinks and digs in the ribs—a strong woman like that take such treatment lying down?

In the end he grew certain she would have her revenge. He remembered that women are said to like the last word: he considered this afresh, and began to believe it. He remembered the adage about he who laughs last laughing longest: he believed that too. And when he mixed the two ideas, substituting a "she" for a "he," the significance grew appalling.

But what form could such revenge take? Whichever way he looked at it, his apprehension grew. He knew that the ways of women were profound and unpredictable, their veiled wiles a labyrinth, their capacity for innuendo prodigious. Yet on the other hand there was the fact that when women fought, when the battle-cry was really raised, then they fought with the gloves off. His mind grew confused with visions of the Wives of Kings and Fishwives with Arms Akimbo. But since his own capacities for innuendo were small, his mind attached itself to, and enlarged upon, the latter conception.

She would slap his face in public! She would tear the house down— shatter the windows, slash the furniture, flood the baths, fire the curtains— (If that were only all . . . !) But what among these oversize visions he really feared was that she would invent a story against him, perhaps make some appalling charge. Assault. Rape. Or what was that word even worse? . . .

Interference! She would say he had Interfered with Her. No proof, no witnesses? No such luck—he knew that two women can get together, and that there would be one or two others dissatisfied with the result of the Contest.

He became overwrought. He dared not go home: but nor could he bear the anticipation.

Finally, less from courage than from a simpler impulse to "go and see what it's all about," he excused himself from Evans and the others ("Ho, the Homing Pigeon!" "Bye Bye Bluebeard! Love to the Misses!") and made his way home. Less certainly from courage, for he made his way in by the back door.

Excusing himself round the maid in the kitchen, who looked at him with surprise and suspicion mixed (another black mark? "Miss Abercrombie, a temporary domestic in the employ of the accused, was called to the witness stand"), he tiptoed into the hall and listened.

No one downstairs.

Upstairs, sounds that might have meant packing.

What voices he now heard spoke in their own languages. No more need of a common language? Getting into groups? Not too good.

Then suddenly down the stairs the sounds of running rustling skirts, heels! In panic he looked each way—impossible to return to the kitchen, no time to cross to the lounge! He was cornered! However, thank Heavens, it was only one of them—Miss Amsterdam, first prize-winner, a friend!

She gave a cry of delight, flung her arms round him and kissed him.

"Oh you dear good kind man," she cried, hugging him, "thank you, thank you, *thank* you!"

If anyone comes in now, Morley thought, then Evidence, Witnesses, Deeper than Ever . . . gently and quickly he disengaged himself, more formally congratulating her.

"But I am so glad you're here," she went on to say, "we've been looking all over for you! Now I must tell you . . . " And she went into details of how some girls would leave on the morrow, by what trains, and the rest on the following day. She made no mention of Miss Great-Belt's intention. But as an afterthought, turning her head back from the front-door: "Oh by the way, that Danish girl wants to see you—urgently, she said."

He was left alone with this. He went on standing in the hall, too centrally for simply standing. The maid came in to ring the gong. He threw out a hand, giving the barometer a great thud, nearly knocking it from the wall. Simultaneously as he went on pounding that thing, the old brass gong rang out. The house echoed with huge sudden noise. And for once, all at once, all the girls seemed to pile out of their rooms together. They came tripping down the stairs at him.

He was cornered with greetings. He could not opt but to go into dinner with them.

Miss Great-Belt nearly forced Miss Sauerkraut out of her chair in order to sit next to him. And of all others her smile was the most welcoming, throughout dinner she was charming.

Naturally, he made himself most gracious to her in return. But he distrusted her, he distrusted every flutter of her lovely eyelids. It must all be a cover for something terrible to come.

And after dinner, after all valedictory speeches had been made, Miss Great-Belt went so far as to suggest that he take her out for some coffee, perhaps even to dance. "But I know dancing must be a sore question between us," she went on to say, "I know it was uncivil of me to go dancing that night you invited me to the theatre. But I *do* apologize. Let's say bygones are bygones? Shall we?"

At that moment Fred Morley could easily have excused himself. His better judgment advised him to. But two other voices spoke inside him. One said that a dance-floor in a hotel was public and therefore safe; the second whispered that perhaps she really was, after all, making her peace with him. The latter voice, though in a whisper, spoke the louder. In fact, engaged again by her charms and never at a loss for respect of his own, he had already begun to believe that she was finally expressing a real attraction towards him.

They took coffee together at Morley's favourite hotel—the very terrace, glass-shaded, where once he had foreseen himself with the Misses Rotterdam and Clermont-Ferrand—and later went in to dance. He took care to act with the greatest propriety and even introduced her to his friend the head-waiter as a professional lady from Denmark, who, with her colleagues, had been billeted by the Town Hall on his house. This would put to rest any wilder speculations as to the nature of his strange and beautiful guest. The bush-telegraph would tap round the room a rational and respectable tune.

As for Miss Great-Belt, she continued to be soft, sweet, charming. All her past animosity had vanished. She seemed to throw open that invisible veil that had hitherto made her so unattainable, so much the woman of "process," and now welcomed him without question into the privacy of her composure. A woman so self-contained is ordinarily an uneasy companion. But when such a woman decides to invite one into her private sympathies, to give exactly her laughter and her confidence in the measure one knows it is withheld from others—then she becomes overwhelming. Without indulgence, with no condescension, but purely and simply, Miss Great-Belt welcomed Morley to herself. He was bowled over.

Quite early in the evening she made one point clear. "Now I do want to say once and for all," she said, opening her great eyes wide for frankness, leaning towards him like a large dark red cat, "that I congratulate you on your decision this afternoon. In my view you were absolutely right. That sweet Dutch girl was obviously the winner. I can see that one of the prizes had to go to an English girl—politics are politics. And there was every reason for poor Nuremburg—she looks so pale, doesn't she? A sick woman, yes she needs encouragement, it was very kind—taking third prize. Who wants to be third anyhow? No, I know you'll suspect I'm jealous—but honestly I'm not. With me justice counts before—whatever is the word?—*self.*"

She said this with great content, purring over her sacrifice, her frank good nature. He did not notice this. His instinct rose to protect a lady in distress. He began instantly to lie that he himself had voted for her for first prize—but what could he do against so many others?

He was surprised to notice that this was not received well. She looked, he thought, even a trifle offended. Why? Ah! . . . And he went straight on to point out that it was exactly because of this out-voting that, momentarily piqued, he simply could not bear to mention so much as her name in his presidential address.

As he stumbled through these paces, Miss Great-Belt watched him keenly. She saw that he was lying, and was satisfied. They finished the evening in high spirit with each other.

When the other ladies left during the next days, Miss Great-Belt stayed on. For propriety's sake she removed to the near-by hotel but she stayed on in the town. She and Morley saw each other every day. They went to the theatre, they dined together, they took motor-trips into the country and they went sailing on the sea.

The weather continued fine, it was a memorable month. Miss Great-Belt wrote to her father and begged permission to remain a few weeks more. Morley was in heaven. Now he avoided the Yacht Club altogether: he spent all his time with his new and lovely companion in places where they might be admired by more discriminating eyes.

It was for him a flirtation *de luxe*. It complimented his years, it redounded satisfactorily to his prowess. Finally, he told himself, he had won the day. Trust an old bachelor! Sometimes, when he thought of it all, he remembered with a reproving chuckle the first days, the very first days when he had unfolded every charm to entice her, when he had sacrificed every self-respect. How had he not realized that it was the exact opposite which would win her? Why—in a dozen musical shows this very process nightly comprised the whole plot! He had played it out himself night after night, year after year—it was the very stuff of life? Why had he never realized . . . ? But then why, damn our eyes, do we all spend our lives delighting in the wisdom of paradox—yet hesitate to apply the risks to ourselves?

He laughed and wagged his doggy head. Silly old fool! But then—hadn't that same silly old fool come through with flying colours? In the end? It took perseverance. He smiled, a little in love with her and himself and with everything else. "He who laughs last," he chuckled.

But then she married him.

On Sansom

William Sansom's life before the Second World War (he was born in 1912) had many of the marks of the conventional middle class: education at Uppingham School and at Bonn in Germany, followed by work in a bank

and later in an advertising agency. He was interested in the arts, attempting to compose music, playing the piano in London clubs, trying to paint,
and writing stories which no one would publish. The outbreak of war
changed his attitudes and his occupation; working as a fireman during the
Battle of Britain and prompted by "The suddenly more serious texture of
life and the foreshortened expectation of it," he abandoned "formula
writing" and began "to write down what I really thought rather than what I
imagined people wanted" (*Twentieth Century Authors*). His stories found
a welcome among editors and critics alike. After the war he supported
himself by various kinds of writing—stories, novels, travel books, children's
stories, even a coloring book—worked as a script writer for a film company,
and in 1954 married Ruth Grundy. According to his entry in *Who's Who,* his
only hobby is "watching."

Sansom's reputation has always been higher in England than in this
country. Fantasy, whimsy, a concern for manner rather than matter, an
appreciation of the *tour de force* or what Elizabeth Bowen calls the
necessary element of conjuring in a story are not exclusively English, but
the toughness underlying the fantasy in Saki, John Collier, E. M. Forster,
and Miss Bowen herself seems to be inaccessible to many American
writers—Ray Bradbury is typical—who seem unable to do without a strong
dose of sentiment or sentimentality. Other Americans, no doubt reacting
against the machine-tooled formulas of O. Henry and the popular magazines, prefer to use art to conceal it. Sansom not only refuses to conceal his
trickery; he flaunts it. Furthermore, he is consciously a philosophical
writer—even rarer in this country than a fantasist—and in fact the philosophical interest in what John Vickery calls "the ontological status of
sensations" helps to account for the angular, distorted, and yet compelling
pictures of the world which Sansom's fiction presents. Sansom himself has
said that in early stories he was writing "philosophically. . . . The statements I wished to make were allied to the teachings of Lao Tze, who
engrosses me." And finally, Sansom cannot be assigned to a popular or even
a definable school. The writers for whom he has expressed enthusiasm—
Henry Green ("the best novelist writing in the English language"), Franz
Kafka, and Rainer Maria Rilke (*The Notebooks of Malte Laurids
Brigge*)—are not the sort to reflect luster on him in the minds of American
critics or common readers, since Green's vogue in America is minor, if
steady, and since the other two writers are far more serious than Sansom in
the approved modernist tradition—full of *Angst,* personal, even confessional, in form. The kind of critic who admires Kafka tends to find Sansom
frivolous in his detachment while ordinary readers, who find "the ordinary
. . . more restful," shy away from a writer who will not let them "close
[their] eyes to the bewilderment of chance and coincidence that otherwise
would strike [them] every minute of the day."

"Watching," *seeing* "the bewilderment of chance and coincidence"—
these terms emphasize Sansom's interest in the visual. He admires Kafka,
he said, because "his visual eye had the same peculiar clarity as the
surrealists whose way of *isolating* objects and movements, etc., has

always influenced me very strongly! (I am really a painter *manqué*.)" The result of this kind of selection is grotesque, but the grotesque can be an instrument either of comedy or of horror. Altered perspective is always unsettling, as writers like Swift ("Last week I saw a woman flayed, and you will hardly believe how much it altered her person for the worse.") and James Thurber (who refused out of metaphysical, if comic, distress to imagine himself looking at a familiar room from a new angle) have demonstrated. Sansom ranges between the two extremes, almost always mixing them. "A Contest of Ladies," for example, is for the most part comic. Analyzed, however, beauty becomes increasingly grotesque as the story develops and in the climactic scene, it comes to seem cadaverous as the judges find "a new world of hidden detail" in the "blanched and black-lipped procession. . . . " Ironically, this is only an episode in the struggle between Fred Morley and Miss Great-Belt, and after this horrifying vision she raises his desire to a new pitch.

Like those of many Sansom characters, Miss Great-Belt's motives are not entirely clear, but they are obviously sinister. The final sentence is not merely a trick but the fulfillment of a threat, a new stage in the process by which Miss Great-Belt, whom Sansom takes care never to make fully human, secures her prey—who thinks himself the predator, safe from the domesticity against which the hotel was designed to guard him. Perhaps Miss Great-Belt will not devour him; she may only—if that is the word— reduce him to the condition of his male contemporaries who have danced in the envious and ribald chorus. Sansom writes of Doole, who is not eaten by a lion in "Among the Dahlias," "If we are not animals, if the human mind is superior to the simple animal body, then it must be true to say that by not being killed, Doole finally suffered a greater ill." In a sense, of course, Morley only meets the common fate; but while common terms can paralyze and soothe, fact is never common and, for Sansom, seldom consoling.

Textual note:

The text printed here follows that of *The Stories of William Sansom* (Boston: Little, Brown and Company, 1963).

Resources for further study:

Sansom's individual volumes of short stories are *Fireman Flower* (1944), *Something Terrible, Something Lovely* (1948), *South* (1948), *The Passionate North* (1950), *A Touch of the Sun* (1952), *Lord Love Us* (1954), *A Contest of Ladies* (1956), *Among the Dahlias* (1957), and *The Ulcerated Milkman* (1966). Short novel collections are *Three* (1946) and *The Equilibriad* (1948). Novels: *The Body* (1949), *The Face of Innocence* (1951), *A Bed of Roses* (1954), *The Loving Eye* (1956), *The Cautious Heart* (1958), *The Last Hours of Sandra Lee* (1961), and *Goodbye* (1966).

Pleasures Strange and Simple (London: Hogarth Press, 1953) contains, among other essays, "Edgar Allan Poe," which has interesting comments on the form of the short story, and autobiographical essays about his fire-fighting experiences. *Blue Skies and Brown Studies* (Hogarth, 1961) and *Away to It All* (Hogarth, 1964) collect some of his travel essays.

SECONDARY MATERIALS:

There is no bibliography, aside from the preternaturally inaccurate listing in Temple and Tucker's *Twentieth Century British Literature,* nor is there any full length study.

USEFUL SHORT STUDIES ARE:

BAILEY, GILBERT. "Talk with William Sansom," *New York Times Book Review,* 12 August 1951, p. 16.

BOWEN, ELIZABETH. "Introduction," *The Stories of William Sansom.* Boston: Little, Brown and Company, 1963.

KUNITZ, STANLEY, and VINETA COLBY. *Twentieth Century Authors.* First Supplement. New York: H. W. Wilson Co., 1955.

NEUMEYER, PETER F. "Franz Kafka and William Sansom," *Wisconsin Studies in Contemporary Literature,* 7 (Winter-Spring 1966), 76–84.

VICKERY, JOHN. "William Sansom and Logical Positivism," *Thought,* 36 (Summer 1961), 231–245.

DORIS LESSING

A Home for the Highland Cattle

These days, when people emigrate, it is not so much in search of sunshine, or food, or even servants. It is fairly safe to say that the family bound for Australia, or wherever it may be, has in its mind a vision of a nice house, or a flat, with maybe a bit of garden. I don't know how things were a hundred or fifty years ago. It seems, from books, that the colonizers and adventurers went sailing off to a new fine life, a new country, opportunities, and so forth. Now all they want is a roof over their heads.

An interesting thing, this: how is it that otherwise reasonable people come to believe that this same roof, that practically vanishing commodity, is freely obtainable just by packing up and going to another country? After all, headlines like World Housing Shortage are common to the point of tedium; and there is not a brochure or pamphlet issued by immigration departments that does not say (though probably in small print, throwing it away, as it were) that it is undesirable to leave home, without first making sure of a place to live.

Marina Giles left England with her husband in just this frame of mind. They had been living where they could, sharing flats and baths, and kitchens, for some years. If someone remarked enviously: "They say that in Africa the sky is always blue," she was likely to reply absent-mindedly: "Yes, and won't it be nice to have a proper house after all these years."

They arrived in Southern Rhodesia, and there was a choice of an immigrants' camp, consisting of mud huts with a communal water supply, or a hotel; and they chose the hotel, being what are known as people of means. That is to say, they had a few hundred pounds, with which they had

323

intended to buy a house as soon as they arrived. It was quite possible to buy a house, just as it is in England, provided one gives up all idea of buying a home one likes, and at a reasonable price. For years Marina had been inspecting houses. They fell into two groups, those she liked, and those she could afford. Now Marina was a romantic, she had not yet fallen into that passive state of mind which accepts (as nine-tenths of the population do) that one should find a corner to live, anywhere, and then arrange one's whole life around it, schooling for one's children, one's place of work, and so on. And since she refused to accept it, she had been living in extreme discomfort, exclaiming: "Why should we spend all the capital we are ever likely to have tying ourselves down to a place we detest!" Nothing could be more reasonable, on the face of it.

But she had not expected to cross an ocean, enter a new and indubitably romantic-sounding country, and find herself in exactly the same position.

The city, seen from the air, is half-buried in trees. Sixty years ago, this was all bare veld; and even now it appears not as if the veld encloses an area of buildings and streets, but rather as if the houses have forced themselves up, under and among the trees. Flying low over it, one sees greenness, growth, then the white flash of a high building, the fragment of a street that has no beginning or end, for it emerges from trees, and is at once reabsorbed by them. And yet it is a large town, spreading wide and scattered, for here there is no problem of space: pressure scatters people outwards, it does not force them perpendicularly. Driving through it from suburb to suburb, is perhaps fifteen miles—some of the important cities of the world are not much less; but if one asks a person who lives there what the population is, he will say ten thousand, which is very little. Why do so small a number of people need so large a space? The inhabitant will probably shrug, for he has never wondered. The truth is that there are not ten thousand, but more likely 150,000, but the others are black, which means that they are not considered. The blacks do not so much *live* here, as squeeze themselves in as they can—all this is very confusing for the newcomer, and it takes quite a time to adjust oneself.

Perhaps every city has one particular thing by which it is known, something which sums it up, both for the people who live in it, and those who have never known it, save in books or legend. Three hundred miles south, for instance, old Lobengula's kraal had the Big Tree. Under its branches sat the betrayed, sorrowful, magnificent King in his rolls of black fat and beads and gauds, watching his doom approach in the white people's advance from the south, and dispensing life and death according to known and honoured customs. That was only sixty years ago . . .

This town has the *Kopje*. When the Pioneers were sent north, they were told to trek on till they reached a large and noble mountain they could not possibly mistake; and there they must stop and build their city. Twenty miles too soon, due to some confusion of mind, or perhaps to understandable exhaustion, they stopped near a small and less shapely hill. This had rankled ever since. Each year, when the ceremonies are held to honour those pioneers, and the vision of Rhodes who sent them forth, the thought creeps in that this is not really what the Founder intended . . . Standing there, at the foot of that *kopje,* the speech-makers say: Sixty years, look what we have accomplished in sixty years. And in the minds of the listeners springs a vision of that city we all dream of, that planned and shapely city without stain or slum—the city that could in fact have been created in those sixty years.

The town spread from the foot of this hill. Around it are the slums, the narrow and crooked streets where the coloured people eke out their short swarming lives among decaying brick and tin. Five minutes walk to one side, and the street peters out in long, soiled grass, above which a power chimney pours black smoke, and where an old petrol tin lies in a gulley, so that a diving hawk swerves away and up, squawking, scared out of his nature by a flash of sunlight. Ten minutes the other way is the business centre, the dazzling white blocks of concrete, modern buildings like modern buildings the world over. Here are the imported clothes, the glass windows full of cars from America, the neon lights, the counters full of pamphlets advertising flights Home—wherever one's home might be. A few blocks further on, and the business part of the town is left behind. This was once the smart area. People who have grown with the city will drive through here on a Sunday afternoon, and, looking at the bungalows raised on their foundations and ornamented with iron scrollwork, will say: In 1910 there was nothing beyond this house but bare veld.

Now, however, there are more houses, small and ugly houses, until all at once we are in the 'thirties, with tall houses eight to a block, like very big soldiers standing to attention in a small space. The verandahs have gone. Tiny balconies project like eyelids, the roofs are like bowler hats, rimless. Exposed to the blistering sun, these houses crowd together without invitation to shade or coolness, for they were not planned for this climate, and until the trees grow, and the creepers spread, they are extremely uncomfortable. (Though, of course, very smart.) Beyond these? The veld again, wastes of grass clotted with the dung of humans and animals, a vlei that is crossed and criss-crossed by innumerable footpaths where the Africans walk in the afternoon from suburb to suburb, stopping to snatch a mouthful of water in cupped palms from potholes filmed with iridescent oil, for safety against mosquitoes.

Over the vlei (which is rapidly being invaded by building, so that soon there will be no open spaces left) is a new suburb. Now, this is something quite different. Where the houses, only twenty minutes' walk away, stood eight to a block, now there are twenty tiny, flimsy little houses, and the men who planned them had in mind the cheap houses along the ribbon roads of England. Small patches of roofed cement, with room, perhaps, for a couple of chairs, call themselves verandahs. There is a hall a couple of yards square—for otherwise where should one hang one's hat? Each little house is divided into rooms so small that there is no space to move from one wall to the other without circling a table or stumbling over a chair. And white walls, glaring white walls, so that one's eyes turn in relief to the trees.

The trees—these houses are intolerable unless foliage softens and hides them. Any new owner, moving in, says wistfully: It won't be so bad when the shrubs grow up. And they grow very quickly. It is an extraordinary thing that this town, which must be one of the most graceless and inconvenient in existence, considered simply as an association of streets and buildings, is so beautiful that no one fails to fall in love with it at first sight. Every street is lined and double-lined with trees, every house screened with brilliant growth. It is a city of gardens.

Marina was at first enchanted. Then her mood changed. For the only houses they could afford were in those mass-produced suburbs, that were spreading like measles as fast as materials could be imported to build them. She said to Philip: "In England, we did not buy a house because we did not want to live in a suburb. We uproot ourselves, come to a reputedly exotic and wild country, and the only place we can afford to live is another suburb. I'd rather be dead."

Philip listened. He was not as upset as she was. They were rather different. Marina was that liberally-minded person produced so plentifully in England during the 'thirties, while Philip was a scientist, and put his faith in techniques, rather than in the inherent decency of human beings. He was, it is true, in his own way an idealist, for he had come to this continent in a mood of fine optimism. England, it seemed to him, did not offer opportunities to young men equipped, as he was, with enthusiasm and so much training. Things would be different overseas. All that was necessary was a go-ahead Government prepared to vote sufficient money to Science—this was just common sense. (Clearly, a new country was likely to have more common sense than an old one.) He was prepared to make gardens flourish where deserts had been. Africa appeared to him eminently suitable for this treatment; and the more he saw of it, those first few weeks, the more enthusiastic he became.

But he soon came to understand that in the evenings, when he propounded these ideas to Marina, her mind was elsewhere. It seemed to him bad luck that they should be in this hotel, which was uncomfortable, with bad food, and packed by fellow-immigrants all desperately searching for that legendary roof. But a house would turn up sooner or later—he had been convinced of this for years. He would not have objected to buying one of those suburban houses. He did not like them, certainly, but he knew quite well that it was not the house, as such, that Marina revolted against. Ah, this feeling we all have about the suburbs! How we dislike the thought of being just like the fellow next door! Bad luck, when the whole world rapidly fills with suburbs, for what is a British Colony but a sort of highly-flavoured suburb to England itself? Somewhere in the back of Marina's mind has been a vision of herself and Philip living in a group of amiable people, pleasantly interested in the arts, who read the *New Statesman* week by week, and held that discreditable phenomena like the colour bar and the black-white struggle could be solved by sufficient goodwill . . . a delightful picture.

Temporarily Philip turned his mind from thoughts of blossoming deserts, and so on, and tried another approach. Perhaps they could buy a house through one of the Schemes for Immigrants? He would return from this Housing Board or that, and say in a worried voice: "There isn't a hope unless one has three children." At this, Marina was likely to become depressed; for she still held the old-fashioned view that before one has children, one should have a house to put them in.

"It's all very well for you," said Marina. "As far as I can see, you'll be spending half your time gallivanting in your lorry from one end of the country to the other, visiting native reserves, and having a lovely time. I don't *mind,* but I have to make some sort of life for myself while you do it." Philip looked rather guilty; for in fact he was away three or four days a week, on trips with fellow-experts, and Marina would be very often left alone.

"Perhaps we could find somewhere temporary, while we wait for a house to turn up?" he suggested.

This offered itself quite soon. Philip heard from a man he met casually that there was a flat available for three months, but he wouldn't swear to it, because it was only an overheard remark at a sundowner party—Philip followed the trail, clinched the deal, and returned to Marina. "It's only for three months," he comforted her.

138 Cecil John Rhodes Vista was in that part of the town built before the sudden expansion in the 'thirties. These were all old houses, unfashionable, built to no important recipe, but according to the whims of the first owners. On one side of 138 was a house whose roof curved down, Chinese fashion, built on a platform for protection against ants, with wooden steps. Its walls were of wood, and it was possible to hear feet tramping over the wooden floors even in the street outside. The other neighbour was a house whose walls were invisible under a mass of golden shower—thick yellow clusters, like smokey honey, dripped from roof to ground. The houses opposite were hidden by massed shrubs.

From the street, all but the roof of 138 was screened by a tall and straggling hedge. The sidewalks were dusty grass, scattered with faggots of dogs' dirt, so that one had to walk carefully. Outside the gate was a great clump of bamboo reaching high into the sky, and all the year round weaver-birds' nests, like woven-grass cricket balls, dangled there bouncing and swaying in the wind. Near it reached the angled brown sticks of the frangipani, breaking into white and a creamy pink, as if a young coloured girl held armfuls of blossom. The street itself was double-lined with trees, first jacaranda, fine green lace against the blue sky, and behind heavy dark masses of the cedrilatoona. All the way down the street were bursts of colour, a drape of purple bougainvillaea, the sparse scarlet flowers of the hibiscus. It was very beautiful, very peaceful.

Once inside the unkempt hedge, 138 was exposed as a shallow brick building, tin-roofed, like an elongated barn, that occupied the centre of two building stands, leaving plenty of space for front and back yards. It had a history. Some twenty years back, some enterprising businessman had built the place, ignoring every known rule of hygiene, in the interests of economy. By the time the local authorities had come to notice its unfitness to exist, the roof was on. There followed a series of court cases. An exhausted judge had finally remarked that there was a housing shortage; and on this basis the place was allowed to remain.

It was really eight semi-detached houses, stuck together in such a way that, standing before the front door of any one, it was possible to see clear through the two rooms which composed each, to the back yard, where washing flapped over the woodpile. A verandah enclosed the front of the building: eight short flights of steps, eight front doors, eight windows—but these windows illuminated the front rooms only. The back room opened into a porch that was screened in by dull green mosquito gauze; and in this way the architect had achieved the really remarkable feat of producing, in a country continually drenched by sunlight, rooms in which it was necessary to have the lights burning all day.

The back yard, a space of bare dust enclosed by parallel hibiscus hedges, was a triumph of individualism over communal living. Eight separate woodpiles, eight clothes-lines, eight short paths edged with brick leading to the eight lavatories that were built side by side like segments of chocolate, behind an enclosing tin screen: the locks (and therefore the keys) were identical, for the sake of cheapness, a system which guaranteed strife among the inhabitants. On either side of the lavatories were two rooms, built as a unit. In these four rooms lived eight native servants. At least, officially there were eight, in practice far more.

When Marina, a woman who took her responsibilities seriously, as has been indicated, looked inside the room which her servant shared with the servant from next door, she exclaimed helplessly: "Dear me, how awful!" The room was very small. The brick walls were unplastered, the tin of the roof bare, focussing the sun's intensity inwards all day, so that even while she stood on the threshold, she began to feel a little faint, because of the enclosed heat. The floor was cement, and the blankets that served as beds lay directly on it. No cupboards or shelves: these were substituted by a string stretching from corner to corner. Two small, high windows, whose glass was cracked and pasted with paper. On the walls were pictures of the English royal family, torn out of illustrated magazines, and of various female film stars, mostly unclothed.

"Dear me," said Marina again, vaguely. She was feeling very guilty, because of this squalor. She came out of the room with relief, wiping the sweat from her face, and looked around the yard. Seen from the back, 138 Cecil John Rhodes Vista was undeniably picturesque. The yard, enclosed by low-scarlet-flowering hibiscus hedges, was of dull red earth; the piles of grey wood were each surrounded by a patch of scattered chips, yellow, orange, white. The colourful washing lines swung and danced. The servants, in their crisp white, leaned on their axes, or gossiped. There was a little black nurse-girl seated on one of the logs, under a big tree, with a white child in her arms. A delightful scene; it would have done as it was for the opening number of a musical comedy. Marina turned her back on it; and with her stern reformer's eye looked again at the end of the yard. In the spaces between the lavatories and the servants' rooms stood eight rubbish cans, each covered by its cloud of flies, and exuding a stale, sour smell. She walked through them into the sanitary lane. Now, if one drives down the streets of such a city, one sees the trees, the gardens, the flowering hedges; the streets form neat squares. Squares (one might suppose) filled with blossoms and greenness, in which the houses are charmingly arranged. But each block is divided down the middle by a sanitary lane, a dust lane, which is lined by rubbish cans, and in this the servants have their social life. Here they go for a quick smoke, in the middle of the day's work; here they meet their friends, or flirt with the women who sell vegetables. It is as if, between each of the streets of the white man's city, there is a hidden street, ignored, forgotten. Marina, emerging into it, found it swarming with gossiping and laughing Africans. They froze, gave her a long suspicious stare, and all at once seemed to vanish, escaping into their respective back yards. In a moment she was alone.

She walked slowly back across the yard to her back door, picking her way among the soft litter from the woodpiles, ducking her head under the flapping clothes. She was watched, cautiously, by the servants, who were suspicious of this sudden curiosity about their way of life—experience had taught them to be suspicious. She was watched, also, by several of the women, through their kitchen windows. They saw a small Englishwoman, with a neat and composed body, pretty fair hair, and a pink and white face under a large straw hat, which she balanced in position with a hand clothed in a white glove. She moved delicately and with obvious distaste through the dust, as if at any moment she might take wings and fly away altogether.

When she reached her back steps, she stopped and called: "Charlie! Come here a moment, please." It was a high voice, a little querulous. When they heard the accents of that voice, saw the white glove, and noted that *please,* the watching women found all their worst fears confirmed.

A young African emerged from the sanitary lane where he had been gossiping (until interrupted by Marina's appearance) with some passing friends. He ran to his new mistress. He wore white shorts, a scarlet American-style shirt, tartan socks which were secured by mauve suspenders, and white tennis shoes. He stopped before her with a polite smile, which almost at once spread into a grin of pure friendliness. He was an amiable and cheerful young man by temperament. This was Marina's first morning in her new home, and she was already conscious of the disproportion between her strong pity for her servant, and that inveterately cheerful face.

She did not, of course, speak any native language, but Charlie spoke English.

"Charlie, how long have you been working here?"

"Two years, madam."

"Where do you come from?"

"Madam?"

"Where is your home?"

"Nyasaland."

"Oh." For this was hundreds of miles north.

"Do you go home to visit your family?"

"Perhaps this year, madam."

"I see. Do you like it here?"

"Madam?" A pause; and he involuntarily glanced back over the rubbish cans at the sanitary lane. He hoped that his friends, who worked on the other side of the town, and whom he did not often see, would not get tired of waiting for him. He hoped, too, that this new mistress (whose politeness to him he did not trust) was not going to choose this moment to order him to clean the silver or do the washing. He continued to grin, but his face was a little anxious, and his eyes rolled continually backwards at the sanitary lane.

"I hope you will be happy working for me," said Marina.

"Oh, yes, madam," he said at once, disappointedly; for clearly she was going to tell him to work.

"If there is anything you want, you must ask me. I am new to the country, and I may make mistakes."

He hesitated, handling the words in his mind. But they were difficult, and he let them slip. He did not think in terms of countries, of continents. He knew the white man's town—this town. He knew the veld. He knew the village from which he came. He knew, from his educated friends, that there was "a big water" across which the white men came in ships: he had seen pictures of ships in old magazines, but this "big water" was confused in his mind with the great lake in his own country. He understood that these white people came from places called England, Germany, Europe, but these were names to him. Once, a friend of his who had been three years to a mission school had said that Africa was one of several continents, and had shown him a tattered sheet of paper—one half of the map of the world—saying: Here is Africa, here is England, here is India. He pointed out Nyasaland, a tiny strip of country, and Charlie felt confused and diminished, for Nyasaland was what he knew, and it seemed to him so vast. Now, when Marina used the phrase "this country" Charlie saw, for a moment, this flat piece of paper, tinted pink and green and blue—the world. But from the sanitary lane came shouts of laughter—again he glanced anxiously over his shoulder; and Marina was conscious of a feeling remarkably like irritation. "Well, you may go," she said formally; and saw his smile flash white right across his face. He turned, and ran back across the yard like an athlete, clearing the woodpile, then the rubbish cans, in a series of great bounds, and vanished behind the lavatories. Marina went inside her "flat" with what was, had she known it, an angry frown. "Disgraceful," she muttered, including in this condemnation the bare room in which this man was expected to fit his life, the dirty sanitary lane bordered with stinking rubbish cans, and also his unreasonable cheerfulness.

Inside, she forgot him in her own discomfort. It was a truly shocking place. The two small rooms were so made that the inter-leading door was in the centre of the wall. They were more like passages than rooms. She switched on the light in what would be the bedroom, and put her hands to her cheek, for it stung where the sun had caught her unaccustomed skin through the chinks of the straw of her hat. The furniture was really beyond description! Two iron bedsteads, on either side of the door, a vast choco-late-brown wardrobe, whose door would not properly shut, one dingy straw mat that slid this way and that over the slippery boards as one walked on it. And the front room! If possible, it was even worse. An enormous cretonne-covered sofa, like a solidified flower bed, a hard and shiny table stuck in the middle of the floor, so that one must walk carefully around it, and four straight, hard chairs, ranged like soldiers against the wall. And the pictures—she did not know such pictures still existed. There was a desert scene, done in coloured cloth, behind glass; a motto in woven straw, also framed in glass, saying: *Welcome all who come in here, Good luck to you and all good cheer.*

There was also a very large picture of highland cattle. Half a dozen of these shaggy and ferocious creatures glared down at her from where they stood knee-deep in sunset-tinted pools. One might imagine that pictures of highland cattle no longer existed outside of Victorian novels, or remote suburban boarding-houses—but no, here they were. Really, why bother to emigrate?

She almost marched over and wrenched that picture from the wall. A curious inhibition prevented her. It was, though she did not know it, the spirit of the building. Some time later she heard Mrs. Black, who had been living for years in the next flat with her husband and three children, remark grimly: "My front door handle has been stuck for weeks, but I'm not going to mend it. If I start doing the place up, it means I'm here for ever." Marina recognised her own feeling when she heard these words. It accounted for the fact that while the families here were all respectable, in the sense that they owned cars, and could expect a regular monthly income, if one looked through the neglected hedge it was impossible not to conclude that every person in the building was born sloven or slut. No one really lived here. They might have been here for years, without prospect of anything better, but they did not live here.

There was one exception, Mrs. Pond, who painted her walls and mended what broke. It was felt she let everyone else down. In front of *her* steps a narrow path edged with brick led to her segment of yard, which was perhaps two feet across, in which lilies and roses were held upright by trellis work, like a tall, green sandwich standing at random in the dusty yard.

Marina thought: well, what's the point? I'm not going to *live* here. The picture could stay. Similarly, she decided there was no sense in unpacking her nice curtains or her books. And the furniture might remain as it was, for it was too awful to waste effort on it. Her thoughts returned to the servants' rooms at the back: it was a disgrace. The whole system was disgraceful . . .

At this point, Mrs. Pond knocked perfunctorily and entered. She was a short, solid woman, tied in at the waist, like a tight sausage, by the string of her apron. She had hard red cheeks, a full, hard bosom, and energetic red hands. Her eyes were small and inquisitive. Her face was ill-tempered, perhaps because she could not help knowing she was disliked. She was used to the disapproving eyes of her fellow-tenants, watching her attend to her strip of "garden"; or while she swept the narrow strip across the back yard that was her path from the back door to her lavatory. There she stood, every morning, among the washing and the woodpiles, wearing a pink satin dressing-gown trimmed with swan's-down, among the clouds of dust stirred up by her yard broom, returning defiant glances for the disapproving ones; and later she would say: "Two rooms is quite enough for a woman by herself. I'm quite satisfied."

She had no right to be satisfied, or at any rate, to say so . . .

But for a woman contented with her lot, there was a look in those sharp eyes which could too easily be diagnosed as envy; and when she said, much too sweetly: "You are an old friend of Mrs. Skinner, maybe?" Marina recognised, with the exhaustion that comes to everyone who has lived too long in overfull buildings, the existence of conspiracy. "I have never met Mrs. Skinner," she said briefly. "She said she was coming here this morning, to make arrangements."

Now, arrangements had been made already, with Philip; and Marina knew Mrs. Skinner was coming to inspect herself; and this thought irritated her.

"She is a nice lady," said Mrs. Pond. "She's my friend. We two have been living here longer than anyone else." Her voice was sour. Marina followed the direction of her eyes, and saw a large white door set into the wall. A built-in cupboard, in fact. She had already noted that cupboard as the only sensible amenity the "flat" possessed.

"That's a nice cupboard," said Mrs. Pond.

"Have all the flats got built-in cupboards?"

"Oh, no. Mrs. Skinner had this put in special last year. She paid for it. Not the landlord. You don't catch the landlord paying for anything."

"I see," said Marina.

"Mrs. Skinner promised me this flat," said Mrs. Pond.

Marina made no reply. She looked at her wrist-watch. It was a beautiful gesture; she even felt a little guilty because of the pointedness of it; but Mrs. Pond promptly said: "It's eleven o'clock. The clock just struck."

"I must finish the unpacking," said Marina.

Mrs. Pond seated herself on the flowery sofa, and remarked: "There's always plenty to do when you move in. That cupboard will save you plenty of space. Mrs. Skinner kept her linen in it. I was going to put all my clothes in. You're Civil Service, so I hear?"

"Yes," said Marina. She could not account for the grudging tone of that last, apparently irrelevant question. She did not know that in this country the privileged class was the Civil Service, or considered to be. No aristocracy, no class distinctions—but alas, one must have something to hate, and the Civil Service does as well as anything. She added: "My husband chose this country rather than the Gold Coast, because it seems the climate is better, even though the pay is bad."

This remark was received with the same sceptical smile that she would have earned in England had she been tactless enough to say to her charwoman: Death duties spell the doom of the middle classes.

"You have to be in the Service to get what's going," said Mrs. Pond, with what she imagined to be a friendly smile. "The Service gets all the plums." And she glanced at the cupboard.

"I think," said Marina icily, "that you are under some misapprehension. My husband happened to hear of this flat by chance."

"There were plenty of people waiting for this flat," said Mrs. Pond reprovingly. "The lady next door, Mrs. Black, would have been glad of it. And she's got three children, too. You have no children, perhaps?"

"Mrs. Pond, I have no idea at all why Mrs. Skinner gave us this flat when she had promised it to Mrs. Black . . . "

"Oh, no, she had promised it to me. It was a faithful promise."

At this moment another lady entered the room without knocking. She was an ample, middle-aged person, in tight corsets, with rigidly-waved hair, and a sharp, efficient face that was now scarlet from heat. She said peremptorily: "Excuse me for coming in without knocking, but I can't get used to a stranger being here when I've lived here so long." Suddenly she saw Mrs. Pond, and at once stiffened into aggression. "I see you have already made friends with Mrs. Pond," she said, giving that lady a glare.

Mrs. Pond was standing, hands on hips, in the traditional attitude of combat; but she squeezed a smile on to her face and said: "I'm making acquaintance."

"Well," said Mrs. Skinner, dismissing her, "I'm going to discuss business with my tenant."

Mrs. Pond hesitated. Mrs. Skinner gave her a long, quelling stare. Mrs. Pond slowly deflated, and went to the door. From the verandah floated back the words: "When people make promises, they should keep them, that's what I say, instead of giving it to people new to the country, and civil servants . . . "

Mrs. Skinner waited until the loud and angry voice faded, and then said briskly: "If you take my advice, you'll have nothing to do with Mrs. Pond, she's more trouble than she's worth."

Marina now understood that she owed this flat to the fact that this highly-coloured lady decided to let it to a stranger simply in order to spite all her friends in the building who hoped to inherit that beautiful cupboard, if only for three months. Mrs. Skinner was looking suspiciously around her; she said at last: "I wouldn't like to think my things weren't looked after."

"Naturally not," said Marina politely.

"When I spoke to your husband we were rather in a hurry. I hope you will make yourself comfortable, but I don't want to have anything altered."

Marina maintained a polite silence.

Mrs. Skinner marched to the inbuilt cupboard, opened it, and found it empty. "I paid a lot of money to have this fitted," she said in an aggrieved voice.

"We only came in yesterday," said Marina. "I haven't unpacked yet."

"You'll find it very useful," said Mrs. Skinner. "I paid for it myself. Some people would have made allowances in the rent."

"I think the rent is quite high enough," said Marina, joining battle at last.

Clearly, this note of defiance was what Mrs. Skinner had been waiting for. She made use of the familiar weapon: "There are plenty of people who would have been glad of it, I can tell you."

"So I gather."

"I could let it tomorrow."

"But," said Marina, in the high formal voice, "you have in fact let it to us, and the lease has been signed, so there is no more to be said, is there?"

Mrs. Skinner hesitated, and finally contented herself by repeating: "I hope my furniture will be looked after. I said in the lease nothing must be altered."

Suddenly Marina found herself saying: "Well, I shall of course move the furniture to suit myself, and hang my own pictures."

"This flat is let furnished, and I'm very fond of my pictures."

"But you will be away, won't you?" This, a sufficiently crude way of saying: "But it is we who will be looking at the pictures, and not you," misfired completely, for Mrs. Skinner merely said: "Yes, I like my pictures, and I don't like to think of them being packed."

Marina looked at the highland cattle and, though not half an hour before she had decided to leave it, said now: "I should like to take that one down."

Mrs. Skinner clasped her hands together before her, in a pose of simple devotion, compressed her lips, and stood staring mournfully up at the picture. "That picture means a lot to me. It used to hang in the parlour when I was a child, back Home. It was my granny's picture first. When I married Mr. Skinner, my mother packed it and sent it especial over the sea, knowing how I was fond of it. It's moved with me everywhere I've been. I wouldn't like to think of it being treated bad, I wouldn't really."

"Oh, very well," said Marina, suddenly exhausted. What, after all, did it matter?

Mrs. Skinner gave her a doubtful look: was it possible she had won her point so easily? "You must keep an eye on Charlie," she went on. "The number of times I've told him he'd poke his broomhandle through that picture . . . "

Hope flared in Marina. There was an extraordinary amount of glass. It seemed that the entire wall was surfaced by angry, shaggy cattle. Accidents did happen . . .

"You must keep an eye on Charlie, anyway. He never does a stroke more than he has to. He's bred bone lazy. You'd better keep an eye on the food too. He steals. I had to have the police to him only last month, when I lost my garnet brooch. Of course he swore he hadn't taken it, but I've never laid my hands on it since. My husband gave him a good hiding, but Master Charlie came up smiling, as usual."

Marina, revolted by this tale, raised her eyebrows disapprovingly. "Indeed?" she said, in her coolest voice.

Mrs. Skinner looked at her, as if to say: "What are you making that funny face for?" she remarked: "They're all born thieves and liars. You shouldn't trust them further than you can kick them. I'm warning you. Of course, you're new here. Only last week a friend was saying, I'm surprised at you letting to people just from England, they always spoil the servants, with their ideas, and I said: 'Oh, Mr. Giles is a sensible man, I trust him.' " This last was said pointedly.

"I don't think," remarked Marina coldly, "that you would be well-advised to trust my husband to give people 'hidings.' " She delicately isolated this word. "I rather feel, in similar circumstances, that even if he did, he would first make sure whether the man had, in fact, stolen the brooch."

Mrs. Skinner disentangled this sentence and in due course gave Marina a distrustful stare. "Well," she said, "it's too late now, and everyone has his way, but of course this is my furniture, and if it is stolen or damaged, you are responsible."

"That, I should have thought, went without saying," said Marina.

They shook hands, with formality, and Mrs. Skinner went out. She returned from the verandah twice, first to say that Marina must not forget to fumigate the native quarters once a month if she didn't want livestock brought into her own flat . . . ("Not that I care if they want to live with lice, dirty creatures, but you have to protect yourself . . . "); and the second time to say that after you've lived in a place for years, it was hard to leave it, even for a holiday, and she was really regretting the day she let it at all. She gave Marina a final accusing and sorrowful look, as if the flat had been stolen from her, and this time finally departed. Marina was left in a mood of defiant anger, looking at the highland cattle picture, which had assumed, during this exchange, the look of a battleground. "Really," she said aloud to herself. "Really! One might have thought that one would be entitled to pack away a picture, if one rents a place . . . "

Two days later she got a note from Mrs. Skinner, saying that she hoped Marina would be happy in the flat, she must remember to keep an eye on Mrs. Pond, who was a real trouble-maker, and she must remember to look after the picture—Mrs. Skinner positively could not sleep for worrying about it.

Since Marina had decided she was not living here, there was comparatively little unpacking to be done. Things were stored. She had more than ever the appearance of a migrating bird who dislikes the twig it has chosen to alight on, but is rather too exhausted to move to another.

But she did read the advertisement columns every day, which were exactly like those in the papers back home. The *accommodation wanted* occupied a full column, while the *accommodation offered* usually did not figure at all. When houses were advertised they usually cost between five and twelve thousand—Marina saw some of them. They were very beautiful; if one had five thousand pounds, what a happy life one might lead—but the same might be said of any country. She also paid another visit to one of the new suburbs, and returned shuddering. "What!" she exclaimed to Philip. "Have we emigrated in order that I may spend the rest of life gossiping and taking tea with women like Mrs. Black and Mrs. Skinner?"

"Perhaps they aren't all like that," he suggested absent-mindedly. For he was quite absorbed in his work. This country was fascinating! He was spending his days in his Government lorry, rushing over hundreds of miles of veld, visiting native reserves and settlements. Never had soil been so misused! Thousands of acres of it, denuded, robbed, fit for nothing, cattle and human beings crowded together—the solution, of course, was perfectly obvious. All one had to do was—and if the Government had any sense—

Marina understood that Philip was acclimatized. One does not speak of the "Government" with that particular mixture of affection and exasperation unless one feels at home. But she was not at all at home. She found herself playing with the idea of buying one of those revolting little houses. After all, one has to live somewhere . . .

Almost every morning, in 138, one might see a group of women standing outside one or other of the flats, debating how to rearrange the rooms. The plan of the building being so eccentric, no solution could possibly be satisfactory, and as soon as everything had been moved around, it was bound to be just as uncomfortable as before. "If I move the bookcase behind the door, then perhaps . . . " Or: "It might be better if I put it into the bathroom . . . "

The problem was: Where should one eat? If the dining-table was in the front room, then the servant had to come through the bedroom with the food. On the other hand, if one had the front room as bedroom, then visitors had to walk through it to the living-room. Marina kept Mrs. Skinner's arrangement. On the back porch, which was the width of a passage, stood a collapsible card-table. When it was set up, Philip sat crouched under the window that opened inwards over his head, while Marina shrank sideways into the bathroom door as Charlie came past with the vegetables. To serve food, Charlie put on a starched white coat, red fez, and white cotton gloves. In between courses he stood just behind them, in the kitchen door, while Marina and Philip ate in state, if discomfort.

Marina found herself becoming increasingly sensitive to what she imagined was his attitude of tolerance. It seemed ridiculous that the ritual of soup, fish, and sweet, silver and glass and fish-knives, should continue under such circumstances. She began to wonder how it all appeared to this young man, who, as soon as their meal was finished, took an enormous pot of mealie porridge off the stove and retired with it to his room, where he shared it (eating with his fingers and squatting on the floor) with the servant from next door, and any of his friends or relatives who happened to be out of work at the time.

That no such thoughts entered the heads of the other inhabitants was clear; and Marina could understand how necessary it was to banish them as quickly as possible. On the other hand . . .

There was something absurd in a system which allowed a healthy young man to spend his life in her kitchen, so that she might do nothing. Besides, it was more trouble than it was worth. Before she and Philip rose, Charlie walked around the outside of the building, and into the front room, and cleaned it. But as the wall was thin and he energetic, they were awakened every morning by the violent banging of his broom and the scraping of furniture. On the other hand, if it were left till they woke up, where should Marina sit while he cleaned it? On the bed, presumably, in the dark bedroom, till he had finished? It seemed to her that she spent half her time arranging her actions so that she might not get in Charlie's way while he cleaned or cooked. But she had learned better than to suggest doing her own work. On one of Mrs. Pond's visits, she had spoken with disgust of certain immigrants from England, who had so far forgotten what was due to their position as white people as to dispense with servants. Marina felt it was hardly worth while upsetting Mrs. Pond for such a small matter. Particularly, of course, as it was only for three months . . .

But upset Mrs. Pond she did, and almost immediately.

When it came to the end of the month, when Charlie's wages were due, and she laid out the twenty shillings he earned, she was filled with guilt. She really could not pay him such an idiotic sum for a whole month's work. But were twenty-five shillings, or thirty, any less ridiculous? She paid him twenty-five, and saw him beam with amazed surprise. He had been planning to ask for a rise, since this woman was easy-going, and he naturally optimistic; but to get a rise without asking for it, and then a full five shillings! Why, it had taken him three months of hard bargaining with Mrs. Skinner to get raised from seventeen and sixpence to nineteen shillings. "Thank you, madam," he said hastily; grabbing the money as if at any moment she might change her mind and take it back. Later that same day, she saw that he was wearing a new pair of crimson satin garters, and felt rather annoyed. Surely those five shillings might have been more sensibly spent? What these unfortunate people needed was an education in civilised values—but before she could pursue the thought, Mrs. Pond entered, looking aggrieved.

It appeared that Mrs. Pond's servant had also demanded a rise, from his nineteen shillings. If Charlie could earn twenty-five shillings, why not he? Marina understood that Mrs. Pond was speaking for all the women in the building.

"You shouldn't spoil them," she said. "I know you are from England, and all that, but . . . "

"It seems to me they are absurdly underpaid," said Marina.

"Before the war they were lucky to get ten bob. They're never satisfied."

"Well, according to the cost-of-living index, the value of money has halved," said Marina. But as even the Government had not come to terms with this official and indisputable fact, Mrs. Pond could not be expected to, and she said crossly: "All you people are the same, you come here with your fancy ideas."

Marina was conscious that every time she left her rooms, she was followed by resentful eyes. Besides, she was feeling a little ridiculous. Crimson satin garters, really!

She discussed the thing with Philip, and decided that payment in kind was more practical. She arranged that Charlie should be supplied, in addition to a pound of meat twice a week, with vegetables. Once again Mrs.

Pond came on a deputation of protest. All the natives in the building were demanding vegetables. "They aren't used to it," she complained. "Their stomachs aren't like ours. They don't need vegetables. You're just putting ideas into their heads."

"According to the regulations," Marina pointed out in that high clear voice, "Africans should be supplied with vegetables."

"Where did you get that from?" said Mrs. Pond suspiciously.

Marina produced the regulations, which Mrs. Pond read in grim silence. "The Government doesn't have to pay for it," she pointed out, very aggrieved. And then, "They're getting out of hand, that's what it is. There'll be trouble, you mark my words . . . "

Marina completed her disgrace on the day when she bought a second-hand iron bedstead and installed it in Charlie's room. That her servant should have to sleep on the bare cement floor, wrapped in a blanket, this she could no longer tolerate. As for Charlie, he accepted his good fortune fatalistically. He could not understand Marina. She appeared to feel guilty about telling him to do the simplest thing, such as clearing away cobwebs he had forgotten. Mrs. Skinner would have docked his wages, and Mr. Skinner cuffed him. This woman presented him with a new bed on the day that he broke her best cut-glass bowl.

He bought himself some new ties, and began swaggering around the back yard among the other servants, whose attitude towards him was as one might expect; one did not expect justice from the white man, whose ways were incomprehensible, but there should be a certain proportion: why should Charlie be the one to chance on an employer who presented him with a fine bed, extra meat, vegetables, and gave him two afternoons off a week instead of one? They looked unkindly at Charlie, as he swanked across the yard in his fine new clothes; they might even shout sarcastic remarks after him. But Charlie was too good-natured and friendly a person to relish such a situation. He made a joke of it, in self-defence, as Marina soon learned.

She had discovered that there was no need to share the complicated social life of the building in order to find out what went on. If, for instance, Mrs. Pond had quarrelled with a neighbour over some sugar that had not been returned, so that all the women were taking sides, there was no need to listen to Mrs. Pond herself to find the truth. Instead, one went to the kitchen window overlooking the back yard, hid oneself behind the curtain, and peered out at the servants.

There they stood, leaning on their axes, or in the intervals of pegging the washing, a group of laughing and gesticulating men, who were creating the new chapter in that perpetually unrolling saga, the extraordinary life of the white people, their masters, in 138 Cecil John Rhodes Vista . . .

February, Mrs. Pond's servant, stepped forward, while the others fell back in a circle around him, already grinning appreciatively. He thrust out his chest, stuck out his chin, and over a bad-tempered face he stretched his mouth in a smile so poisonously ingratiating that his audience roared and slapped their knees with delight. He was Mrs. Pond, one could not mistake it. He minced over to an invisible person, put on an attitude of supplication, held out his hand, received something in it. He returned to the centre of the circle, and looked at what he held with a triumphant smile. In one hand he held an invisible cup, with the other he spooned in invisible sugar. He was Mrs. Pond, drinking her tea, with immense satisfaction, in small dainty sips. Then he belched, rubbed his belly, smacked his lips. Entering into the game another servant came forward, and acted a falsely amiable woman: hands on hips, the jutting elbows, the whole angry body showing indigna- tion, but the face was smiling. February drew himself up, nodded and smiled, turned himself about, lifted something from the air behind him, and began pouring it out: sugar, one could positively hear it trickling. He took the container, and handed it proudly to the waiting visitor. But just as it was taken from him, he changed his mind. A look of agonised greed came over his face, and he withdrew the sugar. Hastily turning himself back, throwing furtive glances over his shoulder, he poured back some of the sugar, then, slowly, as if it hurt to do it, he forced himself round, held out the sugar, and again—just as it left his hand, he grabbed it and poured back just a little more. The other servants were rolling with laughter, as the two men faced each other in the centre of the yard, one indignant, but still polite, screwing up his eyes at the returned sugar, as if there were too small a quantity to be seen, while February held it out at arm's length, his face contorted with the agony it caused him to return it at all. Suddenly the two sprang together, faced each other like a pair of angry hens, and began screeching and flailing their arms.

"February!" came a shout from Mrs. Pond's flat, in her loud, shrill voice. "February, I told you to do the ironing!"

"Madam!" said February, in his politest voice. He walked backwards to the steps, his face screwed up in a grimace of martyred suffering; as he reached the steps, his body fell into the pose of a willing servant, and he walked hastily into the kitchen, where Mrs. Pond was waiting for him.

But the other servants remained, unwilling to drop the game. There was a moment of indecision. They glanced guiltily at the back of the building: perhaps some of the other women were watching? No, complete silence. It was mid-morning, the sun poured down, the shadows lay deep under the big tree, the sap crystallised into little rivulets like burnt toffee on the wood chips, and sent a warm fragrance mingling into the odours of dust and warmed foliage. For the moment, they could not think of anything to do, they might as well go on with the wood-chopping. One yawned, another lifted his axe and let it fall into a log of wood, where it was held, vibrating. He plucked the handle, and it thrummed like a deep guitar note. At once, delightedly, the men gathered around the embedded axe. One twanged it, and the others began to sing. At first Marina was unable to make out the words. Then she heard:

> *There's a man who comes to our house,*
> *When poppa goes away,*
> *Poppa comes back, and . . .*

The men were laughing, and looking at No. 4 of the flats, where a certain lady was housed whose husband worked on the railways. They sang it again:

> *There's a man who comes to this house,*
> *Every single day,*
> *The baas comes back, and*
> *The man goes away . . .*

Marina found that she was angry. Really! The thing had turned into another drama. Charlie, her own servant, was driving an imaginary engine across the yard, chuff chuff, like a child, while two of the others, seated on a log of wood were—really, it was positively obscene!

Marina came away from the window, and reasoned with herself. She was using, in her mind, one of the formulae of the country: *What can one expect?*

At this moment, while she was standing beside the kitchen-table, arguing with her anger, she heard the shrill cry: "Peas! Nice potatoes! Cabbage! Ver' chip!"

Yes, she needed vegetables. She went to the back door. There stood a native woman, with a baby on her back, carefully unslinging the sacks of vegetables which she had supported over her shoulder. She opened the mouth of one, displaying the soft mass of green pea-pods.

"How much?"

"Only one sheeling," said the woman hopefully.

"What!" began Marina, in protest; for this was twice what the shops charged. Then she stopped. Poor woman. No woman should have to carry a heavy child on her back, and great sacks of vegetables from house to house, street to street, all day—"Give me a pound," she said. Using a tin cup, the woman ladled out a small quantity of peas. Marina nearly insisted on weighing them; then she remembered how Mrs. Pond brought her scales out to the back door, on these occasions, shouting abuse at the vendor, if there was short weight. She took in the peas, and brought out a shilling. The woman, who had not expected this, gave Marina a considering look and fell into the pose of a suppliant. She held out her hands, palms upwards, her head bowed, and murmured: "Present, missus, present for my baby."

Again Marina hesitated. She looked at the woman, with her whining face and shifty eyes, and disliked her intensely. The phrase: What can one expect? came to the surface of her mind; and she went indoors and returned with sweets. The woman received them in open, humble palms, and promptly popped half into her own mouth. Then she said: "Dress, missus?"

"No," said Marina, with energy. Why should she?

Without a sign of disappointment, the woman twisted the necks of the sacks around her hand, and dragged them after her over the dust of the yard, and joined the group of servants who were watching this scene with interest. They exchanged greetings. The woman sat down on a log, easing her strained back, and moved the baby around under her armpit, still in its sling, so it could reach her breast. Charlie, the dandy, bent over her, and they began a flirtation. The others fell back. Who, indeed, could compete with that rainbow tie, the satin garters? Charlie was persuasive and assured, the woman bridling and laughing. It went on for some minutes until the baby let the nipple fall from its mouth. Then the woman got up, still laughing, shrugged the baby back into position in the small of her back, pulled the great sacks over one shoulder, and walked off, calling shrilly back to Charlie, so that all the men laughed. Suddenly they all became silent. The nurse-girl emerged from Mrs. Black's flat, and sauntered slowly past them. She was a little creature, a child, in a tight pink cotton dress, her hair braided into a dozen tiny plaits that stuck out all over her head, with a childish face that was usually vivacious and mischievous. But now she looked mournful. She dragged her feet as she walked past Charlie, and gave him a long reproachful look. Jealousy, thought Marina, there was no doubt of that! And Charlie was looking uncomfortable—one could not mistake that either. But surely not! Why, she wasn't old enough for this sort of thing. The phrase, *this sort of thing,* struck Marina herself as a shameful evasion, and she examined it. Then she shrugged and said to herself: All the same, where did the girl sleep? Presumably in one of these rooms, with the men of the place?

Theresa (she had been named after Saint Theresa at the mission school where she had been educated) tossed her head in the direction of the departing seller of vegetables, gave Charlie a final supplicating glance, and disappeared into the sanitary lane.

The men began laughing again, and this time the laughter was directed at Charlie, who received it grinning self-consciously.

Now February, who had finished the ironing, came from Mrs. Pond's flat and began hanging clothes over the line to air. The white things dazzled in the sun and made sharp, black shadows across the red dust. He called out to the others—what interesting events had happened since he went indoors? They laughed, shouted back. He finished pegging the clothes and went over to the others. The group stood under the big tree, talking; Marina, still watching, suddenly felt her cheeks grow hot. Charlie had separated himself off and, with a condensing, bowed movement of his body, had become the African woman, the seller of vegetables. Bent sideways with the weight of sacks, his belly thrust out to balance the heavy baby, he approached a log of wood—her own back step. Then he straightened, sprang back, stretched upward, and pulled from the tree a frond of leaves. These he balanced on his head, and suddenly Marina saw herself. Very straight, precise, finicky, with a prim little face peering this way and that under the broad hat, hands clasped in front of her, she advanced to the log of wood and stood looking downwards.

"Peas, cabbage, potatoes," said Charlie, in a shrill female voice.

"How much?" he answered himself, in Marina's precise, nervous voice.

"Ten sheelings a pound, missus, only ten sheelings a pound!" said Charlie, suddenly writhing on the log in an ecstasy of humility.

"How ridiculous!" said Marina, in that high, alas, absurdly high voice.

Marina watched herself hesitate, her face showing mixed indignation and guilt and, finally, indecision. Charlie nodded twice, said nervously: "Of course, but certainly." Then, in a hurried, embarrassed way, he retreated, and came back, his arms full. He opened them and stood aside to avoid a falling shower of money. For a moment he mimed the African woman and, squatting on the ground, hastily raked in the money and stuffed it into his shirt. Then he stood up—Marina again. He bent uncertainly, with a cross, uncomfortable face, looking down. Then he bent stiffly and picked up a leaf—a single pea-pod, Marina realized—and marched off, looking at the leaf, saying: "Cheap, very cheap!" one hand balancing the leaves on his head, his two feet set prim and precise in front of him.

As the laughter broke out from all the servants, Marina, who was not far from tears, stood by the window and said to herself: Serve you right for eavesdropping.

A clock struck. Various female voices shouted from their respective kitchens:

"February!" "Noah!" "Thursday!" "Sixpence!" "Blackbird!"

The morning lull was over. Time to prepare the midday meal for the white people. The yard was deserted, save for Theresa the nurse-girl returning disconsolately from the sanitary lane, dragging her feet through the dust. Among the stiff quills of hair on her head she had perched a half-faded yellow flower that she had found in one of the rubbish-cans. She looked hopefully at Marina's flat for a glimpse of Charlie; then slowly entered Mrs. Black's.

It happened that Philip was away on one of his trips. Marina ate her lunch by herself, while Charlie, attired in his waiter's outfit, served her food. Not a trace of the cheerful clown remained in his manner. He appeared friendly, though nervous; at any moment, he seemed to be thinking, this strange white woman might revert to type and start scolding and shouting.

As Marina rose from the card-table, being careful not to bump her head on the window, she happened to glance out at the yard and saw Theresa, who was standing under the tree with the youngest of her charges in her arms. The baby was reaching up to play with the leaves. Theresa's eyes were fixed on Charlie's kitchen.

"Charlie," said Marina, "where does Theresa sleep?"

Charlie was startled. He avoided her eyes and muttered: "I don't know, madam."

"But you must know, surely," said Marina, and heard her own voice climb to that high, insistent tone which Charlie had so successfully imitated.

He did not answer.

"How old is Theresa?"

"I don't know." This was true, for he did not even know his own age. As for Theresa, he saw the spindly, little-girl body, with the sharp young breasts pushing out the pink stuff of the dress she wore; he saw the new languor of her walk as she passed him. "She is nurse for Mrs. Black," he said sullenly, meaning: "Ask Mrs. Black. What's it got to do with me?"

Marina said: "Very well," and went out. As she did so she saw Charlie wave to Theresa through the gauze of the porch. Theresa pretended not to see. She was punishing him, because of the vegetable woman.

In the front room the light was falling full on the highland cattle, so that the glass was a square, blinding glitter. Marina shifted her seat, so that her eyes were no longer troubled by it, and contemplated those odious cattle. Why was it that Charlie, who broke a quite fantastic number of cups, saucers, and vases, never—as Mrs. Skinner said he might—put that vigorously-jerking broom-handle through the glass? But it seemed he liked the picture. Marina had seen him standing in front of it, admiring it. Cattle, Marina knew from Philip, played a part in native tribal life that could only be described as religious—might it be that . . .

Some letters slapped on to the cement of the verandah, slid over its polished surface, and came to rest in the doorway. Two letters. Marina watched the uniformed postboy cycle slowly down the front of the building, flinging in the letters, eight times, slap, slap, slap, grinning with pleasure at his own skill. There was a shout of rage. One of the women yelled after him: "You lazy black bastard, can't you even get off your bicycle to deliver the letters?" The postman, without taking any notice, cycled slowly off to the next house.

This was the hour of heat, when all activity faded into somnolence. The servants were away at the back, eating their midday meal. In the eight flats, separated by the flimsy walls which allowed every sound to be heard, the women reclined, sleeping, or lazily gossiping. Marina could hear Mrs. Pond, three rooms away, saying: "The fuss she made over a half a pound of sugar, you would think . . . "

Marina yawned. What a lazy life this was! She decided, at that moment, that she would put an end to this nonsense of hoping, year after year, for some miracle that would provide her, Marina Giles, with a nice house, a garden, and the other vanishing amenities of life. They would buy one of those suburban houses and she would have a baby. She would have several babies. Why not? Nursemaids cost practically nothing. She would become a domestic creature and learn to discuss servants and children with women like Mrs. Black and Mrs. Skinner. Why not? What had she expected? Ah, what had she not expected! For a moment she allowed herself to dream of that large house, that fine exotic garden, the free and amiable life released from the tensions and pressures of modern existence. She dreamed quite absurdly—but then, if no one dreamed these dreams, no one would emigrate, continents would remain undeveloped, and then what would happen to Charlie, whose salvation was (so the statesmen and newspapers continually proclaimed) contact with Mrs. Pond and Mrs. Skinner—white civilisation, in short.

But the phrase "white civilisation" was already coming to affect Marina as violently as it affects everyone else in that violent continent. It is a phrase like "white man's burden," "way of life" or "colour bar"—all of which are certain to touch off emotions better not classified. Marina was alarmed to find that these phrases were beginning to produce in her a feeling of fatigued distaste. For the liberal, so vociferously disapproving in the first six months, is quite certain to turn his back on the whole affair before the end of a year. Marina would soon be finding herself profoundly bored by politics.

But at this moment, having taken the momentous decision, she was quite light-hearted. After all, the house next door to this building was an eyesore, with its corrugated iron and brick and wood flung hastily together; and yet it was beautiful, covered with the yellow and purple and crimson creepers. Yes, they would buy a house in the suburbs, shroud it with greenery, and have four children; and Philip would be perfectly happy rushing violently around the country in a permanent state of moral indignation, and thus they would both be usefully occupied.

Marina reached for the two letters, which still lay just inside the door, where they had been so expertly flung, and opened the first. It was from Mrs. Skinner, written from Cape Town, where she was, rather uneasily, it seemed, on holiday.

> I can't help worrying if everything is all right, and the furniture. Perhaps I ought to have packed away the things, because no stranger understands. I hope Charlie is not getting cheeky, he needs a firm hand, and I forgot to tell you you must deduct one shilling from his wages because he came back late one afternoon, instead of five o'clock as I said, and I had to teach him a lesson.
>
> Yours truly,
> *Emily Skinner*
>
> P.S. I hope the picture is continuing all right.

The second was from Philip.

> I'm afraid I shan't be back tomorrow as Smith suggests while we are here we might as well run over to the Nwenze reserve. It's only just across the river, about seventy miles as the crow flies, but the roads are anybody's guess, after the wet season. Spent this morning as planned, trying to persuade these blacks it is better to have one fat ox than ten all skin and bone, never seen such erosion in my life, gullies twenty feet deep, and the whole tribe will starve next dry season, but you can talk till you are blue, they won't kill a beast till they're forced, and that's what it will come to, and then imagine the outcry from the people back home . . .

At this point Marina remarked to herself: Well, well; and continued:

> You can imagine Screech-Jones or one of them shouting in the House: Compulsion of the poor natives. My eye. It's for their own good. Until all this mystical nonsense about cattle is driven out of their fat heads, we might as well save our breath. You should have seen where I was this morning! To get the reserve back in use, alone, would take the entire vote this year for the whole country,

otherwise the whole place will be a desert, it's all perfectly obvious, but you'll never get this damned Government to see that in a hundred years, and it'll be too late in five.

In haste,
Phil

P.S. I do hope everything is all right, dear, I'll try not to be late.

That night Marina took her evening meal early so that Charlie might finish the washing-up and get off. She was reading in the front room when she understood that her ear was straining through the noise from the wirelesses all around her for a quite different sort of music. Yes, it was a banjo, and loud singing, coming from the servants' rooms, and there was a quality in it that was not to be heard from any wireless set. Marina went through the rooms to the kitchen window. The deserted yard, roofed high with moon and stars, was slatted and barred with light from the eight back doors. The windows of the four servants' rooms gleamed dully; and from the room Charlie shared with February came laughter and singing and the thrumming of the banjo.

> *There's a man who comes to our house,*
> *When poppa goes away . . .*

Marina smiled. It was a maternal smile. (As Mrs. Pond might remark, in a good mood: They are nothing but children.) She liked to think that these men were having a party. And women too: she could hear shrill female voices. How on earth did they all fit into that tiny room? As she returned through the back porch, she heard a man's voice shouting: "Shut up there! Shut up, I say!" Mr. Black from his back porch: "Don't make so much noise."

Complete silence. Marina could see Mr. Black's long, black shadow poised motionless: he was listening. Marina heard him grumble: "Can't hear yourself think with these bastards . . . " He went back into his front room, and the sound of his heavy feet on the wood floor was absorbed by their wireless playing: I love you, Yes I do, I love you . . . Slam! Mr. Black was in a rage.

Marina continued to read. It was not long before once more her distracted ear warned her that riotous music had begun again. They were singing: Congo Conga Conga, we do it in the Congo . . .

Steps on the verandah, a loud knock, and Mr. Black entered.

"Mrs. Giles, your boy's gone haywire. Listen to the din."

Marina said politely: "Do sit down, Mr. Black."

Mr. Black, who in England (from whence he had come as a child) would have been a lanky, pallid, genteel clerk, was in this country an assistant in a haberdasher's; but because of his sun-filled and energetic week-ends, he gave the impression, at first glance, of being that burly young Colonial one sees on advertisements for Empire tobacco. He was thin, bony, muscular, sunburnt; he had the free and easy Colonial manner, the back-slapping air that is always just a little too conscious. "Look," it seems to say, "in this country we are all equal (among the whites, that is—that goes without saying) and I'll fight the first person who suggests anything to the contrary." Democracy, as it were, with one eye on the audience. But alas, he was still a clerk, and felt it; and if there was one class of person he detested it was the civil servant; and if there was another, it was the person new from "Home."

Here they were, united in one person, Marina Giles, wife of Philip Giles, soil expert for the Department of Lands and Afforestation, Marina, whose mere appearance acutely irritated him, every time he saw her moving delicately through the red dust, in her straw hat, white gloves, and touch-me-not manner.

"I say!" he said aggressively, his face flushed, his eyes hot. "I say, what are you going to do about it, because if you don't, I shall."

"I don't doubt it," said Marina precisely; "but I really fail to see why these people should not have a party, if they choose, particularly as it is not yet nine o'clock, and as far as I know there is no law to forbid them."

"Law!" said Mr. Black violently. "Party! They're on our premises, aren't they? It's for us to say. Anyway, if I know anything they're visiting without passes."

"I feel you are being unreasonable," said Marina, with the intention of sounding mildly persuasive; but in fact her voice had lifted to that fatally querulous high note, and her face was as angry and flushed as his.

"Unreasonable! My kids can't sleep with that din."

"It might help if you turned down your own wireless," said Marina sarcastically.

He lifted his fists, clenching them unconsciously. "You people . . . " he began inarticulately. "If you were a man, Mrs. Giles, I tell you straight . . . " He dropped his fists and looked around wildly as Mrs. Pond entered, her face animated with delight in the scene.

"I see Mr. Black is talking to you about your boy," she began, sugarily.

"And your boy too," said Mr. Black.

"Oh, if I had a husband," said Mrs. Pond, putting on an appearance of helpless womanhood, "February would have got what's coming to him long ago."

"For that matter," said Marina, speaking with difficulty because of her loathing for the whole thing, "I don't think you really find a husband necessary for this purpose, since it was only yesterday I saw you hitting February yourself . . ."

"He was cheeky," began Mrs. Pond indignantly.

Marina found words had failed her; but none were necessary for Mr. Black had gone striding out through her own bedroom, followed by Mrs. Pond, and she saw the pair of them cross the shadowy yard to Charlie's room, which was still in darkness, though the music was at a crescendo. As Mr. Black shouted: "Come out of there, you black bastards!" the noise stopped, the door swung in, and half a dozen dark forms ducked under Mr. Black's extended arm and vanished into the sanitary lane. There was a scuffle, and Mr. Black found himself grasping, at arm's length, two people—Charlie and his own nursemaid, Theresa. He let the girl go and she ran after the others. He pushed Charlie against the wall. "What do you mean by making all that noise when I told you not to?" he shouted.

"That's right, that's right," gasped Mrs. Pond from behind him, running this way and that around the pair so as to get a good view.

Charlie, keeping his elbow lifted to shield his head, said: "I'm sorry, baas, I'm sorry, I'm sorry . . . "

"Sorry!" Mr. Black, keeping firm grasp of Charlie's shoulder, lifted his other hand to hit him; Charlie jerked his arm up over his face. Mr. Black's fist, expecting to encounter a cheek, met instead the rising arm and he was thrown off balance and staggered back. "How dare you hit me," he shouted furiously, rushing at Charlie; but Charlie had escaped in a bound over the rubbish-cans and away into the lane.

Mr. Black sent angry shouts after him; then turned and said indignantly to Mrs. Pond: "Did you see that? He hit me!"

"He's out of hand," said Mrs. Pond in a melancholy voice. "What can you expect? He's been spoilt."

They both turned to look accusingly at Marina.

"As a matter of accuracy," said Marina breathlessly, "he did not hit you."

"What, are you taking that nigger's side?" demanded Mr. Black. He was completely taken aback. He looked, amazed, at Mrs. Pond, and said: "She's taking his side!"

"It's not a question of sides," said Marina in that high, precise voice. "I was standing here and saw what happened. You know quite well he did not hit you. He wouldn't dare."

"Yes," said Mr. Black, "that's what a state things have come to, with the Government spoiling them, they can hit us and get away with it, and if we touch them we get fined."

"I don't know how many times I've seen the servants hit since I've been here," said Marina angrily. "If it is the law, it is a remarkably ineffective one."

"Well, I'm going to get the police," shouted Mr. Black, running back to his own flat. "No black bastard is going to hit me and get away with it. Besides, they can all be fined for visiting without passes after nine at night . . . "

"Don't be childish," said Marina, and went inside her rooms. She was crying with rage. Happening to catch a glimpse of herself in the mirror as she passed it she hastily went to splash cold water on her face, for she looked—there was no getting away from it—rather like a particularly genteel school-marm in a temper. When she reached the front room, she found Charlie there throwing terrified glances out into the verandah for fear of Mr. Black or Mrs. Pond.

"Madam," he said. "Madam, I didn't hit him."

"No, of course not," said Marina; and she was astonished to find that she was feeling irritated with him, Charlie. "Really," she said, "must you make such a noise and cause all this fuss."

"But, madam . . . "

"Oh, all right," she said crossly. "All right. But you aren't supposed to . . . who were all those people?"

"My friends."

"Where from?" He was silent. "Did they have passes to be out visiting?" He shifted his eyes uncomfortably. "Well, really," she said irritably, "if the law is that you must have passes, for heaven's sake . . . " Charlie's whole appearance had changed; a moment before he had been a helpless small boy; he had become a sullen young man: this white woman was like all the rest.

Marina controlled her irritation and said gently: "Listen, Charlie, I don't agree with the law and all this nonsense about passes, but I can't change it, and it does seem to me . . . " Once again her irritation rose, once again she suppressed it, and found herself without words. Which was just as well, for Charlie was gazing at her with puzzled suspicion since he saw all white people as a sort of homogeneous mass, a white layer, as it were, spread over the mass of blacks, all concerned in making life as difficult as possible for him and his kind; the idea that a white person might not agree with passes, curfew, and so on was so outrageously new that he could not admit it to his mind at once. Marina said: "Oh, well, Charlie, I know you didn't mean it, and I think you'd better go quietly to bed and keep out of Mr. Black's way, if you can."

"Yes, madam," he said submissively. As he went, she asked: "Does Theresa sleep in the same room as Mr. Black's boy?"

He was silent. "Does she sleep in your room perhaps?" And, as the silence persisted: "Do you mean to tell me she sleeps with you and February?" No reply. "But Charlie . . . " She was about to protest again: But Theresa's nothing but a child; but this did not appear to be an argument which appealed to him.

There were loud voices outside, and Charlie shrank back: "The police!" he said, terrified.

"Ridiculous nonsense," said Marina. But looking out she saw a white policeman; and Charlie fled out through her bedroom and she heard the back door slam. It appeared he had no real confidence in her sympathy.

The policeman entered, alone. "I understand there's been a spot of trouble," he said.

"Over nothing," said Marina.

"A tenant in this building claims he was hit by your servant."

"It's not true. I saw the whole thing."

The policeman looked at her doubtfully and said: "Well, that makes things difficult, doesn't it?" After a moment he said: "Excuse me a moment," and went out. Marina saw him talking to Mr. Black outside her front steps. Soon the policeman came back. "In view of your attitude the charge has been dropped," he said.

"So I should think. I've never heard of anything so silly."

"Well, Mrs. Giles, there was a row going on, and they all ran away, so they must have had guilty consciences about something, probably no passes. And you know they can't have women in their rooms."

"The woman was Mr. Black's own nursemaid."

"He says the girl is supposed to sleep in the location with her father."

"It's a pity Mr. Black takes so little interest in his servants not to know. She sleeps here. How can a child that age be expected to walk five miles here every morning, to be here at seven, and walk five miles back at seven in the evening?"

The policeman gave her a look: "Plenty do it," he said. "It's not the same for them as it is for us. Besides, it's the law."

"The law!" said Marina bitterly.

Again the policeman looked uncertain. He was a pleasant young man, he dealt continually with cases of this kind, he always tried to smooth things over, if he could. He decided on his usual course, despite Marina's hostile manner. "I think the best thing to do," he said, "is if we leave the whole thing. We'll never catch them now, anyway—miles away by this time. And Mr. Black has dropped the charge. You have a talk to your boy and tell him to be careful. Otherwise he'll be getting himself into trouble."

"And what are you going to do about the nurse? It amounts to this: It's convenient for the Blacks to have her here, so they can go out at night, and so on, so they ask no questions. It's a damned disgrace, a girl of that age expected to share a room with the men."

"It's not right, not right at all," said the policeman. "I'll have a word with Mr. Black." And he took his leave, politely.

That night Marina relieved her feelings by writing a long letter about the incident to a friend of hers in England, full of phrases such as "police state," "despotism," and "fascism"; which caused that friend to reply, rather tolerantly, to the effect that she understood these hot climates were rather upsetting and she did so hope Marina was looking after herself, one must have a sense of proportion, after all.

And, in fact, by the morning Marina was wondering why she had allowed herself to be so angry about such an absurd incident. What a country this was! Unless she was very careful she would find herself flying off into hysterical states as easily, for instance, as Mr. Black. If one was going to make a life here, one should adjust oneself . . .

Charlie was grateful and apologetic. He repeated: "Thank you, madam. Thank you." He brought her a present of some vegetables and said: "You are my father and my mother." Marina was deeply touched. He rolled his eyes and made a half-rueful joke: "The police are no good, madam." She discovered that he had spent the night in a friend's room some streets away for fear the police might come and take him to prison. For, in Charlie's mind, the police meant only one thing. Marina tried to explain that one wasn't put in prison without a trial of some sort; but he merely looked at her doubtfully, as if she were making fun of him. So she left it.

And Theresa? She was still working for the Blacks. A few evenings later, when Marina went to turn off the lights before going to bed, she saw Theresa gliding into Charlie's room. She said nothing about it: what could one expect?

Charlie had accepted her as an ally. One day, as he served vegetables, reaching behind her ducked head so that they might be presented, correctly, from the left, he remarked: "That Theresa, she very nice, madam."

"Very nice," said Marina, uncomfortably helping herself to peas from an acute angle, sideways.

"Theresa says, perhaps madam give her a dress?"

"I'll see what I can find," said Marina, after a pause.

"Thank you very much, thank you, madam," he said. He was grateful; but certainly he had expected just that reply: his thanks were not perfunctory, but he thanked her as one might thank one's parents, for instance, from whom one expects such goodness, even takes it a little for granted.

Next morning, when Marina and Philip lay as usual, trying to sleep through the cheerful din of cleaning from the next room, which included a shrill and sprightly whistling, there was a loud crash.

"Oh, damn the man," said Philip, turning over and pulling the clothes over his ears.

"With a bit of luck he's broken that picture," said Marina. She put a dressing-gown on, and went next door. On the floor lay fragments of white porcelain—her favourite vase, which she had brought all the way from England. Charlie was standing over it. "Sorry, madam," he said, cheerfully contrite.

Now that vase had stood on a shelf high above Charlie's head—to break it at all was something of an acrobatic feat . . . Marina pulled herself together. After all, it was only a vase. But her favourite vase, she had had it ten years: she stood there, tightening her lips over all the angry things she would have liked to say, looking at Charlie, who was carelessly sweeping the pieces together. He glanced up, saw her face, and said hastily, really apologetic: "Sorry madam, very, very sorry, madam." Then he added reassuringly: "But the picture is all right." He gazed admiringly up at the highland cattle which he clearly considered the main treasure of the room.

"So it is," said Marina, suppressing the impulse to say: Charlie, if you break that picture I'll give you a present. "Oh, well," she said, "I suppose it doesn't matter. Just sweep the pieces up."

"Yes, missus, thank you," said Charlie cheerfully; and she left, wondering how she had put herself in a position where it became impossible to be legitimately cross with her own servant. Coming back into that room some time later to ask Charlie why the breakfast was so late, she found him still standing under the picture. "Very nice picture," he said, reluctantly leaving the room. "Six oxes. Six fine big oxes, in one picture!"

The work in the flat was finished by mid-morning. Marina told Charlie she wanted to bake; he filled the old-fashioned stove with wood for her, heated the oven and went off into the yard, whistling. She stood at the window, mixing her cake, looking out into the yard.

Charlie came out of his room, sat down on a big log under the tree, stretched his legs before him, and propped a small mirror between his knees. He took a large metal comb and began to work on his thick hair, which he endeavoured to make lie flat, white-man's fashion. He was sitting with his back to the yard.

Soon Theresa came out with a big enamel basin filled with washing. She wore the dress Marina had given her. It was an old black cocktail dress which hung loosely around her calves, and she had tied it at the waist with a big sash of printed cotton. The sophisticated dress, treated thus, hanging full and shapeless, looked grandmotherly and old-fashioned; she looked like an impish child in a matron's garb. She stood beside the washing-line gazing at Charlie's back; then slowly she began pegging the clothes, with long intervals to watch him.

It seemed Charlie did not know she was there. Then his pose of concentrated self-worship froze into a long, close inspection in the mirror, which he began to rock gently between his knees so that the sunlight flashed up from it, first into the branches over his head, then over the dust of the yard to the girl's feet, up her body: the ray of light hovered like a butterfly around her, then settled on her face. She remained still, her eyes shut, with the teasing light flickering on her lids. Then she opened them and exclaimed, indignantly: *"Hau!"*

Charlie did not move. He held the mirror sideways on his knees, where he could see Theresa, and pretended to be hard at work on his parting. For a few seconds they remained thus, Charlie staring into the mirror, Theresa watching him reproachfully. Then he put the mirror back into his pocket, stretched his arms back in a magnificent slow yawn, and remained there, rocking back and forth on his log.

Theresa looked at him thoughtfully; and—since now he could not see her—darted over to the hedge, plucked a scarlet hibiscus flower, and returned to the washing-line, where she continued to hang the washing, the flower held lightly between her lips.

Charlie got up, his arms still locked behind his head, and began a sort of shuffle dance in the sunny dust, among the fallen leaves and chips of wood. It was a crisp, bright morning, the sky was as blue and fresh as the sea: this idyllic scene moved Marina deeply, it must be confessed.

Still dancing, Charlie let his arms fall, turned himself round, and his hands began to move in time with his feet. Jerking, lolling, posing, he slowly approached the centre of the yard, apparently oblivious of Theresa's existence.

There was a shout from the back of the building: "Theresa!" Charlie glanced around, then dived hastily into his room. The girl, left alone, gazed at the dark door into which Charlie had vanished, sighed, and blinked gently at the sunlight. A second shout: "Theresa, are you going to be all day with that washing?"

She tucked the flower among the stiff quills of hair on her head and bent to the basin that stood in the dust. The washing flapped and billowed all around her, so that the small, wiry form appeared to be wrestling with the big, ungainly sheets. Charlie ducked out of his door and ran quickly up the hedge, out of sight of Mrs. Black. He stopped, watching Theresa, who was still fighting with the washing. He whistled, she ignored him. He whistled again, changing key; the long note dissolved into a dance tune, and he sauntered deliberately up the hedge, weight shifting from hip to hip with each step. It was almost a dance: the buttocks sharply protruding and then withdrawn inwards after the prancing, lifting knees. The girl stood motionless, gazing at him, tantalised. She glanced quickly over her shoulder at the building, then ran across the yard to Charlie. The two of them, safe for the moment beside the hedge, looked guiltily for possible spies. They saw Marina behind her curtain—an earnest English face, apparently wrestling with some severe moral problem. But she was a friend. Had she not saved Charlie from the police? Besides, she immediately vanished.

Hidden behind the curtain, Marina saw the couple face each other, smiling. Then the girl tossed her head and turned away. She picked a second flower from the hedge, held it to her lips, and began swinging lightly from the waist, sending Charlie provocative glances over her shoulder that were half disdain and half invitation. To Marina it was as if a mischievous black urchin was playing the part of a coquette; but Charlie was watching with a broad and appreciative smile. He followed her, strolling in an assured and masterful way, as she went into his room. The door closed.

Marina discovered herself to be furious. Really the whole thing was preposterous!

"Philip," she said energetically that night, "we should do something."

"What?" asked Philip, practically. Marina could not think of a sensible answer. Philip gave a short lecture on the problems of the indigenous African peoples who were halfway between the tribal society and modern industrialisation. The thing, of course, should be tackled at its root. Since he was a soil expert, the root, to him, was a sensible organisation of the land. (If he had been a churchman, the root would have been a correct attitude to whichever God he happened to represent; if an authority on money, a mere adjustment of currency would have provided the solution—there is very little comfort from experts these days.) To Philip, it was all as clear as daylight. These people had no idea at all how to farm. They must give up this old attitude of theirs, based on the days when a tribe worked out one piece of ground and moved on to the next; they must learn to conserve their soil and, above all, to regard cattle, not as a sort of spiritual currency, but as an organic part of farm-work. (The word *organic* occurred very frequently in these lectures by Philip.) Once these things were done, everything else would follow . . .

"But in the meantime, Philip, it is quite possible that something may *happen* to Theresa, and she can't be more than fifteen, if that . . . "

Philip looked a little dazed as he adjusted himself from the level on which he had been thinking to the level of Theresa: women always think so personally! He said, rather stiffly: "Well, old girl, in periods of transition, what can one expect?"

What one might expect did in fact occur, and quite soon. One of those long ripples of gossip and delighted indignation passed from one end to the other of 138 Cecil John Rhodes Vista. Mrs. Black's Theresa had got herself into trouble; these girls had no morals; no better than savages; besides, she was a thief. She was wearing clothes that had not been given to her by Mrs. Black. Marina paid a formal visit to Mrs. Black in order to say that she had given Theresa various dresses. The air was not at all cleared. No one cared to what degree Theresa had been corrupted, or by whom. The feeling was: if not Theresa, then someone else. Acts of theft, adultery, and so on were necessary to preserve the proper balance between black and white; the balance was upset, not by Theresa, who played her allotted part, but by Marina, who insisted on introducing these Fabian scruples into a clear-cut situation.

Mrs. Black was polite, grudging, distrustful. She said: "Well, if you've given her the dresses, then it's all right." She added: "But it doesn't alter what she's done, does it now?" Marina could make no reply. The white women of the building continued to gossip and pass judgment for some days: one must, after all, talk about something. It was odd, however, that Mrs. Black made no move at all to sack Theresa, that immoral person, who continued to look after the children with her usual good-natured efficiency, in order that Mrs. Black might have time to gossip and drink tea.

So Marina, who had already made plans to rescue Theresa when she was flung out of her job, found that no rescue was necessary. From time to time Mrs. Black overflowed into reproaches, and lectures about sin. Theresa wept like the child she was, her fists stuck into her eyes. Five minutes afterwards she was helping Mrs. Black bath the baby, or flirting with Charlie in the yard.

For the principals of this scandal seemed the least concerned about it. The days passed, and at last Marina said to Charlie: "Well and what are you going to do now?"

"Madam?" said Charlie. He really did not know what she meant.

"About Theresa," said Marina sternly.

"Theresa she going to have a baby," said Charlie, trying to look penitent, but succeeding only in looking proud.

"It's all very well," said Marina. Charlie continued to sweep the ver- andah, smiling to himself. "But Charlie . . . " began Marina again.

"Madam?" said Charlie, resting on his broom and waiting for her to go on.

"You can't just let things go on, and what will happen to the child when it is born?"

His face puckered, he sighed, and finally he went on sweeping, rather slower than before.

Suddenly Marina stamped her foot and said: "Charlie, this really won't do!" She was really furious.

"Madam!" said Charlie reproachfully.

"Everybody has a good time," said Marina. "You and Theresa enjoy yourselves, all these females have a lovely time, gossiping, and the only thing no one ever thinks about is the baby." After a pause, when he did not reply, she went on: "I suppose you and Theresa think it's quite all right for the baby to be born here, and then you two, and the baby, and February, and all the rest of your friends who have nowhere to go, will all live together in that room. It really is shocking, Charlie."

Charlie shrugged as if to say: "Well, what do you suggest?"

"Can't Theresa go and live with her father?"

Charlie's face tightened into a scowl. "Theresa's father, he no good. Theresa must work, earn money for father."

"I see." Charlie waited; he seemed to be waiting for Marina to solve this problem for him; his attitude said: I have unbounded trust and confidence in you.

"Are any of the other men working here married?"

"Yes, madam."

"Where are their wives?"

"At home." This meant, in their kraals, in the Native Reserves. But Marina had not meant the properly married wives, who usually stayed with the clan, and were visited by their men perhaps one month in a year, or in two years. She meant women like Theresa, who lived in town.

"Now listen, Charlie. Do be sensible. What happens to girls like Theresa when they have babies. Where do they live?"

He shrugged again, meaning: They live as they can, and is it my fault the white people don't let us have our families with us when they work? Suddenly he said grudgingly: "The nanny next door, she has her baby, she works."

"Where is her baby?"

Charlie jerked his head over at the servants' quarters of the next house.

"Does the baas know she has her baby there?"

He looked away, uncomfortably. "Well, and what happens when the police find out?"

He gave her a look which she understood. "Who is the father of that baby?"

He looked away; there was uncomfortable silence; and then he quickly began sweeping the verandah again.

"Charlie!" said Marina, outraged. His whole body had become defensive, sullen; his face was angry. She said energetically: "You should marry Theresa. You can't go on doing this sort of thing."

"I have a wife in my kraal," he said.

"Well, there's nothing to stop you having two wives, is there?"

Charlie pointed out that he had not yet finished paying for his first wife.

Marina thought for a moment. "Theresa's a Christian, isn't she? She was educated at the mission." Charlie shrugged. "If you marry Theresa Christian-fashion, you needn't pay lobola, need you?"

Charlie said: "The Christians only like one wife. And Theresa's father, he wants lobola."

Marina found herself delighted. At any rate he had tried to marry Theresa, and this was evidence of proper feeling. The fact that whether the position was legalized or not the baby's future was still uncertain, did not at once strike her. She was carried away by moral approval. "Well, Charlie, that's much better," she said warmly.

He gave her a rather puzzled look and shrugged again.

"How much lobola does Theresa's father want for her?"

"Plenty. He wants ten cattle."

"What nonsense!" exclaimed Marina energetically. "Where does he suppose you are going to find cattle, working in town, and where's he going to keep them?"

This seemed to annoy Charlie. "In my kraal, I have fine cattle," he pointed out. "I have six fine oxes." He swept, for a while, in silence. "Theresa's father, he mad, he mad old man. I tell him I must give three oxes this year for my own wife. Where do I find ten oxes for Theresa?"

It appeared that Charlie, no more than Theresa's father, found nothing absurd about this desire for cattle on the part of an old man living in the town location. Involuntarily she looked over her shoulder as if Philip might be listening: this conversation would have plunged him into irritated despair. Luckily he was away on one of his trips, and was at this moment almost certain to be exhorting the Africans, in some distant reserve, to abandon this irrational attitude to "fine oxes" which in fact were bound to be nothing but skin and bone, and churning whole tracts of country to dust.

"Why don't you offer Theresa's father some money?" she suggested, glancing down at Charlie's garters which were, this morning, of cherry-coloured silk.

"He wants cattle, not money. He wants Theresa not to marry, he wants her to work for him." Charlie rapidly finished sweeping the verandah and moved off, with relief, tucking the broom under his arm, with an apologetic smile which said: I know you mean well, but I'm glad to end this conversation.

But Marina was not at all inclined to drop the thing. She interviewed Theresa who, amid floods of tears, said Yes, she wanted to marry Charlie, but her father wanted too much lobola. The problem was quite simple to her, merely a question of lobola; Charlie's other wife did not concern her; nor did she, apparently, share Charlie's view that a proper wife in the kraal was one thing, while the women of the town were another.

Marina said: "Shall I come down to the location and talk to your father?"

Theresa hung her head shyly, allowed the last big tears to roll glistening down her cheeks and go splashing to the dust. "Yes, madam," she said gratefully.

Marina returned to Charlie and said she would interview the old man. He appeared restive at this suggestion. "I'll advance you some of your wages and you can pay for Theresa in instalments," she said. He glanced down at his fine shirt, his gay socks, and sighed. If he were going to spend years of life paying five shillings a month, which was all he could afford, for Theresa, then his life as a dandy was over.

Marina said crossly: "Yes, it's all very well, but you can't have it both ways."

He said hastily: "I'll go down and see the father of Theresa, madam. I go soon."

"I think you'd better," she said sternly.

When she told Philip this story he became vigorously indignant. It presented in little, he said, the whole problem of this society. The Government couldn't see an inch in front of its nose. In the first place, by allowing the lobola system to continue, this emotional attitude towards cattle was perpetuated. In the second, by making no proper arrangements for these men to have their families in the towns it made the existence of prostitutes like Theresa inevitable.

"Theresa isn't a prostitute," said Marina indignantly. "It isn't her fault."

"Of course it isn't her fault, that's what I'm saying. But she will be a prostitute, it's inevitable. When Charlie's fed up with her she'll find herself another man and have a child or two by him, and so on . . . "

"You talk about Theresa as if she were a vital statistic," said Marina, and Philip shrugged. That shrug expressed an attitude of mind which Marina would very soon find herself sharing, but she did not yet know that. She was still very worried about Theresa, and after some days she asked Charlie: "Well, and did you see Theresa's father? What did he say?"

"He wants cattle."

"Well, he can't have cattle."

"No," said Charlie, brightening. "My own wife, she cost six cattles. I paid three last year. I pay three more this year, when I go home."

"When are you going home?"

"When Mrs. Skinner comes back. She no good. Not like you, madam, you are my father and mother," he said, giving her his touching, grateful smile.

"And what will happen to Theresa?"

"She stay here." After a long, troubled silence, he said: "She my town wife. I come back to Theresa." This idea seemed to cheer him up.

And it seemed he was genuinely fond of the girl. Looking out of the kitchen window, Marina could see the pair of them, during lulls in the work, seated side by side on the big log under the tree—charming! A charming picture! "It's all very well . . . " said Marina to herself, uneasily.

Some mornings later she found Charlie in the front room, under the picture, and looking at it this time, not with reverent admiration, but rather nervously. As she came in he quickly returned to his work, but Marina could see he wanted to say something to her.

"Madam . . . "

"Well, what is it?"

"This picture costs plenty money?"

"I suppose it did, once."

"Cattles cost plenty money, madam."

"Yes so they do, Charlie."

"If you sell this picture, how much?"

"But it is Mrs. Skinner's picture."

His body drooped with disappointment. "Yes, madam," he said politely, turning away.

"But wait, Charlie—what do you want the picture for?"

"It's all right, madam." He was going out of the room.

"Stop a moment—why do you want it? You do want it, don't you?"

"Oh, yes," he said, his face lit with pleasure. He clasped his hands tight, looking at it. "Oh, yes, yes, madam!"

"What would you do with it? Keep it in your room?"

"I give it to Theresa's father."

"Wha-a-a-t?" said Marina. Slowly she absorbed this idea. "I see." she said. And then, after a pause: "I see . . . " She looked at his hopeful face, thought of Mrs. Skinner, and said suddenly, filled with an undeniably spiteful delight: "I'll give it to you, Charlie."

"Madam!" exclaimed Charlie. He even gave a couple of involuntary little steps, like a dance. "Madam, thank you, thank you."

She was as pleased as he. For a moment they stood smiling delightedly at each other. "I'll tell Mrs. Skinner that I broke it," she said. He went to the picture and lifted his hands gently to the great carved frame. "You must be careful not to break it before you get it to her father." He was staggering as he lifted it down. "Wait!" said Marina suddenly. Checking himself, he stood politely: she saw he expected her to change her mind and take back the gift. "You can't carry that great thing all the way to the location. I'll take it for you in the car!"

"Madam," he said. "Madam . . . " Then, looking helplessly around him for something, someone he could share his joy with, he said: "I'll tell Theresa now . . . " And he ran from the room like a schoolboy.

Marina went to Mrs. Black and asked that Theresa might have the afternoon off. "She had her afternoon off yesterday," said that lady sharply.

"She's going to marry Charlie," said Marina.

"She can marry him next Thursday, can't she?"

"No, because I'm taking them both down in the car to the location, to her father, and . . . "

Mrs. Black said resentfully: "She should have asked me herself."

"It seems to me," said Marina in that high, acid voice, replying not to the words Mrs. Black had used, but to what she had meant: "It seems to me that if one employs a child of fifteen, and under such conditions, the very least one can do is to assume the responsibility for her; and it seems to me quite extraordinary that you never have the slightest idea what she does, where she lives, or even that she is going to get married."

"You swallowed the dictionary?" said Mrs. Black, with an ingratiating smile. "I'm not saying she shouldn't get married; she should have got married before, that's what I'm saying."

Marina returned to her flat, feeling Mrs. Black's resentful eyes on her back: *Who the hell does she think she is, anyway?*

When Marina and Philip reached the lorry that afternoon that was waiting outside the gate, Theresa and Charlie were already sitting in the back, carefully balancing the picture on their knees. The two white people got in the front and Marina glanced anxiously through the window and said to Philip: "Do drive carefully, dear, Theresa shouldn't be bumped around."

"I'd be doing her a favour if I did bump her," said Philip grimly. He was accompanying Marina unwillingly. "Well, I don't know what you think you're going to achieve by it . . . " he had said. However, here he was, looking rather cross.

They drove down the tree-lined, shady streets, through the business area that was all concrete and modernity, past the slums where the half-caste people lived, past the factory sites, where smoke poured and hung, past the cemetery where angels and crosses gleamed white through the trees—they drove five miles, which was the distance Theresa had been expected to walk every morning and evening to her work. They turned off the main road into the location, and at once everything was quite different. No tarmac road, no avenues of beautiful trees here. Dust roads, dust paths, led from all directions inwards to the centre, where the housing area was. Dust lay thick and brown on the veld trees, the great blue sky was seen through a rust-coloured haze, dust gritted on the lips and tongue, and at once the lorry began to jolt and bounce. Marina looked back and saw Charlie and Theresa jerking and sliding with the lorry, under the great picture, clinging to each other for support, and laughing because of the joy-ride. It was the first time Theresa had ridden in a white man's car; and she was waving and calling shrill greetings to the groups of black children who ran after them.

They drove fast, bumping, so as to escape from the rivers of dust that spurted up from the wheels, making a whirling red cloud behind them, from which crowds of loitering Africans ran, cursing and angry. Soon they were in an area that was like a cheap copy of the white man's town; small houses stood in blocks, intersected by dust streets. They were two-roomed shacks with tin roofs, the sun blistering off them; and Marina said angrily: "Isn't it awful, isn't it terrible?"

Had she known that these same houses represented years of campaigning by the liberals of the city, against white public opinion, which obstinately held that houses for natives were merely another manifestation of that *Fabian* spirit from England which was spoiling the fine and uncorrupted savage, she might have been more respectful. Soon they left this new area and were among the sheds and barns that housed dozens of workers each, a state of affairs which caused Marina the acutest indignation. Another glance over her shoulder showed Theresa and Charlie giggling together like a couple of children as they tried to hold the picture still on their knees, for it slid this way and that as if it had a spiteful life of its own. "Ask Charlie where we must go," said Philip; and Marina tapped on the glass till Charlie turned his head and watched her gestures till he understood and pointed onwards with his thumb. More of these brick shacks, with throngs of Africans at their doors, who watched the car indifferently until they saw it was a Government car, and then their eyes grew wary, suspicious. And now, blocking their way, was a wire fence, and Marina looked back at Charlie for instructions, and he indicated they should stop. Philip pulled the lorry up against the fence and Charlie and Theresa jumped down from the back, came forwards and Charlie said apologetically: "Now we must walk, madam." The four went through a gap in the fence and saw a slope of soiled and matted grass that ended in a huddle of buildings on the banks of a small river.

Charlie pointed at it, and went ahead with Theresa. He held the picture on his shoulders, walking bent under it. They passed through the grass, which smelled unpleasant and was covered by a haze of flies, and came to another expanse of dust, in which were scattered buildings—no, not buildings, shacks, extraordinary huts thrown together out of every conceivable substance, with walls perhaps of sacking, or of petrol boxes, roofs of beaten tin, or bits of scrap iron.

"And what happens when it rains?" said Marina, as they wound in and out of these dwellings, among scratching chickens and snarling native mongrels. She found herself profoundly dispirited, as if something inside her said: What's the use? For this area, officially, did not exist. The law was that all the workers, the servants should live inside the location, or in one of the similar townships. But there was never enough room. People overflowed into such makeshift villages everywhere, but as they were not supposed to be there the police might at any moment swoop down and arrest them. Admittedly the police did not often swoop, as the white man must have servants, the servants must live somewhere—and so it all went on, year after year. The Government, from time to time, planned a new housing estate. On paper, all around the white man's city, were fine new townships for the blacks. One had even been built, and to this critical visitors (usually those *Fabians* from overseas) were taken, and came away impressed. They never saw these slums. And so all the time, every day, the black people came from their reserves, their kraals, drawn to the white man's city, to the glitter of money, cinemas, fine clothes; they came in their thousands, no one knew how many, making their own life, as they could, in such hovels. It was all hopeless, as long as Mrs. Black, Mr. Black, Mrs. Pond were the voters with the power; as long as the experts and administrators such as Philip had to work behind Mrs. Pond's back—for nothing is more remarkable than that democratic phenomenon, so clearly shown in this continent, where members of Parliament, civil servants (experts, in short) spend half their time and energy earnestly exhorting Mrs. Pond: For heaven's sake have some sense before it is too late; if you don't let us use enough money to house and feed these people, they'll rise and cut your throats. To which reasonable plea for self-preservation, Mrs. Pond merely turns a sullen and angry stare, muttering: They're getting out of hand, that's what it is, they're getting spoilt.

In a mood of grim despair, Marina found herself standing with Philip in front of a small shack that consisted of sheets of corrugated iron laid loosely together, resting in the dust, like a child's card castle. It was bound at the corners with string, and big stones held the sheet of iron that served as roof from flying away in the first gust of wind.

"Here, madam," said Charlie. He thrust Theresa forward. She went shyly to the dark oblong that was the door, leaned inwards, and spoke some words in her own language. After a moment an old man stooped his way out. He was perhaps not so old—impossible to say. He was lean and tall, with a lined and angry face, and eyes that lifted under heavy lids to peer at Marina and Philip. Towards Charlie he directed a long, deadly stare, then turned away. He wore a pair of old khaki trousers, an old, filthy singlet that left his long, sinewed arms bare: all the bones and muscles of his neck and shoulders showed taut and knotted under the skin.

Theresa, smiling bashfully, indicated Philip and Marina; the old man offered some words of greeting; but he was angry, he did not want to see them, so the two white people fell back a little.

Charlie now came forward with the picture and leaned it gently against the iron of the shack in a way which said: "Here you are, and that's all you are going to get from me." In these surroundings those fierce Scottish cattle seemed to shrink a little. The picture that had dominated a room with its expanse of shining glass, its heavy carved frame, seemed not so enormous now. The cattle seemed even rather absurd, shaggy creatures standing in their wet sunset, glaring with a false challenge at the group of people. The old man looked at the picture, and then said something angry to Theresa. She seemed afraid, and came forward, unknotting a piece of cloth that had lain in the folds at her waist. She handed over some small change—about three shillings in all. The old man took the money, shaking it contemptuously in his hand before he slid it into his pocket. Then he spat, showing contempt. Again he spoke to Theresa, in short, angry sentences, and at the end he flung out his arms, as if throwing something away; and she began to cry and shrank back to Charlie. Charlie laid his hand on her shoulder and pressed it; then left her standing alone and went forward to his father-in-law. He smiled, spoke persuasively, indicated Philip and Marina. The old man listened without speaking, his eyes lowered. Those eyes slid sideways to the big picture, a gleam came into them; Charlie fell silent and they all looked at the picture.

The old man began to speak, in a different voice, sad, and hopeless. He was telling how he had wooed his second wife, Theresa's mother. He spoke of the long courting, according to the old customs, how, with many gifts and courtesies between the clans, the marriage had been agreed on, how the cattle had been chosen, ten great cattle, heavy with good grazing; he told how he had driven them to Theresa's mother's family, carefully across the country, so that they might not be tired and thinned by the journey. As he spoke to the two young people he was reminding them, and himself, of that time when every action had its ritual, its meaning; he was asking them to contrast their graceless behaviour with the dignity of his own marriages, symbolized by the cattle, which were not to be thought of in terms of money, of simply buying a woman—not at all. They meant so much: a sign of good feeling, a token of union between the clans, an earnest that the woman would be looked after, an acknowledgment that she was someone very precious, whose departure would impoverish her family—the cattle were all these things and many more. The old man looked at Charlie and Theresa and seemed to say: "And what about you? What are you in comparison to what we were then?" Finally he spat again, lifted the picture and went into the dark of his hut. They could see him looking at the picture. He liked it: yes, he was pleased, in his way. But soon he left it leaning against the iron and returned to his former pose—he drew a blanket over his head and shoulders and squatted down inside the door, looking out, but not as if he still saw them or intended to make any further sign towards them.

The four were left standing there, in the dust, looking at each other.

Marina was feeling very foolish. Was that all? And Philip answered by saying brusquely, but uncomfortably: "Well, there's your wedding for you."

Theresa and Charlie had linked fingers and were together looking rather awkwardly at the white people. It was an awkward moment indeed—this was the end of it, the two were married, and it was Marina who had arranged the thing. What now?

But there was a more immediate problem. It was still early in the afternoon, the sun slanted overhead, with hours of light in it still, and presumably the newly-married couple would want to be together? Marina said: "Do you want to come back with us in the lorry, or would you rather come later?"

Charlie and Theresa spoke together in their own language, then Charlie said apologetically: "Thank you, madam, we stay."

"With Theresa's father?"

Charlie said: "He won't have Theresa now. He says Theresa can go away. He not want Theresa."

Philip said: "Don't worry, Marina, he'll take her back, he'll take her money all right." He laughed, and Marina was angry with him for laughing.

"He very cross, madam," said Charlie. He even laughed himself, but in a rather anxious way.

The old man still sat quite motionless, looking past them. There were flies at the corners of his eyes; he did not lift his hand to brush them off.

"Well . . ." said Marina. "We can give you a lift back if you like." But it was clear that Theresa was afraid of going back now; Mrs. Black might assume her afternoon off was over and make her work.

Charlie and Theresa smiled again and said, "Goodbye. Thank you, madam. Thank you, baas." They went slowly off across the dusty earth, between the hovels, towards the river, where a group of tall brick huts stood like outsize sentry-boxes. There, though neither Marina nor Philip knew it, was sold illicit liquor; there they would find a tinny gramophone playing dance music from America, there would be singing, dancing, a good time. This was the place the police came first if they were in search of criminals. Marina thought the couple were going down to the river, and she said sentimentally: "Well, they have this afternoon together, that's something."

"Yes," said Philip drily. The two were angry with each other, they did not know why. They walked in silence back to the lorry and drove home, making polite, clear sentences about indifferent topics.

Next day everything was as usual. Theresa back at work with Mrs. Black, Charlie whistling cheerfully in their own flat.

Almost immediately Marina bought a house that seemed passable, about seven miles from the centre of town, in a new suburb. Mrs. Skinner would not be returning for two weeks yes, but it was more convenient for them to move into the new home at once. The problem was Charlie. What would he do during that time? He said he was going home to visit his family. He had heard that his first wife had a new baby and he wanted to see it.

"Then I'll pay you your wages now," said Marina. She paid him, with ten shillings over. It was an uncomfortable moment. This man had been working for them for over two months, intimately, in their home; they had influenced each other's lives—and now he was off, he disappeared, the thing was finished. "Perhaps you'll come and work for me when you come back from your family?" said Marina.

Charlie was very pleased. "Oh, yes, madam," he said. "Mrs. Skinner very bad, she no good, not like you." He gave a comical grimace, and laughed.

"I'll give you our address." Marina wrote it out and saw Charlie fold the piece of paper and place it carefully in an envelope which also held his official pass, a letter from her saying he was travelling to his family, and a further letter, for which he had asked, listing various bits of clothing that Philip had given him, for otherwise, as he explained, the police would catch him and say he had stolen them.

"Well, goodbye, Charlie," said Marina. "I do so hope your wife and your new baby are all right." She thought of Theresa, but did not mention her; she found herself suffering from a curious disinclination to offer further advice or help. What would happen to Theresa? Would she simply move in with the first man who offered her shelter? Almost Marina shrugged.

"Goodbye, madam," said Charlie. He went off to buy himself a new shirt with the ten shillings, and some sweets for Theresa. He was sad to be leaving Theresa. On the other hand, he was looking forward to seeing his new child and his wife; he expected to be home after about a week's walking, perhaps sooner if he could get a lift.

But things did not turn out like this.

Mrs. Skinner returned before she was expected. She found the flat locked and the key with Mrs. Black. Everything was very clean and tidy, but—where was her favourite picture? At first she saw only the lightish square patch on the dimming paint—then she thought of Charlie. Where was he? No sign of him. She came back into the flat and found the letter Marina had left, enclosing eight pounds for the picture "which she had unfortunately broken." The thought came to Mrs. Skinner that she would not have got ten shillings for that picture if she had tried to sell it; then the phrase "sentimental value" came to her rescue, and she was furious. Where was Charlie? For, looking about her, she saw various other articles were missing. Where was her yellow earthen vase? Where was the wooden door-knocker that said *Welcome Friend*? Where was . . . she went off to talk to Mrs. Black, and quite soon all the women dropped in, and she was told many things about Marina. At last she said: "It serves me right for letting to an immigrant. I should have let it to you, dear." The dear in question was Mrs. Pond. The ladies were again emotionally united; the long hostilities that had led to the flat being let to Marina were forgotten; that they were certain to break out again within a week was not to be admitted in this moment of pure friendship.

Mrs. Pond told Mrs. Skinner that she had seen the famous picture being loaded on to the lorry. Probably Mrs. Giles had sold it—but this thought was checked, for both ladies knew what the picture was worth. No, Marina must have disposed of it in some way connected with her *Fabian* outlook—what could one expect from these white kaffirs?

Fuming, Mrs. Skinner went to find Theresa. She saw Charlie, dressed to kill in his new clothes, who had come to say goodbye to Theresa before setting off on his long walk. She flew out, grabbed him by the arm, and dragged him into the flat. "Where's my picture?" she demanded.

At first Charlie denied all knowledge of the picture. Then he said Marina had given it to him. Mrs. Skinner dropped his arm and stared: "But it was my picture . . . " She reflected rapidly: that eight pounds was going to be very useful; she had returned from her holiday, as people do, rather short of money. She exclaimed instead: "What have you done with my yellow vase? Where's my knocker?"

Charlie said he had not seen them. Finally Mrs. Skinner fetched the police. The police found the missing articles in Charlie's bundle. Normally Mrs. Skinner would have cuffed him and fined him five shillings. But there was this business of the picture—she told the police to take him off.

Now, in this city in the heart of what used to be known as the Dark Continent, at any hour of the day, women shopping, typists glancing up from their work out of the window, or the business men passing in their cars, may see (if they choose to look) a file of handcuffed Africans, with two policemen in front and two behind, followed by a straggling group of African women who are accompanying their men to the courts. These are the Africans who have been arrested for visiting without passes, or owning bicycles without lights, or being in possession of clothes or articles without being able to say how they came to own them. These Africans are being marched off to explain themselves to the magistrates. They are given a small fine with the option of prison. They usually choose prison. After all, to pay a ten-shilling fine when one earns perhaps twenty or thirty a month, is no joke, and it is something to be fed and housed, free, for a fortnight. This is an arrangement satisfactory to everyone concerned, for these prisoners mend roads, cut down grass, plant trees: it is as good as having a pool of free labour.

Marina happened to be turning into a shop one morning, where she hoped to buy a table for her new house, and saw, without really seeing them, a file of such handcuffed Africans passing her. They were talking and laughing among themselves, and with the black policemen who herded them, and called back loud and jocular remarks at their women. In Marina's mind the vision of that ideal table (for which she had been searching for some days, without success) was rather stronger than what she actually saw; and it was not until the prisoners had passed that she suddenly said to herself: "Good heavens, that man looks rather like Charlie—and that girl behind there, the plump girl with the spindly legs, there was something about the back view of that girl that was very like Theresa . . . " The file had in the meantime turned a corner and was out of sight. For a moment Marina thought: Perhaps I should follow and see? Then she thought: Nonsense, I'm seeing things, of course it can't be Charlie, he must have reached home by now . . . And she went into the shop to buy her table.

On Lessing

Born in 1919 in Persia, where her father worked in a bank, Doris Tayler (Lessing is her second husband's name) grew up on an isolated Southern Rhodesian farm to which the family moved in 1925. In rebellion against her parents, she refused higher education, left school at the age of fourteen, and educated herself by wide and various reading. Later she moved to Salisbury, worked at various jobs, married twice (in 1939 and 1945, each marriage terminated after four years), and joined the small and ineffectual Rhodesian Communist Party, which seemed to offer hope for reform of a complacent, materialistic, and segregated colonial society. After the war, she decided that the time had come to stop thinking about being a writer and become one. She quit her secretarial job and after a good deal of work produced *The Grass Is Singing,* which was published in 1950, one year after she moved to England. She has lived in England since, supporting herself by writing, taking part in practical politics, deploring at times the provincial and involuted quality of the London literary world but enjoying the privacy, freedom, and comparative detachment impossible in societies like Rhodesia's in which "there is very heavy pressure put on people" and in which "you spend all your time in a torment of conscientiousness" (Newquist, p. 416).

In fact, Mrs. Lessing's ambivalence about her relationship to society pervades her writing. She denies that a writer is obliged to be or should in conscience be uncommitted or apolitical, but she admits that she is "emotionally involved in the basic ethical conflict of communism—what is due to the collective and what to the individual conscience," and the central subject of *Children of Violence,* she has said, is "a study of the individual conscience in its relations with the collective." She rejects both "the pleasurable luxury of despair, the acceptance of disgust," and "the simple economic view of man; both are aspects of cowardice, both fallings away from a central vision, the two easy escapes of our time into false innocence"(*Declaration,* pp. 194, 196). The individual must attempt to maintain a precarious balance between the claims of self and of society, rejecting ivory tower self-absorption as well as submission to the system.

The difficulties of such a position are illustrated in her short story, "The Day Stalin Died" (in *The Habit of Loving*), what in pre-Hemingway times was called a sketch. The narrator, a writer, is distracted all day by her involvement in the complex and trivial affairs of her friends and relatives. The relatives, unthinking Tories who lead sterile lives in a Bournemouth boarding house, are rather tolerant of the narrator's leftist politics but are confused and rather distressed by a visit to a homosexual photographer who reads only the novels of Ronald Firbank. Her friends are doctrinaire communists: one ignores Stalin's death to talk about the Copper Belt; the other, who left her husband when he joined the Labour Party after the Stalin-Hitler treaty and who lives alone with a picture of Stalin over her bed, suspects a capitalist plot and declares that "we will have to pledge ourselves to be worthy of him." "Yes," the narrator replies, "I suppose we will." The whole day's activity has been futile: the friends she hoped to introduce do not meet and in any case disapprove of each other; the photograph is not taken; her writing is always interrupted; everyone ignores the significance of the central event.

In part her reservations about the claims of the collective, especially about its claims over the writer, seem to be a negative reaction to the anti-intellectualism of Stalinist Russia and of many western communists, who "thought writing was inferior to political organizing, that writers should feel ashamed, and apologize for writing books. . . . Active socialists who wanted to write had to make a choice, they had to decide whether they would organize the working class or write books." (See, for example, W. H. Auden's poem, "Spain.") Although she is anxious to write about politics and thinks that "the writer is obligated to dramatize the political conflicts of his time in his fiction," she has a respect for the truth and a distrust of mechanical and schematic presentation which makes it difficult for her "to embody [her] political vision in a novel" (Raskin, p. 174). At least one attempt to do so resulted in "Hunger," a story which has been popular, but which was, in the author's view, a failure. It grew, she recalls, out of a debate between a group of British writers and their Russian hosts. Despite wide divergences of political belief, the British agreed "that writing had to be a product of the individual conscience, or soul," while the Russians demanded "greater simplicity, simple judgment of right and wrong." Reflecting on their position and remembering Dickens, who made simple judgments, who was a great writer, and who lived in "a society as startlingly unjust" as Southern Africa, she decided to write "a story of simple good and bad, with clear-cut choices. . . . " But the story failed: "It wasn't true" ("Preface," *African Stories,* p. 7).

"Truth" in Mrs. Lessing's terms means not only fidelity to private vision but to a conception of man. Perhaps, she writes, "the result of having been a communist is to be a humanist," and she asserts that one should read a novel "for illumination, in order to enlarge one's perception of life," not to encounter certainties but "the warmth, the compassion, the love of people which illuminates the literature of the nineteenth century and which makes all these old novels a statement of faith in man himself." Because of these qualities,

> the highest point of literature was the novel of the nineteenth century, the work of Tolstoy, Stendahl, Dostoevsky, Balzac, Turgenev, Chekhov; the work of the great realists. I define realism as art which springs so vigorously and naturally from a strongly-held, though not necessarily intellectually-defined, view of life that

it absorbs symbolism. I hold the view that the realist novel, the
realist story, is the highest form of prose writing; higher than and
out of the reach of any comparison with expressionism, impres-
sionism, symbolism, naturalism or any other ism." (*Declaration,* p.
188)

This preference for nineteenth-century fiction, accompanied as it often is
by a distaste for (in her case a relative lack of interest in) modern fiction, is
closely related to the larger issues of what fiction is, whether it is composed
of words—an autonomous literary artifact, to be judged by its own laws—or
of things—imitating and making some kind of comment on the real world.
This dichotomy—though it is more often recognized by critics than by
writers and by theorists than by those, readers or writers, engaged with a
specific work—is by no means frivolous, for it deals with some of the central
assumptions about literature in the twentieth century, including the artist's
relationship to his medium, his subject, and his audience. Both in her
fiction and in the theories behind it, Doris Lessing is at the center of the
debate. She has written conventional novels and, to reflect her sense of
despair about their limits and the limits of the imagination, followed one of
them with *The Golden Notebook* to convey the sense that contemporary life
is disintegrating and to answer the question of what conventional fiction
can "actually say about what you've actually experienced" with "absolutely
nothing. Because you can't. I don't know what one does about novels. . . .
You can't get life into [them]. That's all there is to it—no matter how hard
you try" (Howe, pp. 312–313). However, she is also aware that she had at
the beginning of her career two possibilities open: the "intense, careful,
self-conscious, mannered" form which "could have led to the kind of
writing usually described as 'feminine'" (Bowen, Mansfield, Porter,
McCullers) and the "straight, broad, direct" style that "is much less
beguiling" but which leads "to the kind of writing that has the freedom to
develop as it likes" ("Preface," *African Stories,* p. 8). For the most part, as
in "A Home for the Highland Cattle," she has chosen the second.

The fact that she has made a choice may be significant. Most contemporary writers conscious of the two possibilities and faced with a real choice,
as Kingsley Amis and C. P. Snow are not, have inclined towards the first,
and most of the really interesting theoreticians and practical critics of the
novel have followed them. The opposition has only D. H. Lawrence to use
as counterevidence against Joyce, Proust, Mann, and Conrad, and
Lawrence is as uncertain an ally in death as he was in life. Of course, a
good many critics who extol the virtues of Lawrence or of nineteenth-
century fiction take consolation in the fact that no modern work meets their
standard, being no more immune to the pleasures of contemptuous superiority than the rest of us. Those of good will, like Mrs. Lessing, hope that the
novel can retain or regain its position as a dominant form. However, it
remains to be demonstrated that the novel (*not* individual works like
Waugh's *Brideshead Revisited* in 1945 or John Fowles' *The French
Lieutenant's Woman* in 1970, isolated and temporary successes) can be at

once intensely artful and popular in our time. Mimetic critics who believe that the novel should reflect our world would argue that experimental novels, by torturing style and technique and by straining after new, Alexandrian complexities of consciousness, have abandoned the kind of audience that sustained the novel and made it the dominant art form of the nineteenth and early twentieth centuries. Their opponents would argue that conventional techniques, including realism, are inadequate to deal with modern life and therefore cannot enlarge one's perception of life in any but a sociological or journalistic way.

This debate is really about the relevance and function of art; and like most crucial arguments, it seems to be interminable and irresolvable—perhaps because memorable and even great literature has been written out of both assumptions and because there is a good deal of common ground between these apparently irreconcilable positions. Perhaps it is inevitable that contemporary writers like Mrs. Lessing and many of her contemporaries (See Reuben Rabinovitz, *The Reaction Against Experiment in the English Novel, 1950–1960* [New York: Columbia University Press, 1967]) reject the claims of their predecessors, especially if they believe that aesthetic and political theories are indissoluble. However, what is inevitable is not always significant, and the footnotes of literary history are stuffed with works that embody the political conflicts of their time and conform to unimpeachable theories. And the main text has many works of art written out of presuppositions that, stated baldly, modern readers would abhor.

One theoretical defense of Mrs. Lessing's choice of technique which might satisfy even the formalists is that it is adequate to the material even though it is not careful or self-conscious. She once compared Southern Africa to Tolstoy's Russia and added that "For a novelist based on Africa, it is discouraging that so much of what develops there is a repetition of the European nineteenth century" (*Going Home,* pp. 19–21). This may imply the view that a recurrent situation demands conventional methods. At any rate, "A Home for the Highland Cattle" uses the traditional techniques of the omniscient, commenting author and of broad contrasts in support of the theme. Here the narrator serves as intermediary between the subject and the audience, filling in detail, directing our attention and our sympathies, detached, ironic, and aware of the absurdities of Marina's position and of the gradual complicity in the absurdities of the black and white cultures, suspending herself and her audience between hope and despair in an attempt to make us understand. However, the understanding is not primarily sociological, psychological, or even moral. The society portrayed is gone as irretrievably as Kipling's India (one of the risks run by the author who tries "to dramatize the political conflicts of his time"), for emergent Africa flanks Rhodesia geographically and surrounds it psychologically, and the English and Rhodesian governments have denounced and repudiated each other. Nyasaland is foreign territory. Marina's role has disappeared, but her type—in America it used to be called "phony white liberal"—remains, and we are invited more to understand her and her situation than to judge and repudiate. Politically minded readers may with justice see in her attitudes the cause of African unrest, but politics alone will not do justice to the complexity and the essential pathos of Marina's situation. And if the story is to survive, it will do so because Mrs. Lessing has embodied the theme in art—has, in Conrad's phrase, made us *see.*

Marina's plight is in large part a result of her lack of consciousness, of an *idea,* as Conrad put it in *Heart of Darkness,* rather than a sentimental pretense. One of the ways in which Mrs. Lessing hopes to make us see is her use of setting and minor character to support and enrich this contrast. The city and by implication the whole society lack direction and coherence. The site was chosen out of confusion or weariness, and the architecture and layout (planning is too complimentary) are the result of a mélange of misapplied theories and styles, themselves debased, imported from England in defiance of climate and common sense. The secondary characters, like Marina (the name, perhaps, an ironic reference to the heroine of Shakespeare's *Pericles,* who remains uncorrupted in a brothel), are directionless, drifting, self-blinded, caught between English tastes, habits, and morals and the facts of African life, including guilt-induced paranoia. Even Philip, who takes a longer view than any of the characters and who may seem the hero to ecology-conscious readers, is unable to see Theresa and Charlie as human beings with their own lives and values. In sixty years all of this has grown up, displacing the values symbolized at the beginning of the story by old Lobugula's kraal, where the doomed king dispensed "life and death according to known and honored customs" and at the end by Theresa's father, who remembers what the cattle symbolized. It was not sentiment, as for Mrs. Skinner, or superstition, as for Charlie, or ecological imbalance, as for Philip, but rather a coherent and meaningful society. However, Mrs. Lessing denies us the pastoral-utopian consolation of believing that such a past can be revived or indeed any consolation that can be found in a solution. And that is one of the differences between the artist and the writer of tracts.

Textual note:

"A Home for the Highland Cattle" was first collected in *Five* (1953), and reprinted in *African Stories* (1964; U.S. edition, 1965). The text reprinted here follows that of the U.S. edition of *African Stories.*

Resources for further study:

Mrs. Lessing's short fiction has been collected in *This Was the Old Chief's Country* (1951), *Five* (1953), *The Habit of Loving* (1957), *A Man and Two Women* (1963), and *African Stories,* which reprints the stories in the first volume and four of *Five* as well as two previously uncollected stories. The volumes of *Children of Violence (Martha Quest* [1952], *A*

Proper Marriage [1954], *A Ripple from the Storm* [1958], *Landlocked* [1965], and *The Four-Gated City* [1969]), published in this country by Simon and Schuster, are her most considerable work. *The Golden Notebook* (1962) is her most experimental and perhaps her most highly regarded novel.

Some of her essays and interviews important for an understanding of her fiction are:

"The Still Personal Voice," in *Declaration,* Tom Maschler, ed. (New York: E. P. Dutton and Co., Inc., 1958), pp. 187–201.

"Crisis in Central Africa," *Twentieth Century,* 165 (April 1959), 368–376.

Interview by Roy Newquist, *Counterpoint* (New York: Rand McNally & Co., 1964), pp. 414–425.

HOWE, FLORENCE. "Talk with Doris Lessing," *Nation,* 204 (6 March 1967), 311–313.

"Afterword," in *The Story of an African Farm,* by Olive Schreiner (New York: Fawcett World Library, Premier Books, 1968), pp. 273–290.

RASKIN, JONAH. "Doris Lessing at Stony Brook: An Interview," *New American Review,* 8 (1970), 166–179.

BIBLIOGRAPHY:

BURKHAM, SELMA R. "A Doris Lessing Checklist," *Critique,* 11, No. 1 (1969), 69–81.

BIOGRAPHY:

There is no formal biography. See Brewster and Mrs. Lessing's reminiscences in *Going Home* (1957), describing a visit to Rhodesia in 1956; *In Pursuit of the English* (1960; U.S. edition 1961), describing her early days in England; and "All Seething Underneath," *Vogue* [London], 15 February 1954.

CRITICAL:

BREWSTER, DOROTHY. *Doris Lessing.* New York: Twayne Publishers, Inc., 1965.

BURKHAM, SELMA R. "Only Connect: Form and Content in the Works of Doris Lessing," *Critique,* 11, No. 1 (1969), 51–68.

GINDIN, JAMES. "Lessing's Intense Commitment," in *Postwar British Fiction: New Accents and Attitudes.* Berkeley, Calif.: University of California Press, 1962.

MCDOWELL, FREDERICK P. W. "The Fiction of Doris Lessing: An Interim View," *Arizona Quarterly,* 21 (Winter 1965), 314–345.

SCHLEUTER, PAUL. "Doris Lessing: The Free Woman's Commitment," in

Contemporary British Novelists, Charles Shapiro, ed. Carbondale, Illinois: Southern Illinois University Press, 1965.

TUCKER, MARTIN. *Africa in Modern Literature: A Survey of Contemporary Writing in English.* New York: Frederick Ungar Publishing Co., Inc., 1967.

MALCOLM LOWRY
Elephant and Colosseum

It was the early afternoon of a brilliantly sunny day in Rome, a young blue midsummer moon tilted down over the Borghese Gardens, and under the awning on the sidewalk terrace of the Restaurant Rupe Tarpea, crowded by men and women talking, a lone man named Kennish Drumgold Cosnahan sat drinking a glass of milk with an expression of somber panic.

"And this panic, Cosnahan, would you say that this is merely due to the fact that you don't know how to ask for a glass of wine in Italian?"

"Something like that, Drumgold, something like that."

"Or rather, while you can manage a stern 'vino rosso, per favore,' in a wine shop or trattoria, you're afraid that in this place they'd bring you a whole expensive bottle you couldn't afford."

True, Cosnahan did not know how to ask for a glass of milk in Italian either, for all that he'd had a grandmother born in Sicily, but there having appeared a homeless glass upon the tray of a waiter glancing about him, he had cleared his throat, taken his courage and murmured something like "Nel mezzo del cammin di nostra vita mi ritrovai in—" which was about all the other "Italian" he knew (and certainly all the Dante).

His presence upon the terrace validated in this curious fashion, Cosnahan sat waiting for the increase of confidence he felt it should bring about. But no, glancing from time to time at the novel he had laid rather consciously on the table, already he began to be afraid of finishing the wretched glass of milk, for that would bring the ordeal of payment that much closer, another ordeal, also linguistic in character, for it meant speaking to the waiter again, who even now was giving him a renewed fore-and-aft look.

Since it wasn't merely the milk he would be paying for (any more than anyone who bought that book would only pay for the spiritual nourishment

371

it contained) but the commanding site of the Restaurant Rupe Tarpea upon the Via Veneto, to say nothing of the three other sidewalk restaurants on the other three corners created by the crossroads with the Via Sicilia and *their* rent, or their exquisitely dressed female occupants eating ices, to whose charming activities he felt he would be expected also, obscurely, to contribute; as naturally he would be paying also for the view, should he turn around, of the gateway of the Porta Pincia, and finally for the Via Vittorio Veneto itself, with its sidewalks ten feet broad, and its plane trees casting dappled shadows on either side as it swept in great curves down toward the invisible Piazza Barberini; the Via Veneto, which, with its ceaseless traffic of horsecabs and bicycles, combined with expensive American, Italian and English motorcars, gave one not merely the physical sense of its own spaciousness, but produced in him—when now and then he forgot his besetting unease—that expansive feeling of great riches and peace, that purring roaring feeling, yet somehow quiet as a Rolls Royce engine of life being at a sort of permanent flood, as if there had never been a first world war, let alone a second one, which was like an evocation of 1913, of those truly pre-war days from which he retained only this curious yet powerful sensation, when with his parents he must have visited London or Dublin, or at least Weston-super-Mare, at the age of five.

"Yet this deficiency in even the first principles of most foreign languages, Cosnahan, in one whose unconscious mind must be a veritable treasure house of the literature of the Gael—do you not find it strange?—in one whose lineage, if it does not actually go back to Oshin, the—"

"I do, Drumgold! And it makes one wonder sometimes if I am human. Ta dty lhiasagh dty ghoarn!"

"Thy recompense is in thine own hand . . . " Cosnahan picked up the novel that had fallen to the sidewalk and then, with a covert glance at the waiter, the papers which had dropped out of it. He rearranged the wrapper of the novel, regarding as he did so with a suddenly assumed official air the photograph printed on the back; it showed the same face that was reflected in the window, only without the somberness or panic. Happy was the word, and the face appeared considerably younger, though the photograph had been taken only sixteen months before. *Ark from Singapore.* Not a very good title. Arthur should have thought of a better one. On the other side of the cover was pictured the captain of a merchant vessel with his pipe falling out of his mouth, taken aback—and no wonder—before the weather-cloths of the bridge, over which spray was blowing, at the spectacle of a healthy young elephant emerging from his chartroom. High seas were rising about the steamer . . .

Cosnahan searched the face in the photograph. He was disconcerted slightly by the sense of difference, of no longer looking altogether at his own likeness. Yet what was uncanny was the way those eyes looked back at him. He might have been looking at the young Emmanuel Swedenborg, or somebody, in a lighter mood. Yet this afternoon Cosnahan could not wholly think himself back into the happy scene of that snapshot, nor into the whole person it portrayed, of the youngish man, perhaps thirty-five, bronzed, fit, and wearing bathing trunks, arm-in-arm with the pretty gay wild-looking girl wearing shorts and a jersey, smiling and holding up to the camera a tomcat of whiskerando mien, closely resembling Theodore Roosevelt . . . The Cosnahans in Nantucket, it said, beneath it, with Citron-le-Taciturne.

Published by Arthur Wilding and Co., 30th Thousand, the words were added on the flap.

That had been Arthur's idea too, that photograph, Cosnahan reflected, and Arthur who'd taken it, and Arthur also who had named their then nameless new cat, that time he'd flown down to Nantucket for the week end to help them correct the proofs. At midnight, having mistakenly decided that some Danish beer would keep them awake, Cosnahan had said: "For the Lord's sake, let's read something else by someone else!" so Art had picked a book at random, of ancient biography, from the shelves, and read aloud, in a sepulchral voice, some words to this effect: "As a young man I had often brushed against the ghastly wig of the Duke of Brunswick, traversing the corridors of night restaurants, in the hot breath of gas, patchouli, and spiced meats; at Bignons, on the couch at the rear, Citron-le-Taciturne had appeared to me one evening, eating a slice of fois gras . . . "

Whereupon their untitled cat had sprung through the half-open window onto Arthur's shoulder, and had ever after been called Citron-le-Taciturne.

And now a pang struck Cosnahan wondering where the little cat was. Perhaps at this moment, though it was hard to calculate what time it might be in Nantucket, he was having his afternoon snack, prior to making his evening inspection of the ropes and hawsers, and to dropping in, it could be, at the Tavern on the Moors, though they often invented feline hostelries for him, such as the Claw-bar and Grill, or the Ratskeller, or even, when it seemed he might have strayed as far as New York, the Mouseum of Modern Art. Or it could be, since he was devoted to Lovey, that he had followed her to the summer theater where she was playing, and had been adopted by the cast, was even performing in the play.

"Success!——" Cosnahan lit his pipe.

There was something implausible and self-defeating about his particular brand of it, as if—he was thinking of the dream he'd had last night—a play should somehow run for three years on one Saturday matinee. But the rub was that Cosnahan's sales had remained within that inclusive figure of thirty thousand for half a year, most of the copies having been sold in the first few months, most of them actually in the first weeks. Such a success, resembling one of those earthquakes which, by the time one has got used to their roars and jolts, are already subsiding into their equating minor shocks and tremblings, might be all in the day's work to Arthur. Not so to Cosnahan. It had stopped his working altogether. He'd been stopped cold ever since those first few weeks, hadn't been able to do another stroke.

The first edition had contained some advance notices, some even by major writers who, engaged in gloomy and somber strifes of their own, often tend to turn a kindly eye toward humor, in many cases even bad humor, which they may well consider to be better than none. But for the fourth edition—and this was the fourth edition before him—Art's partner, who had not liked the book too well to begin with, insisted on a new idea: he wanted to give the impression that its reception had not been merely highbrow (this anomaly had been known to occur not merely in the realm of light literature but in the movie and the comic strip), but had been spontaneous from Honolulu to the North Pole. So he had quoted from a host of more popular eulogies.

Reading these later eulogies produced in Cosnahan a bizarre mental commotion as of some endless mirrored reduplication, as if it were not merely that all these reviews had been written before of countless other books, but that for a moment he felt like an eternal writer eternally sitting in the eternal city, eternally reading precisely the same sort of notices from which he always derived precisely the same eternal feelings of mingled pleasure, pain, gratitude, sadness, amusement, dismay and beautiful vainglory; though in another way, of course, it could not at all feel like this because, satiated and indeed tottering with praise though he was, when he read any of his reviews, or even, as here, bits of reviews, it was always as if he were reading them for the first time: against this too, was it really possible that any such extraordinary observations as this had ever appeared of any book, possible that he was, after all, a unique case? "Sheer joy"—he read; "if you like a mixture of Conrad and Algernon Blackwood at his best, then Cosnahan's your man." "A mixture of early Conrad and Wodehouse at his funniest—sheer spoofery—I roared!" said another generous fellow. "These bright and breezy pages," another was content with. "And if you can imagine a combination of Jack London, James Stephens and James Oliver Curwood—with a bit of roaring O'Neill thrown in for good measure, there you have Cosnahan!" added another. "Elfin humor—with a robust touch—a miracle!" qualified someone else. While a last good-hearted chap, whom it was invidious to suspect of not having read the beginning either, observed, "There is a passage of rare philosophy at the end." Elsewhere attention was called to the impartiality of the publishers, either that, or it was a mistake, or Art's partner hadn't been able to resist it, by quoting merely the terse subscription to Cosnahan's photograph in the *Time* review, which stated bluntly and ambiguously, "In the Arabian Sea, a Jumbo," and redirected finally back to the author by means of a green detachable slip to the book itself on which was printed: "The world is reading America's new and greatest humorist! Kennish Drumgold Cosnahan! *Ark from Singapore* has now been translated into Italian, French, German, Swedish, etc."

Nor was this all.

Kennish Drumgold Cosnahan [Cosnahan was now informed] was born in Ballaugh in 1908, in the old Kingdom of the Isle of Man. He is a collateral descendant of the renowned Cronkbane family, and another forefather was instrumental in translating the Bible into Manx. Born of strictly Methodist parents, one of his brothers, Matthias Cosnahan, became a Catholic priest. One of his uncles,

however, is a Mohammedan, and he finds the famous name
Drumgold of obscure origin, though there was one other Drumgold
in the Sicilian branch of the family. Another brother disappeared
and is at present a member of the government of St. Helena.
Kennish he believes to be a more autochthonous Manx name than
his surname, though not, he says, as indigenous as Quayne,
Quaggan, Quillish, Qualtrough, Quirk, Quale or Looney. Young
Cosnahan could only speak the old Gaelic until he was nearly nine,
though he had visited England several times. Cosnahan was sent to
a school in England when, in his own words, "A Zeppelin dropped a
bomb on me. This," he adds, "was the beginning and end of all my
war service." [In fact he had spent seven months in the American
merchant marine during the last war, but had seen no action, save
once when his ship ran aground off Venezuela, trying to ram a
nonexistent submarine.]

In 1924 he went to sea before the mast, later serving as a
carpenter's mate, and in *Ark from Singapore* he has reached back
to this early experience, in 1927, on a sailing ship, with a deck
cargo of lions, tigers, and elephants from the Straits Settlements
bound for the Dublin Zoo—

Dear Arthur, Cosnahan thought. Tigers—there had been no tigers, or
lions either. As if the company of one elephant, five black panthers, ten
snakes, and a wild boar had not been enough! As for the sailing ship, it was
just a British tramp steamer exactly like the one on the cover, save that this
one had curiously acquired an American flag.

—two years after which he emigrated to the United States and
settled in the island of Nantucket. It will be recalled that of
Melville's characters in *Moby-Dick* one whaler, described simply
as "grizzled," came from the Isle of Man.

Cosnahan is the recipient of an award for saving life at sea from
the Japanese government, of which he will only say, "Before the
war, of course."

(Yes, quite true. But it had been Mrs. Cosnahan who gave Art that bit of
information; he never would have—he hoped—himself. Just the same, he
rather liked it . . .)

Cosnahan is also the author of several well-known Manx Gaelic
poems, some hymns which are still played in church, and is highly
regarded in jazz circles when he can be persuaded to play as a cool
exponent of bebop upon the bull fiddle. He married Lovey
L'Hirondelle, a young actress, in 1940. They have no children, and
make their home all the year round in Nantucket, swimming,
playing tennis, and in the company of their cat, Citron-le-
Taciturne . . .

Cosnahan laid his pipe aside, took a sip of milk, threw away a crumpled Gauloise from Paris days he found in his pocket and discovered an American cigarette he could not light because he now had no matches. An Italian returning to the next table offered him one, and Cosnahan, bowing his thanks, fleetingly hoped he would somehow manage to identify his beneficiary with the photograph on the cover of the novel, which was lying on the table with that side up: but the man had stooped courteously to retrieve a newspaper clipping that had fluttered out, and himself bowing, turned away.

Cosnahan reseated himself and studied the clipping which, having a more genuine appearance than the others he possessed bearing the clipping bureau's letterhead—it had been culled by himself from a newspaper when in the Isle of Man, after long search—made it all the more painful that it should contain what it did. It was the solitary notice that had appeared on the English edition of his book in his old home, and beneath the pastoral caption, *The Browsing Manxwoman,* ran as follows:

> This book, though bearing upon it the once distinguished native name of Cosnahan—

(Once distinguished, reflected Cosnahan. Who had undistinguished it? Himself? His brother John, in his Napoleonic haunts, or his brother Matthias, in his priestly vestments? The name was less natively Manx than Irish anyhow.)

> —of Cosnahan, and which is reported to have had a considerable vogue in the United States, does not reflect credit upon the citizens of our island, and is of very little interest to our readers. Of a type of humour that was outmoded a dozen years ago, and dealing with the banal subject of a ship carrying a cargo of wild animals that break loose from their cages, instead of being hilarious, it is just deadly dull. Definitely not recommended.

Cosnahan suddenly catching sight of his reflection in the window at this point as he looked up was rewarded by a glimpse of his face as it perhaps essentially was. That Swedenborgian look was still there, but of an elder Swedenborg this time, who worries whether the printer's got an angel in the wrong paragraph; and it had that decidedly Manx look, of the man who knows wood or boats, who wonders if he's made a mistake and if so is prepared to be angry with himself. Cosnahan turned the clipping over. Loch Promenade Conveniences Unsightly, *Suggestion work be stopped. Town Council agrees to carry on.* What? He'd never noticed the reverse side of the clipping before.

> Councillor Eccleshare [he read] declared that the building would have looked better if it were only a couple of feet high instead of forty, and similar to the conveniences on Queens Promenade.

Councillor Timmons considered some machinery should be set in motion to enable the Council to discuss the matter and that now was the time to stop the building if the matter was going to be reconsidered. There was no point in finishing the building and then, on second thoughts, tearing it down. Alderman Shillicorn objected that the conveniences were not only ready to be opened but in fact had been in use for several months. The conveniences were second to none in the British Isles and were a tribute to the engineers who had been working against difficulties.

This indeed added up to a more sensible review of his book than the other, and he put the clipping in his pocket, feeling he might be able to use it, and oddly in a better mood as he brought out the letter written in pencil and begun that morning in the sidewalk café beneath his pension, over a cup of coffee: the letter was to his wife, and reading it over his face reflected in the window became gentle and composed.

What a beastly disappointment she couldn't have come to Europe with him. And yet had she come it would have involved only a worse disappointment for her. Lovey (her nickname came from Lovey Lee, an old recording by the Memphis Five, that she and Cosnahan used to play when they were first in love: first it was only her nickname, then nobody ever called her Margaret, now it was her stage name too) was an actress, who had almost stopped acting after she married him. It was one of those inexplicable runs of bad luck: she was too young, she was too old, the show folded before it reached New York, or once, agonizingly, after weeks of rehearsals, excitement, congratulation, the "chance of a lifetime," after the play opened in Boston the author rewrote the whole thing and changed her part to that of a ten-year-old boy. But now, at the last moment, after all their plans had been made for the trip to Europe they could at last afford, she'd been offered the lead in this show at the Nantucket summer theater. Whether he had his own success partly to blame, or to thank for this, he didn't know, but Cosnahan, seeing her delight outweighed her dismay, would have put off the trip. He hated travel for its own sake, especially without his wife, they could always go next year, whereas the show, if it succeeded, would go on to New York. Cosnahan had stayed long enough to see from the rehearsals there was every indication the play was going to be a hit, but meantime his brother Matthias had cabled to say that their mother, who was very old, was seriously ill in the Isle of Man. And so, after all, he had come over alone, and left three days before the opening night of Lovey's show. And since his own health forbade him to fly he had arrived too late. His mother—a Methodist to the last, to Matt's disappointment—was dead and buried before he even arrived in Liverpool.

Cosnahan wrote his wife a note every day: this was one of his longer letters, though the only one he'd written with any family news other than the sorrowfully inexpressible, or to say how much he regretted his mother had never known her. First he told her, as always, how much he loved her (one proof of which lay in his writing at all, since even the composition of a letter had become difficult) and missed her, congratulated her on the continuing success of the play, answered a few minor questions, asked after the house, and, naturally, Citron-le-Taciturne.

Then he informed her that he still hadn't seen his brother Matt, who had already been obliged to depart for a Catholic congress in Bruges by the time he, Cosnahan, arrived in the Isle of Man. Matt's position as a priest in the island was a bit embarrassing under the circumstances, which had not been made any easier by the antics of their eldest brother John, who, a politician of the extreme left wing, or no wing, some kind of anarchist of the ancient gentle Proudhon persuasion, had just tried, as she had possibly read in the papers, gently to overthrow the government of St. Helena where he was at present incarcerated—unless to say that in regard to St. Helena at all was an overstatement. Matthias could not be visited at present where he was (as for that matter neither could John) but was coming to Rome where he had business and Cosnahan expected to meet him at any moment now. Nor had he seen Art yet, who'd written him from Paris, so Cosnahan knew he was in Europe at least, that *he* would be in Rome at any moment too; anyway Cosnahan was continually on the watch for them both. Then, because he didn't want to say that if Matt didn't show up, he wouldn't have met anybody in Europe he knew who'd ever heard of his great American triumph, and because he thought it might amuse her, he told her about the Pensione Borgnini where he lived . . .

But quite suddenly he laid his letter aside with a sigh. His first thought when he'd received Matt's cable on the ship: *Deeply regret Mother died June sixth writing Matt,* and the cable sent from Bellabella (its little railroad station full of fuchsia!)—Cosnahan's first thought had been: I'll write Mother and explain why I couldn't write her before she died; how my every breath hung on my success—on news of more success, on news of my book, now a best-seller in Dallas, now in Tombstone, and now, God knows, in Eclectic, Alabam! And then on less success, and then on no success, but yet to be translated into Italian, Sanskrit, Esperanto, English! That was the reason I couldn't write you, dearest Mother, why I couldn't find time to send a word, and now I understand that all this I took to myself and wallowed in, you would have transmuted into true gold with the alchemy of your love, and read in it your own simple pride in your son. And then he realized: I'll never write to Mother again, never, never, write that letter I always put off, nor send her a lapis lazuli elephant again, nor tell a lie, nor boast to her, and what shall I do now when that emptiness comes round, the remorse for not having written, what shall I do without staying that remorse, and if I should lose even that remorse, what then?

As a matter of fact it was just such a thought that had stopped him going on with his letter. For the sudden reflection: I haven't written Mother this month, had come to him, quite consciously, before the augmenting and tragic reality had had time to banish it: she'd been dead a month, he'd scarcely written for a year . . . Well, he loved his mother, and there was no sentimentality about it, she was a large-hearted and humorous woman, never mind how eccentric. The practical side of him even considered his mother well out of it, since his father was dead too; though she had all of her senses, indeed more senses than she should have, she was fabulously old, there was little to hope for in the world left to her, and she would certainly be better off in the beyond with the old man: that was exactly how Cosnahan phrased it to himself: "in the beyond with the old man." But was she in the beyond, or, rather, the right sort of beyond with the old man? For the uncomfortable thought lingered that Matt might be right—that in any case it was not surprising he was anxious for his mother's soul, which anxiety had a sounder and rather more complex basis than that she happened to be a Methodist. For the curious thing about all this was, to tell the truth, Cosnahan's mother was a witch . . .

Doubtless the literature is not large regarding the operation of the dark powers among the converts of John Wesley, Cosnahan thought, staring blankly into the orthodox depths of Rome. But he was afraid that what the neighbors said had a foundation in fact. Actually his mother never used these powers save for good and he did not think she could help herself. And, unquestionably, she did not regard them as dark. As for the eerie reputation it gave the Cosnahans in Ballaugh, her gifts were also, in their wry manner, a social asset. Common sense suffered his mother not only to live, but to thrive. From as far back as Cosnahan could remember she was considerably in demand, for in Cosnahan's day poltergeist phenomena were fairly common in the Isle of Man and his mother had the capacity, more properly the attribute or the duty of a Catholic priest, of being able to halt these manifestations. And it was hard in one way to imagine anything more full of profoundly comic possibilities than this: an island beset by the diabolic, in which the phenomenon of coals hurtling out of the kitchen stove to hang in the air and drop one by one at leisure was no unusual occurrence, yet where they had driven out the very force that was capable of canceling the evil: the Catholic priest. Naturam expellas pitchfork, something or other recurret! Throw out nature with a pitchfork but back she always comes! It was much as if God, with that all-wise sense of humor that Cosnahan respected increasingly the longer he remained as a guest upon His earth, had kept Mother Drumgold (as he feared they called her, though she rarely gave any tangential exhibition of her abilities more disturbing than keeping the kettle off the boil on Michaelmas Eve, and this only under extreme social pressure) up His sleeve, an heresiarch so extreme as to function almost like an outsister within the stern enemy camp, a Methodist most wonderfully Methodistic. Though only a Manx Methodist perhaps would be able to see nothing contradictory about it all.

Cosnahan was aware that the subject of witchcraft and the supernatural, by no means always the same thing, had suddenly undergone a startling recrudescence of popularity with the public mind within the last few years, and to him at least this was not strange, that admirable comedian Dostoievsky—for Cosnahan was a well-read man—having long ago hit upon what was, for him, a satisfactory and common-sense solution, at least of the latter, that would have been appreciated by any Tourist Trophy motorbicycle racer in the Isle of Man, briefly that the nearer you approached the goal, the nearer that goal, viewed from another angle (no matter how many circuits of the island you had to make first), approached you; which was to say that so long as man was crouched headlong on his handlebars toward death, the nearer death, and the world of ghosts, approached man: in short, to mix his metaphors with clichés, as his mind always did whether he liked it or not, if man was intent on having one foot in the grave, he must take the consequences. These consequences had been reflected in literature by a preoccupation with the next world, and hence with "dark forces," so enthusiastic that it seemed almost to adumbrate a kind of imminent doom which, on second thoughts, either had already come to pass, was impossible, or unnecessary, and in any case if you believed in the Resurrection and the Life didn't matter so much—unless it was to prophets with a stake in the business. But between merely writing about supernatural or unlawful powers and actually being in possession of them was, to speak literally, a world of difference. And Cosnahan was only too well equipped to say this because he possessed unlawful powers himself, or at least powers not above suspicion. Both Matthias and he had inherited within limits, with Matt it was innate before he found divine ratification, the power to put a stop to the same phenomena, though they discovered this by merest accident when they were quite young. Since the results of these phenomena are sometimes serious (and there is always the poltergeist to be considered) Cosnahan often thought it was this that sent Matt into the Church, though his father had felt differently, maintaining it had something to do with his joining the navy.

For himself Cosnahan found it hard to get away from the suspicion that he was a sort of demon, or a demon in reverse. Ever since that Christmas morning long ago when his mother, with whatever motives, profound, or endearing, or occult plans for his future, had presented him with a gray suède elephant—a trifle large for a periapt—he'd been conscious of something peculiar in his nature. Odd things happened to him. Inexplicable coincidences, and at school geometrical problems beyond his power he had often found solved as by another intelligence, on those occasions, that was, when another human intelligence was not available. True the ineradicable beliefs held to this day upon his island, in the all-dreaded Buggane for example, or the sweet fancy that at the new moon the sea birds that rode the ninth wave from the shore were the souls of the dead, did not exactly tend toward the mundane. "The supernatural," as even the Browsing Manxwoman would admit, "must always be the deepest part of any Manxman's nature . . . " But it was the aroma of frying Cosnahan that more than once had risen to his nostrils during his dreams that sometimes gave him cause for alarm. In ancient days he had comforted himself by the reflection that his expurgatorial talent, inherited as it was from a God-fearing and tender-hearted woman, was of heaven rather than hell. No sooner had he at last found consolation along these lines, however, than the power seemed to fade, to be replaced by another curious faculty, of an almost flawless and Homeric uselessness, when it was considered that soon after it took possession of him he set out on another voyage to sea:

Cosnahan discovered he was a water-diviner. He almost still was. Indeed he still felt the tug sometimes, even without a wand, though much more rarely, for it was as if ever since his book's publication—albeit he wouldn't put it to himself quite like this—"his powers had been falling off," so that he hadn't known whether to be glad or sorry when he experienced that old uneasiness again only the other day in St. Peter's, where they were making excavations in search of St. Peter's tomb, and he had thought of asking a priest were they looking for water too there underground, because in that case he felt he knew where it was. But he had been too shy to do this . . .

Cosnahan sent a mute prayer to heaven for Mother Drumgold's soul and went on reading what he'd written about his pensione; his room, large, clean, airy (the Pensione Borgnini was only a hundred yards from where he sat, in the Via Sicilia—so near, yet in terms of expensiveness and décor, so far), but so noisy he was kept awake half the night. No running water, and the Mexican plumbing a mile away between the dining room and the kitchen. Lack of conveniences didn't bother him much, they were used to that in Nantucket, it was the combination of discomfort, lack of privacy and noise that distracted him: no locks on the doors, and no numbers, so that one was constantly wandering into the wrong room and surprising people: the massive Swedish woman, who worked for an airplane factory, saying: "He said my heart was a fortress," the Englishwoman she lived with, who always wore slacks and couldn't be left alone since her breakdown and who kept trying to make purchases with English money . . . Cosnahan glanced away from his letter down the Via Veneto up which a horsecab, containing Nikolai Gogol, with tragic beaming nose, and smoking a cigar, seemed eternally plodding . . . (But how cruel to make fun of the poor Swedish woman, the consciousness of whose massiveness perhaps stabbed her to the heart, or the poor Englishwoman whose breakdown could not have been any fun for her! No wonder writers stopped writing. Better to make fun of Drumgold Cosnahan, at those times when inscribing his unlikely name for the police in every such pension he had visited in Europe, a species of absolute torture to him, and his flawless incompetence as a linguist, and the unhappy fact of having forgotten so much of the old language, while being condemned half to think in it all the while. Better to write about animals, you could be funny about them without hurting anyone's feelings, not even your own—or could you? Better still not write at all . . .) And the woman who, after supper, he had overheard saying, "My sweet sugar duckling waggle-tailed plum!"

Next he was trying to describe for his wife, because she particulary liked this kind of thing, the atmosphere of Rome: the peculiar flavor of the Roman mornings, the fresh cool air and hot sun, and the afternoons hot, and the "unique golden quality of the Roman sunlight." "And the Corso Umberto, narrow, with screaming jammed trolley-buses, for the Via Veneto, where traffic is limited, is an exception, and the sidewalks only two feet wide that you can't stay on because of the crowd, and can't step off either, or you step under one of the buses, driven at terrific speed, one right behind another!" What on earth was this? Certainly this wasn't the way to keep Lovey's mind at rest about him, the poor girl would be worrying enough about his fear of traffic as it was, and he was about to cross the sentence out when he saw the next one was even worse: "The Piazza Venezia is an inferno, with twelve different kinds of buses coming at you from every direction, and swarms of motor-scooters hurtling at you!"

Cosnahan crossed out both these sentences in such a way that the "Unique golden quality of the Roman sunlight" managed to flow with reasonable excuse into a description of the Forum, with its white marble steps leading to nothing, and broken pillars among which the grass was green, and another sentence where he became rather grandiose about the "sweep and grandeur of the Eternal City," which was nonetheless "proud and cruel as it was beautiful," and the tall dark columns, and dark red brick arches, and here were the broken pillars again, on the ground this time, like fallen trees, and the lovers among the flowers, lying or sitting on the ground in the sunlight, just as he would have liked to be lying or sitting on the ground with her. Finally, since it didn't seem a particularly thoughtful idea to describe the remarkable beauty of Italian women, he described instead the young monks, if they were monks, to be seen everywhere, with their brown eyes and beards and saintly faces, in their coarse brown robes, striding down the avenues in their sandals, not failing to add that his identity with them could not have been more complete . . .

After this he abandoned such descriptive flights and tried to tell her what he'd been doing: sitting in Keats' house, sitting in the dungeon once graced by the person of Vercingetorix, and what was worse, for him, sitting every day in the American Express. This was because Lovey's letters would arrive in a bunch; only once in Rome had he received any mail from her, and these letters mostly antedated the ones he had already received in Paris. Though in any event he would have hung around the place, feeling in the American Express a certain connection with Arthur, or even his anything but American brother, Matthias, either of whom might turn up there. And of course he'd been to the Colosseum, which reminded him of Androcles and the Lion and also of the Albert Hall in a dentist's nightmare.—At this point Cosnahan said how odd it felt to have been once a European immigrant yet this to be his own first visit to Rome. But he added that for the rest his visitations must seem singularly pious to her. For, thinking of his mother, and missing his wife as he did, it gave him a great deal of comfort to wander into the Roman churches, and even to light candles within them . . . This was about as far as he'd got in the letter. It was a bit hard to explain that with no inbred belief in the power of masses and holy water, he nonetheless seemed to have a magical belief in the power of holy water and candles to insure him, as well as Mother Drumgold, against the possible consequences of their unorthodoxy. It was too complicated, whereas what he felt was simple.

But he had somehow to tell his wife, which would delight her, how, more impiously, he'd lain on a bench and gazed at the roof of the Sistine Chapel, and otherwise unimpressed by Michelangelo's muscular comic strip (though it was always possible that the introduction of Noah had afflicted him with an obscure form of professional jealousy) he had thought of the time they whitewashed the ceiling of their cottage in Nantucket, and of the dreadful mixture running down their arms and dripping into their eyes. He might report too that in Raphael's tapestry of the Supper at Emmaus he'd noted that the artist with fine human foresight had provided an item which Rembrandt, in his incomparably greater interpretation, had overlooked: a spare carafe of wine cooling by the disciples' side, an observation he hoped would not be considered irreverent, anyway the Pope hadn't considered it irreverent to have the work in the Vatican Museum.

And he could conclude by remarking that neither his besetting heresies, his Protestantism, nor the knowledge that there were few Manx Catholics left—as he made out Matt intended to shepherd most of them to Rome himself next year, Holy Year, which was part of his business here now— had prevented his taking it as a personal injury when he noticed that upon the innumerable confession boxes in St. Peter's almost every known and unknown language was represented except Manx Gaelic.

Which had seemed, Cosnahan laid down his letter and rested his chin on his hand, all the more reason why then and there he should say his Ayr ain t'ayns niau, Casherick dy row dt' ennym. Dy jig dty reeriaght, Dt' aigney dy row jeant er y thalloo myr te ayns niau. Cur dooin nyn arran jiu as gagh laa. As leih dooin nyn loghtyn—just as he had learned, God rest her soul, at Mother Drumgold's knee.

As we are forgiving to those who are committing trespasses us against, said the Manx. Assuming that there they were, those enemies, and, right at that moment, trespassing against one. As well they might assume it, thought Cosnahan looking away from his table and down the Via Veneto again, up which a huge new Cadillac the size of a conservatory was advancing soundlessly, should they recall all the beautiful old cobbled streets and ancient houses of Douglas that were still being destroyed or pulled down, and beautiful St. Matthew's pulled down and the countryside ruined to make a Liverpool holiday. Yet perhaps this kind of assumption was the great fault of the Manx. And his great fault too. The entire population of the Isle of Man seemed to be trespassing against him, for one thing, because nobody recognized him at home now that he'd become so successful in America. By which he didn't mean merely on the plane of the Browsing Manxwoman. He hadn't even seen a familiar face in Douglas, unless you counted Illiam Dhone, a man, it was true, so unique now he thought of it he might be considered a civic welcome in himself.

For Illiam Dhone had been hanged half an age ago on an open plot of ground where St. Barnabas' Church now stood, and by a freak turn of fortune's wheel, survived this unpleasant ordeal.

Later he had been pardoned, and later still proved innocent, which naturally was considered reason enough for his having survived, and this more than Lazarus of a man he'd met outside Derby Castle and they went into a pub and drank a pint of Castletown Manx oyster stout together. But so long had Cosnahan been a stranger to the old ways and the old speech that—standing under the familiar sign *Castletown 1st prize Ales* and regarding over the bar one of those Manx calendars of singular composition for the previous November that said 24th, Last Norse King of Man died 1205, 27th, Nobles Hospital opened 1906, 30th, Winston Churchill born 1874—he had all but forgotten that Illiam Dhone was not his companion's real name, that it was a nickname meaning sandy or fair-haired, to which the companion himself, now bald, gave no clue; all but forgotten too that this nickname wasn't strictly his own but derived, with the quirky sardonic humor of the Manx, from that other Illiam Dhôan, their own monarch martyr and rebel hero, once collogued into cruel death, in fact, which no Manxman ever really forgets, shot, successfully, before his pardon arrived, Illiam Dhôan who was a forefather of that famous navigator and mutineer of the H.M.S. *Bounty,* that later founder of another remoter Isle of Man, Pitcairn, and the bearer too of the great and simple name of Christian. But no relative at all of the only fellow in Europe who'd recognized Cosnahan on his first trip home in twenty years, and even this Illiam Dhone, who was an engineer's artificer and whose hands were covered with pitch, had not congratulated him, and he had been of two minds, under the circumstances, whether to congratulate Illiam Dhone.

Though in fact the latter (who had doubtless not read the Browsing Manxwoman) *had* paid him a sort of back-handed compliment:

"I heard roundabout, Cosnahan, you know, you had been doing quite good work."

And Cosnahan had almost thought of also saying to him:

"Good work, Illiam Dhone—"

So true it was that these dreamed-of moments of recognition never come off, back from the wars, back from sea, famous or in disgrace, the reception at your source was always the same; there was none—

But what did he expect? Had success on another continent really made him such a swellbox, he wondered, putting away his letter in his pocket with an important air, as though it were a sheaf of diplomatic papers (the huge Rupe Tarpea, he decided, was too public a place to finish it, moreover he had plenty of time to add to it for the airmail he aimed to catch didn't go till midnight), so vain that he quite seriously expected to be recognized everywhere he went, quite seriously expected to be recognized here, in the Rupe Tarpea, so infatuated, that in the same breath he cursed that success, such as it was, he lamented it was not enough, or had passed?

Was he really such a preposterous swellfish as all that? . . . Or was it all, just simply, honest-to-God loneliness? That seemed more like it, the endemic affliction of great cities. Europe was the place where he had his connatural being, this its center, and he would have liked to talk to someone he knew of old. That was understandable, if it did not explain his whole feeling.

But looking down the Via Veneto again, for him there was no one save Gogol, in his hansom cab, clopping eternally up the street, with his eternally beaming nose, and his cigar, and that Rolls-Royce-like purring between the trees, and the same Cadillac the size of a conservatory, and behind him the old gateway the Porta Pincia, and before him the bicycles and tricycles and a few priests and many Americans going up and down through the dappled shadows between the plane trees of the avenue sweeping down to the Piazza Barberini, which he couldn't see, and the striped awnings on the four cafés at the four corners of the crossroads, like the sails of yachts at a regatta ruffling at this moment in a catspaw of breeze, lazily lifting too the caparisons of the horses . . . Cosnahan wondered if this was the very place where, if you sat long enough, so they said, you were *certain* to meet someone you knew. Perhaps it was not a café they meant but just some Roman square. Or perhaps not even a square but just Rome itself, or possibly not Rome either, but Paris, or Budapest . . . Come Arthur, come Matt, he thought . . . And now every other person who passed down the Via Veneto seemed to be a priest or an American publisher. Other people were certainly experiencing better luck: he had observed a hearty greeting only a few tables away on the terrace between two folk from Twin Falls, Idaho. Yes, he had read that there'd never been a time in history when, with this flood of tourists, so many encounters between friends and acquaintances were taking place in Rome.

Yet it didn't seem that even that more romantic encounter with somebody already fallen in with in Europe was in store for him, nothing for example—had his loyalty not been complete—like that felicitous meeting in Rome by the hero of a book he'd been reading with a girl named Rosemary. He remembered the name because it was the same as the original of one of his own, though very different, characters in the Ark, so different that as a matter of fact she was an elephant . . . (It was she upon the cover of his book, being, in a manner of speaking, its heroine.) But failing Matt or Arthur, how he would have loved to see, still somehow by some miracle half expected to see, one of the faces from his island, to speak one of the old names again from Laxey or Ballaugh, or Derbyhaven. Where were they? For they could not all have died, or been killed in the war, all their adventurousness subsumed in that. He would have given anything to meet one of those old friends with the crooked, harsh, twiggy names, the marshy, crazy names, craggy souls like tough wildflowers that rooted themselves on rock like eryngo root: where were all those old purists, the carpenters and shipbuilders he knew, whose religion had been handicraft, "to do their best and no shucking on the job" but whose real conformity ended there. Their fathers would be dead, but where were those of only thirty or forty when he'd known them, who would now be three score and ten, men yet of another age, like Quayle, who smuggled a whole hogshead of rum through the Liverpool customs on a bet. Their sons, his boyhood friends, were scattered, but where had they all scattered to? And now to Cosnahan half closing his eyes it was as if he were sitting once more on the esplanade in Douglas, watching, his more distant view blocked no doubt by the finest conveniences in the British Isles, the people pass, all with the same faces of the same capitulated sleath, all wearing, it seemed even, the same sleathy clothes nowadays, saying to himself: where is Quayne, and where is

Quaggan? where is Quillish? where is Qualtrough? where is Quirk and Quayle and Looney? And Illiam Dhone, who had been hanged? And yet lived, because he was innocent . . .

"That will be a hundred lire, sir," said a new waiter in English, smiling and coming up to him.

"Lhiat myr hoilliu!" Cosnahan laughed, rising to his feet so grateful for the smile and the English words he didn't think of the hundred lire.

Quocunque jeceris stabit. That was something he knew how to say too, much good it would do. Cosnahan, stick and book under his arm, and lighting his pipe, walked down the Via Veneto in the direction of the Piazza Barberini. He was glad the waiter, who'd ended by tipping him with the matches, had disturbed him, for paradoxically enough, considering the trend of his thoughts, he had an appointment. Sort of appointment.

For Cosnahan's presence in Rome was not altogether without purpose. Not merely according to the blurb, but to the terms of a contract drawn up in America, an Italian translation should not only have been made, but be upon the Italian bookshelves by now, though he had so far failed to find it. Similarly with those other countries. Just as it was implied in the blurb again, not only Italy but France too, and even Sweden had leaped at the reviews in the New York papers hailing him as America's newest and greatest humorist, leaped, but without of course looking first at the book itself—how could they since their publishers were dependent on their New York agents, who looked solely at the reviews?—nor calculating the difficulties involved in translating a writer who still half thought in Manx Gaelic, yet wrote in English, into Italian, French, Swedish, etc. The result was that his French publishers when he finally found them in Paris, which was not so easy as one might think, having at last to their distress actually read the work, regretted their hastiness and despite having beforehand remitted him a ruinous advance in dollars (spent long ago in America) were still more than willing to suffer this and let the ill-considered thing drop. He was bound to feel that if the book were eventually translated into French his sudden presence had turned the matter into a point of honor. Sweden meantime preserved an arctic and impenetrable silence, as of the Pole. In England, that had not had to translate it exactly, its praise in America had for some reason prejudiced the publishers, who had let it drop silently and stealthily down the drain, which of course accounted for what had happened to the Isle of Man, while his "German" publisher, who'd signed a contract for the largest advance of the lot, and lived in Switzerland— though there was a chance now an honorable firm in Western Germany itself would take it—had decamped to South America without paying a cent. With all this, Cosnahan could not help wondering sometimes what had caused his novel to succeed in America to begin with. It couldn't be entirely because contemporary literature had reached such an absolute nadir of badness that his own book glittered on high by comparison like the Circlet of the Western Fish . . . No, a mystery remained, there was something about the *Ark,* whatever it was—Cosnahan couldn't help hoping his

Italian publishers might have at last seen it, now they'd had time to read the thing, though it happened Cosnahan hadn't heard from them directly, but from Arthur himself, in a postcard only the other day from Paris:

> Am now over on this side and will try to get to Rome quam celerime if you are still there. I heard via the St. Germain grapevine your Italian publishers would be glad of more biographical material—details of family, streets, houses, ancestors—they go in for that kind of thing in Italy—and could use it in publicity apparently—Arrivederci and congratulations on Lovey's hit—ARTHUR. P.S. Hope you are working.

Which seemed to suggest that the book *was* out here after all, although—Cosnahan's heart missed a beat—he didn't dare count on it . . . And naturally Arthur hoped he was working! But had Art considered those very distractions he implied? Had he himself? Considered that Cosnahan's presence in Europe at all was due to this obscure but huge longing *to* find himself, after so much former failure, actually translated (the very word "translated" had a mystical tinge to him) into other European languages. This was partly due to the small curious linguistic recess in which he had dwelt during early years. Primarily, of course, this recess had insulated him from the English language. But this wasn't the half of it. Nearby Wales confronted him with a language Celtic indeed, but incomprehensible as it was magnificent, savage, bass-toned and druidical, and with words as long as its railway stations. And English once learned, a speech greeted him in Liverpool, that somber and neighboring city, that no familiarity with its caught accents in his invaded island itself could prevent sounding more foreign and harsher to his ears than the language of Tibetan priests, twirling prayer wheels. Yet while it saddened him to conform and learn their language to the point of adoption, to that extent too it had represented so much more of a victory for him, not merely to have mastered English, but to have done this so masterfully the result could be translated into——What? into French? Cosnahan and Flaubert! That was great, heroic. But Italian: that had grandeur and nobility too. Drumgold Cosnahan translated into the language of Dante, Garibaldi and Pirandello! Thus it was possible to say that he was actually *in* Europe because he had expected to find himself translated here, and had looked forward beyond words to enjoying the thrill of this realization with his wife.

So it had been, in some measure, he allowed himself to remember, in Paris, where, wrongly directed to his French publishers at the top of some fifteen flights of stairs without an elevator, upon each floor of which, no sooner had he put a light on than the lights of all the floors savagely went off, until groggy with weariness, and afraid of falling seventy feet into a courtyard in the dark, for there was no railing, he had knocked and knocked at a door from behind which came a sound of crime, or stifled laughter, to ask for help, whereupon five minutes of darkness later that could be compared only to the anguished moments of a mountaineer caught in a storm upon an unnegotiable overhang, all the lights in the building went on again with a crisp crash, whistles wailed, and fifteen armed and bewhiskered gendarmes out of Zola came clattering and clanking up the stone stairs, arrested him and took him away in a Black Maria, where, soon discovering a common interest in rugby football, and the gendarmes that Cosnahan had once played scrum-half against the Racing Club de France, they all became the firmest of friends in no time. At last Cosnahan not only had felt a certain reluctance to leave the Bastille of the Seventh Arrondissement, which seemed to him much cheerier than his hotel room, but had decided that in no country in the world was it such a privilege to be arrested.

And so it almost was, what was unseemly about this incident, and the special disappointment it presaged, having been forgotten in the meantime, here in Rome. He had felt, his first day as he walked down this same sunlit street toward the Forum, that a Manx author such as himself should be translated into Italian, and that this author should himself be in the Eternal City, constituted a phenomenon so remarkable it should have been greeted by the firing of cannon from the monument of Vittorio Emmanuele!

But it so happened that though he possessed a copy of his French contract, and the Swedish one, and his German one, he had omitted to bring a copy of his Italian contract with him, so that not remembering the address of his publishers here, nor for the moment their name, and having his own peculiar difficulties about making inquiries, he had allowed himself to be directed at first to the wrong offices, which were housed by the Tiber, and proved a sort of distributing house, like a huge shed or storeroom, but the machinery of whose presses shook the whole building, as if it were an American newspaper office; such was one's impression, or perhaps it was merely the titanic thunder of the tramway outside, the Circolare Sinistra; and the difficulty of finding this place at all, together with the extraordinary complexity of explaining what his business was—which when he at last made contact was instantly and secretively assumed to be connected with the black market, so that he was beckoned out to a back room where he stood among the piles of other American translations being continually carted away in great blocks, among which at any moment he kept expecting to see his own work disappearing, even as he ever more faintheartedly tried to explain what now several Italians, including a poor old beggar and somebody strayed in from the street trying to sell him a lottery ticket, were assuring him was quite impossible, as did a child, who picked his pocket—had left him so discouraged finally that when he saw that just outside the door over the way was the Palace of Justice, an apparition carrying with it a reminiscence that at this moment retained only its threatening aspect, he had all at once felt utterly exhausted and allowed three days to elapse before trying again.

Meantime, walking down the Corso Umberto, it had come to him that his publisher's name was Garibaldi, a name not to be forgotten, one would have thought; they were the only other publishers in Rome who published translations, and, it devolved, were now in the Via Officino del Vicario, where they must have moved from the Corso Umberto; this name he also recalled from his contract; it had taken him the half-hour before his early lunch this morning to locate them by phone with the aid of his kindly padrona di casa, who had been strangely informed that they were not open again till four o'clock this afternoon.

That was some time hence, it was now one, but the fulfillment of even a half-appointment was for him a circumambient operation, the more so when he imagined he had something to prepare for it.

"And so there you are, Cosnahan, my boy—"

"*Where* am I, Drumgold? The book has died, hasn't it?"

"Died, Cosnahan? What! When the Italian translation may be out, a sensation for all you know!"

Rome, he thought, with mild paranoia . . . How right was that historian he must one day read: success invites self-neglect; by means of self-indulgence. For what did he imagine he was doing this afternoon if not still pursuing the uneasy glimmer of this evanescent sprite of yet more fame? What was behind that "further biographical material" of Arthur's that he was already in his mind seeking to prepare for Garibaldi, had given himself three hours to prepare, long enough, more or less, to plot out a *War and Peace?* At this rate he could see another self of his wandering after this will o' the wisp, this ignis fatuus, all over Europe, to Finland, Germany, to Sweden, perhaps, God knows, end up by stalking his German-Swiss translator all the way to South America and never get home at all.

What on earth *was* he after? Was what he really wanted the kind of recognition no one would suspect? A word would do, or not even a word, but some sign, a kindly look, the look that told him, that *had* told him in America, what workmanship, what craftsmanship there might be in his confounded book. Was that what he was waiting for here? And was the final joker this, that he, a Manxman, was being compelled at first hand to endure, and as a "successful American," a "bloated capitalist," and before the scornful judiciary of his own European kin stuffing their eyes full of Spam while Coca-Cola ran out of their nostrils, that treatment known as the "European cold shoulder"?

Perishing Moddey Doo! Yet for what else but that kind word was he waiting? Certainly he'd experienced almost every other benefit to be derived from it all in America, at that moment of "instantaneous success" (and as if an "English" immigrant could be quite without former knowledge of the *American* cold shoulder!)—the people who wouldn't lend him any money when he was poor who now all at once started ringing him up at every hour to borrow some, the people who spoke to him who wouldn't speak to him before, the people who sent him telegrams from Hollywood saying "This is money and I mean big money, Cosnahan," and when they saw there was no money in it or not enough for them, and that his fame was not so great as they had at first supposed, dropped the whole thing, the people who having found out he was going to Europe insisted they were befriending him by giving him five-thousand-franc notes in exchange for dollars, which notes were taken away from him at the customs as illegal tender, and never returned, thus leaving him broke over the week end in Paris, those writers who would never have spoken to him before either, but now just wanted to *look* at him, or wanted him to contribute without payment to their magazines, the thrice-blasted Canadian writer conversely who went out of his way to say "Of course I haven't read your book, Cosnahan," the lady, also a writer, and with far more money than he, he'd met once in a bar before he was married, who seriously put in a legal claim for twenty-five per cent of the profits from Arthur, because he'd remarked jokingly on that occasion ten years before that if he ever wrote a successful book at all, which at that moment seemed most unlikely, by crikey he'd give her a quarter of the proceeds, and what was worse produced an unsteady yet ruthless witness to his rashness, his own handwriting—all this he had experienced, and, moreover, forgiven, or tried to, for what, after all, is more irritating and disturbing than a personal acquaintance who suddenly becomes famous? Hasn't he done that in a way just for *us?* Didn't he ask us to have a drink with him ten years ago, and though we refused, didn't bother to answer his letters, isn't it just like taking things up where we left off? Sure, hasn't he justified, or expunged, in the twinkling of an eye, all we *haven't* done with our lives meantime? And indeed, hadn't we better go and see him for *his* sake, for we know *him,* what a spendthrift he is, and if we don't get there first he'll be ruined again just like he was when we met him, before you can say knife, and besides we have just the kind of work for him that will make *our* name, but at the same time *his* name shine brighter—all this then he had known, as well as that true generosity of the few people who believed in him, the handful of reviewers who meant what they said, and the people like Arthur and Seward and Bill. But the people who believed in him were all American, and over here in Europe—once more came that inexplicable childish pang, yet so deeply he couldn't believe its cause was mean or unworthy—he'd received no word from the heart, no word at all, unless (not counting his civic reception by Illiam Dhone) it was what his brother Matt said over the phone during that one long-distance conversation, mostly taken up after the first two serious and clear minutes by their saying "What!" "I can't hear you"—which was besides disrupted by a mysterious German voice from somewhere that kept repeating through the continental brouhaha something like "Nicht so besonderes schlect!" or "Hamburger Beefsteak mit zwei Eier und Kartoffelnsalad"—oh, to hell with it all!

And how in the old days they had prayed for his success—his mother and father and Matthias and his brother John, now in durance vile in St. Helena (to whom, he wondered, pausing by a kiosk, should he not send a picture postcard with the Mamertine Dungeon upon it, if that would cheer him up, or hurt his feelings, or a Christmas card, perhaps a Christmas card, if he could get one, would arrive in time for Christmas), hoping that he "had something good in him," and that he would "make good over there." Ah, this was what hurt, that his "making good" had come too late; his father was dead, his mother was dead, and though he had at least sent her a copy of *Ark from Singapore* with its glowing advance notices upon it, followed by a lapis lazuli elephant he'd bought for her in Provincetown, it miserably turned out that the copy, being American and new, had somehow been held up, then lost. It could be Mother Drumgold, not knowing what it was, had even refused to pay duty on it. He still hadn't found out why she didn't get it. Matt was a dreadful letter writer. In fact, though a priest, he was almost illiterate. When the English edition, a flat failure, came out a little later, his mother couldn't even have been aware of it. But why go on torturing himself? What a shopworn tradition the dramatics of even this version of a success story belonged to. Yet ungrateful though it sounded, how could the European help looking upon America, under certain circumstances, as primarily his sounding board, his test of strength? If the opportunity was greater, so was the competition. And having at last become "something," not infrequently he would depart back to his native land with the substantial gains earned at the expense of his magnanimous opponent, and never a backward look. Now Cosnahan had become an American, married an American, sent down his roots in American soil. He had not the slightest desire ever to live again in the Isle of Man. But there was still this much of the European left in him, that he could ask the old question: how can a European feel himself American without first making his peace with Europe, without becoming, however deviously, reconciled with his home?

All of which made Matthias' having said, his voice reaching him at intervals with brotherly and secular extravagance over the telephone in Douglas, "No, old man, I didn't say it wasn't funny, because it is. I said . . . " and after a catastrophic whingdinging in several keys, a voice abruptly, "Hamburger Beefsteak mit zwei Eier and Kartoffelnsalad!—" *"What?"* and then his voice clear and laughing again, "I said it reminded me of the times we used to sing "Hear Us O Lord from Heaven Thy Dwelling Place," reminding him of the old Manx fishermen's hymn, more important to him perhaps than anything, though said faintly, and at long distance, and from Bruges.

Deciding not to cross here he resumed his walk on the same side of the Via Veneto, still in the direction of the Piazza Barberini. Cosnahan was not exactly a man who walked without thinking where he was going. On the contrary, he often thought so intensely about it that every time he approached what, to another, would have seemed a logical crossing, his direction was modified by the decision at all costs, if possible, to avoid that crossing. At the same time he liked to drift, steering as by dead reckoning. Cosnahan had met other men who lived in the country, nearly always ex-sailors or prospectors, who combined this love of walking for its own sake with this same invincible suspicion and fear of traffic. With him this fear had become a far more positive thing in Europe, largely, he suspected, because he didn't have his wife with him. And he remembered how she used literally to pilot him across the streets on their rare trips to Boston or New York: "Hurry up, Drumgold," she would say, "there goes a nice perambulator we can get behind." Or, "Here's a dear old lady with a ducky little three-year-old child who'll run interference for us." Lovey's laughter rang clear as a merry bell.

What really made it worse was that he was now deprived of all the fun they used to get out of it, for he liked to exaggerate the whole thing a little, or conversely, have conscious and terrifying bouts of heroism and pilot *her*.

—Cosnahan knew he was absent-minded, and that his absent-mindedness in combination with this Roman traffic scared him out of his wits . . . Meantime, enjoying the sidewalks of the Via Veneto, generous in width and shady beneath the plane trees, he appropriately thought also of the award for bravery the Japanese government had given him.

It was twenty-one years ago, in the typhoon season, at sunset. His ship was lying peacefully in Yokohama harbor when a storm came darkening around the point. Half the crew were ashore, nearly all the rest had turned in, and the second steward, a fireman, and himself were standing outside the second steward's cabin amidships having a drink of Chinese samshaw and watching, amused because it was equipped with a motor horn it proudly tooted at intervals, a Japanese fishing boat, now about a cable's length away, that had been puttering into port for some time, its dinghy behind. At once it was dark, and rough, with a howling wind and rain; then a collision of thunderclaps crashed almost on top of a gigantic discharge of lightning, in whose brilliance the fishing boat seemed pinned against the night; the lightning blazed a little longer, and they saw the vessel break in half like a stick, and as the two halves sank its crew scramble over the stern into the dinghy, which as they cut adrift was instantly half swamped.

Then in the tumult the heartrending wail downwind for help went up, and one seemed to distinguish a woman's voice among those others, rising and falling, of the shipwrecked.

Cosnahan's duty was more properly to stand by the lifeboat's falls, rather than be a saving member of it, but both he and the fireman climbed into it anyhow, an old-fashioned boat with oars, as would have the steward, had he not been ordered below by the captain to warm up blankets, in case they saved anybody, and get whisky, which in his case was redundant.

What seemed most likely was that they'd never get the lifeboat launched and away, and if they did would need saving themselves, for the sea was running so preposterously high that their freighter, tied to buoys fore and aft, was nearly rolling her bulwarks under. Cosnahan smiled at the memory of how important they'd all at once become, that skeleton crew of lonely men, with the captain yelling against the wind, and the wireless operator running up and down companion ladders saying "Aye aye, sir!"

They got all the Japanese, however, taking the dinghy in tow, though they had to cut it loose finally, transferring its shipwrecked occupants to their lifeboat which had become in charge, at last, of a fat quartermaster named Quattras, a cowardly braggart, everyone thought, and the possessor of a Portuguese wife in Surabaya he was reported to mistreat. For this reason his shipmates rarely cared to admit afterwards the heroism of this man. Since, while the Japanese men were all behaving with the stoic courage of their race, a woman is a woman in any language, and nothing could induce this one, who weighed two hundred and fifty pounds, and was besides in hysterics, to leave the dinghy—perhaps courage in itself, for it was all the little family had left in the world. Despite the awe-inspiring sea, and above all the dreadful din, to which the poor woman added her frenzied bellows, making of the whole one esemplastic miserere, wailings from heaven and earth commingling in a single howl, then exploding in livid light, to be resumed into the same uproar once more, Quattras, who could not swim, sprang unhesitatingly into the scending dinghy, and from that position hurled his ponderous and operatic cargo into the lifeboat, itself in danger of capsizing.

Now this quartermaster was also a Manxman, and like all Manxmen imagined he was a writer or a poet, though in English, and every watch below after that incident was to be seen, to the crew's saturnine relish, working on a story which he entitled tersely, on Cosnahan's advice—this was its sole concession to economy—"The Dinghy." But that nobody should make any mistake about his vocation, the quartermaster worked standing up with the door to his room wide open, his papers spread out on the vacant upper bunk, and his hair falling wildly over his face in a tangle of inspiration.

In this story, "The Dinghy," though, there was no hint of the drama of what had occurred. There wasn't enough romance in that for Quattras. There was nothing of the Japanese family who'd lost their possessions, their little boat, even their bloody little motor horn, nothing, to speak fact, of the leachy dinghy itself, that had stayed in sight half that night, lit by intermittent flashes, and drifted under the lee the next morning when Cosnahan himself, who'd been haunted by it and hadn't slept, dived down the gangway and tied it up; nothing of their tragic joy then, nor their gratitude at having been saved by a handful of barbaric foreign seamen: a quartermaster who on duty behaved as though too fat to move, two scared apprentices, and a fireman and a carpenter's mate both of whom were half-cockeyed, scarcely knew what was up, only obeyed instinct and knack and were actually, at the worst point, laughing their heads off. Quattras, his heroism, neither was anywhere to be found. Not from modesty, nor any aversion to the subjective, or even because he had some sage notion the truth wouldn't sell. On the contrary he felt that what he had written *was* the truth, that it *would* sell, but only to a "high-class audience." And if it did not, he was artist enough to admit, that would be only because it was *too* truthful, *too* realistic, too "art for art's sake," and in short, too much like that Sagami Sea of Japan that had all but engulfed them all, "over their heads." So for the sake of this art, this truth, he introduced pirates, opium runners, a beachcomber in decaying white flannels, while the poor old mother aged seventy, whom he himself had rescued, became a pretty American, fleeing from her brutal father, at the connivance of a tall, dark, and slim Frenchman, who had no part in the dashing proceedings, with a fortune in Shanghai.

—What did man know of his own nature? How many people went through life thinking they were other than they were? Not even the evidence of his own essential being right under his red nose would convince him. How many lives were necessary to find out? Heroic old Quattras, now a Canadian, had never lost the illusion that he was a writer—and who was Cosnahan to say him nay?—at long last had even succeeded in getting something published in a Montreal newspaper, a martial item he'd sent in about butterflies, in which, feeling this time a little propaganda might be in order, he had in all seriousness described the insects as "Butterflies manly and strong . . . Righting the wrong." And "fighting the foe" and "about they go" it seemed, triumphantly, right smack into the Kremlin . . .

Yet what did he, Cosnahan, know of himself? Was he a writer? What *was* a writer? Was any clue to what he was to be gained by giving Garibaldi some more elaborate biographical notes as suggested by Arthur, when finally he saw his Italian publishers? There was some sense in it, to be sure, but what would it help to explain of Cosnahan, should he say: My great-great grandfather, Cronkbane, late of Cronkbane . . .

Cosnahan found himself in a long narrow labyrinth of cobbled streets without having come to Barberini at all. It was a region of underground restaurants, sinister steps leading downward to padlocked grottoes, to just the kind of place where he'd have liked to think out his notes over a brandy or a grappa, only none seemed open. Nocturnal haunts. "And as a young man I had often brushed against the ghastly wig of the Duke of Brunswick, traversing the corridors of night restaurants—" It seemed to him too that the other evening at dusk he had come home this way, barred to motor traffic, in a horsecab, and how beautiful it had been, first with the spectacular sunset behind the Arch of Constantine, and the light fading from scarlet to rose, and from rose to violet, and the lights beginning to flash on. Clipperty-clop, in the sideslipping cab over the cobblestones, clipperty-clop, by these narrow alleyways and by-streets, and then suddenly coming upon the Trevi Fountain—how he loved fountains! which was perhaps natural since they were the city cousins of springs and wells—the cool waterfalls and clear green pool seeming to wash away all the dust and heat of the day, and the people, just gazing into it, sitting round the semi-circular low wall.

And then later that night, he had taken another horsecab through the park, and down through the avenue of magnolias, their leaves glittering hard and carved under the lamplight and a deep gold young moon, larger than he ever remembered having seen a new one before (it was the same one that, a little older, was still going strong in mid-afternoon over the Borghese Gardens), hanging beneath black cypresses. And a few little bars with their lights and flowers shone out as he drove by, the cab feeling so undated and impersonal he could imagine himself in any century at all, save when he remembered he was Drumgold Cosnahan . . .

He came out into the heat and light of one of the indeterminate and dangerous streets in the approaches to the monument of Vittorio Emmanuele, and paused before the titanic thunder and confusion of the traffic. How did you go, how did you begin to go? Yet this momentous traffic was scarcely a symptom of the age in which he lived: in the second century, his guidebook had told him, the traffic was so heavy deliveries had to be made at night to avoid congestion, and was even forbidden in certain streets, as in part it was still forbidden in the crepuscular region he'd just traversed, because of the racket on the cobbles. Cosnahan could see the Colosseum from here—it was just over there he got the horsecab. And the moment before he got the horsecab (and this was not getting across the street) a scene had taken place that caused him to feel his loneliness most of all—

Truckloads of Italian soldiers had been coming down the street toward the Arch of Constantine waving branches of green leaves, singing and cheering, truck after truck of them against the spectacular sunset sky, the continually reclouding heavens. And then, as they passed Cosnahan standing there, catching sight of him they waved at him: he waved back, the soldiers in the next truck behind saw and waved too, more and more enthusiastically till all were yelling and waving wildly, and one soldier ripped all the green leaves from his branch and threw them at Cosnahan with both hands upthrown—

What a joyous and heartwarming scene was that, how deliciously ironic this triumphant recognition of Cosnahan for what he was not, or had not participated in, nor could his absurd consciousness of being a "Manxman of distinction" altogether resist this reception as something obscurely purporting to recognize that too, for to his vanity it did not seem extravagant, just for a moment, to imagine that in this way he was being welcomed to Italy, Lovey and himself; then he remembered Lovey was not there, though how could they be waving like that unless they had seen her so prettily standing beside him? And how delighted she would have been by this. "See, they've brought out the army to welcome you, Drumgold," she'd have said. And they would have laughed all the way home.

Cosnahan eyed the chaos of the road, and somehow attaching himself to a sudden excited gaggle of priests careening out of an alleyway, made the awful and dangerous crossing toward the Forum.

Inside the Forum, to which he had to buy a ticket, and into which he was preceded by the same priests who, all unknown to them, had shepherded him across the road, and two jolly monks, or so they seemed to him, he breathed more easily. Here at least there was no traffic. And how many priests there were! He had no idea of the different orders, and of the two whom he'd put down as "jolly monks," one was wearing a white robe with a black cape over it, upon which, seen from behind, was the emblem of the cross, the vertical arm in red, the horizontal in blue: the other, obviously standing him an afternoon treat, was wearing just a dark gown. But there were all kinds of other priests. There were priests clomping along in heavy boots, in shoes and black socks, in shoes and white socks. And here were majestic priests with cobalt blue sashes and cobalt blue buttons marching down the front of their jet black robes, imperial ones in scarlet robes, and tall solemn ones carrying their hats behind their backs. There was every kind of priest, in short, except the priest Cosnahan wanted to see, Father Matthias Cosnahan, who was his brother. Yet it did his heart good to see them. He reflected that those were unusual thoughts for someone to have who had been born in an atmosphere where Catholics were vilified and priests still scaldingly demeaned as pot-bellied parasites—Matt's faith had to survive a day when if a priest could be sneaked in at all he came from Liverpool and had to hold a service in a stable. It gave him the feeling too that Rome, whether it bore out its legends or not, was one place where you didn't really need to be alone. On the other hand the very staggering multiplicity of these men of God came close to unnerving him again: it was almost hallucinatory, so that, advancing slowly, his stick under his arm, toward the Basilica of Constantine, he imagined he saw Matthias everywhere, and he began to feel there must be some mistake, that Matt had already left some later message for him that he had not received. So much had happened, for good or evil, since the brothers had last seen each other, and even so there was not going to be time to go into half of it.

Cosnahan watched the black swallows, or swifts, like bats playing round the Basilica. Like bats? He hoped the Laurentian thought wasn't a bad omen: Lovey's name, L'Hirondelle, meant swallow. And he remembered how they'd grown quite fond of bats ever since during a heat wave they'd found one stranded on a dusty path in the sunlight, with its little hands, and face like a tiny kitten, and he'd put it in the cool deep shade on a branch where it clung upside down hissing at him . . .

And the swallows, black as they might be, seemed to fly out of love, tossing in the summer air like children's darts, about the evocations of vanished splendor, about the Basilica, in which he was now half ashamed to be less interested than in the white convolvulus and morning bride and wild geranium growing everywhere that you didn't read about in the guidebook.

Isle of Man wildflowers! Eryngo root in the north, samphire at St. Anne's Head; pennyroyal in the marlpits at Ballaugh, and sea kale near Peel—

And there in front of him, examining some kind of spiked and hooded flower, blue and white, stood Matthias again, though Matthias would not have been wearing a long brown corded robe with sandals. That a monk had seemed the same thing as a priest, that he couldn't distinguish in his mind between the numerous denominations and orders, that he'd have to go to his dictionary to discover the difference between a priest and a friar, and could confuse a partial dedication with a complete withdrawal from the world of flesh, reminded him nonetheless at what a distance he stood from Matt.

He could see him now, though he had not seen him, his strong and humorous face with the two front teeth broken in an unhieratic fracas at a rugby match, and hear his voice, though he had heard it only on the phone, deep, certain, rich, and full of mischief and unpriestlike comfort. This clear sense of his brother's dedication and belief had the effect for a moment, as it might with a person who has never loved or been loved, of making him think that some great purpose and meaning in life had passed him by. And for a while, not really having any definable religion himself save a belief in its freedom and an appreciation of the prejudices of other people—or was it because he seemed to detect once again, from afar off, that faint but unmistakable odor of frizzling Cosnahan?—he felt excluded, by that very all-embracing tolerance that a moment since was making him appear such a benign and condescending fellow, as from the great circle of religion altogether, and more lonely than ever.

Cosnahan strolled up the Palatine Hill and, tired, sat on a bench halfway up. My great-great grandfather Cronkbane, should he say? was hung for stealing a sheep. Though the sheep itself had not been harmed it appeared in a vision to the next of kin, demanding further revenge. And immediately afterwards the law that required hanging for theft was repealled. What happened then? . . . Did my great-great grandfather start haunting the sheep?

Two lovers were sitting on the grass under the House of Flavia and he could not help watching them; every now and then they would gaze long in each other's eyes, then look away again, then laugh. The boy took a wisp of grass and began to chew it, the girl took it away from him, and then she laughed. Then they took to looking in each other's eyes again. But such notation of these absurd actions, crude as in an old silent movie, did not describe how beautiful they looked, or *how* they looked, or what it said to him.

My great-great grandfather Cronkbane was not only a poet but a successful inventor and engineer. (Up the eternal Palatine Hill more eternal lovers were walking past more eternal monks and eternal smiling priests.) He surveyed the Isthmus of Panama and submitted to the United States, in 1855, a scheme for a canal without locks, for he was the first to assert that the Atlantic and Pacific Oceans were on a level . . . Cronkbane's poetry is admittedly rugged, but it is vigorous . . .

After a while Cosnahan, like a snag of driftwood caught in a current following some colorful boats downstream, found himself joining in the procession. Onid aalid ben. Ah yes, everybody in Rome seemed to be in love or a priest and all the girls were pretty. Pretty? Almost all these Italian women were exquisitely beautiful, and watching them pass, with that slow, heartbreaking saunter, grasses between their lips, with their lovers, these girls picking their feet off the ground and placing them down again so daintily, as if dancing some slow love dance (but always accompanied by some lover), their hair so glossy and silky, or fair as angels, and their long, slim, almost painfully beautiful legs, and their shy glances, you might wish the girl whose hair and whose carriage or whose hands you had already fallen in love with from behind, to turn round and prove ugly; that, you felt, would at least relieve your heartache. And yet—continuing to indulge, half abstractedly, in these pseudo- or rather contra-Proustian reveries—comparison was the only human relief there was, for having already fallen in love with and lost one such exquisite phantom, it was almost necessary to imagine that the next one that passed was more beautiful still, if only not to think of one's wife. So that one was able to say to himself: well, it was not that other one who was destined for me but this one, and take comfort even in this thought from the reflection that one is going to pass who is more lovely still, the one who would say, or would never say, "My sweet sugar duckling waggle-tailed plum," or whatever that was, translated into Italian.

A Negro stood looking somberly at the Temple of Venus, and Cosnahan wanted to speak to him and say something cheerful, though he did not do so; and Cosnahan went back two hundred feet to give a poor beggar woman with one leg (having passed her meanly at first), at whom he smiled, fifty lire: half the price of his milk, and he went on, feeling meaner than he had before giving it to her.

How hot it was, too hot to smoke his pipe; Cosnahan, turning, made for the river where it might be cooler. And here was the yellow, low Tiber with brown people bathing and playing on the sand. Romans were diving off the top of a sort of houseboat in the mud below the bank. Cosnahan would have liked a swim but probably you had to belong to some kind of club. By the riverside the traffic was even more intense and noisy, though the street was narrow and at least defined, with a dividing refuge, and he was not obliged to cross it yet: plenty of time before his publishers opened: just the same, it might be more sensible definitely to locate them well in advance, because he wanted to find a quiet cool pub in which to sit an hour now and try to write down his ideas for those "further biographical notes," and, as all writers know, "where is the publisher, there too is the pub." Some writers never get any further than the pub.

Over the bridges or along the embankment plunged red, glistening motorbicycles with pushbike-sized wheels, all with the same exquisite girl on the pillion, each one a Beatrice, or a Laura; and how reckless were these Romans, people steering naked-wheeled bicycles at full speed without their handlebars through this traffic, more fellows with girls on the crossbars of pushbikes with mudguards whizzing along, and then more priests: mobile priests this time, the most carefree and reckless of the lot, and here was a goggled old priest going hell for leather down the Lungo Tevere, and again Cosnahan mingled in the procession of priests on foot going and coming, priests with bowler hats, with flat-topped hats, with briefcases, with no hats at all, bearded priests carrying brown paper parcels, black-velvet-hatted priests carrying slim briefcases, more tall solemn ones carrying their hats behind their backs, good little priests reading their breviaries along the embankment, prancing priests, almost defrocked by a sudden wind and dust hurling down from St. Peter's. A motorbicycle like a red gnat flashed over the Garibaldi Bridge. And this too was piloted by a priest with an expression he'd seen only once before, upon the countenance of the great George Dance, as in the Isle of Man he negotiated Ballig Bridge, when it seemed he was going to win the Senior Tourist Trophy motorbicycle race upon a Sunbeam with one cylinder. And now there were more priests: priests in rubber soles, in worn-out soles, blue-fringed, scarlet, and even a poor priest who limped and spat, and why shouldn't he, just like anyone else? And here came three more, dressed in white robes with black capes and hoods and wool stockings and black shoes, joking along—ah, he really loved all these priests, especially these three, not because they were funny, but because they seemed to take such a childish delight in making fun of themselves—they were the same ones he'd seen yesterday in the Vatican, he thought, in the mummy room, the eldest lecturing the other two on the glories of ancient Egypt, and Cosnahan bowed and smiled, though they did not recognize him, and he felt momentarily sad; besides, this might augur some worse disappointment . . . Still, surely enough priests altogether there were to waft Mother Drumgold's soul to heaven, and as he walked on alone he prayed they might. But at the sight of a little procession of smiling priests on gray motor-scooters Cosnahan purred to himself: mechanized priests! Good Lord. Matthias must not be allowed to return home without one of those gray motor-scooters. He would insist upon it.

Ha, there was the Palace of Injustice again. Cosnahan remembered his publishers and began to be nervous, wishing he had Arthur with him. Good, good old Art . . . And Cosnahan now imagined that, instead of Matthias, he saw everywhere this man to whom he owed so much; a tall, rangy, cheerful yet sad-eyed Texan, of unending patience, but who always walked as if advancing toward the net to make a forehand drive at tennis. There were benevolent young-looking businessmen on motor-scooters too who might have been Art, and even passengers sitting bolt upright on the carriers of these motor-scooters that might just have been Arthur, nor did he fail to scan the faces of the passengers in the huge green tram-buses, with their sinister antennae aloft charging along on the overhead net of wires.

Cosnahan was thinking so hard of Arthur he somehow survived another crossing; the Tiber left behind, he found himself gratefully in another labyrinth of cobbled streets forbidden to traffic, stumbled upon the antique court that housed his publishers almost immediately, and observing at the same time, just as he had suspected, a place of seclusion, as if put there for the consolation of anxious or rejected authors, he continued toward the almost empty little bar with low benches and tables, sat down and ordered a large grappa, which was something he knew how to order.

By the door facing him was a sign: *Chi ha Ucciso Il Pettirosso?* beyond which in a tiny square two tootling street musicians were wrestling with what looked like ophicleides. That was good: it was as if the band had come to meet him already. They soon went away, however.

"Who killa the cock-a robin?" the barman explained what the sign meant, though why it was there remained a mystery.

Aye, that was a sad piece indeed, it made him cry with anguish when he first learned it. In his youth he had read a queer story by the same name, something about natural beauty and how man had killed it with ugliness and machinery and with his own spirit. Something like that. It had struck him as sentimental then, like a bit he'd written himself about the factory chimneys of Eleusis. But now Cosnahan, drinking his grappa, found himself thinking of the old lines: "I am thy dying mother tongue, the first speech of this island race. 'Twas I who kept the strangers out . . . " And Cosnahan took his pen and wrote:

"My great grandfather, Cosnahan Curghey Cronkbane, of Ballabeg, was born in 1816, in Cronkbane Street, Douglas . . . Also a poet he developed a love . . . of natural history pursuits. At sixteen he entered Edinburgh University . . . In 1832 he investigated the natural history of Man . . . A thoroughly patriotic Manxman who took pride in having only Manx blood in his veins . . . he visited France, Switzerland, Germany, Algiers, always studying natural history . . . he was appointed Government Palaeontologist in 1844 . . . His memory is commemorated . . . a marble bust. His poetry is admittedly rugged, but it is vigorous."

And now, the next moment, his great grandson, with a feeling of genuine relief, and none of the nervousness that Cosnahan expected, with serene confidence indeed, found himself waiting in the enormous silent coolness of his Italian publisher's offices in Rome in the Via Officino del Vicario. Well, he was here, wasn't he? Or was he? For though he hadn't noticed this before, now that a little hard liquor had ascended to his brain, he had become aware that the fumes of unsullied renown must have been lying there dormant all afternoon simply waiting to be aroused again by this pleasant company, and to take full effect themselves, so that while no one could say that he was tight, in terms of quiet elation it was more as if he'd had seven drinks, not just two. Gone was his memory of France, of his disappointment in England, the silence in Sweden, of the abdication of occupied Germany for parts unknown, of his neglect in the Isle of Man itself—it was as though he had never left Arthur's office that extraordinary morning in New York, when he had said deprecatingly: "Arthur, are the reviews good?" And Arthur had replied: *"Good?* Read that, man! I've been up all night . . . " He was even almost oblivious, so entranced by himself was he, that he had been standing absolutely alone in the offices for nearly ten minutes, the American edition of *Ark from Singapore* in hand, half in readiness, together with his notes for the further biographical material, to present to the senior representative of the firm, whose appearance would shortly no doubt be the result of the hidden activities of the pleasant young Italian with the open shirt and loose tie, who was now telephoning in a recess on his account, or to present to this young man himself, should he wish to consult the American copy of his book again, which, at this moment the youth smilingly re-entered, he apparently did—he took it away with him this time thoughtfully tapping the cover.

Perhaps the young Italian was even speaking to the translator himself. Drumgold Cosnahan, at last translated into the language of Boccaccio and Manzoni, and Croce, and Pirandello, who'd written a story about a poltergeist! Quite forgotten was his sadness about the old language in the little bar with the ophicleides playing outside, that he could hear dimly now, as from another world, playing somewhere else. It was overwhelming. And Garibaldi's offices were as overwhelming as the occasion. The walls, hung with paintings in great gold frames, were of dark crimson satin: the ceilings, of some carved polished wood embossed with narrow gold designs, must have been thirty feet high. Sumptuous chairs were arranged around a huge oak desk, while the office beyond, with walls of jade green satin damask, seemed the size of a small railroad station, and was all done up in red and gold too, with carved chairs upholstered in satin about a carved circular table. And all around Cosnahan, in the private office, were arranged the books of the firm, which like those other unfortunate offices near the Palace of Justice, specialized in translations, only instead of being just bound in paper, these were all sumptuously bound. And among these books, if he could but find it, would be his book, only this was what he hadn't quite been able to make clear to the young Italian. Cosnahan had, true, discovered one book with a ship upon its cover that might have been *Ark from Singapore,* but on closer investigation this proved a translation of a volume containing Conrad's *Typhoon*: and he'd just seen another cover that might have been his, unfortunately it was André Obey's *Noah,* when the young Italian returned.

Afterward it seemed their conversation went something like this:

"I'm afraid we don't know your name, I can't find out whether we're publishing your book or not, Signor."

"But I told you—it's Kennish Drumgold Cosnahan—there it is, on the cover of that book you're holding." Cosnahan took *Ark from Singapore* as the other now handed it back to him. "And *this* is the book you've published. This very one!"

"I'm sorry, Signor—what is it again?" he said, screwing his head around and looking at the cover once more, interested and half-deprecative at once, as if the title were slightly beneath his notice, but at the same time, though he spoke excellent English, he were not averse to adding a new word to his vocabulary. "Ark? Ark?"

"Yes, *Ark from Singapore.* You've published it—you, Garibaldi and Company."

"Ah, but we don't have any such *Ark* in stock, no."

"In stock! But you are publishers, Signor, not a bookshop, aren't you? Or have I made some mistake again?"

"Yes, that's it, a mistake," said the young man. "We do publish translations, only the very best—perhaps you are looking for another publisher—Piccoli, down by the Tiber, yes, opposite the Palace of Justice."

Cosnahan winced. "I am *your* author, and in fact you wanted further biograph—but never mind that. Here I am—look, this is me, on the back of the cover. This is my wife, my cat—"

"Yes, but we don't have you *here,* Signor."

"But you've paid for me in dollars!"

"Ah, you want to change American dollars! How much is it you want to change?" said the young man courteously.

"I don't want to change—Tusen tak—muchas gracias, señor," Cosnahan explained patiently. "You've already paid for my novel in dollars. According to my contract the book should not only have been translated into Italian but have been out for a month. Of course I can understand it may have sold out. What I can't understand is that you should never've heard of me or the book either. And what I can understand least of all, Signor, is why in hell if that's so you should have paid any dollars for the goddamn thing in the first place—"

"Do you have a copy of your contract with you, Signor?" said the Italian, patiently too, for his part, and putting on a pair of spectacles.

"That's what I tried to explain before," Cosnahan replied. "I didn't bring my contract to Europe and I couldn't remember your address. It was a little harder to forget your name, and when I found one day I was in the Corso Umberto I recognized the address too. It's true I discovered you were in the Via Officino del Vicario, so I supposed you must have moved."

"No, we haven't moved. But you see, Signor, we're only the sub-office."

"The sub—"

"Yes, you see our main office is in Torino. I think that is where you made your mistake. On the Corso Umberto, Turin . . . "

"In Turin . . . I beg your pardon. Raad erbee cheauys oo eh, hassys eh!"

Kennish Drumgold Cosnahan was walking down the unfortunate, the illusory Corso Umberto that was not in Turin, the Corso Umberto—narrow, with screaming jammed trolley-buses, and the sidewalk two feet wide that you couldn't stay on because of the crowd and you couldn't step off or you'd step under one of the buses driving at terrific speed, one behind the other, that he'd written about to Lovey—though he hadn't noticed it till this minute. For once in his life, Cosnahan had not only lost his sense of humor but felt really desperate.

In a way, he supposed, after what had already happened, he had been prepared for it. He might have been prepared for it anyway by the ophicleides players who moved away as soon as he arrived at that bar, the priests of the mummy room who hadn't recognized him, his thinking that swallows were like bats, and much besides. And yet this was almost worse than anything, worse than not having met anyone he knew, while it extended the feeling unbearably, that in this place of all places where he might have expected at least his name to strike, they hadn't known either him or his book from Adam's off ox. Yes, and now this ridiculous incident—and a sub-office! what pleasure dome of Kubla Khan, what Doges' palace, must house then that main office in Turin?—had upset him so by its very crowning and cunning futility that he wasn't watching where he was going, had even forgotten to bother about traffic.

"Cosnahan?"

"Yes, Drumgold."

"It is vanity, Cosnahan. The incident is without point, or at least the point you see in it. But that you're not looking where you're going is not without point . . . "

"—And it doesn't seem likely I'm being published in Turin either, whether they've paid me or not."

"What does it matter? You're not going there anyhow. Go and look at the peacocks—"

"No peacocks, Drumgold. I don't want any more bad omens!"

"—so that you may see how vain some of God's creatures can really be!"

Nel mezzo del cammin di nostra vita mi ritrovai in . . . And here was the bosca oscura, the obscure boskage. It was the Borghese Gardens, or perhaps this section was called the Park of Umberto, a spacious park of dark cypresses, dark evergreens, and brittle-leaved trees that looked as though they never shed their leaves, and where the sunlight and shadow were intense. Cosnahan had made almost an exact circuit from the point where he started, and he was not five minutes' walk, possibly, from the Porta Pincia and the Restaurant Rupe Tarpea again, but it had never occurred to him to come to the Borghese Gardens before. A wonder he hadn't, for he soon began to lose his gloomy thoughts. A few lovers were twined in the deep grass among flowers and poppies. Mounted policemen, like equestrian statues in slow motion, lingeringly paraded the transverse streets of the park under the trees, where a few motor-scooters scooted, though there was little cross traffic. The shadows cast by the cypresses were intensely black, not light and airy as he had noticed the shadows in the Bois de Boulogne, and this green grass full of poppies, for there was nothing like a lawn here, was wiry, and in patches grew a foot high. And above still palely tilted the afternoon moon. Vota Garibaldi, Vota de Gasperi, it said again on a wall. Garibaldi. H'm. Poor old John. He *would* send him a Christmas card. Cosnahan crossed a road. He had been looking for the peacocks strutting among the trees as he'd once seen them in Burton Woods, in England, though he hadn't seen any yet (he'd overheard the phrase "such lovely peacocks in the gardens" at the pensione and surmised the famous Borghese Gardens were meant) and at that moment he felt a twinge, a sort of tug at his being, much as one felt divining water, not when the twig turned downward, but when he felt that water was near—not the same, yet like that. And here, all at once, as if in answer to it, beyond a Renaissance gateway like half a sphere that bulged out with iron spikes into a garden with a pretty lawn full of stone satyrs, was a zoo.

Cosnahan entered behind some nuns escorting a dozen little children. But undoubtedly it was *the* Zoo, and how stupid of him, and how unlike him, not to have known this, not to have found it out and come here before, for come he would have; as it was something unconscious, or even stronger and more mysterious, seemed to have propelled him hither, whereas normally a zoo, after a bar, was about the first place he made for when alone in any big city, upon which the zoo would be found to include most of the other's amenities too. For though Cosnahan was hurt by the idea of animals and birds in cages, their being captured or shot no less (and he himself was a first-rate shot who never hunted), his love of wild animals and everything wild, dating from his childhood upon a then wild island, was implicit and genuine. He acknowledged that there were wicked animals, as there were wicked people—yes, he would go that far—aye, and further maybe—with the Swedenborgians. Citron-le-Taciturne himself was a bit wicked, downright sinister in some respects but, that did not prevent one from loving the little cat, or from recognizing his lunar accomplishments, his nocturnal rituals and pomposities, as all representing the special magic of his moonkind . . . But however that might be, or whatever, even some ironic sense of his own extraordinary rarity, had drawn his steps inexorably toward this place, what empathy, abysmal or divine or both, the zoo was evidently where Cosnahan was going and he was glad of it, to seek comfort, and who knows to give some comfort to the porpoise-playing seals, the searching bewildered polar bears, and perhaps even the poor endlessly pacing schizophrenic lions, within each of whom lay trapped, no doubt, the soul of a Manx-American author. And here were the peacocks. They were white ones, in two separate adjoining cages, with a pair of birds in each: alack, the wrong pair; it was an international cartoon, an imbroglio of pure peacock: for while the peahen in one cage and the royal peacock in the other exchanged arrant kisses through the wire meshes, the abandoned peahen cowered, and the corresponding alienated peacock now gorgeously crowding on full sail with a cry part bray and part meorw, screeched, the keeper all this time was quietly gathering up from their common roosting quarters the rival peahens' eggs . . .

ORARIO DEI PASTI

Antropomorfi	9:30	19
Scimmie	10	19:15
Carnivori	18:45	
Orsi Bianchi	20	
Elefanti	19	
Rapaci	18	
Foche	10:30	18:30

Having made out from this that it was too early to see any of the animals fed, Cosnahan, who had turned away feeling he was intruding on the peacocks' privacy, such as it was, followed the direction roughly indicated by two white signs placed one above the other, the upper saying *Rapaci,* the lower *Equidi.* Rapacious animals, he thought, and equus, equi, a horse; from this he deduced zebras and the like. Cosnahan smiled, was pleased by his intelligence, and felt much better already. He was looking at the lion over a carpet of wildflowers. For little white daisies and poppies and lilac-colored bellflowers were growing here sometimes right into the cages. Beyond the flowers, beyond an abyss, and within a scenical rocky lair, the lion lay asleep in the heat of the afternoon. Though it was nearly five by the clock on the façade of the restaurant the sun was scorching, and Cosnahan remembered his tropic days at sea, and how grateful he always was, being a carpenter and thus a day worker, to knock off just as the day was hottest, which wasn't midday, but anywhere between six and eight bells in the afternoon, or about an hour and a half ago—and at this moment he felt again, more strongly, that same familiar twinge or pull at his being—when, on that voyage he was thinking about, he would——*Elefanti,* he read. Cosnahan advanced more rapidly through a smell of elephants and roses. The walk to the elephants' cages was shaded though the beasts themselves were moving in the sun. And then, suddenly, marvelously—could it be?—he saw——

Well, he saw that two elephants were being thrown hay by a man outside their cages pitchforking the fodder from a pile over to them. It was not their dinner hour but they were getting a snack anyway, which was a good thing. The elephants stood in two cages, roofless enclosures, well and sensibly built, with a high stout iron fence outside, spiked on top, and separated from the walk by a few feet. In unison they swung their trunks out, down to the pile of hay, then up, with a benign and refined gesture, feeding the fodder into their kindly, sardonic mouths. Between times they would salute, through the bars, with a practiced intellectual twirl of their trunks, as though conducting, the man with the pitchfork, or in a sterner but still friendly manner, two children who, doubtless without intentional maligni-ty, were trying to feed them paper. Of this the two elephants appeared outwardly tolerant, but, disgusted, would drop the paper and return to the hay. One of them now gently kicked over the footstool with which he was provided, as to say: too bad you weren't better brought up, little boy! But even that silent rebuke was administered with dignity, it seemed, and an extraordinary patience.

The elephant! he thought. If ever there was a creation that testified to the existence of almighty God, and His wide wild humor, it was the elephant, that marvelous juxtaposition of the grotesque and the sublime, even if, according to Victor Hugo, that would make the Almighty a Romantic, as indeed one might ask without offense, how could He help but be, among other things?

It was usual to sentimentalize about elephants, and much has been written about their memory, longevity, fidelity, their patience and sapience, their enlightened compassion toward their offspring, and their unlimited capacity as bond slaves, whether in peace or war, in the service of man. Because in captivity they permitted year in and year out without complain-ing little children to ride on their backs, or to feed them paper—Cosnahan was glad to see the keeper had stopped these brats doing this for he was reluctant to fling them a punishing look in Italian—it was common to ascribe to them the virtues of patience and love and gratitude, in the human sense, as though the elephant existed for the benefit or amusement of man alone. Then when an accident happened, and someone was hurt or killed, the elephant was called a bad elephant and was shot, and his kind was discredited. And this was unfair.

Because an elephant, by the way, is an elephant, and, as with man, no one knows how or why he first came into the world, save that, in Cos-nahan's opinion, one could be sure it was not as generally supposed. (For with our notions of evolution, was it not as with so many of our specula-tions, just as the great Manzoni said, that from the inventions of the common people, the educated borrowed what they could accommodate to their ideas; from the inventions of the educated, the uneducated borrowed what they could understand, and as best they could, and of all an un-digested, barbarous jumble was formed of public irrationality that was called public opinion?)

And an elephant, as itself, within its own paradisal and thundery being as an elephant, among other elephants, in its own princely and poignant and oblique world, had its own elephantine virtues which, if they happened to resemble human ones, was an accident unless, as seemed the truth, it simply attested in this case to a common divinity. If it so happened then that an elephant showed you a love or an intelligence you were wont to say was "almost human," as usual you were flattering to yourself.

Since must there not have been some principle of goodness and sagaciousness first, existing in the elephants' perceptions, that the elephant was able to recognize too in the very different moral climate of captivity or slavery to man in which he found himself later obliged to live, some principle of tolerance, or above all pity, for his captor, who could not help himself, and a certain sense of interest or sportive adventure about whatever he was doing that he recognized as amusing and instructive to his elephantish faculties, monotonous though it might all seem to us?

In a human being this acceptance of slavery would be thoroughly ignoble, but there was no reason to believe an elephant saw matters that way, Cosnahan thought. The jungle is one thing, captivity another. Freedom was of the spirit. So reasoned the elephant, long before news magazines were invented, although Cosnahan, who liked to think he possessed a tragic sense, and in addition was incorrigibly on the side of bad behavior, would have liked to let out the elephant he was looking at, if that would have helped.

But perhaps he would have reckoned without the true nature of the elephant, which even in its wild state was a profoundly meditative animal. Like the sacred ibis who has the habit of standing on one leg for hours at a time by the Nile, in a manner which can only strike most human beings as idiotic, so in its state of deep abstraction, with the elephant. Moreover watch elephants engaged in something calmly destructive in a movie, notice their faces closely, do we not observe that they are as if, ibis-like, smiling softly to themselves, enjoying at the same time some transcendental joke? And so perhaps they are . . . Compassionate creature of titanic orisons! Who are we to say that the elephant does not have some higher comprehension of the will, as do those great mystics who inhabit some of the regions whence they come? To Cosnahan the kind of animism that could read such qualities into an elephant was not based on superstition, but on personal experience. An elephant may serve man, or as a spectacle for man, and as a friend to man, but what he really serves is elephant, his higher elephant.

But in order to understand these things it was perhaps first necessary to have loved an elephant, perhaps in a measure, more than oneself, to have shared, in a measure, the maelstrom, yet also the strange primal peace an elephant inhabited, even perhaps, as Cosnahan had once done, an elephant's very environment of imprisonment, if it can be true here, as it is said of human beings, that in certain common adversities the spirit of concord, comradeship and understanding is manifested at its highest. If you would know the elephant, therefore, O mahouts and maharajahs, try going through the tail-end of a typhoon with one upon a British tramp steamer capable of eight knots an hour in the year 1927, if possible at the age of nineteen, share also with the elephant the calms and the stupendous heat and the boredom, the unendurable monotony of the Oriental seas, the immeasurable length of that voyage over half the map of the the world, over that endless desert of sapphire, on that ship capable of half the speed of a pushbike, whose engine's song is only Frère *Jac*ques: Frère *Jac*ques: Frère *Jac*ques:—stand on the black-oiled foredeck with the lonely creature during the monsoon, in the tremendous shadow of the rain . . . Then indeed, like some ocean-going Renan, you may find the elephant communing with you in regard to your origin and destiny!

And because it was precisely these incredible things that it occurred to him he had once actually done with an elephant, it was the elephant on the left, the one with more luxuriant ideas about the usage of her food apparently, who had taken Cosnahan's attention, though to say this is not to express his feelings: for Jung, Logic and Philosophy to the contrary, if Cosnahan was right, here was one elephant that was not merely true because she existed, not merely a phenomenon, but a conclusion, a statement, and a subjective judgment of a creator all at once. And how could that be? Yet, from time to time, while he watched, there! she would pick up a wisp of hay from her food and place it accurately on the top of her head where, more refreshing wisps continually being added to the lofty pile—for their touching purpose was to cool her—something waggish sat finally like an exfoliating straw hat. Cosnahan advanced softly.

Could it be?—it could—she was—it was, and he had no need to ask, if he could have asked, and he had meant to try, but the keeper had gone—yet how could he have forgotten? And as it seemed now he never really could have forgotten. It took him back of course all those twenty-odd years to the experience that had informed *Ark from Singapore* itself, to a time when the British tramp steamer on which he was the carpenter's mate, the same voyage that had provided him with his meritorious adventure in the Yokohama harbor, only several ports later homeward bound, had loaded that freight as mentioned of heterogeneous wild animals at a Straits Settlement port, that is to say, it was not Malaya at all but Siam, at Bangkok: numerous black panthers, a quantity of snakes, a wild boar, and a young lady elephant. This unusual cargo which located itself on the foredeck, in the forepeak, and even on the fo'c'sle head, the fo'c'sle proper being aft, had been accompanied by a keeper, but the immediate problem was to find a seaman to help him. By British law it is possible to refuse such a job once at sea and despite the faint prospect of some extra cash in London, in addition to overtime at the rate of one shilling per hour, refused it was by the entire fo'c'sle after the first casualty; Cosnahan's senior, the carpenter himself, claimed that while he was lashing the cages, the elephant, with innocent eye, had deliberately tweaked him: thereafter few of the crew, plain superstition in Cosnahan's opinion, would venture forward beyond the rope barrier unless absolutely necessary, and the job of keeper's assistant devolved on Cosnahan alone. It occupied most of his time homeward bound.

Nearly all the other animals were going to the Dublin Zoo, but were to be unloaded at London, the chief exception being the elephant, who was lading for Rome. Since the ship didn't dock in Rome the beast was to be transferred to an Italian vessel at Port Said. But the ship very nearly didn't get to Port Said, or finally, anywhere else.

Yes, yes, yes, it could not be otherwise. It may be that many elephants have this habit of using their afternoon tea as headgear, but there had only been this one elephant in Cosnahan's life. And what he remembered, or remembered again, was this very incident of the elephant's departure from them at Port Said, her destiny at length in Rome's Tyrrhenian port yet again to be transferred, from Ostia—was it?—to be transferred, where else but here? To no lesser place than the Rome Zoo. To this very place.

It was even so. And that parting had been executed in like, though reverse manner, to that of their first meeting, as with crushing indignity, harnessed like an infant and, alas, squealing like one, she had been lowered into a lighter opposite the Casino Palace Hotel, while behind her in the wicked city of Port Said the advertisements for *Thé Lipton* winked on and off, and up the slanting swaying planks from other lighters, up the sides of a neighboring vessel, an endless procession of blackened human slaves bearing baskets of coal had toiled all night, chanting from the Koran.

It had not been easy to forget, any more than how the searchlights in the Suez Canal, where they had tied up eleven times during the previous night, had bothered her before that, nor how the cries of the panthers had maddened her with fright during the tempestuous part of the voyage, nor how, only a little while before Suez, they had looked at the moon hanging in a sky of green above Mount Sinai together at five o'clock in the morning, from the Bitter Lakes or wherever it exactly was, knowing that their friendship would soon be at an end. Nor how, several times, when the lifelines were stretched fore and aft, and the battling scending steamer was working only three knots against Himalayan seas, and not even a look-out would venture forward, he had taken over from the keeper to sit up with her all night—because though she was not too young to be without her she still sadly, it seemed, missed her mother—Cosnahan having lashed himself to her cage at one point to prevent his being washed overboard, and at that both of them were nearly drowned. And then—and might he ever be forgiven for this?—he had but safely conducted her into slavery.

No, it was not something easy to forget, that parting before the voyage was completed, but forget it he had—and the odd thing was he never *could* have forgotten it had he not written *Ark from Singapore*. For in order that his book should be brought to a satisfactory close, or for the sake of unity, all the animals without exception had to be manipulated, after their brief hour of victorious and absurd freedom, successfully to London. And what was the origin in fact of the escape, in which the fictionalized Rosemary, having escaped herself, had gone around kicking in the other cages, and letting the other animals out? It was partly the fear of the other seamen that just this would happen during the storm, and partly that Rosemary had indeed escaped from her cage once, and had kicked in the companion cage of the wild boar who had escaped too; but Rosemary had heeded Cosnahan's voice and returned at last . . .

Cosnahan smiled. Unity, yes, but how much greater a unity was this! To think that all these years, the duration of a coming of age, Rosemary had been patiently waiting here, serving him in her way, going through her daily performances regularly as the pendulum of a clock, despite Mussolini, Fascism, wars, disasters, triumphs, Abyssinia, the Germans, Pirandello,

Marinetti, the American liberation, Garibaldi, de Gasperi and Roberto Rossellini, eating her hay and then at seven o'clock drinking her buckets of milk, and munching her celery and carrots, gathering her strength and growing older unselfishly, as if just waiting for Cosnahan to find his way back to her, first in his mind, then, as if it were not enough that thus she had provided him for the first time with the basis of a living wage, in order that he might meet his benefactor in the flesh again, had actually paid his fare for him back across the Atlantic!

And had heeded Cosnahan's voice at last . . . Cosnahan advanced softly, he patted that accurate questing trunk. "Rosemary," he said, "how could I have forgotten you must be here? . . . My lord, old girl, how you've grown . . . Ah, well, no melancholy now. Jean traagh choud as ta'en ghrian soilshean!"

And Rosemary flapped her ears, which were not very large because she was an Indian elephant, and regarding Cosnahan with her shrewd small intelligent eyes, suddenly trumpeted

"—"

Cosnahan stood speechless.

Naturam, expellas, pitchfork. Nature!—talk about Nature coming back, there was the pitchfork too. Rosemary . . . No preposterous recognition in literature, or fact, to ancient mahout, to John Carter after long jungle separation in *Tarzan of the Apes,* to Sabu—recognition, it was anagnorisis!—and now he knew why he'd thought of Androcles and the Lion—could have been more complete, or, he thought, as if more utterly in conscious defiance of those who would claim that after all the elephant's long memory, unless of injury, is a fable. Or more dramatic, in its way, for it seemed to him, didn't it even have a certain flavor of Aristotle about it?

—Ah, Rosemary, repository of my ancient youthful secrets, sharer of my dream in the violet Indian Ocean (in which you were violently seasick), how often, figuratively speaking, have I held your head, comforted you, while you announced your elephantine misery to the monsoon? How many times washed you, placed the huge soogie sponge full of water so that, when you became too hot, even as now, you could lift it with your trunk and give yourself a nice shower, how often fed you your afternoon hat—ah, dear Rosemary, what times we had! So as it were truncated our friendship, and yet so deep, so, as we see, irrefragable, almost eternal. And how will you fare, perhaps have fared already, translated into Italian? Who knows but that even now you are the rage of Turin, in the land of the Piedmontese!— Though for the moment the less said about that the better.

But now it was as if Rosemary was changing before his eyes into an elephant in a wooden cage, between the scuppers and the number two hatch, to port on the foredeck of that old merchantman. The deck after the storm was all a sleepy idle heave and susurration with intermittently somnolent flingings of spray through the scuppers. At the silently turning wheel above on the bridge a dilatory man stood with his eye on wilder tropes than that of the compass: Quattras. High up there too, pondered the officer on watch, a bored chin in a corner of the weathercloths. Somewhere the engine murmured to itself: *Frère* Jacques: *Frère* Jacques: *Frère* Jacques . . . One bell; and a flying fish, to Rosemary's grave inquiry, fell suddenly on top of her cage, and Cosnahan caught the quivering celestial thing swiftly, and choosing his moment, flung it far back into an ecstasy of its following brothers and sisters. Rosemary was changing into a lapis lazuli elephant. And the lapis lazuli elephant changing into a portrait of a young elephant, on the cover of a novel named *Ark from Singapore,* confronting a ship's captain at the entrance to his chartroom gazing at her with astonishment, much as the author gazed at the same portrait as, still laughing silently to himself, he sat once more under the awning of the Restaurant Rupe Tarpea on the Via Vittorio Veneto, in the twilight of Rome.

. . . Indeed, Cosnahan had changed himself, was aware, quite apart from the extraordinary sense of well-being he felt, of one of those changes which, fiction to the contrary, it is given to very few to remark exactly when they take place, for the good reason, he thought, that maybe they take place in sleep. And Cosnahan felt that he'd woken up. The waiter, the one he'd paid this noontime for the milk, advancing, had said with a welcoming tone: "And where have you been all this beautiful afternoon?" To which he replied merrily: "Cha bee breagerey creidit, ga dy ninsh eh y n'irriney!" a remark having nothing to do with credit but meaning simply, "A liar will not be believed, even though he speak the truth!" And with complete confidence he had ordered, as suitable to the occasion, the bottle of spumante he was drinking with such consummate enjoyment. But first to give some report of all this to his wife, and Cosnahan brought out his letter again, no longer reluctant to finish it here, yet looking away from it down the Via Veneto wondering what he should say.

Still the same ceaseless traffic, yet still that same queer old feeling of riches and peace and grace about the flow of it within the Via Veneto itself, between the plane trees and the sidewalks ten feet wide: but why hadn't he noticed before that this was caused in part by the incidence that neither buses nor trams ran up or down the Via Veneto, they merely crossed it width-ways, as here at the Via Sicilia?

And now the heat of the day had gone and the light of the sky was fading from scarlet to rose and from cobalt to powdered violet and as the lights began to flash on Cosnahan asked himself: What was so theatrical about a swift flurry of figures or one lone figure under an arc light in a great city?

He would have liked "to get it," to capture too—he felt an almost passionate desire to capture—the beauty of the unending processions beneath Rome's high electric flambeaux. And now its marathon moon of tangerine. Arcturus. Spica. Fomalhaut. The Eagle; and the Lyre. But what to say to Lovey?

And Cosnahan glanced away from his letter again to where, the half-hallucination still persisting, a shadowy horsecab containing a twilit Gogol, visible now only as a cigar coal, seemed still plodding up the hill.

Yes, what should he say? That the discovery of Rosemary (and of course, how could Lovey, since he had forgotten, know that their heroine's original had been going to Rome?) had reminded him—as if he needed reminding!—by bringing back those days of longing for home at sea, those more recent warlike days as well in the untenanted submarineless Caribbean, how he longed *now* to return to her, Nantucket, Citron-le-Taciturne? Or, which was true too, that had it not been for Rosemary he might never have met Lovey, since but for his duty to Rosemary he would have transferred in those days to a sister ship at Penang, whereas later it had been the animal's keeper, as he now remembered, who had first counseled him to emigrate to America? Perhaps he should mention in half-serious jest that Rosemary, other adolescent trivialities having passed his naive soul by, was in truth his first great unselfish love, and hence perhaps responsible for who knows what qualities Cosnahan might in Lovey's eyes possess. Or—but what did it *mean,* his meeting with Rosemary? None of this was what he wanted to say, and some of it she already knew. No, it was all far stranger, more mysterious, more wonderful, more *miraculous* than this somehow! And far more complicated than anything he could so obviously say, even though the truth, about its having been a little like meeting himself. Suddenly Cosnahan, who would have had no difficulty at all in attributing the same faculty to an outside agency, felt as if there were some power deep within his own mind capable of thinking of a hundred things at once, each one of which was funnier than the last, more purely ludicrous, while at the same time more purely serious, even solemn, so that gripped at last by the huge comicality of the whole thing on the one hand, and on the other by the equally huge stateliness of its interlinked and profound counterpart, he felt, closing his eyes, that he was going to burst asunder from some attack of gigantic silent laughter. Moreover now a hundred ideas, a hundred meanings seemed spiraling up from the same depths, from the same source in his mind: like a concourse of irreverent angels they spiraled up as through a mental ether, on which he had turned his inward eye, and this no sooner imaged than angels in sort they were, and as though now the heavens without were drawn within him too, among these angels he seemed to detect Mother Drumgold floating upwards on her celestial journey. His mother? But the answer came before Cosnahan had time to question.

For was not Rosemary like a signal *from* his mother, nay, was it not almost as if his mother had herself produced Rosemary or at least guided his steps to her, his meek and impossible elephant, to a meeting in its gently buffoonish manner nearly sublime. And sublime because didn't it seem almost to tell him that life, all life, must have a happy ending, that it was our tragic sense that was the more frivolous, having been given us for aesthetic reasons alone, that beyond tragedy, beyond the world, if not altogether beyond art—naturally one hoped not too soon—reconciliation beyond our wildest dreams of optimism, that Cosnahan, though admittedly a lesser writer, was a more serious one than Shakespeare or somebody? And what was a further motive of this signal, this meeting, this guidance? Why to tell him that by accepting his mother's death, and now he had for the first time fully accepted it, he had released her, and he seemed to see her now flying up through the blue Roman evening clouds, beyond the young gold tangerine moon in the southern sky, ascending, accompanied by these angels of fact or thought; to be greeted by her St. Peter with just a shade of a pained smile, in Manx Gaelic, at that gate . . . Cosnahan lit his pipe. He was trembling a little. He was moved. And a moment later it did not seem that he had had these thoughts, which were a bit primitive even by primitive standards. Yet it was no less difficult to express in words for Lovey merely the mundane effect his encounter with Rosemary appeared to have had on him.

In a way, though it was hard to see why, it had been like one of those forgotten but universal aftermaths to some quarrel of early marriage, arising from having drunk too much at some stupid party, escaping from which into the inevitable bar one ran into some friend of one's youth, down on his luck perhaps, but who instead of borrowing money or showing signs of renewing the friendship beyond a point said, surprisingly and kindly, "What sympathy do you expect to get in a place like this you can't get at home, you old bastard?" so that, although one didn't go home immediately, a little later one found that this advice, "Why don't you go home, you can't handle the stuff," must really have taken root on the spot: but in this case it was not alcohol he could not handle, it was—and so his earlier train of thought, like Cosnahan himself in his walk around Rome, came full circle—

It was success itself, oh, he'd known it, something about its effect he couldn't handle, and the futile search for which he must abandon, let them translate his wretched book back into Manx if they wanted to: that is to say, it was just this vanity he had to abandon, for who wouldn't be honestly proud to be translated into Italian?

And abandon for what? What but his work! Yes, his precious, ridiculous, second-rate, and yet to him, and to his wife too if they must live, all-important work: it was this he had been missing all along, seeking some stimulus, somewhere, anywhere, to begin again, and in the act of seeking, the excuse to postpone that beginning; and now, at one of those rare points where life and poetry meet, Rosemary had appeared; for Rosemary, so to say, *was* his work—Cosnahan glanced down at the cover of his book again—Ah, Rosemary, unique elephant, certainly the only one who turned out to be the bluebird too.

Tomorrow, to that uniqueness of yours, I shall make an offering of the choicest Roman carrots, a bouquet of the freshest and crispest cisalpine celery. And sometimes it is true, so hapless does man seem to me, that I feel that if there is evolution, it must be to such as you. But great and wise though you are, Rosemary, I am bound to point out, our star being low, that man is more various.

Cosnahan took a sip of wine and watched the evening scene for a minute, feeling his sense of kinship deepening: the tricyclists, the bicyclists, the motor-scooters, the many tourists, the far fewer priests, the large number of Americans in uniform, the poor he could not succor, the diseased he could only direct a prayer at, the two carabinieri opposite who, with their eyes downcast, seemed intent rather on some invisible Mamertine scene beneath the earth, or as if brooding upon the multitudinous caryatids of human anguish that upheld the street at all, sealed away from the gaze of happiness and humor, the Swedish woman returning to the Pensione Borgnini, drawing back, half fearful too, before the mighty scission of a crossflowing bus . . . Come Matthias, come Arthur . . . But they would come in their good time, he would see them. He would introduce them to Rosemary, and how delighted they'd be. And he would ask Arthur which Huxley it was who wrote that men should not seek for their differences, rather that which draws them together, which of that very variousness, uniqueness, he'd just been thinking about; no matter, both were right, and which was the one who would have said: but can Rosemary laugh?

But it was not from the knowledge that he would now work again—though he would—that his deepest satisfaction sprang, that was now making him feel as happy as—why, as happy as some old magician who had just recovered his powers and brought off a masterstroke!

The words had almost slipped out of his mouth. And suddenly, at the realization of what he meant, a pure delight in all its renewed and ludicrous implications got the better of him, so that Cosnahan laughed aloud.

Good God, he really *was* a magician. Or this was the real wild fount of his feeling, shared suddenly, human (at the same time more than just universally ancestral), though it seemed to be; this was the real antique and secret source of his present pride, of his future salvation; this that would have caused his book to be translated, and by that, more than that, himself to be translated—his mother's son at last—into a conscious member of the human race.

And who might that be? Who was he? Who was anybody?

For the papers said that man was Smithers, they might even say that he was Drumgold. Cosnahan, they might say that man was. And somewhere they had got the notion that he was as common as the century . . .

But man was Quayne, and man was Quaggan, man was Quillish, man was Qualtrough, man was Quirk and Quayle and Looney, and Illiam Dhone, who had been hanged. And yet lived—because he was innocent?

On Lowry

Born in 1909 to a wealthy Liverpool family (and christened Clarence), Malcolm Lowry began his search for adventure at eighteen when he shipped as cabin boy to the Orient. He then entered Cambridge University, where he took a third-class degree in 1932. A year later he published *Ultramarine,* a novel based on his sea experiences, married Jan Gabrial, an American, and began wanderings, with and without his wife, to New York, Los Angeles, Mexico, Vancouver, and points between, living for the most part on an allowance from his family, drinking, sometimes despairing, writing steadily and occasionally publishing, in and out of hospitals and jails. In 1940 he settled, if that is the word, in Dollarton, near Vancouver, divorced his first wife, married Margerie Bonner, and began serious efforts to publish the third version of *Under the Volcano.* After twelve rejections, he began to rewrite the novel, interrupted by a fire which burned his house and most of his manuscripts and by a series of lesser physical and psychic disasters. The novel was finally published in 1947, and immediately won him a considerable reputation. Although continually busy with projects for novels, collections of stories, poems, and even a film script of F. Scott Fitzgerald's *Tender Is the Night,* he published no more books in his lifetime. Since his death in 1957 his reputation has grown steadily if modestly, aided by the publication of paperback editions of *Under the Volcano,* of *Hear Us O Lord From Heaven Thy Dwelling Place* (1961), and of materials assembled or edited by others from fugitive work or from unfinished manuscripts.

In his life, in his art, and especially in his life becoming legend become art, Lowry embodied most characteristics of the romantic-symbolist artist. For him art was not so much an end as a means, and only one of the available means, toward a higher truth. As a young man, he recognized that he must "identify a finer scene: I must in other words give an imaginary scene identity through the immediate sensation of actual experience etc." and "rub off more prejudice . . . use more hardship, load myself with finer mountains and strengthen more my reach" in ways not possible to one "stopping home among books . . . " (*Letters,* p. 8). This impulse led to his wanderings, his alcoholism, his wide and curious reading in Cabbalistic and occult works as well as more conventional literature, and to his attempt to integrate and provide coherence for this material in his writing. Both ambitious and painstaking, he projected a three- (or five- or six- or seven-) volume series of novels titled *The Voyage That Never Ends*—a post-romantic title in the vein of Rimbaud, Eugene O'Neill, Hart Crane, and Conrad Aiken, whose *Blue Voyage* he much admired. Another or an alternate plan projected "a Dantean trilogy" of which *Under the Volcano* was the inferno, *Lunar Caustic* in one version or another the purgatorio, and *In Ballast to the White Sea,* lost in the fire, the paradiso. The only fully realized work is *Under the Volcano,* which accounts for Harvey Breit's judgment that "Though Lowry knew Heaven, he knew Hell best. Though he knew hope, he knew despair better" (Introduction, *Letters,* p. xiii). Powerful though *Under the Volcano* may be as a portrait of Geoffrey Firmin, the Consul, a man who misuses great powers and suffers greatly— and Lowry invites, in fact insists upon, comparison with the major writers of this or any century—he always intended to conclude the series "in triumph. (The Consul is brought to life again, that is the real Consul; *Under the Volcano* itself functions as a sort of battery in the middle [of the series of novels] but only as a work of the imagination of the protagonist)" (*Letters,* p. 267). Like the alchemist or magician, the artist is to work by transmuting the commonplace. Lowry's metaphor is more plebian: "Sometimes I had the feeling that I was attacking the past rationally with a clawbar and hammer while trying to make it into something else for a supernatural end" (Quoted in Janeway, p. 16).

The stories in *Hear Us O Lord* were drafted, if not completed, between

1950 and 1954. Lowry thought the collection "less like an ordinary book of tales than a sort of novel or an odd aeolian kind itself, i.e., it is more interrelated than it looks" (*Letters,* p. 320). Later, he called it "a kind of—often far less serious, often much more so—*Volcano* in reverse, with a triumphant ending . . . " (*Letters,* p. 338). Among the obvious links between stories are the refrains "Frère Jacques" and the Manx Fisherman's Hymn which gives the book its title. More complex and more deeply felt is the linking theme of the artist, creating out of his own confusion and pain, in fact using that pain as material. Still more fundamental is the theme of reconciliation, of ultimate peace and harmony.

In these stories as in *Under the Volcano,* the solution as well as the problem lies within the self. Kennish Drumgold Cosnahan is a familiar figure in Romantic and modern literature: the victim of writer's block, like Coleridge, and the victim of his own success, like F. Scott Fitzgerald. Unlike most treatments of such figures, including *Volcano,* "Elephant and Colosseum" is comic rather than tragic. Lowry called it "a comic classic, or at least a masterpiece of nature. . . . a kind of short story for Titans, a Moby Jumbo, a comic strip for the infant Panurge, of philosophic trend . . . " (*Letters,* p. 226). It is comic for the same reasons that *Ulysses, Tom Jones, Twelfth Night,* and *Way of the World* are comic: all deal with reprieves from death and sterility and with the conversion of coincidence into pattern and harmony.

For James Joyce and to a great extent for Lowry, who read *Ulysses* carefully for the first time in 1952, pattern was less a function of the plot than of puns and parallels. Thus Rosemary, the elephant who inspires a work of art, is set off by Cosnahan's cat, named from a book; she is presaged by the elephants which Cosnahan and his mother exchanged; and she is ironically paralleled by Fitzgerald's Rosemary, who encounters the hero in Rome in *Tender Is the Night.* Furthermore, as Ophelia said, rosemary is for remembrance, and this elephant does not forget. And the process by which she becomes Maeterlinck's bluebird of happiness proves that Lowry, if not Cosnahan, is a kind of magician. Even more farfetched is the allusion buried in the final series of names. "Qualtrough" was the name given by the mysterious man who telephoned William Herbert Wallace the day before his wife was murdered. Wallace was convicted of murder, but released because a higher court found the evidence insufficient. (See Julian Symons, *Critical Occasions* [London: Hamish Hamilton, 1966], pp. 161–162.) Like Illiam Dhone, and unlike Illiam Dhôan and Cosnahan Cronkbane, therefore, he is reprieved from death. Furthermore, Cosnahan's final release comes from his recognition of the beauty and harmony of the animal considered in and for itself, like the Ancient Mariner, Androcles, more dubiously, Sabu (the Hollywood "Elephant Boy" of the 1940's), and more dubiously still (since he figures in Edgar Rice Burroughs' Mars Books rather than the Tarzan series), John Carter. One need not recognize all of the allusions and parallels to understand the story (though not to do so is to miss a good deal of the wit, both in the modern and metaphysical senses), but awareness of the method and of its implication of higher levels of meaning and being are essential to an understanding of Lowry's theme and technique, both of which are implied in the final pun on "translate."

Lowry said that this novella "breaks all the rules, save that, I hope, of being interesting and amusing" (*Letters,* p. 266), but he may have been writing of an early version. As published, the story has (again like Ulysses) many neoclassical attributes of unity: time (less than a day), place (one city), and action. As Cosnahan is aware, this action is more perfectly unified than the plot of his book, for it ends with a recognition in the best Aristotelian fashion. The story ends where it began, though by no means *as* it began. Cosnahan can let go of his success, of his worries, of the memory of his mother, and of his "expression of sombre panic" because he has discovered in his moment of vision that nothing is ever lost.

Textual note:

The only printed version of "Elephant and Colosseum" is that in *Hear Us O Lord From Heaven Thy Dwelling Place* (Philadelphia: J. B. Lippincott Co., 1961), which is followed here. The paperback edition published by Capricorn apparently reproduces the Lippincott text by photolithography.

Resources for further study:

"Through the Panama" and "The Forest Path to the Spring," also in *Hear Us O Lord,* deal with many of the same themes as "Elephant and Colosseum." *Under the Volcano* is Lowry's major work. Posthumous fiction: *Dark as the Grave Wherein My Friend Is Laid,* Douglas Day and Margerie Bonner Lowry, eds. (1968); *Lunar Caustic,* Conrad Knickerbocker, ed. (1968); *October Ferry to Gabriola,* Day and Lowry, eds. (1970). See also *Selected Poems,* Earle Birney, ed. (1962). *Selected Letters of Malcolm Lowry,* Harvey Breit and Margerie Bonner Lowry, eds. (1964), is invaluable for the study of his work. It contains "A Biographical Chronology."

BIBLIOGRAPHICAL:

BIRNEY, EARLE. "Malcolm Lowry (1909–1957)," *Canadian Literature,* no. 8 (1961), 81–88; no. 9 (1961), 80–84.

SECONDARY MATERIAL:

DOUGLAS DAY is writing a biography. Most of the criticism focuses on *Under the Volcano,* but some of it can be useful to students of the shorter work.
AIKEN, CONRAD. "Malcolm Lowry," *Times Literary Supplement,* 16 February 1967, p. 127. See also 13 April 1967, p. 317.

BOATWRIGHT, JAMES. "The Sequel to Lowry's *Under the Volcano,*" *Shenandoah,* 13 (Winter 1962), 65–70.

Canadian Literature, no. 44 (Spring 1970) is devoted almost entirely to Lowry's work.

COSTA, RICHARD HAUER. "Malcolm Lowry and the Addictions of an Era," *University of Windsor Review,* 5 (Spring 1970), 1–10.

EDMONDS, DALE. "The Short Fiction of Malcolm Lowry," *Tulane Studies in English,* 15 (1967), 59–80.

EPSTEIN, PERLE S. *The Private Labyrinth of Malcolm Lowry: "Under the Volcano" and the Cabbala.* New York: Holt, Rinehart & Winston, Inc., 1969.

HEILMAN, ROBERT B. "The Possessed Artist and the Ailing Soul," *Canadian Literature,* no. 8 (1961), 7–16. In a special issue devoted to Lowry.

JANEWAY, ELIZABETH. "A Legacy, a Man and a Legend," *New York Times Book Review,* 21 May 1961, pp. 1, 16.

KIRK, DOWNIE. "More Than Music: Glimpses of Malcolm Lowry," *Canadian Literature,* no. 8 (1961), 31–38.

KNICKERBOCKER, CONRAD. "Malcolm Lowry in England," *Paris Review,* 10 (Summer 1966), 13–38.

KNICKERBOCKER, CONRAD. "The Voyages of Malcolm Lowry," *Prairie Schooner,* 37 (Winter 1963–1964), 301–314. In a special issue devoted to Lowry.

STERN, JAMES. "Malcolm Lowry—A First Impression," *Encounter,* 29 (1968), 658–668.